FIREBORN

Published by Paused Books 2015

Fireborn
ISBN 978-1508901488

A statutory catalogue deposit of this book can be found at the required libraries as required by the Copyright and Related Rights Act, 2000.

First Edition

www.pausedbooks.com

For Lorraine and Natalie,

for helping us fight each day to become better Fureath'i.

CHAPTER ONE

Lost

Amadis was losing his mind.

His grasp on what was real unravelled more with every moment. Memories that were not his would arrive without warning and dominate his every perception, saturating his senses with false reality. His hands trembled at how powerless he was to stop this. The visions had him question not only his strength, but also any confidence he had in his current surroundings. How could he know that anything was real? Could he even be certain he was losing his mind?

'Amadis, you have been lost in thought for some time now.' Lyat hesitated before asking, 'My friend, are you well?'

Amadis turned to glare at his companion.

'I meant no disrespect,' Lyat said quickly, 'but... we should keep moving, or we will be discovered.'

Lyat was right, but Amadis did not tell him that. Instead he turned and left without speaking. He could hear Lyat grumble about his arrogance as he was forced to follow after. Lyat was an intelligent man, but without Amadis he would become lost in the maze.

Every room of the maze was identical to the last - in structure, if not content - and without the knowledge Amadis possessed, escape was impossible. The rooms were all composed of the same crumbling limestone, with wall carvings of ancient warriors battling demonic creatures, and statues of those warriors also decorating the room. The statues were stone, but their weapons, shields, armour or masks were all real, made of metal or wood. All four walls held an archway to another chamber, and each of those chambers held four more identical archways leading to four more identical rooms. The guardian of the maze constructed it to drive his captives to despair, to take away any spirit they may still possess before he took their lives.

If Amadis was not so terrified his mind would fail him, then he would have summoned the guardian immediately and killed him, so they could continue their journey without delay. Lyat often called Amadis arrogant without peer, but Amadis would shrug this off and say he was simply without peer. What made him so formidable was his ability to kill anyone of his choosing. He had the power to know where someone was, appear instantly at their location and kill them if they needed to be killed. It was this power that held the entire world at peace. It kept each ruler in enough dread of Amadis's wrath, that they could not become tyrants in their own lands, or create war with the lands of others. Amadis had all of this power, so much that the gods themselves feared him, and still, he was losing his mind. The absurdity of it would be enough to drive him to madness if it was not already happening.

Amadis pulled out of his own private torture long enough to see Lyat reaching to touch a statue as they passed it: a female warrior of stone, frozen in mid-fight, her metal blade reflecting the torchlight flickering from each wall.

'Do not touch anything, Lyat, and do not use any power inside this maze. The guardian will feel it, and he will twist this maze until we end up in his hall.'

Lyat frowned. 'And do we fear this guardian? Even you?'

Amadis tightened his jaw. He never had to explain himself to anyone else, but Lyat was different. For years he and Lyat shared a unique friendship, one that neither man could have with any other, their power and positions affording little opportunity for companionship: Lyat was a king of millions, and Amadis was the king of kings. He first met Lyat when he had intended to kill him, to stop Lyat's armies from advancing on weaker nations. Instead they formed a friendship. Amadis wanted to tell his friend why he was here, to explain the fears he fought about losing his mind. But he could not. He could not say the words aloud. Amadis was clutching what little sanity he still possessed, tightly to his heart, and if he opened the truth to Lyat now, he feared that it would be the end of him completely.

'We will not waste our time killing him, Lyat. We will find what we have come here to find and we will leave.'

Lyat stepped closer. He was taller and broader than Amadis's slim frame. Lyat's thick black beard added to the size of his jaw and his wild hair added to his height, each one in contrast with Amadis who was always clean shaven to show the sharp lines of his stone-like face, and Amadis's hair was longer, but tied back tightly to a tail. They were almost complete opposites: Lyat wore thick fur cloaks, and dressed richly; Amadis wore only a shirt, a sword, breeches and boots, dressed plainly and for function. Lyat decorated himself generously with brooches and fine silken clothing, but it did not hide the brutal danger of the person beneath. Having Lyat step so close would be enough to make any man anxious. Amadis was not any man.

'Amadis, are you certain that these doorways even exist? Of course I trust your wisdom, but...' Lyat struggled for words before frowning and spinning away. His boots echoed on the silent stone around them, the air became heavier, and dust began to fall from the ceiling. Amadis recognised this as Lyat's powers struggling to be contained. He rounded on Amadis.

'Never before, Amadis, have you asked this of me! It is precisely your power that you alone can travel where you wish, appear where you will, and kill who you want. If you want to kill this tyrant Aerath then why not just do it! Why have you brought me to this maze, to search with you for some soul-stealing doorways from a forgotten time? Why am I here, Amadis?'

Amadis closed his eyes. The Iceborn Aerath was the latest ruler to dream of world domination. Under normal circumstances, Amadis would know the tyrant's location and travel to him through a plane of existence known as the life-stream. But when he had last journeyed there, it was a trap. Aerath must have discovered some way to poison it, and infected Amadis's mind with a preternatural toxin. Now he was crumbling from within. So he asked Lyat to accompany him here to help battle Aerath because if Amadis's mind faltered at the wrong moment then he would need his friend to save him. It was a humbling thing to need, something Amadis had never before encountered in his life, and he did not know how to handle it.

He should give some explanation. He could simply say that the life-stream he usually travelled was now poisoned. He did not even need to say that the poison was causing him to lose his mind. He did not need to say how he knew Aerath must be the man responsible for tainting his method of travel, and that he now needed to kill Aerath to remove the power behind the dark venom killing him. Once that power was removed, Amadis hoped his mind would heal. It was a delicate hope.

His damaged mind now searched desperately for a solution. Lyat deserved some answer, deserved even some lie. Perhaps he could say the mountain of ice where Aerath resided was unable to be pierced by any other method of travel. But it still did not answer why Lyat was with him. Amadis struggled, he tried to blame the madness for his hesitations, for his irritability, his loss of control, but there was more. For as long as he could remember he had dominated anyone he faced. People would either obey him or be killed by him. He tried to recall the years he and Lyat had spent together as friends. Were those memories being taken from him? Or did they ever happen?

The answer would not come, so Amadis reacted like he would to anyone else. He opened his eyes and his voice went cold. 'You are here because I have asked you here. You do not need another reason and do not question me again.'

Amadis waited. His hands stopped trembling and stayed near the hilt of his sword. A part of him knew it was a mistake to bring Lyat, and a larger mistake to speak to him like this. He may need to kill his friend now. Perhaps not as arrogant as Amadis, Lyat still demanded respect. Amadis's memories were unravelling but he knew enough that Lyat had once been on the path to becoming a warlord. He was known the world over as Lyat the Destroyer of Armies. They had helped each other in that way. Amadis had stopped Lyat from further drowning his soul in the blood of innocent men, and Lyat had taught Amadis that not everyone was so far beneath him. That lesson felt a distant thing now as he reverted to his baser instincts: he felt threatened by Lyat's power; felt his own weakness amplified by his proximity.

Neither man moved. Both were capable of destroying the other in less than a heartbeat if needed. If Lyat choose that moment to attack, to forget their years of friendship like Amadis was appearing to do, if he chose to rid the world of the unbearable Amadis Yeda, to free it of his ceaseless watch, and if at that same moment Amadis's mind should falter...

'Lead on, oh mighty Amadis,' Lyat finally growled through gritted teeth. 'Your lowly servant, Lyat, will follow at your heels.'

Amadis closed his eyes once more to search for peace. Of course Lyat would not attack him. They had been friends for so many years. Had he imagined the tension only moments ago? He had not imagined Lyat's reply in any case, so Amadis would tolerate the contempt of his only friend when the alternative was to kill him. But why did it need to be the only alternative? Why could he not just speak the truth! Why could he not just admit aloud that he was losing his mind! To tell his friend that he was not Amadis anymore, that he was the weak and frightened memory of the man instead.

His mouth would not move, and it took every ounce of control he had not to break down and weep for what he once had been. Amadis turned and left the room.

As they walked in silence, the statues began to disorientate Amadis. He still knew where he was going - his mind had at least not yet robbed him of that - but he was becoming dizzy. Was this the magic of the guardian or the degradation of Amadis's consciousness? From what he knew of the guardian, he was a creature who despised magic. The guardian came from a time when there was no magic, only weapons of exceptional power - weapons like the sword Amadis wore. In that time, no gods existed; something had killed them all... but what?

Amadis panicked. He was certain he knew this. What had killed the gods? And why had more gods returned again, new ones, young, all afraid of Amadis. Did they conspire with Aerath now to kill him? The room around him began to fade. Drawing his sword in alarm, Amadis turned to see Lyat was no longer with him and he was no longer in the guardian's maze.

He was standing next to an underground lake and the smell of damp from the cave walls assaulted him. *This is not real*, he tried telling himself. There was an island in the middle of the lake, but it did not rest in the water; it floated above it. There was nothing that he could see supporting the land mass, its unnatural and massive weight seeming to press down on Amadis's mind. He turned away to look at stepping stones that hovered in a pathway up to the island's top.

I know what is up there.

A flash of red appeared and Amadis spun to face it. He was presented with a man of fire holding a sword of flames. Amadis turned his own sword slightly, a thin, single-edged blade of deep black, with silver flames of its own etched along its deadly curve. He called his sword The Jaguar, because it killed with one touch.

Amadis whipped his blade down and ran it through his enemy's neck without thought. But the creature did not die as it should. Worse, the sword became tangled in the fire instead of passing through. The thing in front of him did not have a face, but it looked like it smiled before sticking its own sword of fire deeply into Amadis's flesh.

Pain exploded, but not where the sword had struck. It burnt his mind, searing through the deepest parts of him. Realisation hit and Amadis remembered with great clarity that this was the poison he had encountered. He had entered the life-stream, ready to travel to the mountain where Aerath waited, ready to kill the man who was trying to turn the world to ice, but inside the life-stream he had met this creature of fire.

A hand grabbed his shoulder and Amadis spun around, his sword suddenly free from the man of flames, stopping it only inches from Lyat's face. The sword shook with fragile control as Amadis struggled to clear his mind. He was back in the maze. There was no lake. There was no spectre of fire. His friend Lyat was frozen in place, staring at the black blade quivering inches from his eyes. As powerful as Lyat was, if that metal touched his skin, then he would be dead. It was the power of the sword, a power from another age, from another life.

Amadis slammed the sword back into his sheath and Lyat began to breathe again. Sweat soaked his skin and Lyat's eyes shone with the realisation that he had almost died. Amadis's hands were trembling again, but as far as he could tell, he was back in control.

'Amadis,' Lyat said, clearing his throat, 'what are you not telling me?'

He would tell him. He needed to tell him. Lyat, my friend, I am losing my mind. I need you now, to protect me, if my mind should fail when we battle Aerath. Please, I beg your help in my weakest hour. Amadis opened his mouth and again could not give life to the words, either to Lyat, or to himself. He could not.

Looking around at anything other than the hurt and confusion on his friend's face, Amadis tried to make sure this was real. His eyes darted around and immediately caught the figure of a statue protruding above an archway. It was of the goddess Am'bril, her naked torso thrusting out from the stone, her arms spread to either side and sinking back to the wall. The statue's fingers trailed into long vines before sinking into rock and becoming narrow groves. Those groves spiralled down the walls and along the floor to underneath where Amadis and Lyat both stood.

'The guardian has found us,' Amadis said softly.

Lyat looked around, the air becoming heavy and the room groaning under its force. Lyat could crush the chamber to rubble if he let out the full strength of his magic, but the guardian was not there. Amadis's eyes drifted down one of the path of archways, looking to where a darkness waited.

'Come, let us kill the thing and be done,' Amadis whispered and began walking towards the darkness.

'Amadis, you...' Lyat started but then changed what he was going to say. He sighed. Perhaps having a common enemy to confront would assuage all the questions that were being left unanswered. 'Tell me this at least, how do we kill him?'

'We do not.' Amadis looked his friend in the eyes and saw all of his questions there. But he also saw something else, he saw both a concern and a trust that he did not deserve. He saw a friend that was being led blindly in a maze, being disrespected at every turn, and yet still remained loyal. Amadis was endlessly grateful to have such a man with him, to give him this strength, but Lyat would be of no use in the coming fight. 'You will be powerless in his hall, my friend. The guardian is from another age, Lyat, before the heavens were breached and its power bled back into this world. When we enter his hall, there will be no magic.'

Pieces of Amadis's memories slowly returned, and with it, confidence. A man named Brijnok had broken through to the heavens all those centuries ago, and allowed gods and magic back into the world. Some of the more dramatic scholars believed that the world was now dying, drowning from the power the heavens flooded into it. Amadis killed anyone that drank too deeply from that power and right now he needed to kill Aerath, but if the guardian of the maze wanted Amadis Yeda to kill him too, then so be it.

They began walking once more, and as they advanced through the different chambers of statues, Amadis turned to see other rooms of darkness in different directions. It would be usual for the trapped warriors of this maze to try to flee, to avoid the hall of shadows and race mindlessly in vain. Amadis, however, walked directly to the darkness that was closest. They journeyed swiftly and in silence, and when they reached the final archway, a black nothingness waited for them. Amadis paused so Lyat could compose himself.

'I have never been without my power before, Amadis,' he confided. Hints of fear trickled through his dangerous exterior. How much stronger was Lyat that he could speak of his weakness with such ease? Admit it openly to his friend. But it was no longer appropriate for Amadis to do the same. Lyat needed him to be strong now. They both did.

'Do not worry, Lyat; I will kill him quickly. I will not give him a single chance to hurt you. Just keep your wits about you and do not lose your mind at what you are about to see.'

Whether those last words were for Lyat or himself, Amadis could not decide. He drew his sword and stepped into the darkness.

· CHAPTER TWO ·

Forgotten

As soon as Amadis entered the darkness, his vision pierced through it and the shadows began to fade. The gloom fled further and further back from his gaze, revealing a hall far larger than the temple should have been able to contain. Pillars lined every direction, making vision of the vast hall difficult, and still the darkness faded further to reveal an ever greater distance. There was no end to it, Amadis knew, so they would keep the entrance in sight and wait for the guardian to come to them. The view of eternity was unsettling, but Lyat handled it well.

'No walls, no ceiling, no end to the hall, and you tell me there is no magic in this place?' Lyat grumbled and stepped about cautiously, his hands working for something to do. His power and strength would already have been taken from him, just as Amadis's was, but at least Amadis had the comfort of his sword. Lyat carried no weapons. His magic was so formidable that he never needed them. His fingers curled in and out of fists now wishing they held one. He turned and smiled to break some of his unease, 'At least there is a floor.'

The distorted reality of the room had nothing to do with magic. The guardian was trapped in this place, caught in a power between broken times. Memories returned to Amadis unbidden as he recalled the terrible creature that destroyed all the gods and created a new age, an age where this guardian had flourished, revelling in the thrill of a world without magic, gifting warriors instead with weapons of power to create war and chaos. Then Brijnok breached the heavens. The magic of flesh could once more compete with the magic of blade, and the guardian was imprisoned here in this hall of shadowed reality. Now all he could do was lure victims to his web with the promise of ancient weapons to those that defeated him. Amadis's hand rested on the hilt of one.

'We shall not be here long,' Amadis said back.

'Such confidence!' a voice spoke from the darkness. It was a hollow, grating whisper that sounded like rusted metal if it could speak. 'Am I so lowly when faced with the mighty Amadis that he shall be done with me and gone so quickly?'

'Show yourself and do not waste my time,' Amadis replied.

The guardian laughed and stepped out from behind a pillar.

'So arrogant,' he said. 'Was I once like you, brother?' The guardian puzzled over his own question and regarded them curiously. His face was a skull wrapped in silver skin, with black hollows in place of eyes and mouth. He wore thick black armour with a blue mask at its centre in the shape of a shield. It was the symbol of Moi'dan's defence against all things magic, except Moi'dan would wear it on his face and not on his chest. The guardian was making a bold claim to display a mask of Moi'dan so blatantly, and to think he had the audacity to call Amadis arrogant. To add to the guardian's conceit, he wore a broad sword on his hip and he had foolishly not drawn it yet. The guardian's silver skin pulled tightly on his skull as he smiled.

'You have become more since we last met, Amadis! I am impressed.'

Amadis did not even bother to frown at the guardian's riddles, he had wasted enough time. But as soon as he had formed the intention to step forward and kill the creature, he found that his sword was gone. Was this a trick of his mind or a trick of the guardian? The rasping laughter that echoed from the guardian gave Amadis his answer.

'Oh the powerful Amadis robbed of all his power. Let me ask you, brother, what are you if not your power? What are any of us? If you take everything of note away from a man, what is left that we can even see? This world has forgotten that.'

'This is not your world and I am not your brother,' Amadis said, trying to control his intentions so as not to give warning. 'And without sword or power I am still more than enough to kill a thing such as you.'

The guardian stepped forward, the movement causing the metal of his body to sound loudly. The silver skin of his skull wrinkled again as he smiled, but this time the black hollow of his mouth grew darker as he spoke. 'That is where you are wrong, brother. That is exactly all we are, you and I. You are more because another of our brothers has joined you, I can feel that now, and you are drawn to us, trying to become complete once more."

The guardian was a broken creature, lost and forgotten, so Amadis paid his comments no heed, but Lyat shifted uncomfortably at the strange speech. The guardian's head snapped at the movement, not realising Lyat was there he had been so intently focused on Amadis. The surprise was clear even on a face that did not have any features.

'But perhaps you are right!' the guardian announced. 'As you stand here unarmed and without power, and still claim to be my better. Perhaps you are correct when you say you are enough to kill me, so let me make it even. Let me be like you and become *more...*'

Eight identical guardians stepped out from behind the pillars and surrounded Lyat and Amadis. Each wore the same armour and each moved with the same motions, but the moment the first one appeared, Amadis attacked. He charged toward the real guardian and without ceremony shouldered the creature to the floor, while at the same time drawing out the guardian's own blade from its sheath. In a single motion he had the armoured warrior slammed to the ground, his sword drawn, and Amadis did not hesitate as he plunged the blade into the guardian's chest. The sword struck cleanly through where he had the image of a shield decorated, and the irony of it pleased Amadis greatly.

The eight other guardians turned as one to see Amadis kill their ninth, and the number of them only enflamed his fury further. Nine guardians wearing the mask of Moi'dan on their chests in mimic of the nine real masks that Moi'dan possessed. It was an outrage. Moi'dan was the greatest warrior of every history and this creature was claiming to be his slayer. Well there were only eight now and as Amadis reached down to pull out the sword he had killed the first with, he was pleased to see a different sword returned to his hands. It had been a great show of strength for the guardian to take it from him in the first place, but clearly that strength had vanished with his life.

Lyat shifted his feet again, nervously waiting for the charge to come from the other eight guardians who were for now still in shock at the sudden death of their first. Amadis turned the Jaguar blade in his hand, letting the silver flames shine, and charged them instead. All eight drew their blades, not matching their first's mistake of keeping it sheathed, but it did not matter. Even without his powers there was no matching Amadis. The second was dead before any had time to make another move, and only then did the fighting begin.

The guardians fought with greater strength and speed than Amadis, their swords were wider and doubled edged, they had full armour to protect everything but their heads, and yet all these things did not stop the third and fourth from falling loudly to the floor.

Lyat made a run for Amadis's back, both to protect it and to stay clear of the faster guardians. They were certainly capable of killing Lyat while he was stripped of power, but as the fifth and sixth dropped with a dead clang, there were less and less threats to Lyat's life. Even fighting together to best Amadis, the guardians were not enough. He fought and the guardians died because he held the Jaguar blade. He had only to touch their silver skin and they dropped to their deaths.

The sword did not swallow life into its power or anything as grand as that; the sword was simply the antithesis to life. Where a thing lived the sword would make it dead. It was a simple power embedded with tremendous strength from an age long vanished. It was the sword that killed with one touch and Amadis was the killer that let it.

It was not long before the hall was littered with nine dead guardians and Amadis thought about plunging their own swords into the mocking shields on their chests just as he did the first. Perhaps that would destroy the guardian for once and for all. But now that he was defeated the guardian would appear anew and offer Amadis his prize. Memory flared unwanted, confirming that he had killed this creature many times before and that The Jaguar was never the prize. Then where did he get it? Amadis had always possessed the sword. It had been a gift from his brother...

Pain pierced into his mind as things he did not understand tried to break free. None of it made sense. He did not have a brother. The poison inside him was burning as fiercely as the spectre of fire who gave it to him. Amadis began to feel light headed, his vision fading to white. *No, not again, please!* A large hand pressed down on his shoulder, and Amadis snapped his eyes to see Lyat looking at him with concern. The hallucination did not come, and it was because of his friend. He had done the right thing in bringing him.

'Thank you, Lyat.'

'For what?'

'For coming here with me.' The gratitude seemed to make Lyat as uncomfortable as it made Amadis. Neither man knew what to say next, so Amadis returned his sword to its sheath and looked to the exit. 'Come, let us leave here. I care not for any prize this creature might offer.'

'You wish to leave as quickly as you defeat me, brother?'

Amadis looked back to see the guardian standing whole again. The nine fallen bodies gone and this time, wisely, he was unarmed. He even had his arms extended in a gesture of surrender.

'You are not my brother.'

The guardian smiled. 'You are right, we are not brothers. We are more.'

'You are defeated. Bring me to the room where you hold the world wounds. I will leave this place.'

'You will leave without your prize?'

'You have nothing I need.'

'Are you so sure?' He asked as a sword appeared in one of his hands. It was long and narrow, single bladed, and almost exact to The Jaguar in every appearance except with one stark difference: the blade was white from hilt to tip. It even had the same silver flames along its edge. 'Have you heard of this sword?'

Amadis paused. 'Yes.'

The Jaguar blade was probably the deadliest blade in the world, but the one that the guardian held, The Lion, had the potential to be worse. If it got into the wrong hands then it could cause catastrophe but in the hands of Amadis...

'Then you know that you cannot hold them both, Amadis, not even you. If you accept this blade then you must relinquish your precious Jaguar.'

The guardian did not lie. If Amadis held them both, or even touched The Jaguar after touching The Lion, they would negate each other, killing him in the process. But he could not risk anyone else claiming it. The new sword was more powerful, but The Jaguar was his.

'What is your answer, Amadis? Will you give up your beloved sword?'

'I will not.'

'Then alas, this will become lost to the histories once more.'

'No.'

The guardian titled his head and stared at Amadis. 'Oh? Do you truly believe that you can hold them both? I fear your arrogance has broken your mind. I would not see you destroyed by such foolish misadventure. So I will not give it to you unless you give me The Jaguar, and even killing me for it will not help you, the sword will vanish, only to reappear to be granted to any warriors that defeat me. We will be left with the same dilemma.' The guardian smiled in clever triumph.

'You choose your words well, guardian. It is precisely warriors that have defeated you. There were two of us in this battle and you may hand the sword to Lyat.'

Lyat's brow lifted in surprise and the guardian's deepened in displeasure. It did not matter that Lyat had not fought. He had been involved in the battle on the side of the victor and so could join him in that victory. The god of battle made the rules for the guardian, and there was nothing he could do to circumvent them, no matter how clever he thought he was. The only problem was of course that Lyat would possess a sword of greater power than The Jaguar, but the blade of black was Amadis's sword, and he would never part with it.

Lyat shrugged his shoulders and reached out to receive the gift. The guardian hesitated for as long as he could, desperate to find a way around the bargain, but eventually relented. He pressed the white handle into Lyat's palm and Amadis realised he was holding his breath to see what would happen.

Lyat looked at the sword with curiosity and Amadis hoped that his friend did not know of its power. Lyat was an extremely intelligent man. He was so deceptively subtle that many thought him simple, but it was as much his sharp mind as his great strength that got him to the position of power he now held. His intelligence could keep other crime lords, kings and entire countries running in rings while he sat back and ruled them. Now Amadis hoped that his dangerous mind did not include knowledge of ancient weapons or the potential they possessed.

'Now that we have accepted our sword, we would like to entrust it to you, Arathema, to keep safe.' The request, as much as the use of the guardian's true name, threw both men into confusion. Amadis's tone did not leave room for doubt though; it was a command, not a request. He elaborated, 'Lyat does not use a sword, and so will give it to you to give to another.'

Lyat said nothing, just eyeing the sword he held and then Amadis. It was a moment of concern because if Lyat knew the true value of the sword, then he would not agree to what Amadis was proposing. He would have to kill his friend to stop him from holding such a dangerous weapon. It was the second time in a short period where Amadis had considered murdering his only friend, but his mind felt clear. He would do what he must. The guardian watched the exchange perplexed, not able to conceive of a man giving away such a powerful weapon, but had to know that Amadis would kill Lyat if he did not. The fact Lyat might not know the power of the sword could be the only thing to save his life.

'I suppose you are right, Amadis, I do not use a sword so what reason is there for me to keep this?'

'Thank you, my friend,' Amadis said and did not realise how much tension he had been holding before relaxing at the words. 'Arathema, take this sword and bring it to my daughter Eva. I do not doubt you will be able to find her.' Lyat handed the bone white sword back to the armoured guardian, but he did so cautiously. Once back in his silver hand, the guardian could still not quite grasp what had happened. Amadis did not care. He would do as he was commanded and it was time to leave. 'Now, bring us to the chamber of mirrors you have created out of the world wounds. We are leaving this place.'

The guardian was still staring at the white sword in his hands with disbelief, and it took Amadis drawing his black sword to break him from his trance. The hollow of his mouth twitched, wanting to speak but not knowing what to say. Amadis had never seen the guardian act like this before. Everything was a game to this creature, always ready with a mocking smile and a clever trick, and Amadis was simply his favourite player.

'You will return again, my brother?' The question sounded more like a plea.

'I will not.'

'I beg you, become more again and free me.'

'No.'

There was finality to Amadis's voice that snapped the guardian out of whatever weakness he was experiencing. He was acting very strangely, but Amadis had greater concerns than the welfare of a beast of Brijnok's. Some strength returned to the silver skinned face and he spread his hands making the white sword disappear. The hall of pillars and shadow began to vanish with it, Amadis watching as the pillars closest to him bent and twisted down to form arches. It was difficult not to feel alarmed at the distorted perception of his surroundings. He fought back creeping doubts that his mind was crumbling and it took most of his strength to stop from closing his eyes to deny it. Amadis forced himself to watch the world deform, before focusing his gaze on the guardian. The silver skull was smiling at him again.

'This is not your world either, brother. Do not forget what he did to us.'

The hall of darkness disappeared, and in its place became the maze of archways once more. Where the guardian stood, there was now a stone statue of his image. The echoes of his last words tried to worm their way into Amadis's mind, to create even more doubts and questions than he already had. He glared at the stone figure until the air in the room became heavy and the statue crushed to dust before his eyes. Lyat slapped his hands together and then clapped one of his palms on Amadis's back.

'That felt good,' Lyat said and Amadis could still feel the weight of his magic making the chamber groan. 'Now, if it had been a fair fight, and he had not robbed me of my power, I could've crushed all nine of those grinning metal bastards into chamber pots to piss in.'

Amadis smiled. With the statue reduced to rubble, he had a clear view of the chamber of mirrors in front. He gave a cursory glance down the other three archways, but it was the room of world wounds that held his attention. These were the doorways that could bring him to where he needed to be, but they did not come without cost. Already he could feel their pull, taking whatever strength he tried to muster. They would take much from him when he walked through, but perhaps they would also take his madness, like the leeching of a festering wound. The thought brought him comfort.

Then his eyes turned cold and he surveyed the mirrors as he would any enemy he was about to conquer. Amadis had seen the world wounds, or cuts, shaped as mirrors before, but they were not always like that. Sometimes they would be a slash through the air, or a whirlpool in the earth or the sky. They were the manifestations of Brijnok's breach, where the power of the heavens flooded through, but in return they fed on life and flesh. The guardian was wise to place them in a circle to face against each other. The wounds pulled in from everything around them and could be shaped and manipulated to a man's will if he was strong enough. If a man was not strong enough then he would be devoured absolutely. Amadis and Lyat would lose years from their lives and quite a bit of their power from walking through them, but fortune had it that both he and Lyat had an abundance of power from which to draw. If the world wounds wanted to drink from their strength, then let the things drown.

'Is this what the rest of the world feels when they stand beside me?' Lyat asked him with a grin. Amadis did indeed feel similarities to the pull and push of force from the two powers. He could still feel Lyat's weight pressing down on his shoulders now that the man was no longer attempting to hide it, but the pull from the mirrors was worse. He was almost dragged forward from where he stood.

'I cannot speak for the world but I will say that I am glad I stand beside you now. Believe me when I offer my gratitude for what you did for me in there.'

Lyat shrugged. 'All I did was stop you from trying to kill me.'

Now it was Amadis's turn to smile. '*Try* to kill you?'

Suddenly Amadis was pushed down to one knee, and in alarm was very close to drawing his sword to strike out. Lyat was grinning down at him.

'Yes, my friend, *try* to kill me. And do not forget it.'

Amadis stood back up. 'I will not. Neither will I forget the power you gave up for me. I will find a way to repay you.'

'You could repay me now by changing your mind and not forcing us to travel by these soul-stealing abominations.'

'I will not change my mind.'

'And I did not think you would.' Lyat sighed. 'Well if we are to die then it might as well be in the most pain-filled and torturous manner known to us.'

'It will not kill us.'

'But you are not denying anything about the pain and torture?'

'I have been through them twice before and I have never known a pain that is worse.'

'You warm my heart with every word, Amadis. Come. Let us go to this ice prison so that my heart can be warmed further.'

Amadis nodded. There was no more room for hesitation. He marched forward and stood in the centre of the circle of mirrors. Immediately he could feel each one ripping at him trying to draw greedily from everything he possessed. So he stepped closer to one and he fed to it his will.

'Aerath,' he said.

The mirror shifted and colours began forming. Amadis wondered if the world wounds could pierce instead Lae Noan's cells, or if it was only magic from the world of flesh that could not exist within its walls. What the image showed was a hall of ice with a single throne in its centre. A giant sat on that throne, easily eight feet in height, and wider than Lyat and Amadis combined. He had the bright blond hair and frozen blue eyes of every one of his race, the Prae'surlas, but Aerath's eyes blazed with power. This was a tyrant who had made his king, and an entire room of Iceborn, kneel to him, the warmaster Drethit and champion Frind'aal among them, and declared himself their new god. That the other gods did not strike him down for heresy said much for his power, but the gods were cowards. They would leave it to Amadis to kill this man and kill him he would.

He turned to Lyat and nodded it was time. They stepped inside the wound.

· CHAPTER THREE ·

Ice

Amadis entered the cut between worlds and immediately his flesh was ripped apart by a thousand hands. Worse, he was robbed of any power he might use to fight it. His mind did not escape the brutal tearing but he was left with enough to recognise the agony that was being inflicted. The pain was nothing that flesh could feel, or that even power could. The pain that ravaged him was piercing directly into his very life. If he had lungs he would scream for death, and if he had hands he would claw through his skull to end the pain. The suffering was more than he could take but it was that he was helpless to do anything about it; that was the torture Amadis felt most.

A floor of ice pressed against his face then. The act itself did not cause pain but the sensation of flesh caused an explosion of pain remembered. His body had not inflicted any damage through the world wound, yet now it desperately tried to reconcile his untouched flesh with the agony just experienced. At least in this reality he had the power to fight it. Amadis forced himself to a stand and drew his sword, ready to deliver death to Aerath. But the cavern of ice was empty, a vacant crystalline throne it's only occupant.

Hoping the vision of Aerath the mirror had shown was not just a figment of his failing mind, Amadis frowned and balled his fists. He looked around expecting to see something, but all he saw was his reflection in the ice looking back. Amadis turned his gaze down to his friend instead who was still suffering on the floor. Lyat's entire body was trembling with shock but there was nothing Amadis could do for him. His own limbs wavered unsteadily from the trauma it had been through, but he would stand guard until they were both recovered.

'Amadis...' Lyat uttered from where he lay.

'Do not speak,' he said back. 'Concentrate your energy on recovery.'

'Amadis...' he insisted on repeating. 'Do not bring me through those cursed things again.'

'I will not my friend. You have my word.'

It was never an option to return by means of the cuts. He was not familiar enough with the wounds to hold them open as he could the life-stream. Nor did he wish to become so familiar. No, once they killed Aerath, Amadis would return them both to Amidon City through the life-stream. He would risk one journey and encountering the poison inside, but only because there was no other choice. Since there was the option of getting into Lae Noan by other means, no matter how dangerous, he had taken it. He had no such luxury with getting out.

The ice mountain of Lae Noan was fiercely guarded by the Prae'surlas. It was both a holy shrine where they worshipped and also a prison for the powerful. It had cells that stripped any man, no matter how great, of every shred of power he might possess. No one had ever escaped from there, and no one had ever been released. Everyone who had tried to sneak inside had been swallowed by the mountain, their life becoming part of the ice. And here he ran such a risk by willingly stepping foot inside.

The ice did more than steal your power though. It was not like the world wound where both life and power were swallowed as one. The mountain was different. It preserved life so you could continue to supply it power. For hundreds of years any beings of power who ventured into the lands of Surlas were taken to the mountain as prizes and contained there for the centuries that passed. They were proudly announced to the world as evidence of Prae'surlas superiority. Worse than that, other fool nations sent their criminals there, some that might be too powerful to hold or kill, others that they just wanted to suffer. The mountain gave you eternal life, but it was a life of oblivion. You needed no food or drink, but also no sleep. Try as you might the mountain would not allow it. A single cell was all you would be given, as far removed from any others as they could manage. Preserved for an eternity of nothingness, there was no greater torture that Amadis could imagine.

Looking around at the glistening walls, Amadis began to see more reflections of his own image appear. Some were startlingly clear, and others were skulking shadows. But he did not think they were guards hiding behind the ice, for all the protectors of the prison were stationed outside. It was not supposed to be possible to gain entry by any other means. It created more doubts that Amadis would not be able to leave through the life-stream, that he might become swallowed into the mountain if he tried, but those same doubts created confidence that it must have been Aerath who poisoned him. The mountain was like a carnivorous rock, feeding on magic from the world, and it had spread its roots into the flowing currents of power from the heavens. The mountain Connected itself to the life-stream and Aerath had Connected himself with the mountain.

Amadis looked to the various tunnels leading out of the cavern, leading to the cells where the mountain fed, and he saw phantoms drift in and out of sight in the reflection of the ice. Some held out begging hands to him and others screamed wildly, tearing at their mouths as they did. Amadis turned away. He would not allow his mind to fail him now. Looking to Lyat again, he saw the man still did not rise, although he did look like he was recovering. Amadis attempted to control his patience but began walking around the ice cavern to vent his rising fury. Where was Aerath? Why did he not strike while they were at their weakest, fresh from the cut?

Amadis approached the different tunnels and casually touched his sword to every spirit that was wailing there. It satisfied him that the apparitions were not real, because if they were then The Jaguar would have destroyed them. It still disturbed him though to confirm that the images were his delusions. He should keep his attention to protecting Lyat until he was recovered, it would focus his mind. Amadis turned back to where Lyat lay, only to find a figure standing above him.

This was no illusion and Amadis's rage was so sudden that he struggled with the need to rush forward and kill the god there and then.

'Kill him, Brijnok, and know no end to my vengeance!' Amadis roared. 'I will follow you to the heavens and slay you there!'

But the man standing by Lyat spread his hands out in peace. He was even unarmed. Amadis had never seen the creature without an obscene decoration of weaponry draped about his body. He had dark hair pulled back in mimicry of Amadis, with a white streak where a single scar ran from his mouth up over his ear and behind his head. Brijnok - the self-proclaimed First God - the god of battle, smiled at him, his scar making it look grotesque. Amadis often wondered why a god so vain about his weapons would not change his appearance. But then Amadis did not care a whit for the mind of Brijnok.

The battle god often attempted to trouble the great Amadis, pathetically trying to test him with words and gifts rather than facing him in battle. Although Amadis did not consider himself a god, nor did he wish to be, he still knew as Brijnok knew: that he could kill one if he wished. The more he considered Brijnok the angrier he became. Other gods remained in their heavens and protected the lands of their worshippers in return for the worship that they gave. But Brijnok did not, and in his vanity he claimed all lands. He walked the earth and meddled in the lives of fleshborn out of petty amusement. He would grant some poor farmer a great power and set him off on a murderous rampage just to celebrate in the carnage it would create. The guardian was his creature, offering similar gifts for the same results, and Brijnok was likely here to mock Amadis for turning down the white sword.

'Amadis, my brother,' Brijnok said. 'You offend me to think I would kill a man without cause.'

Must everyone call me brother this day? I have no brother.

'Do not call me brother and your mere presence is enough to offend me, Brijnok. Be gone before I finally kill you, or worse, before I throw you into one of Lae Noan's cells. This magic is older than even you, *First God*, and it will hold you without discrimination.'

The idea of a god trapped inside Lae Noan was one that pleased Amadis, but he would not become distracted by it. Lyat rose to his hands and knees then, and Amadis lifted his sword to order Brijnok to step back. The god of battle did so with a grin as Lyat the Destroyer of Armies stumbled weakly forward. Once Lyat was behind Amadis, the god spoke again.

'You intrigue me, Amadis, risking so much to come here. You refuse my guardian's gift, you decimate your power by travelling through the cuts, and you then risk capture into one of these cells that, as you have said, can hold anyone regardless of their... *supremacy.*'

He bowed in mockery as he spoke that last word. Amadis longed to speed forward and kill the god but he knew Brijnok would vanish the moment he attacked. He was also concerned about Aerath's absence. The man claiming to be an ice god would have to know of their presence, more so now that Brijnok had deemed to join them. But why did he not act? Did he fear the god of battle or did he belong to him?

'You risk more coming here, unarmed, as a vulnerable thing of flesh. Do you not fear this Aerath as the other gods must. Tell me, god of battle, where is Aerune while this Iceborn commits blasphemy?' Aerune was the real god of the moon and ice, while Aerath was the older name from the dead god of ages past. Brijnok's face darkened at the question though and Amadis became curious. 'You do not know, do you? The question of why Aerath's heresy is left unpunished is one beyond your heavenly omniscience.'

'Aerath is a man of flesh. Why should he concern the gods?' Brijnok tried but Amadis did not believe him. 'Why I bother concerning myself with you is a better question to ask. But perhaps I am here to watch this Aerath put an end to your arrogance. You have not been yourself lately, Amadis, have you? Are you seeing places that are not there? Remembering things that no longer exist?'

'You have done this to me!' Amadis threw the accusation wishing it were his blade, but as he formed the words, he knew they did not ring true. Brijnok was many things, but to kill an enemy by poison was abhorrent to him. He did not see pragmatism or cunning as a weapon as others did; Brijnok's weapons were never so subtle.

The scarred god laughed. 'You have done this to yourself. You have seen fit to become a tyrant to the world, in the pretence of ridding the world of others like you. You are not maintaining peace with your slaughter; you are only denying freedom, eliminating your competitors so that your rule may be eternal. And you claim to hate the gods. At least this Aerath has the honesty to proclaim his divinity, instead of denying it. Come, brother, claim your rightful place at my side, and we will slay all our adversaries together.'

Amadis's patience had run out. He did not care if Aerath was laying a trap here and that Brijnok was the bait. He could stomach no more time in the god's presence.

'Leave my sight now, Brijnok, or challenge me to battle.'

Amadis felt Lyat reposition himself behind him. His power would certainly aid in this fight, but there was the danger Lyat would bring down the mountain on top of them. If Brijnok fled to the heavens, would Amadis risk travelling the poisoned life-stream to follow? For every tyrant he killed in this world, there were always a thousand more with a willing ear for Brijnok's whisper. If he could finally remove the god, remove all the gods; then the world would be right. The echoes of that thought resonated from another age, when the great destroyer did just that. Memories flickered and vanished in his vision, and Amadis held back panic, praying that his mind would not leave him now. But to whom did he pray? The gods?

'Oh how loud the dog barks to the master that feeds him,' Brijnok said back with a sneer. 'You test my patience too far, brother. When Aerath feeds you to his mountain, do not think I will come to your aid.'

Amadis relaxed but kept his contempt fresh in his voice. 'I will not, as you clearly cower from this Aerath as much as you cower from me. Remember, First God, that you gave this power to us. You gave us this strength that you now tremble from with fear. Would that you never breached the heavens and cursed our world with gods again. I dream of a day where we return to a world without you.'

Brijnok did not lash back with further posturing as Amadis expected. His face did not curl up with the familiar snarl of disdain he had been the cause of so often. Instead there was a look of consideration upon the god of battle. When his eyes met Amadis's they seemed to be searching for something. Apparently he did not find whatever he had been looking for and then gave his mocking half-smile.

'Perhaps one day we shall indeed return to that time. But for now I wish you fortune in your endeavours. May all your enemies die screaming, brother.'

Brijnok vanished and left Amadis standing in a daze of lost memory. He had heard that saying before but from whom? Why did the battle god now mock him with it?

'Amadis,' Lyat said with urgency, 'the tunnels.'

Amadis turned and saw the shadows still dancing in his vision, gathering in greater numbers, the spectres of tormented souls lost to the mountain.

'You see them too?'

'Of course,' Lyat said, and frowned. 'Amadis, I know enough that Brijnok's tongue is his sharpest blade, but he spoke of your... changes. Will you tell me now, what has happened to you? Why you have become so distracted? Losing control, even with me?'

I am losing more than my control, Amadis thought. He looked earnestly at his friend but watched as a scar grew out of Lyat's mouth. It trailed a streak a white as it made its way through Lyat's beard and up over his ear. Brijnok's twisted smile looked back from Lyat's face and already Amadis's mind was falling too swiftly. He saw movement then from one of the tunnels, the flash of blond hair and white tunic of an Iceborn. The figure fled and Amadis would have dismissed it if Lyat's head had not shot in that direction also.

'I need to kill Aerath, Lyat, or all is lost.' It was the best he could give.

Lyat let out a long breath, deciding whether to demand more while Amadis was so weak. Venturing into this mountain risked more than life, and Lyat deserved the truth.

'I have never known an Iceborn to flee from anything,' Lyat said instead. 'He is leading us into a trap.'

'We must follow him.'

'I could destroy this mountain now and force him to come to us.'

'This mountain is sacred to the Prae'surlas. If we destroyed it, I would need to kill every last one of them before peace could return to the world.'

'More sacred than killing their new god?' Lyat countered.

'They can claim he ascended to the heavens, taking his ambitions to turn the world to ice with him.'

'Will they claim the same for us when we are swallowed by this mountain?'

'Come,' Amadis said, 'together, what enemy could defeat us?'

Lyat did not seem mollified but he followed loyally as Amadis ventured into the tunnel of ice. The phantoms began to fade and it was not long before they saw a corridor of cells stretch out before them, with sheets of blue ice acting as doors against the pure white of the walls. Amadis knew the doors were Prae'surlas magic layered on top the older power of the mountain. Any magic inside those cells would feed straight to the mountain, but the ice outside created sufficient barriers to anyone within, stripped of all their strength. They walked carefully down the tunnel, eyeing the empty cells without any doors of ice, and eyeing the small barred windows that had been given to those that did. One door interested Amadis, in that it had no window, but clearly the blue of ice rather than the white of the walls. It was curious they would create one cell with a prisoner so dangerous that not even a window was allowed. It was the empty ones that Amadis was wary of though, both that they could hide enemies and that they could take away everything from him. His mind was already trying to do that, but if he could just kill Aerath...

Three giants stepped out from empty cells ahead, all clad in pale blue tunics, with identical bright blond hair, frozen eyes, and all carried spears of ice. They were only Frostborn, a fragment of what power an Iceborn held, and Amadis knew they were merely a distraction. He looked around for Aerath, but Lyat took his gesture as a signal to act. The world dropped as Lyat released his power, all air and substance around them turning into a weight that could crush diamonds into dust. Every man was pressed to the ground, Amadis included, while only Lyat stood and then every cell of ice exploded under the force. The ceiling above shattered, revealing more corridors of prison cells above, and it was only when the ceiling above that began to give that Lyat reigned back his might. Lyat could not use his power in this place. It would bury him as quickly as it buried everything else.

Amadis threw his friend a meaningful look of displeasure, to make sure he did not try that again, before racing to his feet to finish off the three enemies. The Frostborns were also rising, but

Amadis moved with preternatural speed and was on top of them before they could strike out with full magic.

The first glow of blue ice was only beginning to shine from the lead Frostborn's hand, when Amadis promptly sliced it off with an upward strike. The Jaguar's touch made the Frostborn drop dead to the floor no matter how much power he might have previously held. The other two Frostborns were in so much shock at the sudden death of their comrade that they followed his fate without fight. The first received a downward cut along his face before Amadis reversed the hilt of his sword and slammed it through the ribs of the next.

All three were dead in an instant, but Amadis would not take any chances with Powerborn. With the exception of the Jaguar sword, no blade would kill them so easily. The power they were Connected with could heal flesh too quickly for a normal sword to be effective. Magic or power weapons were the only real possibilities, unless there was a small army of archers or pike men that could be used to give them too many wounds to deal with at once. So, keeping an eye for any prisoners that might try to flee now that Lyat had smashed every door, Amadis started cutting off heads. That was when he saw his mistake.

A giant Prae'surlas, dressed in white with blazing blue eyes, now stood behind Lyat. It was the Iceborn Aerath. The trap had been to remove Amadis from his friend's side, so Aerath could deal with them separately. Before Amadis could react, Aerath attacked and so too did Lyat the Destroyer of Armies. Their magics clashed in a blaze of white, but as Amadis's eyes could make out Aerath getting crushed into the ground beneath him, he could also see Lyat being blown into one of the open cells of Lae Noan.

Amadis sprinted forward immediately and through his eyes, time slowed to comprehend the speed of his movements. He could see the glow of white magic burst free from Aerath and expand out in a bubble of ice. The projection was creating a wall to contain Lyat within the cell but it was also to immobilise Amadis. He reached the bubble instantly, swinging his sword to cut up through the attack but, before it could hit him, the white bubble disappeared. Not caring what fortune granted this, Amadis sped over the threshold of magic and was on top of the Iceborn ready to pierce his skin with the Jaguar's blade. But as the white magic faded from sight, the sword swung to meet only air. The Iceborn was gone.

Amadis looked around and held his blade ready. He noticed tiny white flames spreading out in a circle in the crater beneath him, dissipating before they hit the edges. Did the Iceborn enter the life-stream? Powerborn could not do that.

Amadis prepared to smash through the prison cell to free Lyat but before he could, the corridor came alive as spears of ice fired out from every direction. Amadis's blade met each one as it was formed from the floor, the ceiling and walls, shattering each attack with a blinding speed as they tried to kill him. The assault was over as suddenly as it started, leaving the spears he had not smashed to create a web down the corridor in both directions, linking everything together in a tangle of ice. The new magic restricted his vision and Amadis paused for a moment, before breaking through enough to form a clearing. The clatter of ice it created was distracting but Amadis kept his senses sharp, and when the sound finished rebounding through the corridors, a frozen voice broke the silence.

'No one leaves Lae Noan,' Aerath said, his voice rich and deep, but with a sharp crack to every word as if a frozen lake was about to shatter. He appeared further down the corridor, the colour of his frame visible through the web of ice. 'Not even the great Amadis.'

'You are not the only one who can travel the life-stream, Aerath. I go where I will.'

Aerath smiled and it made his face look colder. The irises of his eyes glazed over with white now and his flesh glistened sharply as if he had recreated his entire body out of ice. For a giant, the sharpness made his face look gaunt, void of any meat that might make him human. Perhaps that was how he gained his power, whatever foul ritual he had undergone to forsake his soul, had drained him of life and replaced it with ice. But Amadis did not care. The only thing he cared about was the one rule he used to govern the world of flesh: *a thing must be flesh to exist in the world, and if a thing is flesh then it can be killed.*

'If you can leave as you please, then why do you not?' Aerath asked. There was a look in his dead eyes that seemed to want Amadis to try. Yes, there was the poisoned spectre of fire, but

Amadis also considered if Aerath had created a different trap: that if he tried to open a doorway to the life-stream, the mountain would swallow his power. Amadis did not think it was possible, more likely the Iceborn feared for his life and played games in an attempt to get Amadis to leave, to soak up more of the poison that was already killing him.

'Iceborn,' he said. 'I hold nothing but contempt for the gods, but what I find worse is a man of flesh walking our world and pretending he is one of them.'

'Then it is fortunate that I do not pretend,' Aerath said with a growing power in his voice. 'Kneel, mighty Amadis. Kneel before your god!'

Amadis dropped as an overwhelming power washed over him, and if he had not the Jaguar blade already in his hand, then his knees might actually have touched the ground. As it happened he slammed the blade down and pushed with every muscle in his body to stop the magic from debasing him. Amadis felt his jaw would crack from the rage he contained within as he slowly pushed himself back to a stand. The slightest squinting from the Iceborn's eyes told Amadis that he had shaken the man with his defiance. And that was all this Aerath was; just a man.

Amadis ran forward and crashed through every spear in his way, and they did not slow him. Aerath sent out rapid waves of white magic that weaved through the ice-web and the Jaguar blade ripped up through these as well as the spears without prejudice. Nothing Aerath did would slow Amadis's advance. He felt the floors try to grab him from underneath and saw the walls send down more spears of ice to pierce his skin, but none of it was fast enough or strong enough. Before Aerath could have the sense to register terror in his eyes, Amadis was upon him and slashed down with his sword of death. All the blade had to do was touch the Iceborn's skin and he would be no more. But instead of meeting flesh, the ancient black blade met an aura of energy surrounding Aerath.

It did not cut through the aura, but neither did it bounce off it either. Instead the speed and strength of the strike was caught in the protective power. It was like trying to cut through a raging current, but that river of power was not pushing the sword back. It was the blade that pushed steadily with every ounce of rage Amadis possessed fuelling its efforts. There was nothing that Aerath could do to stop it, because if he diverted any of his power from defending himself, to try to kill Amadis in return, then the Jaguar blade would slam straight down onto his flesh the moment he did. Equally it was only a matter of time before the blade reached its target so Aerath had nothing to lose in the attempt. Amadis did not care what he tried. He would be just as dead no matter what.

The Iceborn's eyes flared then with a sudden light and he was gone. Amadis's sword fell with such power that he was thrown off balance by his own force. Feeling open to assault he turned immediately to meet what would come but nothing did. The same white flames danced subtly along the floor where Aerath had been and Amadis snorted in contempt for the Iceborn's cowardice.

Amadis marched back down to free Lyat or to wait until the craven Iceborn appeared again. He passed empty cells and wondered why Aerath had bothered to create doors on them for Lyat to shatter. He spotted one door that had not shattered, but dismissed it as the shine from his sword caught his eye. Some of his critics would ask what power Amadis had if he did not have his blade. To these critics he laughed and said exactly that it was *his* blade, let them try and take it from him. The guardian had attempted that already and had the agony of nine deaths for his reward. Amadis idly noticed that the black of his ancient weapon looked more silver now as he walked down the corridor, the reflecting ice of the cells almost tarnishing its appearance, but he discarded the notion as more madness. Amadis flexed his fingers around the Jaguar's hilt in irritation of the cold inside the ice mountain. Rarely did he feel the cold. The world did not touch him as it did any other.

Realisation struck as Amadis looked once more at his sword. It was turning to ice. He almost dropped it in revulsion but gripped it harder instead.

'Aerath you coward! Come and fight me if you are truly a god!'

His fingers were freezing along with the sword they held. He should leave. Until he could follow Aerath into the life-stream, this fight would be meaningless, just as it would be with Brijnok, but how could he travel the life-stream until Aerath was destroyed? He clenched his fist harder and wanted to roar his frustration. He would not leave. He would not flee from any enemy, even if it meant killing Aerath with a sword of ice.

Suddenly his sword was almost pulled from his grasp as the ice in the walls called out to the ice of the sword. Amadis held onto the blade but that did not stop its tip from touching the wall. The ice warped out of the wall, wrapping itself around The Jaguar like a snake and Amadis had to rip it free with a snarl. His head spun around wildly, searching for his enemy but all he could see was white and blue staring back. The defining shapes of the cells and corridor merged as one, and Amadis was no longer standing in the mountain of Lae Noan.

'No!' he cried. His mind could not falter now.

Figures appeared in front of him and walked around as if made of mist. Their bodies drifted in and out of focus, with different parts appearing and disappearing. He was not in any place. There were no surroundings, only blank infinity in all directions. The urgency at which he needed to return to his reality, and the rage he felt at his mind's weakness, made it incredibly difficult to remain calm. Amadis closed his eyes and fought for strength.

'...make it sleep...'

Someone whispered to him but he did not open his eyes. Amadis concentrated on what was reality. He was in Lae Noan. He was battling an Iceborn named Aerath.

'...it should never have woken up...'

Amadis could feel the breath on his cheek of whoever it was whispering to him, but he did not know the voice and he did not open his eyes. He imagined it was the spectre of fire tormenting him once more but he needed to visualise the feel of his sword in his hand. He needed to leave whatever delusion his mind had forced upon him and return to Lae Noan. He needed to return and he needed to kill Aerath.

'It will destroy us all!'

The voice screamed in Amadis's ears and he snapped open his eyes to see a host of figures crowded around him. They had all stopped moving and were gathered to stare intensely at Amadis. A man missing both eyes was directly in front of him. A woman with bright green hair stood to his side. Another woman stood beside her with one half of her face withered with old age and the other half as youthful as a child. A man stood behind her and he had tear drops of skin flowing out in every direction from his eyes. More and more figures pressed in on him. Every one of them looked to him demanding action.

Amadis did not look back; instead he looked down to his hand and laughed out. He would show them action. Swinging his sword as hard as he could, Amadis was back in Lae Noan. The Jaguar sword sailed through empty air and cut deeply into the blue of a windowless cell door, one of only two left intact. One contained Lyat, but who was being held in the other? Amadis started to pull his blade free as the ice of the cell crawled out like a swarm of insects to swallow the black blade. He renewed his efforts with fresh urgency but before Amadis could free his sword, Aerath appeared again.

The Iceborn wasted no time, creating a spear of ice from his hand, and plunging it deep into Amadis's chest. Once inside his chest the ice from the spear shot out in every direction creating a thousand more wounds. Blood fled from his body freely and still Amadis did not let go of his sword. He tensed and pulled, resolved to make a final effort to free The Jaguar and put an end to Aerath. But the Iceborn created a second spear and drove that deep within too causing the same terrible injuries. A thousand more wounds burst free from inside his body and although his hand did not drop from his sword, all strength was gone from it.

The flesh of his body hung useless to the demands of his will and his power. He barely had the strength to move his eyes to regard Aerath. Who was this Iceborn that had defeated him? What manner of power had he come to possess that he could be the one to best Amadis Yeda? As if in answer to the unspoken question, Aerath smiled at what little life was left behind Amadis's eyes. Letting go of one of the spears, Aerath gestured towards the strange cell door without a window and slowly the ice at the top began to melt down. With agonising patience, Amadis held onto life, hoping he might still free his sword if the ice melted enough, or at least witness what might be the mystery of Aerath's unexplained power. As the ice drifted downward he could see the shape of a man begin to form. First the hair and then the face but as the figure inside saw the ice unravel, he suddenly rushed forward for freedom. Aerath sealed up the cell door in an instant.

Amadis watched as more and more ice was created to barricade that figure inside. Then he turned and looked at Aerath once more. He was only left with more questions by the strange revelation and his mind trudged through what he had seen but it did not make sense. The figure that was held within the cell: was Aerath himself.

It had not simply been a man that looked exactly like Aerath; it *was* Aerath. Amadis's eyes still had enough power in them to know for certain that it was. But what did it mean? If the Iceborn was about to open his mouth to explain, then he did not hear it. Amadis made one final attempt to free his blade, the effort costing him all of what little strength he had left, but Aerath's spears burst free instead, striking out with a thousand new blades to shred his flesh. The attack was enough to finally force Amadis's hand to drop from his blade and the last thing he saw were the spears of ice becoming serpents, dragging him backwards into a cell. Then everything vanished, as the great Amadis Yeda was swallowed by the mountain.

CHAPTER FOUR

The future

'Amadis is dead! Dallid, did you hear?'

It was always the case where you could hear Thisian before you saw him.

'The sun god sees you, Thisian. How did he die this time?'

'You don't believe me? This time it's the truth!'

Dallid barked a laugh and continued packing what supplies he would need for the journey ahead. He was in his cabin, with most of his things readily arranged by his sleeping pallet. Thisian walked into his chambers without waiting for an invitation.

'The last time, Thisian, when Amadis was turned into a magician's puppet; it was the truth,' Dallid recalled. 'The time before that, when Amadis was eaten by a Jhakral; it was the truth. What was the time before that one? The Prae'surlas claiming to have him in their mountain? The Ihnhaarat burying him under a thousand feet of earth? Or in the ocean? Well whatever it was, Thisian; it was the truth.'

'If you think it's more important, Dallid, to make jokes than be told about news that will change the world, then that's your decision. But you can beg me all you want now and I won't tell you what really happened.'

'Fureath'i do not lie, Thisian,' Dallid explained, still with his back to him. 'And what you have just said, is a lie.'

'That Amadis is dead? But I've told you it's the truth this time!'

'No, Thisian, not that - although I'm sure that's also a lie - but what I meant is that you're going to tell me no matter what I say or do. You're incapable of not talking.'

'Well you can go burn your balls off if you think I'm telling you after that!'

Dallid didn't reply. He just waited. Returning his mind to his task, it was difficult to pack for a journey when you didn't know the route. Phira would choose their path and Dallid couldn't decide how she would decide. It was likely she would opt for the fastest course to Rath'Nor and so they would be going through the mountains, followed by the foothill deserts. It was equally likely though that she would chose to go by tour of the border forts, familiarising herself with each of the fortifications and their commanders along the way. That route would keep them in the forests almost all the way to Rath'Nor.

Phira was impossible to predict and try as he might, Dallid would not be able to get a direct answer from her. She would think it a game of mental capability to make him pack appropriately without knowing where she would lead them. He hated her sometimes because of those games, but he was allowed to hate her; she was his wife after all.

'I know what you're thinking, Dallid. You're thinking if you stay quiet long enough then I will tell you what happened, but not this time.'

Dallid just laughed again and could only imagine the contrived look of outrage on Thisian's face. He continued packing. Then a thought occurred and he finally turned around to face his friend. Much taller than most Fureath'i, Thisian also had wide shoulders and wiry arms - which were now crossed angrily in front of his chest. A frown lined the golden skin of his face, a face that Thisian considered to be the most beautiful in the land - male or female - under his gloriously long black hair (which was styled all to one side). Thisian was doing his very best to appear very serious indeed.

'Did Phira tell you what route we're taking to Rath'Nor?'

'What? No. But why wouldn't we be following the River Midanna all the way?'

'Probably because that route is neither the quickest way nor the best use of her time.'

Thisian cringed dramatically. 'Why? Why can't she just pick the easiest flaming route and let us enjoy the last flaming days of our flaming freedom before we lose it all forever to the flaming army!'

Dallid gave Thisian a quick frown for his over-use of the word flaming.

'Well you have two flaming options there, Thisian. You can challenge Phira to the right to lead the group, or you can challenge

Yiran and Lord Chrial'thau about our entire Fureath'i way of life so we wouldn't have to join the army at all.'

'Two great options, Dallid, both likely to get me killed quicker than actually joining the army. But why didn't Phira-bloody-almighty tell you what route we're taking?'

'Because she was too busy telling me about how Lyat the Destroyer of Armies suddenly appeared down south of the Amalgamation and killed Amadis the Powerful in front of everyone watching.'

The look of shock and disappointment on Thisian's face was worth a hundred days of uncomfortable travel to come.

'How did she -'

'How did she manage to tell everyone the news before you could? Well, Thisian, Phira actually rises with the dawn, like every other sun-worshipping Fureath'i does - except for you. So just think of it, not only could you have not insulted our god, but if you had gotten up when Frehep wanted you to, then you might have had everyone attending to your every word. As it happens I might even believe it this time, but Amadis has been dead before and it is never true. Phira got the news from Yiran. Where did you hear it?'

'Ryat,' he said, still sulking, but he snapped back to himself quickly. 'You would think Phira should have more important things to concern herself with than spreading rumours about Foreign warriors.'

This made Dallid laugh more than anything else. He was definitely enjoying his morning. 'I thought the rumour was complete truth this time, Thisian? And since when is Amadis the Powerful just a Foreign warrior? He's been the unofficial ruler of the world outside of Furea for as long as we've lived, and with him gone to enforce order who knows what will happen. All kinds of idiotic Foreigners might think it a good idea to attack our borders now, so by the time we reach Rath'Nor to enlist, we could be coming straight back here as part of the army to fight.'

'Yes, well, look, none of that matters right now. Ryat didn't just tell me about Amadis, he also wanted me to get the four of us together so he and Yiran can wish us farewell. That's why I'm really here.'

Dallid looked down at his pack, still not complete, and sighed.

'I'll just have to finish this evening.'

Phira wanted them to leave tomorrow morning the moment the light hit the sky. Frehep was the Fureath'i god of the sun and fire, and his rebirth every morning was a holy time. It was the only time such a journey could begin so they would need to be up and ready to go before the dawn arrived. He wanted to dedicate more time to his packing, to impress his wife and her challenge, but he could not keep Yiran or Ryat waiting.

Ryat was Thisian's grandfather, often called Ryat the Large for his impressive girth. He had a few songs and Tellings about his time in the army, and then came back to their village to serve as an elder when he retired. Ryat was a good teacher and a good warrior but Yiran was an entirely different case.

Yiran had no family, having joined the Fureath'i army at the age of twelve - four years earlier than anyone was ever allowed to join - but he retired in their home village of Coruln because he had become friends with Ryat during their time in the army. Yiran was far better known as: Yiran the Unconquered, perhaps the single greatest fleshborn warrior the Fureath'i have ever had. His songs and Tellings were without end and even after years of being trained by him, Dallid and his friends were very uncomfortable in his presence - apart from Phira.

Thisian opened his mouth to say something, but then seeing Dallid's difficulty in packing, he stopped and grinned instead. 'You know, Dallid, a true Fureath'i needs only the fire in his heart and a sabre in his hand. There is no need to bring anything else.'

'Oh and that's all you'll be bringing is it? Nothing but a sword? So I suppose you'll not even be wearing clothes or riding on a horse tomorrow when we go?' Dallid was joking of course, but that wasn't the answer to Phira's challenge, was it? It had better not be.

Thisian grabbed his balls at that idea. 'Why would you even joke about riding on a horse naked? Can you imagine how painful that might be? But no, I have to keep my clothes on. It's only fair to any females we might pass. Even Phira wouldn't be able to concentrate if she could see what she's missing. Don't forget, you are the shortest Fureath'i in our history, Dallid.'

He managed to dodge out of the way of Dallid's punch with a grin, and then turned to run out of the cabin when Dallid followed it up with a kick. Suppressing a curse, Dallid followed his hilarious friend outside. Just because Thisian was as lanky as an ice-giant, did not mean that Dallid was short. Well, yes he was short, and no there was not anyone in his village fully grown that was shorter but there were many millions of Fureath'i in the lands of Furea. Dallid was certain there would be many that were shorter. And he would be very happy when he finds one.

Rolling his shoulders and wishing he had connected with that punch, Dallid re-affirmed that whatever he may lack in height, he made up for in strength and muscle. His chest, his shoulders, and his arms were all much larger and heavier than anyone else in the village. Well apart from Yiran, but Yiran was a living legend and did not need to be compared. Giving his shoulders one last roll, Dallid set out at a run after Thisian.

His short legs were still able to catch up to Thisian's longer, lazy ones and Dallid only tried one more time to kick his friend before they relaxed into a walk. If Ryat and Yiran wanted to see all four of them, then they would have to find Phira and Kris. Dallid was confident he could find his wife in one of a few locations but Kris was a different matter. He was often very strange and preferred to be away from other people when at all possible. So that meant he could be anywhere at all in the miles of forest that surrounded them. Dallid and Thisian kept a look out between the trees as they walked to the village.

'I reckon he'll be busy killing everyone he's been thinking about killing for the last couple of years. Today might be his last chance after all.'

Dallid considered it. 'Well, in that case we could just stay still and he'll find us to kill you, right?'

A look of worry passed over his friend's face and he was thankfully silent for a time. Dallid shook his head again. Kris was definitely strange - and he could be murderously violent, there was no argument there - but he was not the lunatic killer Thisian made him out to be. In the few years Dallid had known Kris, he had found him to be a loyal and honourable friend. There was undoubtedly a dark, vicious side to him, but in Dallid's opinion he kept it under control. There had only been sporadic instances where that control lapsed over the years, too few to even comment upon if they had not been so memorable. But unfortunately each time that control did lapse it had been excessively memorable, even traumatising to any who witnessed. Dallid did not like to think on such things.

'It would be quicker if we just went to find Phira, and left Kris alone,' Thisian offered. 'He prefers being alone anyway right? And Phira should be easy to find. We only need to go to Yiran's cabin and she'll probably be on her back with her legs in the air, giving him one last rut before we leave for the army!'

This time Dallid did connect with his punch. He had been expecting the comment, it was such an old joke of Thisian's by now, and he had planned accordingly. Thisian tried to dodge away as he laughed, but Dallid aimed low to his kidneys instead of high to his big laughing face. The blow to the kidneys dropped the gangly fool quicker than a shot to the jaw would have anyway. Thisian grabbed his side and moaned.

When Phira was younger she had trouble with her family, and Yiran had adopted her under his care. She had become his only family from that moment onward and he had become hers too. Their relationship was very close and their constant proximity to each other was the main reason Phira became as great a warrior as she did, Yiran often proclaiming that she was far better than even him. Dallid did not doubt it but he found their bond troubling. When he married Phira, he did not realise he would have to share her with another man. There was nothing sexual in Phira's relationship with Yiran, but that did not change how close they were to one another. It was a source of private pain for Dallid and a source of public hilarity for Thisian.

'I can only wait, Thisian, until the day that Phira hears you making one of those jokes. She'll do more than punch you, I can tell you that.'

Thisian got up and stretched his torso to ease the pain of the blow. 'More? Do you think she'd rut me too after she was finished with Yiran?'

He jumped away again as soon as he said it, and Dallid should have known better than to react. Thisian would mock Frehep himself if he was bored enough that he needed the entertainment. The sun god or any of his walking-blood Powerborn could burn Thisian to a crisp for hearing it, but Thisian would die laughing.

There was a Fureath'i saying that if you could not eat it, drink it, kill it, or rut it, then burn it. Thisian had his own alteration, getting rid of the "eat, kill and non-alcohol drink" parts of it, leaving just: *if you cannot drink it, mock it or rut it, then rut it.*

'Dallid, I apologise,' Thisian said solemnly. 'You have enough pain in your life being married to her. I should not add to your misery with mockery.'

'Listening to you say anything at all causes me pain, Thisian, not just the mockery.'

'Now it is your turn to wound me. My voice is as beautiful as the rest of me and you know it.'

'On that point we'll agree but I don't think we have the same meaning behind it.' Thisian's voice was about as beautiful as a horse shitting in your ear.

'That's alright, Dallid, I know what your idea of beauty is; after all, I have seen your wife.'

Thisian was poised and ready for flight but Dallid remained calm. He would try a new tactic instead.

'That reminds me, Thisian, of a tale Phira told me only recently. She told me that when you were both thirteen summers, you took out your cock and asked her to marry you.'

'That's a lie!'

'And she answered you by grabbing your balls and nearly twisting them off to make sure you fully understood the strength of her rejection.'

'That never happened!'

'So what I think is you constantly mock her because you're deeply and secretly in love with her.' Now it was Thisian's turn to swing for Dallid and Dallid's turn to dodge back with laughter. 'Aha, it's true then!'

'It is the furthest thing that has ever been from truth and you know it! Dallid, for the love of Frehep and all the Foreign gods outside our lands, do not say such a thing again. If people started thinking that then how could I ever mock her again? Say that I'm in love with Kris before that woman. Burn my balls, Dallid, that's going too far.'

Dallid enjoyed some peaceful silence for the next few minutes as they walked. Thisian would need time to decide what he could say now that Dallid would twist his words into devotion to Phira. Why had he never thought of this before? Embracing the quiet harmony, Dallid's eyes wandered through the trees and admired the rays of light that found their way through. There was little to see but that did not mean he should not look. It could be the last day he ever saw the forests of his home and he should be memorising them. Thisian would say that trees were trees, but to Dallid these were *his* trees. He followed a ray of light up to the sky and then spotted glimpses of the ancient stone structure through the leaves. The great Tower of Frehep would need no memorising. It was one of the marvels of the world.

It was mostly hidden from where he now walked, but the great tower loomed over everything near his village. The surrounding huts and cabins were called Coruln, which Phira had told him was not part of the Fureath'i language at all. Instead she said it was ancient battle scrit and it meant "the guarded shadow." Dallid was not sure if that meant the village was founded originally to protect the tower from its shadow, or that the tower's shadow protected the village, but he could guess which one it meant now. The Tower of Frehep had always housed a Powerborn. Usually it was even a Fireborn, one of the strongest types of Powerborn. But recently the tower was home to Lord Chrial'thau, the strongest of them all.

Tellings and imaginings began to form inside Dallid's mind, seeing the warrior of fire vanquishing numberless enemies, but the sound of steel clashing against steel broke him from his reverie. Dallid and Thisian headed off the path without saying anything, towards where the combat was coming from. There would not be Foreign raiders so deep into Fureath'i territory so the sound was not alarming, and there were few enough villagers who would have the freedom at that time of day to engage in swordplay. The youths would be working and the elders would be instructing them, so if there were two people practicing swordplay then it would be Kris and Phira.

Soon enough they came into view by the stream and as soon as he saw them both in action, Dallid had to stop and watch. Thisian frowned at their halt but even he had to admit such a fight was worth viewing. He did not think it was anything like a blood-fight, but it certainly did not look like any sparring match. Kris was stripped to the waist and fought with a crazed strength that made him look like he wanted to kill Phira. And Phira fought with a speed that made her look like she could kill Kris at any moment of her pleasing.

'I'll wager you the middle watch tomorrow night that Kris will take her this time,' Thisian whispered.

'Phira will win,' Dallid said back. 'She always wins.'

Kris was much stronger than Phira. Although not as tall as Thisian and not as wide as Dallid, Kris looked like a man made entirely of muscle. There was no size or meat to him that would make him look strong while wearing clothes, but bare-chested as he was now, he looked like he had never known rest or relaxation in his entire life; it looked like he just spent his full life training and working. Knowing Kris there was a likely chance he did do just that. Dallid did not think Kris even slept.

Phira on the other hand looked almost fragile in everything but her face. Her body was slim and quick, her clothes hiding all the tight muscle Dallid knew she had, but there was a hardness around her eyes and cheeks that spoke of the strength she possessed. She had light brown hair that was tied tightly and ran inside her clothes down her back so it would not hinder her movements. She moved so quickly it was as if she anticipated Kris's every motion before he made it.

Enjoying the show, Dallid sat down and stretched back, thinking about their last night together in the village. They would have the long journey to Rath'Nor tomorrow but it would be with Kris and Thisian so there would be little privacy. Once they reached the fortress then, it was custom for the marriages of youth to be disbanded. Soldiers were expected to show commitment to their country and nothing else. It also allowed all warriors to take pleasure with whoever they wanted as it was likely they would die sooner rather than later. Dallid and Phira had decided not to disband their marriage. They would try as best they could but Dallid knew the army would take them in different directions very quickly. Phira was destined for command and greatness, Dallid was destined to die at the end of a Prae'surlas spear. But they would have their last night, and Dallid let himself enjoy those more pleasant thoughts.

'Dallid, I want to apologise for all those jokes about Phira earlier.'

He turned to his friend and raised an eyebrow, suspicious.

'Is this a trade so that I don't humiliate you in front of her and Kris with tales of your forbidden love?'

Thisian pressed his mouth together to hold back some clever retort and to Dallid's surprise, he remained serious. 'No, but you and I need to stick together.'

'We do?'

'Yes. Look at those two.'

Dallid looked and saw them continue to batter each other with sweat rolling down them both. Kris was attacking again and Phira was avoiding his blows, throwing him off balance every time she did. It was only a matter of time before she ended it. He turned back to Thisian.

'And?'

'Well look at how they've decided to spend their last day of freedom? If we don't bloody stick together then they'll have us training and working all the flaming way to Rath'Nor. If we don't work together, Dallid, to upset their every plan, then how in the name of Frehep are we supposed to enjoy ourselves?'

'For a moment there I thought you were going to suggest we follow their example and become better Fureath'i,' Dallid said but understood his meaning. Both Phira and Kris were going to thrive within the army. They would be promoted to rank within weeks and Dallid and Thisian would remain as simple warriors without notice. Even though they were all trained by Yiran the Unconquered, Dallid had lived so much of his life with Phira that he could never see himself as anything but ordinary.

'Become better Fureath'i?' Thisian scoffed. 'I'm already the best looking Fureath'i in the world, how much better am I supposed to get?'

At least Thisian had that delusion to hold onto, Dallid thought glumly. He went back to watching his wife fight, and when he saw her turn her sword subtly in her wrist, he knew it was about to end.

'A full night's watch that Phira will win,' he said to Thisian suddenly. His friend eyed the fight sceptically trying to see why

Dallid was so certain but all he saw was Kris continue to hammer relentless assaults.

'Done,' he said with a nod and the moment he spoke the words, Phira spun and slashed Kris across the stomach. The scantest trace of blood showed from the hit, but it was enough to finish their fight. Dallid turned to revel in his victory and saw Thisian with a broad smile of his own. 'Look,' he said, pointing down to Phira.

Both fighters had stopped. Kris was inspecting the expert cut across his stomach, knowing that Phira could have killed him if she had less control. But Phira was also touching the side of her neck, looking at the red that came away with her hand. It looked like Phira might've killed Kris with her spin, but while she did it Kris had killed her with his cut to the neck.

In one way it meant that the sparring match was not over, since a winner had not been cleanly decided. But in another, much more dangerous way, Dallid knew that the fight was absolutely over.

'There is going to be trouble,' he said.

'Why?' Thisian asked. 'Because now that Kris has seen his own blood he'll want to see everyone else's in the village? I'm telling you, Dallid, there is a thin film of nothing holding that lunatic back from slaughtering us all in our sleep. But at least he's going to win me a full night's sleep for tomorrow night!'

Dallid did not even bother frowning at Thisian. He was too busy staring at the expression on Phira's face. She was smiling and although he could not fully hear her words, he imagined that she congratulated Kris on a well-placed strike. But what Dallid knew she was thinking was that Kris was now going to pay dearly for even that slight defeat he had given her.

'I'll wager you now, Thisian, that by the time it takes you to list off all nine Masks of Moi'dan, Phira will have beaten Kris unconscious. I'll even wager a full week's watch.'

'If you say so,' Thisian said and then immediately began reciting each of the famed masks, its name, its appearance and what power each one held beneath. Phira took the same instant to lunge forward, circle her sword around Kris's own and cut into the hand to make him drop his sabre. She followed up by butting him in the face with the handle of her sword and it took three strikes to knock the man from his feet. Thisian was on his forth mask when he stopped to curse.

'Burn Frehep's flaming balls! He can go rut the moon for all the luck he's bloody given me today!'

Thisian's cursing continued to escalate but Dallid grinned and ignored him as Phira spotted them. She waved and turned her palm before lifting and shouting out the sun-god's greeting. Dallid was about to return the gesture when he broke into a curse of his own. Kris was getting back up.

'You have to knock him unconscious, Phira!' he shouted down in a hurry. The shout unfortunately got Thisian's attention too though and, with a laugh, cut his abuse of the gods short, launching straight back into Moi'dan's masks of power.

Dallid got up and ran down to his wife who was just looking at him with confusion. He agreed that it might have looked odd, that he was roaring at her to knock their friend unconscious while Thisian shouted down a recitation of Foreign folklore. But he did not have time to explain himself. 'Kick him in the face, Phira, quick!'

Phira turned to see if Kris was about to throw a knife at her or something else as urgent, but the man was just groggily shaking sense back into his head and trying to get up. When he looked like he was becoming coherent again, Dallid could see that Kris might also think it odd that Dallid was shouting for Phira to crack open his skull. The absurdity of the situation finally outweighed the urgency of it, as Thisian shouted his final mask loud enough for everyone to hear it.

'...and one to blunt all weapons that may attack him. In the shape of a blade it stands on the mask, because with it all other blades and their users become useless!'

Dallid stopped his run and let out a long breath. Phira walked calmly up to him, while still eyeing Kris with suspicion. When her eyes took in the delighted form of Thisian still up by the tree line, she assumed Dallid's moment of madness had been born of some childish nonsense.

'Should I ask?' she offered at least.

Dallid just shook his head. An entire week's watch... he rethought his plans for his last night with Phira and wondered should he spend it storing up sleep instead. His wife wrapped her arms around his neck and kissed him. She was warm and breathing heavy, and there was sweat flowing onto her lips where she kissed him, but it tasted of Phira. Dallid loved every part of it and there was no amount of sleepless nights ahead that would stop him from spending this one with her.

Kris stood up, his face bloodied and swollen from where Phira had smashed her sword into it, and he staggered over to them. He was clenching his fist over and over, but there seemed no anger in it. It looked like he was just testing how badly Phira had injured his wrist. Dallid moved away from their embrace all the same. He did trust Kris, but a warrior was always ready to fight.

'The sun god sees you, Dallid,' Kris said formally.

'The sun god sees you too, Kris. You fought well.'

'As Phira will point out, the only one left alive to enjoy a good fight is the one that wins it.'

He did not smile as he said the words, and neither did he look like he held any resentment towards his loss. Kris could be very strange to judge when it came to how he felt about things. Phira was smiling though. It was clear to see at least she was extremely pleased with her win. It could have just as easily been a loss if Kris's cut to the neck had hit and hers to the stomach had not. Thisian ran down to join them and was sure to remind Dallid of his own recent loss.

'The sun gods see you, Phira, Kris,' he said with unexpected formality. 'He sees you, Phira, with great control to not injure our good friend Kris here too badly and he sees you, Kris, with great determination to be sure and stay conscious no matter how many times Phira smashed you in the face.'

Kris looked at him blankly. He would be forgiven for not understanding Thisian's odd words but to Dallid he just looked like he did not care. Phira looked deeper into Thisian's strange praise, and it was a look of mistrust.

'If you think you might do better, Thisian,' Phira said. 'I am happy to spar with you.'

Thisian laughed as if it was the funniest thing anyone had ever said in the world. 'Good gods no. You would want to be completely out of your mind to raise a sword against you, Phira. No offence intended, Kris.'

Dallid doubted that. Thisian was highly convinced that Kris was indeed completely out of his mind and that every moment of sunlight people survived in his presence was a thing to be celebrated.

Phira snorted her opinion of Thisian's refusal. 'For a man who has claimed to father so many children, Thisian, you would think you'd have a pair of balls hanging down between those legs.'

'It's exactly that I've fathered so many children that my balls must have disappeared, Phira. A man only has so much seed so they're just shrunken and empty right now.'

'It's funny that you've brought up the topic of Thisian's balls though,' Dallid added with a smile. 'Kris, have I ever told you a tale of when Phira and Thisian were thirteen summers old -'

'Yiran!' Thisian shouted to interrupt Dallid's fine Telling, and all three youths turned to see the legend actually walking into view. He was leaving the same path Dallid and Thisian had used earlier, and as he walked into the clearing towards the stream, Ryat emerged with him. It was odd that they had not waited for the four of them to come, but knowing Thisian, Ryat could have given him the charge of summoning them at dawn, only for Thisian to act on it hours later.

Both men were large for Fureath'i, Ryat being large of belly for any race, and so it was not before they had come several steps forward that Dallid could see another smaller figure walking behind them. The smaller figure was an old man with bone white hair hanging long to his shoulders. He looked thin and frail but walked with a perfect posture and a strong stride. Dallid was able to take in one other important feature before he dropped to his knees in reverence; the elder wore the red and yellow flamed tunic of a Fireborn. It was Lord Chrial'thau.

Kris and Phira followed Dallid as soon as they spotted the lord, and even Thisian jumped down and pressed his head to the dirt with immediate respect. The great Fireborn rarely left his tower and Dallid had never seen him before, despite living so close for all his life. He dared not look at him again and Dallid closed his eyes tight as he waited for them to arrive. It could have been his mind playing with his senses but, as he waited, it felt like the sun was shining brighter on his back and neck. The sensation on his skin grew with each step the great Fireborn must have been taking towards them.

'Rise.'

The voice did not belong to Yiran or Ryat, but neither should it belong to a man who looked so old. No, he was not a man, he was the closest thing to a walking god within Furea and he had a voice that suited such a title. Dallid wanted nothing more than to stay where he was and not be seen, but the command had power in it and he was obliged to obey.

One by one the four of them rose, although still with their heads bowed low. Dallid would not risk darting his eyes upward in case they found Chrial'thau staring back. Some of the discomfort was eased by Yiran, only slightly, when he said,

'Frehep's mercy, Kris, what have you done to your face?'

Kris remained silent. Yiran was as highly ranked as any fleshborn could ever hope to achieve, but in the presence of a Powerborn, none of them could speak or move unless they were given his permission. Knowing this, Lord Chrial'thau did his best to allow them to relax.

'For this day, young warriors, you may be at ease in my presence. Speak and act as you would with each other.'

Dallid hoped to every flame of Frehep that Thisian would not take up that offer. It was Phira who spoke first though.

'You honour us too greatly, my lord,' she said. 'We are not worthy to even stand in your company.'

'Do not make me repeat my offer,' Chrial'thau replied.

Somehow, that forceful reminder of his generous concession that they could relax, did very little to make anyone relax. Dallid wanted more than ever to prostrate himself to the dirt until the great Fireborn was gone. Movement to his left made Dallid almost want to turn his head and look, but he did not. From what little he could see though, it seemed as if Phira had obeyed Chrial'thau's command, and was actually standing up straight. Dallid hoped she was not looking the Lord Fireborn in the eye. If Chrial'thau felt she was being disrespectful to him then her career within the army would be finished. No amount of training or talent would help her.

Yiran cleared his throat. 'Let me introduce the four young warriors that we have trained, Lord Chrial'thau. Together they will bring a new age to our great nation, and individually they are among the finest Fureath'i I have ever had the privilege to know.'

Those were extremely kind words. Did he forget that Thisian and Dallid were standing in front of him also?

'This is Thisian,' Yiran announced to answer Dallid's doubts. 'The grandson of Ryat the Large. He has a good height and uses his reach well when in combat. This one's mind is sharp and from what I hear, my lord, he has done his Fureath'i duty extremely well.'

Dallid could not believe how causally Yiran was speaking to Lord Chrial'thau. Thisian's Fureath'i duty was to sire at least four children before reaching army age, and by all accounts - but mainly Thisian's - he had fathered at least forty. Why would Yiran mention something like that to a Lord Fireborn of all people!

'This is Dallid,' he continued. 'The grandson of Derrin the Heart. He has received much of the same fire in his heart that his grandfather was known for and he has arms strong enough to take both myself and Ryat on at once.'

He noted that Yiran did not detail how badly Dallid would lose if he took both of them on at once. Still though, he was pleased at the words about his grandfather.

'This then is Kris, if you can see him under all that blood and bruising. His grandfather was Kirit Fureath'i. He has exceptional talent in explosive fighting and has an even greater strength in the will power he uses to keep it under control.'

Little was known of Kris's grandfather Kirit. The two of them had lived alone for most of their lives in a cabin so well hidden that none of the villagers even knew it was there.

'And finally we have Phira, granddaughter to Yiran. Now here, my lord is our future. She has already surpassed my skill with a blade and I have never had her talent for strategy or tactics. She will be our nation's greatest leader in years to come and if he was not already dead, she would be dangerous enough to kill Amadis himself.'

Yiran finished his grand words, and Dallid knew each of his friends had to be swelling with just as much pride as he was feeling. Ryat remained silent, perhaps not comfortable in speaking around a Lord Fireborn, but the fact the words had come from Yiran the Unconquered, and that they had been spoken to Lord Chrial'thau, it was a great thing.

Chrial'thau remained silent too during each Telling and Dallid could feel that all four young warriors waited anxiously to hear his opinion of them. When he spoke though, it was not to them.

'I would not be so quick, Yiran, to accept the death of Amadis Yeda. He is neither Powerborn nor god. He is something entirely different. When we first fought, new powers would emerge for him as each new threat to his life was considered. Whatever he may be, he is certainly not dead.'

Yiran cleared his throat again. His displeasure at Chrial'thau's dismissal of the four fleshborn warriors poorly masked. 'Whether he is dead or not, my lord, in his absence the world will change. And helping our great country stand ready against that change will be these young warriors. Perhaps a few words of encouragement from you would spark their fires brighter for the journey to come.'

'Very well,' Chrial'thau agreed. 'The sun god sees you, young warriors. May he see you killing Prae'surlas.'

With that the Lord Fireborn left, and Yiran motioned for Ryat to accompany him. It had been the barest of formal farewells and yet coming from a Fireborn, it still felt exhilarating. Perhaps after Yiran's unexpected words, Dallid had been hoping for more but he was foolish to expect anything from a being of power like Chrial'thau. Chrial'thau had fought at Frehep's side when the creation of power had torn the world to war. And now as Frehep reigned over them as their god in the heavens, Chrial'thau walked among them as his equal on earth. As much as Yiran might have appeared displeased at Chrial'thau's courtesy, he showed no inclination now.

'Few fleshborn will ever be offered the opportunity to stand in the presence of a Fireborn. Fewer still will ever have the great Chrial'thau wish them fortune on their futures. I hope that this day will burn bright in your memories for years to come and fuel you all to greatness within the army. With such sentiment in mind, Phira, I would like to offer you a parting gift.'

Yiran reached behind his back and pulled out a slender sword that Dallid did not even see strapped there. It was not thick and curved like a Fureath'i sabre; it was long and slender, with only the smallest of hilts guarding the handle. Yiran's large frame made the blade look weak by comparison but when Phira wrapped her fingers around the grip it took on a much more dangerous edge. Her eyes were wide with excitement as she slipped the sheath slowly down the sword, and when free, she turned her new weapon over and over causing the sun to glare into Dallid's eyes. The type of blade was like the katana the Mordec used, it had longer reach and more versatility than the Fureath'i sabre, but it was not as strong. In Phira's hands though, that did not matter.

'I received it as a gift from Aevad during my time spent there. My name is engraved on the blade but it is yours now. I know it will bring our nation great glory in your hands, Phira.'

Kris moved closer to admire the gift as Phira and Yiran started discussing the advantages and disadvantages of the different kind of sword. Thisian took the opportunity to move closer to Dallid.

'Do you think being Yiran the Unconquered's adopted granddaughter, being highly trained in everything he knows and can do, and now walking around with a sword with his name bloody written on it, will affect how quickly Phira-bloody-almighty rises through the ranks of the army?'

Dallid frowned. 'Phira was always destined for greater things than us, Thisian. There is no-one that has worked harder these last few years.'

'Apart from Kris, I don't think he even sleeps,' Thisian pointed out. 'All I am saying is that we need to stick together now more than ever. Those two will be promoted in charge of people like us within days, and I don't care which of them you're rutting, Dallid, they will order you to die as quickly as every other warrior of limited ability. So if we're not always there for each other, to help us gain whatever advantage we can, then we are ash.'

Dallid said nothing and watched his wife. As Thisian whispered to him his fears, Phira was already ignoring him for excited discussions with Kris and Yiran. He had always known she was too great for him. But it did not matter how well prepared he was for the idea; the reality forming in front of him still melted his heart.

'You are right, my friend,' he said placing a hand on Thisian's shoulder. 'If we do not remain together, then we will die nameless and forgotten. We will never leave each other's side.'

Thisian returned the gesture and placed his hand on Dallid's shoulder. 'It is good to know. But I wouldn't say *never* leave each other's side, after all how else am I to sleep while you're enjoying your week's worth of guard duty!'

Dallid kicked out and managed to catch Thisian in the thigh before he danced away laughing, and at the motion Phira's eyes turned to him. He met her gaze and they smiled at each other. Their love might still be enough. No-one could say for certain what the future would bring.

• CHAPTER FIVE •

Waste

'I should have never left Dallid.'

Thisian found himself grumbling a lot more these days, and that sentiment reflected the heart of all of it. It was five years since he made his pact with Dallid to never leave each other, and four of those years had been gloriously filled with witty conversation, dazzling swordplay, drunken debauchery with even drunker women - and Dallid had been there to watch Thisian enjoy it all. Together there had been no end to their amused lifestyle, no insult left unspoken, no face left un-punched, no day left un-lived. Then Kris became an ember class and Phira-bloody-almighty became a bloody blaze commander, so suddenly Dallid wanted to get serious about his career in the army. That meant no more good times with Thisian, oh no, Dallid transferred to a new squad, so Thisian picked a new one too; one as far away from Dallid, Kris and Phira-bloody-almighty as he could, to the eastern border forts.

For some reason, Thisian thought it would be wildly interesting living at the frontier - a land ripe with peril and adventure; a land where heroes could be born! But with endless stretches of empty land to all sides, Thisian revised his thought that this was a land where heroes could only be bored. It was five years since Amadis died - the latest rumour saying that he tried to shave himself with his Jaguar sword - and the whole world had broken into chaos and war, full of excitement and glory at every turn, but not here at the border forts, and certainly not on look-out duty. How was Thisian ever to gain fortune and fame - to inspire wild Tellings that would have women kneeling at his feet, their mouths dropped open with awe and ready to be put to good use - if all his squad leader had him do was stand still and do nothing, watching more nothing stand still. Madness!

'Stand still and stay quiet,' Thisian mimicked out loud. It was all Gryle, his squad leader, ever said to him. No matter how intelligent the argument, or how clever the reason, the simple brute just dismissed Thisian as a waste of his time. But how was Thisian to become a Fureath'i hero if he was not ever given the right opportunity to prove himself?

His last squad with Dallid had been just as bad. The leader there was so beaten by all of his and Dallid's quick and witty insults that in the end he refused to let them even talk to each other when off duty. 'A Fureath'i is never off duty' was what he would preach. Thisian reckoned he should practice spouting stubborn sayings if he was ever to advance. Not that he wanted to be a squad leader of course; there was far too much work involved. No, Thisian would settle for being a simple world-famous travelling hero, nothing too renowned, just enough to elicit wonder and admiration in everyone he met.

Desperation was all he could drag out of his old squad leader in the end. The man had near pleaded that Thisian and Dallid try life in another squad, but of course he tried unsuccessfully to mask it as important advice: 'You want adventure and heroism, Thisian? Then go to the frontier. You want to prove your worth, Dallid? Then go as far from this ice-blooded snow-dog as you can. A new squad for a new beginning.' The frontier he had meant for Thisian was of course the north and western one that bordered Surlas, where warriors battled in constant skirmishes with Prae'surlas spear fighters, where every day meant kill or die. But that was far too cold for a man to live comfortably.

Not that the eastern border forts were much better. Thisian was used to a hot and wet climate; it was how he preferred his women and it was how he preferred his weather. He had grown up in the eastern forests after all, so was it too much to expect that if he were to amazingly kill a dozen Prae'surlas that they come to him and fight somewhere that was warm? Wrapping his arms around his cloak - if just for the memory of what warmth was - Thisian shuddered at the wind. All of Furea was supposed to blessed with Frehep's heated touch, but it was so cold lately that Thisian wondered if someone had moved the bloody borders and not bothered to tell the sun god about it.

Leaning down on the rail of his look-out post, Thisian considered joining a squad in the western desert. That would definitely be hot. But would it be too hot? Squinting hard he strained to see if a small blur of movement in the distance was actually something or just more nothing. But of course it was nothing. That was all he ever saw.

Movement from below woke him up slightly as he spotted his squad leader Gryle strolling idly about the fort barracks, trying to blind people with the bald shine off his skull. The squad leader was so short and bald and boring and ugly that Thisian could not understand why the man could not take a liking to him. Because, after all, Thisian was tall, interesting, handsome, with beautiful flowing locks of long black hair, so what was there not to like? He should be befriending Thisian if only to ask for advice on how to be better looking.

Thisian had always been the best looking person he knew, and had done enough to better his country by making many more beautiful Fureath'i before he left to join the army. There should be at least a hundred small Thisians toddling around the eastern forests by now, and only so few because he had run out of good looking women. Some of those memories drifted into his mind right then to try warming his blood and it almost worked before the naked women all started to look like Gryle. Smooth hips, toned flat stomach and pert breasts pointing up to a big dirty head of a man who looked like a horse had shit on his face. Why in the name of Frehep would his bloody mind want to show him something as awful as that!

Thisian turned off his brain to stop it from ever imagining anything like that again. So he kept his eyes on the empty waste land instead. He was a dutiful Fureath'i and served his country no matter how pointless the task. There was of course still nothing to see but after what he had just seen in his head, "nothing" was a welcome sight. The land was flat and void of even vegetation for miles, a perfect natural border, but an idiotic place to attack. Foreigners were as stupid as Prae'surlas sometimes, but even they would not try to attack a place so heavily fortified and so able to see an enemy coming for miles. It seemed that everyone was an idiot but him.

Gryle had moved away, continuing his patrol on men that in turn patrolled for him, and would most likely soon go to Matchiek, the ember class that made the squad leaders do his work for him also. Maybe becoming a squad leader was stupid, but being an ember seemed a bit easier. There had to be a way to climb up that high while skipping a few steps. His lunatic friend Kris had managed it, but Thisian tried not to think of him if he could help it. Dallid and Phira had always gotten on much better with the dull, depressing and terrifying man, while Kris had just never quite gotten Thisian's talented sense of humour. He had probably only achieved ember class because he frightened all of his superior officers and they wanted rid of him. Kris certainly frightened Thisian.

'Burn my balls but these forts are boring,' Thisian announced to the world, already growing tired of his own thoughts. 'The sun god sees you warrior Thisian only because there is nothing else to see.'

His delusional mind got the better of him then as he saw two moving shadows in the distance. Whistling over to the next watch tower, the Fureath'i standing there looked to where Thisian pointed. He nodded to confirm the shadows existed, and Thisian wasn't just losing his mind, before whistling down to another. The fort did sometimes get traders and peddlers from the wildlands, or even the Mordec Empire, but it was not much to get excited about.

Resting his hand on his sabre like a good Fureath'i should, Thisian examined the tiny figures as they walked steadily towards them. They had two pack horses as well as the mounts they rode, which was rare in the lands outside Furea, since it was full of bands of raiders looking to prey on the slow or the weak. Merchant trains often looked like small armies as they travelled the lawless lands, but of these two, one of them looked almost an army by himself. The closer he got, the bigger he got and rut was he big. He was as large as a Prae'surlas, a giant compared to a Fureath'i. He was too dark haired and too fat to be Prae'surlas though, the other man with him was dark haired too, though fair skinned, and looked like a small girl when standing next to the other. Thisian hoped they would be interesting.

In all likelihood he would not find out because traders never stayed long in Furea, they were too afraid of the Fureath'i savages. Those yellow skinned barbarians, with their fat pockets of yellow gold, were not to be trusted by honest Foreigners. The Foreign traders would stand skittishly and trade quickly, fearful that at any moment the Fureath'i speaking to them would jump forward and cut their guts open. It was much like the way any sane man would feel while standing in front of Kris. How that violent lunatic outranked Thisian so dramatically was outrageous. Phira-bloody-almighty outranked both of them even more, but Thisian had his own ideas of how she got so successful so quickly.

Word reached for miles of how skilfully she handled a sabre and Thisian knew that must really mean she skilfully handled the sabres Fureath'i men held between their legs. She could sword-play her way all the way up to the heights of power with skills like those. She'd be King soon, but it was their country's own fault for having eight bloody kings in a ruling council and calling them all "The King". Thisian had so many other sordid explanations for how she was so nearly 'king-Phira-bloody-almighty' and he longed to explain them all to someone. He could never do it in his old squad in front of Dallid, not if he didn't want his head broken open, and no-one in his new squad wanted to hear them either. They were all good Fureath'i, too good for the likes of Thisian.

So, going back to being a good Fureath'i, Thisian continued his watch. He watched the two Foreigners get painfully closer and closer, at a speed that made Thisian think about falling asleep. When they were finally at the north gate, he could see a gigantic sword strapped to the back of the fat warrior. Thisian had never seen a blade that big before and wondered if he could even lift it with three other men helping him. The tiny-girl looking one had no weapons that Thisian could see, and the small bit of fluff on his face unfortunately meant he was not a girl after all. Or at least a girl that was too hairy for Thisian to be interested in - and those standards had become very low of late. Either way Thisian found it hard to trust a woman with a beard, not when there were so many mountain Fureath'i around (both the men and women of the mountains all shaved their heads just to play with Thisian's head, because he couldn't tell which were which - the bastards).

Looking back down to the Foreigners, he wondered how the guards would react to them. His Fureath'i brothers never trusted a man without a weapon, and would likely be less than hospitable.

Both were being questioned by someone Thisian could not see, and he guessed what questions were being asked:

'Are you Prae'surlas?' Thisian said in his best Gryle voice.

'Oh no, not us,' he said back in a feminine Foreign voice.

'Are you sure?' he persisted, the Prae'surlas are filthy liars after all.

'How could we be?' they answered. 'If we were Prae'surlas then wouldn't we be off rutting a goat somewhere?'

'Hmmm.' Gryle would nod. 'Prae'surlas do like to rut goats. Very well then, come on in.'

Thisian beamed wide as the two travellers actually entered the fort to link in with his mimicry. Looking around excitedly, and pointlessly, to see if anyone had witnessed the gifted timing, Thisian laughed when he remembered there was absolutely no-one around, anywhere, and definitely no-one as childish as him to find such small things so amusing.

His mind used to be sharp, his intellect fierce and a match for anyone. But he reckoned that the less use his cock was getting, the smaller it was shrinking and everything was shrinking with it. Maybe reverting to childish ways was his mind's way of helping get his mouth back around more tits. Or else boredom had finally driven him insane. It was not a bad thing he guessed, Phira was as mad and reckless as they come and she was a bloody blaze commander. Kris then was the most psychotically violent person ever to be born in Furea and he was an ember class. And Dallid was just a nice guy, who thought a little too much about things, but definitely not insane, and so he was as unimportant as Thisian. Yes, insanity was the way to go. Unfortunately, standing still all day and staring at nothing, to Thisian, was the very definition of insanity. 'Frehep's balls, there is no escape.'

The travellers would most likely be gone before he was finished his shift yet Thisian held onto hope that they would not. He looked expectantly to see where Frehep's journey stood, and found the ball of fire descending but was still a long way off its final farewell. A day in the life of the sun marked the story of Frehep's own life, each stage a wondrous legend of the Fureath'i god, a wondrous story that Thisian was as sick as rotted meat for hearing.

He threw his head back dramatically and blinked patiently for the sun to just disappear already. His head kept going further and further back until Thisian was almost doubled over and could see the warrior in the watch tower opposite him staring. Thisian shot back upright and nodded solemnly at the other man. Cursing in king's tongue, Thisian decided he already looked insane. Why was he the only Fureath'i he had ever met to be some way normal and have a sense of humour? Was he the only person that thought being a better Fureath'i meant becoming worse? He looked up once more at the slowly falling sun.

It was going to be a long wait.

The hours had passed and Thisian had died at least three times of boredom, only to be revived by the intruding cold and start his slow death once more. The warrior that finally relieved Thisian was attractive but she was from the desert. Not only did they all look down on forest Fureath'i but also: they were cunts.

Thisian watched her bare arms as she climbed up to the look-out post. He had always been fascinated with female hands, never being able to look at them without imagining what their soft slender fingers could be wrapping around. He should at least try. His legend could be that he populated every corner of Furea with more attractive Fureath'i.

'If you get bored I can always come back and keep you company.' He said, his smile letting her know that he knew how stupid it sounded, but he had enough humour to get it through as half serious. Speaking to women in the right way was complicated business and Thisian knew he would never be able to fully explain the true art of it to anyone. Especially not a woman.

She looked back at him though as if he had just pulled down his breeches and did a shit right on the watch tower.

'Fureath'i do not get bored.' She twisted her face as if the word tasted bitter. 'Fureath'i use every heartbeat to better themselves and their country.'

'They do? Are you sure?'

She frowned, not getting his humour at all, 'Yes, of course.'

'And don't you feel better from spending these few heartbeats with me?' Thisian smiled. 'I think we could both make our country better by warming each other up, what I have in mind would even increase your heartbeat. Surely that will give you more time to make everything better?'

'You dance with words instead of a sword,' she said in disgust.

Would she prefer me to hit her over the head with my sword? Well she is from the desert. 'Indeed I have a skilled tongue, which has its benefits. My sword is as equally skilled if you would like to find out?'

Her hand drifted over to her sabre. 'Are you challenging me to combat?'

Oh for the love of the gods. 'No. The sword I was referring to was my cock. Look, you have obviously hit your head on some stone in that desert of yours and I would only feel bad rutting a simpleton.' He looked at how attractive she was again, even if she was frowning in terrible confusion at what Thisian was saying. Would he really feel that bad? Probably not, but he was giving up anyway. 'I will leave you in the company of your own wit then, make sure it keeps a sharp eye on all that darkness. The sun god sees you clearer when it's dark.'

The fool woman looked around at see who he was talking about and Thisian shook his head. He should have given up when he saw she was western. Desert women were funny, but not in a good way. There was a saying that a desert woman was only as wet as the blood on your sabre. Maybe he should have challenged her to combat after all. It seemed to Thisian that Fureath'i women followed their birth-lands too literally if all desert women were going to have dry sand in their heads as well as between their legs. All of the forest women he had known, as well as being able to understand words, they all had luscious wet forests between their legs. *What did that leave the mountain women? A pair of stones hanging down in a wrinkly sack?*

Hopping down from the tower with a smile and rubbing his hands together to warm away the cold, Thisian headed towards the fort tavern. He had not seen the two travellers leave which meant they could be proper people and remained for some ale. Thisian ached for entertaining company and made vividly detailed promises to every god that would listen what he would do in return for pleasant and intelligent companions.

When he reached the tavern, Thisian was slightly disappointed
not to hear raucous laughter and music pounding, but he kept his
hopes high and walked inside. For such a dull and depressing place
as the border fort, he would have figured that almost everyone
there would need a good drink as often as possible, but when he
walked in he saw only three tables full, although one of those were
the two travellers. The other tables were Fureath'i keeping to
themselves and eyeing the two traders every second moment to
make sure they did not do anything Foreign.

Thisian sat down right next to the two men.

'The sun god sees you, travellers. I am Thisian Fureath'i, warm
welcome to our fort.' He turned his palm in greeting and the two
traders made half gestures back to do the same. The smaller one
spoke back first, and up closer Thisian decided he was pretty
enough to be a girl after all, if not for the wispy patches of stray hair
around his mouth.

'Ah, the sun god is indeed gifted to see us at night. My name is
Griffil, ah, Lightouch.' He smiled to his large companion as if
sharing a private joke. He spoke Fureath'i fairly passably which
impressed Thisian. The big man spoke next.

'And I'm Krife bloody ice-pissing Foreigner. If you have come to
rut my friend here, I won't sell her cheap.'

Griffil turned to Thisian with a forced smile. 'Do not listen to my
fat friend, I am a man and he is just jealous that I am not as goat-
ugly as he is.'

'The Prae'surlas rut goats,' Thisian said without thinking, but it
produced a burst of laughter from both men.

'Well then that decides that, our next stop sure as bloody hell
isn't Surlas! I'm not going to get bent over by any lusty ice-man. We
get enough of that selling this young girl here to whatever Inn we're
staying at.' Krife slapped Griffil hard on the back and nearly
knocked the small man off the stool.

Again Griffil forced a smile. 'We do not do that. Krife just tries
to mask his own desire for handsome boys with crude jokes at my
expense.'

'There's at least two parts of that description wrong about you,
Griff - handsome and boy.'

Thisian decided he liked both of them straight away.

'Where have you come from?'

The big man took a drink from his mug and Griffil hesitated. Eventually Krife said, 'I thought every place outside of Furea was just called Foreign.'

'Except for Surlas,' Griffil corrected.

'Right, except for the one place you people hate more than anywhere else, yet it's the only country you call by name, and the only bloody language and culture you learn by heart. It's a funny way of hating something if you ask me.'

'I speak some king's tongue,' Thisian said brokenly, but whatever Griffil said back to him was too fast for him to understand. They went back to Fureath'i then.

'I said you are probably the first Fureath'i we've ever met that has an interest in anything outside of Furea, other than where to spit, that is.'

'So what brings you to Furea then?' Thisian asked back.

Krife slammed his hand down hard on the table and Thisian saw several of the other Fureath'i reach for their sabres. 'We've come here to sample some of the finest, cheapest, worst damn ale this world of light has to offer. You can't beat a night of Fureath'i ale. You'll feel like you've been punched in the face by two dozen little rutters, and looking around tonight that's probably what will happen too. More ale!'

One of the fort elders came down and frowned at the two Foreigners for being so loud, and had a separate frown for Thisian for associating with them. Krife either did not notice or did not care, he had his ale and that was all he wanted.

'I was hoping to escape the damned cold, personally,' Griffil said.

Thisian nodded. 'Apologies you have not come at a better time. We are not usually this cold.'

Krife spat out his drank all over the table he laughed so hard. Griffil laughed too. If Thisian was going to be so hilarious with them all the time, he would need to wait until their mouths were empty before saying anything. He wiped some ale and spit off his cloak while Griffil explained. 'Thisian, this is possibly the hottest place in the world right now. Have you not heard how bad it is outside in the wildlands? Or the Mordec Empire? It's as if every land has turned into bloody Surlas. Ice and snow and damn freezing winds are all there is these days, and it just keeps getting worse.'

Thisian didn't like that idea. Maybe Am'bril the Foreign goddess of tempest was dead, or lazy or rutting Aerune. Either way, he guessed it didn't matter to Furea. 'Was that what you said to gain entrance to the fort? That you were tired of the cold and wanted bad ale? I can just imagine the response you got for that.'

Krife barked a cynical laugh and kept drinking. Griffil shook his head.

'No we had some casks of Kel Sheran brandy that your ember ordered off Lady Eva. We offered to sell some of our own collected weapons but none of you people seem interested in anything but a sabre.'

'A Fureath'i is a weapon in himself,' Thisian said dryly. 'What kind of weapons do you have?' he asked, but he really wasn't that interested either.

'Everything. We find and collect ancient and exotic weapons and artefacts. Krife here is actually famous in the wildlands as Krife the Treasure Hunter. He's probably more famous for his quick mouth and his slow fists though than his actual treasure.'

'I'm rich enough,' Krife grunted and rubbed his fists. 'Griffil here is nearly better known than me by now, what did you call yourself earlier? Griffil Light-touch? That doesn't mean he's a skilful whore, Fureath'i, it means he's a dirty, stinking, thief.'

'Fureath'i don't steal,' Thisian said diligently and scolded himself for acting like a squad leader. What was that word they used before Fureath'i? Whore? He had no idea what the word meant. He tried to save some face by expanding on his last statement though. 'And they don't smile, or laugh, or go anywhere or do anything,' he added a little excessively. 'But you're not Fureath'i, so you're free to be as clean or as filthy a thief as you wish.'

'I should bloody hope that I'm not Fureath'i! Can you imagine a Fureath'i as big as me? I've hocked up bigger lumps of phlegm than I've seen of you people. Some of you even come close to being as small as Griffil here.' Krife slapped the small thief across the face and laughed. 'Slow fists eh? My next one won't be such a light-touch! Get it? Light-touch!' He slapped Thisian on the arm while laughing. The bastard had arms as big as most men had legs and Thisian could already feel the bruise forming.

'Well, anyway, there you have it,' Griffil said rubbing his face protectively. 'Just a couple of travelling adventurers trying to make a living.'

'What I wouldn't give to go with you,' Thisian said absently, but the two men were looking at him with consideration. 'No. I didn't mean that, I mean, we cannot leave Furea except to kill Prae'surlas. If we did we would be exiled and never allowed to return.'

Krife scratched his chin, bristled with white stubble, and stared Thisian in the eyes. 'I'll tell you now, son, we'd be more than happy to have a young Fureath'i warrior like you travel with us. It'd be good for our image. Good to be seen to have more men than women in our group.' He turned to frown at Griffil for emphasis. 'How about this, we let you travel with us, and we'll give you a good price for it, let's say one gold piece a day. That's all you have to pay us and you can adventure as much as your heart desires.'

Thisian raised an eyebrow at the offer. 'It's true that most Fureath'i have more gold than sense, but I'm not most Fureath'i.'

'We can see that,' Griffil said, seeming genuinely interested, despite Krife's mock offer.

'If I was to travel with you then you should pay heavily for my services, I am a highly trained soldier after all.' Thisian turned his head as if he was really thinking about it, but he couldn't. Could he?

'I bet you are. Well, think on it, we'll be staying in a town called Lyanat north of here for the next few days, waiting for some damn useless magic to arrive.' Krife spat on the floor with the word magic, and Thisian cringed. Fureath'i weren't the savage barbarians Foreigners thought them to be, but that didn't mean they weren't explosively violent. They were all born with fire in their blood after all, but Thisian was thankful that the elder didn't see the brown coloured spit.

'What do you mean waiting for magic to arrive? A Powerborn?'

Krife spat again and Thisian almost put his hands to his head in reaction. Griffil answered. 'No, no, nothing as grand as a Powerborn, do you really think one of those would sell themselves as magic for hire? No, Thisian, what we have is a waste of gold following us around just in case we run into a real Powerborn. So we can push the damn magician at him and run!'

Krife nodded. 'We'll do our best to get him killed alright, means we won't have to pay him!' He banged his hand on the table again to punctuate his laughter. 'But don't worry lad, if you join with us we'll treat you better, you're not a magic right?'

Thisian shook his head.

'See? Just an honest fleshborn like the rest of us, not trying to get above yourself by messing with all that holy lord god-blood nonsense.'

The warriors at the table nearest to them did overhear that part, and Thisian saw them move to stand up.

'Ah, yes, those Foreign magic users should be hunted down and killed,' Thisian said quickly and loudly. 'It's blasphemy that they try to touch what was not born to them. They are all just insects when compared to the glory of Fireborn.'

It seemed to settle the warriors a little but they still shuffled in their seats, waiting for the smallest reason to start the fight. Krife looked over to them and then back to Thisian. He leaned forward and motioned for Thisian to do the same.

'You don't have to bloody shout!' he roared into Thisian's face. 'I'm rutting sitting right here!' He finished his shout with sitting back and laughing again, before taking another long drink from his mug. Thisian brushed his hand by his ear, which was ringing from the bellow, and tried to change the subject to something that would not get the three of them killed.

'So when you leave holy Furea,' he said loudly before lowering his voice, 'where are you going that you need to hire a magic user? A true Powerborn would easily kill any false magicker.'

'I wouldn't be so sure, Thisian,' Griffil said. 'I've seen a lot of different warriors that can focus magic in a lot of different ways. They mightn't have the same speed, strength or healing as a Powerborn, but their magic can be good enough.'

'Not the one we're buying though,' Krife chipped in. 'Bought the cheapest bastard we could find.'

'So what do you need him for? Where are you going?'

Griffil looked to Krife and the big man just shrugged. 'Well, Thisian, have you ever heard a Telling about the Segments of

Ahmar?' When Thisian shook his head, Griffil went on excitedly. 'Well, basically they are three stone pieces from a bracelet -'

'That doesn't sound like a particularly interesting Telling, Griffil,' Thisian said losing interest immediately. Krife laughed at Thisian's remark, but Griffil went on undeterred.

'- and that bracelet, Thisian, when completed, will give you the power to rule the entire world!'

Thisian raised his eyebrows in disbelief. 'So you mean to collect all three and rule the world? Like Amadis did? Is that what happened then, Amadis owned this bracelet and someone smashed it?'

'No, no, all that happened to Amadis was: he was as sick of his own greatness, as much as the rest of us were, and shoved that sword of his up his own arse,' Krife said. 'And who would want to rule this rotting pile of swamp anyway? No wonder Amadis killed himself, probably sick of the place. No, we're just going to find the damn thing and sell it for all the gold in the world.'

'A noble goal,' Thisian said. 'So where is it?'

'Ah, the only way you'll find that out is if you join us, Fureath'i, another man to keep Griffil from eyeing me up on the cold nights will suit me fine.'

'You're too fat and ugly to be my type, Krife.'

Krife patted his large belly and looked down in consideration. 'I'm not too fat.'

Griffil just laughed but then turned to Thisian. 'So what do you say, Fureath'i? Will you join us?'

· CHAPTER SIX ·

Fureath'i blood

Thisian woke up and worked out a pain in his neck. He had not slept comfortably, but he endured the hardship. Standing up and stretching, a chorus of creaks and clicks added music to his mood as he thought ahead and eagerly anticipated the new day full of exciting possibilities. Possibilities such as: nothing happening; the weather getting colder; the other Fureath'i ignoring him; or possibilities of his squad leader Gryle berating him for no reason other than for something to do. All of these Thisian anticipated with cleverly masked excitement, so much so that if anyone were to look at him they might even think that he was not excited at all.

Not for the first time Thisian cursed himself for not taking those two travellers up on their offer, and not for the first time he reminded himself it was not too late. All it would take was to leave everything he had ever known and set out alone to a land wild with bandits and raiders, hoping that Krife and Griffil would, first, still be at the town and, second, had been genuine in their invitation. It was foolishness. Thisian went about his morning ritual.

When it was time he stepped out of his barracks, which he irritatingly shared with nine others, and greeted the morning sun as did everyone else in the fort. Perhaps two hundred Fureath'i stood either naked, in their small clothes, or intelligently fully dressed to keep off the damned cold as Thisian was. They were all standing and staring at the sun bursting over the horizon bringing Frehep's glory to the new day. The children's stories said that Frehep spent the night battling Aerune and in the morning when he rose it meant he was once again victorious. How the sun could battle the moon always confused Thisian since you could quite clearly see the moon all night, but like every other Fureath'i, watching the glory of Frehep's rebirth still filled his heart to the brim with pride and strength. How could he ever consider leaving Furea?

Easily, he reminded himself and shook off the strange trance the sun held over him. Thisian made a point of noticing how foolish everyone looked, standing like statues to watch something that happened every morning without fail. *One day Frehep will not rise and then what will they do? Stand forever until they die of thirst? More like die from the cold if the sun doesn't rise.* Thisian shivered from the morning cold to add emphasis to his thoughts but still he did not move from where he stood. If he did move, then all the others would surely kill him for being a Prae'surlas. *Well at least I am nearly as tall as one*, he thought sourly, *maybe that is why the others look at me with such envy.*

The final flare of sunburst came into view, and tradition allowed people to move and breathe again. Thisian went to his post without hurry, and did not speak with the man he was relieving, merely whistling at him that he was there. The look-out post held a supply of bread and cheese and Thisian ate without conviction, chewing the over-hard bread methodically. Some watered wine helped soften the meal, but even the idea of drinking it all did not help to improve Thisian's mood. *I should have gone with them,* he thought to himself for the thousandth time.

It was two nights since he had conversed pleasantly with Krife the treasure hunter and Griffil the thief. All of his jokes that night had been met with appropriately boisterous laughter and all of his clever conversation had been met with almost as clever retorts. The Fureath'i at the other tables did not end up trying to attack the two travellers. It was the other way around. Krife had grown bored of the warriors teasing him about starting a fight and he said he would help them be about it. When he lifted his tankard of ale, Thisian thought he would throw the drink on them, but instead Krife downed the full mug and then used the metal cup to clatter one of the warriors across the head. The resulting fight was mayhem.

Thisian wisely had not gotten involved, and Griffil too stayed well out of harm's way, actually hiding behind Thisian. The five Fureath'i at the tables, even the one dazed by the tankard blow, all ran for Krife at the same time. When Griffil jumped out of the way, pulling Thisian with him, he thanked the slender thief's timing as Krife choose that moment to pick up the whole table and use it to club back the assault. The Fureath'i warriors, as highly trained as they were, were all sent landing on their asses. The next time Thisian saw Yiran he would ask why he was never trained in how to fight a table.

The soldiers recovered and began their own barrage of blunt attacks, landing heavy blows with their feet and fists, but kept their sabres sheathed. There was a lot of Krife to hit and the warriors did their best to hit as much of him as they could, but it did not look like Krife even felt them. His massive girth was a weapon in itself as every time he turned around it seemed his bulk pushed a man off balance or an elbow made contact with a face, and when he connected with a punch, Thisian did not think the Fureath'i on the receiving end would ever get back up.

Half way into the great fight, the elder that worked the tavern stormed in and ordered them all out. The Fureath'i warriors were too well disciplined to disobey an elder and like mindless slaves immediately stopped what they were doing. Krife frowned at them all in disbelief and took a bit longer to stop, clobbering one of the passive warriors right across the jaw a few moments after they all stopped fighting. That man did not get up, not until much later the next day. The strange behaviour of all of them though only made Krife burst out laughing again, as he was prone to do, and the impressive cursing from the elder at the big man only made him laugh more. He was so pleased with his night that he invited everyone to share a cask of Kel Sheran brandy that he and Griffil had kept back from the shipment, but of course he did not tell the Fureath'i that. They would neither understand nor approve of the entertaining ways of Foreigners.

But what started as a good night of lively conversation and even a good brawl, soon turned sour for Thisian as the four other Fureath'i quickly got drunk on the strong brandy. The drink had burned his throat like liquid fire when Thisian tried to drink it and he only took careful sips afterwards, but the four warriors devoured the brandy, being encouraged by Krife. But then the drunken Fureath'i turned into drunken singing Fureath'i, Telling the same old stories that Thisian was tired of hearing. Krife and Griffil seemed politely interested but Thisian had to leave, he was too experienced in such situations and knew the four would not stop singing until absolutely every boring Telling about the same few boring Fureath'i were told out loudly and fully.

The next day Thisian watched the two treasure hunters leave without him. They did not seem to be wondering where he was, but they did wait until late in the day before leaving. Perhaps that was because they wanted to see if he would join them or perhaps they had just slept too long from the night of brandy - being the fat and lazy Foreigners that they were. There was no such thing as a fat Fureath'i, apart from Ryat his grandfather of course, but Ryat had earned the right to get fat with years of bettering his country in the army.

None of it mattered any more anyway. Thisian had missed his opportunity and had hence doomed himself to a life of repetitive meaninglessness. His old friend - the sweeping plains of barren dirt - was still there for him though, that friend would never leave him. Thisian did not blame Dallid for leaving him; he just missed him. Each and every Fureath'i needed to put away their first life of youth and when they joined the army they started a new one.

With luck and talent, Thisian would live long enough to survive his army years to retire back to a village and spend the third part of his life bettering his society. He would certainly have enough grandchildren to raise, if all two hundred of the children he had left each left another two hundred then he would have his own army. Perhaps he would still be good looking enough to get a few more young Fureath'i with child. The thought only mildly cheered up his mood.

But how could he lift his mood when the sun was always there to remind him of how low he was. *The sun god sees you, Thisian.*

He refused to let himself be admonished by its disapproving stare. 'Who are you to judge me?' Thisian said out loud. 'You are just a sun! Slave to the goddess of time!'

He did not admit at that moment of course that Frehep was actually the sun. He reasoned that Frehep simply powered the sun, and that the sun was again powered by time itself. Rhyserias the goddess of time made sure it rose every day to keep everyone dying of old age, if the sun did not rise then maybe no one would grow old. Thisian had to rethink his earlier thought about all the

Fureath'i dying while waiting for a sun that did not rise, maybe they would just be standing there forever after all?

Such thoughts belonged to a Scholar. Maybe if he asked to become a Scholar it would mean doing something more interesting than staring out at blank nothing all day. Instead he could spend hours just contemplating what exactly nothing was, if anything. He was certainly too clever to be only a warrior - even as supremely skilled at being a warrior as he was - and he was already scorned by his fellow Fureath'i because of how much taller, smarter and better looking he was than them. So becoming a Scholar would not make him any more of an outcast, really, and in the same line becoming an Exile would also not make him any worse. *Were Krife and Griffil serious in their offer? Are they still at that town?*

Thisian cast the thought out, and tried to direct his wandering mind to warmer climates, like his opulent youth spent outwitting so many girls into rutting him. He was only helping them do their Fureath'i duty after all. Thisian shuddered at the idea that even Kris had done his Fureath'i duty and fathered four children before he left for the army. The idea of four more unpredictable silent lunatics in the world was unsettling enough, but what was more disturbing were the actual women that Kris had bedded. From all reports they were the most awful females that any village had to offer, most being used as monsters to scare little children into becoming better, and or else left to wander the forest to scare off wolves and bears with their musty scents. And Kris had rutted them.

Thisian adjusted himself in his breeches and decided that he really needed to uncover the way to bed western women - smart western women anyway. He had only bedded three or four average looking women since coming to the cursed fort and that was purely because all the above average females stationed there were from the desert. Western women did not seem to understand, or even try to appreciate, his unique intelligence and humour. All of them seemed to look at him like he was covered in goat faeces and most likely being rutted by a Prae'surlas at the same time. How could they see how obviously attractive he was while picturing that? It was madness.

Thisian continued to keep his mind exercised with plenty more circles of reason and unreasonableness, and the hours came and went. Frehep's journey through the sky passed by each and every stage of his life without incident and Thisian drank all the wine to celebrate. There was enough to have kept two more watches supplied, so to hide the fact he'd drank it all, Thisian had to eat all the disgusting hard bread and cheese too. That way at least they could assume it ran out when it was supposed to run out. He had not enjoyed any of it but it was something to do.

Patting his tender stomach, Thisian contemplated getting fat as recreation. It was certainly something he could do while on the lookout posts. He pictured what it would be like to become as large as Krife and smiled at how huge he would be. But then he would not be so extremely attractive any more. Thisian was so dismayed, that when he heard whistling from the southern posts he did not even turn around to see who was arriving.

Anyone coming from the south were just more Fureath'i, and more Fureath'i did not interest Thisian. *Unless there are eastern women in those squads,* his cock suggested helpfully. Thisian jumped around and strained his eyes to see through the solid wall of wood that protected the fort, but the treacherous structure was unrevealing. Turning back to the sun with hope, Thisian let out a shout to see that his watch was almost over. Whoever was approaching from the south, he would be free to help them with whatever needs they had - and Gryle might even congratulate him on his initiative!

There was still no sign of the damned lazy warrior that was to relieve him though when the southern squad entered the border fort. With his back completely turned from the direction he was meant to be surveying, Thisian's sharp eyes searched expertly first for women and then for attractive women. He knew his pride would have to be pushed aside for the occasion. The rarity of willing women in the border fort meant that he would have to consider rutting just the mildly beautiful women, a true step down from his usual standard but he would be generous to them for helping him out so greatly in his time of need.

His first scan only spotted one female warrior in the whole squad though, and from her look and demeanour she was the bloody squad leader. Thisian cursed and invented some new oaths but did not lose heart. Another scan gave him two more members of the squad that could be mountain women. Would it be worth the risk? "A mountain man's luck" was meant to describe good fortune in the face of danger, but Thisian knew it really meant that those poor mountain men took great risk when bedding each other, never knowing if one of them was a woman or a man until it was too late.

The squad leader was at least very attractive and more importantly she was eastern. Thisian watched as she met with some of the other squad leaders of the fort. The ember class Matchiek was nowhere to be seen as usual. Thisian's own squad leader Gryle was there though, and he seemed almost as overly interested in the new squad leader as Thisian was. She had very fair hair, the lightest brown that he had seen in a while, and even her skin seemed lighter than everyone else's. If he was not so fascinated by her then he might have thought she was half Foreign. But for the task at hand she was perfect in every single way. To Thisian she would be the only woman in the world for the next day or two, however long it took.

A whistle turned Thisian back to his position and he nodded eagerly to the warrior that took his post from him. Then he practically jumped down from the watch tower, landing with a painful thud, and raised up clouds of dust making him cough. Wiping a hand across his mouth, Thisian pushed off towards the new squad at a run. The short distance was covered too quickly though and when he arrived he had to stop suddenly and awkwardly. Having come from such a run all the squad leaders turned to him expecting to hear some news or report, instead he just scratched the back of his head with embarrassment.

'Is there some reason you are here, warrior?' Gryle growled at Thisian, clearly angered that he was embarrassing him. That only emboldened Thisian more.

'I heard one of the most fearsome squad leaders this side of the Fire Wall had arrived,' Thisian turned to meet the eyes of the woman. 'But I see she is also one of the most beautiful.'

He purposely did not smile, but she did. He could be seen as simply stating what he saw as fact, nothing Gryle could punish him for, but she certainly found it amusing. Amusing and hopefully intriguing. Gryle was definitely not amused, especially since the other squad leaders there were now all looking at him to explain Thisian's sudden odd presence among them.

'Warrior, turn your heel and -'

'Squad leader,' Thisian interrupted before he could dismiss him, 'I wish to offer my assistance to the newly arrived squad.'

Gryle had a curse ready and he looked like he was about to strike Thisian to accompany it, but the female squad leader interrupted him this time. 'Then look after the horses, warrior.' She handed him her reins and their hands touched for a moment. Oh how Thisian loved girl-hands, so slender and delicate and so capable of such great things. He thought he saw a glimmer of a smile in her eyes.

'You are from Coruln are you not? They have good horses down there,' Gryle conceded. 'Make sure you do a good job.' Thisian wondered why Gryle would care whether or not he did a good job looking after some other squad's horses, and the squat man was eyeing the woman strangely as he spoke.

Gods but he was ugly, the squashed bald head and old broken nose, Thisian almost cringed when Gryle turned his look back to him. The squad leader opened his mouth as if to say more, but then decided against it, looking once again at the newly arrived female squad leader instead. Thisian thought he was acting very strange but did not care to waste time pondering about the man's moods. All Gryle managed to say in the end was low mutterings, impossible to distinguish and was still grumbling about Thisian as all the squad leaders turned and walked away.

More Fureath'i arrived to help the rest of the squad with their mounts, but Thisian led the squad leader's mare to a separate stable where the best were kept. The ember's own stallion was there, as was Gryle's war horse and the other squad leaders' respective animals. Thisian brought the mare to a free stall and began removing the saddle. The horse had a very fair colour just like its rider and was comfortable around him while he brushed her down. Gryle had been right when he spoke about what good horses they bred in Coruln. Time on those horse farms meant Thisian was well experienced in how to look after them properly.

'So what does it feel like to be between those legs?' he asked the horse. There were no other Fureath'i in the stables so he was free to ask the beast a few personal questions, to get to know the new squad leader better. 'Do you think she likes handsome men? I wonder what her name is.'

'Her name is Jaina.' Thisian just about caught himself from jumping and managed a calm sideways glance with a smile as Jaina herself walked into the stable. 'And yes, she does like handsome men, so please tell me if you find any. What was the first question you asked before that? I think I missed that one.'

'Apologies squad leader, I did not think anyone was listening.' He bowed his head in cautious respect but knew he would have to push his luck to achieve any fortune. 'I should apologise for blurting out how beautiful you were earlier too. I was simply taken off guard when I saw you.'

'Oh I doubt that,' Jaina said as she strolled around the stable, running a hand down her horse's neck. 'A young warrior with your smile, I think, would have much practice in saying what he thinks young women like to hear.'

If he was feeling more daring Thisian might have ventured replying: "and what about a woman of your age" but he needed to be careful. The situation was already better than he had hoped. The woman even appeared to be trying to charm *him*.

'And a young woman as beautiful as you, I think, would have much practice in hearing just how beautiful she is.'

'You would be surprised,' Jaina said as she turned to look him in the eyes, 'how the rank of squad leader would encourage most men to caution about saying such things.'

Thisian thought it was time to flash one of his best smiles. 'Personally I have never held much respect for the rank of squad leader.'

Thankfully Jaina smiled back at him instead of drawing her sabre. He still could not believe his luck but was now worrying that perhaps it was a little easy, was she maybe too forward? Did he like that in a woman? She stepped in closer to him and ran her hands through his hair. *Yes*, he thought, *I definitely like that in a woman*.

'Then how fortunate for you, warrior, that you are as handsome as you think you are.'

'Thisian, my name is Thisian.'

'I do not need to know your name, just remove your clothes.'

There was a moment where he paused to consider if he had truly heard her correctly, but as she began to remove her shirt, Thisian speedily undressed himself. He finished much quicker than she did and was pleased by her appreciative smile at his appearance. When she was finally undressed Thisian marvelled at her breasts and the perfect muscle of her entire body. When she casually turned around to slide shut the outside stable doors his gaze clung to her legs and hips. He was barely able to remove his eyes even when she was standing right in front of him and wrapping her arms around his neck.

She guided him over to a different stall and pulled him down to her on the straw. It was then that he forced himself to snap back to the present and concentrate on what he was doing. Jaina curled her long glorious legs around his back and Thisian lost himself in the moment.

When it was over they both lay there for a time, enjoying the residual sensations of what had just happened. Eventually though, Thisian became anxious about the stable doors and someone walking in. Unless it was one of the western women, maybe they would be hypnotised by his body and want to join them. And if it was anyone from Jaina's squad of course they would just kill him.

'Will your squad be in the tavern?' he asked, innocently.

Jaina seemed to have forgotten Thisian was even there. 'Hmm? Oh yes, most likely, it has been a hard few days with harder ones to come. We take what pleasures we can while we can.' She smiled at him again and reminded Thisian of a cat.

'Where have you been?'

She eyed him first and then sighed as she resigned herself that Thisian actually did want a conversation instead of just enjoying lying there. In Thisian's defence though, good conversation was hard to come by.

'We were travelling up along the eastern border these last few days, but tomorrow we are heading into the wildlands proper. Just to harry the bands of raiders that think to stalk our perimeters, keep them from thinking they can escape the cold by coming into our land, kill them if we can.'

'I was asked to join some travellers heading in to the wildlands two days ago, two travelling adventurers.' He said it absently, not really sure why he was telling her.

'*Foreigners*,' Jaina said. It always surprised Thisian how Fureath'i could say the word like a curse. 'How could they think any Fureath'i would join them in such a meaningless life? How are they living to better themselves or their people? How Foreign nations have even survived in the world is a mystery to me. Especially now with Amadis gone, and even the crime-lord Lyat, without them everyone is just killing each other.'

True, but to Thisian it was a mystery he would not mind finding out. Fureath'i knew almost nothing about outside nations other than Surlas, and in a twisted way he toyed with the idea that such knowledge could help to better his people if he went out to learn it. Of course if he became an Exile he would never be allowed back into Furea to share the knowledge gained but his intentions would remain sound.

'Still, I think I would like to see the world outside,' he said before quickly adding, 'if only to better appreciate holy Furea because of it.'

'Well,' she said stretching her arms behind her head and sticking her breasts up high and in front of Thisian's face. 'I could take you into my squad and you could join us. My brother would most definitely not like it, but at least if you were part of my squad you could continue to pleasure me at my request.'

She smiled to tell him she was jesting, but he suspected there was more than some truth in her suggestion.

'Your brother? Is he in your squad then? I do not think I would like to get killed for rutting a man's sister in front of his face.'

'In my squad? Of course not, my brother is your squad leader is he not? Gryle?'

A long list of complex emotions flickered into Thisian's head at that news. A feeling of dread, that Gryle would most certainly murder him, entered Thisian's mind, followed quickly by triumphant joy that he had just bedded the man's sister, flashing back to panic, and again to exultation. If he told Gryle he had his cock up his sister, then the man would kill him, but on the other hand he really did *have* to tell Gryle that he had his cock up the man's sister. Not yet admitting which feeling won through, his pragmatism to stay alive started acting by itself. Thisian got up and began dressing himself. Jaina laughed at him.

'You are still a young warrior but the fire in our blood does not always have to lead us to violence, we have many other passions that it can fuel.' Seeing that Thisian was not convinced she shrugged. 'If my brother is angered by this then I can say it was my wish, he did ask you to look after my needs did he not?'

'That is of course why I am dressing so quickly, so I can run off to immediately tell Gryle about this.' He was not sure if he was not joking. 'My squad leader is a very understanding Fureath'i after all, but he has plenty of fire in his blood. I would even welcome his violence on me considering you have suggested his rutting me as the alternative.'

Jaina laughed again and slowly began getting dressed too. 'I like you, Thisian. You have a clever tongue.'

'And I like you, Jaina. You are the first squad leader to find my tongue a skill rather than a flaw.'

'Well then, you will simply have to start bedding those other squad leaders.'

'Of course, starting with your brother.'

Their laughter was cut short by the stable doors being pulled open and Thisian's breath caught as a warrior walked inside. Thankfully it was just one of the other Fureath'i that had been seeing to the rest of the squad's horses, but the smile he gave the two of them after a quick survey was still suspicious. Those suspicions were then given full life as Gryle walked in behind him.

Time stood still as the tiny brain inside Gryle's ugly head worked through the facts it was presented with. In front of him stood Thisian, not doing any apparent work and putting back on his last boot, his shirt still undone. Behind Thisian then was Gryle's sister Jaina who had her shirt fully laced, but wore nothing else.

Inside his own head Thisian was shouting to run as fast as he could but his moronic legs were in a world of their own. Did they not realise what was about to happen?

Gryle's sabre flashed out of his sheath and everything in Thisian's body jumped to attention. He instinctively grabbed his sword belt and ran down the stable to the back way out. He heard

Jaina's voice try to shout something but he could feel Gryle's ugly bulk right behind him and guessed that her reasoning did not work as well as she thought it would.

Running through the hinged door, Thisian spun around and shouldered it back into Gryle's face. The thud, grunt, and curse told him he had hurt the man but that only made Thisian turn and run faster. Several other Fureath'i stood and gave him strange looks as he ran for his life, and to the gods Thisian had no idea exactly where he was running to.

'Rut this!' he shouted and turned suddenly to find Gryle right on top of him. The lunatic swung his sabre down to split his skull in two and Thisian met the swing but barely.

Gryle did not stop with that and swung again, this time trying to hack Thisian in half from the waist down and he defended frantically as best he could against the blood-crazed squad leader. Thisian had never been as good as Kris or Phira with a sabre, or even Dallid really for that matter, but he had still been trained by Yiran the Unconquered, and a Fureath'i could not do that without learning some skill. Thisian gestured behind the squad leader and shouted, 'Jaina no!'

Gryle turned his head to see what his sister was about to do, but there was no-one there. He turned his head back in time to see Thisian launch an attack of his own. The first one nearly took off the man's ugly ear and more followed that. With his squad leader on the back foot, whatever wild swings Gryle tried to make between blocks, became easier to deflect as more confidence returned to Thisian. Perhaps he could wear the older man down and disarm him. The glory of it would become a legend in itself: the simple warrior that humiliated his squad leader by defeating him in public combat after riding his sister. Gryle swung low against Thisian's legs and the dirty move was barely deflected in time. A large ugly fist followed that and crunched into Thisian's face. It knocked him flat to the ground.

A great cheer came up from some gathering Fureath'i who were in no way trying to help, but simply stood and watched. This angered Thisian into action and he kicked his legs around, sweeping the short squad leader to the ground. Throwing himself forward then he punched into Gryle's groin twice in quick succession. There was no cheer this time and that caused Thisian even more anger.

Standing up he stamped down on Gryle's hand and kicked the sabre away through the dry dirt. Lowering his own sword to rest it on Gryle's neck, Thisian tried not to grin in victory. He needed to appear humble if he was to receive celebration from the other Fureath'i. And still there was no cheer. What did he need to do? Squat down and take a shit on his face? Would that be enough of a definitive victory? Thisian conceded that maybe rutting Jaina on top of Gryle's face would be just as dominating and he was not sure why his mind had gone that other way first.

Gryle swatted Thisian's blade away and rolled to the side, quickly coming back to his feet. The insane man did not even try to retrieve his sword and simply faced Thisian in a crouch with fists ready. Thinking about throwing his own sabre away to make it a fairer fight, Thisian decided against it and instead reversed the blade, slamming the butt hard into Gryle's temple. At the same time though Gryle rushed forward and drove a fierce punch into Thisian's gut, before punching the veins on his forearm making him open his palm and drop the sabre.

The fight became messy then with Gryle bearing Thisian down to the ground, his injured skull bleeding disgustingly all over Thisian's face. Gryle mounted him, much the way his sister had earlier, and bombarded him with punches before Thisian was able to throw him to the side. Thisian's longer arms found their way to Gryle's head then, concentrating on the same area where he had hit him with the sabre hilt. The first two punches dazed him and allowed Thisian to get much closer and use a stronger elbow strike to the same place. He pushed himself clear then and stood over his bleeding squad leader, breathing hard.

Gryle tried to get up and faltered once, before supporting himself with his arms. The bleeding from his head was much worse now and Thisian would have felt bad if Gryle's eyes did not still burn with murderous intent. As it was, the old squad leader stood unsteadily, swaying from side to side, blinking blood out of his eyes. He swung for Thisian and who quickly slid back out of the way, shifting his feet on instinct and throwing a full force kick right into Gryle's head. His shin made contact with the same point on his squad leader's skull where all the rest of his blows had, and Gryle hit the ground heavily. He did not get back up. His eyes were closed and the bleeding was bad, but his back moved up and down to show the man still breathed. Still there was no cheering.

'What in the name of the gods do I need to do...' Thisian cut his muttering short when he looked up and saw the ember class Matchiek standing there and watching him sternly. His first thoughts were to think that Matchiek's presence must have been the reason why the other Fureath'i did not cheer for him. His second thought was that he was in for a lot of punishment for this. Or would he get promoted? Thisian never fully understood how the heights of power worked.

'Warrior, a Fureath'i can never raise a hand against his commander.' Thisian hung his head in penance. It was a fool stupid rule since the only way warriors ever seemed to get promoted was by directly challenging their commanders. If only half the stories he had heard about Phira were true... Thisian shook his head. It did not matter what Phira-bloody-almighty did, it was him that was about to suffer for months on end. He subtly looked around to see if Jaina was nearby, perhaps she could get him off the worst of it. The ember class Matchiek went on, 'If a commander thinks it is best to beat a warrior then the Fureath'i will accept the punishment and thank Frehep for making him stronger for it.'

Thisian knew all this, there was no need to start preaching it, but then by the look in Matchiek's eyes, Thisian thought that the ember was saying it because he intended to beat Thisian right then in front of everyone. That was too much.

'Ember class, Gryle was trying to kill me.'

'Do not speak warrior.'

'But if I had not -'

'Do not speak!'

Matchiek shook with rage at Thisian's lack of discipline, speaking to someone so far above his station, but right then a moment of clarity arrived. The Fureath'i were always taught that a man could be as great as he could make himself, that to be better took constant dedication as well as moments of brilliant bravery. The man standing in front of Thisian did not seem much better than him, and neither did his squad leader Gryle, they were all just men like him, flawed in as many ways but yet had excelled in the Fureath'i society. If Thisian was to ever excel it would have to be far from that same society. So if he was to become better, then it would not be as a Fureath'i. It was time for Thisian to start his own path to greatness.

'I will speak to who I please,' Thisian said boldly, and walked over to where his sabre lay. Picking it up and sheathing it he turned to stare his commander in the eyes. Matchiek could not speak, he simply trembled with outrage. An impetuous grin crossed Thisian's face as he saw the lazy ember class had not taken the time to arm himself, and if he was to try disciplining him in front of everyone now he would be against Thisian with a sabre. The ember must have been still considering it as his eyes flickered down to the unconscious Gryle, a battle hardened squad leader who many had considered a formidable fighter. Thisian wasted no more time and shouted out loud for all to listen, 'My name is Thisian Fureath'i! Remember that name for you will soon hear it on every Teller's lips across the world. I go to begin my legend!'

And on that dramatic statement, Thisian turned his back on his Fureath'i blood.

CHAPTER SEVEN

The watchful sun

I should never have left Thisian.

Dallid's thoughts should have been on his surroundings, on what he was doing and how dangerous the men were that he was approaching, but he could not. Instead he was trying to distract himself from the fact that he might die shortly, and all he thought about was that if he was still in the same squad as Thisian then he would not be in this kind of danger. But it was almost a year since he had seen Thisian and almost three years since he had seen Phira. Dallid tried to concentrate as he crept forward, as unseen and silent as any Fureath'i warrior could, and he was getting very close to the enemies ahead, but also very close to the spears they held. The north-men and their spears would not care how much he missed his wife or his friends and they would kill him if he was not concentrating. Dallid needed to focus.

His squad, *the Watchful Sun*, had surrounded the group of Prae'surlas completely. The subtlest of movements within the forest were the only signs that nearly thirty Fureath'i warriors were about to erupt upon the unprepared northerners. The Prae'surlas had not set any sentries, and did not look if they cared they were deep within their enemy's lands. Ever since the death of Amadis, the world and war had almost become synonymous, so it was not surprising that these northern giants were in Furea, but they had no horses and little supplies, and it was a mystery how they had gotten so far inside the borders. That there could be some greater unknown force at work only made Dallid more nervous.

Dragging his body slowly forward through the wet muck, Dallid considered that it was possible the north-men had been hunted and driven in all the way. It could mean that soon another squad of Fureath'i could arrive as reinforcements. The group of north-men certainly looked weary enough to have been chased for miles. With every one of them looking aged and exhausted, Dallid tried to muster his confidence, surveying his prey. They all looked the same. They all had the same yellow hair the colour of piss; blue eyes the colour of ice; lanky enough to trip over their own legs; and three times as large as a Fureath'i which only meant there were more places to stick a blade. If he asked any other Fureath'i, that would be their exact description too, the hatred burnt into each heart from birth. It was known to all that the Prae'surlas actually bedded their own mothers and sisters to keep their blood line pure, and that kept them all looking exactly alike.

Movement to his right and Dallid swung his head in alarm until he spotted Emylias creeping towards his location. Her face was still partially hidden but her eyes caught his and he could see the smile in them. Foreigners had a term that they called a "Fureath'i smile", but it was a term of warning. It meant whenever you saw a Fureath'i smile, you were about to get a red one across your neck. Emylias had that smile now and she looked impatient for their squad leader to give the signal to attack.

As if just as eager for the assault, one of the northern giants chose that moment to get up to his feet, his big boots nosily crunching their way straight towards the overgrowth where Dallid was hiding. None of the other Prae'surlas even stirred at the sudden movement and their over-confidence only served to drain Dallid of what little confidence he possessed in the first place. Flexing the fingers around his sabre, Dallid wondered if he should leap out before he was discovered. He needed to wait as long as he could until his squad leader ordered the attack, but being a good soldier did him no good if he was a dead one.

The north-man who had gotten up, kept getting closer and did not look as if he was checking the perimeter; his sole intent seemed to be to just lumber straight for Dallid's position. He trudged as if every step was a gruelling effort and his frozen eyes were half lidded, looking ready for sleep. Dallid tried not to worry about being discovered by the man, he was well concealed and the north-man was half asleep. He would not be seen. But then the man started unlacing his breeches and Dallid became very bloody worried. What foul fortune would make the north-man choose that exact location to relieve his bladder? Dallid had to stop himself from moving away but he was about to get pissed on by a damned

Prae'surlas! Dallid's squad leader would kill him if he broke cover early, and the north-man might well kill him if he jumped out to attack, but as the northerner had his manhood already out, there seemed little choice left. Dallid turned the leather strap of his wrist and kissed the coin with Phira's image on it underneath.

'May I see you soon,' he whispered.

Before the first drop of frozen piss could dribble out, Dallid sent his sabre up and into the man's leg. The Prae'surlas roared and every other north-man sprung to attention just before the forest came alive with Fureath'i warriors. Dallid leapt up and plunged his sabre into the side of the same north-man just as Emylias appeared, adding her own blade into the man's stomach. The giant was good and dead from those but Dallid still held his sabre guardedly, anxious of one last attack in his death throes.

None arrived and so he turned quickly to survey the rest of his surroundings. The ambush had turned into a fight, with the larger Prae'surlas swinging and stabbing their spears at the smaller Fureath'i, but Dallid had been right in his estimation that they were weary. The north-men fought for their lives, but it was with muscles that no longer seemed to hold any strength. It was possible Frehep had drained the Prae'surlas of all their strength, as punishment for entering his sacred land, but the sun god did not work that way. Instead, the sun brightened as one of the Prae'surlas saw Dallid in his daze of uncertainty and thought to give him a quick death for it. A lazy spear swipe came and Dallid ducked under it trying to thrust his sabre forward as he did, but the ice-man had stepped forward into the attack too, turning Dallid's blade to only graze along the ribs. To make matters worse, the giant then grabbed his monstrous spear and thought it would be a good idea to crush Dallid with it.

Caught between the spear haft and the chest of the Prae'surlas, Dallid tried to move his arm as much as he could to frantically stab his blade again. Both his arms were caught tightly in the deadly grip though, with the north-man breaking his spine with the spear and squeezing all life and air out of Dallid with his big brute arms from either side. The best Dallid could do was turn his wrist to burrow the tip of his sabre into the graze he had already made. It became a test then of who could kill the other first: if Dallid could work his sabre in deeper and deeper to hit sometime vital, or if the

Prae'surlas could snap Dallid like a twig once all the air had left his body. The agony in his spine gave indications to which was most likely to happen, but then Dallid thanked Frehep as his fellow Fureath'i Jathen arrived. His friend's sabre entered the Prae'surlas in the back and Dallid hoped it had been the north-man's bloody spine that Jathen stabbed. The Prae'surlas gurgled something as he convulsed forward, releasing his crushing grip and Dallid had just enough energy to jump free as he fell.

Arching his back painfully, Dallid looked around to make sure no others were about to take him unaware but there was no need. The Fureath'i warriors had the surprise and the superior numbers. They had been enough for the north-men, all now lying dead or dying, and those were quickly dispatched. Even if the Prae'surlas had not been so aged or weary, the sudden viciousness of the Fureath'i warriors would have won victorious.

Jathen was grinning at Dallid as he tried to stretch away the pain and bruising along his back and sides. He knew he would have to suffer for a long time over what had just happened, and it would have little to do with the physical pain he was now experiencing. To avoid the smug look of his friend, Dallid scanned the remains of the camp spotting Emylias. She eyed him with her half smile and looked away coyly, which brought Dallid's gaze to their squad leader Terik. He too was eyeing Dallid, but it was not with the same alluring promise that Emylias gave him. Terik glared his uncontained displeasure, but, for the time did not give it voice. Instead he ordered out rangers to make sure there were no more Prae'surlas close by, and set the others to stripping the bodies for anything of use.

'Do you want to take the spear for this one, Dallid?' Jathen asked with an irritating grin. 'After all, you did look like you were about to win. Perhaps I should not have interfered?'

Other warriors were snapping off the spear heads of the Prae'surlas they killed as trophies. There was great importance in recording how many ice-men you slew. Some warriors cut a scar into their skin to represent a spear for each one, others took the actual weapons. Some would even take the north-man's head but none looked to be doing that now at least.

'No, Jathen, I will let you have this one, you need the extra spears after all.' Dallid nodded towards the other one he had killed to gain back some standing. 'I have many more that I can add to my tally.'

Jathen laughed when he looked to see the man had died on his back with his breeches still unlaced. It was not particularly dignified.

'Well, Dallid, you can take his spear if you want, but looking at the only one he is holding it is not something I would want!'

Dallid had to laugh with his friend at that, which earned him another severe look from their squad leader Terik. Sighing, Dallid busied himself with stripping anything of value from the dead. They would leave the exposed flesh of their bodies to rot under the sun.

'The sun god sees you, north-men,' Dallid said softly to himself. 'And he sees you dead by Fureath'i blades greater than mine.'

The rangers returned later without sign of any other Prae'surlas, so Dallid and his squad continued their patrol south and made camp as standard. None of the Fureath'i warriors in his squad had been killed or badly injured so it was only camp fires that greeted them that night and not funeral pyres. The same as every Foreigner deserved to rot; every Fureath'i deserved to die by fire. It was said to light your way and raise you up to the heights of power. It was where every warrior, who had been the best that they could be, came back a step better, to see how much more they could become again when born anew into the Fureath'i Life of Fire.

The ultimate goal of every Fureath'i was to come back as Powerborn of course, to not just have a figurative fire in your heart, but to physically be Connected with it. To be Flameborn, or the even stronger Fireborn, was to have the power of the gods flooding your every limb, to have so much that it healed flesh without limit, and erupted outward from your skin. To be Powerborn not only gave you the strength of a dozen men but also the power to burn a dozen men to ash with a gesture. Watching his own camp fire with wonder, Dallid could not even contemplate how it would feel to command such an element, to have it become a part of his very being.

'The sun god sees you, Dallid. Does he see you hiding from Terik?'

Dallid looked up to see Emylias smiling down on him. 'A Fureath'i warrior hides from no man,' he said, smiling back.

Emylias sat down beside him and warmed her hands from his small fire. 'So that is why you sit here instead of the heart fire.'

It was true that the majority of his squad were situated around the central heart fire, but every Fureath'i camp held a good number of fires, especially since the weather had become so cold lately. There could never be too many fires for a Fureath'i. Each one had a large number of uses such as heat, cooking, keeping predators away, some were for prayer and others for hiding from squad leaders.

'Terik is a skilled hunter,' Dallid said smoothly. 'The fault cannot be mine if he is unable to find me.'

'Much the way that north-man's cock found you today?'

Dallid laughed with her. 'What kind of twisted fate makes a north-man chose my exact location to relieve his bladder?'

'Perhaps you smell of piss, Dallid!' Jathen suddenly bellowed as he joined them. 'And like the dogs they are, the north-man wanted to add his scent to your own.' For a small man - the smallest Dallid had ever met in fact - Jathen was certainly loud and as he thumped down between Dallid and Emylias, he seemed to take up much more space than he needed. The fact that he was shorter than Dallid though made him love Jathen enough to forgive any number of irritations. He longed to pick the tiny man up and carry him off to Thisian to prove that there was actually a Fureath'i in the world smaller than Dallid. 'So,' Jathen continued, 'has Terik skinned you yet? Have I missed it?'

'The sun god sees you, Jathen,' Emylias said back. 'And he sees our friend Dallid here spending his time in solitary prayer to him, which means he has so far avoided our good squad leader.'

'So I haven't missed it!' Jathen roared. 'Frehep be praised!'

Dallid did love Jathen's shortness, but he also wished that Jathen was not so damned loud all the time. And he wished Emylias did not always have that damned playful grin of hers. The grin that always added a special spark to her green eyes, and the way her hair would fall down over her face, it painfully reminded Dallid of Phira. It had been three years since he had seen his wife.

Dallid had enough pain between the bruises of his back and sides, Jathen roaring in his ear, and Emylias smiling her way into his head, so he did not need to bring back the pain of Phira in his heart. He was about to demand of them what he should have done instead, if he should have let the blasted Prae'surlas piss all over him, when he spotted a strange flash from the darkness.

Flickers of red light danced all around the camp, but for a moment he thought he saw one of bright green. Too bright and too vivid to be his imagination, and placed too much like a pair of unnatural eyes. Whatever kind of creature would have green eyes so bright that could be seen in the dark, it was a creature that seemed to be looking straight at Dallid.

He was brought back to the present by a rough elbow from Jathen. Turning around to strike back, Dallid was halted when he saw the arrival of Terik.

'Warrior Dallid,' he said simply. 'I must speak to you of your actions today.'

Perhaps other warriors would have left Dallid and Terik alone for a private reprimand, lessening his shame somewhat, but not Jathen and Emylias. They would enjoy this too much.

'Yes, squad leader,' was all Dallid could think to say back.

Frowning down at him Terik took a breath to think where he could start. Terik was from the west of Furea, from the wastelands and the deserts on the other side of the mountains. Strictly speaking all western Fureath'i disliked easterners, thinking them soft from a life of ease within the bountiful forests. Terik however seemed to take his dislike of Dallid to glorious new heights.

'You grew up around these trees did you not?'

Dallid nodded.

'And you are Fureath'i are you not?'

Holding back the urge to sigh he spoke firmly instead, 'Yes, squad leader.'

'It is said a western Fureath'i can conceal themselves behind a single grain of sand if they wished...' Dallid tried to be an attentive soldier but as soon as Terik started that speech, he had to block off the rest. He was just so sick of hearing it: the desert warriors could hide behind a grain of sand, the mountain warriors behind a pebble, so why could a forest warrior with miles and miles of trees not remain hidden?

So Dallid used the time to think up curses for Terik instead, and Jathen and Emylias too. He left only just enough attention to know when to nod, know when to hang his head in shame and know when to proudly respond with a "yes, squad leader." It was going to be a degrading tirade of rhetoric and it was not going to be brief. At least his two friends were present to share in his humiliation and help him relive any parts that he might forget. Dallid accepted it was the sole purpose of friends to torment him and laugh at him at every opportunity. The three friends he had grown up with had certainly done just that. He missed Thisian.

Thisian had always been the quickest and the bawdiest. Kris had always been grim and serious but would show his dry sense of humour whenever the situation would merit it. As for Phira - he missed her so much that he found himself kissing a picture of her on a coin every night before he slept and every morning when he woke. He needed to be stronger. Demanding himself to be a better Fureath'i he readied himself to pay full attention to whatever patronising wisdom Terik was offering, but the bright green light flashed again from the woods. This time Dallid stood up and grabbed his sabre.

'What is it?' Terik asked looking in the direction Dallid was staring. 'What did you see?'

Jathen and Emylias picked up on Dallid's unease but the green light was gone. What could he say he had seen that the squad's scouts and sentries had not?

'Apologies, squad leader, I thought I saw something... green.'

There was a moment of silence around the fire to let the absurdity of his statement sink in. As much as they might have wished it, Jathen and Emylias could not be the first to comment. Terik actually looked pained when he spoke.

'Here stands the man that is married to a blaze commander. Phira the Unrivalled, a woman who has tens of thousands of warriors at her command, who is the youngest Fureath'i ever to assume such a title and soon to be the only woman to ever become a general, and you stand here in the middle of a forest and tell me you have seen something green?'

Dallid opened his mouth but was worried he would only laugh. Terik shook his head unable to comprehend that he had such a warrior under his command. The squad leader turned on his heel and left. Jathen and Emylias waited until he was out of hearing before falling over with laughter and only barely containing it behind their hands. Dallid buried his head into his own hands as he half laughed, half sobbed at his life.

'Dallid, my friend, do not despair,' Jathen consoled. 'If this thing is really as green as you say, then we shall fight it together as brothers. I will fight the entire eastern forest and they will sing songs and speak Tellings of our battle against this colour!'

Dallid wanted nothing better than to punch his brother warrior, but instead looked over at Emylias to see her eyeing him. Her laughter had faded and her look was not with the usual spark that she saved for him. Dallid knew it was the mention of his legendary wife that had done it. If Emylias truly wanted to bed Dallid then a marriage would not necessarily stop her. A Fureath'i woman could take a mate as she pleased and discard them just as easily. The only consequence might be to fight the wife of the man she had just bedded. The largest problem with that of course was that Phira had not achieved her rank as blaze commander, and the name of Unrivalled, without being absolute in her supremacy as a warrior. Phira could kill every man and woman in Dallid's squad if she wanted, and all at the same time.

Sometimes he could not believe that his wife was a blaze commander. Dallid often thought that Terik was young to have even the small command of thirty, and there was Phira a woman years younger in command of tens of thousands. His friend Kris too was ember class having several squads under his instruction, but both Kris and Phira had earned their rank by fanatic dedication and, of course, mountains of dead Prae'surlas.

That was one reason why it was important to mark how many spears you killed, Terik had only gotten his position as squad leader because he had killed more than ten. That was called a flare. Kris, he had heard, had recently achieved a roar of spears, having killed more than a hundred, hence his elevation to ember class. But Phira, through her own skill with a sword but also from ceaseless expeditions and planned attacks with each of her squads, could claim responsibility for more than a thousand dead north-men. A firestorm of spears made her the youngest blaze commander in history and Dallid had just killed his forth Prae'surlas a few hours ago.

So Dallid was married to a legend and wanted nothing more than to escape his own inadequacies by taking comfort in the arms of another woman. Emylias was no longer looking at him anymore and was instead joining Jathen in coming up with new and clever ways to make hilarious insults at Dallid's expense. He ignored them and was content to just watch Emylias as she laughed.

She was beautiful but they were only friends. Whatever stronger feelings they might sometimes imagine, it would not affect their friendship. It was the same as when Dallid sometimes had strong desires to punch Jathen right in the face and that did not affect their friendship. The only difference of course was that Dallid quite regularly punched Jathen in the face.

'Come,' he said, interrupting the current tirade of mockery. 'Let us join the heart fire and listen to the Tellings to save me from listening to you both amuse yourselves on my misfortune.'

Emylias smiled at Dallid and softly voiced her agreement. Jathen voiced his much louder and said, 'You are right, my brother, we have days ahead of us yet to amuse ourselves on your misfortune. It would be foolish for us to burn all that fuel so fast!'

With such things to look forward to, Dallid laboured over to join his fellow squad members in the listening of a Telling. It was Fureath'i custom to sing songs and speak Tellings at every camp fire, a custom founded by Frehep himself. Before he had become a god and was a Fireborn that walked the earth, Frehep had decreed that all great warriors and their deeds needed to be remembered so that all others could hear them and become better for the hearing.

There was even some Fureath'i that took the decree so far as to make it their life's work to create and spread those stories, calling themselves Tellers. Most of those even still thought of themselves as warriors, firing the hearts of their brothers wherever they travelled. Some Tellers were more historical Scholars or philosophical priests than story-tellers, and most Fureath'i saw them all as needing to just pick up a bloody sabre and join the army. But Dallid found it very enjoyable to hear the professional Tellings. Perhaps he had missed his calling. He could just imagine the look on Phira's face if it was found out her husband had become a Teller. Was being the lowest of warriors still better than being the highest of Tellers?

The Telling he was listening to now was just from a warrior in his squad, a woman named Panthera, and she was speaking about two Foreigners that Dallid did not much care about. One was called Protharik the Demonmaster, and he was an assassin with ghost-white hair and blood-red eyes. He summoned demons to do his bidding and could not himself die. Well he could die, but would always reappear over his still dead body and kill you in your surprise. It is said that you could kill the Demonlord a thousand times and stand atop a mountain of his corpses, and he would just reappear once more and kill you when you were too exhausted to fight any longer.

The other Foreigner in the story then was Valhar the Madman or Valhar the Bastard as he was sometimes known. The mad assassin liked to claim he was the bastard son of the great Amadis. The fact that he based that claim simply on the fact he wore the man's sword, spoke towards why he was also called Valhar the Madman. No-one knew exactly how Amadis died, or if he did die, despite the Prae'surlas and every other nation saying they were the ones to slay him (the latest rumour said that Amadis had spent the last five years meditating on a mountain top, waiting to reach his full power so he could slay all the gods) but regardless, he was far too powerful for someone like Valhar to kill. The fact remained however that the madman did wear the legend's sword.

The tale Panthera was speaking of concerning those two Foreign warriors was of Valhar hunting Protharik to see if his Jaguar sword could finally kill the demon lord. Dallid had joined the story where Valhar had just skinned one of the corpses of Protharik and the madman was dressing up in the skin. The reasoning was that he could trick Protharik into thinking he had killed himself, if Valhar stabbed him while wearing the Protharik skin-suit. It did not work. The next ludicrous plan was that Valhar sawed off an arm of one of the dead Prothariks, and then put his Jaguar sword into the dead hand, to try and slay the live Protharik with it. Needless to say that did not work either.

Panthera went to describe more and more plans, each more insane than the last. At one point Valhar gathered as many dead bodies of Protharik that he could find and sat them all down to discuss how exactly they could kill the bastard. It ended with Valhar simply capturing Protharik alive and deciding the only way to kill him was to never kill him. The squad cheered politely when the Telling finished but Dallid could see they were unimpressed.

Panthera's brother then, Parna, offered up his version of something better. Dallid always found it amusing to look at the brother and sister though as they both could have passed as the other. As all mountain Fureath'i did, they kept their heads shaved tightly. So with the same bald head, small eyes and same shade of golden dark skin, it was often impossible to tell them apart. He wished Thisian was there just so he could watch him try to seduce them both without knowing which the female was. The closer he got to his home village of Coruln, the more it seemed that Dallid's thoughts drifted back to his three friends from youth. It was not becoming of a warrior to dwell on the memories of childhood though, so Dallid fixed his attention back to the present. A fire burns what it can now and does not linger on the ashes of the past.

Concentrating on Parna's new Telling, Dallid was only mildly pleased to see that it was a Telling about Fureath'i at least and not about Foreigners or demons like his sister's had been. Parna had chosen a topical Telling too: it was about the Tower of Frehep that they were soon to arrive at, or the Tower of Guardians as it had been known in the tale being Told.

Growing up in the village right next to that tower, Dallid had heard the tale many times. He struggled to become interested because to him the only good Tellings were ones that had great amounts of Prae'surlas insults and even more Prae'surlas dead. Dallid was a fighter however and he would fight his boredom and disinterest if only to avoid leaving and becoming victim to more insults and abuse from Jathen and Emylias.

Parna's Telling was one of both Frehep the Holy and Chrial'thau the Great. It was set in the last years of Frehep as a man, after he had united all of the Fureath'i tribes, joining the desert warriors to the mountain warriors and then joining them all further east to the forest warriors. It was at the end of Frehep's reign as leader of their people that Chrial'thau's power had begun to shine through.

Both were Powerborn, and both were Fireborn, the most powerful of the Fureath'i warriors. Dallid knew that this particular story told of Chrial'thau's first legend and of Frehep's last before becoming a god. The title was called *'Chrial'thau and the Tower Guardian'*, where an army of Fureath'i journeyed further east than they had ever been before. Through the hot and raining forests they came upon an ancient stone tower standing far above all of the trees. They went to explore this tower but were met by a Guardian. Dallid stopped listening.

Try as he might, it was just too boring. He had heard so many versions of the Telling he had to stop himself from blurting out the ending to just put an end to it. In summary, Chrial'thau defeats the mysterious guardian and then replaces him for some reason while Frehep ascends to godhood. Some claim the guardian was Amadis, others say it was Brijnok or Moi'dan, it changed from story to story but the rest of the Telling always remained the same.

When Dallid grew up, it had not always been Chrial'thau who had lived in the tower; it had been Rhisean the Scarred for most of the years. Chrial'thau was the first but he left soon after and there were many others that replaced him as towerguard over the centuries, with each one honouring the role that a Guardian always be within the tower. It did not seem to matter that they had never had to guard it from anything. Then recently, almost two hundred years later, as an old man Chrial'thau the Great had returned to the tower, to stand guard once more and honour the role that he had founded. Dallid could still remember the day he had met the great Fireborn before they left for the army. It had been an honour.

Dallid's squad was getting close to the Tower of Frehep now and he was confident they would begin to see it over the trees tomorrow. Growing up next to the ancient building, along with living in such close proximity to legends like Rhisean, Chrial'thau, and Yiran, Dallid often wondered why he was so content with mediocrity. Perhaps he had no choice and was just incapable of greatness. An army cannot be filled with generals he supposed. Was it even worthwhile to become a squad leader if it meant being as large a pain as Terik?

Looking up to see where his squad leader's attention was, Dallid frowned to see it focused on him. In fact, looking around it seemed that all of the watchful sun's attention was on him. He really needed to stop becoming so lost in his own thoughts. Unclear about why everyone was staring at him, Dallid did not have many options available to him. His friend Kris would always just stare intensely at people until they answered their own questions or went away, so it was as good an option as any. Trying to remove any challenge from his look but keeping as much strength as he could, Dallid just sat there and met the eyes of Terik. Thankfully the squad leader spoke first.

'Well, warrior Dallid?' Terik said, giving the impression he had already spoken and Dallid had not been listening. 'Are you going to give your Telling or would you prefer to wait until the next time we are sneaking up on an enemy to do it?'

Why is everyone so bloody funny today? Dallid wanted to say, but at the same time he conceded that giving a Telling was not so bad. Growing up with Phira who was obsessed with every great Fureath'i, and with Thisian who was obsessed with every great Foreigner, Dallid had a well-stocked supply of Tellings at his disposal. But his greatest fortune had been that he had known a professional Teller named Nureail. She was a friend of Yiran's and would visit often, both to see the retired general and to pass word between the temples and the tower. Dallid had memorised her words.

He considered which story to tell and could see the looks in the other warrior's faces that they wished it was not another Telling about Phira. He did like to Tell those at every opportunity so he could spread her fame, but this time Dallid decided on Phira's master for a change.

'As you command, squad leader,' he said dutifully. He would give them the tale of when Yiran saved the mountain sanctuary of Il-Yu. It was when a mountain cat made of stone had been brought over from Sherah by some idiot squad of Prae'surlas. The cat had of course broken free and killed them all but it ended up heading for the closest mountains which were unfortunately in Furea. It would be a good Telling, plenty of Prae'surlas insults and deaths, and growing Yiran's legend for when they might meet him in the days to come. There was even a Fireborn in it too, Jaiha the Decider of Fates...

Another green flash appeared in the darkness and Dallid was certain this time they were eyes. He had no choice but to ignore it. The sentries on duty would find anything of danger, so it meant Dallid was just losing his mind. Turning to the familiar red of the heart fire for comfort, he was further dismayed as the bloody flames danced in front of his eyes to create what looked like a man with a burning sword. Dallid closed his eyes. Having them open was causing him nothing but trouble.

He took a deep breath.

'Did you know there is something uglier than a goat-rutting Prae'surlas?' he asked to the waiting squad. They looked back with understandable scepticism. '*Two* goat-rutting Prae'surlas!' This made the squad smile. 'And both rutting the same bloody goat!'

They all laughed at that. He had them. 'Now imagine if you can, twenty of these bastards, all still alive as outrageous as that sounds, and all thinking it is a good idea to travel to Sherah and bring back a monster made of stone! Well this is the tale that I will Tell you now...'

With his squad's full attention, Dallid began to enjoy his Telling. His gaze drifted to the woods briefly to see that two glowing green eyes still stared at him from a distance and he looked down to the fire to see that the swordsman of flames still looked at him too. His hand reached to Phira's coin that was strapped to his wrist, holding it to give him strength, and as he continued to give his Telling, Dallid made a silent prayer to Frehep that he could be better. Tomorrow could only be a better day. Then Dallid screamed as the creature of fire lunged forward and stabbed him with a sword of flames.

CHAPTER EIGHT

To be better

No-one else had seen the creature of fire. All they saw was a stray flame flare out and a grown man screech. Even though Dallid had a scar on his arm because of it, his reaction had been thoroughly mocked and he was made to continue his Telling, only with less screeching. When he had finally lain down to sleep later, it was with several parts of him crying for attention. His pride, his heart, his mind, all hurt, and the scar on his arm was the least of them. When the morning came, each pain remained.

'The sun god sees you, Dallid,' he said softly to himself. 'May he see you become better today...'

Every warrior within the watchful sun squad stood and greeted the new day with appropriate veneration. As a nation of warriors, their light might go out at any time, so they celebrated each new day as a fresh victory. Breathing in the sight deeply, Dallid closed his eyes to savour the feeling.

When he opened them he was greeted with Emylias. Her smile was as warm as the sun itself and she was a view just as welcome.

'The sun god sees you, Dallid. We will reach your home village today,' she said. 'How do you feel about your return?'

The question was asked kindly, but it was not a simple answer. Every Fureath'i was expected to sire at least four children by the time they reached an age to join the army. Female warriors were allowed remain longer to see a child through the first few months, but in the end all Fureath'i children were raised by grandparents who had retired from the army and returned to their villages as elders. So here was Dallid returning not as an elder, and neither did he have any children awaiting his return, which meant when the time came that he actually did retire, he would not have any grandchildren waiting for him either. But he smiled at Emylias and said, 'It warms my heart.'

'Perhaps I should stay close to your heart then to help battle this cold.' She laughed at her joke and Dallid laughed at how he was reading too much into her wording. The holy land of Furea was usually blessed with eternal heat. Even in the raining forests of the east the water that fell would be hot, and yet all of Furea was now growing colder by the day. It was worrying but many believed Frehep was merely testing their strength. The fact that the cold was getting worse, did not matter. It was pushed roughly from each warrior's mind. Dallid should have been pushing those thoughts away that instant and pulling Emylias closer to his body so they actually could warm each other up.

'Perhaps we have caused this cold by killing too many Prae'surlas,' he said back to her. 'With everyone we kill we are releasing the ice from their hearts out into the world.'

'I would not let other Fureath'i hear you saying it is possible to kill too many Prae'surlas, Dallid.'

'So I should not discuss my theory with Terik then?'

'No I think you should wait until you see something green again before speaking or screaming with Terik.'

For a moment they just smiled at each other and Dallid felt content. Jathen announced himself loudly then to destroy that feeling.

'The sun god sees you my friends, and he has just seen me take the longest piss I have ever taken in my life. Apologies, Dallid, that I could not find you in time to scream or ask if you wanted me to piss on top of you! But I had found something green in the forest to piss on instead and could not let the opportunity pass.'

'I would accept your apology if you could tell our squad leader of your finding,' Dallid said and hesitated before adding, 'and it was something bright green in the middle of the night and it looked to me like eyes.' He knew he would only receive more ridicule for it - and he had even refrained from speaking about the swordsman in the flames - but if there was some danger in the forest around them he would prefer they knew what to look for at least. It might give them some advantage if an attack came.

Jathen put his arm around Emylias's shoulders, he had to balance up on his toes to do it the man was so tiny, and Dallid wondered again how such a small man could be so damned loud.

'Well then,' he roared. 'I have found it. Are these not the brightest green eyes you have ever seen? And you certainly stare at them often enough! Emylias please, just take him, rut him, and be done with it.' And with that Jathen left them alone to their shared discomfort. Dallid opened his mouth to try breaking the unease but to his surprise Emylias became as blunt as Jathen.

'In the west, Dallid, we can take a man without word or reason,' she said boldly. 'But we have fewer marriages there. Perhaps I have simply spent too much time here in the east. Your forests have made me soft, Dallid. I think I am more interested in such a marriage now. Disband your marriage to Phira and marry me instead.' She lost some of her boldness at how vulnerable that statement left her.

Dallid wanted to say something as she stood there exposed but what was he to say? The silence grew longer until finally Emylias put back her defences and flashed him one of her impetuous smiles. 'But do not take too long to decide because I will bed you soon whether you wish it or not.'

She turned and left him there to deal with that last statement and Dallid felt like he had just been punched in the stomach. He had always known there was a hidden feeling of desire between them and knew that nothing would come of it more than playful flirting. And now she was speaking of marriage?

He was tremendously relieved to hear Terik call their squad to quick march. He was not on scouting or ranging duty and some simple running would do fine to clear his head. *She would bed me soon whether I wish it or not?* Dallid ran. The sun shone brilliantly and the forest path they travelled was good. There was every reason for Dallid to feel well and instead as they ran south he had a feeling of running to his doom. That doom was not just returning to his village as a mediocre Fureath'i either, and having great men look down on him with disappointment. It was facing Emylias again after what she had just said.

As rare as it was for the marriages of youth to not disband within the army, it was rarer still for two warriors to marry while of fighting age. Some elders married when retired, bettering the next generation of Fureath'i together, but active soldiers within the army? It was madness. *Madder than seeing eyes of green and swordsmen of fire?* Dallid looked ahead to his brothers of the watchful sun and hoped that Emylias was not close. He would accept any distraction to stop that next confrontation.

Describing Tellings to himself had always been a past time to give such distraction. He felt it helped him to perfect how he might perform them at a heart fire some night and that made his thoughts return to becoming a professional Teller. He could be free to go where he wanted and bed who he wanted as Tellers never married. And story Telling seemed to at least be something he was actually good at.

Even after Dallid's humiliating scream, his Telling had gone on to be a great success. So much so that Panthera had taken challenge from the failure of her own. But unable to see why hers had failed she told yet another one about Protharik the Demonmaster. It looked clear that she herself had some great interest in all things to do with demons and the world of darkness. At least she had the sense to set it in Surlas this time, where Protharik was summoning every kind of demon imaginable to kill and insult the Prae'surlas.

But Panthera's detailed descriptions had only been met with polite cheering every time the demons killed a north-man, and in the end it had bored the warriors in the squad to sleep. Dallid began to think of others he could Tell in future camp fires, if only to irritate Panthera, and show her how misguided and stubborn she was. The first good Tellings that usually came to Dallid's mind were of course of Phira. For such a short career she had been explosive in her living of it. As a blaze commander her face had even been printed onto the gold coins that the army were given. Turning the coin he had strapped to his wrist, it only reminded Dallid that he and Thisian had never done anything worthy of song, but his other friend Kris had, many times.

His favourite Telling of Kris's had to be the *Sword That Walks*, where while retreating from a much larger Prae'surlas host, after causing great mayhem from a night raid, a member of Kris's squad had become injured with his ankle broken. The squad could not stop, nor had they anything with which to make a stretcher. All they had were their swords and their wills, and that was always the way Kris preferred it.

For a time the man kept going, amazingly keeping pace with the squad, but eventually even an iron will can be undone by the weakness of flesh. Kris was unwilling to leave him behind, even if it was to grant him his last regret - to die killing Prae'surlas - and the man was unwilling to let Kris carry him. It would only slow down the squad despite Kris's insistence that it would not. Eventually Kris decided to make a casting out of their sabres, using the hilts under foot and tying the blades around the leg for support with strips from their clothing.

Dallid had heard from one or two Fureath'i that what actually happened was Kris had knocked the man unconscious and carried him anyway, forcing himself to keep up with the rest of squad running tirelessly for day and night. To Dallid, that sounded exactly like what Kris would do. But most Tellings say that the injured man struggled on, and that when eventually they reached the safety of Furea he needed to have his leg amputated of gangrene.

The last part at least is agreed by all, since now there really was a man in Kris's squad that had a peg leg of the melted down blades, made of Kris's and the other squad member's sabres. It was even grafted together and into the man's flesh by the fire magic of a Flameborn who had become inspired by the story of it all. They say now that the man could fight with the blade in his hand and the blade in his leg with the same ability, but Dallid was not so sure how much to believe that either. Perhaps he could use the metal peg leg as much as a man might kick during a sword fight, but nothing as far as some Tellers made it out to be.

The other Tellings of Kris were a little less fantastic, there was of course the *Blood of Frehep* where Kris ended up killing two of his own men in the heat of battle. They were a squad of fourteen at that stage and they ambushed a squad of twenty Prae'surlas. Kris killed half of them himself but in his fervour was unable to halt his swing when it came down upon Fureath'i flesh. Dallid did not like hearing that Telling, but it was admittedly more believable than the Sword That Walks.

One last Telling then that was well known was the *Fire That Sleeps* - ironic since Dallid was certain Kris never sleeps - where Kris and his men planned another ambush by burying themselves under the earth with just enough cleared to let them breathe. They had scouted the area and judged it the most likely place for the Prae'surlas party they were hunting to make camp. The least dramatic Tellings say his squad waited there for two entire days, with no food or water, just air and patience.

When the Prae'surlas party arrived and actually did make camp as Kris had calculated, still the waiting Fureath'i did not move. It is said that a Prae'surlas had even stood with his full weight upon Kris's head without the Fureath'i moving or reacting. He and his squad waited until dark when the larger Prae'surlas party was sleeping, their lookouts watching in the wrong direction and only then did Kris stir from the earth silently and slit the throat of every north-man in the camp. There was close to fifty Prae'surlas reported to have been in that party, and even the north-men standing guard and patrolling were hunted down by the Fureath'i squad after the slaughter was done. Kris was an impressive Fureath'i but a frightening one.

Dallid was about to launch into his recollections of Phira's Tellings, particularly the *Lighting of Hrosvidar*, but became distracted as sudden recognition came to him about the surrounding terrain. From where he ran, not only could he make out the stone tower in the distance, but the trees were thinning along the path they were following and Dallid could hear the sound of a waterfall close by. His history with the area was a more painful distraction than reciting Tellings to himself, but it would still serve his purpose to clear his mind of Emylias.

The squad would soon approach a canyon where the River Midanna cut deep into the land. It was one of the largest rivers in the world, running almost the full length of eastern Furea, and the sheer size of it to behold always left Dallid speechless. The canyon his squad was approaching then was a place that he and his brothers would often come to as youths with their grandfather. Where the river broke into waterfall was magnificent and as a family they would travel out to marvel at it. But any of the memories he could recall of that canyon would always be stained with the pain of one significant memory in particular:

He had three brothers at one time, and the four of them had been inseparable. Family had been the most important thing in bettering yourself as a Fureath'i according to their grandfather. All four brothers were close in age and all from the same mother and father which was very uncommon in a small village. Young men were encouraged to travel out far to mix their blood with the young women of other villages, leaving as many children behind before leaving for the army. But Dallid's parents had married young and stayed committed, much as he and Phira had done. But unlike them, his parents had served together in the same squad and he heard they even died together in the same skirmish against the Prae'surlas. It was a pleasing thought for Dallid but he did not know either of them and so could never muster feelings of loss. His grandfather though, he was a great man.

It was hard to recollect what age his grandfather might have been when it happened, but Dallid knew that he himself was only thirteen summers. Quite simply, his youngest brother Fredrin had tripped while playing with Dallid and fallen into the canyon. The tragedy was that he had managed to grip onto some roots and vines a way down, trapping him for a torturous time instead of giving him a clean death. His grandfather despaired at the situation and tried to judge how likely a rescue could be. The last thing he remembered of his grandfather was the look he had given Dallid.

He did not speak any words with that look and there had been no blame in those eyes, but the worst part of it was there had not even been the hint of asking Dallid to be the one to climb down. Even at thirteen he was strong, and the more he thought of that day, the more Dallid knew that he could have climbed down and pulled Fredrin up from the cliff.

But instead his grandfather had climbed down, had reached Fredrin and in trying to come back up they had both fallen to their deaths. He was too old to have been able to succeed and Dallid knew it, but he had hesitated. Going over the details of the day again and again, it was the hesitation that he hated the most.

He had taken the look his grandfather left him as leaving him the responsibility for his remaining brothers. Rhain and Royin were each a summer younger and again Dallid should have known better than to think they would accept his guardianship. He was not enough to compare with their grandfather, or even any other Fureath'i in the village. They were raised by other elders like Ryat and Yiran, but each night they still remained a family in the same wooden cabin, and Dallid tried to keep them close. They needed each other's strength to survive the tragedy but not only did his two brothers reject his gestures, they blamed him for everything. It was Dallid who had been playing with Fredrin so close to the canyon mouth. It was Dallid who was the only one strong enough to pull him back up. The bitterness and resentment grew stronger and stronger until it began to take violent form.

Dallid accepted the first attacks they gave him, hoping that it would vent their rage and return them to their family. But as Dallid continued to not fight back, the attacks only grew worse. It all ended then one day when they had come at Dallid with their sabres, he had to fight back but only to defend himself. Their intentions were clear however, that they wanted to kill him. Dallid never reconciled how they could have brought themselves to that point.

Kris had come across the scene and could also see that Rhain and Royin were intent on killing Dallid. Kris killed them both in an instant. He gutted Rhain and opened Royin's throat.

It was difficult for Dallid to describe how he felt about it. He had lost what was left of his family that day but it had brought him and Kris as close as brothers - not in the way that every Fureath'i warrior was his brother, but in a way that did not need words spoken between them to understand. Kris was a cold and distant man, yet Dallid took great strength in his presence and in his friendship. He had become part of Dallid's family from that day. There were four in his family again, him, Kris, Thisian and Phira.

Phira had her own problems with older brothers that beat her, and Dallid wondered if that played a factor in her wish to not want any children. She claimed her decision was purely because it would interfere with her training. But like it or not both Kris and Thisian had become their family. It made him smile to think of what Phira's reaction might be to that idea.

Looking to the tower in the distance, Dallid knew he would not have to come across the canyon using the path that they travelled, but still he turned his head in that direction and a flash of bright green caught him. He stopped immediately. That time had been no trick of his mind and it was certainly not the eyes of Emylias. He thought about bringing others of his squad to investigate the fey occurrence, but did not want to draw anymore ridicule on himself.

Dragging up the memories of what his weakness and inaction had brought before, Dallid made a rash decision - anything rather than hesitate. Knowing it was foolish, he darted off the path and deeper into the forest towards those green lights.

His youth had not been all violence and tragedy. Like every other warrior, he trained with every day to make himself a better Fureath'i. Being able to sprint through thick overgrowth, and not make a sound, was one of a number of skills from such dedication, even if his ability in other areas were lacking. Whatever those green eyes belonged to would not be able to hear him approach.

Spotting a clearing ahead, he slowed, bringing more caution into his movements. Alarming shapes began to form in his vision, and Dallid crouched to conceal himself. The bright yellow hair and blue clothing of the Prae'surlas were unmistakeable. He had no illusions that he could defeat more than one, let alone a full group of north-men by himself, but there was something about the scene that kept him approaching. None of them were moving.

The Prae'surlas were stupid, but even they could not be so witless to think they could sleep in the middle of the day in Furea. Then Dallid saw the source of the green flash and he had been right when he thought they were eyes. Where everyone else was on the ground, this single figure stood. His long black hair hung down over his face, but it could not conceal his eyes. They burned like green fire and made his skin look grey and dead by comparison. Power burned with frightening intensity from those eyes, and they were looking directly at Dallid.

No. The thing could not be looking at him. He was hidden. Not even another Fureath'i would be able to spot him from such a distance. The fact the strange creature was staring in his direction was pure chance. It was true that Dallid's fortune had not been good recently, so doubts, as always, started to creep into his head. Why would the man, who he could assume killed all of the Prae'surlas, be just standing there and staring at nothing? He was staring at Dallid.

Blinking the sweat of fear out of his eyes, Dallid grit his teeth and stood up from his concealment. The creature made no reaction. Ridiculously, to Dallid's mind, one man was not as dangerous as an entire squad of Prae'surlas - even if that one man had just killed the entire squad - and remarkably Dallid took some shaky steps forward.

The man with the burning green eyes was not armed, so neither did Dallid draw his sabre. When he entered the clearing it was evident that all of the Prae'surlas were indeed dead. They had visible sword wounds which at least meant the man in front of Dallid was not magic, but where was his sword? And the power that roared out from the man's eyes immediately contradicted Dallid's judgement about not being magic. What did he know about anything like this? He should not rush to conclusions.

'The sun god sees you, stranger,' he greeted in the hope that any man willing to kill Prae'surlas might be a friend to the Fureath'i.

The grey skinned man looked up towards the sun and then back down to Dallid.

'The sun god sees me.'

He repeated the words as if tasting them in his mouth. His voice sounded wrong. It sounded like an echo of another man's voice. Dallid began to wonder if the creature standing before him was a man at all. He could of course be some kind of Foreign magic, if not a Powerborn, some kind of sorcerer. But he suspected the thing came from a different place than the world of light.

'Yes, he sees you killing Prae'surlas and he is pleased,' Dallid said carefully. 'I also am pleased to see them dead. Did you kill them all yourself?'

'They killed themselves by attacking me.' His green-fire gaze drifted down to where Dallid's sabre lay still at his hip. Dallid was grateful for the intensity of the thing's stare to move away. With its wrong voice and dead grey skin, Dallid could think of only one thing the creature could be.

'You are a demon.'

The green eyes flashed back up with what could have been amusement but the creature did not smile.

'I am a demon,' it repeated softly. The creature then turned up its palm in mimic of a Fureath'i greeting.

The skin on the palm started to bulge and blister, and something pierced out in a flow of thick green blood. Dallid was horrified to see it keep coming, as a jagged blade ripped and tore its way through the demon's skin, growing longer and longer until the full length was held in the demon's hand. The sword was white where it was not stained with blood and skin, and it looked to be made out of bone.

Dallid had to struggle not to throw up, and in his shame he almost wet his breeches. His head told him to run, but his body had the final say as always and did nothing. He did not know if it was from hesitation, from horror or from cowardice. He just stood there and stared down the terrifying demon while trying to express an appearance of confidence and calm. He wanted to touch the coin on his wrist for strength but did not dare to move.

When the demon darted forward, Dallid immediately knew he had made a mistake in not drawing his sabre. But the creature was so quick that even if he had his steel ready he was not sure it would have done any good.

The demonic sword entered flesh and a Prae'surlas let out a final noise.

The demon remained where it was, in a kneeling position, with his sword plunged deep into the freshly stabbed north-man. The Prae'surlas's hand had been wrapped around the broken haft of a spear and it rolled free when the demon pounced. Dallid had been so terrified of the devil he did not even notice the ice-man moving to grasp it. The green eyes lifted up to meet him again, lingering on Dallid's sabre as if wanting him to draw.

'What is your name?' Dallid asked instead, his voice cracking. If there was a demon from the world of darkness in the land of Furea, he would need to tell people. Even if it was killing Prae'surlas, it was still a demon and would have to be driven out. So as a warrior he needed this information, but as a living person he wanted to keep the creature talking in the hopes that its friendship might spare him his life.

'My name.'

It spoke the words as if they were an answer and stood up slowly pulling the sword free. The devil returned to staring at Dallid.

'Attro'phass,' the demon said finally as if thinking about whether or not it was right.

'My name is Dallid Fureath'i,' he said back. He even smiled to show the demon that they had just become friends. The Attro'phass demon cocked its head in confusion at the gesture. 'Why are you in Furea?'

The devil turned his head the other way before answering slowly. 'The Tower of Guardians, that is next.'

Dallid waited for it to say more but the demon seemed to think that it had answered the question. The Tower of Guardians was the older name for the Tower of Frehep, dating back before the forests were part of Furea. For a moment Dallid considered if the demon was the tower's original guardian returned to reclaim the structure, but it was foolishness. Despite the idea being a mere flight of fancy, none of the Tellings he had heard ever hinted that the guardian had been a demon.

For a demon though, the creature was certainly being civil. It did not appear to want to hurt Dallid and seemed content to answer his questions. Opening his mouth to ask another, Dallid was transfixed by the devil's stare for a moment. The bright green light of its eyes looked to pulse with power and Dallid could not believe the reality of the situation he was in. Then the green eyes darted behind him and without thinking Dallid turned to see what it was. He immediately spun back realising his mistake but the demon had not used the distraction to attack. Instead the thing had simply disappeared.

He looked around in bafflement. The demon had been fast but there was nothing that was so fast as to disappear into a forest in so short a moment.

'Dallid!'

He turned to see Jathen run into view, his sabre ready. The tiny man looked around with his own bafflement to see Dallid standing in the company of so many dead Prae'surlas. He looked to his friend with an eyebrow raised.

'Stand witness to my might, Jathen, and know never to cross me,' he tried at first before breaking the effect with a nervous grin. The release almost made him cry instead of laugh. 'I did not kill these men.'

Jathen let out his breath with a laugh. It was good to know he had actually thought Dallid capable of such a feat. 'Dallid, how did you find them? When I noticed you gone I followed your tracks but it was only by hearing your voice that I came here.'

Dallid was shamed he had left tracks for Jathen to follow but tried to remain focused. Perhaps there was nothing he was skilled at.

'Well, Jathen, I saw something green and I followed it here. It was a demon, with green fires instead of eyes. It killed all of these north-men by itself.' He looked down to examine the ice-men and saw they were as similarly aged as the group his squad had encountered the day previous. Had it become a new Prae'surlas tradition to send their elders down to Furea to die?

'A demon? Are you certain? How could it survive in the world of light? Was it summoned?'

'I am not a Scholar of demons, Jathen, neither do I obsess about them like Panthera. All I know is what I saw and heard it speak. The thing pushed a sword made of bone right out of its hand and declared itself to be an Attro'phass demon.'

'The same ones that will come and take you away if you do not care for those of your own blood?' Jathen said the words in jest, but Dallid frowned at them. Could it simply be more ill fortune that Dallid had been recollecting how he had been responsible for the deaths of at least two if not all of his own family? Why then did the Attro'phass demon not attack him? It was a fool's thought and he was about to suggest to Jathen that they search the bodies when the squad's war horn sounded: one long blast to recall all scouts and rangers back to camp and two quick blasts to say they were engaged in battle. Giving each other a quick look of concern, both Fureath'i warriors turned and ran into the forest, leaving the north-men to wither and rot under Frehep's sun.

They spared no time for further conversation with each other, and even Dallid's mind was too focused on the battle to come to try making sense of what had happened. There were demons and north-men in his lands, with the demon at least having indicated it was going to the Tower of Frehep and, by extension, Dallid's home village of Coruln. It made sense the Prae'surlas had the same destination in mind, but the guardian of the tower was Chrial'thau the Great. Any Prae'surlas or demons that reached the tower would only be destroyed by the Fireborn. Dallid's head began to hurt at the confusion of it all and tried to focus his mind like a warrior: *If you cannot eat it, drink it, kill it or rut it, then let it burn.*

The war horn sounded again, followed by two quick blasts the same as before. They were getting close and Dallid took out his sabre to be ready. Perhaps this time he would finally be killed but what else could he do except keep running? He heard shouting from ahead and both he and Jathen pushed harder to reach the battle in time. A flash of green appeared to his left and Dallid panicked thinking the demon was following. Would it help in the killing of the Prae'surlas? As much as it might save Fureath'i lives, Dallid still hoped the demon would not. The thing terrified him.

He made out the images of Fureath'i fighting Prae'surlas through the trees and all thoughts thankfully disappeared from Dallid's mind. He lifted up Phira's coin to his lips and kissed it. There would be no hesitation. Hesitation came from thinking, so he would act; not think. Dallid burst out of the tree line with a roar.

CHAPTER NINE

To kill Prae'surlas

When Dallid entered the battle, the only warriors left standing were Fureath'i. Jathen was seconds behind him and was greeted with the same sight. The battle was over. His squad had not needed him. The ground was decorated with northern dead, but there were also Fureath'i bodies among them. Dallid's eyes swiftly went to every warrior still standing and he did not see Emylias. Trying to hold back panic he looked to the dead but it was difficult to identify them all. The green flash appeared at the edge of his vision again and Dallid thought he would burst from frustration. Was Emylias dead? Why did the demon not show itself? Was it stalking them? The burn scar on his arm flared with fresh pain and all that was missing was for the swordsman of fire to appear and steal his mind.

'Dallid, what is wrong?' Jathen looked at him with concern. 'I don't think I've ever seen you this frightened. Some of our brothers are dead but they have died killing Prae'surlas. They can have no regrets and are now rising up the heights of power as we speak.'

Dallid did not answer, his eyes continued to search everywhere, looking for the demon in the trees, looking for Emylias in the dead. He could hear Terik giving orders to the men, but Dallid ignored him as he ignored Jathen. Warriors began stripping the north-men of valuables and dragging their corpses away. Others were gathering the fallen Fureath'i to prepare the funeral pyres for later. He saw Terik look at him and say something but then two more Fureath'i arrived from the forest. Dallid's entire body sagged with relief when one of them was Emylias. She went straight to Terik.

'Squad leader, we have sighted three more parties of Prae'surlas, all heading south towards the tower.'

Dallid's eyes automatically went to where the tower peered above the forest in the distance. He could see smoke a short way west of the giant stone structure. The Tower of Frehep could not burn, so that meant it was his home village of Coruln that was in flames. Everyone else saw it too and the conclusion was quickly reached. Terik signalled which way for the rangers to go, ordered one more call from the war horn and then, as a squad, they ran. If the small wooden huts of the village were burning then it meant north-men attacking the elders and children that lived inside them. There could be no greater motivation to give strength to the legs of every warrior in the Watchful Sun. All thoughts of Emylias or Phira, his family and his friends, the demon, the swordsman of fire, each vanished as Dallid ran. They would return and burn the fallen dead after, but for now only one thing consumed the mind of each warrior: there were Fureath'i to defend and Prae'surlas to kill.

Dallid's legs burned as he kept pushing himself harder in the run, but he did not know how long he could keep the pace. They all ran at a sprint. They were not far from the village when they saw the smoke, but sprinting at full speed through forests was testing, yet not one of his squad showed any sign of slowing. Thankfully, it was not long before they reached the village, and when they did smoke began to choke Dallid's ragged breath. He could hear the roar of the fire even above the shouts and screams of people fighting and dying. The final sound that greeted him was of steel meeting steel.

Raging flames and corpse-filled streets slammed into Dallid's view. Running past a blazing building and even leaping over a dead Fureath'i, he saw the first of the enemy Prae'surlas. The giant was swinging his spear widely, keeping his much smaller opponents at bay - the other Fureath'i barely coming up to the chest of the monster. Dallid was shorter than them all and was not sure what he could add to the fight, but he would not hesitate.

Charging straight in without thought or plan, Dallid had to throw himself to the ground to avoid the sweeping blade of the giant's spear. Finding himself down at the northerner's feet, he cut his sabre into the man's ankle, and then dived upwards to ram his blade right into the thigh. He scrambled backwards and drove one final blow into the small of his back. That third blow killed the Prae'surlas, just before he was able to pin his heavy spear down on top of Dallid.

Rolling free, Dallid stood up and looked down in shock at the giant he had just killed. The elders and youths that had fought with him did not waste any time to congratulate Dallid on a good kill or in asking where he had come from, they were already charging at the next enemy. All over the burning street there stood giants, each fighting off three times their number in Fureath'i warriors, with many more dead at their feet.

Hesitating a while to consider where he should go next or what he should do, that same hesitation fired up a burning rage at himself. He would act, not think. This was his home village! Dallid reached down and caught a hold of the long spear the dead Prae'surlas had used, finding it awkward and heavy. But it would also be unexpected and once his grip was secure, Dallid simply picked the north-man nearest to him and charged.

Surprised to have to defend against a charging spear thrust, the giant was thrown off balance just enough for a Fureath'i blade to find its way to his ribs. The ice-man let out a roar and picked up the warrior who had stabbed him, head butting her to the ground with a loud and wet crunch. Dallid then stuck his spear into the north-man and let go of it just as the Prae'surlas turned his attention on him, swiping his own spear with greater skill. It caught Dallid's cheek even as he dived to the ground, tearing a sizeable chunk out of his face. Had he not let go of the spear then it would have most likely swept clean through his skull.

Only minutes into the battle and I am almost killed.

Pushing back to his feet, Dallid tried not to let the injury slow him down. His enemy still stood and awkwardly Dallid lunged back in with his sabre. The attack came at the same time as a sword from a different Fureath'i. She struck the kidney while Dallid struck under the armpit. Roaring out like a brainless beast again, the big Prae'surlas kicked the young woman in the chest, with a snapping sound of broken ribs coming just before her scream of pain. Dallid then got the haft of the north-man's spear slammed into his face, flaring fresh agony in his wound and breaking his nose by the feel of it. Blood sprayed from his face and his vision blurred with tears as he fell to the earth.

Dallid knew he needed to move. His enemy still stood and would kill him if he did not. Blinking his vision back to some normality, Dallid looked up fearfully at the Prae'surlas he had stabbed. The wounds they had given the northerner were many though and he looked like he was feeling the effects. The giant wavered on his feet for a moment, making testing motions with his twin gripped spear against the other Fureath'i warriors that were now harassing him. Looking around to be sure no more would show up, the warriors seem to reckon they could wait the dying Prae'surlas out. But they did not have to wait long as the giant soon fell to his knees with blood pouring from his mouth, his wounds becoming too much.

The Fureath'i wasted no time and dove in to stab the fallen giant. Dallid followed them with his eyes as they ran to find more enemies. The heat from the fires blurred his vision as much as the tears from his broken nose, but motions of battle swung from all directions. Roars of victory and of death filled his ears and the stench of blood and of emptied bowels filled his nostrils.

A familiar figure stood out to him then, his vision gladly clearing. Finding courage from somewhere, Dallid got back on his feet and ran over to assist the village elder he had spotted. Ryat was fat for as long as Dallid could remember, but he was also as strong as a bull. Dallid arrived to the fight just as the old fat man ducked nimbly under a spear head and blocked the swinging return. Two other young warriors fought on the other side and as the giant swung again for Ryat, the back end of his spear caught a youngling in the head.

The giant then kicked Ryat in the gut and turned to stab the remaining youth in the chest. The blade got temporarily stuck in the poor youth's ribs but still Dallid did not have an open target for his sabre. This Prae'surlas was well armoured, perhaps even a squad leader of the invaders, and seeing Dallid he let go of his captured long spear. Instead he pulled out two single-handed short spears from his belt and turned to face Dallid head on. Before he had the chance to use the new spears though, Dallid decided to drop to the ground again, using his small height to his advantage, and slid in to crash a kick onto the north-man's knee, with a satisfying crack. Howling in pain but backhanding his spear to reply, the Prae'surlas sliced across the top of Dallid's leg. It did not seem a deep cut but the flesh pulled apart all too easily. Ryat was back on his feet by then and shouldered his bulk into the giant, against the same disjointed knee cap. There was another howl as the man fell and both Dallid and Ryat dived atop him stabbing as quickly as they could. Dallid did not feel the injury in his leg. Everything was fire. It surrounded him and it was inside him.

Their blades slick and their clothes sticky with gore, the two warriors only nodded their respect to the other. Dallid had never felt so proud. He tried to follow after Ryat as the elder ran off in search for more Prae'surlas to fight but the cut on Dallid's leg made him stumble. The adrenalin of battle seemed to push him onwards for a time but the fire he had felt inside of him soon began to burn only in the wound of Dallid's leg. Ironically all that fire seemed to turn his muscle into water. His face throbbed, his nose stung and his leg needed stitching. He could not keep fighting.

From a distance he spotted the last three Prae'surlas that remained in the burning village. The giant's fought side by side now, as Dallid's squad and the remaining villagers closed in. He saw it was Terik who killed the first, showing a display of speed and skill, feinting high and then spinning in low, coming in across the leg and back up along the stomach. He met two spear attacks with solid blocks as he removed himself from the proximity and straight away went back in to finish the job.

All the Fureath'i charged then, two of them taking full spear thrusts straight through and capturing the north-man's weapons. Brave acts but perhaps foolish when considering the fight was soon to be won. Dallid managed to arrive just in time for the fight to be over. When it was done everyone looked around for signs of more, their gazes avoiding the ground that held so many dead or dying brothers. Instead they kept their chins high to scan for the frozen-eyed giants. Dallid and his squad had arrived at the west end of the village so when no more Prae'surlas were visible, Dallid started to hobble east.

He was worried that if he stopped moving he might not be able to begin again. His mind thrashed from thinking about the injuries he had received to looking between every burning building where a dozen Prae'surlas could suddenly charge. When he turned a corner to confront a group of Fureath'i warriors, he had to halt his attack, almost falling when he put weight on the wrong leg.

'Are there others to the west?' the lead warrior shouted at Dallid, but Dallid did not reply. The lead warrior was Yiran the

Unconquered. He was drenched in far more blood than Dallid, and not any of it looked like his own. Yiran strode threatening towards him. 'Answer me, man! Where are the rest?'

It was not hesitation that stilled Dallid's tongue. It was the closure to thought that he had done to protect himself. To make hesitation impossible, he needed to act and keep moving, not stop and begin thinking. Yiran's eyes squinted with impatient rage and he was about to strike some answers from Dallid, when the Watchful Sun and the remaining villagers arrived behind him. Ryat stepped forward and clasped arms with Yiran.

'It is good to see that you are not so old the north-men could conquer you, Yiran. Although I could hear the creaking of your bones from the other side of the village!'

'And it is as I suspected, old man, that you have become so fat that a north-man's spear cannot cut you!'

Both men laughed and it seemed incongruent to the burning buildings and scattering of bodies, but such was their humour.

'Yiran the Unconquered, it is an honour to meet you.' Terik strode up and bowed his head in respect, before offering his arm to greet the legend as Ryat had done.

The old warrior raised his eyebrow and grinned at Ryat. 'You can honour me later, lad, right now the sun god sees us and sees we still have more ice-men to kill. You have cleared them from the west I can presume? Well, as sure as Ryat has the biggest tits I've ever seen, I can tell you there are more of those ice-eyed bastards around.'

Terik smiled uncomfortably and withdrew his waiting hand, not wanting to appear foolish. Dallid gave a soft laugh that Terik would need to do more than that to not appear foolish. But this turned everyone's heads toward Dallid, in particular Ryat and Yiran's. Their eyes seemed to look right into his heart and Dallid shrank beneath the veterans' stare. Both men dwarfed him equally in width of shoulder and depth of chest, Yiran almost a full head taller, and Ryat with such a large stomach that incredibly made him look even stronger. Dallid had never felt so small, in so many ways, but Ryat saved his discomfort by gesturing toward him.

'Yiran, look who Frehep has sent to us, young Dallid the boy has returned a man!' Up until that point he had been a little unsure if the elder had really recognised him before. But the smile Yiran gave him made Dallid's soul soar up to the heights.

'Dallid, my lad, I thought it might be you underneath all that ice-man's blood. It warms my heart to have you fight at my side. Would that we had Phira and Kris with us now, and yes even Thisian, we could march all the way to Surlas!' He turned to the warriors of Terik's squad and went on. 'Here stands one among the finest warriors I have had honour to teach, and never one with more heart.'

Dallid could barely stand but took strength from the looks of respect Yiran's words drew out of his fellow warriors. Many even nodded as if they had always known such a thing about Dallid. Without thinking he searched out for Jathen and Emylias to see what expression they held but was interrupted by Yiran's call to action.

'Come! If those inbred ice-dogs are not busy rutting with their goats or their mothers, then they will be at the Tower of Frehep. Let us see how Lord Chrial'thau will punish them for attacking our land!'

Yiran slapped Dallid on the back, almost knocking him over and began the run for the tower. Ryat and the villagers followed suit, and after a moment Terik nodded to the squad that they should of course follow. He even gave Dallid a separate nod of respect. It was a heady mix of blissful pride and exhausted delirium. Then to make matters worse Dallid found Emylias as she lingered to place a hand on his chest.

The rest of the squad was already out of sight, Jathen running with his head turned to laugh at Dallid. He was pleased Jathen had not been hurt in the battle but only as far as he could punch him in the face later. Soon he too was lost as the squad of warriors turned a corner, following the path towards the imposing tower. It loomed over them now but that was not what Dallid was concentrating on.

Emylias held his face in her hands, shaking her head at his blood soaked body. His friend Thisian had a vulgar saying that western women were only as wet as the Prae'surlas blood on your blade. It was true that western women had a reputation for getting sexually excited by slaughter, but he had never thought Emylias was one of those. She smiled at him and leaned in uncomfortably close. Her breasts pressed up against his chest, and her face brushed lightly against his ear.

'Do not die this day, Dallid. You have much to live for if you survive.'

Her smile was enough to heal all his wounds and fuel his body for another full week of fighting, and as she ran after their squad, she was an easy target to follow. Dallid's leg still sent a jolt of pain up through him every time it landed in the run, and breathing was hard as his throat filled up with blood from his mouth, but Dallid kept Emylias in his sight. Her tight leggings had come away with surprisingly little blood from the battle and her hips from behind were a very pleasing sight. He supposed she was so clean because she did not fight as bluntly as he did. She would not need to charge in head first and hope for the best, she would be able to deflect and strike, as gracefully as an eagle, much the same way Phira did.

Thoughts of his long-missed wife dispelled any fantasies he humoured about taking comfort with Emylias. He did not count himself as much, but he was a better man than to ever betray his wife.

The dissolution of those thoughts brought him back to the reality of his wounds. He could no longer run, so broke down to a laboured walk. Even moving his thigh as slowly as he did was agony now and he ended up having to drag it to the side, no longer able to move his knee. Emylias vanished from his view, but there was no mistaking how close the Tower of Frehep stood. The gigantic structure dominated most of the sky and he would soon be there. The shame of his late arrival would perhaps not fully extinguish the honour his acts and Yiran's praise had given. He might still die a warrior. The roar of battle sounded ahead and made Dallid grit his teeth to force a run once more. He fell after three steps. It was too much weight on his injured leg. But he pushed back up to an angry stand, and, dragging his foot again, Dallid kept going.

He thought he could make out Yiran's roar and that of Ryat, since he had grown up listening to them, and one or two female shouts sounded out too, but he could not know if they were Emylias. The brothers and sisters in his squad and his village could be dying right now beneath the spear of a north-man and all Dallid could do was limp and drag his weakness at a speed to shame a child.

His fist tightened and re-tightened around his sabre, becoming angrier and angrier with each step, trying to focus that into swiftness. A green flash came from the forest to his left and Dallid's rage fled to become terror. Not allowing himself to stop, but not allowing himself to foolishly believe he had seen nothing, Dallid kept going and turned his head to all sides as he limped. If the demon attacked him in his injured state, it would be the end of him, but then what good would he be against the Prae'surlas if he was so feeble?

Thoughts of the demon vanished then as the forest ended. A tranquil lake spread out in front of him, stretching up north with the woodlands following along its edge. The clear blue sky coloured it brightly, with the exception of a great shadow down its centre. The dark stone of the Tower of Frehep imprinted itself onto the lake, and as Dallid kept going the earth of the tower grounds opened before him.

Back in the village the Fureath'i had outnumbered the Prae'surlas giants and had still paid a high cost in the fight. This time it was the northern spearmen that outnumbered the Fureath'i, and his countrymen were paying far more dearly for it. The fight could not be won. Dallid limped on regardless. His leg tried to give way underneath but he would not let it, instead he made it to an enemy and chopped down hard with his sabre making the nearest Prae'surlas raise his spear to block and expose his stomach. Terik dived in and cut open his guts in a lightning manoeuvre. These north-men were not armoured, and would pay for their arrogance.

Terik ran off and Dallid had not even realised it was his squad leader he had been fighting with, but tried to plan as Phira would. It was not hesitation but there was no chance of victory without a plan. Scanning the grounds he saw Yiran fighting on his own against two north-men and Dallid's plan was formed. If they had one chance of winning at all it was Yiran the Unconquered.

Limping over at a broken run, Dallid's plan was to keep Yiran alive and keep him killing Prae'surlas. If he could gather others and keep them together in the same way then they stood a chance, but fighting individually as they did meant certain death. Terik may be talented at killing north-men, but he was a poor squad leader to let his men fight so scattered. Ryat had at least kept some villagers with him, and the dead brothers lying at Yiran's feet meant he had begun with the same.

When he arrived he saw Yiran take a cut on the arm but keep fighting. Those arms had always looked like they were made of iron and for a moment it even surprised Dallid that they could bleed. A third Prae'surlas circled around Yiran then and tried to stick him from behind. It was Dallid's sabre that stabbed the back of the Prae'surlas instead and the falling giant almost wrenched the blade out of his hands. Not an honourable kill but the north-men did not deserve one.

Yiran turned to see Dallid's dispatching of the Prae'surlas behind and quickly went back to the two he had in front. One of those moved to attack Dallid but taking his attention off Yiran was the last mistake he made. Yiran's speed and strength where the stuff of legend and even past his sixtieth year he was able to stab the Prae'surlas in the side and punch the other in the face before either could react. Dallid rammed his blade forward to the stomach of one but was not fast enough. The giant knocked the sabre clear and went to punch Dallid with his other hand. Yiran was fast enough however and his sabre cut down into the swinging arm of the north-man, before spinning behind and plunging the weapon between his shoulder blades.

Awkwardly picking up his fallen sword, Dallid laboured back to a stand and staggered after Yiran. Seeing that Ryat and his two younglings had finished with their fight he yelled over to them.

'Ryat! All to Yiran! To Yiran the Unconquered!'

Ryat understood what Dallid was thinking and began to repeat the shout around to the other Fureath'i. Dallid could see Terik turn his head to hear the shout but ignored it as he concentrated on his own fight. Yiran had already run straight for another fight too, three more Prae'surlas, so Dallid and Ryat followed after to aid him. Trying only to distract and to throw the Prae'surlas off balance, Dallid almost laughed at some of the attacks he delivered. None had any real chance of inflicting damage but the Prae'surlas on instinct would still meet the assault, leaving them open to Yiran's more deadly precision. The old legend's every move either came away with a spray of blood, or forcibly knocked back the far larger warriors who tried to defend. His power was so great that Dallid even watched him in one movement knock a spear fully out of a giant's hands before ramming the butt of his blade into the giant's throat, crushing the windpipe and killing him.

One youngling of Ryat's went down but another three came over, and Dallid was even glad that his own squad still fought as individuals. If the remaining Prae'surlas gathered in numbers and attacked them, then Yiran might be killed, but as it was the warriors of the Watchful Sun took away two to three Prae'surlas each, even if it did mean their deaths. Dallid watched one of the mountain warriors fall to a spear, not knowing if it was Parna or Panthera, but had no time to grieve. Yiran did not stop, so neither would those that defended him. The man was a relentless whirlwind of death and wherever he went, Prae'surlas died.

More and more he killed, but it seemed more and more Prae'surlas remained in front of him. The northerners were not as stupid as Dallid thought and had indeed decided to muster together to kill Yiran. A spear flew in from the side and Dallid turned in time to see it catch another youngling. It had been aimed for Yiran.

A different north-man circled behind and Dallid turned to meet him. He gave four tired swipes of his sabre to give pause to the giant, but the north-man just smiled and slammed the haft of his spear into Dallid's injured leg. A white flash appeared before his eyes and Dallid howled before falling. He still managed to jam his sabre down into the man's giant boot as he landed though. Pulling it out he rolled over and reached in to do the same to his calf, and again to his leg. The giant fell and Dallid was able to call enough energy to dive over and continue finding places to put his sabre. The small sword found willing flesh again and again, and Dallid had to force himself to stop.

Standing was as much a victory as was staying alive, and Dallid lifted his sabre with a weak victory cry. Other voices echoed the call, but too few to bring hope. Not allowing himself to see how many of his squad still fought, he stumbled into Yiran's defence again. Hacking at flesh and pushing at spears, a blackness started to creep behind Dallid's eyes, and a new battle began to remain conscious. At that moment more Prae'surlas charged in from the left.

A spear entered Ryat in the stomach and another in his side. The elder was able to hack off a hand of one of his killers, before lodging his sabre down the collar bone of the other. The fat old elder, always so warm of heart and quick of tongue, fell to the ground and did not get up.

A paralysing pain entered Dallid's shoulder from behind then and he was lifted from the ground. He was sent flying forwards causing him to land painfully on his good arm, twisting the wrist. The impact made blood gush out of his leg wound and Dallid felt dirt and earth enter the hole in his cheek. He could not move the arm where the spear had taken him in the shoulder and closing his eyes became the only thing he could do.

No!

Dallid balled his right hand into a fist, challenging the pain in his wrist to compete with the rest of his body. He opened his eyes and saw Phira staring back at him from the coin attached to his vambrace. Dallid nodded to her and through bleary eyes looked up to see the end of the fight. Yiran still fought, now against six Prae'surlas, and impeded as his vision was, Dallid could not see any others standing. Grasping about uselessly for his sabre, Dallid spotted one several feet away, although not sure if it was his. He pushed himself with his right elbow towards it, leaving his left arm hang loose and right leg with the wound turned away from the ground.

If I am to die then I will die better than I lived, he insisted. *Kris would not give up, Phira would not give up, Yiran would not give up, so neither will I!*

The Unconquered legend downed one of the six Prae'surlas he fought and was rewarded with a spear in the hip. Then another figure bounded in and Dallid thought it was Terik. He fought like a snake darting in and out too quickly for a Prae'surlas spear to meet, and Dallid turned his head to see the north-man that had stabbed Yiran in the hip was now lying dead with the legend standing over him. Yiran the Unconquered let out a roar that should have sent every last north-man running in terror. But the fools remained.

Reaching down to grab a second sabre from a fallen brother, Yiran strode forward at the last four Prae'surlas, with two ready blades, both hungry for blood. Terik still harassed the enemy but they paid far more attention to the striding death of Yiran that now approached. In one swing a spear was down and with the other the giant that had held it. The Fureath'i legend looked like he had been possessed by Frehep himself, still moving with immense strength, batting away spears of far stronger enemies with ease and contempt. Dallid smiled a drunken smile that the sword Yiran was using might perhaps be Dallid's fallen one, and he smiled again in his earlier estimation that the Prae'surlas were indeed fools for not running.

Terik snuck in and cut one of them, while Yiran barged in and killed two. Even Terik stood back in fear as Yiran moved forward to kill the last. He hacked both blades down viciously at the north-man and did not stop, sending up a storm of blood to the skies, painting the heavens with every swing of his blade.

Then it was done. The sun even chose that moment to break out from behind a cloud, bathing everything in fresh light. The omen was not lost on Yiran and so he half-fell and half-knelt, to give praise to Frehep. Terik mimicked the act but it seemed to Dallid that he bowed more to Yiran than to the sun. The sight even gave Dallid renewed strength to lift himself from where he lay in his crawl and turn towards the sun. He was not able to kneel but he still bowed his head in thanks to Frehep for gifting his people with a man such as Yiran.

Once they had paid their respects Terik began running around to each of the bodies, slitting the throat of every Prae'surlas who still had a head. When he came across a brother or sister who had climbed all that they could in this life, he had the grace to take their own blade and ease it down into their hearts. It was a good death for a warrior to have. Later they would be burnt to help them journey the heights faster, but each one had died killing Prae'surlas and would die without regret.

A shadow made Dallid look up to see a legend above him. Yiran knelt down and gently helped him to a stand. He did not think he would have been able to, but in the presence of such greatness, Dallid found some extra strength somewhere.

'The blood of Frehep runs strong today,' Yiran said as he supported Dallid with one arm. Dallid looked around at all of the dead and was able to guess that maybe sixty Prae'surlas lay there. If he included the others back in the village - the number both from what his squad had killed and from what Yiran had killed - it could come far past a hundred. How had one hundred Prae'surlas made it so deep into Furea?

It would make for a great Telling none the less, where a small few Fureath'i killed one hundred Prae'surlas. The count of the children and elders unable to fight would probably bring the Fureath'i dead to much higher than that, but still the battle at the tower alone was deserving of song. If Dallid were to Tell it, he would say Yiran killed all one hundred himself. Absently Dallid realised that he had probably made his flare of spears, having killed more than ten Prae'surlas, but even though it was a goal he had long sought to achieve, the price he had paid seemed too great. His friends, his squad, and the villagers he had grown up with, had all been killed. They were all more deserving of life than he was, and yet he lived.

Dallid's mood lifted then as Terik returned with two others. His squad leader helped one man to stand much as Yiran did with Dallid. It was one of the younglings of the village that Dallid did not know. Perhaps he had changed much since Dallid lived there or perhaps he was just a young man come to find a mate from a surrounding village. The other Fureath'i still alive though was Emylias. This brought a broad smile of disbelief from Dallid and she smiled back to him.

'Perhaps I will have to be gentle with you later,' she said with a soft laugh, but grimaced in pain as she held a hand to a wet patch of blood at her side.

This even brought a laugh from Yiran which encouraged the others to join in, but there was little energy in it. Dallid would not say the words yet but Terik's return meant the death of his friend Jathen. The five of them were incredibly lucky to still be alive and Jathen was just one more fallen brother upon a list of many. Still he had been a good friend. Dallid could not even remember seeing or hearing the loud and tiny warrior during the last battle. He did not remember much other than blood and pain. He would mourn him later and even create a Telling for him. That would bring a smile to Jathen while he looked down from the heights of power, and might even let him climb one step higher before returning back to the world.

Looking around Terik opened his mouth as if to take command but he sounded unsure when saying it to Yiran. 'We should create funeral pyres for our brothers before the worms can drag them down.'

Yiran nodded but said nothing. Instead he turned to look up at the Tower of Frehep. 'I fear our fight might not yet be over.'

'But there is not a Prae'surlas left standing in sight.' Terik was not a coward, he had shown that in the battle, and the thought of more fighting in their injured states was definitely not something Dallid wished for either. But he should not have voiced it. Kris always said that a fool speaks when a man thinks. It was then that he realised what Yiran spoke of.

'Lord Chrial'thau,' Dallid said. 'He did not come to our aid.'

Yiran nodded at the statement and gave words to what it meant, 'Iceborn.'

All five of them said nothing, but Dallid could feel their thoughts. In their combined conditions, they would struggle to kill another Prae'surlas fleshborn, and if they were in full health, then they would struggle significantly against a lesser of the Prae'surlas Powerborn. But if Chrial'thau the Great fought, and had not yet defeated his foe, then it meant they were not the lesser Frostborn, but the greater Iceborn that he faced. Even if Dallid and the others were fifty instead of five, and had full battle armour and short bows, still they would all likely die against a single Iceborn.

But if Chrial'thau the Great still fought, then they would die to help him. Dallid laughed again and said, 'My only regret is that I do not die killing Prae'surlas.'

Everyone else laughed and this time did give heart to it. Dallid had another regret that he would always say softly to himself before facing death though, and that was that he would not see his wife again. He missed Phira more than anything, and selfishly Dallid prayed to Frehep for the strength to survive whatever lay ahead, so that one day, perhaps many years from now, he might see her again. It was a warming dream.

Yiran patted him on the chest, then led the way towards the Tower of Frehep and what waited for them all within.

CHAPTER TEN

Fire and ice

Yiran eased the doors open with one arm, Dallid still being held up by the other. The remaining three warriors stayed behind as Yiran surveyed what was inside. Dallid was granted sight with him but he almost wished that he had not. A tranquil sun shone on the day outside, but a storm was raging within the great hall of the tower. It was the largest structure Dallid had known and yet seven men looked like they took up its entirety.

Six of those men were northern giants, all looking exactly alike apart from one that was larger than the others. He had his back turned to the battle that went on and was leaving the chamber just as Dallid and Yiran peered in. He was going into one of two rooms that were on the eastern side of the tower. The door to the other room was already smashed open, lying in shards. On the western side two spiral stairways mirrored the rooms in location, but more importantly on the western side stood the seventh man whom all of the others fought. He was Chrial'thau the Great.

He looked like a frail old man, his bone white hair hanging down loose over dark and withered skin, yet he stood alone and fought what looked like five Iceborn. Dallid could only guess they were Iceborn from the white tunics they wore with silver spears climbing up the sides, but also from the displays of power they were producing. Chrial'thau matched their tunics with his own of red and yellow flames, but all of these details Dallid had taken in with a glance. What consumed the entire chamber was the war of fire and ice that erupted everywhere at once.

Bubbles of ice would appear in the air only to explode into deadly spears flying down towards Chrial'thau. The Fireborn in turn made bright red fire-bursts flare out from the walls, the floor, and from the air itself, to demolish the ice magic and attack his five opponents. Shields of white appeared around the Iceborns to block flows of fire that looked certain to kill them and giant spears of ice grew from the stone floor in return, shooting towards Chrial'thau only to dissolve into flames. Serpents of fire grew out from the ground in similar fashion to the spears of ice and these too were stopped in mid-flight, becoming frozen solid and shattering. So much power being created and destroyed so swiftly and explosively, it was too much to take in.

Thankfully none of that power was directed at Dallid or Yiran. All the Powerborn were too engrossed in their own fight of magic to notice two half-dead fleshborns entering the hall, except for Chrial'thau. The Fireborn Lord's eyes darted over to spot Yiran and he smiled. A great wall of fire followed that smile, rising up to take Chrial'thau away from their sight. It made every other show of magic look insignificant by comparison as the five Iceborn stepped back from the colossal power. Then the wall rushed forward and all five Prae'surlas raised their hands as one. It was not to cower in fear, but to create their own wall of ice in answer. The ugly wall of twisted ice shot up to meet the fire and, amazingly, it held.

Unlike Chrial'thau's, the Prae'surlas shield of ice grew to take up the entire chamber. It crept out and crawled up the walls, touching the ceiling and the floor, halving the tower hall leaving Chrial'thau on one side and the five Iceborn on the other. Dallid and Yiran of course ended up on the side with the Iceborns.

Yiran turned to Emylias, Terik and the youth the squad leader was holding. 'Now is our chance. We all attack the Iceborn closest while they are distracted, this will draw the attention of the others and give Lord Chrial'thau advantage.' He looked each of them in the eye. 'The sun god has seen us this day, and he has seen us soar to the heights of power in his light. Today we die without regret.'

He removed his arm from Dallid and Dallid found he suddenly had the strength to stand again, enough for one last charge. Terik let go of the injured youth and Emylias gave Dallid a smile. Then as one, they charged without sound. The roaring of Chrial'thau's fire and the cracking of the Prae'surlas ice was loud enough to mask their approach, and all five Fureath'i ran with silent determination.

The injured youth had made it five or six steps before falling. Dallid had not even made it that far. His torn leg collapsed the instant he put weight on it and he fell uselessly to the cold stone floor. All he could do was watch in frustrated agony as Yiran, Terik and Emylias reached the first of the Iceborn and all three plunged their sabres deeply into the north-man's back. So enthralled in whatever ritual of ice magic they were creating, the other four Iceborn did not even turn their heads to look at the fleshborn arrivals, and the one who had been stabbed by the three killing blows, simply turned his head in annoyance. Keeping one arm stretched towards the enormous wall of ice, he turned his other palm in mimic of a Fureath'i greeting. A sphere of white appeared and from it shot three spears. They entered each of his Fureath'i attackers in the chest and killed all three.

Dallid's mind reeled that Emylias, Terik and Yiran had all been killed so suddenly and so unnaturally by a single Prae'surlas. He heard a sabre drop to the floor, and then another, denial and disbelief making him want to pass out. After all they had been through, to be murdered so casually, it was not true. It could not be true. Emylias could not be dead. Yiran the Unconquered could not be dead. Then Dallid looked up in hope as he had only heard two sabres fall.

Yiran still held his sword, even with a spear of ice striking out from his back and an Iceborn smiling at his futile resilience. When Yiran lifted his sword arm up, the Iceborn sighed and let the other two spears - holding the corpses of Terik and Emylias - disappear. They were replaced by a second spear of ice that pierced through Yiran's stomach, but not before Yiran had plunged his own blade into the Iceborn's neck.

It was a strange sight to see, two men standing in front of the other, one with two spears through his body, the other with a sword in his neck. Dallid could not see Yiran's face, but he could see the look of pain and outrage in the frozen eyes of the Iceborn, and more importantly he could see panic. Then Dallid saw Yiran rip his sword forward and chop back again before both men fell to the ground. Yiran fell awkwardly and broke the spears of ice sticking out of him. He did not cry out in pain as he fell and did not move when he landed. The Iceborn followed him to the ground and the man's head rolled free of his body as he landed. All four other Iceborns turned their heads in astonishment.

Dallid could barely think for his own shock. Not in hundreds of years, since the long war where armies of Fireborn fought armies of

Iceborn, before Amadis enforced his brutal peace upon the world, had either a Fireborn or Iceborn been killed. Even in the old Tellings it had taken several greater Powerborn to kill another. To kill a lesser Powerborn would take dozens of fleshborn, but never was it heard of a fleshborn killing a greater Powerborn, no matter what their number. In his death, Yiran the Unconquered had become the first.

All four Iceborns' horror was short lived then as their protective shield of ice shattered and the wall of fire it was holding back rushed forward to consume them. Dallid could feel the heat from where he lay but the wall did not reach him. Instead it divided and wrapped around each of the remaining Iceborns, burning them all alive.

Their screams could just be heard from under the roar of the flames, but Chrial'thau was not finished. He ran to the nearest one with his two fists held under his arm, both hands glowing with the blood-dark magic of impending fire, and then thrust them forward to unleash a ferocious blast of flame. It sent the Iceborn sailing through the chamber, the curtain of fire enveloping him still wrapped tightly. When the Iceborn landed the fire went out and revealed a figure of melted flesh and with half its torso missing from where Chrial'thau had hit. That just left three still screaming, and Dallid marvelled how one Fireborn could kill four Iceborn. Even if his brother warriors had given Chrial'thau the advantage by distracting them, it was still an unbelievable feat. Chrial'thau the Great was probably the only man alive that could achieve such a thing.

The great legend ran towards his next victim, this time with both his hands outstretched to the sides. His fists burned brightly with growing fire, their flames leaving a trail behind as he moved. He slammed both hands together near the head of the burning Iceborn and an explosion sent the ice giant flying. When he hit the ground like the other, the fire went out, but different to the other, there was nothing where once there had been a head.

The fire around the remaining two Iceborns disappeared also however, their skin scarred and blistered but both men strongly alive. Spheres of white appeared in front of them and shattered into hundreds of tiny spears, the weapons flying out in every direction, the ice sticking through stone like steel through flesh. Three of the cursed things landed into the injured youth that had come with Dallid, but he did not cry out from their impact and Dallid tried to mourn his death but could not. Too much else had happened and he himself had miraculously avoided any of the deadly spears. Even Chrial'thau was not so lucky. He had fallen to one knee from the impact, having taken several shards into his head and body. A quick wave of fire covered his body and melted the unholy ice, but the wounds and blood remained.

More spheres of the same magic formed but Chrial'thau waved his hand angrily turning them all to flames. They exploded with similar effect except that this time knives of fire flew out, and they all directed themselves at the Iceborns. Flickering white arcs appeared to block some, but more pierced deeply into northern flesh.

Chrial'thau stood up and set both his fists on fire again. The flames grew up his arms and looked about to consume his entire body when suddenly, it went out. The two Iceborns had stopped their roars of pain and became still, before they both dropped down to their knees. Chrial'thau stood in amazement, frowning at the two Prae'surlas but also at his own hands. He looked at them as if he had never seen them before in his life.

The entire chamber grew cold, and the more Dallid looked the more he could see the colour of Chrial'thau's skin grow pale. The Fireborn's hands turned to ice with horrifying speed, followed just as quickly by the rest of his arms. More ice had formed around his boots, capturing his legs and continuing until Chrial'thau's whole body had become frozen solid. It happened so quickly, only moments before there stood a being of fire and now he was a thing of ice.

The larger Prae'surlas from the start had returned, his Iceborn tunic untarnished by blade or flame, his eyes burning brightly with blue and white light. He strolled like a king in his own throne room and glanced about the hall with disinterest. His eyes rested on the three fallen Iceborn, two without their heads, the other missing most of his torso, but they swept on without care. The dead fleshborn lying around he did not even give consideration and

Dallid realised that he himself, with the amount of blood he was covered in, must have looked like just another corpse.

The large Iceborn's regard passed over the two that were kneeling and his eyes came to rest on the frozen figure of Chrial'thau the Great. If he was responsible for defeating Chrial'thau in such a fashion then he did not smile in triumph, the barest of sneers was all Dallid could see on his lips. Then the giant's eyes flashed brightly and circles of blue and white fire formed around all five other Iceborn.

The two kneeling were lifted from their feet and held suspended in the air, the light from the blue and white flames colouring them completely. Dallid watched with dismay as he saw their burns and wounds heal, and even tears in their clothing were replaced with what he guessed were fibres of ice. Then another of the Iceborns became lifted from their feet. It was the one who had half of his body blown apart by Chrial'thau but the ice-fire created new flesh right in front of Dallid's eyes.

He had thought he knew about Powerborn healing, how the lesser could heal mortal wounds within days and the greater could heal them within hours, but the healing he witnessed right now was unheard of. Shifting his gaze nervously to the remaining two Iceborns who had both been beheaded, Dallid wondered if the sacrifice of his fleshborn brothers had all been in vain. Yiran the Unconquered's last stand gave the world the first man of flesh to kill a Demi-god of power, and it could all be worthless.

He watched the blue and white fires burn and its light soak into the Iceborn bodies, but thankfully those two at least did not stir. The ice-like fires disappeared and the two Iceborn who had been kneeling looked completely refreshed. The one who had lost half his body was standing whole again but not very steadily. An armour of ice had been created where his tunic was destroyed. The large Iceborn who had healed the other three flicked his fingers and all of them knelt once more. He then stepped over to the frozen form of Chrial'thau,

'How mighty he once thought himself,' the Iceborn spoke to the room. 'And now he stands as insignificant as all others. The greatest that this race of fire-rats can throw forth and yet he has been turned to ice like everything else. This infested land will freeze like the rest of the world, and here is the proof. Their god does not dare face me and so in his cowardice has forsaken his people. Who is left to stop me if almighty Frehep will not?'

A tower of fire erupted from Chrial'thau, forcing the large Prae'surlas back and then four more towers of flame burst into creation around each of the surviving Iceborns. The fires were so powerful that this time, Dallid could not hear the Prae'surlas scream. Every one of them was surrounded by a hurricane of fire, nothing compared to the blankets of flame they had previously been victim to. These fires did not just cover their bodies but soared to the very roof of the great hall. They spun with such ferocity that Dallid could feel his skin burn even from such a distance. A show of power like that could only be the great sun god Frehep answering the Iceborn's challenge. Even if he had decreed that he would never interfere in the lives of his people, there were some insults that were too great to bear.

Chrial'thau's tower of fire was the first to vanish, leaving the old man standing, but doubled over in pain. When he reached out his hand towards one of the other towers, Dallid began to wonder if this was Frehep's work or if it was the work of Chrial'thau himself. From what little Dallid knew of such things, any one of the acts he witnessed in the battle could take Flameborns days to prepare, and even any other Fireborn would need time to invoke lengthy rituals to unleash those kinds of magic. Yet Chrial'thau looked to manage them with a moment's thought and concentration, centuries of knowledge and experience aiding his every act.

The old Fireborn crushed his fist over the furthest of the fire towers and it disappeared leaving nothing but bone and ash. That had been the Iceborn who lost half his body. Dallid watched everything with amazement and awe but could not help to laugh weakly at the idea of the Iceborn trying to recover from that. He had seen the man grow a new stomach and chest, but what Chrial'thau had made of him now was nothing but dust.

He turned to the two towers where the kneeling Iceborns had been. Chrial'thau lifted his arms again and crushed them into fists towards those. The towers disappeared to leave what remained inside fall free. It was more than bone and ash this time, but not by much. Blackened skeletons fell to the floor, their smoking flesh twitching violently as they lay on the ground. The things had to be dead. Chrial'thau must have thought so too as he now gave his final attention to the last tower of fire that blazed within the hall. His arms were held out towards it and pressed inward with struggling intensity. The Fireborn looked as if he was trying to bring his hands together to crush the figure inside, as he had the others, but with far greater resistance.

His hands shook under the strain and Chrial'thau even fell to one knee from the effort it cost him. He kept his gaze fixed on the last remaining tower, both hands still Connected with it. Fire broke free from Chrial'thau's skin during the struggle, bursting free from everywhere at once. The frail old Fureath'i turned into a being of fire in front of Dallid, looking much more god than man.

Still he knelt though, unable to rise from the power he was focusing on killing the final Iceborn. The Fireborn lord let out a roar with one last surge of power and the flames flared brighter in the spinning inferno. Then it was over. The fire that covered Chrial'thau disappeared and left an old man once more where the Fireborn had been. He knelt on both knees now with his head sagged from exhaustion. The tower of fire around the Iceborn disappeared also and what it revealed brought a gasp of horror from Dallid.

The Iceborn stood unharmed. Not even his clothing had been touched by the flames. The giant's eyes flashed brightly as he smiled.

'You forget yourself, Chrial'thau,' he said. 'You forget that you are but a man playing with the power of gods, whereas I have truly become a god.'

The old Fureath'i's shoulders heaved with the effort of speaking. He could not rise, but his voice was strong and full of command. His eyes blazed with red fire as he looked up at the giant Iceborn with contempt.

'It is you that forget yourself, Aerath. You forget how I once showed you mercy and left you live. How pathetically weak you once were and so far beneath me that I did not kill you. Now you forget that you are not a god, but someone who has stolen the power of one. Whatever cowardly deal you have done with Aerune to grant you this new strength, know that it is not yours. At best you have become his puppet.'

Aerath laughed. 'I have bargained no deal with Aerune, old man; I have killed him. Something you should have done to Frehep long ago if you ever wished to become more than you are.'

'Everything I am I have made of myself and whether or not you have found some way to slay Aerune, you are still not a god, Aerath. The birth of gods came only once when the heavens were breached, and you and I were not among them. The fact that you still walk the realm of flesh instead of the world of power should be enough to show you your conceit. Even now with all this false power that you try to claim as your own, it is still not enough, Aerath. *You* are not enough, and the moment you realise that is the moment you will become *more*.'

Aerath just stared at Chrial'thau, his face trying to hold back either anger or confusion at the Fireborn's insults. Then his eyes flashed bright once more. 'Witness that you are on your knees before me and know my power, old man. Watch and tell me that I am not a god.'

Two more circles of blue and white fire appeared around the twitching remains of the charred skeletons and Dallid's stomach went cold at what was to come, as both skeletons were lifted from their feet and enveloped in light. Flesh began to grow back over bone and full armours of ice formed as clothing. The Iceborns became warriors of living ice, with the flesh of their skin shining to show the artifice of their creation. But still they stood, three Iceborn including Aerath, in the Tower of Frehep, with its guardian on his knees.

Chrial'thau did not respond to witnessing Aerath's power and Aerath seemed pleased by the Fireborn's silence. Then the giant reached inside his tunic with a grin and pulled out a trinket that he was wearing around his neck. It was a curved piece of broken stone that was raised in parts with ridges and what looked like engraved writing upon it. Aerath's smile this time was indeed triumphant.

'You have witnessed my power, old man, and now look upon its future. You still claim that I am not a god? Then we shall see how that may change. Is this not the very thing you are here to guard Chrial'thau? The very reason this Tower of Guardians was created?

And here I stand with the tower's guardian defeated and its
treasure in my hand.'

Chrial'thau started to laugh.

It was a broken sound, but one that sounded rich with relief.
'You truly are a fool, Aerath. Now that you have touched that thing
it does not matter if I am defeated and it does not matter what new
powers you may possess. Even Aerune cannot save you now; your
destruction is certain. The only question is how soon it will show
itself.' The Fireborn's eyes blazed bright with satisfaction. 'The sun
god sees you, Aerath, and he sees you doomed.'

'Your sun god can try to destroy me if he wishes,' Aerath
sneered, putting the stone segment away. 'But there is only one
person here that is doomed.'

He created a halberd of ice in his hand, white fabrics of magic
appearing from nowhere and circling around each other to forge
the weapon. The spearhead was as long and wide as any sword, and
holding the shaft in one hand, Aerath lifted the blade underneath
Chrial'thau's neck.

'I die without regret, Iceborn,' Chrial'thau said proudly. 'And it
is not Frehep who will destroy you for holding that segment. It is a
power older and more dangerous than any god, and I look forward
to watching your destruction from my place upon the heights.' He
stared boldly into the face of his executioner and Aerath remained
still, hesitation creeping in. Dallid felt a mixture of pride and dread
at Chrial'thau's imminent death. Looking down at his own wounds
Dallid did not doubt he would shortly follow. It would take the
intervention of a god to save Chrial'thau now and hope as he may,
Dallid knew that Frehep would never do that

Then a figure walked through the doors behind him to join the
combatants within.

CHAPTER ELEVEN

Darkness and light

The movement from the doors gave Dallid sudden hope but it came with an equal mix of fear. As a figure walked into the blood drenched Tower of Frehep, Dallid would have laughed had it been more Prae'surlas, others perhaps out in the forest that they had missed.

It was not more north-men though, and neither was it holy Frehep come to offer salvation. Just as beings of power were not meant to walk the world of flesh, neither were creatures of darkness allowed to walk the world of light. But still a demon entered into the tower, its long black hair and pale grey skin acting as stark contrast to the burning green of its eyes. The Attro'phass stepped calmly into the hall and stopped to look around. There were pools of blood and melt-water filling half the hall, with scorch marks and dead bodies decorating the rest. The demon looked at the Fireborn on his knees and the Iceborn giant about to execute him. He gazed at the two sentries made of ice standing behind, and then returned his frightening eyes to Chrial'thau and Aerath.

'You do not belong here, demon,' Aerath growled. 'Be gone from my world.'

The Attro'phass cocked its head and softly replied, 'I do not belong here...'

'Be gone!' Aerath roared and swung to face the demon with his halberd of ice. His eyes flashed bright enough to challenge those of the Attro'phass and as he did the other two Iceborn raced forward to attack. Dallid held back hope but remembered the demon standing over a whole squad of dead Prae'surlas. They had all been fleshborn but he had no idea of what capabilities the demon might possess.

Two swords ripped free from the Attro'phass's hands, much quicker than the slow and deliberate tearing of flesh it had performed for Dallid the last time. Green blood flicked out and sizzled against the stone floor as the blades appeared and then the demon also ran to attack. It was not towards the two Iceborn though, it was towards Aerath.

Dallid wondered if the thing killed Aerath then would the other two Iceborn fall dead also, without Aerath's magic to sustain them. But Dallid was left with no more time to wonder as almost immediately the Attro'phass reached Aerath, who swung his spear out to behead the beast. The demon rolled neatly underneath without breaking momentum and came up to a stand in front of Chrial'thau. Then, without explanation, he plunged both swords straight down into Chrial'thau's chest. The battered Fireborn roared out before collapsing to the floor. Dallid reasoned desperately that he could not be dead. But why did the demon do that? It was supposed to be here to kill Prae'surlas.

Aerath seemed just as surprised to see the demon inexplicably stab Chrial'thau through the chest. Two more swords tore free from the flesh of the Attro'phass, and just as it was set to plunge those into the Fireborn's body as well, Aerath swung his spear to stop it. The demon lifted back its blades in time to meet the halberd of ice but the force of the impact sent the Attro'phass staggering across the room. Then the other two Iceborn were upon it, one fighting with two short spears of ice created from his fists, and the other fighting with one long spear of ice created as part of his forearm - one blade far in front and another sticking back behind the elbow.

For the start the Attro'phass demon just dodged and weaved his body away out of each strike, his frightening green eyes locked on whichever Iceborn was attacking him. Then he lifted up the first of his swords and sliced straight through the weapons of ice. The north-men stumbled for a moment before quickly reforming the blades, reinforcing whatever strength they could give the spears. The next time the swords of bone met ice, they only hacked free small chunks which were quickly re-grown. Then all three began to dance in a dizzying display of speed and skill.

For large warriors the Prae'surlas Iceborns were able to move with unexpected alacrity. Dallid had seen the strength of the larger one, Aerath, knock the demon backwards with one strike, so the demon slid and avoided direct contact with the other stronger warriors now. But whatever other demonic power the Attro'phass possessed, it was a highly skilled swordsman. Phira was widely regarded as the best in Furea, if not the world, but Dallid could not help wondering if this demon was better.

As swiftly as the fighters moved, their weapons found flesh as often as they clashed against each other. The Attro'phass's sword cut through the Powerborn flesh easily, just as it had through their ice. It looked like the sword would go straight through where ever it cut, making Dallid expect to see limbs begin to fall free, until he saw that the wounds the sword created were flashing bright blue and turning to back ice, repelling the devil's blade. Looking to Aerath watching the fight, Dallid thought he knew where that power was coming from.

The smaller wounds the demon took then looked like they damaged the Iceborns more than the demon. The green blood that spilled would melt the weapons and, still Connected to the ice, make the Prae'surlas grunt in pain. And those green-blooded wounds also just disappeared moments after being inflicted.

Again Dallid tried to get his head around that only greater Powerborn were celebrated for having quick healing like that, mending wounds within hours. The demon was healing them in seconds. Even the ice magic Aerath used to heal the wounds of his two Iceborn was not as fast as the demon's. So it looked only a matter of time before the Attro'phass was victorious.

Perhaps it was just as evident to Aerath, because his eyes began to flash again and he held out a hand towards the demon. The Attro'phass's movements slowed and at first it took more injuries from the two Iceborn because of it. Then the Iceborn warriors stepped back and the demon struggled to move at all. A skin of ice was growing around the creature and the Attro'phass turned its burning green eyes accusingly at Aerath before becoming completely encapsulated. More and more ice grew until the demonic statue became a featureless block, with only the demon's eyes visible from within.

'Who could summon such a thing to this place?' Aerath asked, turning his head towards the body of Chrial'thau and then looking down to the segment underneath his tunic. When he lifted his head once more, Aerath looked shaken. 'It matters not. Take the creature back to the mountain. Chrial'thau too. As little power as he has left it can still serve me.'

The two Iceborn stepped forward to comply and the block of ice beside them exploded. The demon burst free with both his swords ready, ramming them up into the sides of the nearest Prae'surlas. Two more bone-swords ripped free from his hands and he crossed them around the same Iceborn's throat. The Attro'phass slashed them together, leaving the head to drop free and bounce along the floor.

Aerath had perhaps been stunned at the sudden speed of the demon but quickly recovered turning the devil's swords to ice. Once frozen Aerath controlled the ice and flung the blades across the room with a wave of his hand. The Attro'phass turned and snarled at him, growing a single sword from his hand, shorter and thicker than before. Aerath gestured to control it but whatever new sword the demon had created, it would not turn to ice.

Instead of running forward to attack Aerath though, the demon turned and stabbed the blade into the skull of the final Iceborn. The man tottered unstably with the sword of bone sticking out from his head. Aerath's eyes flashed to heal the Iceborn but the Attro'phass's own eyes flashed too. The single sword divided into four, with each one breaking free and flying in a different direction, blowing apart the Iceborn's head. The swords flew straight and with such force that when they hit the walls of the tower they became stuck within the stone.

The last of Aerath's Iceborn followers dropped dead to the floor and the Attro'phass threw down his hands to let two new swords burst free. These ones he grew slowly and let the sickening sound of his own flesh ripping fill the chamber. The devil's eyes burned much brighter than Aerath's now, either fuelled by anger or some other power. The Iceborn lifted his hand, creating an explosion of ice and the Attro'phass was blown backwards through the air.

The demon hit the tower wall with a force almost equal to that of its swords and remained fixed in the stone in an equal manner. Ice wrapped around the devil again but this time with far greater speed and with a disturbing warped movement. Darkness beckoned at Dallid's vision but he forced himself to watch the events until all hope was lost. Chrial'thau was not dead yet and however much time

Aerath spent dealing with the Attro'phass demon, it meant more time that Chrial'thau could be healing. Dallid glanced at the still form of the fallen Fireborn but had to turn away, the sight too grim, so he looked back to the captured demon instead.

He was a distance away and his vision was failing, but to Dallid the ice wrapping around the demon looked like it was constantly forming and reforming. It seemed to circle out from the wall and around the limbs of the Attro'phass, binding both arms and legs. The demon did not explode to freedom like the last time, but viciously thrashed from side to side. Aerath strolled over to his captive and stood right in front of the struggling demon. Dallid held his breath waiting for the moment when the demon would burst free and plunge his swords into the giant's neck, but for now the Attro'phass only snarled. Aerath's ice continued to circle, to form and reform against whatever resistance the devil's magic was able to conjure.

'It is my understanding that you can only be killed by another of your kind,' Aerath said with consideration. 'But that you kill your own kind with such tenacity that less than a handful still exist. Tell me, how many Attro'phass demons are left?'

'Soon there will be none left,' the demon said from behind gritted teeth. 'Soon they will be next!'

Aerath leaned closer. 'You are right that soon there will be none left, because once I have created this world into a paradise of ice, your world, demon, will be next.' He turned his back on the creature and walked over to Chrial'thau. His footsteps sounded loudly in the now near lifeless hall. Chrial'thau the Great looked like any of the other corpses when Aerath stood over him, but Dallid knew he could not be dead. 'Tell me, old man, what enemies have you made that they summon an Attro'phass demon to kill you? I believe there are only three left from what had once been an army of thousands. For a creature that cannot be killed by anything else, they kill each other quite capably do they not? Shall we see how they fare against a god?'

Chrial'thau did not answer nor did Aerath wait to see if he would. The Iceborn strode back to the demon and while walking cast his hand out to the side. Dallid did not dare turn his head in case Aerath would notice he was not actually dead, but what he saw fly into view was a long shard of ice. Once the Iceborn caught hold of the shard, the ice disappeared to reveal one of the demon's swords of bone. The Attro'phass had stopped struggling now and just stared at Aerath. Gone was the fury or struggle, and it was replaced by an unnerving curiosity. The devil cocked his head at what was to happen as if quite intrigued at the outcome. Aerath held the sword like it was a thing of filth, his upper lip curling.

'You can command your flesh to create anything and you create a *sword*.' Aerath waved it as he spoke and it looked like a dagger in his gigantic grip. 'Does it frustrate you that you cannot command your flesh free of my ice?'

'I cannot command my flesh free of your ice...' The Attro'phass smiled as he repeated Aerath's words, but he still did not burst free and slay the giant. Aerath frowned at the devil and then stuck it through the stomach with its own sword. The demon did not shout out in pain. The demon did not react at all. It watched Aerath stab him with fascination. Angered by the lack of reaction, Aerath twisted the sword and cut it from side to side. Nothing happened other than green blood seeping out and burning down through the stone below. When Aerath took out the sword, there was no sign of a wound, only the clothing remained torn. Then that too seemed to grow back, a grey shirt and black waistcoat appearing as good as new, not even stained with blood. What kind of creature was the demon that he could create his own clothing at will? Aerath had said it could command its flesh to do anything - was the appearance of clothes just the demon's own flesh?

With a grunt of sudden dissatisfaction Aerath swiped the bone sword through the neck of the Attro'phass. The sword cut through the flesh sharply, and the strength of Aerath's arm carried the blade straight through. But the head did not roll free. It remained where it was, green eyes burning brightly and staring at Aerath. A few drops of green blood could be seen flowing down the neck of the demon but Dallid could not make out any cut at all. It was as if the blade had not just beheaded the creature, as Dallid had clearly seen.

Grabbing the bone sword this time in two hands, Aerath pushed it through the front of the devil's neck. The blade cut in easily and then disappeared to view behind whole flesh. It was then Dallid realised that the reason the Attro'phass's head did not fall off was because the flesh healed the same instant it was cut. Such a creature indeed looked impossible to kill but at least it could bleed. He did not see Aerath take a single wound throughout the battle with Chrial'thau or the demon.

It was a fight of worlds above and below him, and both so far beyond him that he wondered why he still fought to remain conscious. But it was because Chrial'thau still lived, and it was soon approaching when Chrial'thau would rise and destroy them both. Just as he was sure Yiran could kill any man of flesh, Dallid knew Chrial'thau could defeat any being of power, of darkness or light.

'I could continue to find a way to kill you or I could feed you to my mountain and kill you that way. But I fear I do not have time to engage in my own amusement, demon, I have what I came for.' Aerath turned his head over to where Chrial'thau lay. Did the Iceborn come to defeat Chrial'thau or did he come to take the piece of stone that he spoke of earlier? Dallid's vision was beginning to grow dark again. He closed his eyes for a moment but then opened them in a panic. It was not yet over, he would not lose hope. 'Or perhaps I shall still have my amusement,' Aerath said cryptically. 'And perhaps you shall still die by one of your own kind after all.'

He lifted the bone sword and dug it into the demon's chest. The Attro'phass watched as Aerath scooped the sword back out, bringing with it a heavy gush of green blood. The Iceborn went back over to Chrial'thau then, leaving a trail of hissing stone from where the blood dripped from the blade. Enough remained however to fall on the still form of Chrial'thau the Great. Aerath held it over the Fireborn's face and when the first drop touched his mouth Chrial'thau spasmed upward in a roar of pain. Aerath grinned at the reaction and then drove the blood stained sword down into the Fireborn's heart.

'Your pathetic power will not feed my mountain, old man. Your torment will instead feed my delight. You spared me once out of mercy, I now return the deed. Kill this demon and then you are free to live out the rest of your life brutalising your own people. They will hunt you and they will hate you more than any of the Prae'surlas. This is my gift to you. Your sun god sees you, Chrial'thau, and he sees you breath glory to my power!'

Aerath laughed and a blue light flashed from his hand where it pressed the demonic sword into Chrial'thau the Great. The Fireborn of legend did not fight back. There was nothing left. Hope was finally lost. Feeling the warm comfort of letting go, Dallid had no regrets for killing Prae'surlas. It had never been in him to be a great warrior and he hoped the small few he had killed would light him up the heights of power, high enough only that he might look down on Phira as she lived. He regretted not spending every minute of his life with her and it was with that thought that darkness took him.

CHAPTER TWELVE

Fireborn

Dallid opened his eyes and took a moment to remember where he lay. The ceiling was smooth grey with ancient craft, but had become blackened by the battle. *The battle!* Awareness and panic flooded all at once and Dallid shot to his feet. Trying to look everywhere at the same time, Dallid saw little of what he searched for, but after a moment he forced himself to calmness, steadying his breathing.

Everything was how it had been before he blacked out.

Terik and Emylias still lay dead, Yiran also, and the unnamed youth. Jathen and the rest of his squad would still be dead outside. The Fureath'i bodies inside had been burnt but nowhere near as badly as the five Iceborn corpses. Aerath was gone and the Attro'phass demon had vanished too, thankfully, but Chrial'thau still lay defeated in the centre of the grand hall. The swords that had been thrust into his chest were now removed. Perhaps the demon took them back. Dallid wondered if the devil had finally broken free and killed Aerath, but he did not think so. Neither of their bodies were among those scattered in the Tower of Frehep.

It was difficult to believe he had witnessed such an intense battle. How he had been the only one to survive? And then suddenly, distracted with all of his other observations, Dallid realised that something was wrong.

His hand flew to his shoulder and then down to his leg. He cupped and examined his face before going back down to the tear in his breeches. The wounds were gone. They were not healed, not a little better, but completely gone. It was as if Dallid had imagined them, but then the tears in his clothing brought back some sanity to the madness. It was not just the wounds that had been healed though, his exhaustion was no more, and even his vision was sharper as his whole body seemed full with fresh energy. So many dead bodies and dead friends surrounding him, coupled with the head spinning confusion of his recovery, it was too much. Dallid doubled over and retched.

It did not help. Hoping to find some hope or answers Dallid ran towards where Chrial'thau lay. Maybe he was still alive. The Iceborns had only been killed when their heads were removed, and Chrial'thau still had his. Afraid of what he would find when he got close to the great Fireborn, Dallid let himself become distracted. How long had he been unconscious? If it had been days then perhaps his wounds might have healed, but would he not be starving and weak with hunger? Would not the corpses be stinking of rot?

Taking a deep breath to strengthen him, Dallid focused once more towards Lord Chrial'thau. Tales of immortal Fireborn were bred early into young Fureath'i minds, and the idea that the lord of power might be dead was not something easy for Dallid to consider. What had Aerath done to him before Dallid lost consciousness? Would the Iceborn be arrogant enough to leave Chrial'thau alive?

Standing over the fallen Fireborn, Dallid paused to look at his withered face. The old man already looked long dead, but he had looked that way even while demonstrating god-like power during the battle. The lord's skin was worse than it had been though, still thin and brittle looking, it was now grey like rotted meat, and lined with sunken black veins. To Dallid's horror it looked much the way the demon's face had looked. What did Aerath say about the Attro'phass demon dying by one of his own kind? Did he use Chrial'thau's power to summon another demon? Dallid hoped they both turned on Aerath and dragged him back to the hell they came from. The world of darkness would be a fitting place for the Prae'surlas.

Looking down at the sword wounds in Chrial'thau's chest, Dallid was distressed to see they had not even begun to heal. The great Fireborn had to be dead. The healing abilities of a Powerborn were a thing of legend. A disturbing thought came to Dallid then.

Did Aerath heal me?

It made sense in a vile way that the Iceborn would think it amusing to allow one fleshborn to live if only to tell the tale of what he had done, spreading fear to the Fureath'i people. Dallid doubted the Iceborn would have noticed one dying fleshborn out of so many dead ones, but how else was he healed? It made as little sense as everything else did. Dallid needed to tell someone what happened, but he would not terrorise simple villagers with the news. He needed to go to the nearest border fort and tell the officer in charge there. With luck he might find the fort Thisian was stationed in; it would be good to see a friend.

Then another option entered his mind. He could bypass the border forts and go directly to Rath'Nor. The officer at the fort would only do the same, sending a messenger by horse, but they would also send word by raven. Dallid tried to reason that the saved time he spent going direct to Rath'Nor would almost equal the speed a raven from a border fort would accomplish. The difference would only be a few days.

If Dallid did go to Rath'Nor, he would be arriving as a warrior without a squad, and the thought of joining one of Kris or Phira's squads came unbidden to his mind. So much had happened and he was so close to death that he needed to be with his wife and friends again. Phira would not say no if he asked it of her, but he knew she would hate him for it. It would undermine her authority to have a husband to worry about in her squads, but they could find a way to make it work. Dallid's head continued to swim and he knew these plans made no sense, but he had to cling to something, to see some sign of comfort in his future.

If Phira was to be his new blaze commander though, then Dallid would need to become stronger, become better. Decisions chopped their way into Dallid's head and clear tasks presented themselves in order. He would gather the bodies, both Fureath'i and Prae'surlas, stacking the Fureath'i high upon a funeral pyre and throwing the Prae'surlas to rot in the forest. Then he would burn Yiran and Chrial'thau. Both deserved their own pyres a hundred times higher than every other warrior, even Terik and Emylias. But since Dallid was restricted by urgency, he would just have to do the best he could.

Then he would resupply and take a horse from Yiran's own cabin south of the tower. It was likely untouched from the attack and it was the closest stable. With luck he would be at Rath'Nor before the next moon.

Looking back down to the dead legend of Chrial'thau, Dallid nodded farewell and knelt down to take the Fireborn's hand in his own. If the great Powerborn was in truth not dead, then the funeral pyre would not burn him but empower him. If however it was as it seemed, then the fire would burn his body as any other. He touched the great legend's hand and said, 'You have died in the same tower as Frehep when he gave up his life and power, my lord. He did so to live as a god and empower his people with his legend, and I feel certain that you will do the same. Farewell, Lord Chrial'thau.'

Dallid contemplated that Furea could have two deities after this day, perhaps one of fire and one of the sun, but that was a thing for the Scholars to decide. If Aerath could claim to be a god then why not Chrial'thau? There had not been a new god since the creation of power, but if the highest Powerborn had done it once, then why not a second time. If Chrial'thau replaced Frehep in the upmost height of power, then it could even mean Frehep's rebirth among his people.

Now that would be a thing to witness.

A flame burst to life from Chrial'thau's hand and caught hold of Dallid's skin. He jumped up and tried to pat it out desperately, but the fire only caught further. The sleeve of his arm combusted to flames and Dallid looked around for any kind of water or liquid he could use. Whatever melt water had been there during the battle had disappeared along with the rest of the ice magic though. Panicking, Dallid ran out of the tower but he knew he would not make it to the lake in time.

Frantically trying to pat out the fire on his arm, the blaze suddenly caught hold of his entire shirt. There was no time to take it off so he dropped to the ground to roll it out. The fire burned greater. Dallid's mouth filled with dirt as he started crying his alarm. The smoke from his burning clothes began to fill his lungs along with all the dirt. The coughing and shouting together made Dallid vomit, but he still continued to roll in desperation. His clothes were almost burned through, and soon his skin would blister up to die a painful death. Tears flowed down his cheeks and Dallid began to laugh mindlessly amidst it all.

There is no pain.

'There is no pain!' he roared, and made himself lie still. He watched as fire danced on his body and covered his face. It was like a sick dream but he had never had a dream as real as this.

The fire was all he could see, all he could feel, but why was there no pain? His mind felt close to breaking and shakily he stood up. Burnt tatters of clothes fell off of him and when the last of his clothing fell away, only his hands were aflame.

This is a dream.

He commanded the dream to put out the flames and the fire disappeared. Turning and working his fingers nervously, Dallid examined them for scars or blisters, anything at all to tell him that he stood in reality. His skin prickled against the blowing wind, he could feel that it was biting cold, but he was not cold. It made no sense.

Feeling foolish he moved back into the tower, bizarrely worried that someone might see him standing there naked. He had greater things to worry about. His sanity, his grasp of reality, the safety of his land, the deaths of his countrymen - all of these were what should concern him. *Why the fire did not burn me and how I made it stop.*

There was no explanation other than madness and hallucination. But in order to force his thoughts onto anything else, getting more clothes became the pressing priority.

The great hall was dark compared to the bright day outside, although the torches still burned along the walls. They had always burned for as long as he could remember. It was part of the magic of the tower, maybe a remnant of Frehep's own power as he gave it up. For a moment they made him feel like he was not alone, but that was absurd, there was no imagined life in the fires, probably just some magic. All the dim lights could show him were death and shadows.

Focusing once more on his immediate distraction, Dallid surveyed the dead bodies. He could not bring himself to remove their clothes. The burns, blood stains and stab wounds were only part of the reason. So he moved for the spiral staircases. It took courage to step past so many dead bodies while naked, the eerie silence and uncertainty of things pressing on his mind. But if Dallid was to soldier under Phira, or Kris, he would need to make righteous decisions at a moment's glance. Kris's philosophy was that if you had a just reason in your heart then you could justify any decision. It had never been that easy for Dallid, there were too many different reasons for several different options most of the time, how could anyone coldly pick one in an instant. But he needed to be dressed and Chrial'thau's chambers were the closest place to find clothing.

As he ran up the steps, Dallid passed other floors in the tower, each for their own ritual function, none as large as the entrance hall at the base. Half way up he stopped to look out a window and tried to admire the forest view. He forced himself to search for peace in its tranquil familiarity. His search returned with failure. The view was to the west showing only the burning ruin of his home. He was fretting over the hardships of life like a Scholar would, and Dallid knew that to be a warrior he would need to battle them instead.

Lord Chrial'thau's chambers were at the very top of the tower, not that Dallid had ever been, but he knew from stories involving the different towerguards. Sometimes more than one guardian remained there, and there were several guest chambers on the floors preceding the top one, but Dallid did not stop until he arrived at the summit.

The door was ajar, and again Dallid unreasonably worried if Aerath remained within. He pushed open the door with more force than he intended, and it made a large clatter as the frame slammed against the wall behind. If anyone was there, they would now know that Dallid was there too.

He crept in with careful steps. Looking around Dallid noticed light everywhere, but could not quite identify the source. Everything appeared to glow with some kind of aura, some magic of Chrial'thau's that Dallid did not understand. He kept going towards the bed and a chest that sat beside it.

Parchments lined the wall behind the simple bed, four on either side of a single wooden mask, and Dallid recognised the masks of Moi'dan depicted there, the ancient warrior who had ruled an empire in ages past. The pictures of those masked faces stared at him with empty eyes, one a wolf, a sword, a shield, a hammer, helmet, turtle, demon, full helm, but it was the actual mask, the one of an eagle that bothered him the most. They were all aglow with impossible light the same as everything else, but the eagle felt alive.

Frustration began to ache within Dallid's limbs and it seemed he was holding his mind together with an unstable grip. Reality was threatening to unravel at any moment and Dallid could feel the threads slipping from his fingers. There were things he could feel in his mind and flesh that pushed to burst free: frustration, panic, madness. The scar on his arm chose that moment to flare with pain, reminding Dallid of the swordsman of fire that had struck him the previous night. It had all unravelled from that point, as if all confidence and understanding of the world were consumed in those flames. Dallid pressed his hands down onto the solid chest and clenched his teeth. Calming breaths would not come so he quickly threw back the clothes chest and pulled out the first thing he found. It was of course the tunic of a Fireborn.

Hesitating, he anxiously placed it on the bed and searched for anything less sacrilegious. The chest contained more formal outfits for Fireborn, full length robes, heavy cloaks, decorative shirts, none of them were any better. He threw them angrily to the floor, furious that there was nothing a fleshborn could wear. But why would there be?

The thought was meant to reason some calm into his blood but it only goaded him into greater frustration. So Dallid let out a curse that Thisian would have been proud of and went with the first simple tunic he had pulled out, feeling like a criminal for wearing it. Rushing to find leggings and knee high boots to match, he found the great Fireborn at least to be of a similar size to his own. The boots were a little too tight, and the tunic too small for the width of his shoulders, but he was pleased he had something to wear until he reached Yiran's cabin at least. Dallid even found a sabre and sheath in Chrial'thau's chambers. He thought it an odd thing for a Fireborn to keep, but it was the least strange thing he had encountered of late.

Dallid needed to be out of the tower soon. The walls were beginning to feel like they pressed in on top of him as he wore Chrial'thau's clothes, stood in his boots, armed with his sabre. He looked around the dead man's chamber and every one of the masks whispered to the other how foolish Dallid looked. What would the

Lord Chrial'thau do to him when he found out? Turning his head he swung to confront the walls who began to add their own whispers. With a nervous laugh Dallid could almost imagine an actual feeling within the walls. He could feel its pulse, the heartbeat of the tower. He needed to get out.

There was an arch leading to a balcony and Dallid ran to it. Once out of the chamber, he let out a gasp for air as if he had just been held under water. Turning a corner and out a further archway, Dallid stepped onto the balcony fully.

Wind howled at him and gusted roughly through his clothes, and he suddenly found the open air lifesaving. A small wall bordered the balcony, which circled completely around the outside of Chrial'thau's chambers. The thick forest of eastern Furea mapped out before him in all directions and seemed to go on forever. The woods were where he grew up, where he felt at home, and still the disturbing tower was nagging at his bones to go back inside, as if the Foreign stone was his true home.

What is happening to me? Have I died? Is this my test upon the heights of power?

Turning around Dallid embraced the wind trying to lift him from the tower, the sensations on his skin anchoring him to his own mind. Should the wind not be cold? Of course it was cold, he was just too distracted by his own rambling madness to realise it.

Drinking in the view of his heart's land one last time, Dallid turned his back on the sprawling beauty and went back inside. He ran down the stairs with new energy and was not even out of breath when he approached the bottom. If he found out Aerath had healed him then he would have to kill himself, but if it was all just a dream he did not need to be concerned with why the fire did not burn. What happened in dreams were simply to be accepted. Accepted and then forgotten.

Dallid froze when he reached the bottom of the stairs. A creeping dread crawled its way up his spine and he fought for courage. Chrial'thau still lay motionless in the centre of the hall, but above him stood the Attro'phass demon. The long black hair looked as if it did not move, as the demon leaned its head forward to regard the fallen Fireborn. A sword of bone and flesh slid smoothly from the devil's palm and Dallid stepped forward

'No!'

The demon turned its head to Dallid's roar.

'Don't touch him! Leave him be.'

Green eyes flashed with power in the dead stare the demon gave Dallid, but remarkably the bone sword slid back into the flesh of the beast and disappeared.

'I cannot touch him...' the demon said softly, 'not yet.' When it looked at Dallid there was pain and confusion in its features. 'I am told to kill him, and now that he is killed I cannot touch him. What torture is this?'

Its words sounded wrong. It was not Fureath'i being spoke, but how then could Dallid understand it? Unsure why the creature had obeyed his command to leave Chrial'thau alone, Dallid just nodded slowly, frowning at the Attro'phass demon.

'Who told you to kill Chrial'thau? Why?'

'Chrial'thau is the first to die, by my blood if not by my sword,' the devil looked down at the dead Fireborn as it spoke. 'I must kill him again, but I cannot until he wakes up. There are others in this land that I am to kill instead, those that are next.' The demon looked back up at Dallid, its eyes drifting down to the sabre at his hip. 'You are not next.'

'What? What others in my land do you intend to kill? Why are you here? Why are you doing this? What do you mean I am not next?'

The demon tilted its head the other way as if the questions puzzled it. It answered as best it could. 'I am here because I was to destroy Chrial'thau the Great, Fureath'i Fireborn. I do so because I am commanded, and by chance here lies Chrial'thau destroyed, though I would advise you kill him further since I cannot.' The demon smiled sickeningly. 'You are not next. Next is Jaiha the Decider of Fates, she is in the Temple of Fire in the mountain town of Il-Yu. Then I can kill Miral'thau the Wise, he is in the fortress city of Rath'Nor. Then I can...'

'Stop.' Dallid put his hands to his head. 'Why are trying to destroy these great warriors? They will only kill you!'

'They will only kill me...' the devil repeated. Then Dallid remembered what Aerath had said.

'Is what Aerath said true? Can you only be killed by another of your kind?'

The demon glanced down on Chrial'thau again before answering. 'I am the only thing that can kill another of my kind. Only one man of flesh has ever killed an Attro'phass demon, and he was not Fireborn.'

He assumed it was Amadis, though describing the world ruler as a man of flesh seemed an injustice. Still, Dallid did not know what to say to that. How could a thing not be killed? Even Powerborn could be killed. How was there even a demon allowed to exist in the world of light? Who was commanding it to kill Fireborn and why? There were too many questions and in the end he blurted out, 'Why do you not kill me?' Dallid thought it was a stupid question, but he wanted to know, 'Now, or before, or even back in the forest? Why were you killing Prae'surlas and Fireborn but not me?'

'You are not next.' It answered as if no further explanation was needed.

'I do not know what you mean. The Prae'surlas in the forest, why did you kill them? Were they *next*?'

The demon smiled. 'The *fleshborn*? They are not important enough to command me to kill. But they were foolish enough to waste my time and attack me. There is never enough shadow in this place to remain hidden. How can you exist here?'

'How can *you* exist here in the world of light at all? You are a demon!' Dallid felt ridiculous having a conversation with a devil of shadow, but it appeared as long as he did not attack the thing, it would not attack him. That seemed like a fair trade for the time, but if the thing was going to go after more Fireborn, what could Dallid do? Should he try and fight it? 'Why are you commanded to kill Fireborn?'

The Attro'phass shrugged. 'All Fireborn must die.' It turned its head at Dallid again and seemed as equally amused by their civil conversation. 'You must die too, but you are not next, so it is allowed to not kill you yet. It is not often that I can speak with a thing that I do not need to kill.'

'Why must I die?'

'Because all Fireborn must die.'

'But I am not...' It was all too much for Dallid, what was the demon talking about? How could such a beast even speak the Fureath'i language? The ice-men sometimes learnt part of it to question and torture prisoners, the same way the Fureath'i learned the Prae'surlas language to better insult them, but where could a beast from a world of darkness learn to talk? It had to be a dream. There was no other explanation. A tingling screamed out from underneath Dallid's skin and the heartbeat of the tower walls became louder.

'I did not say I would not kill you if you threaten me, Fireborn. I simply said I do not need to kill you now.' The amusement was gone, and the demon looked at him with menace.

Dallid did nothing. He held back treacherous thoughts from his mind and he held back phantom sensations he was receiving from the tower. He held back the urgent sense of exploding frustration that drove him to the brink of madness in his every limb. But he feared that if he did not hold back, then he would lose himself to whatever force was trying to destroy him from within. The Attro'phass seemed to take his stillness as peace, because the impending violence was gone from its stature once more.

'You should kill this one again while it rests.' It nodded to Chrial'thau and at the same time turned and walked away. 'When it wakes up it will be much more *difficult* to kill.'

The demon strolled out of the Tower of Frehep and Dallid stood rooted to the spot. Trickles of reason tried to flow slowly through his mind. Aerath had put demon blood into Chrial'thau, could that turn a man into one? He did not know enough of demon lore to say one way or the other, but the Attro'phass was both saying Chrial'thau was killed and that Chrial'thau was about to wake up. It was the demon's goal apparently to ensure the great Fireborn was indeed killed, and since the demon was content to leave made Dallid conclude that whatever woke up in that body would not be Chrial'thau.

More thoughts broke through. The demon had called Dallid a Fireborn. As ludicrous as that was, it explained why the fire had not burnt his skin, and why his wounds were healed. It was just as preposterous as taking this reasoning from the words of a shadowborn, but it did not change the reality. Chrial'thau could have Transferred his power to Dallid before Aerath killed him with the demon blood. It was implausible, but it could have happened.

Transfers were extremely rare, and for numerous reasons, the first being that not many Powerborn ever died in such a planned and natural way to give time to organise the ritual. In the few cases where that did happen it was supposed to be for dying Fireborns to give their power to surviving Flameborns and so on, never to a fleshborn. You were either born of flesh or born of power. That was what he had always been told.

Dallid looked down at his fists. The earlier sensations he had felt were not as urgent as before but they were still there.

'Fire,' he commanded and his fists exploded into flames. Dallid jumped at the reaction and fought not to extinguish his hands on his tunic. Watching his hands swim with flames was like watching a swarm of poisonous spiders swarm over your skin. He could not take his eyes away.

Fire had never looked so beautiful before to his eyes. Every inch of every flicker held a thousand colours that only his eyes could see. The fire did have life within it and Dallid could feel his Connection to it, and his Connection to the torches on the walls, to the tower itself. None of it made sense to his mind, but his heart embraced the gift completely. Tears would have stained his face if he was not in such a trance of disbelief.

Eager to explore the fascinating magic, Dallid pushed his hands forward to send a fireball across the hall as he had seen Chrial'thau do. The flames from his hands drifted out slowly into the air and swirled for a moment before vanishing. His disappointment made all the fire vanish and with it all light seemed to disappear from the world. The comfort of the torches along the wall calmed his melodrama, but the absence of his own flame also allowed him to question his new theory.

From what he had heard, a Powerborn could only Transfer by touch, and although he did burst into flames first when he laid hand to Chrial'thau, how had his wounds healed? None of it made any sense, and his plan of action of what to do next was shattered. He should still burn the dead, and with that thought Dallid's eyes drifted towards Chrial'thau.

I should burn Chrial'thau now.

A growing feeling of dread told him the demon was right and that what was about to wake up was not anything Dallid wanted to fight. He did not even know any rituals to command his new magic. How could he hope to fight a demon that had the fused powers of the most powerful Fireborn in history? A flicker of movement from Chrial'thau's body made Dallid's breath catch. The motion was Chrial'thau opening his eyes.

The old Fireborn sat up slowly and looked around in a daze. An innocent confusion was all Dallid could see, and his heart began to beat again when he saw that it actually was Chrial'thau, and not some dark monster.

'Chrial'thau, my lord, how do you feel?'

Dallid remembered himself suddenly and dropped down to his knees as he spoke, pressing his head to the stone and tried not to think about the fact he was wearing the legend's own clothes. Chrial'thau did not answer straight away, but when Dallid raised his head he saw that the old Fireborn was indeed looking at him. The eyes did not recognise Dallid, but why would they? Was he staring at the fact Dallid wore his clothing? He was not supposed to speak to a Powerborn without their permission, but he could not let the silence go on.

'My Lord Fireborn, I apologise for the blasphemy. Much has happened that I do not understand. I can explain why I now wear your clothing.'

The old legend still did not speak, but gathered himself up to a stand. He patted his chest where the swords had been stuck, the wounds were no more. When he looked back at Dallid he smiled. The smile was over large and twisted up unnaturally. Things began to crawl along the sides of his face. It was like a spider web of coloured veins creeping over the Fireborn's skin. On one side the veins were black and on the other side they were the colour of ice. The whites of Chrial'thau's eyes went blood red and both his iris's changed in front of Dallid. On the side of his face where ice rooted its way in and out of his skin the eye was spiralling red and blue. On the side of his face where dead and rotted black veins stained his skin, the eye was bright green, just like the Attro'phass. Fire erupted from the creature and flames danced their way all over his body. The fire was the colour of purest darkness and a black shimmering distorted the image of Chrial'thau. It distorted everything but the single green eye which began to pulse with light. That eye still stared at Dallid.

Slowly the demon that had been Chrial'thau lifted from the ground, the black fire somehow powering him into the air. He floated there, smiling down at Dallid who was gone numb from the horror that unfolded before him. The fiery demon screamed out a laugh of hysteria then, and black flames flared outward from his aura. Its smile fixed, its staring eyes unmoving, a withered hand slowly lowered towards Dallid where he knelt and dark fire rained down.

With a speed he did not know he possessed, Dallid threw himself to the side, rolling clear and coming back about. Another wave of fire roared out against him and Dallid dodged it with equal agility. Drawing out his sabre on instinct it did not occur to him to try fighting back with magic. The feeling of solid steel gave him some small strength instead. The demon Chrial'thau roared and more dark flames erupted, clouding into the air like a sickness.

Dallid dropped to the ground letting the wave pass over him. He swiftly sprang to his feet and remarkably, he rushed forward. He was on the demon before it could react and honest steel sliced corrupted flesh along its ribs. Jumping clear and away Dallid could not believe what he had just done, but still readied himself to avoid the next assault.

Chrial'thau did not immediately fight back. He simply cradled his wound, snarling. Staring hatred at Dallid, the aura of fire darkened further around the creature, and he rose higher into the air. Almost brushing the ceiling of the great hall, the demon whimpered like a beast over his wound, breaking occasionally to snarl at Dallid.

Then a storm of fire showered down without warning and without enough time to get clear. On instinct Dallid cowered, lifted his hands protectively in front of his face and waited to see what impact the black magic would have on him. Instead he saw the flames stopped in mid-stream and Dallid could feel the black fire.

Dallid felt as if *he* controlled that fire, and not the demon. Throwing his hands to the side, he was elated to witness that the flames followed. The demon screamed and more terrible magic lashed down on him. But Dallid's reaction was to Connect with this fire also.

He did not know what he did, or how he did it, but his entire body was now Connected with fire, so it came naturally to him to grab a hold of the flames and deflect them away. A mixture of disbelief and confidence filled Dallid's chest. The demonic Chrial'thau howled in frustration, acting so much like an actual animal, that when he spoke Dallid was shocked.

'I will kill you!' it screamed. 'I will you boil your blood until your eyeballs melt! I will burn every last bit of you and sink my teeth into your blistering heart!'

'Then do it!' Dallid screamed back. 'And do not waste time poisoning my ears with your foul voice!'

The demon looked at Dallid holding his sabre and it smiled. Feeling safe in its high perch, it even glanced about the hall casually. 'You are powered by fire and you fight with steel.' The devil sneered in derision. 'I know enough of the soul I have taken, to know that you are harmless. It will take you years to learn how to use your new gift. Chrial'thau knows why you were created, but he also knows that you do not use it because you cannot!'

'Then come down,' Dallid said shakily, 'And I will show you how harmless I am.'

The demon just stared at Dallid with a grim smile. It lifted a withered grey arm, crawling with black fire like maggots through rotted flesh and its smile grew deeper. 'Are you like me I wonder? Do you feel it?'

'I am nothing like you.'

'Do you feel the curse inside your head?' The demonic Chrial'thau seemed to be speaking to itself instead of Dallid, but Dallid did feel something inside his head. It was like a burning presence and it felt like it was the demon who was inside his mind. 'What does it whisper to you? Does it tell you who you have to kill?'

'My mind has not been poisoned with dark magic, demon, I am nothing like you. I do not have a creature inside my mind telling me who to kill. I will kill you and after I am finished there is only one other person I will kill and that is Aerath for creating you.'

The devil laughed. Dallid bristled with anger, and that only made it laugh all the more. 'Maybe we should kill the Attro'phass you and I? Hunt down demons instead of Prae'surlas? Was that not why Aerath created me? To kill my own kind? But the Attro'phass is nothing like me, I am far more. Maybe we should kill Rhisean and every other Fireborn until they all know who is the most powerful? Do I feel some of the Attro'phass's command to kill all Fireborn?' It leered hungrily at Dallid then before gesturing down to the dead bodies that decorated the hall. 'Or maybe we should leave those of darkness and power be, and instead wipe the land clean of weakness. Will we kill all the fleshborn?'

Dallid's face twisted in disgust. Why the demon thought they would do anything together was insanity. The devil smiled at Dallid's discomfort. 'Yes, let us do that then rather than try to burn a thing of fire with more fire. The land is full of those who do not deserve their place in it. Tens of thousands of defenceless peasants infest these forests, and we will grow fat on their delicious blood. We will slaughter them all!' The screech resonated in the great hall of the tower for a time, as the creature stared intensely at Dallid. 'So I ask you, Fireborn, are you like me? Do you hear the curse inside you as I do? Will we kill *Aerath* together? We have no choice! We will both grow stronger with every day he lives, until we finally destroy him! Join with me and I will teach you how to use your true power. You and I *are* the same!'

'I am nothing like you!' Dallid shouted back. 'The sun god sees you, demon! And he will see you dead by my blade!'

The entire hall became fire. It was not Dallid who did it, it was not almighty Frehep come to destroy the demon - it was the demon's own power that filled up the great hall with black flame. Dallid cowered down at its intensity, and a paltry glow of red fire surrounded him to keep the black flames out. Whatever Chrial'thau had become, he had become something much more powerful than the Fireborn had been. The thought was made worse that Chrial'thau had been the strongest of all Powerborn. Where Chrial'thau the Fireborn had struggled to burn five glorious towers of flame, Chrial'thau the demon filled the entire hall. Air had been changed to black fire and Dallid did not know how his own power held it back. He could feel the tainted magic tear at his, picking it apart and feeding on it. Just as he thought he would finally be consumed by it, the black fire disappeared. The demon laughed.

'Do you still claim we are not the same? The curse will not let me feed on you because you are born of the same destruction.' The demonic Chrial'thau cocked its head the way the Attro'phass did, its green eye blazing just as brightly, but its eye of spiralled blue and red grew brighter too. 'I am stronger though, than the curse that created me. I will kill Aerath for his hand in making this but it does not mean I will not devour every life I find from here to Lae Noan.' Its smile twisted again unnaturally up its deformed face as it spoke down to Dallid. 'And that, includes even *you*.'

Two great blasts of flames flashed out, and Dallid caught a hold of the one directed at him. The other burst the wooden entrance to the tower into bits and the demon Chrial'thau was already flying towards it. Dallid tried to send the fire he gripped in pursuit of the devil, but he had not the strength it needed. The throw of fire fell much shorter and spread harmlessly over the stone floor. Pushing as fast as he could Dallid ran to follow.

He was met at the doors by another explosion of black flame and sent rolling backwards into the hall. The dark fire stayed and formed a wall to stop Dallid from leaving. Readying himself to try rushing through the magic anyway, Dallid was once more thrown off balance as the ground began to shake beneath him. Looking around and feeling like his head was about to be crushed Dallid changed his mind. It was not the ground shaking but the tower.

The pulsing heartbeat he had felt earlier now raced alarmingly. For no reason he could think of Dallid doubled over, as if someone had just made him swallow something foul and poisoned. Another explosion came and it punched a hole right through one of the stone walls of the ancient tower. More black fire filled that breach and in his disorientation Dallid thought he could see the dark flames going into the actual walls. If there had really been power embedded into the Tower of Frehep, then the black flames of the demon were now trying to corrupt it.

As well as trying to seep into the thick stone of the walls, the fire spread out along the floor and the ceiling, burning as fiercely as if the entire structure was made of wood. Another piece of the wall was blown inward and Dallid knew he had to find some way to escape. The devil possessing Chrial'thau may not have wanted to kill Dallid by fire, but it seemed more than happy to bring down the entire tower to kill him instead. The demon-fire covered every inch of the hall, choking up everything but a small space where Dallid's own red fire had appeared to hold it back. It was nothing he was doing intentionally and he was terrified that his flames would suddenly vanish, leaving him to become enveloped by the darkness.

The black flames roared and lashed out in every direction like demonic snakes. If Dallid had ever wondered what hell within the world of darkness would be like, then he was standing right in the centre of it. Unable to move for fear that the black fire would make him into something akin to Chrial'thau, Dallid also knew the entire tower was about to be crushed down on top of him. He had never felt such panic. It was not hesitation when there were no options, but in the end it was better to die fighting than to die in fear of it.

Turning his wrist to give the melted coin of Phira one last kiss, Dallid realised he was crying. He was glad she could not see how weak he was now in his final hour. He gave out a roar, pushed so that his red flames blazed brighter, and then ran into the storm of hell-fire. His plan started to work as the shield of red flames barged their way through the blackness and Dallid dared to hope he might even make it.

More explosions sounded out from all directions then and Dallid looked up in time to see the ceiling crash down on top of him. It was followed by the rest of the building as the ancient Tower of Frehep crumbled to the earth in a hail of black fire.

• CHAPTER THIRTEEN •

The blood of Frehep

The wind challenged his every step, his footing shifted with loose and moving stones - some were even covered in ice - but Kris persisted up the mountain trail. His squads were patrolling below him but neither he nor they belonged to the task. The mountains were for men of more idle skills. His men were skilled at one thing and that was killing Prae'surlas. Why then had his superiors thought it reasonable to reward them with access to the mountain Scholar-town of Il-Yu?

A stone arch approached ahead, worn and blasted from the winds where it was not green with overgrowth or white with an infestation of frost and ice. An elder wrapped in a woollen cloak waited there to greet him, but Kris did not rush to go any faster. He went as hard as any man should but some things were not worth his dedication. He should be with his squad leaders. He had ten full squads of the best Prae'surlas killers the country had ever seen, and here they were, wasted with pointless time forced upon them for peaceful reflection.

All Fureath'i needed to be better in all areas of life, but Kris felt peaceful reflection was simply an indulgence to self-pity. A Fureath'i should be able to identify his short comings in an instant and be strong enough to keep going while trying to better them. A full month of visiting temples would make his men weak, and Kris was only there to respectfully inform the priestess that they would not be staying. The elder watched him as he arrived at the gate, but Kris gave him nothing to watch.

'The sun god sees you, elder.'

'May he shine brightly on us all,' the old man replied. But when Kris raised his palm in greeting and bowed his head in respect, the old man at the arch did not return the courtesy. Instead he said, 'You frown, my son.'

Kris frowned further at the man for pointing out the obvious, but he would not be disrespectful. 'I am Kris Fureath'i, ember class, I am here to visit the High Priestess Jaiha Fireborn on bequest of the King.'

'All you have spoken is true.'

Kris needed to clench his fist but would not let his anger control him. His voice was as even as always. 'Fureath'i do not lie.'

The old man nodded slowly. 'Again you state what is clear, but it seems they do not always tell every truth either. You did not say why you are frowning.'

'You did not ask,' Kris returned.

For a time there was nothing said, while both men just met the eyes of the other. It was a contest Kris had been in before and one he was skilled at winning. Intense silence made most people uncomfortable, Kris however found what seldom comfort he ever took in it. It was conversation that made Kris uncomfortable, useless noise to reassure insecure people that they still lived. This old man though, did not look like most people.

He was most likely a Scholar if he resided in the temple town of Il-Yu. There were some temple warriors of course, chosen by Jaiha Fireborn who was the Decider of Fates, but they were chosen to go through life as a Fureath'i with a sabre that would never run wet with Prae'surlas blood. It was a life almost as doomed as that of a priest, and as much as Kris doubted the fighting competence of any of the temple warriors, he could still safely judge that the old man was not one.

So if he was a Scholar, he would be well used to long times spent doing nothing. A Scholar's entire life was just one long time spent doing nothing. The stare of Kris's dark eyes pushed at the weaker pale eyes of the old man, which were already watering from the wind. But inside those eyes, Kris saw the look of a very patient man - a man who did not have ten squads of impatient warriors waiting for him. Kris needed to be done with the place so, uncharacteristically, he initiated the exchange.

'I frown because the wind blows strongly,' he said finally. 'And I frown because I contemplate the famous beauty of these mountains.'

He purposely did not indicate what judgements he had drawn from that contemplation, but how could anyone find a place that was so cold, and that was even covered in snow and ice, a place of beauty? The very idea of snow in Furea was an insult. The blessed land should be confined to the deserts and the forests. The mountains were simply what divided them.

'I believe you frown because you fight a battle inside you, young warrior, and when you do not have a battle to fight outside, it becomes harder to keep control within, does it not?' Kris frowned at the old man and this made him laugh. 'Come my son, it is a common tale for the heart of a warrior.' Only then did he turn his palm in greeting and bow his head slightly. 'Please follow me to the high priestess. I believe, young warrior, you will find this place to be a deep well of calm that you may draw upon to your strength.'

He followed the old man in silence and strangely began to wish that some of his childhood friends were there. It was odd for Kris to desire companionship of any kind but Dallid or Thisian would have the perfect humorous remark to insult the condescending elder, and Phira, well she would most likely have punched him in the face. Maybe as a squad leader he might have been excused the act himself, but not as an ember class, he had too much standing and responsibility now to indulge in such foolishness. Phira would not have cared though. Perhaps that clarity of righteousness was why she still vastly outranked Kris despite their equal service. Kris had many flaws but envy was not one of them. Phira outranked him because she was better skilled, and he would just have to keep working hard to better himself until he compared.

They reached the first temple quickly and unfortunately the priestess was not there, so the old man continued his steady shuffle without pause and Kris took a cursory glance at the inside. The masonry and artwork were indeed superb, but only by a Foreigner's standards. For every Fureath'i that wasted their life in the pursuit of art, knowledge and enlightenment, it meant one less warrior to fight the Prae'surlas. To Kris, that was equal to the Scholar killing a Fureath'i warrior. As soon as he formed the thought however, Kris forced himself to dismiss it. Instead he began to wonder how much the priestess might know of him.

The Telling of the Sword that Walks was widely known and Kris could tolerate it for the benefit of his men, but others he certainly did not wish heard, in particular the Blood of Frehep. He could not allow himself to be ashamed of his actions, for they had all been as how a proper Fureath'i should act, but he did not need constant reminding.

Stepping outside of the first temple and back into the ice bitten wind, Kris looked over his shoulder to see the building worked into the mountain. He had heard as much from descriptions of the place and turning his gaze forward, the entire temple village spread out before his eyes. They had reached a trailing wooden bridge, one of several he could see that connected similar stone temples built somehow into the mountain peaks themselves. The land dropped and disappeared making it look like they were a number of islands connected to each other but instead of water there was only air. There was a distant nothingness beneath him trailing off into mist in places, and looking up he saw the bridge in front spanned for an incredible length. How had this place even been built all those years ago? It defied reason, but he could only take answer that a god's acts were beyond the reason of men.

Realising that the temple village of Il-Yu was already beginning to get him to think like a Scholar, Kris simply concentrated on crossing the bridge. It was odd that he did not hear of more accidental deaths occurring in the place, but then again even if he had heard he doubted he would have paid much attention. The potential for his own death at this simple crossing did not concern him either. Death was just another step upon the heights of power. Perhaps in his next life he would come back better.

Death could only be warmer than it was at that moment in any case. Without rock walls for shelter, the freezing wind cut right through him. Many believed Frehep was strengthening his people before a time of great testing, and the arrival of the cold gripping the country was an omen to finally wage all-out war upon the Prae'surlas. It had been perhaps a hundred years since the two nations had clashed fully, and from all reports both countries had been almost obliterated by it, some saying the war itself lasted more than three decades. The need to repel other nations from encroaching into both borders was how the war had ended. Now there were only constant skirmishes, neither people willing to cripple their nations so severely again.

That had been the time the eight members of the King decreed the need for more children left in the villages for elders to raise - to recover the losses of the long war - yet the tradition remained. In the first stage of a warrior's life he needed to better himself with knowledge and training but he also needed to sire at least four children. Then when he began the second stage of his life to better his nation in the army, the next generation would be doubled. Finally at retirement a warrior had to return to the village of his birth and raise whatever grandchildren his own children had left. Bettering your society and the future Fureath'i was the last task of a warrior before climbing the heights of power.

Kris had done his duty and left four of his blood in different villages, although he had struggled to allow it. Often he contemplated going back to those villages and killing the children. To be a better Fureath'i was his goal but he did not wish to pass on his blood to anyone. The fact Dallid and Phira did not have any children had been the deciding factor for him. Phira had needed to concentrate on her training but if every Fureath'i did that then there would be no next generation. Thisian of course claimed he had at least two hundred young girls from the surrounding villages pregnant with his seed and hence Kris did not need to add any more. But the idea of two hundred more Thisians in the world had also contributed to Kris's difficult decision to reproduce.

So with the tradition in place for so many years, Fureath'i warriors now outnumbered the Prae'surlas by at least five to one. A war would not be so devastating this time, at least not to the Fureath'i.

'The priestess waits within.'

Kris did not like being taken by surprise, and so frowned when he saw the old man had stopped and spoken. It was simply his need to distract his thoughts that had caused it, nothing more, the upcoming war needed to be considered by all leaders and Kris tried to feel justified for his lapse in awareness. His thanks to the old man was a grunt.

The elder smiled and gestured for Kris to proceed inside. The temple he was entering was called the Temple of Zenith, one of the three Great Temples of Furea. From the outside it blended seamlessly into the mountain as all the others did, and turning around Kris spotted that they had crossed two more bridges during his distraction. It was enough to harden him to full concentration. The High Priestess Jaiha was a Fireborn and his words needed to be perfect.

If the outside of the Temple of Zenith was modest and understated, then the inside overcompensated greatly. Large pillars and arches grew out of the floors and walls. They looked like fire made stone, twisting and flowing with tendrils of flames sticking out all along them. Windows of stained glass designs took up entire walls and gave the stone-made fires the impression of movement when the coloured light touched them. Torches burned at every location, accompanied by pedestals of pointless relics. A miniature wooden shield made into the shape of a sword caught Kris's eye as particularly useless. There were also Foreign suits of armour or encased weaponry lining the walls in places, with rugs and wall hangings of past battles and the men that fought them in others.

He was alone in the temple as far as he could see. The sound of his footsteps echoed harshly throughout the over-large chambers as he marched, enough to make a lesser man feel self-conscious about the way that he walked. The grand murals of great men looked down upon him as he went. He paid them no mind but knew who would be there. Frehep the Holy, as well as Chrial'thau the Great, but other lords of power that held mantle among them would be such as Lao Sin the Deadly, Rhisean the Scarred, Miral'thau the Wise and the priestess herself, Jaiha the Decider of Fates. All hundreds of years old and still burning brightly, Chrial'thau being the oldest, said to have been born almost at the same time as Frehep, at the very beginning of the age of power.

The giant chamber divided into three when he approached the end. Taking cursory glances down all avenues, Kris had already decided his direction but hesitated upon seeing a strange sight. A fire burned wildly in a chamber far to his right, and although he had spotted a priestess if he continued straight, the wild fire seemed more likely to be the Lady Fireborn's work. Turning on his heel, Kris strode quickly towards the flames, ignoring any further decoration.

When he reached the chamber of fire, there were no rocks or trinkets paraded around the room, or even torches on the walls. There were no windows, or wall hangings, and it was bare of everything but the fire itself, and what was at its centre. The fire burned in a ring around what looked to be a long rectangle of glass standing upright. Moving around to the front of the thing, Kris saw that it was a type of mirror, but instead of showing his own image back to him it showed a Prae'surlas. It was the largest Prae'surlas he had ever seen and he was dressed as their Iceborn dress, in a tunic of white and silver. Both those pale colours were overpowered by the brightness of the Iceborn's blue and white eyes. It was an intense image.

When the Iceborn moved, Kris's hand shot for his sabre, but common sense told him the Iceborn was not real. It was simply some fashioning of magic that allowed the image to be there, and the magical antics of Powerborn had nothing to do with Kris. He conceded it was at least very convincing magic, since the Iceborn was staring directly at him, the sneer of derision and disgust very real. Kris turned without giving it another thought and let the Iceborn image continue to burn in the fire that surrounded it.

Going back to the junction he had been at before, Kris continued straight to where he spotted a female figure sitting in meditation by an altar. He had heard the Fireborn priestess shaved her hair tight in the style of the mountain women, but the priestess he could see now had long hair. Kris reserved his judgement until he was close enough to see that it was in fact a man, albeit wearing women's robes.

Dismissing prejudice thoughts, Kris cleared his head and steeled his heart to feel and think nothing. He was a man of will, not of emotion and not of body. Standing with his arms folded behind his back, he stood with military precision awaiting the man to finish whatever meditation he was involved in and to register Kris's arrival. He would not interrupt the priest to demand the location of Lady Jaiha as he felt no urgency to meet the Fireborn. If she wished to meet with him then she would wait or the priest would fetch her. Either way Kris would not wander aimlessly through the temple.

Time passed then, with no movement in the least, neither from the mediating man nor from the arrival of the Lady Jaiha. Kris did not dwell on it. He was solid and strong and would stay in position for as long as it took.

More time went by and the cold finally began to get to Kris. He had survived the blasted ice-lands of Surlas several times, but in each case he had been dressed appropriately. The standard Fureath'i garb that he currently wore - little more than a loin cloth and armour - was better suited to the heat that normally bathed the lands of Furea. The cold of the mountains caused him a moment of weakness then as he reconsidered if where he stood was indeed the place he should be waiting for the Lady Fireborn.

To his relief the Fireborn priestess actually arrived not long after, strolling majestically into view. It had been the right choice to wait it seemed and there was no confusion this time. The air of command that a Powerborn emanated was unmistakeable. She was a being gifted with the blood of gods and she was a lord of all that she surveyed. Kris dropped to his knees in reverence, forehead touching the floor, and awaited her approval.

'Nureail wishes to rename you the frozen fire, did you know that?'

Kris remained silent. Did she mean the Teller Nureail? She was a friend of Yiran's and had often performed for his home village when she visited. Was she here? If she was, then the fact she was discussing renaming him did not bode well. The Lady Jaiha stopped in front of Kris and took a time to study him before allowing him to rise.

'The sun god sees you, warrior,' she said with remembered formality.

'May he find me killing Prae'surlas, my lady,' Kris answered to the floor. It was the martial answer that a solider gave to his commanding officer, not the formal one that he perhaps should have used. The answer suited his mind though so he could not regret saying it.

'Stand with me as equal this day, warrior, an ember class can often be the same rank as Flameborn can it not? Then let us talk as two lords.'

Kris did not allow himself to become uncomfortable at the prospect, so he stood up to meet her eyes. He could feel his cold eyes of black clash against the light of her spiralling irises of gold and red. She was magnificent. The shaven hair against her head only served to show how perfectly she was formed.

'Thank you, Lady Jaiha Fireborn, for this honour.'

'Your thanks have been accepted. Now tell me, does it describe you? Nureail's idea of the frozen fire?'

He frowned before he realised who he was frowning at, but did not compromise his honesty. 'If we are to speak as equals then I will answer that it insults me greatly. There is nothing frozen in the heart of a Fureath'i.'

Another woman walked in to join them at his words, and Kris regarded Nureail without reaction. Her light brown hair hung past her shoulders in curls, and bounced subtly as she walked. At the same point the man sitting down near them stood up and turned his palm in greeting. Kris did the same and bowed slightly to both as respect to their station. He had an estimation of who the man was. Although he had never accompanied Nureail to Kris's home village of Coruln, it was said that her brother Tereail was never far away. It was Nureail that spoke.

'I did not mean it as insult, Kris, please understand that. What I have simply done is taken what Tellings I know of you and created a picture for our priestess. I believe you are a fire held - if not frozen - then, held restricted; a fierce fire that is only unleashed in battle, and then wrapped up in chains for everyday life.'

'The Blood of Frehep,' Tereail said, nodding.

Kris turned his gaze sharply to the man but did not speak. Tereail was the brother of a Teller, so would of course have heard every Telling several times, what did it matter to Kris that he knew of the Blood of Frehep. He still wanted to kill the man though.

The Lady Jaiha smiled at Kris's reaction. 'It cannot be easy for you, Kris, to have every Fureath'i hear of you killing your own kind, using it both as warning and as exemplar. That to unleash the blood of Frehep is to kill many Prae'surlas, but if it is not controlled then the blood of Frehep from your brothers and sisters in battle can also be spilled.'

'But he did kill many Prae'surlas,' Tereail smiled. 'I hear he is already over the hundred.'

Already Kris could not stand the man. More than his usual abhorrence for people, every time this man opened his mouth, Kris wanted to shove his sabre down there. His sister Nureail seemed to be studying Kris in much the same way as the Lady Jaiha did, which also did not warm her to his *frozen* heart. Kris did not wonder why they took such an interest in him, the bored life of a Scholar perhaps. It was time to leave.

'I have come here not to discuss my exploits, but to thank you for inviting me into your sanctuary. It is an honour rarely achieved for any Fureath'i. My men are too humble to accept this, as am I. So it is for this reason that we will not remain here, but will return to our posts on the Surlas border.'

Nureail seemed alarmed by this. The Lady Jaiha was more controlled. 'I do not yet accept your thanks for that honour.' She allowed herself a small grin. 'So you will remain here a while longer, as I consider it.'

It took a lot of control not to frown or clench a fist, but Kris had a lot of control. So he nodded his understanding and returned to his silent stance, armed crossed behind his back, eyes held forward. Tereail and Nureail kept meeting each other's eyes looking to urge the other to say something, not thinking Kris would notice. It was Nureail who finally spoke. The Fireborn Jaiha was content to match Kris's silent regard.

Standing so close to the Fireborn he felt himself weakening slightly. The power that she radiated was bordering on intoxicating, leaving him beginning to feel both drunk of body and will. The idea that he could be influenced so easily by her power only made him redouble the strength inside that held him together.

'Kris, have you ever killed a Powerborn?' The Teller Nureail stepped closer to whisper the question, as if Jaiha Fireborn would not hear. Powerborn were not mortal as fleshborn were, with prolonged life and almost limitless healing, but they were not immortal. Enough fleshborn fighting together could kill one. For every injury you inflicted on a Powerborn, their strength of attack faded as their power was used to mend their bodies. Kris had studied, planned and taken part in such attritions. He was even certain that given the right circumstances he might be able to defeat one in single combat. Kris figured that if he stabbed anyone fast enough and long enough, they would die eventually.

Looking at the Lady Jaiha, Kris felt that certainty burn to ash from the purest awe of her presence. It was difficult to feel so small and weak next to another being. Kris prided himself greatly on his strength; it was all that stopped him from killing everyone he met.

Turning away from the glory of the Fireborn's eyes, Kris moved his dark gaze to Nureail's eyes of sparkling green. The Teller's closeness had its own intoxication as Kris was made aware of the perfumed scent she wore on her neck. When not compared to the Fireborn priestess, the Teller herself was extremely beautiful. She recoiled on instinct at the darkness of his eyes though, and quickly tried to mask her reaction. Kris did not care. He knew he frightened people when he looked at them, and they were right to be frightened. He answered Nureail.

'I have been part of five successful assaults and executions of Frostborn, yes.'

'But not an Iceborn?' Tereail asked, also moving closer. His scent was not so intoxicating.

Kris turned to throw a look of disdain at the man, the slightest trace of irritation in his dark eyes but none in his voice when he spoke. 'It is not possible for a fleshborn to kill an Iceborn.'

Tereail nodded as if he had known this, which he of course should have unless he was completely simple, but there was a trace of disappointment in his manner. When Nureail asked the next question, the Fireborn priestess Jaiha was still just staring at Kris intently. She would definitely have been able to see the surprise on Kris's face at what Nureail asked next:

'Would you like to kill one?'

At first he frowned, and then he considered, was it simply a question of his Fureath'i heart? To test his integrity? If so then she was lucky that he did not demand a duel that instant - Fureath'i custom let him kill as many people as he wanted that way - but something in the way she said it, it was almost an offer. Kris considered his words but was saved by Jaiha's intervention.

'Kris, are you aware of Tereail and Nureail's abilities as Scholars?'

'Nureail is a Teller as well as a Scholar,' he said simply. 'I know less of Tereail.'

The Fireborn priestess nodded. 'They are regarded as lords because of services they can offer to the Powerborn and to the King.'

He almost looked at Tereail to question if such a man was truly held as lord, but instead he looked to Nureail, and was pleased at the more pleasant sight. He could tolerate her status as lord as long as she stopped insulting him. The true lord of power Jaiha then continued. 'Born to a Fureath'i father, their hearts are true, but their mother, was of Foreign blood. It was from her that they were gifted other power, very different to that of the Powerborn. They may not possess our strength or healing, but they certainly possess power. Whereas mine is a Connection to fire; theirs is a joining with time - Nureail with the past and Tereail with the future.

'And this is where we have need of you, Kris. Tereail's connection with the future is by no means a certainty, every viewing that he has changes in a thousand different ways with the passing of each heartbeat, but sometimes certain things do not change. Your involvement in what we plan, Kris, is one of those things that did not change. In every possibility where we have a chance of success, it is you who we have chosen. Would you like to hear what we plan?'

'My men are born to better serve our lords, our King, and our country,' he replied flatly, not particularly wanting to get involved in the whimsical plans of Scholars, but he remembered again the hint of offer in Nureail's voice at killing an Iceborn. That was indeed something Kris was interested in doing so he met the Fireborn's eyes and said, 'Only speak the command and it will be done.'

The Fireborn priestess began to stroll then instead of answering straight. She considered the right words to explain to Kris his mission, and when she began she did so without looking at him. 'Have you wondered at the change in the weather, Kris?'

'A warrior leaves such wonderment to Scholars.'

Jaiha smiled. 'Well then, we Scholars have indeed wondered, and what we have found concerns every warrior. It concerns every Fureath'i, and it concerns every living being who is not a Prae'surlas.' She turned to look at him then. 'The world is turning to ice, Kris. We believe it will only take a matter of years, but in a matter of days it will be too late to stop it.'

Kris frowned. 'Frehep would not let the blessed land of Furea turn to ice. His power is the sun.'

'Frehep fights,' Jaiha conceded. 'And that is why our lands have not seen much change. But there are those that are trying to weaken him, to kill his warriors, bleed his power, and if you were to journey outside our borders you would indeed see how much Frehep fights. Those lands are already covered in winter, waiting desperately for a spring that will never come. There will be no new crops planted, or harvests gathered, game will no longer be found, children will no longer survive their births. In a short time everyone will die. The snow and ice will continue until all the world is a mirror of Surlas, frozen and dead.'

She paused to let the words sink in.

'We should go to war. Destroy the Prae'surlas now.' Kris said, more certain than ever that this was the correct action.

'We could. We could send every warrior to the north, and we could even kill every Prae'surlas we find. But it would not stop the ice. Such a war would take years, and as I have said we have a matter of days, ten days to be precise. You see, it is not the Prae'surlas who are responsible, but one man, one Iceborn named Aerath.'

Kris's mind went back to the image of the Iceborn he had seen in the chamber of fire. Could that have been why the magic they used showed his image? It did not matter. 'Then we shall go to the King, and gather every Lord Fireborn and Flameborn. They will storm into Surlas, kill this Aerath, it would be done within ten days.'

'Aerath would not let himself be killed,' Jaiha explained patiently, as if the fate of Furea did not rest vitally on every moment's use. 'He would hide and he would wait, letting his countrymen fight for him instead, knowing that the weather will eventually be the death of Furea and all that live there. Aerath need not kill another single Fureath'i and he will still be responsible for the death of us all.'

Frustration crept into the muscles of his arms and fists. The only thing Kris disliked more than Scholars, was being near them and having to listen to them. 'Then what *should* we do.'

Nureail placed a calming hand upon his shoulder. Her touch was gentle and Kris felt he was defiling her by it touching him. 'We have asked ourselves the same questions, Kris, searching in all the wrong ways to find out how we can stop this terrible fate. It was only by a gift of Frehep that we stumbled upon our one chance. My brother visited the futures of all our great warriors, trying to merge the possibility of our salvation to their fates. It was only when I asked him to look at you, Kris, that we found our answer and requested you to come at once.'

Her brother explained further. 'When you first showed me the way we could stop Aerath, Kris, I did try to link that way with more powerful warriors. You are after all only a simple fleshborn.' Tereail spoke with no regard at how he risked Kris killing him with every word. 'But all of our Powerborn met their end, even Jaiha. There is a destruction linked to Aerath that pulled all of the great warriors to their different dooms. I am still struggling to understand it, but it seems there are forces at work in the world, perhaps even separate to Aerath's plans, that are seeking out and destroying greatness. I feel that you somehow avoid that destruction, Kris, perhaps because you are not... well, of any greatness.'

Nureail winced at Tereail's words, but Jaiha explained further. 'Regardless of why the fates have chosen you, Kris, here is what you must do: you will travel from here to an ancient temple where once Jhakral worshipped the gods of another age, there you will acquire an artefact that Tereail has seen can stop the age of ice bearing down on us. You will travel from the Jhakral temple to the Temple of Ice. It is much alike to the Temple of Fire we are now in, but the difference being it has been lost to the Prae'surlas for some years. Aerath has somehow found a way in. In this ice temple then, you will not find Aerune the ice god, but instead you will find Am'bril the goddess of tempest. A Foreign god as you might call her but one that has a Connection to every land and its weather, even Furea. Aerath has found a way to kill her and use that Connection to turn the world to ice.

'She is not dead yet however and the artefact we have found in Tereail's vision can release her from Aerath's hold. That is why we have ten days, Kris, because in every vision after this time, the goddess dies and the ritual to turn the world to ice unstoppable. It is our hope that once we have released Am'bril she will do what we cannot and begin restoring the world to its natural state. But it is not enough to save her. You must also kill Aerath or there is nothing to stop him recapturing the goddess and beginning the ritual anew. I know this is a lot to be told at once, Kris, but we have little time. Yours will be an impossible fight of a fleshborn against an Iceborn, but Tereail has viewed many times the image of you cutting off Aerath's head. The details of how you accomplish this thing have not been clear, such is the uncertainty of Tereail's vision, but I think you will agree with me when I say it is enough that we are certain it can be done. We have seen you do it and so it is possible.'

Kris remained silent. The Lady Jaiha would need to give him a much more comprehensive briefing before they were to leave, and it would take time to gather his squads and bring them all up to the temple. While he still went through the necessary preparation in his head, Tereail unnecessarily spoke again. 'You must know, Kris, that many times I have viewed this future and it is you that has died. Aerath is an Iceborn after all. You must already know what he did to the Prae'surlas champion Frind'aal, how he made the ice king kneel to him. He is worshipped in Surlas as a god.'

'Aerath is just another Prae'surlas,' Kris said back. 'And killing Prae'surlas is what my squads do best. You said that we have ten days? Can such a journey be done in that time? Where are these temples located?'

'It must be ten days because that is how long the goddess Am'bril has left to live,' Nureail spoke with hesitation. 'She fights Aerath's power, but he has become too strong for her, and we have been unable to discover how he has become so strong as to challenge the gods, even claiming to become one. There have not been any new gods since the creation of power. You would think that surely even the real Aerune would try to stop what he plans. Or if Amadis was still alive.' She bit her lip and looked away before returning with more strength to meet his dark eyes. 'Kris, you should know, your squads, they cannot go with you.'

He dismissed the statement. 'My men go where I go.'

'I have viewed this mission many times, Kris,' Tereail said. 'If your men go with you they will die.'

'Then they die to better their country while killing Prae'surlas, there is no other way a man could wish to die.'

'What about in his bed after a long and fulfilling life?' Tereail must have seen the disgust in Kris's eyes at such a notion, so he swiftly continued, his voice firmer and with false authority. 'In any case in the viewings where your men accompany you, you have not succeeded. That many warriors at once was enough it seemed to bring the same notice and destruction that all the great warriors brought by themselves. It has only succeeded where lesser men go, avoiding the detection from whatever force is causing this destruction.'

Kris frowned. 'Lesser *men*? Who else is going?'

'Nureail and Tereail will accompany you,' Jaiha answered and Kris immediately wanted to kill himself rather than allow that to happen. He tried to be reasonable, to object peacefully, but the Fireborn did not let him. 'They have not been seen to interfere with the mission or its success and they will help you locate the artefact in the first temple as well as show you how to travel between the temples. Both of these are tasks that will speed your journey and both are tasks that can only be completed by a Scholar. So unless you are indeed a Scholar in disguise, Kris, they are to accompany you'

Kris could think of no greater torture than to journey alone with two half-blood Foreign Scholars. But in doing this he would save his land and his people, and he would be given the chance to kill an Iceborn. His personal feelings should not be an issue. A Fireborn has requested his service and honouring him greatly in the asking. He was strong enough for this. He needed to be.

'I accept your terms, my lady,' he said with a bow that brought him to one knee. 'We will leave immediately. Please send word to my men that I leave Prothrin the Sword in charge as acting ember.'

Jaiha nodded, pleased with his decision and Nureail practically beamed with excitement. 'I had hoped to meet your man: the Sword

That Walks.' Her smile made her look much younger than she was. 'It is a pity he did not accompany you. Did your squad really-'

Kris raised his hand to stop Nureail mid-sentence. 'I am sure there will be plenty of time for idle conversation during our journey, Lady Nureail.' The fact that was true made Kris want to sigh. 'If we have only ten days to achieve our goals then you will need to change into clothing more suited to travel and out of your dresses.' He turned to Tereail as he said, 'Both of you.'

The man looked abashed as he did not seem to realise what he was wearing. With muttered agreement, and brief farewells to the Lady Fireborn, both Nureail and Tereail went to get ready and Kris was left alone with the legendary Jaiha the Decider of Fates. He had only been with her minutes and she had already involved him in events far beyond his station. To stop the entire world turning to ice, to save the goddess that was being used to do it, and to kill the Powerborn that was strong enough to kill that god. It was like hearing a bad Telling.

'You are doing the world a great service, Kris,' Jaiha said, her voice washing over him with a wave of calm.

'All I do is in service to better Furea, my lady,' he said back to her. 'The rest of the world, and everyone in it, can freeze and die for all I care.'

• CHAPTER FOURTEEN •

Waiting

Kris waited. Not for the first time during this patient wait, he reasoned that he could have gone down to his men in person and come back in the time it took the two Scholars to ready themselves. He would have been able to journey down to the camps, join them in a barrel of ale, spend the night singing with them, then head north and kill a dozen Prae'surlas, before returning still with enough time to die of old age before either Scholar deemed it time for them to leave.

They would both be in for shocking changes when the journey got underway and he became their squad leader. *If the journey gets underway,* he added dryly. When he was told he had only ten days to accomplish his task, they had failed to inform him that all ten of those would be spent waiting for Nureail and Tereail to pack their belongings. If they did not pack lightly enough to travel with speed then their first camp fire would be a large one.

What made it more infuriating was that Nureail was even a Teller. She should have more experience with travel than she was showing. And could Tereail not view the future? Could he not use his apparent mantic talents to see what he would need and pack swiftly? Kris watched a growing shadow along the floor.

He himself had nothing more than his sword and some supplies given to him by the priests of the temple. What more would he need if they were merely travelling from temple to temple without a fresh breeze of air to touch their skins. He was dressed as any other Fureath'i should, with simple tunic and some protective armour, leather straps to protect his forearms, and knee high greaves attached to his boots. He wore a belt of rank around his waist that gave him some protection along his stomach. It was large enough for supply pouches and holdings of weapons. He had heard that the border forts had gotten so cold that some warriors were using cloaks like Foreigners, but Kris did not think he would ever let himself look so weak in the blessed lands of Furea. The shadow from the window's light continued to grow, and as it reached Kris's boot it meant he would wait no longer.

Marching off to the nearest Scholar with a righteous pace, it was Nureail's apartments that he set out for. She at least had the greater chance of being ready, but Tellers were leisurely, always being asked to stay another night in a village, with everyone hanging on their every word. If Kris caught Nureail giving a Telling at that moment to some priest then he would drag her by the hair to their departure.

No priests or monks loitered by her apartments though, and Kris entered unchallenged. All the rooms of the temple were wide and open, with grand pillared archways spreading out to form the entrances. There were no doors or divisions for privacy, so when Kris walked in on her bathing he had no way to know what he would see.

The pool took up half the room and no barriers stood erect to shield her from view. She was not even washing herself but simply floating in its luxury. Kris was speechless, and not at the sight of her nakedness, but at the fact he waited for her and there she was lounging in a pool of water. Her eyes opened to greet him and she did not try to cover herself from view. Kris turned his back to save her shame.

'How long have you been looking at me?' Nureail asked, with no hint of outrage or embarrassment in her voice. 'I did not hear you come in.'

'A better question to ask is how long have I been waiting for you. We were to leave immediately.'

'Ah, so you have been looking at me for quite some time then. There is no need to apologise.'

Kris could hear the smile in her voice, and heard sounds of water dropping from her body as she stood up. Her disrespect to the urgency of the mission angered him.

'If I am to apologise then it should perhaps be to the people of Furea. Will I explain to them that we did not act in time because Lady Nureail wished to bathe? If you are to travel with me, as Jaiha Fireborn has asked, then it will be as a squad, and as your squad leader I will not permit you any luxuries.'

'It is exactly because there will be no luxuries that I indulge in my last one now. And do not think to lecture me on life on the road, I am a Teller after all or has my nudity washed your brain clean of that knowledge?'

'You overrate your own nudity, Teller.' He almost growled the last word but refrained. 'Life as a Scholar and a Teller, Lady Nureail, is much different to life as a Fureath'i.'

The patting of wet feet announced her angry march up to him. Kris did not turn around.

'You dare to claim I am not Fureath'i!' Her shouting echoed in the open chamber. 'Just because I do not kill a Prae'surlas for every hour there is in the day, does not mean that I do not fight for my country. Our country will only survive because of the study we have done in this temple. You do not... Kris, I demand that you turn around and face me when I am shouting at you!'

Kris turned around and looked down to see she was still naked. Water dripped from her bare skin, with wet beads visible on her hips and breasts. Kris moved his eyes to hers. They were light green with traces of brown and Kris would not move his eyes from them until she became dressed. The angry Teller faltered at his level gaze and seemed to lose what she wished to shout at him. Kris thought he would assist her if only to speed things up.

'You may shout at me all you wish during our journey but we will leave immediately. We have only ten days to achieve our goal and the task is long. Put on your clothes.'

'I will not! Not if it makes you uncomfortable. And have you not even asked how we will travel to the other temples? We could journey to both and return back today if we wished. But Tereail has seen our deaths in this endeavour more times than our success and if I am to die today then I will spend it as I wish.'

'As much as you will burden me, Nureail, I will not let you die.' Kris was surprised by the words. There was no way he could promise that. If there were things that could kill a Fireborn ahead of him then what chance did he stand? He added quickly, 'I will die before I let harm come to you.' That at least was achievable. Nureail seemed mollified by the words and even looked at him with a tenderness that was not appropriate. The speed in which she flared to rage was matched in how fast it disappeared again. Such an emotionally unstable person was going to be difficult company. Kris continued to look into her eyes.

'None of us know what will happen, Kris.' Her hand almost reached up for his face. 'Many squad leaders hold the responsibility for losing men. What difference should it make if it was their blade or their bad decision? The result is the same. The men are still dead. So since you are not alone in your situation, you should forgive yourself.'

Kris's black eyes grew fierce and Nureail stepped back at their intensity. Her mouth even dropped at the sudden rage Kris was staring at her. The knowledge she might have of him killing his own men had nothing to do with their current situation. He held no guilt for his actions so there was nothing to forgive. The Teller was mistaken if she inferred that Kris suddenly wished to discuss it. His voice held nothing but cold indifference when he spoke back to her.

'I will find Tereail and send for you when we are leaving. If you do not arrive in time then we leave without you.'

He turned and exited the apartments. The heels of his boots sounded loudly as he thundered through the cavernous temple. This time he did pass some priests and they shied away from his violent stride. Some even turned and fled while others had the fool idea to cower down where they stood. As if Kris would waste his time hurting them.

He would certainly hurt Tereail if he found the man as idle as Nureail had been. He would drag the Scholar out by his skirts rather than his hair, if he did not share his sister's habit and was at least dressed. Thankfully Kris walked past a bathing pool in the man's apartments and found it empty, although when he did come across Tereail it was not much better. The Scholar was still wearing a dress and was just sitting down, reading a book. It was too much.

'We leave now, Tereail.'

The man raised his head slightly to acknowledge Kris but did not stop reading. He was mouthing the words as he read them and did not look as if he rushed.

'Put down the book and put on clothing more appropriate to travel. Do it now, Tereail, or I will strike you unconscious and carry you over my shoulder.'

Still Tereail did not stir. He even had the audacity to wave his hand at Kris dismissively. 'Yes, yes, will you see if my sister is ready? I shall join you then.'

Kris took out his sabre but Tereail did not notice. He calmly levelled the blade at the Scholar's neck, which made him jerk in shock and almost cut himself in the act. Kris was in control however and pulled the blade enough to account for the motion. A small cut would serve as reminder for future conversations. Tereail's eyes were wide with disbelief and Kris lowered the blade only enough so he could swipe the sabre away and send the book flying across the room.

'You fool! That book is over four hundred years old!' Tereail scurried over to where it landed and carefully picked the thing up, caring for it like a babe.

'I feel that is how old I have become waiting for you both. We leave now or you do not accompany me.'

Tereail's anger did not quickly fade and he wrapped his arms around the wounded paper. 'And how will you find the artefact you need without me, Kris?'

'I will take your books of course and they will tell me.' Kris did not like the way the two Scholars made him act. Already they had discovered ways to push his patience beyond its limit. If they were warriors, or if he was holding himself under any less control, then they would both be dead now, and brutally abused before it.

'It is precisely that reason that I must painfully decide which of these we can afford to carry.'

'I will carry no books, Tereail.'

'But you must! I could not possibly carry them all. Even Nureail will need to carry some.'

Kris frowned in amazement. How many books did Tereail intend to bring that it would take three of them to carry? 'You will not bring so many. Only as many as you can carry and that will not slow us down. You should not need them in any case. Have you not seen this artefact and its use in your visions?'

Tereail muttered to himself in answer and began sorting through a mountain of books that were stacked on the table. Surely he had not thought he could bring that many? Kris wondered how Scholars could be so stupid. 'Not that I need to explain my gift to you, Kris, but as with everything else, the artefact shifts and changes with each vision. Some similarities remain, but already I have found two dozen relics in these books that could be confused with it. The futures that I travel are not as clear as your sight in the present, it is blurred and shifting, distorted and dizzying, I do not expect you to understand but I do expect you to respect my judgement. We need all these books.'

Kris did not frown or clench a fist in frustration. He was back in control. 'If you cannot select ten,' he told Tereail, 'then I will burn all these books right now.'

Tereail laughed and searched Kris's face for humour. The only thing humorous was the changing expression on the Scholar's own face as he realised how serious Kris was being.

'You will not. Lady Jaiha would not allow you.'

'I will. And unless she arrives in the next few heartbeats, she will not stop me.'

Still Tereail stared in disbelief at Kris. Perhaps if he managed to fetch enough water to extinguish all the fires in the chamber, then Tereail himself would be able to stop the act. But Kris did not think a Scholar's mind worked that way. He would not be searching for an action of his own; he would be searching for some reasoning that might change Kris's action. The determined set to Kris's jaw must have made him see reason about that.

'You are a madman. How can you expect us to succeed if you cripple us before we even begin?' Tereail was at least sorting through his books in a panic as he spoke. 'We will need all the books on the relics similar to the one we search for.' Kris nodded to this. 'And of course the books on the Jhakral language will take up most of my pack!'

'You do not need books on how the Jhakral speak.'

'The temple we are going to first is the Jhakral temple.' Tereail seemed always to speak as if lecturing an infant. 'There will be translations that I might not be able to decipher alone.'

'So you can read the Jhakral language.'

'Yes, but -'

'What other languages do you know?'

Tereail hesitated. 'Well, all of them of course, maybe my understanding of battle-scrit and demon rune is not as detailed as the modern languages but what kind of a Scholar would I be if I could not read the books of other nations?'

'If you were a Scholar who could not read, then you might almost be a Fureath'i,' Kris said coldly. 'But from what you have told me, I see no need for any of the language books to be taken with you.'

'But!' Tereail looked around for aid from someone or something against Kris's cruel demands. 'There will be different dialects! Different eras of language that are almost so obscure that I could not possibly -'

'You have until the time it takes me to walk over and grab that torch from the wall, to decide which ten books you may bring. I suggest the ones about what we are actually seeking.'

'Kris! Please listen to me. You have to understand what I am telling you!'

Kris turned around and walked steadily towards the torch he had indicated. It was not a fast walk, but it was by no means languid. When he placed his hand over its base and remove it from its holding, he saw Tereail finally realise that Kris would actually do it. The Scholar jumped and began tossing away books with only a quick glance at their titles and no regard for their condition once he had thrown them to the floor.

Again Kris's returning pace was fair, the speed not leaning in favour for either outcome. The Scholar, who was considered a lord because of his talents, equal in rank to a Powerborn almost, was sweating from the stress Kris was putting him through. When he returned to the books with the torch, Tereail was looking frantically along the remaining titles still lying on the table. Kris lowered the torch to the nearest book, not particularly wishing to start a fire in the sacred temple, but he would delay no longer.

'Wait! I have narrowed it to twelve and I simply cannot choose further! Please, I will carry them all, it will not slow us down. Kris you cannot do this!'

Kris nodded his acceptance and returned the torch to its holding. His pace was much swifter now for it was time to leave. When he returned he saw that three more books had found their way back onto the table, but reducing them to fifteen from what had looked like fifty was enough of a success for today. He could lose the other books while they journeyed.

'Now, pack your things and change out of your dress, it is long past time to leave.' Kris crossed his arms behind his back, settling himself to wait and stare at the man to hurry him. Tereail went about his business, muttering about how it was the robe of office that he wore and not a dress, and how Kris was the most simpleminded and stubborn man he had ever met, needlessly destructive, and no wonder she would like him.

This made Kris raise an eyebrow of unexpected curiosity. It was not like him to show an interest in anything that was not immediately important, but he could not help wondering who he meant. Was it the Lady Jaiha? The Fireborn had certainly shown Kris much respect by allowing him to address her as an equal. He could not have possibly been referring to his sister. Kris and Nureail had just demonstrated how much they could not tolerate each other in the Teller's recent dramatic outburst. As soon as his thoughts drifted to possibilities of other women they might encounter in a future Tereail had viewed, Kris made himself stop caring.

His attention went back to the Scholar to make sure his every move was as economic as could be. The man moved with the hurried clumsiness of harassment but he was still moving smoothly enough to satisfy Kris. At one point he picked up another fallen book and Kris withdrew his sabre with a frightening speed. Tereail jumped and the book went flying out of his hands, but Kris simply began sharpening his blade calmly as if he had not been watching Tereail at all. The steady ring of stone against steel set an effective rhythm to make the Scholar finish the rest of his preparations quickly.

When he was finally dressed and ready to leave he confronted Kris with an accusing stare. 'I still do not see why you need to hurry so much.' He said while stuffing the last book into the travel pack. 'Our dinner with Lady Jaiha will not be for another hour yet at least.'

Kris almost laughed with disbelief. But he never laughed, and rarely smiled, instead he kept his demeanour grim. 'There will be no dinner. We leave now.'

Tereail was more confident with his arguments when concerning the Fireborn however. 'I would like to see you try your bully tactics with the Priestess, *ember*.' He tried to make the title sound demeaning but such a high role could never be seen to look low, if anything it only further emphasised Kris's authority. Tereail seemed to realise this but continued regardless. 'I will not tell her of your madness here. It would only serve to sully our last moments with the great Fireborn.'

'A Fureath'i should not be so dramatic. You even have Nureail convinced of her own death at this venture. If you have seen that I can succeed then I will ensure that it is so. You will not die if there is anything I can do to prevent it.' Those words were strongly aimed at the efforts Kris would need to ensure he did not kill the man himself.

'It is not my own death that I speak about, though a likely possibility that seems to be, but of Lady Jaiha herself. There were only the fewest traces of hope when I viewed into her futures. In almost certitude, the Priestess will be killed before we return. A demon with green eyes that has already killed Lord Chrial'thau is coming for Lady Jaiha. This she knows, and she bravely waits to meet the creature. Someone is trying to destroy the strongest Fireborns to weaken Frehep's power, and we do not think it is Aerath but someone even more malevolent.'

Kris wondered if Tereail used such flowery language to mimic his own sister in her Tellings, and he did not believe that Chrial'thau was dead, that a demon could kill him or any Fireborn, or even survive in the world of light at all. But it did not matter to him if it was true. Everyone dies.

'We all stand ready to meet our deaths. Such is the strength we take from bettering our people with our every breath.' Still though, Kris did not like the idea of a demon in the heart of Furea. He should order his men to remain at the temple, to offer what protection they could. He hated asking a question of a Scholar, for fear of the length in answer, but it might be important. 'What manner of demon is it?'

Tereail hung his head and looked shamed. Kris did not think such a feeling could exist in a Scholar. 'I did not look at it,' he whined. 'When I begin to see it, I... I can feel my own destruction approach. Perhaps I am a coward in your eyes, but what I do is not safe. When I enter a person's future, I am there as much as I am here in the present. If I were to die there, then, it would be my end. Perhaps my body would live on, but my mind would be lost. So I flee when it turns its eyes on me, and return to see the death of a Fireborn. Can you now see why I do not rush to abandon her?'

Kris was not moved. 'What we do is worth more than one life and we are not waiting any longer. I will tell the Priestess the same.' Let her regret her own decision to let him speak as an equal. She was now just one more Scholar he had to convince it was time to go.

Shouldering Tereail's pack, largely to prevent the man from stuffing anything else into it, Kris left the apartments. He carried the weight easily but could tell that a few hours of travel with it would test most men. Kris was not most men, but unfortunately neither was Tereail. The Scholar reached out as if to stop Kris from touching the pack, maybe fearful that he would still toss the whole thing into the fire. The idea almost brought a smile to Kris's face.

The pace he set was brisk and even without the burden of the heavy pack load, Tereail struggled to keep up. Nothing that had happened in the last hour boded well for the next few days of travel, but Kris did not generally allow himself to dwell on what could be. There would be plenty time to dwell on them when they actually happened. If Dallid were with him he would find a way to turn it to positive, and suggest that Kris's influence would serve to strengthen both Scholars and make them better Fureath'i. Kris would have gladly read every book in the temple if it meant Dallid and Phira were going on the journey with him instead.

His eyebrows raised when he spotted Nureail ahead, surprised that she was dressed and fully kitted out for travel. She turned her palm in greeting to Tereail but did not greet Kris. Perhaps it was petty but he spoke anyway. 'The sun god sees you, Lady Nureail, and he is surprised to see you have chosen to wear clothes for this trip. I did not think Tellers needed them.'

Tereail turned to face Kris in outrage at the insult to his sister's honour, but Nureail did not even blush.

'Well perhaps I would not have, if it were not for you being unable to take your lustful eyes off me. I thought you had stronger will than to allow yourself a slave to your more base desires, Kris.'

Kris opened his mouth, indignation and bewilderment blazing to life, but at Nureail's smile he knew better than to defend himself. She was simply trying to goad him into an emotional reaction and he would not be a party to it. Keeping his voice at its neutral best he replied. 'It is good then that you have not made any effort to appear attractive for our trip, I would not have my lustful desires get in the way of our goal.'

Tereail let out a loud sigh and Kris turned to frown at its meaning. Wisely the Scholar did not elaborate, just giving Kris a smug and knowing smile. Neither was Nureail given opportunity to return insult for the Fireborn Priestess came into view at that moment, burning away all childish acts within the room and reminding them of the greater power that they served. She appeared to glide along the marble flooring, making not a sound, and emanating glorious light. Kris dropped to his knees in respect, the heavy pack still balanced upon his shoulder. His two Scholar companions did not mirror his act of respect.

They simply turned their palms in greeting, the way they might if seeing any Fureath'i. Kris bowed his head lower to make up for their indecency. The Lady Jaiha stopped before him and asked him to rise. He met her sunburst eyes again as an equal, and her smile ignited his soul.

'The sun god sees you, my warrior.'

'May he see me killing Prae'surlas, my lady.'

His same reply made her smile. It was a sight to behold. 'I see you are already to leave. I expected little else from you, Kris.' She turned to Tereail and Nureail. 'It seems our dinner will have to wait for another time my friends.'

'But, Jaiha, I would see our last evening together a memorable one.'

The Lady turned to Tereail and cupped his chin with her hand. 'You should know more than anyone that the future is not certain. I go to my fate just as you go to yours, if we have the heart and will to make it so, then we will meet again. Besides, I do not think Kris can postpone for another moment. His determination is what we need right now, it is what will save our people.'

'My thanks, Jaiha Fireborn.' Kris nodded to her wisdom. 'Tereail has told me of what you stay to meet. My men, I will order them to remain and provide what help their hearts can add.'

'Exceptional warriors all of them I am sure, but this is my battle and I would not have good blood spilt when it can be avoided.' She gave a weak smile as she joked: 'Now it seems I decide my own fate, and that is to remain here and wait for my destruction.' The smile did not hide the sadness in her eyes, and even the smile itself soon faded. 'Come let me show you how you will travel.'

She gave Nureail a private smile, and another for Tereail, before she turned to lead the way. With her back to them as they walked, she began explaining about the temple.

'The Temple of Dawn in the east and the Temple of Dusk in the west are but copies of this temple, Kris. The Temple of Zenith is called so not just because it is highest in truth, but it lies highest in power and history also. Even the Tower of Frehep does not pre-date this temple, and that tower was built long before the Fureath'i journeyed into the forests, long before even the last age began, let alone this one.

'The true name for where we stand would be the Temple of Fire, and within it there is a Connection to the stream of life that provides those of us, gifted with the blood of gods, with the energy needed to power our bodies and create the magics of pyromancy. Through this Connection the temple is then joined to the other greater temples secreted about the world, some lost to any other ways of locating them.'

They turned a corner and entered the main chamber of the temple, where vast pillars held aloft the impossibly high ceiling. Men of flesh could not have constructed such a thing. Even the altar which they approached was decorated and built in such a way that it looked like the creator had first turned the stone to liquid before crafting unbelievable twists and design. Walking up past the altar, the Fireborn came to a stop looking down upon a spiralling platform on the floor behind.

'These are the doorways that link the Great Temples, Kris, a threshold to the stream of life energy that will transport you to the next temple within seconds. They are gateways torn through the world of gods.' She gestured and the spiralled lines of stone on the decorative platform lit up with glowing power, pulsing between red and gold and back again. 'With this I can shift the pattern to bring you to the precise temple. When you reach there the platform you arrive at can return you here. You will have to search out smaller flowstones like these to bring you to the next temple, the Temple of Ice. Tereail and Nureail will know the designs for this. There will of course be a master dais like this one where you can dictate your destination, but you need to be a Powerborn to work it. Ironic since we cannot step onto these platforms. If we did then the life-stream would tear our bodies apart, our own power rushing out to join its source. That is why thankfully, although Nureail and Tereail are gifted and hold power, they are not Powerborn. And as fleshborns, you are all able to pass through without notice.'

She turned to look at Kris again. 'Yet another reason why I cannot accompany you. The paths we would need to take would be far more time consuming and dangerous. Despite your imposing skills as a warrior, Kris, it will be your stealth and speed that we need. Pass through these pathways unnoticed and save our world from its demise.'

Kris nodded his acceptance. He had put meaning into the gesture and hoped the priestess did not need words from him to express the honour and responsibility she had given him. The warm smile that lit her eyes as well as his heart said she understood and Kris turned to nod to his companions that they would leave. Both Scholars moved forward to hug the Fireborn farewell and then stood beside Kris taking deep breaths to steady their hearts. Waiting to see what the future held, Kris placed one hand upon the hilt of his sabre and stepped onto the platform, vanishing from the Temple of Fire.

• CHAPTER FIFTEEN •

Fire

Phira watched the burning fire and thought of home. Not just her village of Coruln, but home as any footstep on Fureath'i soil. The fortress city of Rath'Nor had become as much a home to her as Coruln, and her marriage to her country as important as her marriage to her husband. Dallid was the love that made her heart beat, but every beat of it was to better serve her country. She wished that Dallid was there to serve her now.

'Oh it has been too bloody long,' she said, even though there was no-one to hear.

She was alone and staring at the fire in the room, wishing the one in her heart would stop thinking of Dallid and wishing the real one in front of her was bigger. The fires that they made were the only things of familiar comfort her squads had while in Surlas, even indoors in an acquired building, the fires were a blessing. Smoke filled their lungs for the past three days as they remained hidden, but a Fureath'i perseveres. Fire and smoke did not harm them as it might have others. In the larger room down the corridor behind her, far more fires burned, and breathing in the smoke of this single fire was as close to fresh air as she would get.

The building was empty of furnishings and the walls and flooring were made of stone, so she had little fear of the building catching. Say one good thing about the Prae'surlas, they built good houses. Perhaps years of having the Fureath'i burn them down had finally taught the north-men to become smarter.

She pealed back some fabric curtain they had fashioned and watched the city full of Prae'surlas stride about their day. Fureath'i did not have or need glass windows since they lived in a land of eternal heat, but she appreciated that the Prae'surlas did have them. It thankfully meant she did not have to feel the full chill of outside. It had gotten cold in Furea, and eternal winter in the wildlands surrounding the borders, but there could be no place in the world as cold as Surlas.

The Surlas city she and her squads were in now was called Grwenilthen, a word you needed to spit to even think of pronouncing. A more common name for it was the City of Statues. The Prae'surlas loved giving their cities grand titles like that, to try to elevate their worth above the rest of the world: Grwenilthen the City of Statues; Dowrathel the City of Towers; Hrosvidar the City of Ships; Aeris the City of Walls; they will all burn the same when the war comes. With enough fire it might even make the temperature of Surlas bearable.

The City of Statues was a trading city near the wildlands border, usually not so cold, but this winter was different. It should be well into spring approaching summer now and still the weather grew worse. The Prae'surlas did not seem to notice. They sauntered about, the layers of fat that made them so huge protecting them from the bitterness. Phira closed the curtain again.

She took off the white porcelain mask she was wearing. They had entered the city in disguise naturally, as stupid as the Prae'surlas were, four squads of armed Fureath'i would at least cause a little notice. So they had come as Ihnhaarat slave traders: the Foreign nation from far east beyond the Mordec Empire, who conveniently kept their faces covered at all times.

The traders mostly wore blank white masks without marking and the warriors wore skull designs upon theirs. The Foreigners even had their own Powerborn, who could call down lightning from the skies or from their hands. Those ones had skull masks also, but further decorated with either a lightning bolt or teardrops of blood. Phira's reports had not been able to determine what the difference in symbols meant yet. It was most likely the difference between greater and lesser Powerborn. It was a lesser Powerborn she was now going to meet; a Frostborn.

Pulling out her sword - a jagged thing with the serrated blade of the Ihnhaarat - Phira looked at it with dismay. It was so ugly. She longed to hold the beautiful curve of her Fureath'i sabre again or the narrow elegance of her katana, *Unrivalled*, that Yiran had given her. Still, Phira did enjoy a variety of weapon and the crude instrument would do.

She entered the back room and was overcome with the heat. It was wonderful. The smoke did not even bother her since the warmth was such a welcome pleasure. Torches lined each of the walls, the oiled rags not giving off much smoke at all, but underneath them lay fire pits that did. Those were formed from anything her scouts could find without drawing attention and so the smoke was erratic depending on what it burned. It was the larger pit in the centre of the room that was such splendour though. It almost reminded her of a heart fire. There was one man in the room that was not enjoying the roaring heat, and that was the Frostborn she had come to see.

They had captured him without incident, her men being expert in such things. A Frostborn could not do much when peppered with arrows all aimed for his head and heart. It did not kill the Powerborn, but the amount of energy taken to heal his mind and body was enough to leave him too weak and addled to fight back. They had kept most of the arrows in him, to keep the thing injured and bleeding, sapping his strength. The fires did as much as the injuries to stop him from using magic, the heat too great for even the smallest trace of ice to form.

Phira stood in front of the battered prisoner, and the man tried to stare back with defiance. She swung her sword across and hacked out a chunk of the man's cheek. The large Prae'surlas did not fall from his chair, but simply swung his head to take the blow. His blonde hair was matted over his face with sweat and his cold blue eyes stared something like hatred. The Prae'surlas did not hate the Fureath'i though, they viewed the Fureath'i as too far beneath them to be worthy of hate. One of her embers, Lei, laughed at her.

'That is the first question you have to ask him then?'

Phira raised an eyebrow at Lei's impudence for breaking rank in front of the enemy but then grinned at him.

'Was it not a good question?' she asked back.

'I thought it too subtle.'

Her other ember Gravren shook his head at their behaviour and kept his eyes on the Frostborn, ready to plunge his blade into its heart at any moment. Gravren was always very serious, much like her childhood friend Kris she thought. She had heard much of Kris recently with his promotion to ember class and when she returned to Rath'Nor she would request his squads to come under her command. He was building quite a reputation and she could use a man like that.

The thought worried her then, about whether Dallid would take insult that she did not request for him to join with her. She could not though, as much as her flesh wanted him to join with her, that alone told her he would be too distracting and she needed full commitment to her career. She would just have to survive on love for her country instead of from her husband, and take her fleshly pleasure in giving others pain. The Frostborn was fortunate that she would get to take it out on him.

'Your name?' she asked.

The Frostborn tried to spit but could not form the moisture to do so. Instead he answered, his cracked dry throat sounding like a man already dead from thirst. 'The Powerful do not answer to vermin.'

The Powerful and the Demi-gods: the Prae'surlas's own grandiose titles for their Frostborn and Iceborn.

'Are not all vermin when compared to the Powerful?' she asked innocently. 'How then do you answer what food you would like? Or answer how you would like your ass to be cleaned?'

He bore his teeth at her mockery. 'The Powerful order, they do not answer.'

'It seems to me that you just answered my question.' Again Lei laughed, as well as some of the other men in the room, but not Gravren of course. Phira continued, 'So we have gotten past that first obstacle, the next should not be so hard. What do you know about this weather? This winter that does not relent. If it does not stop soon then every land will turn into Surlas will it not? Now I know I am bias but that to me sounds like something the Prae'surlas would try to do.'

The Frostborn said nothing, which only convinced Phira more that she had found someone who could tell her something. She and her squads had been tasked with gathering information about the growing cold that was choking the world. It was not so evident in Furea yet, but the King knew of its effect on every other land. It was not natural, and if anyone was to blame then it would be the

Prae'surlas. Admittedly, the Fureath'i did blame the Prae'surlas for most things.

'I don't see why you will not talk to me. We have even learnt your language to make it easier for you. It feels like I'm out of breath all the time, your words go up and down so much, but we have learnt it. Listen to how perfectly the animals can mimic your highborn speech. All you need do to be rid of us is tell us what divine plans your Demi-gods have devised and you can be on your way.'

The Frostborn gave a pained laugh. 'Do you expect me to believe you will let me live?'

Phira threw her eyes to Frehep. 'Well alright, you've caught me, we are going to kill you, but once you tell us what you know you can be on your way to that death quickly. Imagine it, away from all this fire, and away from all these flea infested Fureath'i.' She picked something from her hair and pretended to eat it. 'Or are we the fleas? Really, you Prae'surlas insult so badly that I can't follow.'

'You are not worthy to hear of our god's divine plans.'

'Oh then, it is not King Rohlan or the Demi-gods who are responsible, but your actual god? So is it Aerath or Aerune? They are both the same name are they not? Or is my Prae'surlas not as good as I believe.'

'Your animal tongue chews up the words like a cow chews cud.' The man tried to spit again but was left denied.

'Here,' Phira said. 'Let me help you with that.' She hooked the man across the jaw with the butt of her sword, knocking out one of his teeth and filling his mouth with blood. 'There, now you have something to spit.' She was surprised he did not have stronger teeth. Perhaps he was more beaten that she thought.

The Frostborn spat out the blood from his mouth without thinking, and then upon hearing her words stopped himself from doing it again. He could not accept her help, or perhaps he could not accept that such a blow had come from a fleshborn Fureath'i, and from a woman at that.

'So we were saying, is it Aerath or Aerune? Do you believe Aerath is really Aerune reborn? Surely if he was an imposter the real god would strike him down. Luckily we have no such confusion between Lord Chrial'thau and Holy Frehep because both were alive at the same time. Is Aerath that old?'

The Frostborn coughed as he tried to laugh again. 'He is more ancient than your pathetic Chrial'thau, who will soon be dead, and you can thank the only true god *Aerath* for that.'

The emphasis on the name let Phira know at least who was behind the weather ritual. All she needed to know now were the details and how to stop it. She could try to question him until he told her everything, even if it took weeks or months, unless what the Frostborn was saying about Chrial'thau was true.

'Chrial'thau has humbled Aerath before, we have a famous Telling about it actually, the *Grand Mercy of Pity* it is called. During the long war when we'd laid siege to Dowrathel, after we defeated the mighty towers that protect it, and after growing bored at your cowardice, we offered you a way out. We offered single combat between champions for our entertainment and out you sent Aerath. We had expected Grelit, your champion of the east, but all you had to offer was the champion of a city. I think the fight might have lasted all of a heartbeat before Chrial'thau won. I also hear Aerath soiled himself and wept like a babe for mercy. In disgust Chrial'thau granted it. That was just over a hundred years ago, and I don't think Aerath could have grown so much in power to be a danger to Chrial'thau now, or to be responsible for this foul weather.'

'I was at that siege, fool girl, and Chrial'thau only left because he could not kill Aerath, because he is our god reborn and he will cleanse the world of your kind. If you think the cold is bad now you are a fool, it will get much worse for you and none but the chosen Prae'surlas will be left alive to paradise in its glory.'

'That's twice you've called me a fool in the same breath, which seems a bit unnecessary. You are older than I thought though. Tell me, how does it feel to be that old and know that you are about to be killed by a fleshborn just over twenty summers old? Summers, not winters. It must be galling. It must make you want to show me exactly how little time I have left to live in this soon to be frozen world. What do you think one such as me could even do with that information? Don't you think it worth explaining so that I could spread terror among my people? So that I can send all the little

Fureath'i fire-rats scurrying about in a panic? Surely that is worth the words of the Powerful.'

He said nothing, but the blazing blue of his eyes let Phira know he was considering it. The Frostborn's eyes spiralled with dark and light blue, but they did not burn the way a Fureath'i Powerborn's did. Phira met his gaze and considered what the man had to lose by telling her what she wished to know. What could they possibly do to stop one such as Aerath? Well with one word from her, the eight Kings of Furea would rally up two hundred Powerborn and send them all charging into Surlas. Before the north-men had a chance to gather a similar force of Iceborn to meet it, the Fureath'i host would have found Aerath and destroyed him, returning as quickly as they left and standing ready for any doomed attempt of retaliation. All the Frostborn needed to do was say the words and his god would be killed.

'Very well,' he growled. 'But only so I can be done with you. I welcome the cold embrace of my god. He will return me to greatness and I will repay you for your insolence.'

'My balls are shaking in fear, but go on.'

The Frostborn sneered, changing his mind about talking to such an obscene woman. His disgust for being held in room full of obscene Fureath'i must have been greater though. He wished to be killed and done. He spat. 'First of your feeble Chrial'thau, he is most likely already dead. My lord has plans to journey there by means you could not understand to make an example of your people's *champion*.'

'Journey where?'

'A pathetic rat's nest called Coruln, next to your stolen tower. This he will destroy too. Just the first of many ways he will bring ruin to your kind.'

Phira did not show the alarm she felt at the details this Frostborn knew. It was fortunate that Aerath felt the need to boast his grand plans to a lowly Frostborn, fortunate and foolish. But still, her father Yiran lived in that village. The idea that Aerath planned to murder her village was enraging but she was correct in her estimation of Chrial'thau to Aerath. The Iceborn may have recently been strutting around declaring himself a god, he may have made the ice king kneel to him and he may even have bested Frind'aal the most powerful of the Iceborn, but that did not change the fact Aerath was still just an Iceborn. Chrial'thau was equalled in power only by the gods.

'What else.'

'He will see your citadel frozen and smashed, he will bring new religion to your three temples and he will have your people kept as pets and slaves -'

'Yes, yes, all very ambitious, Frostborn, but how? How does he plan to do this? How can he alone change the weather of an entire world?'

'He is a god.'

'There are other gods, true gods raised up at the creation of power, why would they allow him to do this?'

'The other gods are weak. They cower in fear of his might.'

Phira turned around in frustration. 'This is pointless. If you have nothing useful to tell me, then I will just have to not kill you. We will wait here and enjoy the heat. I have nowhere I need to go, my country is already doomed to ruin, so why not stay here? Tell me how, Frostborn! How will Aerath do it?'

He rasped a broken laugh. 'The mind of a fleshborn cannot fathom the infinity of a god. You would not understand even if you were told.'

The smoke was getting to her, even with Lei's alterations to the building to vent it all towards the chimneys. If any Prae'surlas wondered why the mysterious Ihnhaarat traders made so much smoke, they would just reason the Ihnhaarat behaved mysteriously. Phira left the room, followed by her ember Lei. Gravren remained guard with the other men, his grim stare fixed on the laughing Frostborn.

She struggled to contain her sudden anger and was very close to striking Lei just to have some release. It would not have been the first time and she was well known by all her men for being volatile. But it was the same passion - that she did such a poor job at containing on an everyday basis - that made her great as a warrior and commander. It did not matter how she achieved results, all that mattered was she did. Anyone that wished to challenge her methods was welcome to do so at their own risk. Lei must have sensed her violent intentions as he stepped back before speaking.

'We could keep him here another week, blaze commander, but not much longer.' He scratched the back of his head and lowered his eyes to avoid her anger. Lei always felt uncomfortable giving her advice but it was the job of the embers to challenge their blaze commander as much as to follow their orders. Of course Phira knew she could be very domineering. She may have been arrogant and over powering, but all of it was rightly justified. She thundered her glare at Lei as he continued, growing more uncomfortable with each word. 'Even the most self-involved Prae'surlas will notice a band of Ihnhaarat traders that spend a month without trading anything.' He scratched his head again. 'Do you think he will talk?'

'Frostborn don't feel pain as fleshborn do,' Phira conceded but stepped closer to get within striking distance of Lei should she need to backhand him. 'And eventually the fires will not hold him.'

'Then what are your orders?'

Phira turned and glanced out the windows again, risking it without her porcelain mask. Blue eyed giants passed by in their hundreds. They all looked the same, even the women. All brutishly tall and wide, with the same foppish long pale hair, their only differences were eyes of either pale ice or dark ice. How the Prae'surlas still defended they were not all inbred was madness. Every Foreigner with ears knew the Prae'surlas bedded their own mothers and sisters.

All Fureath'i had the same golden skin as each other of course, the desert warriors darker than the forest ones, but it was there the similarities ended. The Fureath'i race was varied with height and width, eyes and hair, with millions of warriors and every one distinctly individual. The Prae'surlas race was like a group of players running around with mirrors showing the same god-ugly north-man over and over.

'We will go home, Lei, get some sun back on top of us and some women underneath us.' She smiled at him as she repeated the words she heard every soldier mutter over the last few weeks.

Lei opened his mouth and closed it again. Phira thought he would have stopped getting shocked by her at this stage. Foolishly he said instead, 'But our mission, blaze commander, we need to complete it.'

Phira moved slowly towards him and he stepped back involuntarily. This made Phira smile again and Lei cursed for his reaction.

'Am I that frightful?'

'To look at? Certainly not. To disagree with? Most definitely.'

'I am pleased that you do not find me *frightful* to look at, Lei.' This made the man blush. Phira's fondness of him was part in how easily she intimidated him and part in how he still tried to fight it. He was not a weak man by any means. She was simply too much for him. 'But we have completed our mission. We have discovered Aerath is directly behind the continued change in the weather, and that he plans a series of attacks within Furea beginning with Chrial'thau at the Tower of Frehep. Both of these problems can be solved with Aerath's death. The quicker we return to Rath'Nor to order this death, the better for all.'

The better for Coruln especially, she thought. Yiran was more than a master to her, more even than a father. He held an equal part of her heart as did Dallid and her country. If she could prevent the Iceborn's attack on her village, then she would do so immediately. It did not matter she had not discovered how Aerath had become so powerful or how he was hoping to manage a journey into the heart of Furea unchallenged. It did not even matter how Aerath was turning the world to ice. There was a single answer for all the questions and that was to remove the Iceborn's head.

'Come. Let us tell our friend he is in luck. We will kill him today.'

'Your mercy is equalled only by your beauty, blaze commander.'

Phira eyed him. 'Do you think I'm beautiful, Lei? Would you like to bed me?'

As always the battle of lust and fear was amusing to watch on his face. She eased over to him and ran her hand down his stomach. She felt his manhood already swelling with desire. She moved past this and grabbed him by the balls, Lei's entire body paralysed with pain.

'Oh you do have these do you?' She let go of them and the back of her fist cracked into the side of his face, knocking him to one side. 'You should use them some time. But only a blaze commander can bed her ember, Lei, not the other way around. So I will not tolerate idle compliments, however heavily laced with irony as they are.' She waited for a moment, to see if he would actually fight back. If she was in his position she would have killed her by now.

'Yes, blaze commander,' Lei replied, his head held down to his chest. It was a pity he was as fond of her as she was of him. So he would not fight, no matter how much she wanted him to. Phira wondered if Lei enjoyed the abuse as much as she did. The half-smile he gave her as she left indicated he did. Or did she imagine that?

She returned back to the room of fire and Phira presented herself before the imprisoned Frostborn one last time.

She sighed. 'The sun god sees you, Frostborn, and he grows weary of your sight. I have decided I will indeed grant you your wish and kill you this day. Have you any regrets you wish to speak?'

The prospect of death did indeed seem to delight him and he smiled up at her. 'My only regret is that I do not die killing Prae'surlas.' He laughed. 'Is that not your pathetic Fureath'i tradition to utter as your dying words? Do you not realise the stupidity of it? That you are actually wishing for a Prae'surlas to kill you?'

'To be killed by a Prae'surlas and to die killing Prae'surlas are two distinctly different things. Have your simple minded people not a death ritual or do we kill you too quickly for one?'

The shine behind his eyes seemed to grow brighter as he stared at her. Maybe the eyes could begin to resemble fire given enough power. 'With my last breath,' he hissed at her, 'I breathe glory to my god!' He spat blood on her boots and bore his teeth at her one final time.

'Very well then, I hereby charge you with the crime of being a Prae'surlas, the punishment: death.' She turned to her second ember and offered him the act. 'Gravren, your squads tracked and found him. I will give you the honour of his kill.'

The look of surprise and gratitude in Gravren's eyes was a rewarding one for Phira. Of her two embers, Lei could be controlled with violence and sexual abuse, but with Gravren she would either have to earn his unwavering respect and loyalty or she would have to kill him. Killing a Frostborn was one of the highest honours a Fureath'i could achieve and she did not need another spear upon her rank, she already had enough to satisfy her needs. To bring fruition to her goal of soon becoming general, she had much grander plans set in place. Killing one more Frostborn would not benefit that goal, but compounding the loyalty of men like Gravren certainly would.

Gravren was not much for words so after the look of appreciation, he lifted his own Ihnhaarat blade. Everyman in the room was dressed in the black trader robes, and all of them armed with the serrated swords. It was an odd sight as she looked around, seeing so many black clad warriors surrounded by fire, then something even stranger caught her eye.

The faintest trickle of frost had appeared at the corners of the room. Focusing on it she could even see the tendrils of ice spreading. The breath in front of her mouth misted and despite all of the roaring fires, she began to feel cold. Turning her head to their Frostborn prisoner she had enough time to see him smile at her. Then half the fires in the room went out and the Frostborn burst free from his bindings. If her squads had not been armed then the single Powerborn would have killed them all, even in his injured state. Their healing, their strength, their speed, all surpassed that of a fleshborn greatly. That did not mean fleshborn were without speed though.

The moment the Frostborn moved, so had Phira's blade. It was an ugly thick weapon but her sword arm was strong enough to use it like any other. It pierced into the Powerborn's gut and she withdrew it immediately to spin and sink the blade into the side of the man's neck. In the time she had struck those two blows, Gravren had yet to strike once, plunging his sword fully down into the Frostborn's chest just as Phira ripped her sword free from the throat.

Her warriors had taken a step forward to intervene but now looked like they stood frozen from the sudden speed of it all, both at the sudden strength of the Frostborn to break free, but also at how swiftly Phira's sword had defeated him. The Powerborn wavered on his feet, his mouth opening and closing like a dying fish. Gravren's sword was still embedded in his lungs to stop any words from coming out, but the Frostborn's head looked ready to fall off from the half of his neck Phira had torn free.

If he had not been still riddled with arrows, beaten and weary by the heat of the fires, and further weakened by the strength it must have taken to out the flames, then Phira would not have been able to cut him apart so easily. It was not something she would point out to her men though. She would let them see their blaze commander strike with greater speed than a Powerborn, and she would now let them see her own loyalty to her men.

'Gravren, the kill is still yours.'

He frowned at her, his eyes darting to the two wounds she had inflicted before he had been able to achieve one. She could see he wanted to protest, to explain that had it not been for her, the Frostborn might have killed him. The sword wound Gravren had given him was severe but it would not have stopped the Frostborn from breaking Gravren's neck. Phira could see her ember's thoughts even if he never gave them words, and she nodded her approval when he obediently held out his hand to his men for another sword.

He wisely did not risk taking out the one already in the Frostborn. It was always difficult to tell how much sudden strength they could muster - as just witnessed. Even with half his head hanging off the Powerborn was no less dangerous, no one knew exactly how much their magic cost them. With half of the fires now dead it was possible he could suddenly summon shards of ice to fly into the flesh of every Fureath'i there. Gravren knew this as much as Phira did so it was without further ceremony that he hacked into the other side of the Frostborn's neck and the head dropped to the floor.

The stoic ember did not speak as he handed his sword back to his men, and retrieved his own from the chest of the dead Prae'surlas. The slightest watering of his eyes spoke of the intense emotion Gravren was feeling. Phira turned to see Lei's reaction and as she turned, one of the squad leaders stepped forward to gather up the severed head of the Frostborn, wrapping it with cloth before stuffing it in a bag.

Fureath'i did not generally collect heads as the Prae'surlas did, but a Powerborn head was something special. They had beetles that would strip the flesh and stop it spreading disease. The man who took the head had been the leader of the squad under Gravren who had hunted the Frostborn down in the first place, so that honour could be his. He looked to Phira for permission before storing it and she nodded her approval.

She preferred to collect weapons instead of heads and went over to the belongings of the now dead Powerborn. She had already spotted previously which one she wished to collect and picked it up without pause. It was odd for a Frostborn to carry weapons when they did not need them, but she knew of some Flameborns that still preferred to use a sabre when in combat too.

The spear she picked up was perhaps not something she wished to be seen wearing as an Ihnhaarat, or even as a Fureath'i when they returned, but maybe she could wear it during an expedition into the waste lands between Surlas and the Mordec Empire. It was a small double sided spear that could be strapped to a forearm. Too big for her arm by far, but could still be useful. She already had quite a prized collection that she seldom ever got to use, but had a good feeling that she would have opportunity to try this one.

Strapping back the serrated Ihnhaarat sword to her waste, Phira slipped the short spear through her belt under her robes. She would collect the Ihnhaarat sword also, but it was not likely she would use it if they experienced trouble on their return journey. It was ugly and ill-designed. It might have been created to induce fear from its grisly appearance, but had little practical use other than for sawing meat.

Knowing it was time to leave, her men began putting out the remaining fires and gathering their gear. They would be glad to be free of the smoke finally. Every man knew what was needed to be done without her ordering it. Even the embers and squad leaders simply supervised with stern silence and only sped things up with their own hands every now and again. In little time the four squads were packed and ready, her lookouts given word to return. Both embers neatly inspected two squads each, and Phira left them to their jobs. She had the highest faith in their abilities and that was why she had chosen them for this mission. She had eleven more embers waiting back in Rath'Nor, and even Lei and Gravren each had several other squads under their command back in Furea. She had needed stealth and speed for this mission though, and had come with just the best. Nodding that the embers were ready to leave, Phira donned her own mask and finally left the smoke-filled building.

The cold air stung them, but for a time it was refreshing. The group of near fifty Fureath'i warriors walked casually down the street full of Prae'surlas, passing soldiers and civilians alike. The high collared black coats and all concealing cloaks of the same colour were too perfect for disguise. The only thing that could go wrong was of course if they walked into another group of Ihnhaarat traders, but for now the subterfuge worked as it should.

Gravren and Lei sent off their men to retrieve the horses stored in a different Inn. It was where they all had stayed before capturing the Frostborn. She had left only a minimum of warriors behind to ensure nothing happened to their mounts, needing the rest to stand guard over their captive during the torture. Rather than delay any longer she ordered a rendezvous in Breel's square.

She would wait until they were reunited with their horses and out of the city before giving her squads their orders. She would have to split them up, each going a different route to increase the likelihood of speed and success. The sooner the King was told of Aerath, the sooner Aerath would be killed, and the sooner the world, her country and her village of Coruln would be safe. She knew that Frehep could not hear her so deeply into Surlas, but Phira said a silent prayer to the sun god anyway. She prayed that she would not be too late.

CHAPTER SIXTEEN

The rise to greatness

Phira once again sat alone and stared at a fire. She had her belt knife out, paused from making a carving out of wood, and just sat staring at the flames. Her rank demanded that she stay separated from the rest of her warriors, but Phira had learned to enjoy the time. She used it to gather her thoughts and plan ahead while the two squads under Lei's command sang softly and spoke Tellings to each other at the larger fire. The *Unseen Blade* and the *Revealing Light* were the two squads she had chosen to keep close to her, not just because Lei was their commander though.

Those two squads were best at remaining unseen and tracking enemies. Gravren and his two squads were better at breaking command and killing Prae'surlas rather than obeying complex orders. But if it were not for them she would never have captured that Frostborn and discovered how badly the Iceborn Aerath needed to be killed. Shivering, Phira wrapped the thick black wools of her Ihnhaarat costume around tighter and continued her wood carving.

Dallid would warm me up.

Phira closed her eyes and imagined his large arms wrapped around her. She imagined them at a camp fire back in Furea where neither of them would need to wear any clothes. It was not good to let her mind stray to such thoughts though, Lei would only eventually get abused in return. So instead she opened her eyes and went back to the wooden carving of Dallid she was making. She could never get his eyes right. Idly she wished his face could be on a coin like her own bloody was. Then she could see him every day.

Picking up her Ihnhaarat mask, Phira stared at the blank expression it wore and thought of Lei's mask that had the painted visage of a sneer. Part of the convenience about their disguises as Ihnhaarat was, not just the warmth, but to help their subterfuge near to all the Ihnhaarat did not speak. Slave traders usually had one to three nominated officials that were allowed speak and wore the painted mask that Lei wore, and only they could barter or speak with clients. The sneering face was to remind people that they wanted to buy what the Ihnhaarat had to sell and not the other way around. Phira did not think it helped them with their trading, but she was glad of the sneering mask. They had to deal with a situation requiring its use while leaving the city previously.

A Prae'surlas squad challenged them as her horses and wagons were steadily leaving the city. The sole reason it had happened was because of the amount of refugees going the other way. They were all fleeing the freezing wildlands for the ironic warmth and security of a Prae'surlas city. It made Phira and her troupe the only travellers actually heading away from the place. She tried to curse their panic and ignorance, but the families were starving and they sought the protection of the Prae'surlas because the northern swine actually had food.

The weather made it impossible to farm anymore. The earth everywhere Phira had seen was nearly always frozen solid. The refugees would have been better off making the longer journey to the Mordec Empire rather than Surlas, but the farms in the Empire would most likely not be any better than in the wildlands. As far she knew the Mordish hatred for the Ihnhaarat still assured they did not use slaves, but without slaves how could anyone grow enough food to survive?

Other information she had gathered while in Grwenilthen told her that the Mordec armies had gathered north to confront an Ihnhaarat host that was spotted travelling west. Although the Ihnhaarat were headed towards Amidon City, the Mordish had ridden to intercept. Skirmishes between the two nations were as constant as those between Furea and Surlas, but if all of the Mordec armies had gathered then it could mean a more substantial war. Such a war would never happen if Amadis was still alive, and such a war had already started between Furea and Surlas in Phira's mind. The acts of Aerath assured that. Still though, the Mordec armies invading Ihnhaarah would be beneficial to Furea as it would cut off a large portion of the Prae'surlas slave supplies.

The Ihnhaarat bred and sold creatures that looked like humans but acted like animals, called Chuabhotari, and the things could

Connect with plant life and vegetation much the way a Fureath'i Powerborn could Connect with fire. Phira had no idea how the Prae'surlas survived before they discovered the slaves, but for the last few hundred years the fey creatures were the only way farms could exist in the forbidding climate of Surlas. That was why thousands of other Foreigners were leaving their towns and villages, accepting life under Prae'surlas rule just to ensure they would not starve to death in the cold ravaging the world.

They would live but it would not be much of a life. The Prae'surlas saw themselves as better than everyone else and structured their entire society on that basis. Blood and position made everyone superior to someone else, all men were naturally superior to women, and all Prae'surlas were vastly superior to Foreigners. So any honest fleshborns seeking sanctuary in the cities of Surlas were only going to find cruelty, poverty and misery.

It angered Phira greatly that Furea was the only nation that saw the heart of a woman just as worthy as a man. They were the only army to allow women to join in battle. It should not have caused her such rage of course since that was exactly what made the Fureath'i army the largest in the world, and in all likelihood the same reason it was the best. In the Mordec Empire women were not as badly treated as in Surlas, in those lands at least the women made up the bulk of the merchant class, but even there it was seen as ridiculous to have a woman want to take up sword. Fingering her own blade Phira knew the world was full of fools.

That was why Lei had been selected as the Speaker in their Ihnhaarat trading party, Phira could not because she was a woman, and Gravren could not because he was a stubborn fool. If Gravren had been the Speaker when the Prae'surlas squad had challenged them outside the gates of Grwenilthen, then his first words would have been a sabre blade across the Prae'surlas's neck. Fine words, Phira had to admit, but a Fureath'i needed to see beyond the Prae'surlas in front of her to the greater goal behind.

Lei had been perfect in his dealings with the Prae'surlas squad. He was even able to clip his accent to make it sound from far to the east. The insults he produced in outrage to their challenge was just enough not to get them arrested but sufficient to make the Prae'surlas let them be about their business. One of the northerners had then spotted smoke coming from the city and rode off to assist. The fire was almost certainly the building where they had left the beheaded Frostborn. It would be characteristic of Gravren to have constructed fires in the upstairs rooms, packed as full of flammable material as was needed to burn the stone buildings, and all in order to bring down half the city as they left. His only answer to her questioning was to say that the Fureath'i were fire and the Prae'surlas were there to burn. Lei had helpfully pointed out that she had never specifically ordered Gravren not to burn the city to the ground.

She was displeased with Gravren but she hoped the blaze had spread widely and killed many. Death by fire was too good an honour to give a dead Prae'surlas but she had no problem delivering such a gift to a live one.

Looking back to her campfire she put away the wooden carving of Dallid. Phira took out the short spear she had taken as a token from the Frostborn they killed and began examining it. It was an interesting weapon, long enough to use as a sword if she wished to. The only way to ensure she would get to try out the new weapon was to remove the serrated sword from her scabbard right then and replace it with the spear. But instead she laughed softly and returned the spear back into the cluttered sack where she stored the rest of her collection.

Taking her mind away from the sack of trophies, Phira thought to where the other collected item of their expedition might be. The severed head of the Frostborn was still in the possession of Gravren's squad leader. They were a twisted bunch but she knew they were capable. She had ordered Gravren's two squads south and west to the port town of Hrosvidar, where they were to buy passage across the Ice Sea to Kel Sherah. When on board the vessel, they were to bribe the captain to drop them off at Rath'Nor. It might not seem odd that the Ihnhaarat wanted to avoid Prae'surlas knowing they were trading with Fureath'i. Still, she knew Gravren would disobey those orders.

The wagons were slowing her down so she had given them all to Gravren. It would slow him down instead but it had doubled her chances of success. She and her two squads would continue south and east to Dowrathel, then enter the wildlands before doubling back west to Furea. If all went as planned she would be back in Rath'Nor within seven days, and Gravren would not be long after, perhaps a day or two later. That was of course if he followed her orders.

But Gravren was just as ambitious as Phira and knew that to gain advantage he needed to show arrogance at every opportunity. Capturing the Frostborn was an example of that, but blatantly disobeying orders was only going to get him killed by Phira herself. She tried to put herself in his boots and figured he would want to reach Rath'Nor with the news of Aerath first. The only way he could do that would be to cut straight for the fortress of Aeris and then barge his way through the Prae'surlas defences. That plan might even work but their disguise as Ihnhaarat would become common knowledge and ruin future covert operations within Surlas.

Phira hoped Gravren would follow her orders or she really would have to kill him. Lei would have been the smarter choice to send alone with two squads, and better able to negotiate his way through challenge. But she liked to keep Lei close. Partly because of the pleasure she took in abusing him.

Her trusted ember even chose that moment to sit down beside her and it made Phira smile. Every time Lei made her smile however, her heart ached for Dallid. The constant battle kept her strong and affirmed her resolve. It was probably for that reason that she valued Lei's company more than anything. He was a constant reminder of the price Phira paid to get where she was, and that kept her focused.

'You missed a lively Telling about Ahrthuru the Defender,' Lei said. 'And you will never guess who spoke it.'

'Well if you are reprimanding me about missing such a lively Telling, then I can only assume it was told by the sweet feminine vocals of ember class Lei.'

'Then you would be wrong in your assumption, blaze commander.'

'Oh?' Phira's eyebrows lifted and she scanned behind her to read which one of the warriors it might have been. Ahrthuru the Defender was a boring tale, about one Kel Sheran with courage who died to save the rest of his cowardly people. The person who told it would have to be slightly boring themselves, taking quiet pride in the simple story. Lei gave her the answer before she could guess.

'You will never guess correctly, blaze commander, it was Drayilus.' Lei grinned at the look of disbelief Phira must have had on her face.

'Drayilus speaks? This is a first.' Admittedly the Unseen Blade had not been with her long, but in the few weeks she had soldiered with them, the large squad leader had not spoken at all. He seemed able to give orders with a variety of looks and frowns, sometimes even venturing a quick hand signal. 'Thank you greatly for bringing this news to my attention, Lei. I can imagine just how lively that might have been.'

'You imagine correctly, blaze commander. He was pressured into it by our other squad leader Pellix.' Lei always ignored her insults well, just as she ignored the hidden meanings in his words, and so he continued his conversation despite Phira's clear dismissal of it. 'The version that Drayilus gave us, it was low in pace but high in graphic and detail. Especially about what the Jhakral did to the dead.'

Phira sighed. 'Well that is good to know. After all it is often that we encounter Jhakral in these parts and so it is good that all of the soldiers know exactly how they will be violated when killed by one. If you are going to waste your time with useless Tellings, then maybe I should Tell one that is worthwhile.' She said it absently but considered it a good idea. It was not common for a blaze commander to give camp fire Tellings the way simple soldiers did. Lei seemed to think it a bad idea anyway.

'I have heard you sing, blaze commander. You do not sound as beautiful as you look.'

He moved out of striking distance again as he made the compliment. It seemed these were to be his new challenges. Perhaps his balls were not as small as she had thought. Phira was never so subtle when challenging her previous blaze commander. She always found the most inconvenient times for him and persistently unmanned him in front of as many warriors as possible.

'I did not say I would sing, Lei. I will give a Telling.'

'Do you think it wise?' Lei frowned at first but then his face lit up with an idea. 'Maybe you should Tell the Lighting of Hrosvidar! It would show our brothers how humble a warrior you are.'

Phira shook her head at his constant impertinence. Gravren challenged her with his disobedience and Lei did it with his insolence. They could be punished with death for committing either against a blaze commander, but it was also the only way they would ever gain promotion. It was a dangerous position to be in of course, Phira could kill them for challenging her authority and she could kill them for being too weak and never challenging it. Climbing the heights of power was a deadly game and it was one that Phira delighted in playing.

She considered Lei's suggestion though about Telling the Lighting of Hrosvidar. It was one of Phira's earlier exploits on her rise up through the ranks. She was just promoted to ember class and the first time she had more than one squad at her command. Using the extra men she immediately orchestrated a deception where they first travelled to Kel Sherah over sea and purchased several barrels of whale oil, ostensibly for delivery back to Rath'Nor. Instead she had waited for a Prae'surlas vessel to arrive that was small enough for her men to sail. When it came, she captured the ship without the Kel Sheran traders noticing and filled it with as many of the oil barrels as she could fit.

She had only intended for the flaming ship to set fire to some few other ships in the port of Hrosvidar, but what had happened had far exceeded her expectations. From reports, after they abandoned the fire-ship on a collision course for the city, close to every ship in the harbour was caught up in the damage. It had simply been good fortune that the winds had blown the flames from the sails of ship to ship, but when the barrels of oil fully exploded even the warehouses on the docks caught alight. The fire had run wild for days. After being impressed with the stone of Grwenilthen, Phira still marvelled that most other of the Prae'surlas cities were not better defended against attack by fire. After all, who did they think they were at war with?

'No, Lei, I will not be Telling that one,' she answered. 'Come. Let us join our warriors.'

Phira walked over to the second camp fire and every soldier stood to attention immediately. She told them to be at ease, but as they sat down she still received cautious looks from them. Phira was infamous for testing her men without their knowledge, and equally known for sudden acts of violence against them when they failed those tests. But even with those intentions far from her mind now, she knew the other warriors would never be comfortable around her. Her rank demanded the same deference and respect as a Lord Flameborn would. She even outranked any Flameborn lords who did not hold official title within the army. When she became general, she would even rival a Fireborn for martial rank.

As she sat down, all was silent, and Phira waited for Lei to join her at the fire before she began. 'My fellow warriors, Lei has informed me I have missed a momentous Telling from Drayilus.' Some men laughed until the serious stare of the thickly muscled squad leader fell upon them. Only Pellix kept her mocking grin. Phira continued. 'So I have decided I shall add to the occasion with a Telling as well as a warning. Many of you have been in this puss-coloured land of snow before, so you know what it feels to be without Frehep's hand upon your shoulder. But soon we shall enter the wildlands, and in them we enter the realm of Foreign gods.

'These gods are not like holy Frehep, who gives us the fire in our hearts at birth and lets us burn as brightly as we can make ourselves in life, never interfering. Neither are they like Aerune who is too fat, lazy, and disgusted, to involve himself in the everyday goat rutting of the Prae'surlas. No these Foreign gods in the wildlands, they are not powerful enough to rule a kingdom from above, these Foreign gods need to walk the earth below in order to maintain their rule.'

She looked around to her soldiers, who were all dutifully listening and most likely knew some of what she was saying, but she had a tale to follow that few others than Dallid knew, one that she had only heard from Yiran.

'As you can see, Am'bril is busy wrapping her legs around Aerune with all this snow, but that does not mean the next old hag you see will not be Rhyserias the goddess of time, or the next thief you roll dice with will not be Di Thorel the god of fortune. All of these gods have little better to do than meddle with fleshborn. They at least stand wary of Powerborn, but for simple warriors like us, they love nothing better than to play with our lives for their fleeting amusement.

'Now, there is one god above all others that you will need to be watchful. Scholars record him as the First God, and his priests proclaim him as the creator of gods. It is argued he is worshipped by every living being that fights for survival in this world and his name is Brijnok the god of battle. I have little doubt the moment we step outside of Surlas, he will sense immediately the flaming hearts of thirty of the brightest warriors ever to step foot upon the forsaken soil of the wildlands. He will try to claim you for his own, for he does not realise how strongly Frehep is already in our hearts, but I will Tell you now a tale about this Brijnok, so you may know what kind of man he was before he became a god.

'Two brothers of battle journeyed centuries ago, searching for three stone relics that could grant them unthinkable power. These warriors were of course Brijnok the Battlelord, and his brother - although many have forgotten that they were - Moi'dan the Masked. Moi'dan and his masks have a dozen Tellings each, and Brijnok's battles could keep us here for another week, but this Telling is the only one where the two brothers are together in the heights of their power, each ruling half the world in empire.

'Toward the end of the Age of Might, it is said that Moi'dan sent word to his brother Brijnok, asking that they meet, even though both warriors had agreed to keep distance from the other. The world is large and great warriors can carve great legends into it when left alone, but when two great warriors meet then it is near always the case that the world is then denied one forever after. This is why the brothers agreed to stay apart, and when Brijnok heard of Moi'dan's request he was understandably ill at ease.

'But his love for his brother was great and he agreed to leave the battles he was engaged in expanding his empire. Moi'dan had nine kingdoms of his own that he left and when he faced Brijnok he went without his masks as an act of trust. Brijnok was moved by his brother's gesture, and the Battlelord in turn cast off his weapons, the powerful blades of magic and legend, that claimed thousands of souls throughout the years. So stripped of power and stripped of pride, the two brothers embraced as they met, rejoicing in the union.

'It was then that Moi'dan told Brijnok of the three stone pieces he had started to collect, each one more powerful than his masks, and that to collect the third and final piece, he would need his brother's help. Moi'dan explained that with all three pieces they would have the power to control this world, even travel to others, and they could rule it all together. Brijnok was sceptical, saying that they already had great empires to rule, and the rest of the world was but a matter of time. But Moi'dan explained if they both kept expanding in power as they were, then their armies would have nowhere left to go except against each other. He went on to say that with the power of the three segments they would not need an army, that they could simply claim the world. Still unconvinced, but out of loyalty to his brother, Brijnok agreed that he would help Moi'dan.

'So Moi'dan, once more armed with his masks of power, and Brijnok, once more armed with his weapons of devastation, together they fought against a being of unspeakable destruction. The creature was the protector of the stone segments, and linked with their very creation. Its destruction descended down on anyone who held even one of the stones, and Moi'dan and Brijnok held two! But they were able to combine their amazing power to defeat this creature, and collect the third stone segment.

'Moi'dan rejoiced and congratulated his brother on their epic battle. Brijnok said nothing and watched as Moi'dan completed the ritual they had started. He fused together all three stones and just as he was about to unlock all the power of the world, a blade of betrayal sliced into his heart. Brijnok took the completed segments and left Moi'dan standing, hands empty, and with a sword sticking from his chest. The cruel Battlelord examined his new power and spoke to his brother, "thank you" he said, "for bringing this to me. I agreed we would conquer the world together, but only I will rule it." So as Moi'dan died, Brijnok used the new power to become a god.

'But a man that betrays his own brother is not a man, and a god that was created from such a man, is no god. You should never trust any god apart from almighty Frehep, but most of all not the god of battle. He will smile at you and offer you gifts, he will convince you that he wants you only to live as a warrior asking nothing in return.

He will ask for nothing and that is all you are to him, it is all you will become if you listen to him and become his. So listen to me my warriors and remind yourselves what you already know to be true. A Fureath'i needs nothing but the sabre in her hand, the fire in her heart and a Prae'surlas to kill!'

This brought a great cheer to mark the end of the Telling and Phira watched as everyone considered what they had heard. Phira may not be as good at Tellings as Dallid was but she got her point across. All knew that Brijnok was a Foreign god, but few had known how it came to be. They would have naturally assumed it was as Fureath'i believed and that Brijnok climbed the heights of power through betterment and honest combat. Perhaps he would even have achieved that eventually but it was important for them to know Brijnok achieved his godhood through treachery and deceit. Bad enough to kill his own brother, but Phira doubted any of them had known Brijnok's brother had even been Moi'dan. Tellings about the Masks of Moi'dan were famous separate to any of Brijnok, and Yiran had told Phira it was not well known because it was not spoken of in the wildlands. It was said that Brijnok walked the lands and would slay any that spoke such lies. Yiran had heard it from the Teller named Nureail, a lady of power who doubled as a Scholar.

Looking up to the sky, Phira knew Brijnok had as little power in Surlas as he had in Furea, but still if they were to get into battle in the wildlands and the god did appear, she wanted her men prepared to deny any gifts he might offer. Each one came with its own curse. Lei cleared his throat and broke the contemplative silence Phira had created.

'Thank you, blaze commander, there is much that we did not know and much that we need to remember. It seems Foreign gods are just as despicable as everything else that is Foreign!' This caused a round of agreement from the others. Then a light appeared in Lei's eyes and Phira frowned at what his thoughts might be. 'Blaze commander, your Telling was so welcome, we would have another!'

More agreement and requests chorused around the fire and as Phira opened her mouth to decline, Lei spoke first and failed at hiding the enjoyment that sounded in his own voice. 'Blaze commander, if I may be so bold, could you give us your Telling of the Lighting of Hrosvidar! It is a favourite of ours.'

A great cheer went out from the warriors at the prospect and Phira smiled, to stop herself from punching Lei's teeth down his throat. It was understandable for a blaze to take pride in their commander's exploits, and everyone enjoyed Tellings where large amounts of Prae'surlas got killed. So Phira began the Telling, and at the same time began planning just how she was to repay Lei. The ideas she came up with were extravagant enough to fill up half a dozen Tellings of their own, most involving wild curses and plagues sent down by the gods themselves. Flicking her eyes up to the heavens again, she wondered briefly if the gods could hear her prayer and if they would answer.

Let them not, she thought, *let them keep to their world of power and let them stay out of my way.*

• CHAPTER SEVENTEEN •

Understanding

It was over a year since Kris had spilt any Fureath'i blood, but he wanted nothing more than to do so now. It had taken all of his control not to kill Tereail a dozen times already and Kris was only too glad to simply be away from him as he stood in the empty room. He sought for peace in the serene surroundings, the comforting silence and absolute calm. It did not come.

After stepping through the dais in the Temple of Zenith, they had entered the Jhakral temple and found it abandoned. It was uselessly filled with relics and artefacts as the Scholars said it would be, but so far there had been no sign of any Jhakral beasts there to kill them. The untouched dust that lined the floors told Kris no one had set foot in the temple for what could have been an age. He could walk for minutes and feel like he was alone for miles. He rarely felt peace apart from when engaged in violence, but if he had any chance of achieving it, it would have been in a place like this. It could have been perfect if his blood did not boil from the two helpless children he had been burdened with.

In a different chamber, the very first one they had entered, Tereail studied each and every scrap of dust as if it held all the secrets of the world. Whereas Nureail marvelled at every broken statue, and every rusted sword, as if she could see the actual warriors ascribed to them. Of course it just so happened that she could, but she did not need to explain it all to Kris and Tereail in time wasting detail. Kris felt his head was full of so much useless information already that he would soon wake up and grab his sabre by the blade, having forgotten how to hold a sword. Nureail could be even more aggravating than Tereail, who at least spoke only to himself some of the time. But Nureail seemed to have made it her mission to not let a single breath pass from her lips without it being used to educate Kris about something needless.

'Burn all Scholars and let the Tellers follow,' he said in a growl. The words filled up the empty room for a moment and then faded back to nothing. A fire pit burned in the centre, but it should not have been enough to light the whole room by itself. Not without any natural light to aid it, and there was not any fuel that Kris could see for the flames either. It was a false fire giving false light. The sound and heat were genuine enough but he could feel nothing from it. He had not the Connection to fire that Powerborn did, nor even the mastery of it that priests could summon, but as a Fureath'i he could usually look at a fire and take something from it. That something could often bring a faint light to his darkened heart so he treasured what it felt like to be Fureath'i.

But his heart was now busy containing a rage that screamed to be released. Kris had tried to ease it by smashing the useless artefacts which had previously filled the room. Even that simple act strove to frustrate him, with stones that would not break, masks that would not crack or burn, even pottery that would not shatter. So it was with mixed satisfaction he had lined all the debris against the wall at the end of the task. It meant there was one room searched in a practical manner and could be marked off against a hundred others. The Jhakral temple was colossal, just as the beasts themselves were reputed to be, but the task of searching every room was made impossible by his two companions and their unrealistic methods.

It was the third day of their exploration within the temple and while Kris had eliminated many rooms, the two Scholars still loitered in the same one. He had to hold Tereail at sword point to get the man to describe the relic they were trying to find instead of describing excuses why he could not. The Scholar had attempted to convince Kris that it was too specific for anyone other than him to uncover, but Kris had been persuasive. So Tereail explained as much as he could, and Kris had given him two new scars to add to the one he had already left on his neck.

Having the description now at least meant Kris was able to leave them for short times to make more useful scouting of the surrounding rooms. But he could not leave them alone for too long. The temple may have been long abandoned but if they three could suddenly rediscover it then why not others. He wondered if the unknown destruction they were meant to avoid would be a hoard of Jhakral beasts. It did not especially matter to him who he had to stop from killing Nureail or Tereail, only that he would, partly because if anyone was going to be the one to kill them it should be him.

Peace would not come, as it never did, and Kris had to admit he was wasting as much time as the two Scholars, just standing and doing nothing. There were three more rooms in the circumference he had allowed himself, and after he had searched and smashed everything in those rooms, he would have to drag Tereail by his hair to another room to create a new centre point. Kris almost smiled when he imagined Tereail's reaction to all the smashed and destroyed artefacts he would see while being dragged to a new room. In a moment of confidence from Tereail yesterday, he had jeered about how Kris never smiled, how he never laughed, how he never slept and how he rarely ate, he had thought he was extremely clever by asking what, if anything, Kris actually did do. Kris just replied that he killed people. That kept the Scholar quiet for a few hours at least.

Walking to the edge room he looked into the new centre point for tomorrow but did not enter it. The room would have to remain intact in order for Tereail to examine it. Everywhere else Kris would do the inspecting. It was the only way to make the task even mildly achievable. Thankfully not every room he had found held the same needless abundance of ancient clutter. After his few days of mapping and examining the Jhakral temple, Kris had found that each room had the same unnatural fire pit in the centre, but where some were inexplicably filled with ancient relics, other rooms were completely empty. Some had statues in them, often still intact, and one room he had found even held a series of mirrors.

In that room nine identical mirrors were arrayed in a circle around the centre fire. To his eyes it looked like frost was forming underneath the strange looking glasses despite the fire, and as Kris entered the room he did feel significantly colder. Then colours started to swirl and images began to form in the mirrors. Kris ignored them and left the room as soon as the magic began. The item they were searching for was not a mirror and he would not let the other two waste time by entering that room either, even if he had to knock them both unconscious to do it.

With that in mind Kris thought to how Nureail had taken to wearing a sabre at his command, and she even moved as if she knew how to use it. Tereail smiled condescendingly at Kris's direct order to wear a sabre, ignored it, and then continued with what he was doing before being interrupted. It had been difficult not to kill Tereail then, but Kris had controlled his urge. He told himself he only allowed the Scholar's insolence because the sabre would just get caught in Tereail's skirts. So where it would be easy to knock out the brother, Kris was concerned that Nureail would try to put up a fight. He hoped he would not have to hurt her too much, but he had hurt far more people for far less reason in the past and knew he would not hesitate if he had to do it.

Moving back to his chosen limit of the patrol area, Kris looked around to see how many rooms were left. It was still too many so he set about smashing and gathering as much as he could. If it was made of stone he used the butt of his sabre to crack it. If it was made of glass, pewter, porcelain, or pottery, he would use the blade of his sabre to smash it. The noise was not ideal, but the work had to be done. Anything he could not break or smash, he kicked into the fire to burn.

Halfway through a sword swing toward one particular piece, Kris stopped his blade and knelt down to examine it. Part of Tereail's description of the relic was that it was in the shape of fire, but made of ice, the Scholar had flustered over the precise wording but Kris did not find the concept so confusing. He knew what fire looked like, and he knew what ice was, what else mattered? The item he picked up was bulbous at the bottom and spiralled up to a sharp and narrow point at the top. The artefact appeared to be made out of glass and did not especially look like fire, but Kris added it to his pack of similar shaped pieces. He would present his findings to Tereail at their evening meal and patiently sit through the man laughing self-righteously at how wrong Kris had been in his search.

Kris kicked another book into the fire in the middle of the room and wondered if he should hold onto the book covers to present to Tereail in the evenings also. It would help Kris know if it was an important book he had burned, and would benefit his searching greatly knowing his work was worthwhile.

If he were allowed his squads the same three days in the temple, the task would be finished. That all he had was the word of a Scholar and a Priestess to say bringing his squads would lead to certain destruction was not enough to comfort him. There could be an army of Jhakral in the temple and they would not know about it, the rooms were certainly large enough to house them. Thinking about his options, Kris knew that Nureail had some connection to the past that he was not interested in understanding, and Tereail would have read a thousand or so books on the place, so he could always ask them to give him more information about the temple. They could tell him where about in the world it was situated, how long ago had it been more commonly used, and how large it might be. But as concerned as he was about the size and potential dangers of the temple, he was far more concerned of the size of the answer he would receive from either of them. The next time he was torturing a Prae'surlas, Kris thought he would try teaching it pointless subjects. It was an interesting idea, to see if he could make an ice-man rip off his own ears just to stop the lecture.

Tereail had thankfully started cutting whatever speeches he attempted short, saying that Kris would not understand it even if he was trying to set fire to it, but Nureail was getting worse. She had taken it as her personal mission to change Kris's view about knowledge and the wasted lives of Scholars. Why she bothered was the only mystery Kris wanted to discover. He should interrupt her the next time to say that if he did not think it possible to change them into warriors then they should not think it possible to change him into a Scholar. Either that or he should allow himself to lose his control with one of them. Kris's fingers twitched at the idea but as reasonable as it sounded it was too risky. After one showing of what he was capable of, both Scholars would jump to obey his commands, but there was an equal chance he would end up killing them both in his frenzy.

Looking around, Kris suppressed the idea and nodded with satisfaction that the room was searched. It had not been filled with much, and he had destroyed it quickly. It irritated him that the clutter was so inconsistently placed, but how had so many items come to gather so haphazardly in one temple anyway? He did not believe that ancient Jhakral had collected them. The beasts were reported to be giants, twice as large as a Prae'surlas, and if the statues in some of the rooms were any indications, those reports were understated. The sometimes tiny items he was smashing in the different chambers would never have fit into the giant hand of a Jhakral and even the larger ones were brittle enough to be crushed at a touch. It was simply another question to which Kris did not care about the answer.

As he worked his way through the next room, he let his mind drift to something useful and began going through what a battle with a Jhakral would entail. He was unsure if they were considered Powerborn or not. He knew the difference between a magicker and a Powerborn was one of strength of flesh instead of power. A Foreign magicker could summon tricks and attacks, but were essentially fleshborn. They were not faster or stronger and they died easily. A Powerborn then was someone who was always Connected to magic, it filled their veins.

Jhakral were not Powerborn. They were simply large creatures with great strength, their skin as tough as rock, and bones that lined the outside of their bodies. The size would certainly be difficult, but his greater speed and agility could stand up. Not many had ever fought a Jhakral and lived, so Kris did not want to think himself arrogant to assume he would win. No matter what he promised Nureail, a Jhakral was almost certain to kill him and them both with ease. He would do his best to make that task difficult though, and the Scholars would of course make Kris's job of doing that as difficult as they could too.

If the beasts did appear, he would be fighting them merely to give the Scholars time to hide. They had no way out yet as Tereail was the only one who could read the stone platforms and although Kris had discovered two of them, Tereail had bluntly said they were not for the Ice Temple. It would disrupt Kris's own search pattern too much to bring all three of them on an expedition specifically to locate the right platform, so he was content to find the relic first. If they did not find it within seven days then it did not matter if they had a way out or not, Furea would be doomed.

Kris clenched his fist around the handle of his sabre and reassured himself that it would cut a Jhakral's skin if struck with enough force. The skin of the beasts may be akin to rock, but metal could scratch rock, and given enough persistence it could cut. If there was a way for a man and his sword to kill a Jhakral, then Kris would find it.

A distant noise echoed then and Kris went still. He strained his ears to judge the direction and distance but the sound was gone. It had been so slight that he struggled even to put a source on it. Could it have been a roar? How big was the temple that a roar could sound so slight?

Either way it was as good a time as any to head back. Nureail and Tereail were both without any semblance of common sense but he did not think they would have left the room, especially not so far away as that roar would have been. He mostly assumed that because of the speed in which they examined each object. Sometimes when they found one that excited them they began to talk in a different language entirely, it was still Fureath'i, but it was not anything that Kris understood. So he was both relieved and annoyed when he saw they were still where he left them. He had been gone hours and they had shifted only minutely in their position.

'It is time for evening meal,' he announced after frowning at them for a while, but neither Scholar moved. They did not even look up when he marched into the room. If he had been five Jhakral he doubted they would have noticed.

Kris dropped his relic findings of the day next to Tereail for him to scoff at in his own time, and then calmly walked over to a large vase that was complexly decorated with a tight-scripted Foreign language. He smashed it loudly. Nureail startled but smiled when she saw Kris was responsible, whereas Tereail's entire face dropped with disbelief.

'You idiot! Every single item in this temple has information more valuable than a thousand warriors' weight in gold! You have no right!' Tereail cried out with dramatic anguish and was torn between going over to gather up the broken pottery, and standing protectively over the vase he was currently reading.

'It is time for evening meal,' Kris repeated.

'How can you tell?' Nureail asked, still holding her grin of amusement. If she was open to finding Kris's pragmatic abuse of Tereail amusing, then perhaps he could begin to like her.

'I have enough control of my body to know the passing of time,' he explained first and then added. 'A true Fureath'i can know the sun's location no matter where he is.'

'And where are we?' Nureail asked.

Kris had no idea where the temple of the Jhakral was located, it was most likely in the mountains north of Kel Sherah, but the world of light was vast enough to hide any manner of strange building.

'Not in Furea,' Kris settled for, 'And the sooner we do what we have been charged to do, the sooner we can return. It is time to eat.'

Tereail waved his hand angrily at Kris and muttered, 'I will eat later.'

'I will smash every vase in this room, Tereail. You will do as I command.'

Nureail laughed at the horror on her brother's face. She at least travelled over to the fire pit to begin preparing the meal. Tereail took a moment to stare at Kris as if not being able to believe he could exist. His hand reached up to the cuts on his neck, face and head.

'No-one should so willingly destroy something so precious and ancient. It is in our blood to respect our ancestors. You should not dishonour their history.'

'They are not my ancestors,' Kris said and thought about when Tereail would see the trail of destruction he had left throughout the temple. How they did not hear it, was a wonder, but then they did not seem to hear or see anything any normal Fureath'i would. Tereail decided he was hungry after all and grudgingly left his study.

All three of them were actually able to work in a cohesive manner when it came to the meals. Nureail's experience at travelling had apparently brushed off upon Tereail. The stew they ate was warm and filling, and the conversation was blessedly absent. Some small few words needed to be said however.

'Tomorrow we will leave this room and go to another of my choosing. From there I will begin my new perimeter of patrol.'

'Out of the question,' Tereail said with his mouth full of bread. 'Our work here is not yet done.'

'You have spent three days in this one room when the Jhakral temple houses hundreds. We have seven days remaining to achieve our task.'

'I am confident we will find the artefact, Kris. In the different futures, we find the relic nearly every time.' Tereail's relaxed attitude to such a momentous mission, made Kris question the man's grasp on reality. For someone who could connect with time, he had little understanding of it.

'What about in the ones where we do not? What can you tell me of those? Do we face enemies? Describe the room where we find the artefact.'

Tereail shook his head slowly with a smile and continued eating. 'You don't understand. It doesn't work like that. Really, Nureail, can you explain to him at least that he will never understand?'

'No he is right, Tereail, we waste precious time with self-indulgent discovery.' Nureail smiled at whatever brief look of amazement found its way onto Kris's face. She continued, 'But you are also right, brother, that Kris will never understand. If it is something that he cannot stick with a sabre then it is something his mind does not want to know about.'

'Ah, sister, you do him an injustice, his mind is also open to burning things! How does that warrior saying go? If you cannot eat, drink, kill or rut it, then burn it!' The two Scholars laughed at their own hilarity and Kris remained passive. Perhaps he would allow himself to smile tomorrow when they saw precisely how right they were.

'You have two more days to search in the manner that you believe your visions have shown you, but you will do so in a way that allows me to patrol and protect you best. That means we are moving both tomorrow and the day after. Then we will change our strategy and all three of us will move swiftly together to search every room with brutal efficiency to find both the relic and the platform that will bring us to the Ice Temple.'

Tereail's mouth hung open but remained silent as his mind raced to find the right reasoning to explain how unreasonable Kris was being. He turned to Nureail with a pleading look.

'That sounds reasonable, ember,' Nureail finally said, and Tereail looked as if he had been kicked in the stomach.

'You do not need to call me ember, Teller, you do not have martial rank.'

'And you do not need to call me Teller, ember, as you do not hang on my every word.'

'Wait!' Tereail cried out. 'We're not finished with this discussion. I insist that you defer to my superior knowledge in this aspect, Kris. I have seen I will find the relic and so I must behave in the manner that best resembles my true nature, to actualise the probable reality of my possible future. It doesn't matter that you don't understand me but you will leave me to my research without harassment!'

'No.'

Tereail frowned. 'What do you mean no?'

'Now it is you who does not understand me? I thought you were a Scholar, Tereail. No means that everything you have said, will not be.'

'You insufferable imbecile! Have you -'

Kris took out his sabre and Tereail jumped before trying to regain his composure. Shamed at his reaction, Tereail put on an act of bravado.

'If you are going to kill me, Kris, then do it. Stop going on and on about how you'd love to do it, and could do it, at any moment of your pleasing, and just bloody do it! Do it and see our nation of Furea destroyed by your violent idiocy.'

'I will not kill you, Tereail.' The man relaxed visibly. 'But that does not mean you will need to be uninjured to complete your task. For instance, you do not need two hands, or even your tongue.'

'Oh you will cut off my tongue and one of my hands? That would still kill me. Your threats will not work with me.'

'I do not make threats and losing a tongue or a hand will not kill you. After you have passed out from the pain of it, I will seal the wounds with fire and in addition to stopping you bleeding to death, the fresh pain will even bring you back to consciousness so you can continue your work. I have done this before, Tereail, ask your sister.'

Tereail tried to laugh, half in disbelief and half in hysteria, he looked to Nureail with incredulity forced onto his face, but his sister just nodded.

'Kris does not make threats, Tereail, and his squads are among those with the greatest discipline and swiftest obedience.' She smiled caustically at him. 'I wager that it is all from heart-felt affection.'

Kris did not respond to her remark but stared levelly at Tereail to make sure the man understood him. The Scholar's mind seemed slow to accept things that he did not like and Kris idly considered that life as a Scholar might not even be suited to him. A Scholar was supposed to be open to all sides of every argument, but on the other hand, that would help explain why it took so long for Tereail to come to decisions. Kris had heard arguments go on for weeks between simple soldiers with neither one really listening to the other's way of attacking the topic, but only focusing on how they could further defend theirs. Life as a Scholar was a wasted life indeed. Tereail stood up.

'Well, if I'm to be out numbered in this then I had better get back to work.' He bowed dramatically to Kris. 'That is of course if my king allows it?'

'Your King demands that you always be a better Fureath'i,' Kris said simply.

Tereail snorted, and sulked back over to his examination. Kris noted with some satisfaction that the man only gave a passing look to the vase he had been inspecting for the last few hours. At least now he might contain his search to items that were actually to do with their task. Nureail laughed. 'I think he is starting to like you, Kris.'

'I am easily liked.'

• CHAPTER EIGHTEEN •

Reason

'Was that a joke, Kris? Perhaps we are having an influence on you after all?' Nureail sat there just looking at him, and Kris considered getting up to go back to his own searching. There was something about Nureail's gaze that made him feel she was looking for the right way to ask something. It only made him move quicker to rise, but she lifted up a hand to stop him. 'It is Fureath'i tradition to give a Telling at every fire is it not?'

'This temple has too many fires.'

'You will like this one. It is to do with reason and understanding.'

Kris sat back down with reluctance. 'I think you may be misguided in your assumption of what I like. I will remain out of courtesy only if it is brief.'

'It is always warming for a Teller to know her audience sits purely out of courtesy. But yes I shall cut out all theatrics and embellishments and everything that makes a good Telling, and I shall keep it brief and boring so it will be further to your liking.' She smiled at him and he was watching how her eyes could light up from such a simple gesture. He rarely bothered with looking at his reflection but he knew his own dark eyes would never shine so bright even if he did ever smile. Kris settled himself to look anywhere but her eyes when she began the Telling. 'This tale is of Lord Miral'thau the Wise and how he destroyed reasoning with understanding:

'Three Scholars from Kel Sherah came to visit the great Fureath'i fortress of Rath'Nor many years ago. I shall spare you their journey,' she said with irritation, 'and so will start in the middle. That of course will make the Telling so short as to almost become the story's end, and yet we use it as a beginning. As you can see, already reason wavers and threatens to unravel, because this

Telling bares so much defiance toward it, but it will be wise Miral'thau that gets the Kel Sherans to make the final cut.

'Where Fureath'i have games of strength and sabre, so too do Kel Sherans have games of mind and reason. While feasting with the eight Kings of Furea, these three Scholars from Kel Sherah offered to demonstrate such a game which they called the snake that eats its own tail. It began with them asking for a subject and one warrior said in derision, *"the purpose of scholars."* Everyone laughed, including the three Kel Sherans as they began the game. They asked: *"When training a warrior, is it better for the warrior to listen to the instruction of one single master who has greatest knowledge on the subject or to listen to several instructors at the same time who each would only have lesser knowledge when compared to the master."* Singling out the man who had thought to mock them, they asked him for answer:

"The master" he said.

"So the other instructors," the Kel Sherans asked, *"they would continue to go on as warriors and not train as instructors any longer then?"*

"If there is a master there to teach as you described, yes"

"Good," the Kel Sherans said with smiles upon their face, *"so this master, is it better that he train one student or several students?"*

"If he is able," the warrior answered, *"then his mastery would make many better rather than just one."*

"Then he would be able to better do this if he spent his time only instructing and not being a warrior himself?"

"An elder would have that ability, yes," the warrior agreed.

"So we are agreed that he would no longer have time to be a warrior himself but instead would train others to become better warriors? And we are agreed that this person would create the best warrior, dedicating all his time to instruction?"

Fearful of a trick, the Fureath'i considered it but finally said, *"Yes, what you have described would create the best warrior."*

"Let us change the subject slightly and ask you another question, how would you describe a man who never used a sabre in violence?"

"A Scholar," the warrior laughed, thinking he had cleverly found an unexpected way to insult them.

"What about a man who had spent years learning everything he could about one thing and then spent all his days teaching it to others?"

"You still describe a Scholar," he answered.

This was when all three Scholars laughed at the Fureath'i: *"So by your agreement, if we have a man who does not use a sabre in violence, because he spends all of his time teaching others how to use it, then this master of fighting, who you have agreed is the best person to train a warrior, has now become a scholar! So by your own agreement you have told us that scholars make better warriors than warriors do!"*

'Every Fureath'i at the feast was understandably outraged by the conclusion, and began shouting insults and threats, but the Kel Sherans did not listen they were so caught up in amusement at their own cleverness. This was when Lord Miral'thau cleared his throat and asked if he could take a turn playing the game. The three Kel Sherans were delighted he would want to and eagerly agreed, but before they could begin the lord of power Miral'thau clarified that he did not wish to be played by the game, but that he would play it himself, asking questions of the three men from Kel Sherah. Intrigued by the situation they agreed and let him ask his first question:

"To play your game," he said, *"you take a statement that is not true and then prove it true. So in this last case you took the untrue statement that Scholars make the best warriors and then turned it into truth? Am I correct?"*

"That is the broad basis of the game, yes."

"And you do this by reason, am I right?"

"Yes logic and deduction can both be termed as reason."

Lord Miral'thau took his time with the Kel Sherans, considering his words each time before posing it to them, *"And the first statement when held as untrue, must be untrue first by reason for the game to work, yes?"*

"Yes, that is the fun of the game," they answered joyfully.

Lord Miral'thau smiled too, joining them in their mirth, *"So by starting with something that is known as untrue by reason, and using that same reason you prove it is in fact true? It is like a blacksmith with only one hammer, who tries to use that same hammer to take itself apart and reconstruct itself again. That is an impossible thing. And rather than show us how grand reason is, you have shown us how flawed it is, because it can be used to contradict itself so completely, and thus negate itself, does it not? It contradicts reason even more that you use it to mock men who would kill you without thought. So the conclusion I draw from your reasoning is that there is no such thing as reason, thus negated by your own game, and you cannot prove me otherwise since you would have to use reason to do so, and I have just claimed that reason does not exist. So my Kel Sheran friends, it is my opinion that you spend your lives studying something that does not exist and there is no way to prove me wrong, since to do so you would have to assume that reason exists in order to use it to prove that reason exists."*

"But you have just used reason to disprove that it exists!" one protested.

"To my understanding it is only more proof that it destroys itself out of existence. But you forget that I will not accept any argument that uses reason to challenge my conclusion."

The three Scholars had nothing they could reply to that. Everything they thought of was of course immediately dismissed because it contained reasoning. How could they possibly reason a counter argument that did not contain reason? So eventually they resigned themselves to defeat and instead of challenging his argument, they challenged Miral'thau.

"If our lives are so wasted, spent studying something that does not exist, then what makes your lives so much better?"

"Because we spend it killing Prae'surlas." he answered to a great cheer from the feast.

Kris sat in silence for a time when Nureail finished her Telling. That last line would normally get her listeners cheering at the closing but she should know by now that he did not cheer. He was not the best of people to give Tellings to and he wondered why she persisted. Her Telling had been good though, as all of hers were. Perhaps it was not so useless having a professional Teller as company on this journey.

'Thank you for the Telling,' he said finally. 'I am glad that I have heard it.' It was as much praise as he was likely to give for any tale. If her point had been to help him understand the reasoning of Scholars then she had failed, but it had pleased him to hear of Lord Miral'thau explain to the Kel Sherans how their lives were a waste. He stood up and made to leave. 'I will return in a few hours before you sleep.'

'I will accompany you to the other rooms,' she said and got up to go with him. Kris quickly tried to think of reasons why she should not. He looked over to Tereail but Nureail pre-empted his objections. 'He will prefer time to himself to wallow in self-pity,' she said with a sigh. 'And if there are any Jhakral here then I will not make a difference in defending him.'

'Fleshborn warriors could arrive,' Kris argued. 'By the same method we did, and against them you would prove invaluable.' She looked at him strangely for the compliment, so he added, 'any Fureath'i would.'

'So Tereail will be fine,' she reasoned. 'Since as a Fureath'i he will naturally be able to fight off at least five Foreigners, correct?'

'Any Fureath'i with a sabre,' Kris amended.

'And that includes me?'

Kris nodded and Nureail beamed a proud smile. He could not tell if it was genuine or a pretence to mock him. 'I'm glad you now consider me a Fureath'i and not just a Scholar or Teller. Perhaps with time I'll be promoted further to a woman or even Nureail. What do you think?'

'I think I would prefer to patrol alone.'

Nureail laughed which earned a glare from her brother further down the room. 'Your preference matters as much to me and ours do to you. Unless you have an official reason why I am not to accompany you?'

Kris remained silent. Phira would have been able to concoct a reason that did not border on lying but which was not completely evident as truth either. Kris had not the same creativity, so he just turned and left. He should have taken her Telling as a foreshadowing of the twisting of words that she could unleash on him.

Nureail followed, and even with his back turned, Kris could feel her triumphant grin. He had to consider his route as they travelled, for there were rooms he did not want her curious nature to latch onto. The room with the mirrors was certainly out of the question. There was another room that might distract her away from her attention on him though, so Kris mapped out his patrol towards there.

The first room they entered, where Kris had previously inspected, brought a gasp of horror from Nureail. She knelt down next to some items to cup them in her hands. 'The Jhakral are a brutal race,' she muttered. 'Such destruction.'

Kris did not consider silence as lying; he simply considered it his preferred alternative to conversation. Clearing his throat to indicate they should keep moving, he knew he could not leave her alone to wander free. But if she was not willing to move at his speed then he would take her back to Tereail. She looked up at him and Kris was surprised to see her eyes moist with tears. It did not make Kris feel badly for what he had done. He would do what he must. But he offered her a hand to bring her back to her feet and they walked at a slower pace through the next rooms.

'Some of these artefacts, Kris, are thousands of years old, and survived countless wars and ages, only to get trampled by Jhakral in this blasted temple.'

Kris opened his mouth and then closed it again. Could she not connect with time and travel back to see Kris as the one to smash the ancient pieces? Nureail noticed the motion and asked, 'What is it?'

He changed from what he had been about to say, and instead asked, 'How is it they came to be here? As you say, a Jhakral's hands would crush most of it to dust, so they did not collect these things.'

'You are right. It was a ritual done hundreds of years ago in the last age by Brijnok. Do you know of him?'

'The Foreign god of battle, yes I know of him.'

'Well he is the god of battle everywhere but Furea, and like it or not he is the first among the gods. He even walks the lands of Surlas these days. But yes, before the birth of power, during the wars where he and his brother Moi'dan each carved their own separate empires, Brijnok enacted this ritual. I can Tell you the full song later if you wish, but the summary is Brijnok always feared his brother Moi'dan, feared that he was more powerful, and that he would one day betray him. So that led Brijnok to act first and he powered one of the largest rituals the world of light has ever felt - perhaps apart from the current one where Aerath is turning our world to ice. But what Brijnok did: was remove all the items of power from the lands and confine them to the Great Temples.'

Kris did not know that Moi'dan and Brijnok were brothers. It seemed odd to him that it would never have come up in any Tellings. Did Nureail make a mistake? It did not matter. Out of politeness he pointed out a different flaw to her explanation. 'I thought Brijnok fought with weapons of power, that he was not Powerborn, only fleshborn. He would remove his own power with such an act.'

'Well, yes and no, although weapons of power did give lasting effects to flesh, Brijnok was still essentially fleshborn, as was Moi'dan, and the masks of Moi'dan were the motivation for Brijnok's extreme act. He had protected his own store of weapons and aimed the ritual at every other item hidden or otherwise in the world. The ritual worked and the world was cleansed of all items of power, scattering them to whichever temple was closest. All but the weapons Brijnok fought with, and all but the masks that Moi'dan wore. Perhaps Moi'dan was too powerful for the ritual to affect him, or perhaps he had suspected his brother's treachery and protected them. I do not know, but judging on the later tale of when Brijnok betrays him again, I do not think Moi'dan suspected.'

'How does he betray him the second time?' Kris asked. He had never heard either Telling before.

'He betrayed him by becoming a god,' Nureail said furtively. 'But that is a tale for another day.'

She smiled and Kris frowned. *Always a Teller,* he thought.

They kept walking and turned into another large chamber, with the same open fire pit and had four large Jhakral statues surrounding it. For a moment Kris even thought they looked real. For all he knew Jhakral were actually made from stone and all the statues he had passed could wake up at any moment and rampage through the temple. The beasts of rock did not move however, and they kept going to the room Kris wanted to show Nureail.

When they entered, Nureail's hand went to her chest and she smiled. 'Kris,' she gasped. 'This is beautiful.'

The sizes of the different chambers varied, but this one was perhaps four times as large as any other. Torches lit the sides of the vast room, and the floor lowered down to meet a tranquil lake. It was perfectly still and reflected the unnatural torch light with vivid colour upon the water. Two giant statues stood at the end, both of Jhakral, and positioned as if holding up the ceiling of the temple. Another light came from below the lake, and Kris would not have been surprised if it was a fire pit underneath, burning strongly despite being fully immersed by water.

'I did not think Jhakral could swim,' Kris said as he saw tears come again to Nureail's eyes.

She laughed and added, 'I did not think Jhakral wash either. So this lake must have been built purely for art.'

'I did have my suspicions that Jhakral were all artists.'

Nureail laughed again. 'Have you gone in? Is it warm? What do you think that light is from underneath?'

'I have not gone in, but if you wish it I can give you some privacy while I continue to patrol.'

'So you've brought me here with intentions of seeing me naked again?'

'No.' He said it a little too quickly so added, 'But perhaps I have brought you here because I think you need a wash.'

It did not make sense, but Kris took joy in making Nureail smile. Everything about her seemed designed to irritate and frustrate him, yet he was finding peace from her happiness. It had been a long time since he had found peace in anything other than satisfying his violent urges. Such a new discovery was uncomfortable. Kris's thoughts were interrupted by a hard punch to his ribs, and the Teller laughed at how she had caught him off guard.

'Come, let us bathe together.'

'No, it would not be appropriate.'

Nureail frowned at him. 'How would it not be appropriate?'

'You are free to rest and relax as you deem necessary. I cannot waste time while I have a mission to accomplish. If you wish to bathe I will patrol this area, but we will need to return back to Tereail soon.'

Her smile and enjoyment vanished and Kris felt a moment of loss. He would not apologise for his duty to his country though. Their quest was too important to indulge in frivolous activity.

'I have taken an interest in you, Kris, you know that.' She waited to see if Kris would react. He did not and she sighed before continuing. 'I've learned every Telling and acquired as much information as I could about you. You fascinate me, and you enrage and frustrate me, and yes, you frighten me, but I admire you. I admire your strength and determination, and I admire the struggle within that you battle for control every day. But I also know you're not without feeling, even if you wish to pretend so. I know that you've fathered four children as every *good* Fureath'i should, so I know your blood is not as frozen as you insist it is.'

'There is nothing frozen about my blood,' Kris let anger seep into his voice. 'I am the best Fureath'i that I can be, and better than many others I have encountered.'

'I know you are a Fureath'i, Kris,' Nureail said, throwing her hands in the air. 'You are bloody Fureath'i to a fault! But what I want to know is, are you anything more than just a Fureath'i? Underneath your duty and responsibility are you still a man? Do you not see me as a woman?'

She stood there, waiting for an answer, and Kris had no idea what she wanted to hear. His anger was building, and if there was anything to fight at that moment he would have gladly unleashed all within him, control be damned. She acted as if she knew everything about him, as if he were some book or Telling that she could study. But she had no idea of the things he was capable of doing, of things he had done. He had done things to men, to women, to children that he even he could not bear to think about. All had been done in times when he lost control and still he had darker thoughts that surfaced worse.

She spoke of his struggle, but what did she know of the thoughts that sometimes entered his head, and how he fought to deny them. That was what strength was, it was not having the good fortune to be born with a heart of purity and virtue; it was having a heart full of darkness and dishonourable thoughts, and having the strength to deny that person, to forcibly create a better one each and every day, each and every heartbeat. She would never understand his struggle or how important his control was to him. And he would not waste time trying to explain it.

'I will return in an hour to escort you back to your brother. Do not try to find your way back alone or you will get lost and delay me further in finding you.'

'Kris...'

He looked into her eyes and saw how open and full of emotion they were. He knew that his own had gone darker, and glinted with a dangerous light that his own men had told him of. There was nothing more to say so Kris turned on his heel and left the Teller to her privacy. As he walked past the statues of Jhakral he clenched his fists, wishing that they really would come to life so he would have an outlet for his rage. He said a prayer to Frehep to give him the strength he needed to be better. But if there was one thing that Kris understood more than anything else, it was that strength could only ever come from within.

CHAPTER NINETEEN

The feeling of time

It was time to move. Tereail had not slept at all and held himself with heroic bravery, acting like he was not as exhausted as he looked. He claimed he had regularly spent many days in a row without sleep and often without food if his work demanded it. Thus it was only fitting that he do so now they had such a short time to examine so much important information. Kris was able to put Tereail out of his head but the other Scholar was another matter.

When Kris returned to Nureail the previous evening, he had expected stubborn anger, and vocal irritation from her. What he received instead was gentle compliance. There was no tension between them despite his flash of rage at her personal intrusion, and although Kris regretted it, he wondered if she had accepted it as part of who he was. Nureail even slept close to him by the fire now, an arm or a foot of hers accidentally brushing against him while she turned in her sleep. Kris did not sleep. He rested but remained aware, often coming back to full consciousness every time Tereail moved to a different place in the chamber or began speaking to himself about some fascinating relic.

Perhaps an hour or two before dawn Kris allowed himself some full sleep to recharge, but had awoken soon after to find Nureail's arm draped across his chest. Whether it was innocent or misguided, Nureail's advances were unwelcome and Kris had chosen that moment to rise.

Tereail did not turn to look at him as he walked out of the chamber, and Kris did one last patrol of their first perimeter. The next room he had chosen for them was a straight line down from the edge of the circuit he had created, and most definitely had the thickest inventory of jewels and artefacts out of any other rooms he had seen so far. He still did not enter the room. The dust lining the floors of each chamber was a valuable indicator that they were alone. So Kris tried to follow the same path of his own footprints whenever possible, and if there was a room he could avoid stepping into altogether it was better. He returned to Nureail and Tereail, and once again he found neither had moved.

Kneeling down he carefully shook Nureail's shoulder and she opened her eyes to greet him. She smiled upon seeing him and the light green in her eyes became brighter with it. Kris realised he was crouching inappropriately close and stood up. Turning to Tereail he said, 'Time to leave.'

To Kris's amazement Tereail gave a tired nod, and hefted his bags over his shoulders. He had a new bag that contained items he had found and were not of any use to them beyond being a burden of more weight, but Kris would allow it as far as it did not impede them. Nureail picked up her own baggage, and surprisingly they were all ready to leave the chamber together. They could break their fast later in the new room. That was of course if Tereail would not insist he did not need food as well as sleep. Kris felt some approval for the Scholar's resolve.

That feeling disappeared then as Tereail did not notice the damage and destruction done in the other chambers as they travelled deeper into the temple. Nureail's eyes kept flicking towards her brother to see how he would react, but they then drifted to Kris when she thought he was not looking. She was none of his concern. What was strongly his concern was if Tereail was too fatigued to notice something so obvious, how would he find a single object hidden under a mountain of others?

Suppressing the urge to mutter a curse, Kris settled for a frown and a tightening of his fist. Turning around to keep a keen eye on the view through the chambers they passed, he saw Nureail smiling, which only made him deepen his frown further. Blessedly the Scholars continued to move along without delay or complaint, and they made swift work of the trek to the new room Kris had chosen.

The fresh treasure of ancient objects brought Tereail back to life and his entire face shone with frantic excitement. Gone was the worn look of a man ready to fall down where he stood, and the Scholar even turned to Kris to commend him on his selection.

'This is the room, Kris. I knew Jaiha was right in her measure of you. You have chosen the room where we will find it!'

'You have seen this?' Kris was still sceptical of his supposed powers.

'Yes, yes I have. Many times. It is precisely as I have seen it.'

'Good. I shall begin my patrol then, call out for me when you have found the item and we shall begin searching for the Ice Temple dais.'

Tereail was not listening. He had wandered over to a stone tablet covered with minute symbols before Kris had even finished his sentence. He felt like pointing out that they were not looking for a stone tablet, but a fire made of ice. Placing his hand on the hilt of his sabre sometimes soothed Kris's anger, but only when it gave him a promise of combat. So his anger remained. He clenched his other fist with a loud crack of knuckle.

'Tereail will hear nothing but his own thoughts for the rest of day, do not take insult from his actions.'

Kris turned to Nureail. 'Then I will take comfort as protector to the man, knowing he will hear nothing while I am away.'

'You presume I am going with you then?'

Kris frowned. He had not considered Nureail would leave her brother again to go with Kris. Why would she? And worse, it was now as if he was condoning it.

'Most Fureath'i, when they are surprised, Kris, their eyebrows go up. But not you, your eyebrows go down. Do you know that?'

He managed to control himself from frowning at her, keeping his features without gesture or emotion. 'I have not the time to give thought or notice to such things.'

'And I thought you noticed everything,' she said while staring back at him just as blankly. Kris did not respond. He had many times stared down men twice his size and strength, and made them bend to his will. Kris at least knew the darkness of his own eyes, even if he did not know the habits of his brow. They were a clear message to tell people to stay away.

Nureail's big eyes of light green and brown did not falter, and Kris recalled the last time he had broken to another's stare. It was the old man from Il-Yu, the patient priest who would have stood in front of Kris for years if needed. It seemed Scholars were too stupid to know when a man was about to kill them. He turned and left.

Nureail followed and Kris frowned to himself at her stubborn persistence. He did not turn his head as spoke back to her. 'I do not think it wise to leave Tereail undefended.'

'Well then what better way to protect him than by patrolling his perimeter.'

'That is what I will do. You must remain with him as a last defence.'

They passed through the first chamber which was gladly void of anything but the fire. But it made Kris angry at whatever ritual Brijnok had invoked to manufacture such a thing. The ritual had no order.

'As the better swordsman,' Nureail persisted, 'you are the more reasonable choice to remain by his side. I will patrol and you will remain with Tereail.'

Kris stopped and turned. He expected to see her smiling again, but she was not. He was tired of her games.

'Standing in a room doing nothing is not a task for a warrior. It is the job of a Scholar.'

Nureail patted the sabre at her belt. 'You have promoted me to Fureath'i remember, so no longer a Scholar.'

'We do not have time for this.' Kris's voice did not rise, nor did his anger show in any outward way. Inside of course, it was close to overwhelming him.

'Then you should stop arguing for the sake of arguing, Kris,' Nureail argued back. 'Now that *is* the task of a Scholar.'

Still she did not smile. Was she mocking him? Mimicking his control of emotion? He would not play her games. Kris continued on, and his new shadow followed. The next room did not contain any items either. It was pleasing but concerning. His suspicious nature suspected someone moved all of the objects into the one room as bait, where Tereail now studied alone, but the dust on the floor showed only Fureath'i boot prints.

The current room had a moat of water that surrounded the fire pit, and peering down into it, Kris could see an underground tunnel leading down with a second light coming from below. Kris did not like the fact there could be a second temple hidden beneath him, one submersed in water. If he could trust Nureail to react promptly should Tereail cry out, then he would have dove down to investigate. He did not think Jhakral could swim, but those underwater tunnels provided another entrance for possible threats. Kris only hoped they found no more transport platforms close by. The one leading back to the Fire Temple and the two others - the locations of which Tereail had neglected to educate Kris with - were already too many avenues of sudden assault as it was.

'We are wasting time here, Kris.'

Kris closed his eyes to stop from frowning or clenching his fist. Nureail still did not smile to demonstrate any enjoyment in her torment of him. Her actions were the type of ceaseless irritation he would have expected from his childhood friend Thisian. Thinking of his friends, Kris clutched for how any of them would have reacted. None were helpful. Nureail's childish manner would not have affected Dallid, he was never easily ruffled by anything so he would have just smiled at her good nature. Because Nureail was so beautiful, Thisian would have attempted to bed her. And Phira of course would have punched the Teller's teeth down her throat. Kris considered them all, Phira's response especially, and even Thisian's if he thought it would work to push Nureail away. But Dallid's was the most appropriate. Kris would not let it anger him. He would not let it affect him in the least because Nureail's actions were not important to Kris.

He did not smile, but he did not reply to her provocation either. Calmly, Kris moved to the next room in their circuit, this one at least containing items he could smash. Taking his sabre out of its scabbard, Kris almost felt joy at the prospect of the destruction he would cause, and it could also serve to push the Teller away from him. Nureail took away that joy.

'Kris, I apologise for how I acted last night by the pool.'

Kris did not reply.

'Kris?'

'There is no need to apologise,' he said, grudgingly.

'There is need, it has clearly upset you.'

He turned to her, sabre held ready in his hand. 'I am not upset. Warriors do not have needless emotions like being *upset*.'

'You are acting as if you are upset, Kris.'

A lesser man might have screamed. Instead, Kris said a silent prayer to every flame of Frehep, but he did not ask for strength. He asked for an enemy to fight, for any outlet for his uncontrollable anger. No, there was nothing within him that was so strong he could not control. No matter how fierce the emotion of his heart or mind, Kris himself was stronger. He needed a new tactic.

'I accept your apology.'

'Thank you, but I would like to explain.'

'Very well then,' he said with perfect calm. 'I will listen to your explanation while I examine this room.'

He would let her speak until she was satisfied and then he would nod and agree with everything she had said. It would not be a lie or false agreement if he did not listen to what she had been saying. Dallid had once confided in him that when he angered Phira, letting her talk about it was the quickest solution. The quickest apart from letting her fight it out. But fighting Phira, in even a practice bout, always had the potential for great harm. Kris began sifting through items on the ground with his sabre, strangely hesitant to smash them yet, as Nureail agreed to his terms.

'Well I am sure you know Tellers are different to other Fureath'i women, Kris - apart from western women perhaps - but we travel much and it can be lonely. When we find someone that intrigues us, a Teller will take him to her bed without much consideration. We rarely spend more than a day or two in any one village, so there is not much opportunity to waste time. But with you, Kris, it is different. I am very interested in you, for more than just taking you to bed. Believe it or not I greatly enjoy being around you. I enjoy your strength, your heart, even your sense of humour. But with this ritual Aerath has cursed upon the world, and with the futures Tereail has seen for us, well, I didn't think we had much time and I didn't think you were the type of man to make advances towards a woman casually. So I didn't want to wait or try to entice you towards me with any kind of subtly or tact. I apologise for being so forward. Do you understand?'

She waited for him to respond but he had no idea what he was supposed to say. She grew angry. 'This is not easy for me! You say you are in control of what you do and how you feel, and you say despite how strong you are that the struggle is hard. Then imagine what it is like for someone that is weak! We have the same struggles over our emotions, Kris, but we haven't your strength to help us, making it that much harder! I can't help how I feel about you, and I'm not as strong as you are to simply ignore it. So? Do you have anything to say back to me?'

Kris had to clear his throat after his first attempt at speaking failed. *She wanted to bed me? She enjoyed my sense of humour?* The woman was insane. What was he to say?

'I understand you, Nureail. Thank you for explaining.'

'That's all you have to say?'

Kris's mind raced. 'Tell me more about you.' He wanted to keep her talking so he could continue working. His question might even let her believe he was considering her offer as a mate. But if she truly knew him as she claimed, then she would know that he would never taint the heart of another by chaining his own to it.

Nureail hesitated and continued to stare at Kris. He did not return the look but kept examining the array of relics that lay scattered around the chamber. 'What would you like to know?' she asked cautiously.

'Everything.'

Nureail laughed. 'I don't think we have the time, you are asking a Teller to speak openly on a topic she knows most about.'

'Tell me about your connection to time then.' That was something he was mildly interested in learning about. Powerborn were the gods that walked the earth and he worshipped them as if they were Frehep's own children. A woman who claimed part of that title while still remaining fleshborn was something he would like to understand better.

'Alright.' She looked around and picked up a metal ring. 'What do you think this is?'

Kris cursed internally. This was not going to be the long monologue he had hoped for.

'A woman's bracelet,' he said without really looking at it.

Nureail laughed and shook her head. 'I'm horrified that you both think this would be considered jewellery for a woman, and that you can't recognise a piece of a sword.'

'If that is from a sword then it is a sword too large for any man to hold,' Kris said defensively. If there was one thing he knew better than most, it was swords.

'How strange to find it then in the Jhakral temple; it's from a Jhakral sword, Kris, and by holding it, I can connect with it and follow its history back in time.'

Kris frowned as Nureail began staring intently at the piece. Everything remained the same as it was, but Kris had the strange feeling he had just disappeared from the Jhakral temple and reappeared in the exact same location. When Nureail looked back to Kris a moment later, her face had gone pale and she looked frightened. Something felt wrong. He looked around to try to place the cause of his feeling of discomfort.

'What is it?' he asked Nureail.

'I don't know,' she said back. 'Something feels different. It was as if I was trapped in the past, for... a life time, but the memories are fading now, they always do. I tried to return but I was stopped. I knew the visions I was seeing could not hurt me if I hid from them, but it was a close thing. As the memories fade all I can remember is what felt like years of fear.'

'You only looked at the piece for a moment.' Kris frowned at Nureail's alarm. 'But even I feel like something has changed around us.'

'I thought I would have been in my trance for hours, it felt like...'

'Is it something about the item?' Kris wanted to discover if some kind of magic had occurred, and he needed Nureail to recover her strength. 'Tell me what you can about it.'

'This piece,' she stumbled over the word, 'has quite a power. But I don't think it could hold me in the past. I was nearly so lost.' Nureail clenched her teeth, forcing calm and steady words. 'If this metal ring is attached to a Jhakral sword, Kris, then it grants the user the same strength as one of the beasts. That is all. A useful item if we can find such a sword.'

'That would be a strange thing to find in a Jhakral temple,' Kris said back to Nureail and she grinned at his mimic of her earlier jibe.

'As long as the sword does not have a live Jhakral at the other end of it,' she added.

'What did you see when you went back? Could you see the beasts fight?'

'I saw...' she said and stopped to take a breath, strength returning to her proud face. 'I saw it being used to fight against Jhakral. It was created by the Kel Sherans, back when the Defenders still used swords, perhaps half a millennium ago.'

'You travelled back five hundred years in that one moment? No wonder I feel as if a day has passed.'

She looked at him strangely then, but continued. 'Well it has been here in this room for several hundred years, and in a storage room in Foriton for years before that. I didn't know Kel Sherah was one of Moi'dan's kingdoms before the birth of power. But I stopped travelling back as soon as I passed a battle scene, where ancient Kel Sheran warriors hunted the Jhakral beasts in the mountains. The ways in which the Kel Sherans died were... brutal.'

'I find it strange to hear you speak of Kel Sherans and warriors in the same breath, but it sounds as if they provoked the Jhakral beasts into invading, by hunting them for centuries before.'

'Perhaps,' Nureail did not seem willing to speak further and Kris watched her pocket the metal ring in a separate pouch she had tied around her waist.

'What other items have you found?'

'Between myself and Tereail? Several of great power, and if he can locate the relic we need today then it would not have been time wasted at all and will even aid us in our quest should we need to fight.'

Kris was not convinced. 'How? If we can find a Jhakral sword then I agree, but how else can a bag of trinkets help us if we are attacked?'

Nureail sighed but at least looked more at ease. Arguing with Kris seemed to bring her back to normal. 'They are not just trinkets, Kris. They are items of power that helped carve out empires. We have found weapons also, a wooden Loden Sword that can be used to strike a projectile force of energy in the direction of its swing. That could take out several enemies from a distance and all we need to do is discover how to power it.'

'So it has no power?'

'That is what I've just said. I haven't had time to delve fully into its past yet and find out how we can use it.'

'So it is just a wooden stick.'

'At this moment yes!' Nureail frowned and clenched her fists in frustration and Kris almost smiled. 'But we have others that are still powered, you have heard of a Loden Shield, yes? Well we have found the next best thing. It is an arm brace that acts the same, drawing any magic attack towards the brace and safely away from you. We have another that will repel magic, two godstones like the ones used in the defence of Foriton itself during the Jhakral invasion. They can create the same shield that kept the entire city safe for weeks.

'Another one can translate any script into any language. And every time we used it on that vase in the first room it often elaborated with new information depending on what language it was read, that is why Tereail spent so much time reading it, it spoke of the future and included the coming ice age that Aerath is trying to create.'

'And these are all rocks?'

'No they are stones of power, Kris.'

'It sounds to me that you have collected sticks and rocks, and women's jewellery.'

Nureail let out a scream of frustration and she was answered by a deafening roar.

They both froze, heads turned to stare in the direction of the sound. The beast's roar came from where they left Tereail.

· CHAPTER TWENTY ·

Beasts

Sprinting as hard as he could Kris thundered back towards the chamber. His head jerked in all directions searching every adjacent chamber they passed but he could see nothing of what made the sound. He skidded to a halt when he returned to Tereail and he found the Scholar alone, intently looking upon a golden rod.

Nureail arrived shortly behind and her brother turned to give them both a look of annoyance for their sudden interruption. 'Did you not hear it?' Nureail asked while looking around expecting to see a beast hidden somewhere under the ancient objects.

'Hear what?'

'The roar you book-brained imbecile or are your ears packed with snow?' Nureail was terrified; Kris could hear it in her voice.

'I have heard nothing. Perhaps you imagined it as a memory from one of your visions. It would not be the first time.' He went back to work but continued lecturing. 'Did you know, Kris, that sometimes she has visions in our own time? They are resonant echoes of memories too vivid to fade away and so they plague her struggling senses. I do not know why she continues to use her connection. You always say they frighten you, Nureail, like a Telling by ghosts and corpses. Did you see yourself again? I do not how it is possible, I am never able to view myself in the future. What did she say to you this time?'

Kris put a stop to the revealing of Nureail's private fears, 'What are those?' He pointed with his sabre to behind the Scholar.

Tereail turned around and lowered his lip in curious ignorance. There were footprints leading into the chamber and back out again. They did not lead to Tereail.

'I do not know. Are they yours from when you found this room?'

'No,' Kris said from behind clenched teeth. 'I did not set foot in this place. Are you saying you did not leave this room? That those boot prints are not yours?'

'They are not.' Tereail did not seem as worried as he should be. Someone had been and gone to the room without Tereail noticing and they had taken something with them. The prints almost looked like Fureath'i boots, but they were too light. It would have to have been a child's light touch of foot, but they were as large as a man's. He looked to Nureail who at least had the proper look of fear in her eyes. Kris readjusted his sabre and marched to where the footsteps led.

Nureail followed but Kris turned and shook his head, motioning over to Tereail and the Teller silently agreed that they could not leave him alone again. Not after hearing that roar, and not after finding those foot prints. Kris examined them more intensely when he was closer but they revealed no new information. He should get Nureail to use her power to look back and see who or what made the prints, but was not sure if she would risk it after seeing how shaken she had been just moments earlier. He exited the chamber.

The trail was clear through the otherwise untouched dust, but the man had tried to make his step as light as air. The boot was too large to have been a woman or child, but the touch was still too slight to have been a man. Kris himself was not a large man, Thisian towered above him, and Dallid was much wider of shoulder - although Dallid was very short, even for a Fureath'i. But Kris's boot, no matter how carefully he laid it, left a clear and deep impression much thicker and heavier than the one he followed.

The Chuabhotari - sold as slaves by the Ihnhaarat - were almost insubstantial in their frame. One of those could have made the soft trail. They were meant to have little more than the minds of beasts too, could it have been responsible for the roar? Kris did not think so, he had never heard of one going savage. They were often described as docile to the point of inaction. Those were the tamed ones anyway, the ones raised as slaves. Perhaps a wild one from the jungles in the north east could have been responsible.

The trail turned a corner through the next room and Kris was ready to face anything that threatened their mission. He did not care what it was. He would kill it. But the next chamber was empty and the footsteps lead to a dais.

Kris clenched his fist. Whoever had stolen something from their room had come and gone, and it was all because Kris had begun his search in the wrong direction. He stalked into the surrounding chambers and found no sign that life had ever been there. Whoever the thief was, he had entered by the dais and left immediately having found what he wanted. Or perhaps he had fled upon seeing Tereail. It was unlikely.

Running back to the first chamber, Kris let his rage take flame. He hated things he could not understand, and with his current mission that included everything. His feeling of wrongness from earlier, compounded with the sudden appearance of an intruder. It was too much to be coincidence. The sabre in his hand practically jumped with anticipation for any form of action he could take. Kris's heart pounded with a need for retaliation, his body tensed with strength desperate to be unleashed. He turned into the room and saw Nureail and Tereail standing there, waiting for him to return.

And a beast twice as large as a Prae'surlas filled up the doorway behind them.

At last.

The beast's eyes spotted all three and opened its mouth with a snarl that turned into a roar. It was the same roar they had heard before, and the Jhakral charged forward. Nureail and Tereail turned in horror. Kris sheathed his sabre and in the same fluid motion, as the monster thundered towards them, Kris grabbed a man-sized vase next to him and spun his entire body round. Releasing, it flew through the air with critical precision and the pottery exploded into the face of the beast.

Kris did not wait to see if the thing was blinded. His sabre was once more in his hand, and he charged the creature in return, not caring that it was three times his size. He shouted at the two Scholars who were still too terrified to move.

'Run! Follow the footprints to the dais! Go!'

He turned his shout into a roar then as he engaged the Jhakral. The thing had skin the colour of stone and it felt like just that as Kris ran his sabre along its knee with his first strike. The giant beast was busy rubbing its face clear of the shards, but stopped to swing a heavy arm down to swat Kris away. He ducked it easily and cut into the back of the creature's knee, following with a clean stab to its hamstring.

None of his three attacks had drawn any blood, and did not look close to breaking the thick skin. His strikes had barely left a mark. Large external bones lined the monstrous muscles, as if the skin was not already tough enough. A leather jerkin and loin-cloth were all the clothes the Jhakral wore. The beast kicked out and Kris had to dive back which gave the Jhakral time to remove the heavy sword strapped to its back. In a moment of distraction Kris looked to see if Nureail was still in the room. If he had that metal piece and could somehow disarm the Jhakral, then there was a chance Kris would not die in the next few heartbeats. Perhaps the sword of a Jhakral could actually cut the skin of a Jhakral. Without the piece though, Kris would never be able to lift it. The blade was almost the same size as Kris was, and it flew towards him with furious power.

Ducking underneath, Kris rolled forward coming up to stab at the shins and ankles, trying anywhere different that might be a weakness. The damned beast showed then it was able to hold the giant sword with one arm, as the other arm punched down at Kris. His dodge was too close, and he could even smell the stench of moulding rock off the beast's skin.

Kris's speed and skill were without fault as he dodged certain death to deliver meaningless blows in return. The futility was not lost on Kris, but it was not something he would concern himself with. If Tereail and Nureail had made it to the dais, then he should run to go after them. If Jhakral were Powerborn after all, then they could not step on the dais as Jaiha claimed. Other options were limited and Kris decided to stop trying to think of them. So he went back to focusing on not dying.

Pretending to drop his guard from fatigue, he made the Jhakral over extend and go off balance. Using the opportunity Kris weaved under the legs of the beast and plunged his sabre two-handed up into the creature's groin. There was no roar of pain, no splash of blood, only the same cursed sound of metal striking stone.

The Jhakral even had the intelligence to squeeze its legs together and caught Kris's shoulders as he tried to spin free. His momentum won him through, but the obstruction threw his balance. It allowed the beast to crash a giant fist down on the back of Kris's skull. It had never happened to Kris, but if he were ever to get a boulder smashed down onto his head, he imagined it would feel the same.

His legs disappeared, and so too did his thoughts. Kris fought for enough awareness to feel the floor against his cheek. He had no strength or even muscle in his arms, but he moved them anyway. There was one thing that Kris did for every minute of his entire life and that was fight. It did not matter that what he fought, external or internal, all that mattered was it was constant. He would never stop.

One of his hands slapped down onto something wet and sticky. His other hand was still wrapped around something cold and metal. Kris had to remember where his legs were and what it was like to stand up, because he could not feel them. But still he stood, ready to fight.

The Jhakral was not descending upon him as it should have been. Kris focused on the beast and saw it standing immobile and looking to the distance. Kris turned his disorientated vision to see what it was looking at. There was a tiny figure standing down there, shouting in some language Kris had never heard. It looked absurd for such a small thing to shout so authoritatively at a thing so big. It was Nureail.

The woman would argue with anything.

Kris's blood turned to fire and burned away all traces of injury. The bloody fool woman was standing in front of a monster and trying to berate it. Kris fell more than stepped forward, but kept upright and kept moving. He increased his speed as he approached his target and barrelled all of his strength into the knee of the Jhakral. It was enough to buckle the stance of the beast and gave Kris the time he needed to grab Nureail by the arm and pull her to a run.

She was shouting something at Kris but he felt like his ears were full of blood. They left the chamber and turned towards the dais only to see Tereail still there also, examining some rocks in a doorway of all things. Kris threw Nureail past the door and swung his sabre to knock Tereail in the same direction, and hopefully kill him in the process. But in his daze, he missed the blasted Scholar. Looking back to see the Jhakral charge behind them, Tereail stood up calmly and dusted his hands, oblivious to the death rampaging towards him.

'Get to the dais!' Kris roared but heard it as if he were muffled by a raging river. Neither fool Scholar moved and Tereail was saying something. All Kris cared about was placing himself between the Jhakral and Nureail. He timed his last attack with exhausting concentration and at the right moment launched himself into the air. He would see how tough the beast's throat would be against both their momentums combined. Kris had to leap to nearly double his height to reach the mark but he did it without hesitation. His sabre blade met the Jhakral's throat right underneath the archway that separated the two chambers.

Something flashed and Kris was rebounded back to the ground, his sabre no longer in his hands. But neither did he feel the creature run over him as it should have. Maybe he had killed it. The stone floor hit hard and knocked the air out of him but a warm and gentle hand appeared quickly on his cheek. The softness of her skin was unbearable. The beauty of her eyes leaning over him was agonizing, filled with hurt and concern.

'I am fine,' he said calmly, although a part him muttered that his skull was cracked and he felt like he was bleeding to death. 'Did I kill it?'

Nureail spoke to him from a distance. Kris had only ever let himself get drunk beyond control once, and he remembered vaguely experiencing something similar that night. The blood of Frehep ran thick with shame back then and Kris would not dishonour himself in such a way again. He sat up.

The Jhakral was right in front of them, still standing, and still thrashing violently. There was no sabre lodged within its throat. Kris got to his feet immediately despite both Nureail and Tereail trying to hold him down, and despite his present weakness, he was still too strong for them.

'It cannot hurt us, Kris!'

He turned to frown at Nureail. Why was the Jhakral not attacking them? It had not even left the chamber it had been in. Kris looked down to see his sabre lying on the floor. He walked slowly over to pick it up, never taking his eyes from the raging beast. An unseen force was stopping it from passing through the archway, with each punch and sword swing halted suddenly against nothing.

Tereail's smile was insufferable. 'Nureail tells me you called them useless rocks?'

Looking down to see a coloured stone at either side of the archway, Kris frowned again even though it made his head split with pain. Nureail was still staring at him with panic, but she managed to find words to lecture him.

'Remember, Kris? They are the same power that Foriton used to hold a full city protected. They are called godstones.'

Kris said nothing and lifted his gaze back to the Jhakral.

The creature had stopped thrashing, and now stood staring back at him. Dark monstrous eyes glittered with intelligence and regarded every detail of Kris, but he knew that his own eyes were darker.

'The question now is,' Tereail said, while releasing a long breath, 'how do we retrieve the stones and still escape the Jhakral?'

Kris looked at Tereail and would have tried to strike him if it did not take all his strength just to stay standing.

'The question, Tereail,' he said back slowly, 'is why we are still standing here when we should be gone through that dais and after our intruder.'

It appeared the man had clean forgotten about that, and began to give it some thought. Kris's mind was more than made up as two more Jhakral lumbered into the chamber in front of them and began conversing with the first. The barrier of magic blocked out sound as well as substance, and it was a strange sight to see, three monsters speaking silently to each other, less than ten paces away.

Kris turned. 'We leave.'

'But we have not found the artefact, Kris! We cannot! It is in that room, I am certain!'

'Then we find the thief that has visited there while you were immersed in your studies. If he does not have the item we need, we will return. Perhaps by that time the Jhakral will be elsewhere.'

They reached the dais while Tereail considered his words. Kris turned to Nureail. 'What does it say?'

She squinted her eyes for a moment before speaking. 'It says the Temple of Life.'

'Or wind or air or life's voice, depending on which dialect you wish to use,' Tereail began. 'But Kris what if we -'

Kris caught the man by his hair and threw him on top of the dais, he disappeared the instant he touched it. Nureail looked to him in shock but then stepped voluntarily to follow her brother. Kris did not spare the Jhakral temple any last look before stepping on the dais himself.

His second step did not hit a floor in another temple as it had when he used the strange platforms previously. This time he arrived sprawled across the ground on top of sharp items digging into him. It was a room like the chambers in the Jhakral temple, but as if every single relic were all piled into a series of sand dunes. Nureail and Tereail lay similarly dishevelled and slowly rose to a sit or crouch. Kris craned his neck behind him and could not see any Jhakral following, or even the platform they should have arrived on. Instead it was just masses of jewels and treasure, weapons and artefacts, ranging from glowing hammers to wooden animals. When he turned his head forward again a figure stood before him.

Kris's head was still dizzy, but the man in front of him appeared to glow with what could only be described as raw power. His skin was the purest white Kris had ever seen, and even in his groggy state Kris could clearly see the figure's eyes. They were a swirling sandstorm of light and Kris knew they could only be in the presence of a god.

· CHAPTER TWENTY ONE ·

Strength

His eyes opened to darkness but it was not night. He could just about see the light of day make golden outlines from the dark. *Where am I?* Dallid breathed in and his mouth was filled with dust. Spitting and coughing, his body tried to curl forward and was pressed down from all sides. In a panic he lashed out but found the resistance too great. It felt like a mountain was on top of him. His arms and legs were trapped under weights too large for his flesh. A new power arrived then and suddenly Dallid found the heavy blocks shifting under his strength. He did not know where the power came from but Dallid clutched at it frantically and used it all to get him out from wherever he was. Pushing and kicking, the blocks began to tumble away but it was not enough. He needed to get out! Dizzy with panic, Dallid pushed with every ounce of strength he could steal, and finally the mountain moved and he was able to climb free.

Tears stained his face as he sucked in open air. Dallid stared up to the sun in gratitude and then turned his eyes back down to the earth. He was surrounded by a chaos of stone with massive chunks sticking out from the lake and cutting into the forest.

The Tower of Frehep has fallen.

Dallid looked around as memory returned, seeing bodies now underneath the rocks. Fureath'i clothes crept out from under the ruins as much as Prae'surlas. Dallid looked up to the sky again to where the tower once stood. It was empty and the view was replaced with one of the sun god looking down on him. Dallid turned his head away from it and took another look at the devastation. The Tower of Frehep had survived for many Ages if the Scholars were to be believed and now it was destroyed.

More important facts returned to Dallid then: the Prae'surlas had invaded his village; his entire squad was killed; Jathen and Emylias were dead, Yiran the Unconquered was dead. Chrial'thau the Great had been turned into a demon and another demon calling itself an Attro'phass was loose in the country trying to kill other great Fireborns. An Iceborn named Aerath was somehow responsible for all of it.

Dallid had been killed and had woken up a Fireborn...

He looked down at his hands and only then saw how badly injured his flesh was. Both forearms were heavily mangled and coloured with every kind of injury, and lifting up his tunic Dallid saw that his chest and torso was just as bad. Poking at the battered flesh carefully, he only felt an echo of pain. It made sense that he would be hurt, the Tower of Frehep had been brought down on top of him. So why did it not hurt as it should? No, nothing about it made sense. To prove that point Dallid commanded flames to burst to life from his fists.

'I am Fireborn,' he said testing. It only made him certain he'd gone mad. Or he was dead and this was the heights of power. He was being tested to see if he could cope with the stresses life would throw at him. If he could hunt down and destroy Aerath then he would be reborn in the next life better. *As a Fireborn?*

Dallid shook his head and then amended that it was Chrial'thau he was to hunt down. He was the demon running free through Furea, Aerath had most likely returned to Lae Noan. How was Dallid supposed to get there and kill him? But how was he to do any of it? He was not some mighty warrior, he was below average at best, why did he think he was capable of hunting anything, demon or Iceborn?

For some reason it did not matter to him how it would be done, just that it had to be. Perhaps becoming a Fireborn had burnt away all his hesitation and made him into the warrior he had always wanted to be.

'I am not worthy to be a Fireborn. I am the least deserving of any Fureath'i.'

His voice sounded odd around so much death and destruction. Was being the only survivor of such an event what it meant to be great? He had never dreamed of greatness; that had been Phira and Thisian. Even Kris quietly aspired to prove himself by climbing the ranks. All Dallid had ever wanted was to spend his every day with the woman that he loved, and to create new life in their image - a simple dream, but one that he could not achieve.

Phira could not settle for something so ordinary, her heart burned for the very summit of power. What right did Dallid have to give priority to his desires over hers? That they had the short time they did as man and wife was more than most ever got to experience. It was true happiness and enough to power his heart for a hundred lifetimes. Emylias's death made Dallid feel fresh how much he loved Phira and how utterly destroyed he would be if she were to die.

In a panic he looked to his wrist and saw that the leather wrist strap was gone. It must have burnt through or fallen off. He looked around vainly for it, but there was nothing but rubble and corpses to be seen. The coin was a small thing to lose after so much else, his squad, his friends, his heroes, but it seemed enough of a loss to finally push him over the edge. *How can any of this be real?*

Pressing his hands against his head, Dallid winced as pain lanced through him. The pain he had felt in his bruised body had only been the dull memory of pain, but the one in his head was like a snake of fire burrowing its way through his mind. The sensation stopped shortly after it started and began to pulse slowly inside his mind. It was Chrial'thau. There was no way he could know but he knew it was true. He had to find Chrial'thau.

'I have to *kill* Chrial'thau,' Dallid said. It did not feel right wanting to kill Chrial'thau, but he had to find him. Then they would kill Aerath.

'No!' he roared. Memories of how Chrial'thau had said the same thing came back to him. He would do nothing with the demon except kill him. Then Aerath would meet the end of Dallid's blade. His hands were shaking from the intensity of feelings he was experiencing and only then did he realise they were still on fire.

How quickly I have become used to my own skin burning.

Dallid turned and ran from the thought. He leapt down from the mountain of rubble and soon became part of the forest. Faster and faster he pushed himself, letting some other being's strength power his muscles. He dodged between trees and leapt over roots with an agility he had never before possessed. The speed at which he flew down game trails and avoided thickets was not his. But the clarity of letting himself get lost in the run was too peaceful to disturb. The exhilaration he felt from the empowered muscles was too intoxicating to stop. So Dallid ran.

He felt strong. He had never felt strong before. Yes his arms were thick with muscle, but always he felt weaker than other people. Perhaps he just spent too much time around Phira. Dallid laughed at that thought when only minutes earlier he had mourned that he had never spent enough time with her. How quickly was his new strength changing him? He sought for more.

It was only when realising he ran towards the sensation within his head, that Dallid began to slow. He was running towards Chrial'thau without any thought. He had not burned the bodies of his brothers as he had pledged, he had not gone to Yiran's cabin to find a horse and supplies as he had planned, instead he simply ran to do battle as a warrior of fire.

Pushing speed back into his run, Dallid knew that the longer Chrial'thau was left free to do as he wished then more Fureath'i would die. He tried to push back thoughts of how long he could keep up such a run for. As a fleshborn he might have been able to run one full day and night but would have been exhausted from it. As a Powerborn he no longer knew what his limits might be.

They did not need to eat, or drink, or take strength from air or from blood. A Powerborn needed nothing other than his own power to survive. That was the description he had been given as a youth anyway. Yet he still breathed and felt thirsty, and he had seen that Powerborns need more than their own power to survive: they also need their heads. He had witnessed the deaths of five Iceborns when before he had never even heard of the death of one - not one killed in single combat at least. In the long war they said it would take a thousand men of flesh to kill one man of power. Dallid did not feel like he could kill a thousand Prae'surlas. His fleshborn heart would never find peace with such power.

But he was no longer fleshborn. *Am I truly Powerborn?*

Dallid could not answer his own question, yet he ran without rest and had lived from a battle where a hundred others had not. So if he were to accept that he was really Fireborn then what did that mean for his life? What did that mean for his marriage to Phira? The first answers he could imagine were all negative. As a

Powerborn, his marriage to Phira would be no more. The risk of death or deformity through conception between fleshborn and Powerborn was too dangerous to be tolerated. Their differing stations before had all but annulled their marriage anyway so Dallid did not allow that to distress him too much. In fact his new station as Fireborn should equal hers as blaze commander, within the army at least, since he was still without rank and would not receive it without years of training and by then Phira would probably be King.

If he returned to Rath'Nor with the heads of Aerath and Chrial'thau however, he might be recognised more quickly - well, perhaps not with the head of Chrial'thau. His legend was too strongly ingrained in the hearts of every Fureath'i. The mere fact he had become a demon should even be kept from the majority of men, but such a lie would need to be something he discussed with the King. First he had to catch the creature anyway, then kill it and destroy the body, then enter Surlas, catch and kill Aerath, and then he could worry about those other matters.

Dallid frowned at the strange thoughts. This was not him. He did not go charging forth on quests of vengeance against gods and demons. The thoughts sounded like they belonged to someone else. He began to worry then if Chrial'thau really had transferred his powers to Dallid, had he transferred more? Did these uncharacteristic notions belong to the Fireborn of legend? Was his mind becoming a part of Dallid as his power was?

The thought terrified him. He struggled to find out if what he thought was truly him, or someone else forcing their will on him. *Phira*, he thought, *I will concentrate on Phira*. Those thoughts alone would be his.

His first thought could be asking Phira if she would be his sword. Being a sword of god to a Fireborn, or even a sword of war to a Flameborn, was as great an honour as any fleshborn would dream. But Phira had always held higher dreams than most. Becoming a general as Yiran had been was only her first goal. Even as a youth she had joked often about becoming part of the Fire King, the eight rulers of Furea, but Dallid had never taken that ambition as seriously as he should have. No, she would not be content with simply being the sword of a Fireborn.

A flash of light made Dallid skid to a halt.

It reminded him that not everyone who walked the lands of Furea these days, were Fureath'i. The flash could have been just a beam of sunlight that was focused strangely for a moment, since his viewing of the sun seemed completely different now that he was Powerborn. The sun sang to him and danced to its own music, and it was a music that flowed through everything, including him. Again his fleshborn mind struggled to fully comprehend the feelings it produced but his mind at least told him that the flash of light could also have been from a spear. The mystery of how more than a hundred Prae'surlas got so far into Furea was in the long list of questions that Dallid needed to find answers.

His ears attuned themselves to the forest and his eyes relaxed to take in everything. Even Dallid's sense of smell was different, making many things too strong and distracting. Patiently he waited but nothing moved. There was no presence that he could sense beyond the distant one of Chrial'thau. Dallid moved his foot to resume the run and the flash appeared again. This time he drew his sabre when he saw a being of pure fire standing between the trees in front of him. The thing had no features, but when it moved its head down, Dallid somehow knew it looked at his sabre. Then it was gone.

Spinning around to see where it would appear next Dallid wanted to shout or do something. But he was not sure what he had just seen. Stepping cautiously over to where the image had been he looked down to see no sign of scorched underbrush, no smell of smouldered plant life. In fact Dallid had not felt the fire of the image at all, not the same way he had felt the torches in the tower, or now even the sun. Chrial'thau's tainted fire, fouled by demonic magic, still burned within his mind from the distance, so what had the image been?

It could have been Frehep, come to see who this new Fireborn was that had unrightfully received the power of gods. But Frehep did not walk the earth. That was the core of religion: that every Fureath'i could rely on the strength of his own heart, nothing else. Foreign gods walked the lands, but why would one appear as a being of fire? And Frehep would not have allowed a Foreign god entry to his holy land. But it seemed he now allowed demons of darkness to enter, so why not gods? Aerath claimed to be a god.

Feeling the darkness in his mind moving further and further away, Dallid cursed that every moment he wasted in hesitation was a moment the demon could be causing murder. He broke back into his run. If the image came back he would fight it, but for the moment he had enough enemies to concentrate on.

It could've been the figment of my battered mind, trying to cope with the image of myself as a Fireborn and projecting it out into vision. My mind is trying to reject the idea and wishes to push it out.

Dallid smiled at the thought but the last time he had seen a flash he thought was nothing, it turned into a demon, an Attro'phass demon that had a quest to hunt down and kill every Fireborn in a specific order, going by rank and power by all appearances. *First Lord Chrial'thau, then Lady Jaiha, then Lord Miral'thau, who would be next? When would he come for me?* Dallid did not let the thought enter into his list of questions, any one of those Fireborn would destroy the demon and that would be the end of its misguided mission.

Yet Chrial'thau is now dead and the demon still lives.

Dallid let his mind concoct a sudden possibility of demonic versions of all the great Fireborns, roaming the lands causing mayhem and death. It was a chilling thought. One was bad enough and Dallid was still not certain at all how he would fight it. He would not learn a lifetime of mastery and control in a few days of running. Eventually Chrial'thau would stop, Dallid would catch him and they would do battle. The weight of the sabre at his belt confirmed how he would fight him.

If Protharik the Demonmaster could kill demons with steel then so could Dallid the Fireborn. It was just unfortunate that all the Teller's stories differed on whether Protharik killed them or controlled them. That reminded Dallid that they were just stories. His was real, or at least he thought it was, and it was one he should not try too hard to think about; it would only overwhelm him.

A hero from a story charges in and saves the day. So that is what I will do.

Dallid nearly tripped over a leg as he charged into a clearing of dead Prae'surlas. The sight of so many dead northerners in his forests was almost becoming a common one. The only difference with these Prae'surlas though, was that they were all burnt alive.

It could mean that a real Fireborn, or even a Flameborn was patrolling the area, but the stabbing pain in his skull led Dallid to believe it was the demon that was responsible. If there were other Powerborn nearby would Dallid feel them in his mind the way he felt Chrial'thau? The fact that anything connected him with the foul demon disturbed Dallid but at least he knew where the beast was. Sparing no more thought for the mutilated Prae'surlas, Dallid pressed harder in his run.

It was hard to determine but he thought he could feel the sensation of Chrial'thau getting closer. There were so many new sensations going on in Dallid's mind and body that it was enough to unhinge a man, but it felt good to have a clear goal. He raced towards a just cause with a sabre at his hip and strength in his arms to use it. There could be no better feeling, but it only became lost within the battle of every other emotion inside his mind. *This power should have been given to someone better*.

Smoke drifted above the trees ahead and Dallid pushed anxiously towards it. If it was another Powerborn then he would have much needed help, but if it was Chrial'thau then he would at least have some end to his torment.

The smoke grew thicker the closer he got and Dallid no longer felt like it could be a Powerborn responsible. He had seen similar smoke from his own village and already guessed what he was about to find. The sensation in his mind was close but not close enough to place Chrial'thau at the site of the smoke. Dallid had no idea how long he had been buried underneath the tower. The devil might have a few days lead on him, or only a few hours.

The smoke grew closer and Dallid burst free from the tree line ready to fight any enemy but had to quickly turn away. There was nothing in his stomach to vomit so he empty retched until he got himself under control. He attempted to turn his head back and failed once, before finally making himself look at the scene Chrial'thau had created. It could only have been the demon. Nothing else could create such evil.

Buildings still burned and smouldered, but it was the still smouldering people that Dallid could not take his eyes from. Their flesh was charred and blackened but they were all frozen in mid-life. They stood like statues of ruined flesh, their stench filling the air, and their bodies held distorted in the last agony of life. One woman stood with a sabre burnt to her hand, while another stood trying to rip out her eyes. There were children who were killed while huddling in fear, and men who had tried to shield them. An entire village of murdered Fureath'i, held frozen by fire, in the horror of their last breath.

He could not look at it. Dallid left and ran towards the sensation within his mind. The demon no longer seemed so far ahead now. Fuelled by the need to get away from that horrific village and to find the thing responsible, Dallid moved faster than he thought anything could move. The distance between them started to close quickly. Through gritted teeth he reasoned that it would take the demon time to kill so many people, and it was time that Dallid could use to catch him.

The feeling of the demon began to get alarmingly close. What started as a distant thing now seemed to charge towards Dallid with unstoppable speed as he ran. But a hero did not give time to panic. It was Dallid who was charging with unstoppable speed to the demon, not the other way around.

In the direction he moved, the forest began to thin. More and more trees were cut down and a man-made clearing was forming around a farm. Dallid slowed to a stop and then crept forward to remain unseen. There was a good chance Chrial'thau knew of his location with the same Connection to each other, and so Dallid did not want to rush into an ambush.

Staying to the shelter of the trees, he let his new vision scout around the area. Dallid had never considered himself having poor eyesight before, but now he felt as if the world had only lit up for the first time. It was a beautiful sensation.

The farm house was robust, as it would have housed numerous youths from the surrounding villages at any one time, and apart from animal pens, the barn was the only other building where Chrial'thau could be. The powerful presence of the demon was so strong, that Dallid would have sworn that the thing stood right in front of him, but as there was no-one to be seen, he continued his search.

Craning his head up and around, and moving forward as carefully as he could, Dallid could not understand how Chrial'thau could feel so close and be nowhere to be seen. Movement came then from behind the large farmhouse, and he spotted two youths in thick woollen cloaks working with cattle. Their hoods were drawn and Dallid only then noticed that the further north he was travelling the colder the weather was getting. It was strange that he had not realised it before. Apparently Powerborn did not need any Connection to the flesh, the only Connection that mattered was the one with fire.

A third youth exited the farmhouse, similarly wrapped with a hood hiding his face. Dallid watched as the young warrior moved into the barn and decided he could wait no longer. The Fureath'i working and living there needed to be warned about the danger they were about to face and if that exposed his position to Chrial'thau then so be it. Phira would have a plan of action, expertly crafted and envisioned to perfection. But Dallid preferred to mimic his friend Kris. Kris would just run in and kill his enemy, everything else be damned.

Dallid ran forward from his place of concealment and prepared himself for an attack of dark fire from wherever the demon was hiding. His shoulders were bunched and the muscles on his back were tensed. It would not by any means improve his chances of survival if the dark energy hit him, but he did it anyway. The cautious run from the forest to the farm took only moments and Dallid turned around swiftly to see if Chrial'thau had revealed himself. His stare cut all around him, but the forest and the skies were free of the demon's image. The door behind him opened and Dallid spun to see an elder walk out. The older man quickly moved from surprise to reverence upon seeing Dallid's tunic, and he dropped to the ground with a bow, his forehead touching the earth.

Dallid was speechless.

His shock at the man's reaction matched the man's own shock at suddenly seeing a Fireborn. The threatening existence of Chrial'thau in his mind was enough to help Dallid find his tongue again. He could feel that any moment the devil would appear and slaughter everyone there.

'Get up. Please. You must gather everyone and leave.'

The man did not move and could not seem to hear the words over his shock. 'My Lord,' he stammered. 'You honour our community with your presence. You honour us.'

Dallid caught the man by his shirt and lifted him off his feet. 'Will you listen to me! You and everyone here must leave, there is a demon coming that means you death!'

'My Lord, I do not understand, but it will be as you say. Where shall we go?'

Had the man no sense? Here was an elder, a Fureath'i who had survived life in the army and been returned to deliver wisdom to the next generation, and yet he blithered like a child in front of Dallid. It should have been the other way around.

'It does not matter. Go to the nearest village. You do not appreciate the urgency of this matter, the demon is already here!'

The man's eyes widened and Dallid nodded that he had finally understood the seriousness of the situation. But at the same moment, day turned into night.

Turning around with false courage, Dallid met the evil eyes of the demonic Chrial'thau: one horribly glowing with a disgusting mix of blue and red light, the other blazing with the terrible green of the Attro'phass demon. Black fire swam all around the devil's body and the thing smiled with malice. His frail stature and bone-white hair was incongruous against the deep black of the fire. By just gazing on it, Dallid could feel the goodness of his soul getting devoured by its touch. The demon that Chrial'thau had become was truly a thing of darkest nightmare.

But a hero does not hesitate.

· CHAPTER TWENTY TWO ·

Power

Dallid's sabre swung out with too much speed, too much power, it did not feel right and still missed despite the strength behind it. The demon's speed made his own look ordinary, carelessly swaying back, letting the tip of his sabre glide tauntingly close to the withered skin of its neck. Setting his jaw, Dallid followed with more vicious sabre swings, each one powered with new resolve and focused skill. The demon dodged and drifted back lazily, before floating up into the sky with a minimum of effort.

'You are a child swinging at his father with wooden sticks!' Chrial'thau laughed. 'Any moment the father grows bored and strikes the boy down.'

'Then strike me down!' Dallid shouted back.

'Put away your steel and we shall do battle proper.' The thing licked its lips with anticipation. Dallid did not know why it feared his sword so much, but he would do nothing that the thing wanted.

'You would prefer to die by the magic of a Powerborn than the steel of a fleshborn?'

'You have no magic that is worthy of the name. I would prefer it only so I could laugh at your helplessness.'

The demon broke into laughter anyway, a cruel sound full of evil and madness. The sound echoed loudly and people began to appear from fields and buildings to see what was happening. Youths and elders stood in shock and awe of a seeing both a burning demon in the sky and a Fireborn on the earth to fight it. The demon's own tunic had become burnt and stained. The stains must have been blood from the Fureath'i it had already killed, and the burnt marks from its own cursed black flames. The fact the fabled tunic of a Powerborn was withering under the demon's blaze did not fill Dallid with confidence at how his own stolen tunic would hold out. It would still be more protection than any of the farm workers had. Both he and Chrial'thau looked at them gather and stare. Dallid watched them arrive with sickening panic and Chrial'thau watched them appear with glee. The devil turned its rotted smile to Dallid.

'Watch while the father educates the child on magic.'

One youth had edged his way closer to them, his sabre drawn, his eyes full of determination. He had the same dark eyes as Kris did. Dallid and the demon both turned their head to him and he screamed. Chrial'thau was only staring at him and still was able to take his life. Dallid could even feel what the demon was doing. He was boiling every drop of blood inside of the young Fureath'i's body. Dallid could feel it, sense the ritual that was taking place, identify how much power it took the demon to produce and yet was powerless to stop it. One of his hands reached forward, trying to Connect with the cursed fire, while the other hand tightened around the hilt of his sabre, crushing the metal slightly. All others moved to do something, to run or to fight, when a wide barrier of dark fire erupted out of the earth and circled the entire farm, trapping them.

More flames burst from the farm houses and the barns, and the whole estate was burning with the demon's rage. It was so much. It was more than Dallid had even seen Chrial'thau as a Fireborn conjure. So many people trapped and dying, and the demon wearing Chrial'thau's skin did not even look as if it was exerting itself. The fiery beast had eyes only for the torture of the single Fureath'i whose blood it was boiling.

The youth was long in dying and Chrial'thau was in no hurry to make the death any quicker. Dallid trembled with frustration that his own Connection would not come. There was too much power everywhere and he could not single out the one ritual that he might stop the youth's suffering. With no other choice, Dallid lashed out and hurled his sword forward like a throwing knife. The blade shot straight and plunged into the demon's shoulder with a roar.

Dallid added his own roar as he sprinted forward and launched himself into the air. Chrial'thau's head turned just as Dallid gripped both of his hands around the demon's ankle. His weight bore the demon down to earth, the black fire blessedly not effecting Dallid's own skin. Losing himself in helpless rage Dallid thundered his fists into the body of the beast. Muscles crunched and bones snapped under his attack, and Dallid went to pull his sabre free so he could end the thing.

Chrial'thau's screams reached new heights as Dallid ripped the thick curved blade of the sabre out, but let loose a blast of flame to stop him plunging the sword through its skull. The demon fire blew Dallid back through the air but only caused minor pain, so Dallid rolled to his feet straight away. The demon though, had returned to its perch in the sky, well out of Dallid's reach. A consolation for his efforts was that the fires burning throughout the farm had vanished. Dallid looked around anxiously and had little choice but to crouch, waiting for an opportunity to attack again.

The demon nursed its wounded shoulder and snarled like a rabid dog down at him. Dallid returned the snarl. His entire body still shook at the intensity of the situation, but he had to keep telling himself, the devil's fire could not hurt him. That was why it wanted him to attack using his own fire; it would be just as ineffective.

'Return to the earth and let me put you out of your miserable existence, demon,' he spoke as he thought Phira would. 'If there is anything of Fireborn inside of you then you should beg me for your death.'

'I exist now, *Fireborn*, just to cause you misery!' Letting go of its injured shoulder, the demon threw its hand towards the elders in front of the farm house. The old man was huddled in fear, shaken, just like Dallid was, by the unreality of the situation that they all faced, while others ran. A stream of black fire roared down on him, and Dallid almost dropped his sabre reaching forward to grab hold of the flames.

This time he was able to control it and threw the stream aside to scorch the earth instead. Still the elder did not flee and Dallid clenched his jaw.

'You Connect to every fire but your own!' The demon was laughing with contempt. 'Is the power you were cursed with so pathetic that you shame away from using it?'

'My powers are a gift from Frehep, and they will be the end of you demon.'

'You are a fool. I have Chrial'thau's mind and even he knows that such a thing cannot happen. Maybe it was Aerath who gave you your powers the way he gave me mine? The curse can cause us to do things we would not do. Perhaps he thought you would become another like me!' Chrial'thau laughed at the idea. 'He will die by our hands, but not before we have our fill of Fureath'i flesh.'

'Aerath's hand had nothing to do with my power!' Dallid shouted back. 'You are an abomination to our lands and I am Frehep's answer to destroy you.'

'Then show me his gift if you are so certain that ice will not appear from your hands.'

Dallid had enough of the demon's taunting, he would find a way to pull the thing to the ground and he would hack the beast to pieces. Pushing the strength he felt inside him down to his fists, Dallid set both alight with bright red fire. He stood ready, hands ablaze, flames even dancing up his sword blade. He looked like a true hero from the stories. He looked a true Powerborn, lord of all, defending the light against darkness. Chrial'thau's face lit up with glee.

'At last you have shown me what a fool you are.'

The fire turned from red to black and roared out of Dallid's control. He dropped his sword as he lifted both hands in front of him to try and stop the black flames. The demonic magic surged forward and exploded in front of his face. The world went white and the sensation of flying greeted his skin before the heavy thump of the earth hit.

The pain was excruciating. His hands felt like they had been blown apart and when Dallid tried to move his fingers he could not feel them. His skull screamed with a piercing pain that made him think his sabre had been lodged there, and all the strength that had powered his limbs had disappeared.

Part of him knew he needed to get up, but the other part just lay helplessly waiting for the demon to kill him. It was better that he die. He was not strong enough for this power. He did not deserve it. A woman screamed.

Phira.

Dallid got up. No longer was he Kris, doing what needed to be done simply because he must. He was Dallid the Fireborn, and he fought for the one thing that mattered to him, he fought for Phira. He knew the woman's scream was not his wife, but he made himself imagine it was. Even if he could not fully believe it, he fought because if he did not then he might never see her again.

Vision was slow in returning, but between white flashes, Dallid saw his sabre and stumbled over to retrieve it. He fell to one knee while bending over to pick it up, but with the heated steel in hand, his strength returned. His hands had not been blown apart as he had feared, but looking down at his sword he saw the skin holding it was red and blistered. He searched for Chrial'thau.

The demon stood watching him, in front of the farmhouse with arms held up to either side. In each hand he gripped the throat of a Fureath'i. The elder man and another who looked to be the elder's wife, hung helplessly with the devil's hand held ready to crush both their necks. Others lay dead around the farm, more must have escaped, but it would not be for long if Dallid did not do something. How could the demon hold a man off his feet after getting stabbed in the shoulder moments ago? Was all demonic healing that fast? Dallid's skin felt tight from scarring as he clenched his fists.

'Chrial'thau the Fireborn was a lord of this land was he not?' the demon taunted. 'The Powerborn protector of his fleshborn brothers? How is it then that you just stand there and watch your people die at the hands of Chrial'thau the Demon? Are you not Powerborn at all?' The demon cackled at its own wickedness. 'Take one step towards me and I wash my hands with the blood in their throats.'

'You will kill them anyway.' Dallid tried to sound sure, 'And before your hands have fully closed I will have sliced your skull in two.'

'No, *Fireborn*, you will have killed them. Throw down your sabre and give me your life in return for theirs. Is that not what a true Fireborn would do?'

Dallid had never experienced such strong hatred before as he now felt for this demon. How could such an evil creature wear the face of a Fureath'i legend? He did not know what to do. The demon would kill the fleshborns if Dallid dropped his sabre, but if Dallid ran forward he would kill them too. Every Fureath'i would gladly give their life for the betterment of their country, and ridding the land of that devil was certainly worth it. But how could he move when he knew it would kill two of his blood?

The elder's wife took the decision away.

With skilful subtly that belied her age, Dallid saw without looking that she had begun to withdraw her belt knife. He kept his eyes on the devil and would not even glance towards the woman least it end her life. There was only so long Chrial'thau would allow him the immobility of indecision but he needed to wait until the precise moment. The moment arrived as the knife plunged into the devil's side and Dallid bolted forward. The elder husband was forgotten and tossed aside as Chrial'thau freed his right hand to punch through the skull of the elder wife. Dallid's speed served him well and in the same flash of violence, his sabre sliced up through the devil's fist in mid-flight. The hand flew free from the beast before it touched the woman, and Chrial'thau howled out in pain.

The elder wife was dropped as the wretched creature placed his surviving hand over the stump of where the other had been. But Dallid was not finished. He brought back his thrust and ripped along Chrial'thau's side before swinging a return blow down through the neck. The demon had enough composure to throw itself to safety from that and narrowly escaped with only a small chunk of it torn out. The moment Chrial'thau touched the ground, he ignited himself fully into a being of black fire and roared up into the sky. But he did not flee.

Instead he cradled his wounded hand and stared down at Dallid. The demon's head cocked to the side just the Attro'phass demon had and Chrial'thau's left eye flashed bright green. Slowly a sword of jagged bone cut its way out of the severed stump where the devil's hand had been. Dallid watched in disbelief as the sword continued to grow until a new hand appeared holding the blade.

In the battle of the tower, Dallid had watched both Chrial'thau and the Attro'phass demon kill Iceborn Demi-gods with ease. Now he faced a devil that seemed to have both Chrial'thau's and the Attro'phass's power combined. Whatever Aerath had created was something the world had never seen before. The creature smiled at Dallid before it sped away faster than Dallid's sight could catch.

So Dallid was left there, standing victorious and never feeling so weak. He had hurt the beast, cut off a piece of its arm and its neck, but it simple grew new flesh and escaped. How was he ever to kill the thing? How was he even going to fight it if it was able to escape with flight of such speed?

Taking a better look down at his own hands, Dallid felt the stinging pain in them for the first time. They were raw and blistered with weeping sores. Gently he brought his left hand up to feel his face. The same puckered, ruined skin greeted his touch, and he wondered if it would heal. He was Fireborn after all. But fire should not be able to burn him.

The great general Rhisean had a body covered in burn scars, his eyes were even melted white and it was said he could see only heat. But that had been a result of Connecting with too much fire for his body to handle and his Powerborn healing had never been able to restore his appearance. But was this really something Dallid should be spending time thinking about? How he looked?

Looking down at the elder wife he saw that she had not risen from where she was thrown. With her husband leaning over her helplessly and other survivors gathering, Dallid knew he was being foolish. It did not matter if demon-fire burned him differently to real fire. He was still alive and relatively unharmed. The same did not look to be true for the woman lying on the earth.

Her husband looked up at Dallid then but immediately dropped his gaze back down to the ground. All of the others dropped to their knees too. It was madness that they would act in such a way moments after experiencing such an event. Dallid stood speechless. The elder crouching over his wife tried to say something then but could not find the words for some time. Eventually he said,

'My lord, forgive me... my wife...' He broke down into tears.

It was said that Powerborn could heal. That they could release their power into a fleshborn and give their body a moment of perfect strength that healed broken flesh. Looking down at the unmoving body of the man's wife, Dallid did not know what to do.

If he tried some ritual it could end up burning all the skin off the woman and killing her, or she could end up with boiling blood like the poor youth that still lay by the barn. So he just looked down on the man, weeping over the woman that he loved, and Dallid did nothing.

'Jher.' The woman spoke softly and the man cried louder with disbelief. 'Jher, are you unhurt?'

The man rubbed his bruised neck but shook his head. 'I am unhurt, Glosia. The Lord Fireborn saved us.'

Dallid shifted uncomfortably and saw some blood pooling beneath the woman's head. She must have hit it when thrown to the ground, and the black and red marks around her throat looked much worse than her husband's. Still the woman's eyes were open and she spoke with strength, she spoke to Dallid but still did not meet his eyes.

'Thank you, my lord. May Frehep reward you for your deeds.'

It was too much. 'I did not save you, you saved yourself. If you had not stabbed him then I would not have made it to him in time.'

'You honour us, lord, too greatly, you are the glory of Frehep made flesh and you have saved our lives and our farm.'

The farm was in ruins and an elder thanked him for it. It was not right. Dallid hoped the blood he could see around the woman was just a scalp wound. If he were a real Fireborn then he could make sure she would live, but he was not. Looking over to the dead Fureath'i he had already let die, Dallid had no choice but to turn and leave. He could not look at the dead he was unable to save. He could not look at the fawning elders who thanked him for his same useless efforts.

Not long ago they both would have treated him like the youth he still was, and now they grovelled and wept at his power. Growing up in a village so close to Lord Chrial'thau as towerguard, people would sometimes drop knee and pray at the mention of the Fireborn's name. Dallid was often among them.

And now I have chopped Chrial'thau apart with my sabre and stand above kneeling elders praising my glory.

He shook his head at all the deaths he had not been able to prevent and wondered why Frehep had not gifted Yiran with the Fireborn power, or anyone else. They could only do better than Dallid had done. He looked back at the kneeling Fureath'i and saw that Glosia, the elder wife, was sitting up with the help of a young woman. Dallid was glad to see that she looked strong. Her husband was still weeping in gratitude of her life.

It was a warming picture. That a man and wife's love could survive life in the army to retire on a farm, with perhaps grandchildren waiting for them to raise. Dallid and Phira would not have any grandchildren, or perhaps even a future together, but it was good dream.

Looking in the direction the demon had fled, Dallid searched to judge how far it had gone already. The way the demon could fly, it might be hard to catch up on the beast again. He could feel it already far distant, but in his search northward Dallid came across another feeling of Connection, much larger than the feeling of the demon. It could not have possibly been another Fireborn, although the idea was welcome. The power was too great and he remembered then how far north he had already come.

He would soon be at the Temple of Dawn.

CHAPTER TWENTY THREE

Temple of Dawn

It was approaching dusk when Dallid finally saw the temple. He had been feeling it strongly ever since he left the farm. As well as bringing him a strange sense of comfort, the vivid Connection Dallid had found with the temple had created the illusion that it was much closer. Always he had been certain he would see it as he crested a hill, or cleared a copse of trees, and always it had been nowhere in sight. Dallid came to a stop from his run when it finally did arrive in view, just to make sure his mind was not tricking him.

The entire structure sang to him as much as the sun did, and it burned so brightly in his head that the feeling of Chrial'thau was forgotten. It was difficult, but if he concentrated, he could locate Chrial'thau miles north of the temple. He wondered if the place of power would be an appealing target for the beast. The fiery towers that stood above the temple definitely called out to Dallid, hypnotising him in a strange trance.

He had run for two days after leaving the farm. Ignoring the fact he had not eaten, did not tire, and that the blisters on his hands were already healing, Dallid marvelled at the land. On the second day the forest had begun to thin, and the land became rolling hills and uncultivated terrain. It had been odd for Dallid to see. His experience in the army had only brought him to the forests of the east and to Rath'Nor in the mountains.

The Keren pass connecting the east to the Fureath'i capital was too far south to have land like he was seeing. So for his years he had only three pictures of Furea: The hot, wet forests of his birth; the unforgiving mountains to the west; and the merciless deserts on the other side. All three territories were created by power, both by Frehep's protection and by the Powerborn's constant Connection with the land that they walked. So it was sobering to see that natural landscape existed in Furea, if only when getting close to the borders.

And it was cold.

Dallid did not think Fireborn could feel cold from his earlier experiences, so he amazed to think what fleshborns were feeling. Beyond the temple and the great river that it bridged, lay a scattering of border forts, and beyond those lay the wildlands and other Foreign kingdoms like Surlas and the Mordec Empire. If it was cold in Furea, it must have been freezing in the other nations.

Pulling his eyes away from the north, Dallid managed to look west instead, and could make out the Fire Wall mountain range. It pushed proudly out beyond the northern border, and even pierced into Surlas like a Fureath'i sabre. The Keren pass back south was the closest way to get through to Rath'Nor from the east without leaving Furea, and the fortress itself was actually built into another pass facing north. The mountain range was a natural border for their only city, a fortress that could never be taken with the mountains protecting its east and west, and the desert guarding the south.

Bringing his mind back to the present, Dallid tried to place Chrial'thau on the map he was creating in his mind. It was possible the beast was attacking the border forts. With fortune the demon had left Furea though. Hoping the Temple of Dawn would house actual maps, Dallid broke back into his sprint and raced forward. His speed had improved dramatically since placing foot on clear ground and out of the forests, and without boasting, Dallid reckoned he could outrun any number of the fastest horses in the land. The speed at which he travelled through the lands of Furea should not be possible. Only a few days past he had been at the Tower of Frehep and now he was already at the Temple of Dawn, on the banks of the great River Midanna.

If Dallid had not chosen to head toward the temple, then perhaps the great River Midanna would have stopped his journey short. Even growing up near a lake, Dallid had never been skilled at swimming, nor was he eager to better himself toward it. He might have well been the first Fireborn ever to die by drowning if he had attempted to cross the river at another point. Fireborn did not need to breath but he would have found a way to drown, he was sure.

As the only crossing for many miles the temple had originally been built as a rallying point for the border forts should an enemy army try to invade. In the years since, with no nation foolish enough to attack them, the temple had changed from a place of war to a place of peace, and attracted Scholars instead of warriors. At least it attracted Powerborn also, and looking once more up at the burning fires, Dallid knew why.

The structure was built in a triangular fashion. It had a great tower at each of the three edges, overshadowing the rest of the temple, with part of it branching off in a curve to join in the centre. That became the top of the central building then, and thick stone walls joined each base of the towers to complete the structure. Dallid could only really focus on one aspect of the temple though, and they were what sat atop those towers.

The brightest flames he had ever seen burned there. Three separate flames but all burning close together at the apex of the building. Each one represented the three different kingdoms of Furea, back before they were united, and they were never extinguished. That in itself represented greater philosophy to a Fureath'i, breaking his life into three: youth, maturity and retirement. The fires did not go out, the same as the fire in the heart of a Fureath'i never went out. *A Life of Fire*, was the name Scholar's gave it, but it meant more than any words could explain. The priests and Scholars spent their lives considering the infinite meanings that the circle of betterment could provide.

His legs had already crossed the distance down to them and Dallid arrived at the gates. The Temple of Dawn loomed in front of him and he was no closer to sensing if other Flameborns or Fireborns were inside. All he could feel or even think of was the intensity of the three flaming towers. It was beyond distracting. How could Powerborn be expected to think when such explosions of power burned so fervently above them? What manner of magic even fuelled them? Dallid began to change his idea this place would attract Powerborn warriors, more likely it would repel them.

Had Rhisean truly tried to Connect with one of those fires? The Tellings of how the scarred Fireborn had melted his face and skin often differed, but Dallid wondered if that one might be true.

The large gates opened up before Dallid tried to bang on them, and he did not even register spying the sentries that must have seen him. If Chrial'thau did choose that moment to double back and launch an assault, Dallid would be too distracted to notice. Four Fureath'i warriors, wrapped in woollen clothing instead of the standard garb, pulled back the gates and a Priest of Frehep stood in his own thickly warm robes to greet Dallid. Frowning at the strangely dressed Fureath'i, Dallid spared one last look up at the towers, and stepped under the walls into the Temple of Dawn.

His Connection vanished. Turning around suddenly, suspecting treachery or attack, the only thing stopping Dallid from running back out of the temple was the gentle smile that the priest gave.

'It was engrained into the stones of the temple to shield those within from the fury above,' the priest's grin widened. 'You were expecting it, my lord, were you not?'

Dallid gaped at the man, not having the slightest idea what he was talking about.

His mouth dropped further as the four warriors dropped to their knees and pressed heads against the stone floor. For some reason seeing other warriors bow before him was worse than seeing elders do it. The priest thankfully did not bow. Dallid had no idea why not, but he was greatly relieved that someone would look him in the eye.

'My lord,' he said respectfully. 'I apologise if I have caused offence.'

'What manner of magic are those towers?' Dallid asked. He did not know if he was more confused at the towers or at the feeling of loss when his Connection to them disappeared. He could sense Chrial'thau again much clearer now, and he still felt the same ready explosion of power beneath his skin. So whatever blocked his Connection, it was something specific to the towers. Still, of all the questions he needed answers, it was the least important and the most useless, and yet he asked it first.

'Apologies, my lord, my experience with Lord Fireborns has been limited, but those few that have visited have been well versed on our temple's history. I should not have made such a presumption.'

Was the man apologising or was he mocking him? Dallid always tried to like every man, regardless if they were Scholars or priests, so he thought the best and bowed his head to accept the contrition. Perhaps it was just his low opinion of himself, but he always prided himself on seeing the best in people, unlike any of the friends he grew up with. Thisian only saw people as someone to rut or someone in the way of him rutting, Phira saw people as things she could use to her advantage, and whether or not Dallid liked to admit it, Kris did sometimes act like he saw people as just things that he had to stop himself from killing.

They were all low thoughts and ones not worthy of a friend, so Dallid banished it and brought his focus back to the priest. The first of his problems came to him this time so he asked a sensible question.

'Are there other Powerborn here now?'

The priest spread his hands, palms up in greeting, but out wide in apology. 'There are not. The Lord Kr'une had been here a few weeks past, he stayed for some time.'

Being married to Phira, Dallid had heard her speak of every warrior of greatness in detail, and every Flameborn and Fireborn in even more. Most of it disappeared the moment it hit his ears, but the name Kr'une stood out to him. He was a Flameborn Dallid thought, and there was something different about him.

'What was his purpose in staying here so long?'

'I would not presume to know the mind of a lord of power.' He eyed Dallid for a moment and then decided to continue. 'But if I were to guess then I would say that his heart was empty from spending so much time in the Foreign lands.'

That was why Dallid knew him. He was perhaps one of only a few Fureath'i that regularly spent time outside of Furea, Yiran and Phira being the next two that came to mind. The Flameborn Kr'une patrolled outside the border forts, reporting in and between each fort regularly, as well as rounding up troupes whenever he thought a group of bandits needed convincing to stay further away from Furea's border.

'And what, may I ask, has brought you to our holy temple, my lord?'

Dallid looked at the man in surprise, he had forgotten the priest was there and he did not even have the distraction of the towers to blame for it. He may be Fireborn, but had not been born without respect.

'I apologise for my manner, I have yet to ask you your name and for permission to enter your temple. I am Dallid,' he hesitated before adding, 'Fireborn. The sun god sees you, Priest of Frehep.'

The priest bowed in respect. 'May he look upon one worthy of his service. I am Sindel, and a Lord Fireborn needs no permission to enter anywhere, he is lord of all he sees.'

Dallid stood awkwardly then, the priest standing silent. A real Fireborn would have given command of what his purpose was, and what he required of the priests to assist in it. Instead he looked down at the warriors all kneeling, each one older than him, and more than likely had killed more Prae'surlas than him.

'Please, tell the warriors they can rise. I have come here because I chase an enemy and because I have questions.'

'Has an enemy gotten past our borders, my lord?' The priest frowned. The temple would also be a rallying point for enemies to sack and search for gold if they did ever make it into Furea.

'No, not exactly.' Dallid did not know how much to Tell, he would not lie, but he would not cause panic in his lands. 'Just one demon, and I have already injured it, it will not be long before I kill it.'

He hoped he sounded more confident that he felt but it did not seem to make the priest feel any better. 'A creature of darkness in our world of light is bad enough, but in Furea? Along with this cold, it is but one of many things to worry about. Come, there is a man here that may be of some use. He has battled demons before.'

Dallid was not sure who the priest could mean if there were no other Powerborn at the temple. Unless it was actually Protharik, but he was Powerborn in all but name. A man that could summon, control or kill demons, and could not die, was someone Dallid certainly considered Powerborn, and he was certainly someone who might help him with Chrial'thau. One Telling he had heard told that it took over twenty attempts to kill some giant winged demon before Protharik won. Which meant of course that the battle ground between the two was littered with over twenty identical Protharik corpses, same clothing, same weapons, each one a perfect mirror image. To Dallid it seemed like all Protharik *could* do was die.

Returning from his thoughts, he was pleased that when they began walking, the warriors were able to rise and close the gates behind them. Sindel led him down dark corridors and through wide chambers, all lit by the sparsest of torches. It seemed odd that a temple of the sun had such little light. There were not even windows to allow natural sun inside. The priest was silent as they travelled and Dallid did not want to disturb it. Answers to his questions or satisfaction in his quests were the things that would fully bring him peace, but there was an air in the temple that allowed him traces of what it would feel like.

All he could see apart from closed doors, were empty rooms, and where there was not a warrior patrolling, there was a priest studying. It was all so serene but Dallid knew that the warriors could not have enjoyed such a place. Even Thisian would long for some action if he was posted here, and Thisian was the laziest Fureath'i in the history of Furea. Every warrior had to spend some time in each of the nation's roles however, apart from the select few who proved themselves worthy of promotion, so Dallid hoped that the warriors time spent on duty in the temple would be short.

It was one of the closed doors that Sindel finally brought them to, and knocked before entering. A deep voice answered for them to proceed inside. The man within stood up from his seat and put down the book he had been reading. He smiled a greeting to them both and turned his palm in welcome, but he was not Fureath'i. His skin was as dark as night, and he wore strange clothes of fabrics Dallid was not familiar with. His trousers were baggy and hung out over his boots, and the shirt he wore only covered one arm, with a length of it hanging down above his belt on the other side. It nearly touched his boot on the other. Everything about him was severely Foreign.

'Let me introduce Lord Dallid Fireborn,' Sindel said, turning back to Dallid then. 'My lord, this is Dagen, Captain Defender of Kel Sherah.'

Dagen dropped to one knee and bowed his head in reverence to Dallid's rank, but Dallid himself did not know enough of Dagen's title to guess how to act. He settled for a slight nod of his head, and Dagen's eyebrows lifted at the act. Was it surprise or insult? Dallid did not know and wished he had paid more attention all those times

Phira had tried to lecture him. But at the time, it had seemed as if no one would ever need to know half of the extensive knowledge she had been mouthing on about.

'Lord Fireborn, I am both honoured by, and undeserving, of your respect.' Dagen smiled meekly but still met his eyes. Whatever way the Kel Sherans treated their own Powerborn, it was either not with the same worship that Fureath'i did, or else Dagen's rank did not deem it necessary.

When Dallid said nothing back, Sindel rubbed his hands together anxiously. 'Shall we take meal together and perhaps then Dagen may be able to answer your questions about the demon you pursue.'

'There is a demon in this land?' Dagen's friendly nature changed swiftly. Dallid had always regarded Kel Sherans as weak and cowards, but the Defenders were said to be among the most highly skilled warriors in the world.

'There is.'

'Do you know what kind?'

Dallid hesitated. 'It is a demon of black fire, wearing the face of a Fureath'i.'

'I fear I have never heard of such a demon.'

'I do not think its kind has ever existed before. It was *created*.' Dallid was not sure how much he should say to a Foreigner and a priest, but whatever help they could provide might benefit his mission. 'An Iceborn named Aerath, somehow poisoned a Fireborn with the blood of an Attro'phass demon. The resulting abomination is what I now hunt.'

'A Lord Fireborn? What is their name?' Sindel was shocked but spoke with calm, not panic. Perhaps he could swear the priest to secrecy using his rank as Fireborn. Although, if Dallid was not to journey to Rath'Nor as he first planned, then the temple might be able to deliver the grim news. Sindel would have ravens or they would have riders that could reach the nearest border fort. Dallid was not sure about Dagen however. He was a Foreigner, who had no business knowing of Fureath'i hardship. But he had come for answers, and for those he would need to explain his questions.

'Very well then,' Dallid started with some hesitation, but built in confidence as he went on to explain. He began with the Prae'surlas raiding parties in the lands surrounding the Tower of Frehep. Then he went onto to the deaths of his squad and of Yiran the Unconquered. The death of Chrial'thau brought frenzied distress to the priest, but Dallid did not stop until he detailed everything including his fight with the demon at the farm. The silence that followed his words felt heavy upon them, but Dallid could still feel lighter for having told someone of his experience. At least now if he were to die fighting either Chrial'thau or Aerath, then the tale would not go untold.

'Each of your words are sharp in their Telling, Dallid Fireborn.' Dagen spoke slowly, the Fureath'i language sounding long and drawn out upon his tongue. 'But to my heart, the death of Yiran strikes most painfully. He is the reason I am in your lands, to visit with my old friend, and now I find that it can never again be.'

'There is so much in what you have said, ah, Dallid...' Sindel stumbled over using the proper honorary. 'I apologise. It does not matter how you came to hold the blood of the gods within you, all that matters is that you do. Lord Fireborn forgive me. There is much I would still ask. The news you bring of Chrial'thau is crushing to my Fureath'i heart. And yet...' he paused and looked both Dallid and Dagen squarely before continuing. 'My worship of Frehep allows me some, slight, pyromancy. And several days ago I was granted a vision of Chrial'thau battling the Iceborn Aerath. I thought it but a dream of fancy, detailing the famous combat where he humbled the fiend outside of Dowrathel. And then, last night I was granted another, vision it must be, for this one gave me sight of Lady Jaiha the divine Decider of Fates, the very Lady who directed me towards my path of priesthood and worship. As much of a blessing her image had been, I was shaken to find it also a vision of her death. The green-eyed Attro'phass you described fits well my own dream, Lord Dallid. But why would Frehep show me these things? What can I do? Unless I was meant to meet with you this day? There are so many questions.'

Dallid laughed helplessly. 'And I do not have the answers, Sindel. I came here hoping to find wisdom to my own questions.' Dallid knew how the priest felt, but he had already Told of everything he knew. Perhaps some things were not meant to be fully understood, not by fleshborn or Powerborn, or anyone other than the gods. Dagen's voice, as oddly deep and slow as it was, did not hold the same defeat.

'Let us answer these questions together then, using what knowledge we have all three.' Dagen gestured to Dallid. 'Speak of your first concerns and we shall see where our discussion will grow. In Kel Sherah, reason is the highest skill any citizen or defender can hold. With it we can defeat any circumstance or opponent. Begin, please.'

'A moment.' Sindel walked to the chamber door and craned his neck outside. After looking both ways he disappeared from view but returned soon after. 'Apologies, I have asked one of my brothers to bring some food while we converse. Let us sit.'

He gestured to a cushioned chair and Dallid looked at it with scepticism. He had never seen anything so soft. Approaching it as if it were a wounded Prae'surlas, Dallid placed a cautious hand down on the fabrics. When he eased his weight on the cushions, the soft comfort made Dallid quite uncomfortable. So instead of resting back into it, he leaned forward, his arms resting on his own knees.

Dagen and Sindel were watching him without expression, each sitting back leisurely into the extravagant chairs without trouble. Dallid cleared his throat.

'I have several pressing questions, much as you, Sindel, and I do not know which one to address first. How is it that this power came to me? How did the Prae'surlas get past the border forts and so deep into Furea and why did Aerath do this? Why does the Attro'phass demon do this? If it is true it has killed the Lady Jaiha…, but it was Aerath who had weakened Chrial'thau and then poisoned him with demon blood. I know we cannot conceive what evil swills within the mind of a Prae'surlas, but there had to be a reason he was in Furea to begin with, other than murder and destruction. And I am even unsure of what way I can kill either Aerath, or the beast he has created, when I have yet to perform even the simplest of rituals. I do not even know why I am so driven to try. It would make more sense for me to report immediately back to Rath'Nor but for some reason I cannot. Is it my new power that drives me? You say you know of magic with fire, Sindel, are you able to teach me? Have you a means to send word to Rath'Nor to warn Lord Miral'thau about Jaiha and Chrial'thau?'

'To your last request, of course I will have ravens sent without delay, but to your first I fear you give more worth to my own humble powers than they deserve. It is heard of in priests but not common, and even so the magic we touch is not a hundredth part of the power the weakest Lord Flameborn has. It is not widely spoken among Fureath'i, partly because there is not much of which to speak, but privately what little pyromancy we can claim brings more pride than use. Manipulation of a flame, but never creation, and the visions I will admit are most likely due to our touching the power of one truly Connected, like a Lord Fireborn, instead of touching the source of power Frehep provides.' He must have seen the hope in Dallid's face disappear that he could have a teacher, if even for a night, anything to gain advantage in the battles he must face. The priest tried to smile positively. 'But if we cannot help with that problem, we will do our best for your others. Reasoning out answers is a skill at which our friend Dagen here is quite adept.'

Dagen smiled humbly but shook his head. 'As you would compare your power to the hundredth part of a Lord Flameborn, let me compare my untrained mind to that of the lowest of Scholars within my land. I am simply a Defender against the Jhakral, but I will help as best I can. Tell me, Sindel, what are the ways Fureath'i Powerborn can come to hold power?'

'It is the same as your land, Dagen, they are born to it.'

'Do they not Transfer?'

Sindel laughed. 'Our Powerborn are warriors, Dagen, they do not die in their beds. It is not unheard of that one dying in battle may Transfer their power to another. But if Lord Chrial'thau Transferred his power to Lord Dallid, then how does the demon still have a Connection with fire? If it is purely a demonic magic then Dallid could not join with it, and also I think the poison of the demon's blood would have spread to young Lord Dallid in the act.'

Dallid felt a flash of worry at the mention of the poison. Was that why it thought they were both the same? Was that why his mind gave him thoughts that felt like they were not his?

'Perhaps you are right,' Dagen said. 'Tell me then of the Tower of Frehep. I admit during my friendship with Yiran, I have always wished to see the tower of his home. It seems I have left it too late.'

To Dallid's eyes he could see the smallest traces of emotion behind Dagen's own. He did not think he could have seen them without his empowered eyesight however, nor did he think the dark skinned man would let tears fall. He seemed impressively strong and Dallid was gaining some confidence from the man's calm reasoning.

'The Tower of Frehep is a holder of ancient artefacts and religious items that hold worth to us because of their history, not their power. If any of them had been found to hold power, then they would have been transferred to the Temple of Zenith.'

Dagen nodded. 'I know well that it is a landmark of history, the story of the first guardian is one that fascinates me. It seems strange it was so strongly guarded and yet contained nothing of value, does it not? Perhaps, as you say, since the Fureath'i are in the majority warriors, something could have been overlooked.'

'You may be right.' Sindel frowned, 'But it was priests and other Scholars like myself that examined the tower when first Holy Frehep conquered it.'

'And the Fireborn Frehep chose that same location to ascent into godhood, did he not?'

'Yes. It was the place of his great reckoning. During his battles to secure Furea as one nation of brotherhood and power, he had come into contact with Foreign gods and how they behaved. His battles with Brijnok alone account for several Tellings, but he is said to have clashed with Di Thorel, Am'bril, Rhyserias, Aerune, Creedus, Hesiot, all of them. So when he was ready to ascend to the fullest height of power and become our god, he made his proclamation that he would never again walk the earth; that he would not interfere in the lives of men as did the lesser gods. But with that freedom came his price and so he would not rule us, and he would not protect us from anyone but the other gods. He did not want his people to grow weak with reliance upon him against Foreign enemies, so instead said that he would leave his power for us all to use in ourselves.'

'And did he leave this power in the Tower of Frehep as he died?'

Both Dallid and Sindel looked to each other with a smile. It was the priest who spoke though, Dallid was content to listen.

'You misunderstand, Dagen, the power he left for us is in each of our hearts. Every Fureath'i burns with the blood of Frehep, not just Powerborn.'

'And before Frehep died, were the Fureath'i not warriors?'

'Of course they were but they warred with each other, clan against clan, lord against lord. Frehep's power was uniting us all with his final gift, that all of us held a part of his power. That we all burn as brothers in the Fureath'i Life of Fire.'

Dagen paused then, choosing his words carefully. 'I do not wish to cast doubt upon your beliefs, Sindel, nor do I doubt the unity of brotherhood that the Fureath'i share. All I am thinking is that Frehep had already united the Fureath'i before he died. He did not necessarily need to unite you further in his death. Perhaps what he meant was that he would leave his actual power, rather than his notional power. Perhaps he knew of a way to leave it in the Tower of Frehep, and when his people's need came, his power would be returned.'

All three ran the idea through their heads, trying to come to terms with such a notion. Dallid did not like it in the least. He had already felt unworthy of holding Chrial'thau's power in his veins. That he might hold Frehep's was out of the question.

'But how would this be his people's need?' Dallid asked. 'It would have made better sense had the power gone to Yiran, or even Lord Chrial'thau. Not me. I know what Aerath did was unspeakable, believe me I burn at the thought of it, and I know that two of our nation's most beloved champions have been slain, but I do not think that it is a time of our greatest need.'

'I agree,' Sindel said. 'It has never been known that the power of a Fireborn could be stored like that. Even the fires of this temple are just a self-powering ritual. It could not be used to enter a person. As for our greatest need, when the eight Kings hear of this, it may well result in a full scale war against the Prae'surlas, Lord Dallid. Even the death of Aerath would not stop it.'

'Was that why Aerath did this do you think? To start a war between our two countries?' Dallid knew Phira had devised some plan with Yiran on how Furea could outright win such a war, but everyone else believed that a full war would cripple both countries no matter who won. Foreign armies would take advantage like the last time, and Fureath'i troupes would have to pull out of Surlas to defend.

'It is possible Aerath would wish such a thing,' Dagen said carefully. 'From what I know of the Iceborn he is claiming to be Aerune reborn.' Dagen stopped and looked at Dallid then before continuing. 'If Surlas were under threat of war from Furea he might be able to consolidate his rule as god and protector. But would he need to? Let us not forget that he has already made King Rohlan kneel to him and has banished their great champion Frind'aal. But I have another thought. Dallid Fireborn, you have told us that Aerath took with him a stone segment from the tower?'

'Yes, I think so.' Dallid found it hard to remember everything about that battle, he had been so badly injured. It was difficult to recall specifics. The stone segment did seem strange at the time though. 'I remember him speaking to Chrial'thau about it. He said it would bring destruction.'

'Sindel does your temple have records of what items lay protected in the tower? It is my belief that the first guardian, and every Fireborn that followed, were indeed protecting something of extreme power.'

'We would have scrolls of inventory, yes, but it would take time to retrieve them from the library. I do not know what help they will be. I as well as every other priest have examined those scrolls in my studies. The segment that Lord Dallid speaks of is a broken piece of stone, the only reason it was not thrown away were the ancient runes carved into it. Perhaps the full piece might have been powerful in the past, but not a broken shard.'

'You have a Scholar named Nureail do you not?' Dallid was surprised by Dagen's knowledge of Nureail.

'We do,' Sindel said, 'and although she is more Teller than Scholar, the Lady Nureail does have indispensable talents.'

'And did she use her talents on the items in the tower?'

Sindel shook his head. 'Perhaps Lord Chrial'thau would have allowed her had she requested since his return as towerguard, but her Foreign blood, if you will excuse the term, is not met well by every Fureath'i. Even our lords of power may sometimes become too formal in their allowances. To my knowledge she has attempted to examine those items but has been refused.'

If Dagen was offended by how the Fureath'i treated Foreigners, even ones they considered lords, he did not show it. Instead he continued. 'This is unfortunate, my friend, because I fear that she is the only way to determine the true worth of items of power. Even in my own country, a land filled with academics and learning, we cannot know the true history of the items we find. We know of Lady Nureail because we have tried to purchase her services in the past but in these instances *she* was the one to refuse.'

'So you think the item Aerath took, could be the item Frehep used to store his power? I thought you said it had been given to Lord Dallid. What use then would it be to Aerath?'

Dagen sighed, breathing out loudly through his nose. 'The things I suggest are only that, suggestions. We speak of possibilities to help lift the darkness of ignorance from our eyes and mind. What Dallid Fireborn here has described - and I will wait until I have seen the scrolls you possess before confirming my suspicions - may be a Segment of Ahmar. Are you familiar with this?'

Dallid's eyebrows went up and Sindel's eyebrows went down, but both shook their heads.

'It is a tale of specific interest only to some,' Dagen started, 'And not one well liked in Kel Sherah, or Furea either it seems, but there are those in other lands that continue to hunt for them. It is a tale of such power that it will always find willing ears to hear it but it is more a myth than legend at this stage. Tellings, as you call them, claim that a bracelet of limitless power was created near the beginning of the world. Long before our age or even the age before it, when the beginning of power occurred rather than the beginning of the world. Not the recent rebirth that brought to the world Powerborns such as Lord Dallid, but the very start, before the birth of gods and before Brijnok or Moi'dan ruled the world, there was a more ancient world, filled with power. It was not divided as ours is: where only some are born with power and some are not, and the complete antithesis to our last age when none had power at all. This time in history they deduced that every living creature was born with it.

'The most ancient of those creatures created this bracelet to control her own power, some of the scrolls have named her Fearie. But a thief, whose name I have never discovered, stole the bracelet and was destroyed by Fearie's son. Where the creature herself had power of pure creation, the son held the power of pure destruction. It was why she created him after all, to bring destruction to the bracelet, to stop the thief from using it. So after destroying the stone bracelet, to ensure no one ever tried to reassemble it, the son placed a further curse on the segments. As long as they remained hidden and not held, they would be dormant, but as soon as they were searched for and removed, then the curse would awaken and destruction would reign down upon the holder.'

Dagen eyed Dallid for a moment before speaking again. 'You say that Aerath removed the segment before you received your powers? Then perhaps you are part of the curse of destruction, created to hunt down and destroy Aerath for removing the piece.'

'I do not like that idea any better than the others you have suggested, Dagen,' Dallid said with a frown. 'But tell me, how many of these segments are there? The Attro'phass demon said something about bringing destruction also, to the Fireborns in our country.'

'There are only three, Dallid Fireborn, and I believe the Attro'phass demon appearing at the same time was unfortunate co-incidence. It could be part of the curse, but the only being I have known able to control an Attro'phass was Moi'dan and his Demon Mask. Although, if that piece was truly a Segment of Ahmar, and if Chrial'thau Fireborn or anyone else had moved it or held it for any reason, then Aerath, the demon and the rest of the Prae'surlas could all have been part of the curse of destruction brought down.'

'I must admit,' Dagen said with an embarrassed smile, 'this is an area of interest to me. I believe that the warrior, who Frehep and Chrial'thau fought in the tower as the first guardian, was in fact the son of the creature Fearie. It would then stand to reason that the piece Aerath took was in fact a Segment of Ahmar, and that is why he attacked your village. He seeks to link all three and perhaps become a true god to realise his current claims.'

That still did not answer how Aerath had gotten there in the first place, or really how Dallid received his powers. He did not like the idea of being part of a curse, or that Chrial'thau Transferred to him, or especially that he might be Frehep's power reborn. The food arrived then and Dallid had no appetite for it. It only reminded him of his Powerborn status, and that he did not need food or rest, nor did he have time for it. He stood up.

'I am thankful for your insights but I feel I have spent too much time here. If I cannot learn to control my powers in this place, then I should continue my pursuit of the demon. With fortune I will slay it with a sabre instead of fire and then seek out Aerath. If I am to be his destruction as you say, then I wish I knew how I could do such a thing. But all I know is I cannot stop until it's done.'

'You leave so soon? But it is night and we have so much to discuss,' Dagen said with clear disappointment. 'You said you feel the demon in your mind, has it gone far?'

'It has, but at least while it moves I know it is not hurting anyone. I think the beast is heading for Surlas. It wants to kill Aerath as much as I do.'

'Into Surlas,' Dagen said with a nod. 'That is good, is it not? The ice prison of Lae Noan is a place that fascinates me almost as much as the Tower of Frehep, but it is the place where Aerath is most likely to be found. If I were you, I would chase the demon there and while they do battle, seize advantage and strike first at Aerath as I believe he is the more powerful foe.'

'There is little honour in that,' Sindel said. They were all standing now, the other men anxious that Dallid not leave. 'I would recommend you chase the beast out of our lands and let it be killed by Foreigners. You should report to Rath'Nor, Lord Dallid, only there can you receive the training you need to defeat an Iceborn. Perhaps if you gather more Lords Fireborn, you can enter Surlas together and kill Aerath easily, possibly even preventing the war.'

Dallid looked to be considering both of their advice, and even considering that he might stay and run further circles of words and ideas with them. But even as a fleshborn he would have become restless from doing nothing but talk and think. As a Fireborn he nearly shook with energy and the need for action. Aerath and the demon in his mind needed to be killed. He did not have the planning or the ability to do such a thing and he could not explain why he did not take Sindel's advice. It was the most logical plan of action to succeed in his quest, but he could not go any other direction than north.

'Sindel, has your temple a map I can borrow?' Dallid asked finally. 'I will continue to follow the demon north towards Aerath, but I will try to avoid any Prae'surlas cities if I can.'

Both men nodded seeing that Dallid had set his mind, and Sindel left to find him a map. When they were alone Dallid turned to Dagen and said, 'I think I will take your advice Dagen and try to kill Aerath while he is fighting Chrial'thau.' It would not mean he was fighting Aerath *with* Chrial'thau though. 'Do not tell the priest, as I do not wish to dishonour my name, but if I am to have any chance of cutting off Aerath's head, I do not think it can be done by honourable combat.'

'There is no honour or dishonour when it comes to survival, Dallid Fireborn.'

Dallid was not sure he agreed with that, but could see how the Kel Sherans would tell themselves that when they hid from the world from fear of living in it.

'Regardless of whether that is true, Dagen, or whether your theories are right, I will prove myself worthy of this new power or I will die because I am not. Either way I believe I will have the answer that I am seeking the most.'

When Sindel returned Dallid said his farewells to the priest and the Kel Sheran Defender, storing his map in a travel pouch the priest also provided. Dallid then made an odd request and asked if he could have a coin with Blaze Commander Phira on it. Sindel dutifully went to the temple's coin vaults and returned with a selection of different kings, generals and blaze commanders to choose from. Dallid smiled at how odd his request must have sounded but he took a gold coin with Phira's image on it and felt complete again.

Dallid wondered dryly how long before the coin would melt and before both the map and the pouch were burnt to ash but kept his thoughts to himself as he left the temple.

When he stepped out from underneath the walls again, the fires from the towers crashed down on top of him. They felt like someone was roaring into his ears but in a way that was exhilarating. He needed to get as far as he could from the distraction of such power. Dallid wondered how Frehep would react to one of his lords shying away from fire. The thought made Dallid laugh and he felt his spirits rise slightly from his time within the temple.

Then, as the gates closed behind Dallid, a being of fire suddenly appeared outside the Temple of Dawn. Dallid froze in mid step at the apparition and before he could move, the spectre of flames rushed forward and consumed him.

CHAPTER TWENTY FOUR

Gods

Noise bombarded Dallid from all sides. He felt a thousand bodies press themselves against him. The sensations kept moving, making his head swim, and the sudden thought that he was underwater made him immediately draw breath with panic. It did not feel like water entering his lungs but it was definitely not air. The pressure began to lesson against his skin. Sound drifted away from him. Calm spread out along his body, and it was only then that Dallid opened his eyes.

A being of fire stood in front of him. Taking a step back, Dallid looked around to get his bearings and was greeted with a distorted wilderness of shadow and colour. All around him the air waved with shades of shifting brown and purple. Clouds of shadow drifted to further obscure what little vision he could gather. It seemed he could see empty landscape for miles, and yet had difficultly seeing right in front of his eyes. Dallid returned back to the spectre of fire. This was the thing he had seen in the flames, the thing that had given him a scar that his Fireborn healing did not touch. It had no sword now. It did not even move. It just stood there in the shape of a man but without any substance to make it real. The flames flowed around its shape, flicking out at the air every now and again. The fire stretched out towards Dallid.

The idea that the fire was drawing towards him, made Dallid step back further again and when he did so, the being began to change. The healthy red fire started to darken, and took on the same browns and purples of the land that surrounded them. The strange spectre looked down at this change and carefully moved closer to Dallid again.

It did not move in a threatening way, and even held out its arms to try and calm its approach. Dallid held his ground as the being came forward. The hale red of pure fire grew anew, brighter with every step that it took. When it stopped, it seemed to Dallid that the thing was just looking at him, even though it had no eyes. Then it spoke somehow, even with no mouth.

Disjointed words entered painfully into Dallid's head, some that he understood but made no sense and others that did not sound like any language he had ever heard. Phira was fluent in quite a number of languages and he believed he had heard her practicing enough to recognise them, but still the strange being made no sense.

'Where am I?' Dallid tried, his words making the air move apart as if something unwanted and Foreign passed through them. The being of fire cocked its head trying to understand. When neither one said anything again, the spectre gestured with its hand. It could have been interpreted to come closer, but Dallid thought that it wanted him to keep talking. 'Who are you? Why have you brought me here?' He paused for a nervous moment before asking, 'Are you... Holy Frehep?'

The thing did look like Frehep might, but how could he know? The being had its head still cocked to the side, slowly going lower and lower. Dallid looked around uncomfortably, not sure what to do. If the thing had brought him here, then how was he to escape when he did not know where he was?

'Kill. Brijnok.'

Those words made some sense to Dallid. Brijnok was the Foreign god of battle, but why would anyone think a Fureath'i would be interested in killing him. Not that Dallid could kill a god. A Fireborn was said to have the blood and power of a god made flesh, but that flesh made a significant difference when it came to killing. Were gods not immortals made of pure power? The differences between beings of flesh, beings of power, and beings of both flesh and power, were the day dreams of a Scholar. Dallid was a warrior. No. He was a Fireborn.

'There is only one person that I intend to kill and that is Aerath.'

And Chrial'thau, he added afterwards in his mind. How could he quickly forget the beast? A jumble of words flew into Dallid's mind again: 'Aerath', 'he took him', 'keeps him', 'becomes him', 'Aerune', 'Amadis...'

'You make no sense,' Dallid said in frustration. 'Why have you brought me here? I will not kill Brijnok, even if I could. I have no reason to. My life and power are given to the destruction of Aerath.'

'Kill Brijnok,' the spectre insisted.

'Why do you want Brijnok dead?'

The spectre of fire did not answer. It just stood there and stared at Dallid, its eyeless face a dance of flames. Then the strange world vanished. Sight reappeared as suddenly as it disappeared and revealed a land thick with snow. Breathing in the cold air, to test the reality of what was happening, Dallid looked around at the white capped woods, and the farm house it surrounded. Normally his first thought would have been that they were in Surlas. But if winter covered all the Foreign lands - if he was to believe the tales - then they could be anywhere.

He looked to the spectre of fire next to him and was alarmed to see the thing had changed too. No longer did it burn with pure red flames, it was instead made out of crackling ice. There was still no substance to it. The frost that made up its shape came and went like falling snow. It pulsed with white flowers of ice instead of flowing with fire. At least that meant it was not Frehep that abducted him, but some other strange creature.

Dallid wanted to move away from it, but if the being had meant him harm then it could have done so already. As far as Dallid could tell, the spectre seemed powerful enough to do as it pleased. So what other options were there besides fight it or reason with it? The warrior that Dallid tried to become, constantly battled with the intelligent man that Phira tried to make of him. Both lessons did little to give him confidence in either role. As a compromise Dallid would speak with the thing, but he would do so as a being of fire himself.

He clenched his fists to set them alight but nothing happened. Immediately he reached for his sabre, but that too was gone. Dallid's eyes took on a wild look as he was suddenly defenceless and it seemed he had no other choice than to attack the spectre of ice with his bare hands.

'Not, here,' it said to him, but it was accompanied with a string of other random words, most incomprehensible.

'How are you doing this? Why am I here? Return me to Furea!'

'Kill, Brijnok,' it repeated.

'No!' Dallid roared at the thing, not caring who was around to hear. The spectre of ice did not react though. It just kept looking at Dallid without eyes, keeping perfectly still, while the ice that formed it, kept moving. Finally it pointed down to the farm house and before Dallid knew what was happening they were inside.

'How...' he cut his question short as they were suddenly not alone. The house was filled with Prae'surlas and a Foreign swordsman threatening them. Dallid's hand flew to where his sabre should be again and was only reminded that he had been rendered powerless. Jumping back to gain some room, he prepared himself for unarmed combat against so many opponents. What else could he do?

'Brijnok, warrior,' the spectre of ice said loudly. No one turned at the sudden noise and neither did they turn at their appearance. Dallid looked again at the situation and this time spotted a pair of legs on the floor through a doorway. There had been killing done. Only two of the standing Prae'surlas were male, with five females and three children. He saw that none of the north-men were armed, and were all herded into a corner by the Foreign swordsman. The swordsman had hair that hung down to his jaw, silvered with age at the sides and the man gestured wildly with a black bladed sword. He had his back to Dallid and the ice spectre so that would explain why the Foreigner did not see them. But the Prae'surlas were facing them and they did not appear to see either.

'Can they see us?' Dallid whispered harshly.

'Not, here,' is all the spectre of ice answered.

Gaining slightly more confidence that some kind of magic was keeping them hidden, Dallid only then listened to the words the Foreign swordsman was ranting. He was speaking in Prae'surlas with a thick wildlands accent and everything he said was utter madness.

'... how can you even pretend that the snow is not your fault? I would say something if you at least had the decency to hide it from me, but your entire farm is covered in it! It is clear to anyone that you are growing the bloody snow! What kind of bastards use a farm to grow snow in the middle of an unending winter! I'll tell you what kind: complete and utter bastards! Indecent Prae'surlas whoresons, always getting taller so they can eat the freshest snow -'

The swordsman turned then and looked directly at Dallid and the spectre of ice that stood next to him. For a moment Dallid became caught up in his lunacy and thought that a spectre of ice would merit far more reasonable blame for the winter than the farmers. The madman's eyes drifted away from Dallid though and looked at every other part of the farm house with equal suspicion.

'Bloody ghosts,' he muttered and rounded back on the terrified farmers, 'and that's only another reason to be rid of all this damned snow, inviting bloody ghosts to hide in it!'

'When the true god Aerath has turned the world to ice, spirits will be all that remains of the weak.' One of the male farmers spat on the ground at the swordsman's feet. 'It will be a perfect land where only the purity of Prae'surlas will survive.'

'What did you say?' the swordsman demanded, pointing the tip of his blade in the man's face. Dallid was confounded how one man with one sword could hold so many people twice his size. The Prae'surlas were cowards, and ugly, but they were not that stupid. If they all rushed him then one or two would die but the rest would win out. Even with his sword so committed to one person, none of the others looked as if they would attack. The one who had spoken at least sneered his disgust at the Foreigner. Instead of repeating what he had said, he replied:

'With my last breath I breathe glory to my god.'

The swordsman's blade flicked out, scarcely brushing the north-man's face and yet the seven-foot farmer fell lifeless to the floor. All the others tried to hold back their fear and huddled together for comfort. They tried not to look down on the suddenly deceased man. The insanity of the Foreigner now made sense to Dallid when it was coupled with a sword that could kill with one touch. He was Valhar the Madman, or Valhar the Bastard as he preferred to be called. What was the man doing in Surlas and why was the spectre showing Dallid this?

Valhar laughed at the dead Prae'surlas on the floor. 'What an odd thing to say! Dead people don't breathe.' He pushed his face up closer to the last standing male. 'I'm right aren't I? They don't breathe? Do they?'

Testing his assertion, Valhar crouched down and pressed his ear against the dead man's mouth. It was the ideal opportunity to flee, but with a sword that only needed to tip you once, escape no longer seemed so easy to Dallid. Whoever tried it would be abandoning the children to the madman's brutality. Standing back up, Valhar nodded and smiled at the survivors,

'He was bloody right! He's still breathing something about some bloody Aerath. I know an Iceborn named Aerath you know, I hear he went mad. Everyone in that mountain goes mad. I knew a madman once too, a good friend of mine, Protharik. I know he hates dying, so I decided to show some decency and not kill him. Had to kill him a few times first just to show him I could though. Then I showed how much I could keep him alive. Had to torture him to show him how much I was trying not to kill him too. It might have been the torture that turned him mad. I had them all at the table you see, a full banquet of Prothariks.' Valhar laughed manically at the idea. 'The mad bastard just pretended to be one of the dead ones. Escaped. Or did I kill him? Bloody sword is always killing people.' He pressed his face up against the last standing male again. 'I've never killed anyone in my life! It's always some blood thirsty sword! Look!'

He slapped it down onto the bare arm of one of the women and she dropped dead, then he began striking the children. This at last spurred the male to attack and Dallid was stunned at how fast Valhar reacted. There was no way any normal man could have spun back so quickly and caught the Prae'surlas with his sword the way Valhar did. If Valhar did not continue to move in the same blurred speed of movement, Dallid would have thought that the spectre of ice was distorting his vision. Everyone was dead in the farmhouse within moments and that did not stop Valhar from shouting at them. Uncomfortable and frustrated with the demented scene, Dallid turned to the ice being.

'Why are you showing me this? Take me back to Furea!'

'Kill. Brijnok.'

'What has Valhar to do with Brijnok? Why should I care if he is killing Prae'surlas?'

'Brijnok. Warrior.'

'I am not waging a war on the god of battle. Return me to Furea and I will wage war on the false god of ice instead.'

'Brijnok. Warrior. Kill. Wife.'

The scene changed and they were outside. It was still snowing and Valhar was still there. Only this time they were surrounded by a squad of Ihnhaarat, in a different snow covered farmland. Valhar was shouting about ghosts again and Dallid looked over to see who he was talking to. It was Phira. His wife stood not ten paces away and yet Dallid knew that if he tried to speak with her or touch her that he could not. Whatever magic the ice spectre was using, it seemed to make them truly 'not here' as he claimed. Why was she speaking with Valhar though? Were the Ihnhaarat her squad in disguise? While he struggled with the confusion of his situation, Valhar erupted into action. He flew at Phira with the same terrible speed that Dallid had seen him use to kill eight Prae'surlas in a single heartbeat. Dallid closed his eyes without thinking. There was nothing he could do and he could not watch.

There was no sound to tell him how the encounter had faired, no grunts of fighting and no exchange of steel. No voices spoke to indicate what had happened and after a time Dallid had no choice but to open his eyes. He could see neither Phira nor Valhar. They were back in the strange realm of shifting colour and the spectre had returned once more to a being of fire.

'Kill. Brijnok,' it repeated.

'Are you saying that if I kill Brijnok then I will save Phira? Is she killed by that madman? Tell me!'

'Dies by a sword, dies by a sword,' the words chanted through Dallid's head and told him nothing. Did she die? He could not make himself believe it. Not by a sword. She was the greatest in the world with a sword. She would never fall to one. Dallid had enough of the spectre of fire and its games.

'Take me back to Furea.'

'No.'

'I will kill you if you do not.'

The spectre tilted his head as if comprehending the words. Then it nodded.

'Yes. Destroy. Destroy Brijnok.'

'Why? Why do you think I am capable of doing that? Why do you wish the god dead so badly?'

It turned its head side to side like it was afraid someone would be watching. When it spoke again, through some of the jumble and confusion, Dallid thought he detected a hint of hesitation.

'Words and thoughts get stolen. Swept away. Difficult. Dangerous. Someone could find them. Safer to show.'

If the spectre was trying to learn how to communicate with Dallid, it seemed to be getting better. Less meaningless words drifted in and out of the coherent ones, even if it did still cause Dallid pain to hear them. Then they were somewhere else once more. Up in a mountain range but with everywhere covered in snow like Surlas had been. There was a darkness to the place however that made Dallid think it was not the Prae'surlas country. The spectre was no longer fire or ice either, but made itself up of ripples in the air. It was difficult to see in the darkness of the mountain, and from what movement the spectre made, Dallid guessed he was made out of wind.

Strangely the spectre gestured for them to walk. Why did he not just take them to the place he wished to be? That was what he had done in the previous journey. But Dallid followed and they walked on the snow covered rock and they did not leave a mark. The dark clouds above made it look like a storm was raging, but Dallid did not feel it. He reminded himself about not really being there, but if he could see and hear, then why not feel? Nothing about the last few days of his life had made any sense. Why should his current circumstances be any different?

The rock walls near them started to narrow as they travelled by foot. It quickly took on the look of a small valley and then a small cave. Dallid wondered how small it would get before they reached where they were going and looked around to make sure the spectre was still with him. The distortion of air in the shape of a man followed him now, letting Dallid lead the way. That did not give Dallid confidence.

Seeing he was again without his sabre Dallid vainly searched for a Connection with fire instead. Nothing. Perhaps if he had anything at all to use as a weapon he would be more accepting of his situation. The small cave opened out before him and Dallid halted rather than stepping though.

He could see an old temple built into the rocks ahead, hidden on all sides by a sunken bowl within the mountain. He spotted one or two more cave mouths to suggest other ways of reaching the temple, but his attention did not last long on the surroundings. The spectre had brought him to another man, one who had also just recently done murder.

Sitting outside the weathered temple, was a man of pure white skin and hair. His arms were resting on his legs and his head was hung down heavy. He sat like a man who had blood on his hands, and the red stained snow surrounding him gave easy truth to that judgement. There was enough blood and gore to warrant dozens of bodies but there were no other remains that he could see. The corpses could have been burnt but even that would leave something. The white skinned man lifted his head then and although he did not look in their direction, Dallid could see white fire burning from behind his eyes. The light was so bright that it made his pure white skin and hair seem dull, and the power shining out was so extreme that Dallid wanted to do nothing more than turn and run.

The spectre chose that moment to speak with him and Dallid wanted to strike out at the being to keep it quiet.

'Jherin,' it said clearly. 'Brijnok will wake the monster, Jherin.'

The white skinned man called Jherin hung his head back down and thankfully his eyes were no longer visible, but giving the thing a name did not make Dallid feel any better. Dallid was not a great warrior. He was not even a brave warrior. He was guilty of over thinking things like a Scholar and so, he tried as much as he could to charge body first into all situations like a warrior should, avoiding all thought and the hesitation that came with it. It was that hesitation that had cost him the life of his grandfather, and his brothers, and he was sure if he thought about it hard enough he could find it as the cause of why he and Phira were not together now. But it was his own private struggle and he felt that every day he became better, that every fight and battle he charged into he became stronger. And despite his new power, and everything he had been through in the last few days, all his years of work felt like they had now vanished as he looked at that one man sitting motionless by the old temple.

'The destroyer of power,' the spectre whispered. 'The destroyer of an age.' Dallid shook his head at the intensity of his fear and before he could ask how someone could destroy an age, the spectre showed him.

The first thing Dallid could see was a blinding light in the shape of a man. He thought it was Jherin Connecting his body with the same terrible white light that shone from his eyes, but he was standing right next to Dallid as the spectre would, and they stood atop a hill looking down upon a battle. It was in the centre of that battle where Jherin stood. It was still only his eyes that shone, the rest of his body seemingly flesh, and Dallid gave one last glance towards the strange shape of the light standing next to him. Satisfied it was the spectre taking on another new form, Dallid gave his full attention to the battle below.

Armies charged from all directions. It was impossible to estimate exactly how many but it numbered in the tens of thousands at least. Lights of all colours filled the sky as magic was thrown from one army towards the other, but through all the flashes of power and magic, the shining white eyes of Jherin stood clearest at its centre. He stood with a wide clearing around him as thousands of warriors rushed against each other.

Comprehension dawned on Dallid then as he saw the truth of the scene. The armies were not attacking each other, they were all attacking Jherin.

So many of the warriors looked to be Powerborn it made for a chaotic sight. It was clear enough to see though, that as soon as their flashes of power came close to Jherin it simply disappeared. Then he saw the first of the actual warriors get close to Jherin themselves and they too disappeared in a way. It was not the calm dissolution of the warrior's power that happened in the sky though. When the warrior themselves got too close, they disappeared in an explosion of death. The wide clearing around Jherin was a perimeter of destruction, marked clearly by a constant explosive spray of blood and power. Every warrior that ran into it faced the same fate without exception yet on they ran without fear or falter.

Dallid examined what kinds of men they were that they so wilfully ran to their obvious deaths, and after much searching he had to conclude that all of them were magic. The speed of their charge and the agility of their leaps marked them as more again, not just magics but Powerborn. Yet their armour and their weapons looked to be emitting just as much magic and power as their flesh. So it looked in all appearances to Dallid, that he was witnessing an army of thousands of Powerborn, all armed with powerformed weapons and armour, all waging war on a single being and they were all being destroyed.

'Are they Powerborn?' he asked the spectre. 'What race are they? I see no Fureath'i, no Prae'surlas, no Ihnhaarat, or Kel Sherans. All four races together could not field so many Powerborn as below. Where is this place?'

'The world was once power,' the being of light answered, 'then power was destroyed.'

Frowning down at the carnage, Dallid tried to remember all the lectures Phira would give him. She could put a Scholar and Teller both to shame with her knowledge and she had described to Dallid the last three ages. If this was the Age of Creation he was seeing, then how could the spectre show him something so many centuries ago? It seemed too real to be a dream.

With all their power however, the armies still ran helpless towards whatever Jherin was. Phira told him about how every culture had the antithesis to their god. They had both agreed the stories were just stories, but the creature he was watching below looked to be that very thing. Was Jherin the one who destroyed all the gods and created the Age of Might? Amadis once had a saying: grow powerful and gain the gods favour, grow too powerful and gain the devil's destruction. Amadis had meant destruction by his own hands, but this Jherin was something much worse.

Squinting down at the scene he thought he could see the perimeter of death around Jherin getting smaller. Perhaps the might the armies were throwing at Jherin were slowly wearing down his own power, shrinking down the protective barrier of destruction that he held around him. The white skinned being did not even move however. He just stood, with his arms held down by his sides, and only the blinding fires in his eyes spoke of any power he possessed.

Focusing on it more now, Dallid could definitely see the ring of death getting closer and closer to Jherin, and it could be soon when the Powerborn warriors were able to actually engage with the dreaded creature.

The spectre did not let Dallid find out how the battle concluded. Instead he suddenly brought them to an underground cave. Torches burned along the walls and a waterfall even poured down at the far end feeding a river that disappeared further underground. Jherin was there again, his eyes drawing all attention once more.

Instead of fighting an army this time, he just stood with two men. Both were armed but not positioned for combat. Their stances were relaxed and casual even though they stood in front of certain death. One man had short black hair and a scar that ran all the way from his mouth up along the side of his head. It went back into his hair causing a white line trailing over the ear. He had so many weapons secured around his body it looked like he should fall down from their weight, but he stood tall and strong.

The other man then, to Dallid's surprise, was a Fureath'i, but looked too tall and too wide. The largest Fureath'i he had ever seen certainly, so much so that it almost made him look like a Foreigner. He only carried a single sword but he had something like wooden plates tied along his belts. Turning to see what form the spectre would take in this new vision Dallid was very surprised to see the same Fureath'i man. In every other vision the spectre appeared to take on whatever was the strongest element of the location. It seemed very strange that the large Fureath'i was the strongest element, especially considering Jherin's proximity. Even the waterfall would have made more sense, but Dallid did not claim to understand what was happening so he would not protest.

The spectre turned to look at Dallid and seeing the surprise on his face he must have realised that he looked different. He looked down at the golden coloured skin on his hands, and slowly lifted them to touch his face. If it were anyone else Dallid would have said he looked disturbed but what could he know of a spectre's looks who usually was nothing more than a featureless shape? The spectre frowned at the strange occurrence and pointed at the man with the scar along his face.

'Brijnok.'

'Is this how he wakes Jherin? Is this what you want me to stop?'

The spectre frowned but spoke the clearest he had done so far, perhaps having a mouth and tongue gave some help or perhaps he was just becoming more practiced. 'No. This is where Brijnok sent Jherin to sleep.'

Dallid turned to the three figures and began listening to what they were saying. It was Jherin who was speaking, his voice calm but powerful.

'I asked for you to hide them and yet you have brought them together. What other choice do I have?'

Brijnok's scar made him look like he was already smiling, but he smiled further anyway. Everything about the way he spoke and held himself was thick with arrogance and self-importance.

'I have brought them together my friend, precisely to give you a choice.' Something changed in Jherin's face then, there was confusion but something resembling curiosity also. 'It is constant is it not? No matter how much you destroy, more and more life is created. When I look at you I see a being in despair, my friend, one that has become exhausted by a world that he can never understand. You were created simply to know destruction and nothing else, it must pain you as much as I suspect or else you would have destroyed us both already, would you not?'

'I have never wished to destroy,' he said softly, but not apologetically. 'I have no choice.'

'These segments, my friend, created you for that. With these same segments I can take it all away. I can give you the peace you crave more than anything else. Here is where you have your choice. With the same power that created you, we can destroy you, end your suffering. Finally you can rest, sleep, even die...'

Jherin was silent for a time. The light from his eyes began to fade as he whispered, 'Please, let it be so.'

Brijnok smiled broader and the scene vanished. The spectre became the being of fire and Dallid was back in the realm of shifting light and shadow.

'I will show you no more,' the spectre said suddenly and waved his hand to dismiss Dallid like someone would wave away a begging dog.

When he appeared outside the Temple of Dawn, the comforting weight of his sabre hung at Dallid's belt, and the roaring Connection with the towers of fire flowed through his body. The spectre had followed him but Dallid at least stood before him as a Fireborn again.

'I have returned you to Furea as you have requested. You will do as I request and destroy Brijnok.'

'In that last place you brought me, what did Brijnok do?' Dallid asked back.

'He sent the destroyer to sleep, in mind if not in body, but now he is going to wake him again. You too were created to destroy and you must use that power to destroy Brijnok. Pursue Aerath if you must, if only because Brijnok wishes the Iceborn to succeed. He hates the other gods more than anything else and he waits until Aerath has killed them all, then he will wake up Jherin to kill Aerath, and Jherin will destroy us all.'

Startled at the clarity of the answer, Dallid still could not reconcile his situation with the new addition of the spectre's commands. 'Why do the other gods not kill Aerath or Brijnok?'

'Because they fear them both. Brijnok is the First God and more powerful than any other on their own. Perhaps together they could kill the god of battle, but they are too proud or arrogant to do so. The same is true for Aerath. The Iceborn has already captured two gods, and the others fear they will be next if they challenge.'

Two gods? 'Frehep would not fear Aerath, so why does he not act?" Dallid hesitated before adding, 'Are you Frehep?'

'I am not, nor do I claim to know the god of fire's reasons for not acting. Will you kill Brijnok?'

It felt strange to Dallid having a conversion with a spectre of fire now he was back in reality. Self-consciously he looked around to be sure none of the temple guards had ventured out or were manning the walls above him. Considering the spectre's request, Dallid weighed up the consequences of acceptance and denial. Acceptance would draw him away from returning to a life within the army and the training he needed to become a real Fireborn. Denial then, if he was to believe the spectre, could lead to the destruction of all life in the world of light. Were Aerath and Chrial'thau not villains enough? Did the world need more in the form of Brijnok and Jherin?

Jherin looked certainly capable to accomplish such a thing but why did the spectre think Dallid was able to stop it? The other reason it had given Dallid then was if he killed Brijnok, then Valhar would not kill Phira. There were so many doubts that even Dallid's mind did not where to begin hesitating. How could he kill a god? How did he think he could even kill Aerath or Chrial'thau? If only Amadis were still alive, the world would be simpler. Live in peace, or die by his sword.

Again the voice of the Fireborn within Dallid's head tried to answer but he angrily cut it off. Every inch of power inside his veins was pushing him towards Aerath and Chrial'thau, it would give him no answer towards the strange request to kill Brijnok. So Dallid answered it himself.

If there was anything he could do that even had the slightest chance of saving Phira's life, then he would do it.

'If it means Phira's survival, then I will do all that I can to destroy Brijnok, but only after I have killed Aerath.'

The spectre of fire stood for a time in silence before nodding to Dallid. 'I am pleased.'

'But you need to help me. How am I supposed to kill a god? You showed me how Valhar was going to kill Phira, show me how you expect me to kill Brijnok. Show me how I can kill Aerath.'

'I will not. The futures change. Showing you one would only hinder you in completing any other. You will find a way.' It paused and then added one final thing, 'All I can offer you is this: you will not be able to defeat Aerath because he is too powerful and you will not be able to defeat the god of battle if you fight him. Both are impossible. So you must take Aerath's power away from him, and you must not fight Brijnok. For Aerath: look to a cell within Lae Noan of solid ice, with no bars or windows to see within, and for Brijnok: do not fight him; just kill him. Find a way to do that and you will have your answer.'

CHAPTER TWENTY FIVE

A fire of ice

'Am'bril can go and rut a bloody horse!' Thisian cursed as he wrapped his cloak around tighter again. It did no good though. The cold weather did not suddenly disappear.

He had even been warned by Krife and Griffil that it was so bloody cold outside of Furea, and all Thisian had the good sense to do was pack a slightly thicker cloak for his journey. Back in the heart of Furea he could go months without wearing any more than boots and breeches, so Thisian had felt preposterously overdressed when setting forth on his adventure. Yet now his legend was going to be told as the simple minded Fureath'i who died one day out of Furea because of the unbearable cold. The ground looked like Surlas with the all the bloody snow, but none of it would be half as bad if the ice-cursed wind would just stop. It was going to be a slow, cold, and boring start to his bloody legend.

Thisian the Exile: that could be his name. He would take the title given to him as a mark of shame and wear it with honour. He would be known all over as the one Fureath'i brave enough to excel in exiled life. Even if it meant he would always be the lowest ranking of his friends, he would compensate by being the most infamously famous.

It was only a matter of time before Dallid outranked him anyway. He had spent enough time around Phira for her ambition to rub off on him, while she was busy rubbing everything else off on him. Thisian smiled a private smile trying to picture what it would be like with Phira. Not with her and Dallid of course, that would be inappropriate, Dallid was his friend after all, so out of respect Thisian only imagined doing Phira himself. He bet she was very commanding.

They were his main regrets, that he would never get to see his friends again, never get to mock Dallid over how short he is, never get to finally push Kris over the edge, and never get to stick his cock up Phira like he had always assumed he one day would.

He would never see any of them again now. But more importantly he would never bed a western girl now either. Despite his failures at the border fort, he was confident he would discover the correct approach at some stage. He had heard so much about them and their fiery passions, and experienced nothing but ice growing on their tits from lack of use.

They were simple ambitions he had created, not as grand as becoming a squad leader or ember class, but more substantial ones like bedding eastern, western and mountain women, one or two of each, maybe at the same time. All he was missing from that list was the western and mountain women. Then he could move onto his other lists like bedding a squad leader, an ember class and blaze commander. He'd just done a squad leader, and the other best thing about that list was the only female blaze commander in the army was Phira-bloody-almighty.

Women generally started the army later than men, because some would still be pregnant at the same age that men left. Most women would stay for at least the first year of the child's life before leaving themselves, sometimes longer. So that loss of two or more years often excluded female warriors from possible field experience, not to mind the time they lost in training from being pregnant in the first place. Phira would moan about how it was unfair that a female warrior should have to choose between being a good warrior or a good Fureath'i, but Thisian would always say back that the solution was easy. All women had to do was accept they would never be as good as a man and the difficult decision would be removed. Phira usually answered such well thought philosophies with thoughtless violence.

She thought she had proven him wrong the last time they met in Rath'Nor when Phira was already an ember class and he was still just a warrior. She tried to make him admit that he had been wrong, that she proved women could be just as good as men but he cleverly answered back that if anything she had proven his point for him. He explained that Phira was not just as good as a man; she had gone too far and become better. So technically she could never be as good. He was half-praising her achievements, half-trying to sweet talk her into rutting him, and half-praising his own cleverness, but she did not appreciate any of it.

She always berated him for having a low opinion of women, but it was exactly the opposite was true. He loved everything about women. He loved their hands, their fingers, their arms, their eyes, their hips, their breasts, their hair, their legs, their hair between their legs. There were quite a substantial number of things about women he loved.

But it was time for him to stop dwelling on the past. He was not married to Phira - and thank Frehep's balls for that - so it did not matter what she thought. Thisian would look forward to the cold future of the wildlands and forget the lovely warm past of Furea. There would be new goals for him to achieve such as bedding a girl from every nation - apart from Surlas. Well maybe if the girl only had some Prae'surlas blood, and did not still live there, an exile like him. Then he might consider it. There was also the goal of bedding a girl who was a magicker.

He had never really fantasised about rutting with a Powerborn before, they would just snap it off, but with Foreigners they could be magic users that were not Powerborn at all. They would have no strength or speed to hurt him, just weird magic abilities to add some variety to their debauchery. The world suddenly seemed full of possibilities and not just a cold biting wind in a dull empty landscape.

'I am Thisian the Exile!' he shouted out to his horse and anyone else that wanted to listen. 'Let all men stand back in fear and let all women lie down in preparation! I'll be a legend outside of Furea since I couldn't be one inside, so Frehep be damned.'

A flash of fire appeared in the distance and Thisian's mouth dropped. He slowed his horse to a stop.

Looking up to the heavens sheepishly, he expected to see Frehep come flaming down from the sky to strike him dead for his blasphemy. But he was not in Furea anymore. Frehep had no hold on him in these lands. Looking ahead to where the flash appeared, Thisian wondered what it might have been. He should really circle around it, try to avoid any bandits or raiders that might be lurking about to prey on a lone rider. But if Krife and Griffil could ride alone, just the two of them, and not get harassed, then surely one man on a horse could do the same. If he was approached by raiders then he would just ride away. His horse would be able to run just as fast as their horses. Thisian could not see any faults with his logic.

'I should've been a scholar,' Thisian said. 'I'm too clever to be just a warrior.'

Maybe he would journey to Kel Sherah after he had adventured with Krife and Griffil for a time. They were a nation full of weakly scholars and skittish academics. Ignoring the small few Defenders that were skulking about, Thisian would be regarded as the strongest warrior in the entire land. There they would recognise straight away how quick minded he was, and marvel how he had still become a mighty warrior despite his obvious mental strength. He would have to venture there at some stage anyway if he wished to achieve his new life goal: spreading his fame as a warrior to all men, and then spreading the legs of all their women.

Looking at his immediate decisions and squinting towards where the fire burst had come from, Thisian knew he should avoid it. However, if it was a trap, then any bandit would know a reasonable man would avoid such an obvious ploy, they would be expecting only simpletons. Against such opponents, his wits could win him through, and it might not be bandits at all. It could be a female magicker in distress.

His curiosity got the better of him and Thisian kicked towards the flash. He would only get so close to see what it was and be ready to ride off if any trouble arrived. It was a pity Kris was not there. The pure senselessness, no matter how well reasoned, of such self-indulgent curiosity would drive him to madness. Thisian could picture it in his mind, blood trickling down from Kris's nose from trying to hold in his rage, Thisian's nonsensical arguments disarming Kris's sensible ones with their hilarious absurdity. It would have been glorious.

'What purpose could this possibly serve, Thisian?' he said in his best Kris voice. He was always calm and quiet, no emotion filtering up to the surface, no outward signs that the volcano was about to erupt. 'How will this curiosity make you a better Fureath'i?'

'Well, Kris,' Thisian answered, in a voice much richer and louder with strength and power. 'Are you fearful of what you might find? I thought Fureath'i warriors feared nothing and killed everything? Who knows what exotic dangers await us.'

The idea began to worry Thisian. The flash of magic could of course mean danger, and if it was sorcery then what if Thisian was not able to outrun them with just a horse? Thisian decided to rename his horse Kris then, and refused to back down in front of him.

'Kris,' he said and patted the horse's neck. 'You've no need to worry. I'll protect you should any danger confront us.'

The horse did not respond, just like Kris would not, but Thisian knew he would be inside his head, irritating away the self-control. It was a tough decision to think of which he would miss more, the chance to rut Phira, or the chance to push Kris over the edge. Having famous Tellings of his exploits might be enough to do it anyway. Having all the warriors in his squads Tell them all each night until Kris had ground his teeth done to stubs. And if the Tellings were really good, Phira might even search him out, regretting the opportunity she had missed to experience Thisian's prowess while he was still in Furea. He would grudgingly accept her pleading request and let Phira try her best to pleasure him. Thisian did not think she would be very good, but being a good Fureath'i she would work hard to become better.

Dallid would have to come find him then. After all Thisian would have broken his good friend Kris's mind and bedded his good wife Phira. It would be a fight to the death, and would make another grand Telling. Thisian of course would spare Dallid's life in the end. Their friendship was too strong. Their history too intertwined. Perhaps a complex relationship of brother and enemy would begin, spiralling out into a web of epic tales.

'Thisian, you think with the mind of a child,' Kris said.

'Shut up, horse,' Thisian said back. 'I have a need to entertain myself since my company is so poor.'

The horse did not respond and Thisian nodded with approval. He did take a moment though to do a quick scan of reality and make sure he did not spot any approaching raiders. How could there be so much land without forest? The west of Furea was worse but he knew to expect dried dead nothing over there. Straining his eyes he thought he could see the shadows of a wood further east, and if his map had not told him straight north, he might have considered travelling through it just for familiarity. Everything else was just flat lands, like around the border forts, but decorated with ice and snow, with a border of snow covered hills in the distance. The flash appeared again and Thisian heeled his mount to a quicker pace.

He would tough out the cutting wind in his face if it meant he could kick Kris regularly. The bloody wind was bad though. The useless hood of his useless cloak would not stay on his head no matter how tightly he tied it, and his cheeks started to sting before long. His nose was running and his fingers and toes hurt him, and Thisian regretted coming back to reality almost immediately.

If he were Fireborn then he would Transfer some of his powers to his horse, and then make the beast burn warmly as they rode. Its fire would not hurt either him or the animal, and would strike fear and awe in the hearts of everything that witnessed. He would be a god riding a flaming beast with power-fuelled muscles tearing apart the distance to his every destination. It was such a compelling image - and practical idea - Thisian marvelled at why he had not heard of it being done before.

A figure appeared in the distance then and Thisian nearly got himself thrown from the saddle he stopped the mount so suddenly. Kris stamped his feet with displeasure and tried to pace around, but Thisian held him under control. It was never best to leave Kris have his own way, it might only give him a moment of peace and he would hate that more than anything. Thisian could not reflect on how he did things for his friend's own good right then though, his gaze was locked intently with the colours of the figure's clothing he was seeing ahead of him.

It was man positioned where the flash had appeared - or a large woman - and he was lying on the ground. He did not move and there was no one else in sight, but the colours he wore made Thisian bare his teeth. Bright orange and yellow were the traditional colours worn by a Flameborn in proper garb. The brightness was unmistakeable, but why would a Flameborn be lying on the ground unmoving? Why would he be out here in the wildlands anyway?

If it was a trap, how were the bursts of fire created? If it was really an injured Flameborn and he was looking for help, what in the name of Frehep had injured him? And what could Thisian do to help a lord of power? He decided his curiosity had been satisfied. He knew what the burst of fire had been and he could now continue on his way.

'There's nothing we can do, Kris,' he said to the horse, who gave him a look that voiced clear disapproval. 'How do we know he's even still alive?' he insisted, trying to turn the stubborn horse to his cause. The blasted Flameborn lifted his head towards Thisian and for a moment Thisian held his breath as if it would hide him. A small burst of fire appeared then a few paces in front of the horse to show what good eyesight the damned Powerborn had, and what good hearing he probably had too.

'He could be trying to warn us off from a trap,' Thisian offered but Kris immediately whinnied his condemnation. 'Am'bril really can go and rut a bloody horse, and if I see her I'm giving her you!' Thisian kicked his heels into Kris.

The pace he choose was not fast, and the closer Thisian got the more of a show he made at looking around, making sure there was absolutely no-one around anywhere, looking anywhere but at the man in front. Thisian really should have had some story prepared for the bloody Flameborn. Could he proudly announce that he was Thisian the Exile to a Fureath'i lord?

He did not look down at the injured Flameborn until his horse was almost right on top of him. Then giving one last scan of the surrounding landscape, Thisian dismounted, only to let out a cry on seeing what the injured Flameborn looked like. 'Frehep's balls! What in the name of light happened to you?'

The Flameborn looked like he had been melted into himself, but there was no scarring or burn marks. His head was resting on his shoulder as he lay there, but the skin was joined and even sank inside the collar bone. One of his arms was completing missing, the elbow going into his body and not coming out again until a mangled wrist appeared from the man's hip bone. And the tops of both his legs had become one awkward thigh muscle, with two legs trying to rip it free from just above the knees. Thisian almost vomited.

'I am Lord Kr'une,' the Flameborn said softly, but Thisian could hear a note of anger underneath. Was it the lack of respect he had shown? He had simply been caught by surprise and had not thought to kneel. Anyway, the man was a melted lump of flesh and fabric, how could he kneel in reverence to that? An exile did not bow to anyone.

'Well, what happened to you?' Thisian asked with a shaky voice that purposefully lacked any honorary. He was trying for a lot more confidence than he had managed. But as soon as he asked the question, he saw the broken stubs of arrows in the man's body. Looking around frantically, Thisian still could not see anyone approaching, but at least knew they must be near.

'The goddess,' Kr'une whispered, and Thisian knelt down closer to hear his words. He grimaced openly at getting so close to such a graphic deformity, but Kr'une deemed not to notice. 'Rhyserias. She sent me, but there were other Fureath'i there... they were trapped in time... she brought me to this.'

Thisian did not know why the goddess of time had abused one of Frehep's Flameborns like that but if she was the one behind the attack then Thisian did not want to suffer the same fate. At least if she tried it with Thisian, it would just kill him. The wretched Powerborn would keep surviving in agony having no way to heal or die.

Kr'une began fumbling to retrieve something from his belt pouch then and Thisian watched the action patiently, glad at having something else to look at apart from the disgusting disfigurement. It was not the arm that disappeared into the torso that he was using, but the more or less whole arm that had just a head melted into its shoulder. The movement was arduous all the same, and finally Thisian lost his patience. 'Let me bloody do it,' he said as he swatted the Powerborn's limp hand away.

Thisian easily opened the belt pouch and pulled out the only thing that lay inside. It was a small glass figure shaped like a burning fire. Holding it in front of him for a moment and marvelling at the beauty of the trinket, Thisian felt it begin to stick to his palm. Pulling it free, his skin tore slightly and he frowned at what kind of glass it was. 'What is this?'

'A fire of ice,' Kr'une breathed out painfully. 'You must take it to... Rath'Nor, or one of the temples... Aerath... you must...'

The Flameborn closed his eyes and Thisian stayed crouching where he was. The ice trinket started to hurt his skin again and Thisian frowned with irritation. Looking down at the belt pouch it had been stored in, Thisian flicked his eyes up to Kr'une's awful face, to make sure the Flameborn was still dead, and then looked back down to the belt pouch. Shrugging out of practicality Thisian undid the leather strap and thanked Frehep that it not been melted into the Flameborn's body. Looking up to the sky Thisian also quickly thanked Rhyserias in advance for not doing the same to him. What had he said about Aerath? He had heard of the Iceborn that was strutting around telling everyone he was a god. Thisian wondered if that was who Am'bril was rutting to make everything so cold. Maybe Rhyserias was jealous.

Once the new belt strap was secure and the strange item safely tucked away, Thisian did not consider going back to Rath'Nor or to one of the temples for even a moment. Standing up and looking around, he was more than happy instead to leave as quickly as he could before whoever had lodged those arrows into the Flameborn returned. He may have blamed the goddess of time for doing that to him, but as far as Thisian knew, gods did not use wooden arrows. It was more likely that some bandits thought to take advantage of Kr'une's injured state and he might have killed them in return, but as weak as he was with Thisian, the idea was not convincing.

Fresh blood began to trickle out of Kr'une's arrows wounds then and Thisian wondered if that meant he had truly died, and the Powerborn healing no longer worked. Lifting his boot over to one of the arrows stubs, Thisian jostled it a bit and the Flameborn let out a roar of pain. Jumping back in panic, Thisian relaxed only slightly when the Flameborn's eyes did not reopen, but his confusion grew as the man's chest began to move with ragged breathing.

'I thought Powerborn did not need to breath,' Thisian said out loud, and to that sound the Flameborn's eyes did open, but he did not respond. He looked in too much pain. Now Thisian was truly unsure of what to do. Was he capable of riding away with the Flameborn looking right at him? Probably, but only a few minutes ago the lord of power had been able to throw a flash of fire right next to Thisian. If he rode away, then likely the next one would be at his head.

He could throw the Flameborn over his horse but where would he ride? Eventually Kr'une would regain enough strength to ask where they were. Maybe returning the near dead lord to Furea would pardon Thisian for his crime of exile and even herald him as a hero. He did not think so. Did he even want to go back to the same stale existence of never being good enough? If being Fureath'i was to be better, then Thisian would be better off without other Fureath'i judging him. Even the lowest of Fureath'i were still the highest of Foreigners, and that was where Thisian wanted to be.

Turning back north to the direction he would head, Thisian looked towards the future and he saw a dozen riders watching him from a distance.

'Where did those flaming bastards come from?' Thisian swore an oath against every god he could think of - apart from Rhyserias - and looked at his horse. If he were to try and outride them, the safest direction was back towards Furea. Any other way and he could end up lost, if he did not end up caught. Looking down on the disgusting Flameborn he said. 'This is how I'm rewarded for saving you.'

Kr'une's eyes met his and he worked his mouth silently a few times before words came out. 'I sent them away, perhaps... I can give you time...'

'Are you going to burst into flames and hobble furiously towards them? Oh don't look at me like that. I'm going to die because of you!'

'I will kill...'

'You will kill who? Me or them? You don't look like you can do either right now.' The gravity of the situation was beginning to sink in on Thisian but he defiantly pushed it away. If he did not push it away then he was likely to only start weeping. 'Perhaps I can reason with them. What purpose will it serve to kill me? I hope their Fureath'i is better than my king's tongue.' Looking his horse in the eye he added, 'Kris, I'm going to die.'

The silent bastard said nothing to that and Thisian cursed again. He had no choice but to try and flee. With luck they would waste time killing Kr'une a bit better than he already was. Maybe the Flameborn could not die, but Thisian sure as Frehep's flaming balls could. What was he thinking riding out alone in the wildlands anyway? Why had he not just stayed in Furea? A hand grabbed hold of Thisian's ankle then.

'The sun god sees you, warrior,' Kr'une pushed out forcibly, 'and you are not worthy.' Thisian looked down in confusion and started to say something in return at the unnecessary insult, but the Flameborn's grip tightened painfully. 'Swear to oath that you will see this item to a temple.'

'What item? The lump of glass?'

Kr'une squeezed tighter and Thisian shouted out in pain. 'Swear it!' the Flameborn hissed.

'Yes! Yes! I swear by Frehep and on my soul as a Fureath'i, may I never climb the heights because of it, I will do as you say! For the love of light let me go!'

Kr'une released his crushing strength, but kept hold of Thisian's ankle, looking up at him again he said, 'May you burn brightly, brother.'

A moment of silence followed. It was a moment of taunting calm before a torrent of pain stormed into Thisian's flesh. Kr'une was trying to kill him, the dying Flameborn had taken such offence at Thisian's disrespect that he was burning him alive from the inside. Thisian tried to kick his leg free, but the hold was too firm. Desperately, Thisian stamped on the hand to break it loose, but Kr'une did not release. Instead a stronger wave of pain roared into Thisian and he collapsed to the ground, his body paralysed with unthinkable suffering.

He wanted to roll around in agony, to thrash violently at the assault his body was under, but all that he could do was twitch and Thisian was barely aware that he was doing even that. Pain was everything and in the fleeting moments his mind had glimpses of awareness, Thisian hoped for a death that would quickly come. But Kr'une would not grant him that, instead the torment was prolonged to last a thousand life times. He was consumed by a fire so intense that all that should have remained of him was scattered ash. When the pain did finally stop, Thisian did not dare move in case it would start again.

He was vaguely aware that he was sobbing, and that he had probably soiled himself. Gradually the cold wind began returning sensation to his skin. The sounds of his horse snorting and moving greeted his ears, and when Thisian opened his eyes the sun nearly blinded him. He felt as if he had been thrown into a lake filled with light, and now he was spluttering to get it out of his mouth, nose and ears. It was far too bright for his eyes, and he kept them shielded as he timidly got to his feet. He moved with the slow tenderness as if he had been beaten for days, and when Thisian finally stood straight, he looked down on Kr'une accusingly.

The Flameborn's eyes stared straight up at him, their yellow and orange swirls still bright in colour, but the light that had shined beneath them was gone. Had the fool killed himself in his final act of punishing Thisian? The power must have been too much for him in his weakened state, and while torturing Thisian, there was not enough left to fight off the injuries.

None of that mattered though as the sound of horses approaching made Thisian remember the riders he had seen before. Turning too late, they were already upon him, four of them riding wide to trap him in. Thisian spun around looking at the dirty, scruffy, ugly Foreigners that were about to kill him. His sabre hung at his hip, but Thisian did not consider using it. Already two men in front of him had crossbows drawn and ready. It took him a second glance around to realise that two women were part of the raider party. They were so brutish that even Kris would not have bedded them. But if it would get Thisian out alive he would be willing to do anything.

Before he could try charming the two beasts of women to his left, a fat man with a face like pig-shit spoke to him. If he was the leader, then Thisian thought he had an idea of how they ranked such things. It was either by looks or by stench. The fat man was impressively awful in both categories. The words he spoke were grunted king's tongue, and Thisian thought he understood the words: fire, gold, and girl. It did not necessarily make sense, but Thisian thought he knew the king's tongue for kill and dead, and neither of those had been mentioned yet.

'Do any of you speak Fureath'i?' he said back hopefully, and they all looked at him blankly. It had been a slim chance, but since they said the word gold to him, Thisian thought he should try to buy his way free. He had a heavy purse on his belt, and with fortune he would not even have to give them all of it. Taking another look at how ugly they were though Thisian decided instead that they could all go rut themselves. If a Fureath'i warrior was worth five Foreigners then a tall and handsome Fureath'i warrior could take all these ugly bastards. They would kill him after he gave them his gold anyway so he might as well make them work for it.

So, heroically, Thisian dropped to his knees and started wailing and begging for his life. He fumbled with his purse and spilled the gold out on the ground in front of him. The leader laughed and slid off his horse, stepping forward to collect the gold and kill the weeping Fureath'i. Thisian slid two knives down his sleeves and wondered where the ugliest part of the bastard was that he could stab. There was too much to choose from so when the leader got close enough Thisian jumped up and rammed the blade into his fat neck. He spun the man around to act as a shield while he flung his other knife at one of the two crossbow men. Both bolts had already been released but it was lucky that Thisian had a fine fat Foreigner to get in the way. The only problem was, that with both bolts and Thisian's knife, it meant the fat man was good and dead now and made him rather heavy to hold up. Pushing the lump of meat into a horse, Thisian took out his sabre and slashed down on another horse's face. The beast bucked and knocked off its rider, and Thisian hoped it would panic all the others.

Instead of the sounds of horses panicking though, he heard the twang of bow strings being snapped. Spinning around to kill them next, he turned just in time to see two arrows enter him. They made a strange wet thud and went in further than Thisian thought possible. He supposed when they were fired from such a close range, there was little to stop them. It was an odd thing to think about for a man who just been killed. He should have thinking some clever curses, or about all the beautiful women he had seen naked. Looking up to see it was the two repulsive looking women who had shot him, Thisian laughed.

'My only regret!' he shouted out loud to all of the watching raiders, 'Is that I die...'

He did not finish the traditional quote. His abbreviation seemed more fitting. Thisian dropped his sabre, and wondered why his legs did not drop with it. His hands itched to hold the steel one more time, but he was afraid that if he reached down he would not get back up. While he still stood, he was still alive.

Mortal wounds do not matter to a Fureath'i warrior, Thisian though with irony, but still felt his blood begin to heat at the thought. *A Fureath'i Exile burns bright with his every heart beat and this is my last!* He wanted to laugh and his hands joined his humour by aching for one final act of greatness before he died.

'I am Thisian the Exile!' he roared out and his hands burst into flames.

Every horse jumped and every rider cursed before turning immediately and galloping away. Thisian stood with his mouth open, watching the entire party of raiders flee from him. Except for the dead ones, and the one who had fallen off his horse, that one was running with his arms flailing for people to come back for him.. But they were all odd things for Thisian to focus on when both his hands were on fire.

Closing his fists, Thisian closed his eyes in support, and began taking deep breaths in through his nose. He could still feel the two arrows in his body, but none of it was really real, so what did it matter? This was just another fantasy. He had fallen asleep on his horse, because the horse was so boring. Or else Kr'une had knocked him unconscious from that random act of torture. It was not real.

When he opened his eyes, the fire from his hands had gone out.

'That's better,' he said and turned to find reassurance from Kris, but the horse had bolted with the rest of the animals. He must not have liked the sudden fire any more than the others did. Either that or Kris could not handle the jealousy of such an act.

Ignoring the surreal items sticking out from his body, Thisian instead looked down on the dead Flameborn Kr'une. He was not sure how long he stared at him, but after some time Thisian opened his hands and they sprang into flames again. Putting them out straight away, Thisian took his time before reacting.

It appeared Kr'une had Transferred his Flameborn powers to him, saving his life and all of a sudden making him an immortal lord of fire and power.

'Yeah!' he screamed and jumped up and down on the spot. 'Yes! Finally something has happened to me! Yes! Thank you to whichever horse-rutting god heard me and answered my blasphemous prayers!'

Thisian danced about with excitement and went down to kiss Kr'une on the cheek for his gift, but changed his mind the closer he got to the mangled flesh. So he continued dancing. The arrows dug at his innards painfully at the movement but how could he care? He was a Flameborn now! A few paltry arrows could not kill a Flameborn. His eyes caught Kr'une's peppered body for a minute, but quickly dismissed the contradiction. When he was satisfied enough celebration had been had, Thisian stood still, faced the sun and the world, and planted his fists on his hips.

'Lord Thisian!' he declared with overwhelming pleasure. 'Lord Thisian Flameborn!'

He looked down at Kr'une's clothes just to make sure the man had not been a Fireborn, but it was enough of a dream as it was. If it really was a dream then he did not care. He would enjoy every bloody minute of the damned dream for as long as it lasted.

It was some time before Thisian's excitement wore down enough to make him think of what to do next. He had significantly more options available to him now, even without his horse and supplies. Powerborn did not need anything other than their power. *Powerborn*. The Transfer could have killed him as easily as not, but it seemed Kr'une had had no other choice. Had he ever heard a Telling of a fleshborn being given the blood of the gods? Had he just been a part of his very first Telling? He would need to compose it immediately.

But first he needed to take out the two shafts of wood still sticking inside him. Grabbing hold of one of the arrows, Thisian almost dropped to his knees in pain as his grip moved the thing in some wrong way. He did not want to touch the bloody thing again. How great was the healing of a Flameborn? How long would it take him to recover? Thisian changed his mind about taking them out at all. As long as he did not move, then he did not seem to notice them much.

Perhaps he should try removing Kr'une's clothes first. His own were sure to catch fire at some stage if he was going to be bursting fantastically into flame all the time. He opened his hands one more time and giggled like a child when they lit up with fire. He closed his hands and put them out again.

Looking down at the bits of Kr'une's clothes that were fused into flesh, Thisian did not like the idea much better than the removing of the arrows. Kr'une's tunic was the only thing that would keep him clothed though, despite it being a bit of a mess, and as amazing as Thisian looked naked, it was too bloody cold to be doing anything as stupid as that. The Flameborn tunic was not so bad, it only had one or two rips at the shoulder and ribs, so it would bloody do. Going over to his sabre and picking it up without enthusiasm, Thisian sighed as he tried to steel himself to the task before him.

'There will be no Telling of this part,' he assured himself. 'Once you have his tunic, and get these arrows out of you, then, then your legend will really begin.' Thisian smiled the biggest smile he had ever known. He said the words once more, just to enjoy the taste of them in his mouth.

'Lord Thisian Flameborn,' he said softly at first. Then with his sabre in one hand he threw out both his arms and roared up to the heavens for all the gods to hear,

'Lord Thisian bloody Flameborn!'

· CHAPTER TWENTY SIX ·

Payment

When he first saw the town, Thisian was not sure if anyone lived there. The snow covered everything and his first thoughts were that everyone had abandoned the place to find somewhere warmer. But then he spotted the guardsmen, wrapped up in thick cloaks and furs, covered in the same bloody snow as everything else.

The two warriors looked as run down as the actual town. The walls were only twice Thisian's height, made of rotting wood, and had enough holes in them that someone would not even need to jump over. The guardsmen sat to one side of the gates in a small shelter, huddled around a cook fire. Looking at the long spears they held in their hands and the bows over their shoulders, made Thisian rub the wounds from the arrows he had only recently removed. He could not decide which had been worse, getting the tunic off the mangled flesh of Kr'une, or getting the arrows out. Both had been absolutely disgusting, but the removal of the barbs from his flesh had been excruciating. The idea of receiving more injuries did not appeal to him so he took his time in wondering what way to approach the Foreign warriors.

Fureath'i had a reputation for being unreasonably violent and so were not widely welcomed in most places. On the other hand, Fureath'i were not generally interested in going to most places unless it was with the sole intention of being unreasonably violent. It was a difficult cycle to break and Thisian could picture how his attempts at civility might go. He would stride majestically up to the two men, and announce in his best king's tongue: *'I am Lord Thisian Flameborn, I will be entering your well defended town but you have my word I will not burn it to the ground. Now quickly bow, so I can be on my way.'* Their responses would no doubt vary from either: sticking him with a spear, shooting him with an arrow or laughing at him for pretending to be Powerborn.

Opting to go for the more dignified approach, Thisian simply kept walking straight through the gates and entered the dreary town of Lyanat without drama. At least he hoped it was Lyanat. The detour he had taken to investigate the fire flash had brought him slightly off course, and Kris had of course run off with his map - *bastard horse* - but Thisian was confident he had restored his direction. A real Flameborn might have been able to Connect with the sun and know their way like that but he could make do with his old fleshborn tracking skills.

'Wait a minute,' he said stopping in his tracks. 'I *am* a real Flameborn.' There was no-one out on the frozen streets to hear him and the two guards were not interested. The only response he received to his bold statement was a throbbing pain from his unhealed arrow wounds. Frowning in his best Kris impression, Thisian continued his march down the snowy street.

He might be a real Flameborn but he was becoming really impatient with his new Flameborn powers. From what he had heard, Powerborns could heal any wound straight away, yet he still walked around with two big bloody holes in his chest. Admittedly the two arrow wounds would have fully killed him had he still been fleshborn, but he was Flameborn now. He expected much more co-operation when it came to his great powers actually doing things.

The previous day, after first taking out the arrows and putting on his fireproof clothing - which he then had to cover with a flammable cloak to keep off the flaming cold - Thisian had sprinted as fast as he could to test his new power. Perhaps that excess of energy had stopped his wounds from closing completely. They had certainly bled enough during the run and as powerful as he felt while running, he had been absolutely exhausted afterwards.

Cutting short his recollections, Thisian realised he was possibly wasting time just stomping about in the snow. So, choosing a random building that had three gold coins painted onto a sign post, he headed for that. The dilapidated town was relatively close to Furea, and his nation was well known for being rich in gold, perhaps the sign even represented the three different kingdoms of Furea. Either way Thisian was confident of being greeted warmly inside.

When he pushed open the door, he was pleased to see the tavern was similar to the one at the border fort. There was a big fire at one side, with stools and tables circled around it. At the back of the room was a wooden bar with serving girls dressed delightfully inappropriate for how cold the weather was. Thisian could see nearly all of their breasts and immediately decided that the wildlands were superior to Furea. Making his way towards the lovely young girls, Thisian gave them one of his best smiles.

'The sun god sees you, fair maiden,' he said without adding how much of her he could see. 'I'm looking for a man named Krife.'

His king's tongue had been slow and careful but good other than that. The woman slapped him hard across the face and spat on his feet before storming off with a scowl. A burly man with arms as big as Yiran's stepped up to him then and glared at Thisian as if he had been the one to slap the woman instead of the other way around. Maybe the man was her father - although he was too horse-ugly to sire anyone so luscious - but maybe Thisian had also said something wrong in the king's tongue. The large man spoke to Thisian with a slow, mean voice. 'Fureath'i?' he asked.

Thisian nodded.

'Out of my tavern!'

Two more men just as big as the tavern owner appeared. They definitely looked as if they could have been his sons since they had the same squashed face and crumbled ears.

'You have a very beautiful family,' Thisian said to them in Fureath'i. 'I'll be back to taste your daughter's enormous breasts later.'

The tavern owner just frowned with incomprehension at Thisian's retort, and so Thisian sighed knowing he would have to learn more king's tongue if he was ever to insult anyone properly to their face. A few weeks would be enough, definitely faster than the few years of learning he would need to be a Powerborn back in Rath'Nor. The only thing he needed to learn on how to be a Flameborn was how to get people to bow down - and maybe even take off their clothes in awe - but certainly not spit on your feet.

He turned with a majestic swirl of his plain cloak, over his finer, if torn, Flameborn tunic and left the tavern to step back into the snow-rotted street. Looking further down along, Thisian picked out three to four signs that could be taverns. Other buildings had stalls that were empty or large gates that were closed so he could dismiss those. He knew more than most Fureath'i did about how Foreigners lived their lives, using gold, silver and bronze to buy and sell things to survive. At first it had been hard to imagine, being raised in the Fureath'i brotherhood of every man bettering themselves, their society and their country in every way that they can. But as he got older, read more books, and heard more from Tellers, Thisian took to preferring the idea of every man for themselves. Not having to rely on others to give you food or clothes or weapons, not having to work on a farm for no reward other than you were expected to do it.

Thisian had felt less and less Fureath'i the more he thought about and questioned things. His friends just said he was talking like a Scholar or that he spoke with ice on his tongue, but Thisian knew the truth. He was too clever to be Fureath'i, too tall and too handsome too, but he always felt above doing what others did without thinking. It was ironic that he thought of himself as better than the society that constantly tried to better itself. But Furea tried to better itself by refusing to change. It was idiotic and at least now Thisian knew why he had always felt better. He was destined to become Powerborn. Di Thorel the god of fortune must have found him from under Frehep's watch and chose him to become the great man he was always meant to be.

Frehep sure as rut didn't choose me for this. I've cursed the god's wrinkly old flaming balls far too often for that.

A body flew out of a tavern up the street then and Thisian jumped in fright, both his hands coming up protectively to his face. He froze in the undignified position for a moment, before quickly resuming his usual, much more warrior-like demeanour. The man that had been thrown out of the tavern was slowly rising to his feet and wiping off the snow and muck from his long coat. A bulbous belly pushed out from underneath the coat and Thisian was impressed at who ever had managed to throw such a fat man like that. The person would have to be huge, and so it was a good place to look for Krife.

The fat Foreigner gave Thisian a passing scowl as he marched away and perhaps he needed to reason that to a Foreigner, a frown or a scowl was the same as a bow. He wondered if all Foreigners were going to be fat as well. The buxom serving maids from the last tavern were certainly not the usual lean and muscled Fureath'i women he was used to. Forming a new list of goals in his mind, Thisian began forming ranks of how fat a woman he would like to bed. It would all add to his legend. As much as he hoped the beast that had thrown that last man out of the tavern was Krife, Thisian also hoped that maybe whoever had done it was an enormous woman too. That could be a Telling right there, Thisian and the bedded beast. Kris would love to hear his men Telling that one.

Walking into the new tavern, Thisian had to swing back out of the way of another man sent tumbling out the door with a giant boot. The giant wearing the boots then charged out after him to pick the poor man up again and carry him off somewhere. Thisian turned his palm to Krife as greeting, but the giant treasure hunter did not even see him.

'Fureath'i!' Griffil cried out from inside the tavern. 'You have come!'

Pretending Krife's insult had not happened, Thisian held his chin up high as he moved towards Griffil.

'The sun god sees you, Griffil,' Thisian said in well skilled king's tongue. 'I see Krife is making friends.'

The slender thief smiled. 'And I see you've not practiced your king's tongue. It still sounds like you're chewing on week old meat. Let us talk Fureath'i so these surly louts do not listen. Were your eyes always that colour?'

My eyes? Thisian just nodded and sat down on the stool that Griffil was offering. The tavern was smaller than the first he had visited, less populated, but with the few other patrons all staring at Griffil and Thisian. The serving maids were a good bit fatter than the first though, showing less of their breasts but enough to keep his interest. Thisian made a quick mental note of which level of fat he could place them within his list. They just glared back at his handsome interest, but once he had mastered the king's tongue there would be no stopping him.

'I'd ask why Krife is fighting those men, but I don't think there will be a reason,' Thisian said in Fureath'i, keeping his eyes on the other men that looked ready to start a fight.

'You'd be right,' Griffil agreed. 'We're still waiting for this blasted magician. It has been three days now, Fureath'i! So Krife has begun to blame men for not being magicians. In his defence, he is correct of course, they are not magicians so they can't find flaw in his arguments.'

'This seems a violent town,' Thisian said.

'That is something, coming from a Fureath'i.' Griffil laughed. 'But yes, as rough as this town is usually, the cold has made them worse. Krife is too old and angry for this place at the moment, the magicker had better come quickly or we'll run out of taverns that we've not been barred from.'

The giant treasure hunter stormed back into the room then, the open door behind blowing in a cold wind, and the fire at the edge of the tavern flickered at the intrusion. Thisian eyed the fire as if it had spoken his name. His hands tingled and longed to ignite to join the flames in their dance, but he did not want to set his cloak on fire. The big man Krife was busy staring down each of the other patrons until they all looked away, burying their faces into their cups or into muttered conversation with each other. Krife laughed at the reactions before slamming himself down next to Griffil and Thisian.

'Who's your friend, Griffil?' Krife asked and then roared out laughing at the sight of Thisian's face dropping in dismay. He slapped Thisian on the back as he laughed, and it still hurt, even as a Powerborn. 'I'm joking, lad! I'd recognise a Fureath'i anywhere. Unless you were standing next to another one of you golden bastards, then you'd be as unrecognisable as an Ihnhaarat's arse is to their face. Did you know they wear those masks down their breeches? Griffil told me that.'

The fact that he was speaking in Fureath'i should have alerted Thisian to the joke, but being around the easily distracted man made him feel anxious. *Is this how Kris feels being around me?*

'Thisian here was just telling me how violent he thinks us Foreigners are,' Griffil said with a smile.

Krife sat down and nodded solemnly. 'I know what you mean, lad. I can barely get a minute's peace in this town without one of them wanting to fight me.' He called over a serving girl for some ale. 'Why only yesterday I was attacked by a bloody tavern wench! Dented a fine pitcher of wine off my poor face for no reason.'

'Well,' Griffil elaborated, 'You did slap her rump so hard that she was lifted off the ground. I'm surprised that you didn't break her hip.'

Thisian laughed. 'I might have met her.'

'That is why I never let Krife drink in the same Inn we're staying at.'

'The place smells like shit, vomit, spit, and piss anyway,' Krife protested. 'I should empty my own chamber pot in the common room to give it a better aroma.'

'He's just angry at having to stay in one place for more than a day,' Griffil said to Thisian. 'It's only a coincidence that the places don't like it when Krife is there for more than a day either.'

'I'm a treasure hunter, boy,' Krife growled. 'I should be out hunting, not sitting here waiting for some self-important magician. I say we leave without him, the Fureath'i will have to do instead. You haven't become a magic since we've last spoke, have you?'

Thisian opened his mouth and didn't know what to say. It was only then that it hit him how truly unbelievable his situation was. People do not just suddenly become Powerborn or magic users. They are born with the Connection or they train for years to summon the power. Krife answered his own question.

'Of course you're not. You're a decent fleshborn like the rest of us. Damned magickers thinking they can walk around acting like they're the squirted runts of a god's cock. The next dozen magic users I see I am going to punch right in the face and see how much of a god-bastard's dribble they are then.'

Thisian opened his mouth again but decided to close it. Griffil leaned into him. 'Speaking of bastards, we've heard that Valhar the Bastard was through here a few weeks ago. Compared to him, Krife is as civilised as a Mordec Lady.'

'There you go again, Griffil, trying to get me in a dress. You need to grow a cock before you can stick it up my arse you know.'

Thisian frowned at Krife's needlessly unending use of offensive language and then looked around as if Valhar the Bastard was going to burst into the room right that instant. He needed to be more aware that he was no longer in Furea. In the rest of the lands, gods and warriors walked as one, he was as likely to run into any of them from the stories at any moment. Valhar worried him though. He had that sword that could kill a Powerborn with one touch. And that would just be Thisian's bloody luck to become Flameborn one day and get flaming killed the next. Most lords of power lived for hundreds of years, and his legend would be the one who lived the shortest ever in history.

'How long ago was he here?' Thisian asked coolly, his concerns well masked behind a strong voice.

'He left as soon as he heard I was coming,' Krife announced. 'There's only room for one violent lunatic at a time in this town. And my sword's bigger!'

'Your sword is as fat as the rest of you,' Griffil said and Krife patted his belly considering. Griffil shook his head and continued. 'The few people that were willing to speak to us, before Krife opened his mouth, said that he was on his way to Surlas. They said the madman was sick of the snow and the cold, and was going to find each and every Prae'surlas, demand that they get rid of the cold out of sheer decency, and that he would kill the indecent bastards if they did.'

'I think I'm starting to like Valhar.' Thisian smiled. 'With his sword he might kill all the Prae'surlas in a few months at most.'

'The fool will get a spear jammed up him long before then,' Krife said dismissively. 'How the idiot hasn't been spitted with an arrow before now is a miracle. Still though, I've been getting an urge to go to Surlas myself lately, same way I got me an urge to go into Furea but was sick of it as soon as I got there. Don't ask me why, but now I'm thinking of taking a look at Lae Noan after we finish with this.'

'I've a friend in Lae Noan, Ithnahn remember? I keep meaning to break him out, not that anyone has ever gotten out of there, but one thief should be able to sneak in right? Maybe if Valhar was up there as a distraction it might work. But I hear the reason he hasn't been shot or magicked before now is he actually has magic on him,' Griffil said in a hushed voice even though no-one could understand them anyway. 'I hear he bedded a powerful witch and she was so pleased with his performance that she put a shroud over him making his body invincible but at the cost of his mind.'

'Pah! I've bedded a hundred women that I could call witches and they've all been extremely pleased. I don't have any magic on me, and I don't want any.'

'I don't know, Krife, you do seem to get mysteriously fatter each year, and your hide is so ugly now that no arrow would go near it. I think one of those witches might indeed have given you something other than a rash. How else have you lived to be so old when your mouth is so loud?'

Krife showed him a bronze arm brace on his left forearm then and nodded as if that answered Griffil's question. All the talk of arrows made Thisian put his hand down to his wounds. They were still raw and throbbed with memory of the sudden attack. Griffil watched him cradle his ribs, so Thisian pulled his hand away quickly and tied his cloak around tighter so they did not see his tunic. They might not recognise what it meant, but they seemed a lot smarter than they acted. That damned Griffil seemed to see and notice everything too. He needed to distract the thief's attention.

'I know a Teller - that's a Fureath'i bard - and she thinks that Valhar might really be Amadis,' Thisian said. 'She thinks that when Amadis disappeared, he wasn't killed, but his mind and power was destroyed. So he woke up a madman with a sword that kills with one touch, and the reason he hasn't been killed himself is that he still has Amadis's power, and he's just too insane to use it.'

'Interesting,' Griffil admitted. 'But what I think, is that the madness is just an act, similar to how ugly Krife is. No-one could really be that ugly and survive, the same as no-one could really be that insane.' Krife picked up the metal pitcher of wine and examined his face to check for ugliness. Griffil continued, 'Either that or the sword takes in magic the same way it takes in life. Could be a power weapon from one of Brijnok's tales, or even the battle god himself could be protecting him, pleased to have someone travelling around inciting death and violence. Brijnok must be protecting Krife here too, I can think of at least a hundred people that want to kill him.'

'I've met that bastard Brijnok, and the smiling god sure isn't protecting me. He'd kill me if he could. But do you know what I think?' Griffil and Thisian both shook their heads with a grin, waiting for whatever loud and abusive answer Krife had prepared for them. 'I think that fat man who just walked in is our magicker.'

Krife stood up and matched straight over to a portly man in a black cloak. Griffil winced and said, 'I'm not sure if the poor man is better off being the magician or not being the magician. Krife is likely to batter him for either.'

Thisian turned his head and watched as Krife strode up to the suspect magician. The round man pulled back his hood to reveal puffing cheeks and a sweating brow, and Krife showed his strength by catching him by the shoulders and lifting the fat man straight up off his feet.

'You a magic?' Krife asked eloquently.

'You must be Krife,' the fat man replied levelly. Thisian had to give him credit for the coolness of voice he managed. Krife dropped him back to the ground and the fat man smoothed his fine cloak for a moment before looking very unimpressed at Krife. 'My name is Hane Slighteye, from the Amalgamation of Sorcerers, at your service.' The last part he said with a clear sigh of displeasure.

Krife looked him up and down with an equal look of displeasure. 'I'm docking you for every day that you made us wait in this rat's hole of a town. Even the whores seemed to have something lodged up their arses, and not in the way I like.'

Hane crinkled his nose at Krife's words, and Thisian turned to Griffil. He had followed some of what was being said in king's tongue, but there were a lot of words that he was not sure about.

'What's a whore?' he whispered.

'A woman that beds you for money,' Griffil said while doing his own inspection of the magician.

Thisian was stunned.

'What do you mean beds you for money? As in you pay her gold and she lets you rut her?'

Griffil frowned at Thisian. 'Of course. Even the smallest town in the land has at least two whorehouses, maybe not a Fantaven house, but enough to keep you warm.'

Thisian would have to reconsider his lists. The information he had just been given was perhaps the greatest thing that had ever happened to him. Even greater than becoming a flaming Flameborn! All the Tellings of Foreign life, and not once had anyone mentioned to him about the most important part about the existence of whores. Trying to calculate how much coin he had with him, Thisian did not notice Krife shouting at them to leave and pushing the magician out the door. Griffil grinned as he pulled the Fureath'i out the door with them.

'I have been travelling for days. I will need at least a full night's rest, if not two,' the magician complained to Krife.

'Well, you should have gotten here two nights ago.' Krife growled before turning to grin at Griffil and Thisian. 'I thought magics were supposed to be smart.'

Hane sneered at the insult and looked down his nose at Krife's two companions. Thisian brought himself up to his full height, which was higher than Griffil but still only up to the chest of Krife. The old man was a giant.

I wonder if you are allowed to pay for more than one woman at a time.

'You are fortunate that I have business of my own in the Temple of Wind, if you do indeed know its location, or else I would abandon you to your own offensiveness,' Hane said with a disgusted tone.

If Thisian found the right whorehouse, he could cross off an entire list in one night, maybe even two lists.

'It looks to me that you should be paying us as guides then,' Krife said while crossing his large arms over his larger chest.

As many women as he could have as long as he had enough gold to pay for them. The idea was too fantastic to fully comprehend.

'You will pay the Amalgamation what you have promised them, what I receive from this expedition is my own business and none of yours. Why you even need a magician when you have an exiled Fureath'i Flameborn in your party is beyond me anyway, unless you have more refined magical needs than I have assumed, but somehow I doubt it. Regardless the agreement has been made and we shall see it through.'

If he was able to choose from any of a number of willing women, then what should he base the decision on? Which list of goals did he want to accomplish first? The entire world was spiralling out of control with possibilities for Thisian when he noticed Krife, Griffil, and Hane all staring at him.

'Did I say something out loud about the whores?' he asked innocently. 'Can we go to a whorehouse now?'

Krife and Griffil looked to each other for a moment, before Krife turned back to Hane and prodded him in the shoulder. 'I hope you know this means you're only getting paid half now.'

'I have already said that what you owe the Amalgamation has nothing to do with me...' Hane started to argue but Krife turned his back on him and walked off. Griffil followed and Thisian shambled after the two of them.

'Are we going to the whores?' he asked as they all made their way down the snow covered street. He heard a muttering behind him to say that the magician was following too but Thisian's mind was on nothing but the whores they were going to find. This was to be the greatest day in Thisian's life. Women would willingly let you do what you wanted to them and all you had to give them was gold? It was madness.

It was brilliant, glorious, life-changing, madness.

CHAPTER TWENTY SEVEN

The fall to madness

Phira was going mad. She was sick of looking at nothing but snow. They left their camp in the snow and returned to the road of snow, and all before dawn which did not sit well with her men as it meant that they could not give proper respect to the sunrise. But Phira would not suffer any time lost, so Frehep would just have to survive without one morning's worship. The steady stream of refugees coming towards them from the east had dwindled the further they went from the city but there were still enough to notice if eastern traders began kneeling before the sun.

She almost wished there were more Foreign refugees to see - even if they were all forsaking themselves to a life under Prae'surlas rule - because when there were not any refugees to see, all that remained was snow. Phira was not widely known for having a stable temperament at the best of times and in this single morning the snow already had her on the verge of madness.

Her two squads were wrapped warmly, kept moving atop their mounts, and constantly searched the distance for signs of trouble. Cold fog streamed out from their dead-faced masks, showing that the lifeless gazes still breathed. Phira worked her fingers on the reins, but no matter how warmly she dressed, or how active she kept herself, there seemed little she could do to stop her fingers freezing solid. She would push them all faster if she did not fear the horses breaking legs on ice. Perhaps ice was why her scouts had not returned.

More likely the outriders had not returned because they had nothing to report and did not want to risk speed to come back and speak of nothing. But Phira demanded they come back at regular intervals or how else was she to know they had not been killed. She would kill them herself if they did not return soon.

The road ahead would eventually lead them to the Chaos Gate, a small town, disorderly by Prae'surlas standards, but highly civilised compared to the rest of the wildlands. The town was built around a cross roads where they could turn south to Dowrathel, the trading city they were travelling to, north to Lae Noan, the mountain prison of ice, or continue east to Amidon, a city that probably housed even more criminals than the prison did. Lae Noan at least was bound to have some decent Fureath'i in its population. Phira doubted a Fureath'i had ever willingly set foot in Amidon, and if they did it was to try burning the place down.

Regardless, they would turn south to Dowrathel, staying well clear of both Lae Noan and Amidon. As much as both locations disgusted her, they were also ridiculous concepts for Phira to think on. Understanding of all things was paramount for a general, and Yiran had helped her to understand that the pursuit of knowledge was not always a waste of a warrior's life. It was the goal that determined whether something was worthwhile. Endless reading for fear of action, for simple sloth, or selfish joy, was the unworthy life of a Scholar. But constant learning while on the path to a true goal: that was a worthy thing that could make you better. So she consumed information with the same drive and purpose she gave everything else.

Knowledge of something though, and understanding of it, were two different things. Lae Noan was a prison that housed thousands of criminals, but worse than that, it preserved their lives in the ice, so a villain from hundreds of years ago would still be alive just waiting to escape. No-one had ever escaped from Lae Noan, but the entire concept was profoundly unnecessary. Why not just kill the criminal and be done with it, why give them immortal life in a mountain that took dozens of Powerborn to guard? Yiran explained that for a Prae'surlas, to live in shame was a greater punishment than to die, and that the Lae Noan ice prison was a fate far worse than death.

To Phira though, it seemed there was something missing. There had to be some other purpose why they accepted the worst prisoners of other nations into their care. Some reason other than arrogant pride, although the Prae'surlas had more than enough of that, but the idea of taking such a burden just to show to the world that they could; it was audacity beyond even the Prae'surlas.

It was in Phira's mind to some day break in and discover the secrets of Lae Noan. With an elite group of Powerborn they could even destroy it. But her mind was full of such side-plans and improbable contingencies. She would create them and store them away, keeping them ready if ever one would serve her purpose. And with her current purpose being to assassinate Aerath - and Lae Noan the most likely destination for that to occur - perhaps it was not so improbable.

With the destruction of Lae Noan seeming a little less unlikely, Phira smiled underneath her mask. All she needed to do next was return to Rath'Nor before Gravren, assemble a squad of the most powerful Fireborn she could find, somehow convince the King to give her command of such a squad, and then kill an Iceborn who was powerful enough to turn the whole world into ice.

She wished a scout would return so she could take out her frustration on them, but instead Phira concentrated it on the other abomination in her mind.

Amidon City was a collection of more murderers, rapists, and thieves than anywhere else in the world of light. By any sane reasoning the society should not be able to exist, with everyone killing and stealing from each other until no-one was left. Yet somehow it was one of the largest cities in the world, run by several different powers like a body infected with multiple deceases. Each of the deceases were busy fighting the other and that left none with enough strength to destroy the body full, and so, the city lived on.

When Amadis was alive, he ruled the city with pure strength and awe, even the gods feared to step foot in his land. At the height of his power, the Shakara army of Amadis was large enough to rival any land apart from Furea. But when he disappeared the army fell apart, turning into a thousand different bands of raiders and mercenaries, some settling into fortified villages, others selling their trade to the Mordec Empire, most living off the land and lives of honest fleshborn.

Amadis's adopted daughter, Eva Yeda, the Lady of Amidon City, tried to hold onto his rule, and kept some small part of the Shakara for herself, but the rule was too large for her grip. She acquired quite a merchant empire while her father lived, and then used those funds to finance her private army, but the city had become riddled with a cancer of crime lords, each one dug in too deep for her to burn out. Lyat the Destroyer of Armies had ruled all the crime lords before he disappeared, and his absence from the world caused as much chaos as the absence of Amadis. Phira knew the name of every major crime boss now and what part of the city they controlled. Yiran had described the city as an enemy to Furea, and you needed to know all of your enemies if you were to kill them.

She knew of Harruk the Cripple, whose withered appearance belied his merciless cruelty; of Roque the Puppeteer, who controlled so many people without their knowledge, it was impossible to gage his full power; of Gildas the Poisoned, who assured the loyalty of his men by feeding them poison every day that had the antidote worked into it, so to stay alive they needed to keep taking it; she knew of Hrothlar the Masked; of Cor'dell the Many; of Lyanti the Daughter; of Balfore Thane the Forbidden; of Wolfram the Fire and Ephraim the Beast. The list was endless and Phira knew them all.

She could understand belonging to an army like the Shakara trying to better the city and the lands around it. She could even understand belonging to an army of criminals battling for the complete opposite of what the Shakara were trying to achieve. But it was the others that Phira was unwilling to accept. There were groups that were not trying to change Amidon City or the wildlands at all, but simply wished to keep it the way it was. That idea was so Foreign to a Fureath'i, it had taken Yiran many weeks to explain it fully.

Highly trained warriors would ally themselves to no-one and hire their skills for coin to add further to the chaos. The best of these assassins could command armies themselves and do much to bring stability to the land, and yet they laid back to bask in their own opulence. Protharik the Demonlord, either summoned demons that he would then kill for coin, or else he hunted demons yet still demanded reparations for his service.

A madman, Valhar, who had somehow acquired the Jaguar sword of Amadis, fed hungrily off the world of chaos that the city bred. Valhar was not widely used as an assassin for hire, but his prices fluctuated as much as his mind did, and he was often considered for tasks any reasonable man would turn down.

Then there was Reningal'ad'haustaluthain, who's name took an age to pronounce and who's own love for himself was nearly as vast. He claimed to be the only unmasked Ihnhaarat in the world and claimed to be unmatched with a sword, yet used crossbows or poison or a dagger in the night to kill whoever he was paid to kill. He was hired in equal demand from both the crime lords and the Shakara, as likely to turn cloak and kill one as he was the other. How could a warrior live that way?

The snow was driving her thoughts to distraction. She looked to the sun for help but Frehep could not be seen behind the clouds. *If I cannot see him, does the sun god still see me?*

'Blaze commander, two of your scouts return.'

Phira turned to look on the grim features of Lei's mask without movement or reply. Her voice was almost as cold as the air that carried it. 'They time it well, Lei, for any longer then I would geld them both.'

Lei laughed behind his mask and spread his hand out to encompass the winter surroundings. 'The Guild of Gelders do not run here in Surlas, blaze commander. Please tell me that you do not mean to start one. There is no need! It is so cold here a man's stones can freeze solid and snap off in the saddle, I know mine are close to that.'

'Would you like me to warm your loins, Lei?'

The expressionless mask she was wearing matched the emotionless tone of her voice. Behind that mask, she allowed herself a grin. Lei always knew when to lift her up from threatening darkness. But that did not mean she would not take pleasure in the uncomfortable way Lei repositioned himself before deciding how to answer. The day that she did not test him on the boundaries of his dual relationship, was the day that Kris would laugh. Phira missed Kris, but he could be too serious to be around. Thisian was the complete other side of the scale, lacking any propriety or respectability at all. Lei was capable of finding the right mix - so much like Dallid in many ways - so Phira continued to challenge him, to test his talent and keep it sharp. He finally chose his answer but had taken too long in doing so.

'Blaze commander, the fire of your heart as a Fureath'i is enough to warm us all.'

Phira wanted to shrug her indifference to his attempt but instead went on with, 'Including your loins?'

'If that is what you wish, blaze commander.'

'Is that what you wish, Lei?'

'I wish only for what my blaze commander asks of me.'

Phira smiled again, unseen behind the Ihnhaarat mask. 'A blaze commander expects more from her ember than mere obedience.' He moved to speak again but she was finished with him. 'Go see to the scouts.'

It was amazing Lei's horse did not break all four of its legs the way the man kicked to be away from her. Phira knew Lei's attraction to her was strong, but right at that moment he wished nothing more than to be as far from her as he could be. It was not uncommon for commanders to bed their subordinates, but it could only be the commander's decision, and she would never do it. She would make Lei believe that it could be any day though. She needed to amuse herself somehow.

The report Lei received was brief and he returned to Phira promptly. 'It is bad, blaze commander.'

'Another troupe of Prae'surlas?' she asked, although she did not think it would be.

'Worse, blaze commander, it is another troupe of Ihnhaarat.'

That was indeed worse. The Prae'surlas they could confidence their way past, but the eastern traders would most definitely wish to know their business, and Lei's impression of an Ihnhaarat might not be so good when dealing with real ones. Phira spoke it better than most, but did not know enough of the people to judge how a woman Speaker would be met. If every other nation outside of Furea were a basis, then it would not be met well.

'Do we kill them?' Lei asked, and Phira considered it. He knew well that would be her first thoughts. Killing them would allow her more information about what the traders looked like, and even further legitimise their own deception confiscating more goods to display as trade if they were searched by the Prae'surlas. But a bloody fight between two bands of Ihnhaarat would be seen by someone. Looking south Phira examined the hills and turning north she glanced at the forests. Both were unwelcome delays but the forest was at least closer.

'We head north, off the road. Send word to the scouts of what signs to watch for and follow us. We will return to the road tomorrow. Let us hope the Ihnhaarat have not already seen us.'

Phira turned her mount and her two squads followed neatly. Lei was busy directing men to find the other warriors out ranging, letting them know which bird signals to listen for, which animal track to follow. Hopefully they would not have to journey so deep off road as to necessitate that, but preparing for every possibility was what Phira did.

It took an age for her squads to traverse the dangerously exposed flatland between the road and the forest. Phira expected any moment for the black figures of the Ihnhaarat to appear on the road and see them. Or even a simple Prae'surlas farmer - if such things still existed - to call out to them and demand their business. If a single Foreign settler took notice of their troupe's strange departure, then word of it could reach ears of the other Ihnhaarat.

Fortunately, as the last of her riders took shelter behind the trees, there was still no sign of the other Ihnhaarat. She praised the keen eyes and quick return of her scouts and decided she would commend them later. For now though they would have to keep impressing her, to find a way through the forest that stayed both hidden and close to the road. Given the deep snow visible around the trees, she guessed it would be difficult indeed. Snow in forests held all manner of unseen dangers for a horse's leg. It would be slow and frustrating, and yet another delay.

'Does not this remind you of home, blaze commander?'

Phira looked at Lei and shook her head. 'This place is more home to a sand eater. There are trees, but everywhere else there is the same nothing of the deserts.'

'Then it is good we have so many western Fureath'i in our squads, blaze commander,' Lei said. 'I always find it amusing when we complain about the western Fureath'i because they say all easterners do *is* complain. How does that saying go: if a mountain man kills five ice-men, he would say nothing. If a desert man kills five ice-men, he would roar out in celebration and cut five spears into his flesh. But if a forest man kills five ice-men, he would cut ten spears into his flesh, talk for twenty days about how he killed them, and complain for forty more about being out of breath from all his talking'

Phira sighed. 'Lei, for the love of Frehep, shut up. You are like a woman the way you natter on and on, perhaps you should be braiding my hair while we discuss the boys in our village.' Next he would be talking to her about his feelings instead of about her men. She had a wide variety of warriors under her command, but the eastern ones were the smartest and followed orders the best. Mountain men had discipline but no imagination or initiative. Westerners then were sometimes only as good as setting off a pack of dogs.

It should not matter if any of the men heard her opinions of them. It was healthy for a squad to hate their commander. One such westerner actually chose that moment to come riding back to her. Phira smiled beneath her mask. For a moment she thought the man would challenge her. She would even promote him if he did, assuming he survived the encounter. Her intelligence soon banished the fantasy though and she recognised the man from those sent to scout the forest. Still, Phira's hand did not move from her sword.

The man addressed Lei as was proper. 'Ember, please let my blaze commander know that I have found a Prae'surlas farm close to our position.'

'I did not think the Prae'surlas still had farms.' Lei's words mirrored Phira's own thoughts. 'Is it inhabited?'

'It was, Ember, but they all are dead now.'

Phira's grip tightened around her sword. If Gravren's influence had caused her own scouts to needlessly kill and bring attention, then she would have to publically execute the man. Gravren was held as one of the great warriors in the country, and to kill him would be a waste, but it would consolidate her own reputation as without peer. She pushed the plan to the back of her mind to give it more thought at a later date.

'Did you kill them?' Phira asked coolly.

The scout bowed his head so low from atop his horse that Phira thought he would break his own neck. 'No, blaze commander, I would never disobey your command. They were dead when we discovered the farm, but their deaths look fresh, I judge a few hours.'

Phira looked to the sky. Trying to find the pale imitation of the sun that Surlas kept, she weighed up her need for speed and her need to assess what dangers were surrounding her.

'Bring me to the farm. Lei, if your monthly moon's blood is not causing you too much pain and emotion, then leave me four more scouts and take the rest onwards, we will catch you.'

'Yes, blaze commander.' He bowed in salute, his voice straining to hide the anger at her needless belittling of him in front of the scout. It served him right for behaving like such a woman all the time.

Phira motioned for the scout to lead the way, the four other scouts soon joining them. Heading further north away from the bulk of the forest, the trees began to thin and the ground became less treacherous. Still they reduced their speed instead of increasing it. If there were soldiers around that did this murder, then she did not want to give away her own position too easily.

The farm was little more than a large house and some fenced off fields, large by Fureath'i standards but worthlessly small to the Prae'surlas. Phira's eyes took in the details in passing as she scanned the surroundings for whoever was responsible. There were bodies lying in the fields and in one of the pens, dead goats mainly and some pigs, but there were plenty forms that looked almost like men. She had seen enough slaves with her time in Surlas to recognise the Chuabhotari. The things were tall like a Prae'surlas but unnaturally thin, the arms too long and brittle, and the skin of the waifs the same pale colour as their hair. They looked white from a distance but she knew that closer up it would actually be a pale green. The slave's deaths made Phira frown. To kill a family living in a farm was one thing, but to kill valuable animals and slaves made no sense.

They continued approaching the farm house, and through the half-open door Phira could see an arm lying on the ground from within. There was no pool of blood surrounding it. She turned her horse toward the pen with the dead slaves and made two slight gestures to either side of her that sent men in a circuit of the farm.

Two of the other rangers would keep watchful eyes on the tree line, while the one who had given the report stayed close to her.

Pulling her horse up along the fencing, Phira removed her mask to get a better inspection. It felt good to be free of the thing. The smell of pig shit was strong, but there was something else about the scene. There was no blood and there were no visible wounds. Were the animals poisoned? Why then did the Chuabhotari waifs have no signs of blood or wounds? It was not without possibility that the slaves were made to eat with the pigs. Slaves and animals were ranked the same to a Prae'surlas, both held just slightly higher than a Fureath'i.

Phira jumped down from her horse and drew her sword in the same fluid motion. The scout shadowing her startled at the movement but recovered and quickly followed her. Using the clumsy, jagged, Ihnhaarat blade Phira nudged open the door of the farm house and peered inside to see a man, two women and six children all lying dead on the floor. Some rope lay where four of the children were, and it looked as if it had been cut. It was as if a group of raiders had taken the farm, tied up the occupants, and then cut them free before killing them. Did they hunt them for sport? Why then kill them only a few feet from their release?

'Do you smell anything, warrior?'

'I smell pig shit, blaze commander.'

Phira grinned at his candour. 'But nothing putrid, no rotting flesh, and no released bowels from the time of death. What was it that made you judge the murder done but some hours ago?'

'The colour of their skin, blaze commander, it is still the pale of a Prae'surlas and not the pale of a dead Prae'surlas.'

Lowering her sword Phira pushed the blade into the skin of a dead woman's arm. It entered with ease but with no blood emerging. Looking at the tip of the blade she frowned down at the small stain of red it held, and still nothing seeped out from the hole she made in the flesh. Phira turned and left, going back to her horse. The other scouts signalled for the two patrolling to return, but Phira did not wait for them before riding back to the forest. The Prae'surlas had been as the animals and slaves had been: no wounds, no blood, and no decomposition. Which meant even the flies and maggots stayed away from the bodies. Whatever poison had been used it was one that Phira was not familiar with and that displeased her.

The other scouts re-joined their party and they rode to catch up with the main group in silence. Her mind examined all the possibilities of what they had found but could not easily extract a solution. If the family had been tied up then why poison them? Most poisons were so deadly that it would cause blood or vomit to seep from the victim. But those back at the farm looked almost alive if not for their eyes.

As finely preserved as the corpses were, her scout had been correct in the timing, if not the reasoning. If a night had passed since they were slain then all that flesh would be frozen by now. Unless the poison was so potent to ward off weather as well as rot, but that seemed too unlikely to contemplate. The necks and mouths appeared untouched so death by suffocation did not seem likely either, and even magic would leave some trace of how it killed its prey. Perhaps an Iceborn could have frozen their insides solid, but the woman that Phira cut did not have a frozen arm. There was an ocean of unknown magickers living in the wildlands, as well as south and east of the Mordec Empire, but she prided herself on being extremely well knowledged and knew of no magic that could do that.

A god then, she mused, imagining that Rhyserias the goddess of time could have set foot on the farm and preserved them at the point of death. But it did not explain the rope or the release from same. Nor would a Foreign god enter Aerune's realm, unless of course Aerune was dead and Aerath had actually killed him.

A figure in black appeared ahead of her and for a moment Phira's fantasies made her unable to identify one of her own warriors. It would be easy for someone to infiltrate her squads with everyone hiding their faces as they did. It could even be a real Ihnhaarat from the other band that was sighted near. So, before the approaching masked Ihnhaarat got any closer, Phira signalled with her hands for her own riders to take off their masks. She had not put her own back on despite the cold, and waited patiently for the approaching rider to take off theirs. They did not.

The figure dressed as an Ihnhaarat kept riding towards them, so Phira unsheathed her sword and rested it atop her saddle. The rider stopped immediately, and only then seemed to realise everyone else had their masks off. When the warrior took off her mask she looked shamed that she had not done it sooner. Phira's own suspicions had gotten the better of her though, so she did not let the female warrior burn with shame too long.

'Report.'

'Yes, blaze commander, Ember Lei sends word, we have discovered another farm.'

'Surlas is full of farms,' Phira stated, impatient for the full report.

'Apologies, blaze commander, we have discovered another farm with its occupants dead.'

Phira nodded. 'Take us there.' Turning her head slightly to her five rangers she added, 'Remain without mask until I say otherwise.'

She and Lei had a complex series of gestures and challenges to prevent such an infiltration, but the mystery of the farm deaths had her on guard and she would not take any needless risks. Phira's eyes tracked every detail of the land they passed on their way to meet up with Lei at the other farm, and she was sure every other warrior was doing the same. It would be impossible for anyone other than a magicker to be near without their discovering them.

Prae'surlas were too big to hide anywhere, and could be smelled a mile off regardless, so that only left Foreigners. It made sense that some murderous Foreigners would accompany the honest Foreigners on their refuge into Surlas, to try and feed off their state of weakness and vulnerability. But if a band of raiders had a magicker powerful enough to kill a whole farm without leaving a mark, then they did not need to prey on the weak, they could prey on who they wished.

Lei was waiting for her when they arrived and Phira glanced through the trees behind him to the farm similar to the one they had just left. This one was bigger and the motionless lumps looked like cattle instead of pigs. Perhaps a dozen more dead slaves lay scattered around the surrounding fields.

'Blaze commander, a farm that grows dead Prae'surlas, now here is a venture I can see our countrymen interested in.' Lei's mask came off at the sight of Phira's group no longer wearing them, and his command gestures were filtering throughout the others swiftly. Her eyes flickered to see if she could find any that still wore a mask, and then went back to Lei's smiling face. 'Whose talented business do you think it is?'

'I have not yet decided.' She admitted and then asked, 'What are your thoughts on the corpses?'

'I think it is too few dead Prae'surlas, blaze commander, but then there can never be enough. They look as frozen as their own hearts but our scouts cannot suggest a cause of death other than poison.'

'Or magic,' Phira added and Lei frowned at the thought.

'Here in Surlas? There should be only one kind of magic in this snow-cursed land.'

'We are close to the wildlands.' Phira stated and looked around in thought. 'It matters not. We are not travelling without care regardless and one unseen danger is the same as a hundred unseen dangers for all we can do about it. We continue on.'

'May the sun god see us through all this snow and burn brightly in our hearts,' Lei incanted and every warrior within earshot bowed their head in salute.

Frehep has no power in these lands, Phira thought coldly, *but neither should any of the other gods.*

She would not mention her concerns that a god walked these woods. After her previous Telling on the subject some may begin to think that she was obsessed with the idea. But a god or a magicker was looking like the probable culprit, and either possibility could mean the death of them all. They needed speed.

'We leave this forest and travel behind it on the old road we saw in the open farmlands. If there are any farms still left with living occupants then we shall simply be mysterious Ihnhaarat travelling along the dirt trail instead of the comfort of the new road. Either way by the time they alert Prae'surlas soldiers we shall be far gone.'

'Yes, blaze commander.' All her men chorused the same sentence. She expected such obedience and threw Lei an impatient look to be about their departure. His uptake was quick and they all exited the trees back towards the farm road before kicking off at speed. The risk of ice on the grass and dirt was less than the forest or the new road, even though the snow was sometimes deceptively deep, but Phira was willing to push as much speed as she could until a horse actually did break a leg, and that would only slow down the horse. It would not stop her.

Riding so openly she had been forced to command the masks back on, but took the time to better study the mannerisms of each of her warriors. It was impossible to know the names of everyone within her blaze command, as it numbered almost at ten thousand. But she would study the thirty that she had with her with an intense scrutiny until her paranoia was gone. It could work out well for the warriors having her personal knowledge of their skills and gestures, if they did not prove wanting.

Another farm appeared in the distance but she paid it no heed. Whatever mystery was assaulting Surlas would have to remain so. It would not surprise her if it was the same ritual Aerath was performing to freeze the world that was killing the farmers. *Powering his own grandeur on the lives of his people.* He had to get his new power from somewhere, so why not from a ritual that took the lives of fleshborn and turned it into power for him?

An out-rider came back to the front of the column and Phira raised her head to see if she could determine who it was. It was Lei the outrider was speaking to, that much was clear, and the two warriors flanking Lei were Pellix and Drayilus, their size and posture made that apparent too. Phira slowed her horse as they approached the stopped group and she could induce that the masked out-rider was part of the Revealing Light squad the way he spoke to both Pellix and Lei. The man was small, even on horseback, although not as short as Dallid, no one was, and when Phira rode up he bowed down to make himself look even smaller still.

'What has Henrus to report?'

Lei turned to Phira and paused for a moment, either to hesitate over her correct guess of Henrus or in confusion because Henrus was still out scouting. She remained confident though, the man favoured his left shoulder by the way he held the reigns. There were only two such warriors in the Revealing Light squad and Henrus was the shorter of the two.

'Blaze commander, warrior Henrus has found our killer.' Phira turned her head with interest and Lei continued. 'It seems, blaze commander, that it is not magic as you suspected but a man. The man is, well, he is speaking to the animals in the pen. Henrus is modestly versed in king's tongue, but the things the man is saying, they make no sense.'

'A madman,' Phira said. 'And his sword, the metal is black?'

'Yes, blaze commander,' Henrus bowed. 'How did you know?'

'Because he is Valhar.' She spoke the word and every warrior became tense with unease. How one man could instil such ill comfort simply because he had stolen a sword and pretended to be insane; it was preposterous.

Valhar the Madman, or Valhar the Bastard as he preferred to be known, claiming to be the off spring of some whore the great Amadis Yeda had rutted decades ago. It was his Jaguar sword, the sword that killed with one touch, that was the reason behind the instant preservation of the dead bodies they found. Valhar would not need to break the skin, only place black metal upon it and remove all life from the victim. How the fiend had not been peppered with arrows long ago was a better mystery. Phira cursed that they had none now. The Ihnhaarat did not use them to trade apparently.

'Your orders, blaze commander.' Lei's voice tried to hide his anxiety, but he would not want to see any of his warriors dead at the lucky blow of a Foreign madman.

'We have no business stopping someone from killing Prae'surlas. Let him do as he pleases.'

Lei nodded but Henrus spoke instead, 'Blaze commander...'

Phira turned her gaze on him for speaking out of rank and the man shrank down smaller than she thought any man could. She herself had never been much concerned with the respects of rank when she was a warrior, but she would still have never spoken to a blaze commander without their leave. She nodded to Lei to let him continue.

'You may speak, warrior.' Lei said with the displeasure thick in his voice. He turned his gaze to Pellix also. She would be punished later, just as harshly as Henrus, for not having better control of her squad.

The man Henrus was overwhelmed by his own mistake though; he could not bring himself to even lift his head. Getting any more words out seemed like it would be too great a struggle and most likely he only managed to force them out because his ember had commanded it.

'Apologies, ember, apologies, squad leader.' He was right not to apologise to Phira as it would only be another mistake. 'I did not mean, it is just, I will follow my blaze commander to my death at her order, and I do not mean to be insubordinate, it is just...'

'Speak, Henrus!' Pellix was the one to shout at him, desperately trying to return control to her squad.

'Yes, squad leader, apologies, squad leader.' He seemed to grow in confidence when just addressing her and finally managed to say what he was attempting. 'Children, squad leader, the madman Valhar, he has a dozen children tied up by the animals. They are still alive. They are crying. And they are screaming. I know they are Prae'surlas, but they are still just children.'

Lei turned his head towards Phira, and Phira closed her eyes. Was everyone in her squad turning into an over-emotional woman now? What did any of them care about the deaths of Prae'surlas children? They were children that would just grow up to be Prae'surlas. Killing them now could only mean less spears to kill in ten years' time. She had never had any children, so what affection should she hold towards a young life? A Prae'surlas was a Prae'surlas, and they all deserved to die.

'Every Prae'surlas deserves to die,' Phira said with a sigh. 'But in battle and to a Fureath'i sabre.'

'Yes, blaze commander.' Lei nodded in salute and thankfully did not argue with her.

'When we approach, we will do so with great care. That is why I have chosen your two squads to be with me. We remove the children, but any adults can be left to rot. No-one is to engage Valhar, you are to harass him, and distract him, until I can get close enough to kill him.'

One touch from his sword and she would be dead. One glancing brush and everything she had worked for would be destroyed. But one touch from her sword could be just as deadly, and all she had to do was ensure she got there first. Putting away the awkward tree-saw that the Ihnhaarat called a sword, Phira retrieved a true blade from her saddle packs. Not her Fureath'i sabre, but *Unrivalled*: her longer Mordec katana that Yiran had given her. She would need the extra reach to keep that damned hell-sword away from her.

Phira took a deep breath. She had attempted to resist the temptation of personal glory. She had attempted to put the good of her mission and her nation before her own wild ambitions. And all it took was a single outburst of emotion to give her reason to give in. She had dreamed all her life about testing herself against one of the world's renowned and soon, because of it, she could be dead. But also soon, she could be the slayer of Valhar the Bastard. And then, she would have a new sword. She would have the Jaguar sword. With that, she could better her nation and be able to kill Iceborns with ease. With that, she could better every nation and be able to kill Aerath in particular. With that, she could better the entire world and kill every magicker, Powerborn and even the gods. Then, and only then, could she truly be: Phira the Unrivalled.

CHAPTER TWENTY EIGHT

Valhar the Bastard

Phira trembled with the cold. She had taken off her mask and her cloak, since her leather waistcoat and black shirt would serve her better for ease of movement. Her hair as always was in a single braid that she kept inside her shirt and down the length of her back. She still had her gloves, and she still kept as much skin as she could covered, but the damned cold was making her shake uncontrollably. It was foul fortune that Gravren had taken what small supply of arrows they had, but she had deemed his squads the most likely to become engaged in a battle. So she needed to be free of all other hindrance now if she was to fight the man holding the Jaguar blade. Every peripheral, every instinct, every hour of training in her entire life, everything needed to be perfect if she was to survive. The risk almost outweighed the goal, since it would not better her country if she were dead. But if she acquired that sword... the thought made her shudder with possibility and no longer did she tremble because of the cold.

Her men had surrounded the farm, and those coming from behind would soon be through the clearing. From where she sat with Lei and six others, Phira watched the machinations of a madman in the scene below. An animal pen that housed chickens and goats, also held a circle of ten children all tied together. On the other side of the wooden fencing, a middle aged man with silver streaks colouring the sides of his shoulder-length hair, waved a shining black sword in wild gestures as he shouted at both the animals and children.

Every now and then he would turn suddenly and level the blade towards his own horse, shouting something accusingly, and return to his abusive tirade to the animal pen. A litter of dead beasts lay at the lunatic's feet, and even from the distance she was away, Phira judged that at least four of the children tied up were dead as well. She kicked her horse forward.

If Valhar noticed a dozen Ihnhaarat riders slowly approach from the tree lines, he did not show it. Phira was the only one without her mask. She did not want any of her men thinking about engaging the dangerous assassin, and the restricted vision of the trader masks would serve as a reminder not to try. They were nearly on top of him before Valhar's horse snorted and stamped its hooves in reaction. The madman turned around at the horse in outrage.

'What do you mean they're lying? They haven't said anything! Don't shout at me! Are you as indecent as these north-men now?'

The horse did not argue back and Valhar still did not look like he noticed them. Phira slowly dismounted and six others did the same. Lei was to stay mounted, if anything happened to Phira it was imperative that he retain command and keep them true to the mission. The six others were needed to harry Valhar, to give Phira any advantage she could take. And still he did not register their presence.

'You bastards!' He glared at the terrified children. 'You have infected my own horse with your indecency! What do you have to say for yourselves?' The youths just sobbed or wailed, one of them had to be under the age of three, and Phira could confirm that they were indeed tied up with four dead children. It was horrific. 'Just what I thought you would say. You say my horse was the one to infect *you*. You may be right but my horse is no damned liar.' Valhar propped his boot on the fence ready to jump over into the pig pen. Phira had enough.

'Stop where you are, madman. We have you surrounded. Relinquish your weapons now and you may be allowed to live.'

Valhar turned and jumped at the sight of them. What looked like genuine shock and confusion coloured his face.

'Are you ghosts?' he asked suspiciously.

'We are your death if you do not heed our words,' Phira answered.

'I bloody hate ghosts,' he continued. 'My friend Protharik is a ghost you know, he brings them back with him. My father Amadis is a ghost as well, he made me find out where they all are, but then didn't bother asking me what I found out!'

'Put your sword on the ground or we will kill you,' Phira tried again.

'No,' Valhar said. 'Put your own bloody swords on the ground or *I* will kill *you*. If you had any bloody decency you would kill yourselves. Damned dead ghosts, already dead and needing more killing still. Dead and cold.' His face lit up with a sudden thought. '*You're* the ones who made everything so cold!'

Phira nodded to the four men that had circled behind him, the others on horseback had all gathered around now. Whatever happened, there would be no escape for the man. But when Valhar suddenly moved, it seemed Phira's vision disappeared. A blur of colour replaced where the madman stood. Two of her men tumbled to the ground before she could react, and two more at least managed to meet blades with the assassin, before the deadly black metal of the Jaguar sword met their flesh and their lives disappeared.

Phira's sword hammered down without further delay and she was greatly surprised to find Valhar spinning to block the strike. She did not relent and continued a series of furious blows that kept him moving backwards in defence. He met each of her vicious swings with a frantic speed that made him difficult to see, but Phira's flow of blade did not stop and the madman fought for his life.

She had him steadily moving back to the farm house itself and knew that with nowhere left to retreat to, Valhar would misstep. The numbing cold of the day was forgotten as all that consumed Phira was her sword and his. She could not let herself think about the Jaguar sword and what it could do, she only concentrated on victory.

Then, Valhar's blade bounced off her own with a sudden jolt and came thrusting towards her stomach with unbelievable speed. Phira swayed back in reaction but felt the black sword brush against her coat for a moment before Valhar punched her in the face. On instinct Phira swung away with a return blow that connected with the madman's head and she saw a piece of his flesh come away from the exchange.

Both fighters stood facing each other for a moment, their directions turned away from the farm house again, but still safely surrounded by mounted Fureath'i. Valhar brought his hand up to where his left ear used to be and Phira found her own free hand brushing against the sharp tear in her coat. Paralysing panic welled up in the pit of her stomach as she realised how close that had been. An inch deeper and it would have touched flesh. She would be dead. Phira clenched her jaw in denial, and felt her cheek and eye already begin to swell from the blow she had taken. Her opponent had his jaw hung open, staring at the blood left on his hand after touching where his ear used to be.

'You bastard...' he said in disbelief. 'That was my favourite ear! How could you? What have I done to you to deserve this?'

'I am yet to do worse, madman,' Phira said. She looked to the riders behind and thought about ordering them forward, but she had already lost four warriors to that black sword and could not afford any more. 'Throw down your weapons and I have magic that can restore your ear for you.' Fureath'i did not lie, but to a madman what she spoke was as good as truth.

'What are you saying? I can only hear half your words without my bloody ear! I'll have to take yours,' he snarled and rushed towards Phira with the same blurring speed that had killed her men. The man and sword were indistinguishable and it did not matter how skilled Phira was with a blade if she could not know where to defend against. She had no choice but to throw herself to the ground as the blur of movement came upon her, but swung her legs hard up into the image as she fell. The colour resolved back into a man, and the man fell tumbling to the ground, landing badly on his hands causing him to release his blade temporarily. Phira did not need a second chance.

Jumping to her feet with more urgency that she had ever moved in her life, Phira first kicked the black sword away from the madman, and then kicked Valhar straight across the jaw. The kick sent him spinning, but he turned the movement into a roll and got to his feet with more agility than his age should have allowed. Eyeing the Jaguar sword in the snow behind Phira, and eyeing her own sword levelled towards him, Valhar seemed to be weighing his options. Then he folded his arms and nodded his satisfaction, tipping his head as if the side with the ear was now heavier than the side without. Valhar the Bastard frowned seriously at Phira.

'I have relinquished my weapons as you asked, so give me back my ear and let me continue my work in peace,' he said with sudden calmness, the gleam of madness gone from his eyes, and the froth of hysteria gone from his mouth. 'Although why a ghost needs my ear and weapons is pure madness.'

'The time for surrender has passed,' she replied and stepped forward to kill the man.

Valhar turned and ran. Two of Phira's warriors steered their mounts to block him and Valhar's hands flicked out in two quick motions. One of her men's hands went up to hold his throat, while the other slumped sideways in his saddle, a dagger in his chest. The madman did not stop sprinting. His movements became a blur of colour again and Phira could not believe what she was seeing. Cursing, she had to order back all of her men from pursuing, pointing out just two. She then turned to examine her prize.

The rich black of it looked almost perverted in the frozen white that surrounded. Flexing her fingers from the cold, Phira took her time in admiring the blade. There were the faintest traces of silver flames that ran up the inside of it, almost invisible against the severity of the black. The sword of flame sang to her Fureath'i heart. On the hilt there was a design of two circles touching, creating a small oval between them. The oval was coloured white.

Touching the slash in her coat again, Phira took off the garment, not caring for the cold at that moment, and began wrapping the weapon with the leather waistcoat, careful not to let her skin touch it. Finally happy to pick up the prize, Phira tested the weight before looking back around at her men. Lei was still staring in the direction Valhar had run.

'Have they not caught him yet?' she asked with surprise.

'The madman runs with a crazed speed, blaze commander, he made it to the tree line before the horses could reach him. Our men have followed and it will not be long.'

Phira frowned at the inconvenience, she should have let them all rush upon him when they had tried to and casualties be damned. 'Send two more forest trackers in after and tell them what signs to follow for us.' Lei nodded and rode over to speak with two more riders. Phira turned to find Pellix. 'Have your men free the children and then search Valhar's horse.'

'It is already done, blaze commander,' Pellix said confidently, but cowered down at the look Phira gave her. The squad leader had no doubt been eager to impress due to the earlier failure of squad discipline, but Phira preferred to be in command of all areas. Orders had specific times to be acted out, and turning to the farm house showed the reason why.

The six living children stood huddling, all of them with wide eyes still fresh with terror, and what they saw was a squad of Ihnhaarat traders, who saved them from a Foreign murderer, and with that squad was a Fureath'i woman dressed in the same clothes. The eldest of the children even managed to throw hatred at Phira from behind the tears that still ran. Eventualities, not tears, were what ran through Phira, and none of them were pleasant.

If she did not kill the children then word of Fureath'i dressed as Ihnhaarat would spread. Even tying them back up would be the same as killing them in this cold. If any of the local farmers kept messenger birds, then by the time Phira reached Dowrathel, their disguises would be useless. She had to kill the children. While thinking of the least horrific way to do it, Phira was distracted by a shine of metal from one of her approaching warriors.

'Blaze commander,' Drayilus said. 'We have found maps and supplies that can be of use in the Foreigner's saddle bags, and also, this.' He held up a metal device that was in the shape of an over large diamond. Plates folded into themselves to form points on either end, and a long yellow jewel could be seen slotted through the centre. It was called a Spike, and it could be the answer Phira was searching for. She smiled at the children.

Later that evening Phira sat at her own separate fire once again, to contemplate the things she had done that day. And the things she would need to do the next. The Prae'surlas children still nagged at her. They were so young but their frozen blue eyes shone with enough hatred to place them well beyond their years. Valhar had killed their father, and all three of the women, likely all the sisters, wives and mothers to everyone there. Prae'surlas had peculiar customs when it came to marriage, women were less than men, and being a wife, although increasing the woman's own standing in society, still seemed to mean little more than being owned, and not just the woman but their entire family. One of the women would have been the man's wife, the other two his own or his wife's sisters, who would belong to the man until he sold them off for marriage but was welcome to breed with them until that time. The children would be allowed to breed with their mothers and father too until they themselves bought wives or were sold as them. They were better off dead than having a life like that.

The Fureath'i system was much better: either marry one warrior and mate with just them, or marry none and mate with anyone of your choosing. As long as four or more children were the result, it did not matter. Marriage beyond youth only got in the way of army life, as Phira knew too well, but elders often remarried again. Sometimes it was the same spouse of their youth, but usually just any other surviving elder that returned to the village. The companionship of society and Fureath'i brotherhood should be enough to fill a warrior's heart. What kind of weak person would also need love?

'I should have killed those children,' she said quietly to herself. Turning around to see that none of her squads were nearby, Phira returned to the fire and thought about retrieving the wooden carving she had made of Dallid. It did not do him justice, so instead she found a new branch and began a fresh one. Her belt knife worked at the wood in a calming rhythm and she continued to admire the flames in front of her.

She needed to burn the bodies of her men, but could not do it back at the farm. It would have just drawn attention quicker than the inevitable tales that would be told by the children. The youths would travel as best they could to find a nearby farm that Valhar had not slaughtered, or perhaps a village, and the story of Fureath'i dressed as Ihnhaarat would sweep over the land like a snow storm. Gone was any future use of such a guise, and all because she could not cut the throat of a three year old girl. The Spike had given her one solution, but it did not stop her anger at the weakness she had shown. She had convinced herself that she could do anything that was needed to better herself and her country. She had just been proven wrong.

Kris would have done it, she knew, *and he would not have given the act another thought.*

A fire does not dwell on the ash it has left behind but only looks to the fuel in front of it. Phira put down the branch she was working on and took out the Spike instead, examining the small metal markings that could be moved about the centre of the piece. Around the dull yellow jewel, little notches could be pushed and slid into different patterns and each pattern would be an exact location. They were maps of the stars. Enter the right marking and the device would catch you in a current of power, rushing you to that place under those stars.

Powerborns could not use it, the stream of power the Spike used was the same they were Connected to and it would rip them apart. Similar things existed in the Great Temples of old, but all they could bring you to was another temple, the Spike could bring you anywhere.

All she needed was the correct markings for an area near Rath'Nor and she could transport herself there immediately. Valhar had a parchment with him that must have held such star markings, but they were coded in a way to prevent anyone other than a madman from using them. She would not waste her time trying to decipher that code, but instead would make straight for Amidon City.

That way they would be out of Surlas in enough time before word spread of their disguises and once past the border she would be able to burn the bodies of the men Valhar had killed. One man just killed six of her warriors. The only word to describe such a thing was lunacy.

Even now she could still not believe it had happened.

But they would press on and obtain the codes they needed. Once in Amidon City she would find Lady Eva Yeda. Eva had good relations with the Fureath'i selling them most of their imported alcohol. As a people the Fureath'i bought little from outside Furea, but what they did buy, the trade was with her.

Securely attaching the Spike to her belt straps, Phira took out the Jaguar sword again, still wrapped in her leather waistcoat. Snow had started to fall earlier in the day, but as long as she had her cloak to warm her, she did not need the coat. Cold could sneak in and kill a person without them knowing, it would only be when you began to feel warm that it was too late. Flexing her fingers to make sure they still hurt, Phira put the Jaguar sword back. She had a spare sheath to house the sword but did not like the prospect of it falling free.

And she could not risk touching it until Valhar was dead. All tales told that it would kill anyone with one touch except for its wielder. Phira would not take the chance.

It is only the blade that kills, she tried to reassure herself. *I can hold the handle and test the sword at least.*

As she reached done to unwrap the leather coat, Lei sat down next to her and he did not look pleased.

'Still they have not returned, blaze commander,' Lei said with a seething anger. The four charged with hunting down Valhar were part of the Revealing Light, Pellix's squad, but Lei took strict responsibility for their failures as ember to Pellix. 'Permission to send the Unseen Blade out to track them down.'

Phira drew her hand back from the Jaguar blade. So close to so much power and she could not grasp it even though it was right within reach. One thing she prided herself on, when accepting her own selfishness, was that everything she achieved in life she had earned by strength of heart and not of birth. She had fought to become Yiran's apprentice, and had fought to learn everything from him and earn each promotion that she had achieved since. Earlier that day she had fought for the prize that lay at her feet, risking sudden death in a dangerous sword fight and won victorious. Valhar had killed six other Fureath'i warriors, a highly skilled assassin despite whatever facade of madness he claimed, and Phira had bested him. But as much as true ownership of such a sword would bring her, Phira would not let her own personal glory blind her this time.

'Valhar needs to die, but we cannot afford the time it would take. If four of the best trackers we have cannot find him, kill him, and return to us, then four more will not either.'

'Yes, blaze commander,' Lei said flatly.

Phira turned to regard his anger. 'We will leave one hour before first light. If our men have not returned by that time then they will have to follow us further for I mean to be out of Surlas before sun down tomorrow.' Lei nodded but said nothing. 'Is there something on your mind, Lei? Please, tell me. Do you believe I'm abandoning my men? Do you think I'm an ice-hearted bitch?'

His anger disappeared. 'No, blaze commander, I would never think such a thing. Each man here is able to thrive alone in any terrain; we are abandoning no-one. My anger is simply fresh from today's events.'

'Do you think we should have killed the children?'

'I think we should never have gone near that farm in the first place, Pellix and Henrus have much to answer for. Six from our squads are dead, and our own blaze commander was nearly one of them.'

'You feared I would lose the fight?' Phira asked with one eyebrow raised.

'You have never lost a fight when it is honest steel against steel, but that sword, if it had touched you, or even the speed with which the assassin was able to produce a throwing knife, he could have thrown them at you just as easily.'

'If he had killed me with those knives then he would have had no route of escape. For a madman he is certainly not stupid. But here, you can hug me, Lei, and weep into my warm breasts if you are so glad I am still alive.' Phira let a knife of her own slide unseen down her sleeve, ready to punish Lei for any more of his feminine weakness. 'It would be good to feel your body pressed up against mine...'

Lei shook his head. 'I apologise for my emotions, blaze commander, but I feared we lost you when Valhar made that thrust for your stomach. I... feared *I* had lost you.'

Phira watched the moisture gather in Lei's eyes, the light of the fire sparkling against the held back tears. She certainly cared for Lei, and valued and respected him, and as much as she loved abusing the man, she would not mind using him for other pleasures. But Phira's own selfish ambition had caused Dallid enough suffering without adding this. She could not know if Dallid was lying with other women but would not condemn him if he did. It was her own decision that their lives be this way, and her own weakness that she could not dissolve the marriage altogether.

Dallid may be small, but he was a giant portion of her heart that reminded Phira she did not always dedicate her life to her own selfish needs. There had been a time when her heart beat just for him, before Yiran, and before her grand ambitions to save her country from ruin.

'Lei,' she said, placing her hand tenderly on his cheek. 'For the love of Frehep, grow a pair of balls.'

Lei closed his eyes, he really should not have expected any better and he even laughed. 'One day I might outrank you, then I'll bloody be able to order you to do whatever I want.'

'Not if you keep falling in love with cunts like me,' she smiled back. 'I'd only bite your cock off and shove it up your own arse, Lei. You're not strong enough for me.' Phira wanted to shake her head. She was sounding more and more like Thisian every day. It was a disturbing thought.

Phira had been watching for his hand to move and strike her, so she was remarkably caught off guard when he leaned in and kissed her. Phira was so impressed with his audacity that she let him continue and even kissed him back. His breath tasted good in her mouth and his hands found their way to her hips. When her blood started to heat up, wanting his hands to explore further, she knew it was time to stop. The knife in her hand pressed its way to Lei's throat and he froze. She pushed him back and she sighed at the need for it.

'Try to kiss me again, Lei, and I'll have no choice but to cut off your balls, whether you've grown a pair by then or not. Now return to the men and arrange the watch. I wish to be informed when our riders return with news of Valhar.'

Lei stood up obediently and raised his palm in farewell. 'Yes, blaze commander.' It was a brave show.

When he left she wanted to sob. She wanted nothing more than to jump the fool man and release three years of pent up frustration. It had been so long she could think about nothing else, and then realised that this was exactly what it felt like to be Thisian, no wonder she was starting to sound like him.

Phira closed her eyes and thought of Dallid.

When she woke up it was before dawn. The fires still burned underneath the canvas ceilings they had erected for their camps, but the cold made it near impossible to sleep. Her face throbbed. She cursed her weakness of flesh but the fact that she still breathed showed her strength. Sweeping her cloak back to have the scabbard ready, Phira laid a reassuring hand upon her sword hilt. Her woollen cloak was wet from the damned snow but at least they would be out of Surlas by day's end.

The rest of the world would not yet be as bad, despite what the Frostborn claimed. No one Powerborn could command that much power. If Aerath was to turn the world into ice, then it would take decades. Her urgency was returning to Rath'Nor before Gravren, and if she could not find a way to be a part of the squad sent to destroy Aerath, then she would return to Coruln and ensure Yiran and her village were safe.

Phira got up from the sleeping trench constructed to hold off the cold but try as they might with canvas roofs, snow trenches and extra bedding underneath them, the cold would always be there to try and kill them. Stepping about the camp, Phira spotted one of the sentries by the edge. They were wearing their Ihnhaarat mask, to help keep the frost from their face and nodded to Phira as she passed. Walking over to the second fire, she searched for Lei's lying form to wake him and begin readying their departure. Logs and rocks had been dragged over to surround the fire, and some men slept with their backs pressed against them. There was a spattering of blood on one of the rocks, and out of curiosity Phira stepped over to see why.

A piece of flesh was lying on the rock, which was strange, since she had not noticed any altercation between the warriors the night before. Fighting between squad members was common enough as long as it was not between officers, but the fight was over when blood was spilled, actually cutting off a piece of flesh was rare.

Picking up the red sticky meat, Phira's head flared with panic when she saw she was holding an ear. Turning back to the sentry with immediate suspicion, Phira saw the warrior staring at her.

The dead white face of the mask seemed to glow through the dark of early morning, and the black cloak hid any weapons the sentry might be holding. Phira still had her katana strapped to her belt and drew it out with purpose as she marched over to the warrior. The sentry drew out his own blade, the serrated one of the Ihnhaarat and pretended to look around as if questioning why Phira had drawn hers.

'Your pretence does not fool me, madman,' she spat before readying herself to strike.

The man took off his mask then and revealed the golden skinned face of a Fureath'i.

'Blaze commander?' he asked in confusion, nervously eyeing the lowered blade she had positioned to gut him.

Turning around to scan the area, Phira squeezed her sword fiercely. 'Last night, was there violence between the squads?'

'Violence, blaze commander? No, none, we spoke Tellings of our fallen, and of your victory: Phira the Jaguar.'

He bowed down his head for speaking her name. But his nervous eyes tried to gage her reaction to see if further bowing or apology was necessary. Phira did not care a sheep's tit about what the man said, she was on edge with alarm. That ear belonged to Valhar, unless one of the men had taken it as a trophy.

She relaxed. Of course that was what had happened. Her suspicions and trying to think of every possible threat had blinded her to the obvious. Ignoring the sentry and returning back to the camp fire, Phira found Lei and woke him with a boot in the ribs.

'Blaze commander,' he greeted with a grunt and quickly stood up.

'Wake the men, our riders have not returned and we are leaving without them.'

He nodded and went about waking both squad leaders first, getting them to ready their respective warriors. Phira kept a keen eye on the proceedings, still not fully recovered from the state of alarm she had brought on herself. One by one each warrior rose and went about their tasks as normal, and Phira was about to turn away to prepare her own belongings, when she saw someone had moved the severed ear to another rock across from the fire. It was strange that she had not seen any warrior do it. Phira had been keeping a sharp eye to see who the owner of the trophy had been. Looking back to where first she had seen it, her breath caught to see it still there.

'Blaze commander! Come quickly!' Lei called out and Phira ran across to where the other sentries were placed.

Both were dead. Their left ears had been cut off in mockery after their throats had been slit. She cursed herself a fool for not checking on them as she had the first sentry.

How did the bastard get so close?

'Blaze commander, what are your orders?'

Phira ignored the question and stormed back to her own saddle bags. She saw the wet red colour long before she arrived, and then stood motionless, fuming with overwhelming anger and with nothing to direct it towards. Four more ears were placed neatly upon the canvas sack where she stored her weapons. All left ears, she had no doubt, and she kicked the sack in frustration, scattering the rancid flesh.

Pacing up and down trying to gather her thoughts and release some energy, Phira tried to go through all possible plans of action, but the only thing she could think of was how had the man gotten into a Fureath'i camp and killed two of her men? He had gotten close enough to her that he could leave rotting flesh by her side and then disappear without leaving a single footstep in the snow.

Perhaps the man is really bloody Brijnok and pretends to be a madman so the other gods will not notice, she thought and then a more likely idea occurred to her. Amadis the Powerful, the original owner of the Jaguar sword, and Valhar's claimed sire, had possessed the speed and strength of a Powerborn. *That would explain how his movements could blur during the attack,* but Phira did not fully believe her own thoughts. One problem with her theory was there was no way she would have survived a sword fight with Amadis the Powerful.

Phira stopped pacing. Where she had kicked her canvas sack, some weapons had fallen out, including one wrapped in a leather waistcoat. Using the tip of her katana, Phira carefully lifted the fabric to reveal the shining black blade of the Jaguar sword still underneath, and relief flooded through her.

Either he did not know it was there or he wanted to drive her to madness first before he took it. As well as wishing to torment her with the severed ears of her warriors, Valhar could be taunting her to pick up the deathly blade. Did that confirm if she were to touch it, it would kill her? Did Valhar leave it there as a trap or did he not find it?

Or did it mean that she was the new owner of the sword and Valhar was unable to touch it himself until she was dead.

'But the bastard could have killed me while I slept.'

Her outburst made her notice Lei had followed her when she ignored his question. He looked down and saw the red stain upon the sack, as well as the ears still visible from where she had kicked them.

'Blaze commander, I will not sleep until this fiend has been gutted. Not a single warrior under your command will close their eyes again and risk another failure such as this. Already my best trackers are scouting the area. As soon as full light arrives the villain will have no place in the world that he can hide.'

Phira took a breath and closed her eyes. The swelling around her cheek and eyebrow throbbed painfully at the motion, but it was easy to ignore. 'We will not legitimise his baiting with our reaction, Lei.' Her ember started to protest but she stopped him with a severe look. 'He has killed twelve of our men now. Twelve.' She nearly choked on hearing the words but remained composed. 'Six by the farm, four of our trackers and two of our scouts, but our current mission is more important than personal vengeance. The betterment of our nation comes first above all and we will travel with fire until it is completed. We cannot waste time chasing down a lunatic who wishes to be chased.'

Lei nodded his compliance but she could see his true feelings clearly. Her own eyes wanted to burn with the same sentiments, but her position as commander could allow no doubt or hesitation. Her position as a Fureath'i could tolerate a small compromise however.

'He will not be forgotten, Lei. I have thousands of warriors at my disposal that I can devote towards his death, and when such time allows our dedication to that task, take solace that I will do all that can be done to bring great suffering down upon Valhar the Bastard.'

'Yes, blaze commander,' he said with more conviction, but it would not stop his desire to hunt down the madman and tear out his throat with his bare hands. Twice Valhar had been in a position to kill Phira, and she knew that her life was something worth more to Lei than anything else in the world, the fool that he was.

Turning around as light began to glow from a rising sun, Phira's eyes searched vainly for a hint of the infamous assassin. Any sign at all to make her change her mind towards pursuit. A part of her could even imagine that the madman would show himself to her, just a glimpse to keep her hatred fresh.

But Phira saw nothing but snow.

CHAPTER TWENTY NINE

Hunted

Phira sat atop her horse, refreshingly free of the Ihnhaarat mask. How those people managed to live their whole lives with them on was a thing of idiocy. Any custom that challenged common sense needed to fall to it. Fureath'i customs were not beyond her cut, and she had severe changes that she would make to those, but had to wait until she was in a position to make them. Her people were stuck in a world of tradition and magic, and saw no need to better themselves with reason or mechanics. So when Phira first studied the warfare of the Mordec Empire she had been amazed at how superbly they had developed despite the absence of Powerborn within their race. The siege engines and war machines they had created, along with the science of tactics they had reasoned, made them a fearsome army. But of course, it was an army that would still be swept aside by one with Powerborns. Phira put back on her mask.

A rider approached their position wearing the clothing of the Ihnhaarat, but he was missing his shadow. Phira grit her teeth. Either Valhar had killed the warrior's shadow, the warrior had broken her orders, or the rider was Valhar. Those kinds of constant suspicions were driving Phira as mad as the assassin who hunted her. Every hour she would stop her squads and make them remove their masks, still convinced that the bastard was hiding in plain sight of them. How else was he able to get so close and kill her soldiers? Her right hand rested on the hilt of her sword, and Phira sat patiently for the warrior to arrive.

'Blaze commander!' the rider shouted in recognisable Fureath'i, but Phira's hand did not move. He pulled his horse up inappropriately close. 'Blaze commander, forgive me, but I have urgent news.'

'Have you found, captured, or killed Valhar?' Phira asked.

The ranger dropped his head. 'We have not, blaze commander, but we have sighted a party of Ihnhaarat in the forest, perhaps fifty in total. I believe they are the same party we left the road to avoid and I believe they are hunting for us.'

Could things continue to get worse? Phira pulled out her sword and thrust the butt of it into the ranger's face, knocking the mask clean off. Blood was trailing from his lip and nose from the strike, but he at least did not meet her eyes as he accepted the blow and hung his head.

'Where is your shadow?' she asked.

'She had to remain, blaze commander, to keep watch on the Ihnhaarat.'

'And what were my orders?'

'Never to leave my shadow's side, blaze commander.'

The news of the Ihnhaarat in the forest was important enough for him to risk her ire by disobeying orders. It was a brave thing but orders had to be followed.

'If, because of your absence, her throat is cut by Valhar's hand then I will have no choice but to do the same to yours.'

'I understand, blaze commander.'

She took pride that he indeed did accept the risk involved in giving her the information. It would not stop her from killing him later if she had to, but still, Phira was proud. She left the warrior to his shame and to return to his shadow immediately. Making her way through the trees over to Lei, she saw his mask was also off and noticed him hold back a curse when he saw the look on her face.

'You have heard,' he said with resignation.

'Was I not to?'

'Not by another scout who forgot their place thinking they could speak to a blaze commander, no.' he said. 'It is not common for blaze commanders to ride with their squads like you do. It is easy for them to forget propriety.'

Another outdated Fureath'i custom. She was too frustrated to care about it and she had not struck the scout for speaking to her out of rank, she struck him for abandoning his shadow to the possibility of Valhar's knives. Making the scout report to his squad leader, and then to the ember class and finally to the blaze commander was an absolute waste of time. It was the ember's job to keep the men in line and the blaze commander's job to keep them alive. So she would let Lei punish the man further if she was not forced to kill him later herself.

'Let us escape Surlas first and then we can examine our discipline, Lei.' Results were all that mattered to her.

'You are right as always, blaze commander,' Lei conceded. 'Let us deal with these Prae'surlas, the villain Valhar, and then we can worry about being better Fureath'i.'

'Prae'surlas?'

Lei looked anxiously to his two companions, perhaps rightfully worried that he was about to be assaulted by Phira.

'The Prae'surlas that are hunting us, blaze commander, did the scout not explain that?'

Phira let out a laugh. *Of course things can always get worse.* Her laughter made everyone near her very nervous.

'No, Lei, the scout told me about the Ihnhaarat hunting us from the south.'

This time Lei did curse and immediately bowed his head in submission. Phira stared at him for a time.

'Apologies, blaze commander,' he finally uttered. 'I forget myself.'

Her eyes stayed on him for a time. The horses shifted timidly, picking up on the tension, and Phira could see beads of sweat form on Lei's forehead, unconcerned of the cold surrounding them.

'Tell me about the Prae'surlas hunting us, Lei.'

'They are coming from the west, blaze commander. I would judge they were following Valhar east and came across the farms he had left.'

Lei wisely did not mention that they most likely encountered the children she had left alive too, who in turn would have given as much information as they knew. Phira said nothing for a while, letting her mind sort through the different options. Lei and the other two warriors sat uncomfortably while they waited, never knowing when she was going to become angry, if she would strike them, if she would cut them, or if she would kill them. *Have I always been such an intense and volatile bitch?*

Only since joining the army, Phira decided. She had been a girl without rank or much ability before then. The playfully unpredictable nature of that girl had become something to fear from the woman as a blaze commander. The youngest, and only female, blaze commander in the country, and it could not be easy for these older men to live in such anxiety of her moods. So Phira let their anxiety grow as it would, and did nothing to relieve the tension she had created. Instead she began forming a plan of action.

If they continued as they were, it was possible that Valhar would continue to elude her traps and pick off her men. Or would the other two hunting parties make him keep his distance? It was impossible to figure out what a madman might do. She did not think she would have much time to set traps for Valhar anyway if she was busy avoiding two different hosts hunting them.

Phira was not particularly concerned about the Ihnhaarat. They were traders after all, with only a handful of warriors. Unless they had Powerborns with them, in which case they would be great trouble indeed. But she was confident none of them would be skilled trackers in any case. The traders were doing well to follow them so far, but now that she was aware of them, Phira could avoid them without much effort.

The Prae'surlas though were far better at hunting Fureath'i in the snow than the Fureath'i were at evading them. Given that it was a forest and nearly half her squads were made up of forest Fureath'i did not help when it was drenched with white muck, and it would be hard going keeping vigilant for Valhar and being chased by Prae'surlas at the same time. Phira did not like being chased.

'We kill the Prae'surlas,' she said firmly.

'As you command,' Lei began before letting himself add, 'But they are said to number at least thirty. With our casualties -'

'I am aware of our casualties, Lei.'

Lei cleared his throat. It was his job to point out any dangers Phira was overlooking and if he did not then she would reprimand him for not doing so. The challenge for him was to make those points without Phira turning him into another casualty. And in the mood she was in, he would be wise to stay silent.

'We should call back our scouts,' he decided on. It was half way to saying that they needed every single warrior to ensure her recklessness would work, and it was half way to saying that he fully supported her plan of action. More importantly it said that he was anxious to begin.

'Call them quickly and have everyone ready to move. We have Prae'surlas to kill.'

When everyone had returned, Phira could not resist sneaking up with her rangers to get a look at the Prae'surlas they were about to attack. Lei had nearly blown a blood vessel when she told him, but she had told him, not asked him. He almost contained his frustration but failed with mutterings about going alone to look at north-men and about Valhar finding her. Phira shook her head at him, he really was worse than a woman for worry.

So she had gotten as close as she could to the pack of north-men, as close as anyone dressed all in black could have while surrounded by white. She had made some observations and then returned without incident. Grandmother Lei expressed his surprise and approval that she had decided not to begin the charge by herself, and Blaze Commander Phira punched him in the face for his impropriety. She did not break his nose, but he would not be breathing from it for a few days. All in all she was content that she would hate to have herself as a blaze commander.

As she kept telling him, Lei needed to grow a pair of stones and stand up to Phira, or she would continue to roll him belly up at every opportunity. Thankfully he did not grow his stones today though, because she did not have time to be wasting on such nonsense.

Her men were in position and she stood in front of a small group as if she were discussing orders. Two rangers had been sent out to let themselves be seen by the Prae'surlas, but to do so subtly enough that the Prae'surlas would not be suspicious. If the north-men's own scouts followed them, then they would just have to kill them and keep trying until the Prae'surlas got it right. If the northern scouts got it right straight away and returned to their host, then they would lead the entire party into a trap. Phira and her group were part of the bait, she being the only one facing the direction that the Prae'surlas would come, and her men all standing with good discipline, held their backs to the soon approaching enemy. She did not need to be seen talking, as they all had their masks on, so she stood in silence and waited.

Six Ihnhaarat masks stared back at her, and Phira's treacherous mind kept returning to the possibility that Valhar was one of them. It seemed like something the madman would do, to dress up and pretend to be part of her squad, salute and take orders with amused vigour. It almost made her want to strike the masks off of each of their faces and reveal the bastard finally. She had since strapped the Jaguar blade to her back to ensure it was not taken, but maybe having it so close to her was making her as mad as Valhar. Could that be the secret of the sword? It took the lives of those it touched but it took the mind of the person holding it? Phira stretched her fingers and flexed.

Going over the permutations in her head again, Phira did a quick check that she was not forgetting anything. The plan was for fourteen Fureath'i to kill thirty Prae'surlas in the middle of winter in Surlas. Kris had a Telling about him doing something similar, where he made his men bury themselves in the best camp site, wait until the Prae'surlas unbelievably did actually camp there, then continue to wait before killing them all in their sleep. What Phira wanted to know is how many other times had Kris tried that plan and had it fail? Where were the Tellings about the ten other times he had made his warriors bury themselves for the night and have nothing happen? She had not heard anything to indicate that such failed attempts had ever happened but it was amusing to think it.

Her plan was not as simple and definitely not as stubborn. Out of her fourteen men she had six with her as the main attacking party. Two scouts were luring the Prae'surlas towards them, where only four of her men were waiting buried in the snow. She would let the Tellers decide whose plan was better, and she was just glad that Kris was not her ember.

Kris was exactly the warrior who would kill his commander if he thought their decision was not the best for the blaze command. So Kris was of course sent very far away from his blaze command for that reason, and given as many Prae'surlas to kill as he wanted to make sure he did not come back. It was what had happened to Phira when she was an ember. The only difference was that Kris probably enjoyed the isolation and independence too much to go back and harass his blaze commander like he should. He was stronger than her in many ways but in that one area of necessary persistence, he was weak.

Weak was perhaps a wrong word to describe anything about Kris though and she regretted the thought immediately. Phira owed a lot of her own strength to him. Her skill came from Yiran, and the fire in her heart she owed to Dallid, but Kris had given her all of what little control she possessed.

As a youth she had been the youngest of five brothers, from three different mothers, but all six had been gathered together by Phira's grandmother on her father's side. The elder had been very insistent when rounding up the youths from the three villages, and Phira liked to believe some of her strength as a female warrior came from her too. As an elder though her grandmother had too many other duties within the community and was not always there to discipline the six youths. So Phira, as the only girl, was mercilessly beaten by her brothers most days, often for being slower or weaker than them in training, but sometimes because she was just the only girl. It made her hate them but it made her fight to become better so she could repay them too.

The major turning point in her life was when Yiran the Unconquered retired from the army, coming back to Coruln as an elder to the community. He had joined the army at the age of twelve so he had no children either, and so no grandchildren. When news of him arriving came, the entire region was buzzing about him training the next generation of legendary warriors. Every one of her brothers had planned the rest of their youths around what supreme training they would be receiving from the unconquered legend. Then Yiran had arrived, and when asked by Ryat how soon he would begin training the youths in swordplay, he said that he would not.

Everyone was shocked and Yiran even went on to say that he would train the youths in farming, blacksmithing, and tailoring instead. According to the man, if his country wanted to better itself from his sabre then his country should not have forced him to retire.

Her brothers were devastated but Phira had never expected to be good enough to be trained by the legend anyway. Her dismissal of the traumatising event for her brothers served only to increase their rage towards her and the beatings had increased during those weeks. It somehow became her fault that Yiran had deemed them unworthy. She had not yet known Kris back then but Thisian and Dallid both tried to help her whenever they could. It did not make much of a difference, all five of her brothers were older and stronger, and as a family they did almost everything together. Beating three twelve year olds made little more difference than beating one.

Phira was trying to fight the five of them on her own the day Yiran found her. They were playing their favourite game with her, where they would let her have the first strike, which would be blocked easily and then returned. Only this day they thought it would be funnier if when she struck one; that all five would strike back. They were only using blunted sabres so to them it was merely good fun, training their weakling sister to be better. She did as best as she could, but she had no way of defending against five attackers.

It was Yiran's fault that the worst of them hit her, she had been about to defend her head, letting the others strike at her body, when she saw him striding across the field and her attention was distracted. The blow had cracked open her skull and she had no memory of what happened after. According to Yiran he had taught her brothers what it could mean for five to attack one, and although she did not see them for a time after, Phira had heard they had all been beaten bloody by the man.

The life changing result was that Yiran adopted her as his own daughter, and took her away from her five brothers. Phira's grandmother had been in a rage at the news and demanded she be returned. Yiran flatly told her he would kill the first person to lay a hand on Phira, including her grandmother. So her grandmother could not drag her back, and Phira would not go back by choice. She remained and, once fully recovered, demanded that Yiran train her. He laughed when she said it and told her that she sounded like a general giving orders already. For a time it was just the two of them and Phira cherished it greatly. Soon she returned to the others in the village though.

Thisian and his grandfather had found some boy named Kris alone in the woods and brought him to the village. Apparently

Kris's grandfather had lived alone with him much the way Phira and Yiran were doing, but the main difference was that Kris's grandfather had died when Kris was seven, and so Kris had spent the last five years living on his own.

Thisian could not get over how different the boy was but Dallid and Phira did not mind him. He was quiet and hardworking and fitted into their group well. When they were younger Thisian had always been the one Phira was closest to, but it seemed to come after the arrival of Kris that things began to change. She spent less and less time with the group, training with Yiran instead, and whenever she did return, Thisian seemed more interested in the new breasts Phira was growing underneath her tunic and the new hair he knew she had between her legs, than anything else. So she stayed away from Thisian and grew closer to Dallid and Kris, especially Dallid who she only seemed to be seeing for the first time since she separated from Thisian.

Dallid had always been the more serious one of the group when compared to Thisian and Phira, but with the arrival of Kris it made her see Dallid as the decent Fureath'i that he was. He was not as wild as her, but he was not as obsessed with mating as Thisian was.

She and Dallid grew closer and married, but before that happened, two of her brothers had left to join the army. It came as a surprise when she found out. Phira had been so busy spending time with Yiran and Dallid that she had more or less forgotten about them. She became angry with herself for avoiding them for so long, and decided that with her new training, it was time for a reckoning.

When she arrived at the cabin of her remaining three brothers, they were on their own with no elders or other villagers around. Phira had them all to herself. The three of them were in training when she got there and they were reserved in their initial reactions. They looked behind her to see if Yiran was to follow and they looked down at Phira's hand where she held her sabre. It was not blunted.

Nervous, being only three instead of five, they still tried to laugh at her. Phira did not laugh and told them that she would let them have the first strike. All three were older and stronger than her, with years more training and experience, but the time Phira had spent with Yiran proved their match. Her speed and skill was too much and soon into the fight Phira knew she could begin to toy with them. She started making cuts along their faces to enrage them and more along their forearms to make their grips slick with blood. The more frustrated they grew, the greater their hatred became. They screamed at her as they attacked and she increased the cruelty of her own in return.

Kris suddenly appeared from nowhere, silent as ever, and no-one wanted him there. The three brothers were already losing and did not need another sabre to battle and Phira was winning by herself, she did not need anyone's help. He was roared at by everyone to go away, but none risked turning their sabres on him as they were too heavily committed to the fight already going on. Kris continued to stand there and watch, said nothing and did nothing. Soon Phira forgot about him and with her full concentration on the fight, she saw the opportunity she was looking for. Two of the brothers had moved back which left one fatally vulnerable. Phira disarmed him and followed through with a back hand cut to the throat. Her arm hit something mid swing, and she found she was stopped by Kris's grip.

'You do not want to kill your own blood,' he said, and held her arm unmoving.

In her rage Phira almost tried to kill Kris, but there was something about his eyes that made her stop. They were the blackest eyes she had ever seen on a Fureath'i, but something inside them made her know that he spoke the truth. She even seemed to know that he spoke from personal experience. Phira never found out if Kris had killed his own grandfather, even at the unlikely age of seven, but she did not doubt that he could have.

The brother she was about to kill was shocked by how close her blade stood, but the other two rushed in with outrage of it. Kris stepped back and let Phira make her own decision. She launched into it with a snarl and when she had defeated them both, one with a broken nose and one with a broken arm, Phira realised that she did not need to kill them. She had beaten them and killing them would not make her better, she was already better.

Yiran had taught her that to be better, you could not look at other people for it; the only person you could look at was yourself.

Kris explained to her later the difference between fighting and killing, and that every warrior needed to know how to separate the two. Phira never had much control when compared to some Fureath'i, but she thanked Kris for what little she had. Her wild impulses and reckless plans were responsible for a lot her success but could have easily have been responsible for her death many times. It made her smile to know that Kris would not consider Phira as having any control at all, but she knew deep down that she could be much worse if she tried.

Movement ahead brought her back to the present and it was time to fight. Her warriors were to wound as many Prae'surlas as they could, but the plan was to just fight the northerners so that her squad could get away. She did not want to kill too many yet. Phira watched her returning rangers wade their way through snow and forest, pretending to be ignorant of the Prae'surlas following them. Then she spotted the ice giants lumbering after, the forerunners of what looked to be the full host. Underneath her mask, Phira smiled.

Drawing out her sword, Phira began shouting in Ihnhaarat to try and maintain their disguises for as long as they could. She shouted towards her rangers to warn them of the Prae'surlas following them and they both turned around to see the host approaching. Standing still in surprise for a time, it took more shouting from Phira to get her two men running back to join her. As soon as they merged with her waiting warriors, a different two drifted off and became lost to the forest. The Prae'surlas noticed that her group was not running and did not break into a charge as she would have liked. Instead they carefully picked their way forward, confident that they had the advantage with numbers and home terrain. Phira barged to the front of her warriors to spur on the lazy north-men.

'You dare hunt my men!' she shouted in Prae'surlas. 'The nation of Ihnhaarah will not stand for this!'

'You dare speak to a man in such a way?' the foremost Prae'surlas shouted back, incensed that a woman could talk at all. 'You Ihnhaarat are nothing but whores that serve us for money. Why are you in these forests? You should be back on the road selling us slaves.'

The Prae'surlas must have known from the children that a squad of Fureath'i were dressed as Ihnhaarat. Either the man she was dealing with was good at keeping his suspicions to himself, or they had not met the children and he assumed her group were genuine. She supposed a Fureath'i woman dressed as an Ihnhaarat in the middle of Surlas would never have the audacity to start threatening a host of Prae'surlas twice her number.

'You think we are your whores? You are nothing but our dogs that we throw scraps of food!' she shouted back. 'Without our slaves your nation would be sucking on snow. Be gone and leave us to our business!'

As more and more of them got closer, a different Prae'surlas answered her. 'You do not tell us where to go within our own lands, merchant. It is exactly about your business that we will speak with you. Drop your weapons and remain where you are.'

'Come and get our weapons if you want them so badly!'

Phira judged the distance where the Prae'surlas had come to and decided it was good enough. She wanted them to charge but still they were being cautious, so Phira had no choice but to start the charge herself.

'May Creedus bring light to our blades!' she shouted in Ihnhaarat as her and six Fureath'i ran forward to fight thirty Prae'surlas.

She had been counting on the arrogance of the Prae'surlas, but as they stood there laughing, doubts began to form in her head that she had overestimated their conceit. Then one of the spearmen waved an order and six Prae'surlas were sent forward to deal with the troublesome traders. Most likely the northerners were even ordered to just placate and capture the excitable Ihnhaarat so that they could be questioned.

Then, as the two parties were about to meet, four highly trained shadows of black rose up from the white snow and took the Prae'surlas from the sides. The four men she had in waiting made their first strikes all count and before the north-men could respond she and her six warriors were on them. Looking around Phira was confident that none of her men had been injured and already the thirty Prae'surlas were down to twenty four.

The full host of north-men were standing in outrage when Phira shook her sword at them. 'Look what your whores have done to you! You try to poke us with your spears and we cut off your cocks!'

Phira remembered the first time she had learnt about whores from Yiran, she had been appalled at their existence but taken great joy about never telling Thisian about them. Her amusement was cut short then, when at last the full charge came. Even Phira was not so arrogant as to stand and fight them. All ten Fureath'i turned their heels and ran, weaving in spiral formation in and out the trees to avoid any throwing spears that would be sent. It slowed down their escape needing to dodge like that and with the Prae'surlas having longer legs, and greater experience with traversing the snow, it would only be a matter of time before they bore down on them. So, as her squad ran, two more black cloaks drifted off into the forest and disappeared.

When she heard the first shouts, Phira smiled. The two she had sent out before she charged were already positioned to strike at the Prae'surlas from the rear. They would stab and harass, and then quickly disappear before getting engaged with the host. Two more of her men took their turn and drifted off to either side. Phira wondered if the Prae'surlas would send a group out after them. Turning around she was able to do a quick count and continue back to running. She only counted twenty, but there was no way to tell if some had broken off to catch her lone warriors, or if some had been killed or injured by them. All she could do was to continue running and stick to her plans.

Spotting a sign that her scouts had left her, Phira had to shout in Prae'surlas for all her men to hear. Only some of them could speak Ihnhaarat - and she did not dare to shout in Fureath'i yet. At the command her warriors drifted south, keeping a sharp eye for more signs left by the two scouts she had held back to guide their retreat. Twice more they had to make changes in their course, and she could not risk letting any more of her warriors break off to harass the north-men. She had to rely on those that had already done so to follow orders and return to where they had picketed the horses, ready for the escape when it came.

An alarming time passed then where Phira could not spot any more signs from her two scouts. None of her warriors shouted out that they saw them either, but she was confident that if there were signs, she would have seen them. Doubts began to race alongside her that Valhar had used the opportunity to create greater havoc. That he had found her squad split and ripe for murder. If he had killed the two scouts she had left behind then all could be lost. New plans began to form in her mind to compensate, and she struggled for a way to survive the situation.

Then two black figures appeared ahead but Phira held back her relief. 'The Prae'surlas have attacked us!' she shouted in Ihnhaarat.

'Those goat-rutting bastards!' Pellix shouted back to her.

It was only then that Phira allowed herself smile and her group swept up the two new additions as they continued their run. Risking sporadic glances back, Phira was glad the forest had not thinned through their route or else more than one of her men would have spears through their backs. As it was the Prae'surlas were close but she believed they would have enough time. Pellix lead the way now, having mapped out their path and no longer needing to mark signs to follow. When Phira glanced back again she was startled to see how close the north-men had gotten but luckily she had already reached her goal.

Close to fifty black cloaks with bright white masks were riding carefully though the forest, searching for the mysterious group of fellow traders they had spotted the previous day. Perhaps the real Ihnhaarat had simply been curious as to where their countrymen had gone to or perhaps they had been suspicious of more. Regardless of their reasons, Phira was about to reward their curiosity with a host of northern giants all looking to do murder.

'The Prae'surlas have attacked us!' she shouted in Ihnhaarat again and did not slow down as she reached the traders. Phira and her men kept running, nimbly making their way through the mounted Ihnhaarat and, before any could stop her to challenge them, the Prae'surlas arrived and let loose their spears. The larger host of Ihnhaarat had no choice but to fight back and soon both of Phira's enemies were killing each other. She and her squad did not stop and let the tangled battle continue without them.

The sounds of fighting began to fade the further she ran, the shouts of rage and the screams of pain growing distant, and soon she was leading the way again, familiar with the area where they had left their mounts. Four of her warriors were already there and she ordered them to take off their masks for caution. The four Fureath'i did so without delay, and she and her own men returned the gesture. For a moment of madness Valhar's face flashed out to her instead of a Fureath'i's golden skin, but on second glance it was just her mind playing tricks with her. Only two warriors had failed to come back and she quickly questioned the other four as to their whereabouts.

'I did not see them fall to a Prae'surlas spear, blaze commander,' one warrior answered confidently. 'Unless...' Phira almost drew her sword to strike the man for his hesitation, and seeing the flash of anger in her eyes quickly continued. 'Forgive me, blaze commander, unless the assassin Valhar has taken them while they were separated.'

The thought had entered Phira's mind as well but it did nothing for the morale of the men to have someone word it. How one man had killed so many highly trained warriors...

Gritting her teeth to stop from beating the warrior, Phira turned back to Lei.

'We leave now. If either party gain quick victory they will come searching for the scoundrels that caused the mayhem.'

Lei hesitated and Phira raised an eyebrow in preparation. If she was in his position then she would have loudly declared she was a coward for abandoning their missing warriors. She would have challenged her blaze commander to a dual to assume command and she would have succeeded. Smartly, Phira's old commander had never given any heed to her challenges, knowing that she would kill him, and just as smartly, Lei did not either. She understood how difficult it must be for him to have a blaze commander so unbearable and superior, but he was still letting her abandon his men to the frozen cold of Surlas.

'I will remain and find our missing warriors, blaze commander. We will meet back with the squads as soon as it is possible.'

Phira wished she was wearing her mask again so she could react genuinely to his gesture. But as it was, her face had to show a different mask, one of cold contempt. 'You will do as you are ordered, Lei, or I will bend you over in front of all your soldiers and take you like the woman you are, and I will be using my sword to do it. My orders are to leave and I am not asking you for your suggestions regarding them. We all leave together. I will not send anyone out on their own so Valhar can pick them off. The two warriors have fallen or they would have returned by now. They understood their orders, now it is time for you to understand yours.'

There. She could see him hate her for how she treated him. For how she treated her missing men and for how she looked like she did not care.

'Yes, blaze commander,' he said and did nothing to hide the emotions from his words. Lei would be happier if he hated her and she would do everything she could do to help him.

Every other member of her squad probably hated her too, both for needlessly humiliating Lei, and for leaving the missing men to rot in the snow. Phira wished she could stop comparing herself to Kris, but she knew that he would not have left any of his men behind, the Sword That Walks was proof of that. It was strange to her for a man like Kris, who seemed to hate other people - who seemed to barely tolerate them in fact, to the point of just about not killing them - how he could be so committed to the lives and safety of the men in his squad.

When he is not killing them himself.

Phira regretted the unfair thought but she did not have time to feel guilty about being thoughtless. She did not have time to care about Lei's feelings towards their men or her men's feelings towards her. It did not matter how many men died and that she was the woman to blame for every one of them, all that mattered was the success of her mission.

Putting back on her Ihnhaarat mask, Phira was at least able to let her face sag with the effort her role as commander cost her. Perhaps the difference between her and Kris was that he truly did not care, and yet put on the appearance that he did. It was the opposite for her.

Phira vaulted onto her horse and kicked forward. Thankfully she heard her men follow. They could all hate her if they wished, but as long as the soldier followed orders then it should not matter to Phira who that soldier was. Their thoughts, their feelings, their heart, none of it should matter as long as she could use them as she needed. Blinking away thoughts of Dallid and Yiran, Phira accepted that no-one's life mattered to her but her own.

Looking up to the sun as she rode, Phira knew that the sun god could see her, but he was just one more person that did not matter.

CHAPTER THIRTY

Telling

Looking up at the sun, Thisian saw Frehep looking back at him, and they both knew that neither bloody knew where the hell Thisian was or where the rut he was going. And burn Frehep's bloody wrinkled sagging balls it was cold.

Wherever they were going, it was a long and cold bloody way to go for whores. They had travelled the whole day and not passed a single town or village that might have one. Griffil *promised* him they would find a town of whorehouses every time he asked during the journey but Thisian was only going to keep his patience a short while longer. He was a valuable member of their party, a fearsome Powerborn with the blood of the gods within his flesh. The fact that he had not yet done anything was the fault of there being nothing to do.

'We have to walk our horses because of the snow, we have to go this way because of the snow,' Thisian said, mocking his companions quietly in the Fureath'i tongue. 'The Amalgamation has never been treated so badly; but we have to treat the Amalgamation so badly because of the snow!'

It seemed to Thisian that legendary quests and epic adventures involved an awful lot of walking and doing nothing. At least Griffil was trying to teach him the king's tongue while they rode, but Thisian would quickly get sick of learning, lose interest, grow bored again and ask Griffil to continue. It was indeed a trying journey on a hero's heart.

'We have to stop because of the snow,' Griffil called back and Thisian barked out a laugh. Krife turned around and grinned at him to see why he was laughing but when Thisian just shrugged Krife shook his head and laughed about insane Fureath'i savages.

'*Lord* insane Fureath'i savage,' Thisian muttered, offended that no one had called him lord since he became Powerborn. 'What about you, Kris? Will you call me lord?' The new horse that he had cleverly named Kris again - it was a good name for a horse - did not dignify his demand with a reply. 'Shut up, horse. I should have named you Phira instead of Kris, at least she would speak to me if only to tell me to be quiet.'

If the horse was named Phira though it would most likely kick him off and trample him, but at least he would get to spend his days riding her. As a highly skilled Fureath'i warrior, Thisian had been in many fights, but if he was to name the one person who had hit him the most in his life it was of course Phira-bloody-almighty. She took it upon herself to make striking Thisian an art form.

Before they had left for the army, she had been able to take out her sabre and strike Thisian in the face so fast with the flat that he did not even have time to flinch. It was not natural for one person to be so fast. He grinned then wondering if he was faster than her now he was Powerborn. He was still not sure if he would risk meeting her in a fair fight, but if the odds were in his favour then it would be interesting to find out.

Krife and Griffil had spotted a small cave ahead and that had been the reason for the early halt, but Thisian would not complain. As long as they were on the way to whores then he would tolerate some time out of the snow. They had to dismount to get up to the cave mouth and when they arrived Thisian saw there was not enough room for both them and the horses. He felt bad for the beasts but accepted their fate with a mature outlook.

'Magic,' Krife called out, and Thisian looked to see if it was him. Strange that he would respond to it, but it turned out to be Hane that the fat old treasure hunter was shouting at. 'Bring the horses inside the cave and see to them.'

The fatter younger magician bristled at the command. 'I have not been assigned to your party as a servant.'

'And I'm not paying you to sit around and grow fatter you worthless rut!'

'You are paying the Amalgamation you imbecile, not me. I am here by assignment as my duty to the great Amalgamation of Sorcerers and you would do well not to bring their wrath down on you.'

'You'll be bringing the wrath of my sword right up your fat arse now if you don't pull all that weight of yours!' and Krife took out his gigantic sword to show he was serious. Hane's eyes flashed with murderous rage for a moment before returning to his normal demeanour. As proud as Thisian was for the soft man to show some fire for a second, his thoughts quickly returned to what they were fighting about.

'The cave is not big enough for us and the horses, Krife.'

'That's true, Fireborn. I'm glad we brought you along.'

Cringing at the wrong title, Thisian had already given up on trying to correct him. He had explained the difference between Fireborn and Flameborn in great detail and Krife just laughed at him and said, *whatever you say, Fireborn*. Thisian should have really learnt that talking with Krife was always pointless and often painful. He walked over to Griffil. 'Does that mean we have to sleep out in the snow with nothing but our blankets?'

Griffil shook his head seriously, 'Of course not, Thisian.' Like the fool that he was, Thisian relaxed, and Griffil continued. 'We will have to tie our blankets to those branches there to stop us from getting buried in snow during the night. We will sleep in our cloaks.' He slapped Thisian on the back like Krife would have. 'But we might find some way to keep a fine big fire going for the whole night. What do you think?'

What Thisian thought was that they wanted him to waste his energy staying Connected to a fire all bloody night. Would he even be able to sleep if he was using magic like that? Flameborns did not need to sleep of course, he thought sourly. They sounded a lot like Kris. But if they were like Kris, and did not eat, drink, or sleep, then what joy did they have in life?

As if by destiny his mind cycled back to whores. Nodding with determination, Thisian choose a likely spot for their fire and sat himself down, trying to ignore the watchful eyes of his Foreign companions. Krife would be watching and waiting for the opportunity to abuse him, Hane would be looking and probably trying to steal some of his magic secrets, and Griffil, well Griffil just seemed to look at him too much anyway.

Thisian ignored them all and pushed his cloak well back out of reach of his dangerous hands. They combusted with a powerful display of strength and Thisian amazed himself at his own abilities. Creating the fire seemed relatively easy - as his skin always seemed ready to explode with it - so now all he had to do was get the fire to catch to the ground and maintain it. Looking up at the trees where they would tie their blankets, Thisian considered getting some wood. That would look like weakness though, and any man that grew up with Kris and Phira, knew better than to show any weakness. He was side-tracked for a moment wondering if that was why Dallid worked so hard to get such big arms and chest, to look stronger. But no, Thisian corrected, Dallid only did it because he was so bloody short.

Giving his fine tall arms a flex, Thisian threw his hands forward dramatically to create holy god-fire!

The flames erupted, going straight out, and must have felt some of his intentions since it actually stayed where he wanted it. The snow did not catch fire as he half-thought it might, but the flames settled in mid-air and just created a pool of melt water underneath. Thisian frowned suspiciously and took his time getting used to the feeling of Connection he had with it. The fire felt like it beat at the same time as his heart, pulsing with the same power as his blood.

Breathing out through his mouth in preparation, Thisian closed his fists to out the fire on his hands. He did not intend to close his eyes as well and when he opened them he smiled triumphantly that the camp fire still blazed. He had created his first heart fire from pure power! Standing up to meet the overwhelming congratulations of all his grateful companions, Thisian found none of them even looking at him. They were all seeing to their own tasks, getting ready for camp and the meal.

'Bloody ice drinkers,' he grumbled. 'All probably too busy building goats of snow to rut, I should let the fire go out and let them all freeze since they don't appreciate me.' He guessed what Krife's response to that would be, but Thisian should be able to burn through that thick hide of his before the treasure hunter could swing his tree-trunk of a sword. At the very least he could distract Krife by burning through Griffil's hide and then seize advantage.

Phira would often quote - without anyone asking - that: *opportunity demanded arrogance to seize advantage* but Thisian liked to think that the advantage was always there if you were just willing to do what your enemy was not. He found that having little moral conscience was a large advantage in doing that. Even Kris seemed to have more of a conscience than Thisian. It was a strange thought that he could think of a murdering psychotic having more moral integrity than him. But, the fortunate advantage of having no conscience was, it did not bother him for long.

Hane paddled down to appreciate his fire eventually and stood beside Thisian examining the floating flames. If the fat man was using magic then Thisian had no way of knowing, but he had better not touch Thisian's magic. It just seemed wrong having another man touch your magic with his. He frowned at the intrusive magician.

'Am I to presume that you are not long with your magic?' Hane asked with great presumption.

'You can presume that I will burn your hide to oil if you make insults like that again, fat man.'

He smiled graciously. 'Please, just because we travel with that man does not mean we need all act like him. I am merely observing that you act with a certain hesitation when it comes to your Connection. You remind me of an apprentice.'

Thisian Connected with the fire and flared it up at Hane's face. The fat man screeched and shielded himself with his arms. Thisian laughed and was announced of Krife's arrival by the old man's own bellow of laughter.

'Got you right in the face!' he laughed. 'You better not have damaged our fire with your ugly face, or I'm taking it out of your pay!'

The magician looked like he would stalk away but after a quick consideration of the cold, Hane settled for seating himself on the opposite side of the fire. Krife put up a stand around the flames and placed his pot of stew over it, before thumping down onto the ground next to Thisian. Griffil arrived silently and was already sitting before Thisian realised he was the only one still standing. The fire had cleared away a good area of snowless ground now and casually Thisian moved away from the treasure hunter, to save his arms and back some bruising, sitting himself down between Griffil and Hane instead. He was nudged by the slender thief.

'I have a question, Thisian, if I may?' Griffil asked politely.

'It's for pissing and rutting with,' Krife answered for him.

'Thank you, Krife, for at least admitting I have one, but no, Thisian, I have some questions about the Fureath'i that confuse me.'

'We use ours for pissing and rutting too, Griffil,' Thisian smiled back causing Krife to roar out laughing.

'Yes, well my question is about what the Fureath'i use gold for. They don't seem to use it at all and yet have full purses of it. Why do you have it, and more importantly, if no-one in your country ever uses it, how do you get it?'

'Well,' Thisian said, not sure where to start, 'I suppose the reason we all have full purses is because we never use it. But in the army you spend time in each role to better your nation, and one of those roles is working in the mines, just like road building, and fort construction. So that's where we get the gold I guess.'

'You're allowed to keep the gold you mine?'

'No of course not, it all goes to Rath'Nor,' Thisian was not sure where the confusion was coming from. 'The coins are made in Rath'Nor and given to the army. We only have them in case we are marooned outside of Furea. We'd have much more use of them inside of Furea if someone had told us about the idea of whores. But anything else we need we are given in the army or given from farms.'

'That's what I can't comprehend,' Griffil said. 'You are just given everything?'

'Well we make the things at youth, and only given them in maturity, when we're elders we go back to making it again. So from birth we better ourselves with training and craft, working on the farms when we're not practicing weaponry. We breed livestock, grow harvests, build furniture and tailor clothes. The farms can be as big as that town we were in, and the youths from every village for miles will be made work there and bring back supplies. Some elders live there and some travel with the youths. Look, it changes from village to village, and it's exactly as boring as it sounds. I don't know if Foreigners can understand it.'

'A society without commerce is one that will not survive,' Hane said dismissively. 'Everyone working to better themselves, their country, and their community for nothing in return, it is a child's dream.'

'Didn't you hear him? They get everything they bloody want in return!' Krife smiled at the idea, 'So we make all the children and old people do the work and then get everything we want for free?'

Thisian just shook his head. 'A Foreigner can never understand what it is to be Fureath'i.'

'You do know, Krife, that you would be one of those old people right? It doesn't matter how much bigger and fatter you get every year, it doesn't stop you getting older. But I think I know more than most about Fureath'i, Thisian,' Griffil said confidently. 'For instance, this is your first camp fire with us. Isn't it Fureath'i tradition to sing a song or tell a story?'

'I'll sing a song,' Krife offered. 'I have one about a time when Griffil tried one of my women. She was at least twice as big as I am and when she sat on top of poor Griffil here, well he got lost straight up her! I had to go in and get him out myself.'

There was a good mix of responses to that statement: there was the roaring laughter of Krife, the look of purest revulsion on Hane, the polite laughing of Griffil, and Thisian's own thoughtful contemplation about what it would be like to be with a woman twice the size of Krife. She would have to be a mix between a Jhakral and five horses. It did not sound pleasant but Thisian was curious.

'I'll tell my own one, about me, if that's alright,' Griffil said. 'Not that I don't trust you to tell a good one, Krife. Now let's see, I need to impress my skill and infamy on you, Thisian, and of course our sorcerer friend here, so it will have to be an important one.' Krife groaned and Griffil ignored him. 'So let me begin by saying that I am not as young as I appear, that I am deceptively older than the eye will let you believe.'

'I think you look old enough,' Thisian said helpfully.

Griffil frowned at him. 'As I was saying, you may not believe it but I was a young man when Amadis the Powerful was approaching the height of his power, and I was in Amidon City when the Meeting of the Three Emperors occurred: Amadis the Powerful, emperor of the wildlands, and arbitrator of the world; Motaan the Beloved, emperor of the Mordec Empire; and Lyat the Destroyer of Armies, emperor of thieves. The city was packed full of foreign visitors hoping to catch a glance of any one of three great legends, not to mind the accompanying armies and camp followers. Needless to say the city was ripe for the skilled plucking of a master thief.'

'Needless to say, but you still said it,' Krife pointed out.

'Needless to say, I am the one telling this story and I have set the scene for my great act. Any other thief might have found the opportunity to sneak into some crime lords estate while they were busy treating with Lyat's emissaries, or to secret into the vast camp of the Shakara army while the majority of the men were enjoying the city. The more ambitious might have even tried his luck getting into the army camp of the Mordec Empire knowing what riches the beloved Motaan would have brought. But those were all things that someone might expect a thief to do. So where I chose to go was the one place that no sane thief would ever want to set foot. I broke into the very place where those three dangerous legends were meeting. I went inside the great Shakara mansion, to Amadis's own home, to see what I could find.'

'I can only assume that this story ends with Lyat crushing you to pulp,' Thisian said with a grin. 'Or with Motaan getting his wards to cut you to pieces?'

Griffil patted his body. 'Alas no, at least I do not think I was killed back then, but if I find out different my Fureath'i friend, you will be the first to know.'

Hane let out a snort of disbelief. 'You did not break into the mansion of Amadis Yeda while he was inside. He would immediately know it and kill you.'

'Yet I did, and he did not,' Griffil insisted. Hane did not look convinced and Thisian knew that Amadis and his three armies, instead of attacking Surlas or Furea as was expected, journeyed south after that meeting. That meant he had to force his way past the Amalgamation of Sorcerers who stopped anyone from travelling south. A mighty tarnish on the supposedly fearsome reputation of the Amalgamation.

Griffil continued trying to convince the magician. 'Perhaps Amadis was too distracted with his great company, or perhaps I was too small for his great senses to notice, but into the mansion I went and in search of unknown treasures I did go.'

'Tell them about all the unknown treasures you did find, Griff,' Krife said while trying to keep the roaring laugh back. The annoyed look Griffil threw him broke it free and their camp was assaulted with the old giant's laughter again.

'It is not what I found, but about what I could have found,' Griffil insisted.

'So in other words, he found nothing.'

'I did not find nothing!' Griffil said angrily. 'I came away with my weight in gold and one of the very first Spikes. Amadis was said to have created it with the Kel Sherans, drawing on his ability to sense the presence of other beings, like our magician friend has pointed out. But I believe that the Spikes are remnants of the Age of Might, where a warrior did not need magic or gods,' he said waving dismissively at Hane and Thisian, 'just their own might and the will to wield a powerformed weapon with courage.'

'If it was from the Age of Might, Griffil,' Hane said derisively. 'Then it would in fact be a remnant from the Age of Creation. Because, as you say, there was no magic back then, and so how did they create the powerformed weapons?'

'Does he look like a magic to you, magic?' Krife stepped in threateningly. 'It's not his job to explain your job, so just let him finish his damned story.'

Hane tried to scowl at Krife for his hypocrisy but the mean, ugly look on the old treasure hunter's face was enough to make anyone turn away. Krife then winked at Thisian with a smile, pleased with how he was abusing the poor magician.

'My gratitude, Krife,' Griffil said.

'Save your gratitude and finish this awful story. And for the record your weight in gold is about the same weight as a rabbit's tit.' Krife said back and patted his stomach proudly to show that his weight in gold would be much more. He caught Thisian looking and then patted his own tits for extra emphasis.

'Yes, well, all I wanted to emphasise was what I could have found. I could have come across the deadly Jaguar blade, or even with Motaan's wards Aevad and Pyroas in the building, I might have come across their own powerformed blades."

'I'm pretty sure you wouldn't like coming across those blades Griff.' Krife patted his own monstrous sword. 'Just like mine. There's been lots have tried to take it and there's only been one way

I've been giving it to 'em, and that's right up their arses 'till it reaches their heads.'

'Fine, Krife, if you are so anxious to put yourself in the same level of fame as Amadis or Motaan's swordsmen, let us here one of your tales,' Griffil said sourly. 'Which one will it be? The one where you were too drunk to notice the Ihnhaarat come and arrest us without a fight, only to wake up three days later and blame me for getting us thrown in the dungeon? Or how about the one where you remained asleep as the wild Chuabhotari rampaged through our camp and stole absolutely everything we had?'

'Stole everything except this sword,' Krife said as if Griffil's insults were the ideal set up for his tale. 'So I was up north past the Shadow Wall, and I had gotten so drunk I was passed out for days. When I woke up I found I had been carried off by these little silver haired rats that called themselves the bloody Whirren.' Hane's attention peeked up at the mention of the strange things but Thisian had never heard of them. 'Well I woke up with a bad damn headache and a lot of damn little people, that only stood up to my bloody knees, all staring at me. So naturally, with the silver haired rats looking for a show, the first thing I had to do was take a massive piss. And I'll tell you all, that's quite a thing to have so many little silver haired people all stare at you taking a piss. Must've been near a hundred I reckon.' Krife stopped then and nodded in satisfaction.

'That's your story?' Griffil asked. 'I've never heard you mention these Whirren before and your story is that they captured you and took a long piss and they let you go?'

Krife scratched his crotch. 'I thought it was a good story, how about you, Fireborn?'

'It could have done with more pissing,' Thisian said back. This made Krife roar out laughing again.

'Alright, alright, well the story doesn't end there as it happens. So a few days later, when I had finished my piss, the leader comes up to me and speaks in the worst king's tongue I had ever heard, even worse than yours, Fireborn, and he says: "hey big man, you fight." So I nodded and said "aye, I fight." And he lights up with the brightest smile that I've ever seen and he points to a few small rutters holding spears, just like you, Fireborn, you Fureath'i lot fight with spears don't you? Well anyway he says to me: "you fight them," so I shrugged and said alright.'

Hane snorted his disapproval again and shook his head at Krife's stupidity. 'Do you know anything about the Whirren, Krife? They get their magic from blood, and not just any blood, it has to be their own blood. How many did they let you kill?'

Krife frowned. 'They didn't *let* me kill any. I fought and killed a damn load of them though. Suppose it makes sense now alright, they did seem rightly pleased with the way I slaughtered the lot of 'em. But then again they were small and my sword was big, so would get two or three of them each time I swung it.'

'How did you get out?' Hane asked with interest. 'The Whirren like to reward their guests by introducing them to their god.'

'Yeah,' Krife sighed. 'The bloody Koruk beast, not sure I would call it a god. The place where the Whirren lived, you thought there was giant black grass poking about from everywhere, long thin trees that swayed in the wind, but no, turned out that was the damned Koruk beast. They said it was a reward alright, never did see the beast's head, but just cut my bloody way out of there as fast as I could. The silver haired rats didn't seem too angry at me leaving, more disappointed I reckon.' Krife leaned forward and stirred the cooking stew a bit and then sat back down. 'Well that's my story, at least a hundred times better than Griff's boring tale of piss, didn't even have any bloody piss in it, so what about you, magic? Or you, Fireborn? Think you can beat it?'

Thisian was not sure what one to say, Krife and Griffil had heard a lot of Fureath'i Tellings the night they had stayed at the border fort. *Too many of the same boring old stories.* He had none about himself yet, apart maybe from how he got his powers, but he was not sure he wanted people to know that, even if he had promised he was going to start inventing as many Tellings as he could to spread his fame. It could be useful to come up with an original one now and start Telling it to these three, so they could pass it on and get the fire going. Hane rudely interrupted Thisian's dazed silence though, offering his own Telling.

'Well there is one that I am particularly proud of. I can assume you all have heard of Zaviada Kasia?'

'The sixteen year old witch that makes fools of your Amalgamation at every opportunity?' Krife asked innocently.

'She only wears the body of a sixteen year old girl, she is much older, and she does not make fools of us, she is the daughter of the origin of magic.'

'Heard she was a demon,' Krife interrupted.

'She is not a demon.'

'Well I heard she was.'

'Are you going to let me begin my story, Krife?'

'That depends, is it going to get good any time soon?'

Hane closed his eyes, knowing that Krife was only trying to get him angry. When he opened them he ignored the old treasure hunter and went about his story. It was not about Zaviada making fools of the Amalgamation but it seemed to be about it taking near to twenty other magicians to chase her away, Hane among them. Krife kept interrupting asking why it took so many grown men to chase off one little sixteen year old girl, but Hane diligently ignored him. He seemed obsessed with testifying to the Amalgamation's strength saying they had already stood strong to the wolves of far greater beings, which didn't make any sense. Hane cracked a grin at his own remark anyway, but the important part that Thisian heard was that the story did not get good at any stage.

Thisian muttered something about passing water and left just as they started dishing out the stew. He had thought he was hungry but the idea of eating seemed to make him uncomfortable now. As he walked around their camp he told himself that he did not need food, he had his power to sustain him. No food, no sleep, no drink. Panic hit Thisian then as he wondered if he was still able to get drunk. He would have to find out quickly, but did not know how much Krife might have on him. From his stories it led Thisian to believe that the old treasure hunter constantly had barrels of drink with him.

Looking up to the horses he tried to see what Krife had actually brought. He could see little from so far away but he caught his own horse looking at him and Thisian laughed when he thought about the last time he had tried to get Kris drunk. Kris had refused politely but Thisian insisted saying that it might at least make the man bearable company. Instead of getting angry which is what

Thisian wanted, Kris had actually apologised to him. He said that he knew he was difficult to be around and that he would try to be better. The sudden honesty had made it difficult to mock Kris after that, but not impossible. Thisian explained that all Kris needed to do to be better company was either drink, laugh, or grow a pair of tits. Kris did not do any of those and left.

The only time he had actually been successful in getting Kris drunk was when they were very young. He had only just come to the village, with Thisian and Ryat finding him living alone in the woods. He said his grandfather had been dead for years and Kris had taken care of himself without anyone finding him until Thisian did. Well, as murderously unstable as Kris was now as a man, he had been far worse as a youth.

Raiders had ventured into their lands around that time, sneaking past one of the poorer border forts, looking for some of the famed Fureath'i gold. They had been hunted down and killed by the patrolling squads but not before they had found a village. They killed a lot of elders and youths there, and had done worse to the women. Ryat and the other elders from Coruln had taken in some survivors from the raid, three of them young women who had been raped. Thisian found them uncomfortable to look at, but Kris had frowned intensely at all three.

Thinking it nothing more than strange behaviour, Thisian gave it no more thought until he saw Kris skulking about their huts later that evening. All three had taken rest to recover and it was a few hours past sundown when Kris went to their cabin. He could not have been more than thirteen summers, but he walked in and slit the throats of all three women. They were three Fureath'i women that had survived being raped by Foreigners only to be killed by some lunatic youth and Thisian confronted Kris as he was leaving the scene. Thinking back, he was lucky he was not killed too, but he had wanted to know why Kris had done it.

There was no anger in Kris's eyes when he looked at Thisian, only confusion. Thisian had tried to explain to the strange youth that it was not alright to kill people for their own good and then had to push his wits to their limits in concealing the act. He had to go back into the hut and give each of the women a sabre and huddle them together to make it look like they decided between themselves to end their lives. Still the elders were suspicious and horrified when they found the scene, but no-one really believed that any Fureath'i would kill their own kind, especially three in such an exposed state. Actually, come to think of it, the less Thisian thought about Kris the better. Turning away from his horse he moved to more joyful memories.

Thisian had gotten Phira drunk once too, before she had fully committed herself to a life of boring training and unending success. He had innocently suggested they go swimming and could not believe his luck when she agreed, so they ran to the lake. It was dark but he saw enough in the moon light to make it worth his while. Not that he really wanted Phira of course, he imagined she was too tough, her skin like a leather hide, with muscles growing over where she used to have breasts. But back then she was still young and soft, and whether he liked to admit it, he had wanted her.

He could not remember exactly how young they had been, he thought it was the same year he had found Kris, so they would have been thirteen summers again, but there had seemed no better chance for him to have her, with them both drunk and naked. When he swam over to initiate it though, it did not go to plan.

She let him put his hand on her breasts and just stared at him, she even let him slip a hand down to between her legs. At the start she just frowned at him as he tested how far she would let him go, and then she even moved her hand to between his legs. Was it that memory why he loved women's hands so much? *Well it bloody shouldn't.*

He should have known the whole thing was too good to be true. Her gentle caress had soon turned into a violent crushing and before he had time to acknowledge the pain between his legs, she had head butted him square in the nose, breaking it cleanly.

It was a miracle he still turned out so outrageously handsome, but Thisian should have bloody known Phira would take more pleasure in breaking people's noses than from anything any real woman would. She was lucky that he did not drown because of the attack. So no, he did not want Phira-bloody-almighty, the risk was too great of permanent disfigurement. The bloody woman just seemed to love hurting people for no reason and was almost as unpredictable as Kris who loved to kill people rather than hurt them. No, Kris did not love anything, he just hated some things a little less than others.

Looking back up to his Kris-named-horse, Thisian frowned when, strangely, he saw someone in the cave. The man was too slender to be Hane or Krife, but was too tall to be Griffil. Creeping up closer to see who it was, the man turned and looked at Thisian before disappearing into air. He did not know who the man had been but there was something oddly familiar about him. Confused, Thisian swung his look back to the camp fire and all three of his companions were still there, looking like they were finishing their meal, and two out of the three had their backs to him.

It was Hane who was looking right at him, but when Thisian stared back the magician lowered his gaze to the fire that still floated in mid-air. Thisian walked back to the camp and sat down carefully, eyeing the magician, but trying not to be obvious about it. Krife made some comment about how long it took Thisian to take a piss but Thisian only laughed slightly, not fully listening. He pretended to be transfixed with his fire floating in the air between them, but he was really considering what he had just seen. Then it came to him why the man was familiar. He would look exactly as Hane would look if he was not fat.

Wondering if he should say anything to the rest of his group, Thisian kept quiet for now. He did not trust the magician, but then he did not trust Krife or Griffil either. He would have to bide his time and wait to see which of the two he could trust the least. It could be possible to blackmail Hane by letting him know that he had discovered his secret, that the act of fat useless magician was just an act. Or he could reveal the truth to Krife and demonstrate how much the thieves could trust him.

Was the fat man sitting next to him now an illusion and the slender one in the cave the truth, or was it the other way around? There could always be two magicians, perhaps brothers with one remaining unseen for their journey. Thisian didn't know enough about Foreign magickers to know what they could be capable of. What kind of reaction would Krife have at hearing the strange information? Thisian worked through what he knew of each of them only to find Griffil eyeing him from across the fire. What did the thief know? He seemed to know everything.

Thisian grinned. Suddenly this whore-less trip had gotten interesting. Whatever Hane or Krife or Griffil had planned, Thisian would be ready for it. He was not just a handsome, invincible, god-blooded warrior; he was also extremely clever. Thisian could out smart his companions, always stay a step ahead of them, and Krife chose that moment to let out the longest, loudest, release of gas Thisian had ever experienced.

All four coughed and spluttered against the poisonous fumes, including Krife, who was also busy choking from laughter and pride at the act. Holding back the vomit in his throat, Thisian reaffirmed that surely he was smarter than these people. His companions may be untrustworthy, but they were also too stupid to be dangerous. As a Flameborn, Thisian knew he was, without hesitation, the most dangerous man there. Maybe, even the most dangerous man... in the world.

· CHAPTER THIRTY ONE ·

A dangerous man

Kris's hand moved to his sabre.

A white-skinned being stood in front of him, the light of power shining so fiercely from his eyes that it made Kris's head hurt even more than it already did. He felt certain the being was a god but he had never heard a description of a Foreign god to match the figure. The white-skinned man moved his gaze to Kris's hand and Kris stopped before he touched the metal hilt, testing. The being looked up into Kris's eyes then and Kris held his own dark gaze steady under the piercing light. After a time, the man nodded, as if some agreement had just been reached.

'I am Nureail Fureath'i,' the Teller said suddenly, perhaps trying to disarm whatever violence had been brewing between Kris and the being of light. 'This is my brother Tereail, and this is our protector Kris.'

The man turned his head to study Nureail while she spoke and looked at Tereail and back to Kris with mention of their names. Kris began to wonder if the being would understand the Fureath'i language when it did not respond. He then wondered if his Scholars were about to start repeating themselves in an infinite amount of different languages.

'I am Jherin,' the man said finally, his voice soft.

He sounded tired, and when his eyes were turned, Kris could see the man's body sagged. He thought Jherin might say more but nothing else came, so Kris's hand remained near his sabre, and he brought his other hand up to the back of his skull. Probing the extent of his injuries, Kris was displeased to feel the flesh too tender and still bleeding freely, but if the bone was fractured then he would not be able to stand. In answer, all strength left his body and his vision went white, but Kris did not fall.

'You are hurt,' Jherin said. His head had turned when Kris moved his arm up to inspect his wounds. 'You have been part of violence.'

'We were attacked by Jhakral,' Nureail explained quickly. 'We did not initiate the violence.'

Kris considered if that was entirely true. It had been him who charged the Jhakral and not the other way around. It did not matter either way, if the beasts were intelligent then the three of them would have been seen as thieves stealing from their temple, and worthy of violence all the same. That brought him back to their current priority. 'Has another person travelled here from the Jhakral Temple? Come from the same dais?' Kris turned around again to see if he could locate it, which started Nureail and Tereail doing the same. The latter had been busy ignoring the strange being of power - who was clearly a very serious threat - and so Tereail thought it more important to dart his eyes over each and every little bit of treasure in the cave instead.

Jherin sighed before answering. 'Yes. He brought destruction to the dais, but it destroyed him also. They were never built for his kind to travel.'

'He destroyed the dais? Then how did we arrive here?' Tereail's tone made it clear he thought Jherin was speaking falsely.

'The starstream still exists. Things will still enter this temple but now no longer leave it.'

Kris frowned but it was Nureail who made Jherin elaborate. 'This other person, was he Powerborn? They are unable to use the dais, is that what happened? What did he look like? You said it destroyed him? Is his body still here?'

Jherin's face took on a pained look at so many questions and Kris almost smiled with pity. 'He looked like you: Fureath'i. His power, and the power he travelled, ripped at each other, shattering the stone, and melting his flesh. When last I saw him, he lived, but he would not live for long.'

Nureail turned to Kris. 'Fureath'i? A Fureath'i Powerborn has been here? Did Lady Jaiha send another on our quest in case we failed? Then how did we not see him? How long ago did this happen? Minutes? Hours?'

Jherin looked up to the ceiling as if he could see the sun, and answered, 'Two days I believe. I sometimes cannot perceive time. The goddess, Rhyserias, I could feel her watching him, but she fled when I turned my gaze on her.'

'No,' Kris said simply. 'I examined that room before entering and there were no footprints of any kind, the thief, Fureath'i or not, only entered minutes ago when we left Tereail alone.'

He expected argument but the two Scholars were just looking at each other, not noticing that Kris had even spoken at all. Let them theorise the probabilities, he had a direct course before him.

'My gratitude, Jherin, for your help. If you know which direction the injured man went we would appreciate it further.' With no apparent way back to the Jhakral temple, pursuing the alleged Powerborn thief was now their immediate goal, to see if he had indeed stole what they were searching for.

'He went southwest towards Furea,' Jherin said, the same tone of burden drifting into his voice. 'He asked if I could help him, but I could not, only free him. I was created to destroy.' His eyes drifted back down to Kris's sabre.

Nureail and Tereail had broken free of whatever trance they had been in then, and Kris resisted the urge to place his hand on his sabre. 'You were created?' Nureail asked, 'By whom? Why were you created to destroy? Destroy what?"

Kris sighed at Nureail's intrusive curiosity, and looked around to at least see footprints similar to those in the Jhakral Temple. These were the same size but heavier, and one was dragging. It matched the story that the thief was injured. Kris would not believe it was a Powerborn however, not a Fureath'i one at least. He noticed those footprints were the only ones. Jherin did not seem to create any. No answer came to Nureail's last invasive questions either, as the strange being was now looking up through one of the cave walls.

'What is it?' Kris asked.

'Intruders,' Jherin replied gently.

'Do they mean violence?' Nureail asked as if hinting at some deeper meaning. Kris knew she had an idea of who this Jherin was. There could hardly be a man of such obvious power that the Teller had not heard about through story or her own connection with time and history. The pure white man turned back to her accusingly, as if she had just named him a criminal. Kris could see his eyes tighten with struggle, but his voice remained soft.

'If they do, then I will destroy them.' He spoke the words as if it meant his own destruction and then began to disappear before their eyes. He fell apart in a swirling dust that scattered to nothing, and after he was gone all that remained was a faint figment of light from his eyes.

Kris turned to the two Scholars, 'Tell me what he is.'

Still staring where the man had been, Nureail spoke almost as softly as Jherin did. 'He is destruction made whole, Kris,' she rounded on him then and nodded down to where Kris's hand was placed. 'And we were as close, as your hand is to your sabre, at being destroyed by him had you touched skin upon that sword. We were very fortunate this day.'

***

Let every god piss on Di Thorel and his fortune, Thisian fumed to himself. *I've got to have the least amount of luck that any handsome man has ever had in history.*

It had only taken one more day for them to finish their journey to the Shadow Wall, and Thisian, as clever as he was, had spent that entire day cursing every god at every opportunity he could. His vulgar tirades had earned plenty of disgusted looks from Hane the devious fat magician and plenty of cruel laughter from Krife the obnoxious fat treasure hunter. The skinny liar of a thief at least helped Thisian practice his king's tongue by suggesting an unending supply of other curses. So at this rate Thisian would soon be fluent in insulting everyone, and should also be able to anger every god should the need arise.

'Is Am'bril bloody rutting an iceman's spear? Damn the gods and burn all their balls, it is too bloody cold!' But it was not the gods or the cold that he was angry at, or even the intrigue and deception the fat magician was up to, no, Thisian was livid because Griffil had finally admitted that there would be no towns or villages with whorehouses on their journey, despite constant assurances the previous day that the trek would be filled with them. Trying to make his bad humour worse, Thisian went back to examining the furtive magicker.

Hane was still giving him disapproving looks for all his cursing but apart from that did not look like he suspected Thisian knew his secret. The fat magician played his role very well and even started complaining almost as much as Thisian did. It was all to keep them thinking he was weak and harmless, fat and slow, but Thisian knew it was an illusion. Still not sure why Hane was keeping his appearance as deception - or perhaps keeping a colleague hidden - he began to wonder if the magician's personality was not an act at all. Almost everything was an insult to the Amalgamation, and everything else was not how he was accustomed to being treated. Krife had gotten off his horse at one point. He said nothing but unstrapped his giant sword, and calmly swung it straight for Hane's head.

The fat magician certainly moved fast then, barely avoiding the swing. If his complaining was all just an act then it was an extremely dangerous one. Thisian's anger rose at not knowing why the magician was pretending to be fat and why he was pretending to be so irritating. Then a more important reason to be angry at Hane entered Thisian's head.

'Hey, fat man, why couldn't you have come a day earlier? Then maybe we would've had time for some whores, three at the very least.' It did not matter that Thisian had only arrived minutes before Hane.

The magician snorted with distaste. 'The Powerborn I have encountered prior to you have all acted with far more dignity.'

'Far more dignity *my lord*,' Thisian corrected him, but Hane did not rise to his baiting. Damn but he was bored. And cold, and hungry, and tired, all things bloody Flameborns were not supposed to feel. His arrow wounds were a little better, not as sore as the day before, but not fully healed either. He would patiently wait for whatever ritual was taking his energy and mending his flesh to be over and then if he was still cold, hungry, or tired there would be trouble.

Thisian demanded that he should be bursting with power once the necessary healing was completed, and then all that power was going straight into some lucky whore. When Griffil admitted to him that he had been lying about their journey being packed with whorehouses, Thisian was crestfallen. Krife had even displayed an emotion other than anger or amusement at Thisian's anguish. The old treasure hunter showed genuine compassion when he apologised to Thisian about not having time for whores. The big man had gotten angry then, saying there should always be time for whores.

Trying to take his mind off whores for a time, Thisian felt like he was slowly turning to ice waiting for something to happen in this adventure. All he had seen was snow and all he had done was get cold and complain. Even finding out Hane was up to something did not interest him as much as he thought it might. Everyone was up to something. Looking at the magician again, Thisian glanced at the thick furs the other three had taken to wearing while travelling. The further up the mountain range they went, the colder it got. Thisian had asked to borrow one of the furs and Krife laughed at him, asking if he knew how badly burnt-hair smelled. There was some reasoning in that he supposed. Thisian thought about lighting his hands to keep him warm but then worried that it would spook the horse or his cloak would catch flame. *How the blazes do those real Flameborns do it?*

Other! He quickly amended, *other Flameborns.* But still, there they were, strutting around in just their tunics, all safe and warm back in Furea, none of them had to tough it in the cold like he did. Looking around, Thisian did not see many shadows either as they slowly climbed the base of the frozen Shadow Wall. The never ending winter had just turned it into another Ice Wall.

Apparently the Shadow Wall was supposed to form the border to the north, where demons were said to live. The Teller Nureail had told him that demons were nowhere on the world of light, but in an unseen world of darkness pressed together with their world. Thisian had no idea what she was talking about but she had really big breasts, for a Fureath'i at least. So Thisian had pretended to be interested in the Teller's intellectual ramblings, about a further world of power pressed in where the gods lived, and how the world of light drew from both in equal balance. And the world of light then was not only those two worlds pressing against each other, but a further two again. Thisian had stopped listening to her at that point. He had concluded he would not get to see her naked.

So no, the Shadow Wall did not hold back the demon hoards. There was nothing north of the mountains. If anything it was supposed to hold back the Chuabhotari savages, or the Ihnhaarat slavers from the east, and the whole continent was flooded with both so the useless mountains did not even do that.

Something landed on his nose then and Thisian let out a fresh curse to Aerune for ever inventing snow. If there was one thing that was completely useless it was snow - snow and being a Flameborn who was cold; both useless in their own ways. Krife and Griffil stopped their horses then, and Thisian looked up eagerly to see if they had come to something interesting.

The two thieves stood in front of a rock face, with narrow pathways leading down to either side. With his powerful eyesight, Thisian could see that it was just a boring rock face, covered with useless snow, with nothing there at all.

'Hey, Fireborn!' Krife shouted to him. 'Come over here and wrap your skinny fire arms around me, I'm freezing!'

'I'm not Fireborn,' Thisian sighed but he knew better than to try explaining the difference to Krife anymore. So he just shouted back, 'You're too fat! My arms wouldn't go all the way around.'

'If that's the only reason to stop you cuddling a man, then you've been spending too much time with Griffil!'

Thisian laughed. He was not used to being the one receiving abuse. He had always been the one to deliver it. Kris and Phira were the best to tease, pushing their control and conceited sense of dignity to the limits. Dallid was too friendly to tease sometimes, just laughing good heartedly and only occasionally taking a swing at him.

Thisian and Hane's horses joined the other two up where they had stopped, and for a while Krife just frowned at the magician. Griffil eyed the two of them with a knowing patience, and Thisian seemed to be the only one to notice they were stopped for no reason in the freezing snow in front of nothing. Was it time to stop for food? Thisian's appetite had been strange again. Sometimes he would feel nothing and then suddenly become starving. Not a thing since his decision to leave Furea made sense any more. There were women in the world that would open their legs for you, just for coin. No charm or work needed, just a few coins.

'Why are you smiling like that, Thisian?' Griffil asked suddenly.

'He's probably thinking about whores again,' Krife answered while still staring strangely at Hane. 'But never mind the Fireborn, what about this fat dung heap of magic here, you going to work for your coin or not?'

'It is the Amalgamation that receives payment for my services, not me,' he replied serenely. 'What would you like me to do?'

Krife tipped his head towards the rock face. The magician looked baffled.

'Krife, I require you to use words and not just grunts and gestures.'

'What about fists and swords?' Griffil offered.

Krife's answer, for once, was actually in a reasonably straight forward manner though: 'This wall here,' Krife said to the magician. 'I don't think it's really there.'

Hane turned his attention back to the wall and began muttering a chant of some kind, which must have meant he was using his so-called magic. Thisian thought he might as well be the voice of intelligence, if no-one else would.

'Why in the name of Frehep's burnt and freckled balls have you suddenly decided that flaming wall is not a bloody rutting wall at all?' Thisian blurted out.

Krife turned to Griffil, who looked back with a grin. 'Stop teaching the Fireborn curse words, Griffil, it's like speaking with a Mordec trader.'

'Forgive my colleague, Thisian,' Griffil said. 'He is old and delicate, rough words hurt his soft ears. But to answer your question, we have been here before. The map we acquired marked this exact spot as the entrance to the Temple of Wind, but we have travelled both the pathways beside it, and it only becomes a maze. So Krife, being lazy, decided to take the maps location literally and that is why we needed a magician who uses illusions to find the entrance.'

Krife raised his hands up to his ears and began pinching them to test their toughness. But Thisian could only frown at the logic, and then tried to frown further at the reality. It really could happen that they had travelled to the mountains of nothingness, to do nothing in front of a wall for a while, and then if Di Thorel had heard his curses, they might even be allowed to wander around a maze of nothingness for a time after that. There could be nothing better.

'There is indeed nothing there,' Hane said with a look of concentration on his face and Thisian started laughing. Hane continued on intently, 'I have never encountered something so raw. It is not an illusion of rock, but a destruction of the absence of rock. The reality of the entrance was destroyed, so the reality of its surroundings converged to heal the rift. This is not a magic I am familiar with.'

'Are you saying you can't get us through it?' Griffil asked.

'No,' Krife interrupted. 'What he's saying is I was right!' The old giant beamed triumphantly and shone his satisfaction at everyone.

'Perhaps I can trick the magic into thinking it no longer needs to heal itself, present to it an image of rock and therefore remove the real rock.' It was clear Hane was talking to himself, but Krife nodded to his words anyway.

'Fireborn, blow us a hole through that rock.'

Before Thisian could open his mouth to object, Hane did it for him. 'Do no such thing! You have no idea what kind of magic you are dealing with here. Introducing Connected-Fire to it could leak the destruction to Frehep himself for all we know.'

Krife and Griffil turned to each other nodding, with their lips curled down in curious consideration, as if such a thing would be a sight worth seeing. Thisian backed his horse away from the empty rock face.

'No,' Hane said. The more he spoke the more authority seemed to seep into his voice, becoming deeper and stronger. 'We will use gentle attempts, cut off from causing a greater destruction, if I can even trick the magic into shifting...'

More chanting sounded deep down the throat of the fat man, Thisian did not think it was king's tongue, but the rumblings were too faint for him to be sure. A hole appeared in the rock then and Hane's breath caught. Krife jumped down off his horse in celebration and made straight for the too-small hole without delay. Within a step the fissure was sealed back to rock again. Krife growled and reached for his sword as if he would smash the thing open or smash Hane open, which ever achieved the best result. Thisian and Griffil got off their own mounts slower, and watched Hane who was sweating now.

'That was close,' he said, swallowing loudly between words. 'The instant my magic went near it the destruction enveloped.'

'Well if it caused the hole then do it again,' Krife explained simply to the stupid magician.

'It nearly killed me,' Hane protested.

'This is only making the plan sound better, magician. Hurry up now, I want to swing my sword at something or find some treasure.'

The magician sat for a while in thought and eventually dismounted as well. Thisian had the good sense to gather the horses' reins and locate somewhere to secure them. If they were going to make a run at a magic hole in a wall, then he did not want the horses to run off too. One group of idiots sprinting with panic, fear, and lunacy, was more than enough.

When he returned, some decision had been made and Hane held his hands together with his eyes closed. It was the strangest magic Thisian had ever watched because there was nothing to see only the grumbling of bad song. Flameborn magic was real magic: a man with power burning through every muscle, able to ignite his own skin and anything else at will. The fat magician standing still with his hands pressed against together just looked like he was praying for a way to get away without Krife cutting him in half.

A vortex of colour appeared then to the side of where they stood and Hane opened his eyes.

'Quickly,' he urged and as he spoke the hole appeared again but this time grew larger. The swirling colours that had appeared to their left began trembling and shaking violently, but all four of them were running so Thisian could not see what happened next. They ran into a cave mouth too large to have been hidden behind that rock face, and when Thisian turned around he saw the same rocks slam back into place. All light vanished, and even his empowered eyesight could not make out where the others were. Krife's deep voice rumbled with an echo when he spoke,

'Fireborn?'

'Yes?' Thisian replied.

'Do I really need to ask?'

'Ask what?' Thisian said before it occurred to him, 'Oh.'

Looking around first for no reason, since all he could see was darkness, Thisian made a point of pushing his cloak as far back as he could before stretching his hands out as far as he could. He could feel the power tingling underneath his skin, all he had to do was release it. He closed his fists up by his chest and then threw his arms down, hands opening wide. The cave exploded with light.

Hane jumped back from the fire that appeared almost on top of him, and Thisian saw that Krife and Griffil had already stepped much further into the cave to avoid the flare. The magician tried to gather back some credibility and started explaining the magical ritual he had just summoned. 'I created a conflux of energies that the strange void magic was drawn to,' Hane answered to the question no-one had asked. 'It allowed the reality of the cave mouth to reappear...'

'Shut up, magician,' Krife said bluntly and looked around until he found something that interested him. Further down there were a line of dormant torches secured into the wall and after stamping down to retrieve one, the old giant came back and without ceremony thrust it at Thisian's hands.

Pulling back his hands in reaction, Thisian frowned at Krife, but the ugly treasure hunter just gave him a toothy smile in return. Some of his back teeth were missing. *Burn my balls but he is ugly.*

While Thisian was listing off all of the things that were stomach wrenchingly revolting about Krife's face, his three companions had already began making their way down the tunnel with Krife's new torch leading the way. Their shadows flashed in and out of sight against the walls, as the torch made Thisian's own flaming hands seem redundant.

Flicking his wrists a few times to extinguish the fire, Thisian ran after the others before he got left alone in the dark. It warmed his heart to know that he was so valued as to not just be left standing there, forgotten after what little use he could be was over. After using that magic though, his arrow wounds began hurting again.

Wait until we get into a fight, he thought, *then they will see how useful I can be. They can see how many bloody arrows I can get hit with while I stand there not knowing how to use any flaming fire magic.*

As he caught up with them, Krife straight away lifted a meaty fist to signal them to stop. The dark tunnel reached a bend and opened out to fresh air further on, so they peeked around, past the exit of the cave, and a weathered stone structure loomed into view. It was a temple built into the rock walls, hidden on all sides by a bowl within the mountain. There were some other caves in the stone which made Thisian groan but the temple looked as much a part of the rock to be nearly hidden anyway.

The temple front had too many entrances scattered about too, with steps going up and down everywhere he could see, so that if it was not for one very frightening fact, then they might have been getting lost within a maze after all. But as it happened, the same reason Thisian could guess which was the correct entrance was also the reason Krife had stopped them.

A man stood in front of one entrance, dressed in plain clothes of faded grey, and no weapons that Thisian could see. His skin was white, but it was not the same difference between Thisian's golden skin and his companion's blotched pale and pink skin, the man standing in front of them looked made of snow. He did not have the blonde hair or blue eyes of a Prae'surlas, his hair kept more or less the same dead white as his skin, but the eyes, they swirled and shone with a deadly light. The man terrified Thisian.

'Fireborn,' Krife whispered. 'Go kill him.'

'No!' Thisian and Hane both cried at the same time. Hane's was more a hiss while Thisian's was more a manly shriek. Griffil smiled and looked to Krife.

'Well alright, Hane, you're a magic too, you go kill him.'

'Be quiet you fools.' Hane's eyes would not leave the man in white. 'That thing can kill us any time he wants.'

'He couldn't kill me,' Krife muttered.

'That thing could destroy this entire mountain range if he wished it. Be content that he has not murdered us already and is granting us opportunity to leave.'

Krife looked around at how much of the mountain range he could view from inside the cave mouth. The sky was getting dark, but it was still possible to see how vast the mountains were becoming. Thisian tried to see what he might be looking for but his eyes kept drifting back to the man in white.

'I can still swing a sword faster than a magic can say a spell,' Krife grumbled. 'But I've never met a man that could destroy a mountain before.' His hand reached for the giant blade strapped to his back, before moving further down to scratch the back of his arse. 'Think I'd like to meet a man like that.'

And with that Krife strode confidently out of the cave and into the open air, heading straight for the white-skinned man. Hane's mouth was left open in failed protest and Griffil closed his eyes. When he opened them he turned to Thisian and smiled, 'Well, we've all got to die someway.' And the young thief trotted after his large companion, who was almost upon the guardian of the temple. Thisian knew it was now his turn to show courage and follow his companions to meet certain death.

'They can both rut an iceman's spear if they think I'm going out there.' Thisian turned to Hane for confirmation of his good sense, but the fat magician was not listening. He looked in a trance. Thisian hoped he was not doing any more strange magic, but no sound was coming from him anyway.

When Krife reached the white-skinned man, for a moment he stood there, looming over him. Then Krife's hand shot out and the other man just looked down at the offered limb with confusion. Fureath'i turned their palms in greeting, to show no concealed weapon and no fist held in anger, but he still knew that most other races clasped each other's arms in greeting. The white-skinned man appeared bemused by the entire gesture.

When he finally placed his hand into Krife's, it was with a tentative curiosity, and to Thisian's eyes, the smallest traces of a smile appeared on his face. 'I'm Krife,' the grizzled giant said as he roughly shook arms with the other man.

Drawing back his hand slowly after the action, he looked down upon the white skin of his palm before replying, 'My name is Jherin.'

Even from the relative distance, Thisian found his voice haunting. It sounded like some spirit would, maybe a ghost that suffered from a great tragedy and was cursed to relive it over and over. Thisian's mind ran away with the idea for a while, while Krife continued to show his guile and tact.

'Pleasure to meet you, Jherin. Are you going to kill us?'

Griffil was there now and he raised his eyebrows at Krife for his bluntness, but Jherin just smiled softly. 'No, Krife, I hope that I will not.'

Krife slapped him on the shoulder in celebration, making Jherin stumble slightly off balance. 'Even more pleased to meet you now!' He turned back to the cave entrance and shouted, 'Did you hear that, magics? You can come out if you've finished pissing yourselves!' Turning back to Jherin, he said with a side glance, 'I'll tell you they're both about as useful as a whore without an arse.'

The mention of whores did nothing to improve Thisian's mood, but he felt obliged to leave the false safety of the cave anyway. He held his chin up high as he walked, showing off his full height. He was nowhere near as tall as Krife, or not really as tall as Jherin either, but almost taller than Griffil. Thisian was far better looking than all them either way. And he was a lord, and had the power of the gods...

Thisian's heart stopped when Jherin turned his head to look at him. The power in those eyes seemed barely contained from ripping him apart that instant, and Thisian only began to breathe as he realised that Jherin's dangerous gaze was not on him at all, but behind him, on Hane.

'Thank Frehep's piss covered balls for that,' Thisian whispered to himself, and vainly added that he no longer needed to breathe, or even needed blood as far as he knew. *How can Powerborn be killed if we don't need anything at all to live?* Looking back at Jherin - while stepping to the side so that the man could have a good long uninterrupted look at Hane with Thisian nowhere near - he revisited his last thought.

I could get ripped apart by a roaring power unleashed from a mountain-destroying, white-skinned freak's terrifying eyes!

Krife seemed to notice the new tension between Jherin and Hane, and did his best to disarm the situation. 'You can kill that fat one if you want,' he said reassuringly. 'Just means we don't have to pay him later.'

For once Hane did not try to remind Krife that it was the Amalgamation he was to pay and not Hane himself. The magician just tried to meet the eyes of Jherin, and held himself reasonably well apart from the dripping sweat covering his face.

'Your kind,' Jherin said softly, 'seek me out.'

'I am not them,' Hane replied.

'But you will speak to them of me.'

'Yes, but in many days' time. You can be gone from here by then.'

If Hane was arguing for his life - as it very much seemed to Thisian he was - then he was being extremely calm about it. Calm or else his mind was broken from soiling his breeches under Jherin's terrorizing stare. The white-skinned being's voice was so soft, so empty of hope.

'There are things here that I do not wish them to have.'

'Then you can destroy these things.'

Krife was scratching the back of his head, and making uncomfortable faces at Hane's words. 'Are these things valuable?' he asked. 'Because I can take them away from here rather than have you destroy them.'

Jherin's eyes turned back to Krife, as if he just remembered he was there. 'I do not *wish* to destroy, Krife.'

'Then it's settled,' Krife slapped the man on the shoulder again before turning to enter the temple. 'We can take anything you don't want those rat magicians getting their teeth into.'

Before the fey being had a chance to object, Krife marched confidently into the temple. Griffil immediately followed suit which left the two *magics* standing there nervously waiting to see if Jherin would destroy them. Thisian tried not to look at those sandstorm eyes of swirling white. Too much power and far too much movement in them - just looking at them made Thisian queasy and yet he could not look away.

Jherin's solemn gaze drifted over to Hane again, who tried to mask his terror with confidence. His chin high with false authority, the fat in Hane's cheeks still trembled visibly. The illusion of fat was looking pretty real now, and Thisian had no idea what kind of power Jherin was supposed to have, but something told him Hane was about to die.

'If you're going to kiss him, magician, then do it already!' Krife shouted out from inside the temple, 'But you'll only make Griffil jealous. So get your fat hide in here, Hane, and bring that daydreaming Fireborn with you.'

Hane seemed to breathe again and eyed where Krife and Griffil stood. Jherin's expression did not change. His eyes still shone towards Hane, and the drifting lights flowing in circles inside were the only things that moved. Thisian took the opportunity to very slowly step away. If Jherin was going to destroy Hane, he wanted to be a mountain's distance away just in case.

Then the strange being dropped his gaze, as if the effort of holding his head suddenly became too great. Thisian continued his steady departure and after a moment's consideration, Hane joined him. It took a lot of concentration for Thisian to keep walking without looking back over his shoulder. Griffil and Krife at least were facing that direction so might provide some warning should Jherin change his mind and attack. Or else they would say nothing and laugh about it after.

'Still alive, Hane?' Krife asked with a mocking grin.

'Krife,' the magician sighed. 'What the world presents to you in vision is only food for your mind and nothing more. You know not what you eat and only that you have eaten it.'

'So, you're not alive then?'

'You are the lowest form of worthless,' Hane said as he shook his head at their laughter, and then pushed his way through to continue into the temple.

'How about you, Fireborn?' Krife asked. 'You alive?'

'I'm not sure,' Thisian smiled. 'The dead still shit themselves when they die, right?'

This brought a grin from them both, but also a watchful eye towards Jherin who had not moved from his position outside the temple.

'Jherin seems like someone who is good at both of those, Thisian,' Griffil whispered. 'Making people shit themselves and making people dead.'

'Yeah. We'd better go after that mutton-rutter Hane before he gets himself into trouble again,' Krife said while nodding towards Jherin. 'Come on, Fireborn, welcome to your first treasure trove.'

They walked after the magician, and Thisian idly looked around, not too interested in finding any gold really. Gold was always plentiful in Furea, the mines in the Fire Wall were the most abundant in the world, but then again he never had anything worth spending it on in Furea either. Before his mind could descend once more to the base fantasy of how many whores he could buy, Thisian was slapped sober when they entered the first chamber.

There were mountains of gold and jewels scattered all around the pillared chamber. It was enough for a Foreigner to buy himself an empire, and enough for a Fureath'i to buy himself a kingdom of whorehouses. Griffil had told him about the Fantaven houses, and Thisian could most definitely see himself spending the majority of his legend adventuring there. But the sheer excess of wealth and treasure was not what had slapped Thisian so coldly in the face.

The chamber was full of heaps of treasure, but there was enough cleared in areas to hold a group of people standing around, and in one of those bloody areas stood a man almost as bloody dangerous as Jherin was. He was someone with the same unpredictable violence radiating from him, just waiting to be unleashed. Hane had come to a halt upon finding the man, and even Krife and Griffil stood warily at the sight of the waiting warrior. His weapon was in his hand, and everything about his stance spoke of a readiness to kill them all in a single motion.

Kris's eyes squinted slightly upon seeing Thisian there, wearing the tattered tunic of a Flameborn, with a group of treasure hunting Foreigners. That squint was the same as another man shouting out in hysterical confusion.

'I am surprised to see you here, Thisian,' Kris said flatly.

'That's *Lord* Thisian,' the Flameborn corrected, with what could only be described as *indescribable* satisfaction.

· CHAPTER THIRTY TWO ·

Movement

'You wear the tunic of a Flameborn,' Kris said and he could see Thisian's irritation at his own lack of reaction. But even if Thisian really was a Flameborn - a fact Kris very much doubted - he still would not kneel, his rank did not demand it.

'The sun god sees you too, Kris,' he said back, chastising Kris for foregoing the formal greeting, 'and he sees you wearing the expression of a man looking to kill something.' Thisian nodded down to Kris's sword with indignation. 'Are you going to put that away?'

Kris's eyes swept to the large warrior and monstrous broad sword he had strapped to his back. He then took in the slender youth and the fat man in robes. From the stance of the youth he had knives prepared and ready, and from the impatient frown of the fat man, he was either a blasphemous magician or a fool Scholar, either one would have the same grand ideas about their own superiority. Kris was confident he would kill them all.

So after considering each of the new arrivals, and the fact that Thisian was the company they kept, Kris found his answer. 'I will keep my sabre where it is,' he said. 'Until I find someplace better to put it.'

'Do you see what my life was like?' Thisian exclaimed, throwing his hands out for sympathy from his new companions. 'Imagine an entire nation of that. Millions of them! Maybe not quite as bad as Kris, but still, insufferable all the same.'

'Kris,' Nureail's voice sounded softly from behind, 'perhaps here is the wrong place to do violence.'

She at least had the decency to sound meek while ordering him to put away his blade in front of three unknown enemies. Kris did not think the woman knew what meek meant, and he was even more surprised she was not trying to order them all to stand down and listen to her. Kris turned his head and met her perfect eyes.

When he slammed the blade back into the scabbard, every man jumped in the room apart from the big one. The old warrior just grinned.

'Frehep's balls, Kris! Are you trying to rutting startle us into attacking you? Nureail? What are you doing here? Actually Kris, what the blazing hell are you doing here?'

All three other Fureath'i stared heatedly at Thisian for his use of their god's name in such a derogatory manner, but the imbecile did not even notice. 'We are here by command of Lady Jaiha Fireborn,' Kris replied. 'And you? Who are your companions?'

He had enough shame left in him to scratch the back of his head before launching into a rambling deceit. The fat magician must have decided Kris was not going to kill them right that moment and snorted with contempt at their conversation. He shuffled over to the one of the stockpiles of treasure, not too far away from where Tereail had engrossed himself. The youth accompanying Thisian began drifting away then also, trying to circle behind Kris, but very casually. Kris kept them all in his vision. Nureail stayed where she was, perhaps interested in what Thisian had to say, and the large warrior remained where he was also, never taking his eyes off Kris.

'My companions?' Thisian asked before answering. 'Well we have Krife the Treasure Hunter, he's the giant to your left, next is Griffil the master, ah, well thief, but he's not Fureath'i so we shouldn't judge, and lastly there's Hane, the fat illusionist, as useless as he is useless.' Thisian stopped then as if he had not purposely omitted the main details of his being there. Kris held his gaze. He had done this countless times on Thisian. An intense stare would make him keep talking about everything, hopefully brushing onto what might actually matter. It worked. 'And me, well, this may sound strange, Kris, but, I met a dying Flameborn,' he hesitated before continuing further, 'and, he was in a bit of a mess. So, the bones of the story - as many bones as he had left anyway - is that he Transferred his powers to me, and now I can do this.'

Fire erupted from Thisian's open hands, and Kris hoped that he did not react. Glancing over to the magician to see if it was some trick, Kris moved his vision anywhere but the triumphant smile of Thisian.

'What was the Flameborn's name?' Nureail asked, thankfully. As much as the story did not sit well with Kris, he could not allow himself to show curiosity about it. Let the Scholar elicit all she wanted from Thisian.

'Kr'une. The one that patrols the border forts,' Thisian said, a defensive note to his voice. 'I'm not lying. Fureath'i do not lie,' he said and even tried to sound Fureath'i while saying it. There was too much ice on his tongue for it to work though. The magician had to be responsible for Thisian's fire; it was the only explanation Kris would accept.

'And why did he Transfer to you?' Nureail pressed. 'I apologise if my questions show disrespect, but it is extremely rare for a lord of power to Transfer to a fleshborn. I could list all recorded instances using just my fingers.'

Thisian looked down at her hands then, and incredibly seemed to be lusting at them. Kris felt his fist tighten and fought for control. Had the man no integrity? Could he not restrain himself from leering at the woman? Thisian's gaze moved without subtly from the exposed flesh of her arms to the concealed flesh of her hips and bosom, before finally meeting her eyes and remembering that she had asked a question.

'What? Oh, there were raiders approaching, and he was in no condition to fight them. His flesh had melted into itself. It was disgusting.' Thisian plucked at the torn tunic he wore, the flames on his hands having been extinguished soon after they had lighted. 'As you can see, I had some trouble getting this off of him.' He laughed then at how difficult it had been for him to strip the dead body of a Powerborn after they had Transferred all their power into him.

'I have never heard of a Powerborn so badly injured before. Did he say what happened to him?' Nureail would not relent until she pulled every last drop of information out of Thisian.

'He said Rhyserias, the goddess of time, did it to him, and something about frozen Fureath'i.'

The colour left Nureail's face at the mention of Rhyserias, but she controlled it well. Anyone not as familiar with Nureail's features might even have missed it, but Kris could see a confusing mixture of emotion in the woman. Thisian clearly did not notice as he was glancing about the room, and started to make for the shiniest pile of jewels he could see. Nureail was not finished with him though and Thisian's face dropped when she continued.

'I am still confused -' she began.

'Well, Nureail, I'm not the Teller here,' he interrupted. 'I can't be expected to recall every single detail with dramatic accuracy.'

'No, you are not, but you are now a Lord Flameborn, an event that will need to be Told. The manner of Lord Kr'une's death is unclear, even if as you say he was badly injured, it is the proper option to die as a Flameborn and to assail the heights of power as a lord. Not to Transfer it to someone,' she stumbled over the right way to phrase it, 'untrained.'

Unworthy, undeserving, a person so completely un-Fureath'i that it was a struggle for Kris to accept any of the reality he was being presented. Once more Thisian showed his sharp mind by not picking up the implied insult Nureail had delivered,

'Oh,' was all he said, and then looked around before grinning smugly. 'Well this is a temple isn't it?' He rummaged around in his belt pouch before producing something he then displayed to Kris and Nureail in his palm. 'Kr'une made me take an oath that I'd get this to a temple. I guess he Transferred to me to make sure I had the strength to make it. Or else he must have thought it was time to create the most handsome lord of power the world has ever seen.'

Thisian flipped his womanly long hair all over to one side of his head and tried to smile charmingly at Nureail. Kris's mind was cascading with more and more unreality though until he took a firm grip of it in his will. Was the injury to his skull causing this? No, he would accept what fortune presented and he would fight to make it what it should. The glass figure of fire in Thisian's hand matched precisely what Tereail had described. Nureail's eyes watered at the sight of it. Even the large warrior was eyeing it with interest.

It had settled within Kris that with the dais destroyed they had no way of returning to the Jhakral temple to further search for the item and had placed his attention towards finding the thief. The Fureath'i Powerborn, as Jherin described him, melted and injured, near death, only to run into Thisian outside of Furea, as an Exile in all probability. Thisian then returns, and unwittingly hands them what they need.

'Why isn't anyone saying anything? What is it? Is it valuable? Krife? How much is this worth?'

The large warrior, Krife, shrugged his shoulders and rumbled, 'Depends who's buying. These two look like they'd pay a coin or two for it.'

Kris lifted his eyes up to meet Krife's, and fed the darkness into them to show the man what he would do if he attempted to stop Thisian giving them the relic. Krife grinned back at him, inviting the attack, but Kris knew with certainty that he could plunge his sabre deep into the giant's chest before the man was able to even un-tie the lumbering beast of a sword he had attached to his back.

'Here, just take it,' Thisian said as he prodded it toward Kris and Nureail. 'Will you take it to Rath'Nor? Or to one of the Fureath'i temples?'

'No,' Kris said as he took the item from Thisian and secured it away in his own belt pouch. He turned to Nureail and motioned towards her brother. 'We are leaving.'

'Now?' Thisian burst out. 'Why? Where are you going? Have you heard word from Dallid? Or even Phira-bloody-almighty herself? I can't let you leave until you at least call me Lord Thisian and kneel down in awe of me.' The look of disgust Kris gave him did nothing to dent the joy and amusement painted across *Lord* Thisian's face. 'You have to,' he added with a broad grin, 'I am your lord.'

'As an ember class within the army I outrank a Flameborn outside of military rank,' Kris explained, trying to detach any satisfaction from sounding in it. 'You are a new recruit as I see it, and as far as I know, it will take you the best part of a century to master your power and be allowed take on the title of lord. So if anything you are in the company of a ranking military officer and two actual Fureath'i lords. If we wish it we could order you to kneel.'

'Kris,' Thisian said slowly, 'I don't think I've ever heard you speak that many words in your life. Clearly travelling with a Teller has been rubbing off on you. Well not literally rubbing off on you of course, for obvious reasons.' Kris did not react, but Nureail's cheeks coloured the slightest of red. Perhaps Thisian was not as oblivious as he tried to appear. 'Brijnok's cock, you have! Kris, I've a new found respect for you, but poor Nureail, I must say, I've lost all respect for you. You've left Kris rut you? Truly? Why? How? No, don't tell me, it's already left such a disgusting image in my mind that I mightn't ever be able to grace between your legs myself anymore. I mean -'

'Thisian!' Kris roared. 'You will watch your tongue or I will tear it out with my bare hands!' His head pounded with the sound of blood rushing through his body, screaming for Thisian's. Flameborn or not, he would speak to a Lady with respect or he would get carved up to a thousand pieces. Both Thisian and Nureail were staring at him for his outburst, but he did not care. If he were to lose his control then at least it would be ridding Furea of a Flameborn like Thisian.

Thisian smiled. 'It looks like I'm getting better, Kris. It used to take me weeks of tormenting you to get a reaction like that. He must really love you, Nureail, until he kills you of course. But, Kris, it is good to see you're still made of blood and not ice!'

The large treasure hunter Krife had the audacity to laugh out loud then, and deemed whatever threat Kris had previously been, dealt with. He too wandered off to examine the room of treasures. Nureail choose that time to place her hand inappropriately upon Kris's shoulder, the skin of her hand touching the skin of his neck. It created an explosion of sensation, but it was one of calm that dissolved his rage with unfamiliar ease.

His rage had always needed desperate fighting, the battle hopeless and that was what made Kris fight even harder. He did not feel comfortable under her touch, it was not right. Although he had meant to roughly shake her away, Kris's hand gently removed Nureail's own and he did not meet her eyes. Thisian could not stop smiling and opened his mouth to antagonise further. Kris interrupted him.

'Thisian,' he said. 'Do you wish me to kill you?' Gone again was all emotion, he was back in control, his voice level and deadly.

Posturing his fists on his hips before answering, Thisian tried to look down on Kris to show he could look as tall as an icicle. 'Do you really think you could kill me, Kris? Like it or not, I'm a Flameborn now.'

'Have you mastered so much Thisian, to produce fire quicker than I can draw my blade and stick it in your heart?'

Thisian eyed Kris's sabre and hesitated. 'That wouldn't kill me,' he finally decided on, 'you'd have to stab me more than once.'

'And at what point do you think I would stop?' Kris asked.

Realisation hit Thisian and he transformed his smile from smug to friendly. 'Brother, why are we speaking of such things anyway? Let us Tell of better times. Have you news of Dallid or Phira?'

Kris shook his head. 'You have a false smile for every situation, Thisian. You will need to begin acting like a Flameborn.'

'And Flameborn don't smile? Do they have a different frown for every situation like you?'

Kris frowned at the remark, and then made himself relax his face. He would not show any emotion, negative or otherwise. 'Blaze Commander Phira is in Surlas, and last I heard, Dallid was with you in the *Path of Stone* squad,' Kris said, letting it appear that he too wished to reminisce. He very much did not.

'Surlas? Has Phira-bloody-almighty gone off to kill another thousand ice-men all by herself? Well, Dallid and I left the Path of Stone squad, I went north into the *Sabre's Arc* in the border forts, and he went south into the *Watchful Sun*.'

'And the Sabre's Arc is what brings you here then,' Kris asked, his anger beginning to rise at the idea of Thisian becoming an Exile. 'You will return to Rath'Nor.' He spoke the words strongly and harshly, and received glances from Thisian's Foreign companions at the severity of it. The order was so forceful that Thisian even jumped when caught so off-guard by it. But it was a direct order and the only attempt Kris would make to ignore Thisian's apparent Exile status. It was more for loyalty to Dallid and Phira and their affection towards Thisian, than any that Kris felt himself. 'You will leave now and...'

Kris stopped as Jherin appeared. Everyone in the room stopped where they were and cast nervous glances towards the white-skinned man. Kris clenched his fist instead of reaching for his sabre, but only because Jherin had not shown him any signs of violent intent. He had appeared so suddenly though, Kris had been keeping his eyes on everyone within the room and did not see any movement in the least to mark Jherin's arrival.

The white currents in Jherin's eyes scanned the room, taking in each figure slowly. It was difficult for Kris to meet those eyes without falter but he did it. The supposed Flameborn lowered his. The big man Krife made his way slowly back over, stopping unnecessarily close to Kris. It was at the same side Kris held his sabre. That would make it difficult to draw and strike in that direction, should the need arise. Kris thought about casually repositioning himself, but there was something about Jherin's manner that held his full attention.

Before, when the being had looked at them, it had been with indifference. Even when Kris had almost reached for his sabre, the look perhaps changed to reluctance. Now however, the eyes shone with purpose, so reluctant or otherwise, Jherin had returned to the chamber for a reason.

'I cannot let you take that.'

He was speaking to Hane, the fat man in robes. Hane's expression was a mix of innocence and confusion. The magician was clearly a practiced liar.

'Of what do you speak?' he asked with more composure than Kris thought such a man could possess.

'Remove it from your robes and give it to Krife. He will take it from this place. For a time the curse will not come.'

Krife cleared his throat. Perhaps he too felt the tension in the air and wished to speak carefully.

'You heard the white bastard, ya fat mule. Hand over whatever it is you've found and be sure that I'm deducting it from your pay.'

Strangely to Kris, Hane winced at that last part, while everyone else winced at the first part of Krife's crass announcement. Jherin did not remove his gaze from the magician.

'Krife,' Hane said with a sigh. 'You remind me of stepping in an animal's shit. Even if I come back and kill you, your memory will be like a lingering smell that I fear will always be a taint on me.'

Several things happened at once then. For the briefest of moments, the room was filled with multiple images of Hane. Each identical in form, each in a different pose. Even though it was only an instant, Kris was not sure if he could have pointed to the real magician. The next thing that happened was that on either side of Kris, hands caught his forearms to prevent their movement. On one side Nureail had grabbed onto him, either through shock or for protection, but on the other side a giant's hand had locked the arm closest to his sabre in place.

Kris's reaction to draw the sabre would have been instant had he not been hindered and before he could break his arms free, the next thing happened. Jherin did not move, his hands did not flicker, the brightness of his shining eyes did not alter, and yet Kris knew what had happened was of his doing. In one moment the room was full with illusions of Hane the magician, in the next moment they were gone and in the place of the real Hane, was an explosion of death.

CHAPTER THIRTY THREE

Shadows

Blood and gore burst outward from where the magician stood, but
to Kris's eyes it was not enough to make up an entire man. There
was only one piece that looked like it could have been bone in the
red remains on the ground, so everything else must have been
destroyed completely.

It was humbling to see such power cause that level of
devastation so quickly. If Kris allowed himself, he might have
wondered how anyone could fight such a being. But as it happened,
Kris did not think on it, he simply knew he would fight him if he
must. Nureail's hands relaxed from around his arm, and Kris pulled
his other roughly out of Krife's grip. Jherin turned his head at the
movement and Kris met his eyes with defiance.

'And I was just starting to like Hane,' Krife said. 'Smelling like
animal shit is the best I've smelled in years.'

Jherin moved his attention to the large warrior and gave the
faintest of smiles. 'Goodbye, Krife,' he said faintly. 'Do not carry it
for long. It can only bring you ruin.'

The being of power dissolved again into nothingness before
their eyes, his white light leaving a faint aura in the air before
finally fading. It took several heartbeats before anyone else spoke or
moved. Although his footsteps were light, Kris could make out the
silent approach of Griffil from behind. He went to Krife, and
slapped a thin arm on his shoulder, laughing nervously as he did it.

'A whole world of people who can't stand the sight, sound, or
smell of you, Krife, and you find the one person who actually likes
you. And with absolute perfect timing or we could all be splattered
piles of blood and mess like dear Hane over there.'

'I haven't been exploded yet,' Krife grunted and strode over
where the remains of Hane lay. Bending over to pick up what Kris
had thought was bone, Krife shook as much blood as he could off of
it before stepping over to nearest person which happened to be a

traumatised Tereail. The Scholar was ghost white and staring horrified at the scene. He did not even notice when Krife used the man's robes to wipe off the rest of the blood from the item. The large man gave Tereail a grin of thanks and nodded towards Griffil, 'This is it.'

Griffil walked over to peer at the object Krife was holding and from what Kris could see it was a piece of curved stone with scratches on it and was snapped broken on both ends.

Kris retrieved his own item and for prudence walked over to let Tereail examine it. He allowed a few gentler attempts to catch his attention before Kris finally just caught Tereail by the hair and pulled his head down to see what he had.

'Yes!' he exclaimed looking from Kris to Nureail with excitement. 'This is it! We found it. We are saved!' Nureail joined them and Kris looked back to see Thisian eye their group momentarily before walking over to join Griffil and Krife. 'We must get this to the Ice Temple,' Tereail stated unnecessarily and then he looked up at Kris.

'How can we get there now, Kris?' Nureail asked. 'With the dais gone we cannot get back to the Jhakral temple, and none of Tereail's visions ever brought us here.'

'Yes, something has happened to alter things significantly.' Tereail mused, already becoming lost in thought.

Kris held back a sigh. The Scholars were supposed to be ones with all the knowledge. 'If this temple is like the others, then there will be other platforms, I doubt they were all destroyed. There must be more, perhaps even one straight to the Ice Temple. We have six days to find it.'

Tereail did not even hear him, but Nureail nodded. 'You are right, although,' she paused and looked at her brother, 'I do not think we have six days.'

Kris turned to see what the other three in the chamber were doing while asking Nureail to elaborate. 'Why?'

'The Flameborn Kr'une,' she said. 'If he did take the artefact from the chamber, then how did he give it to Thisian two days before entering the room?'

Kris frowned. 'It does not matter how we have the item; all that matters is that we have it. Our attention should now be on finding the dais to get us to the Temple of Ice.'

'Yes, I understand that, Kris, but what I am saying could be important. When I connected with the past in the Jhakral temple, do you remember I said I could not get back? That has never happened before, and with both Jherin and Thisian mentioning Rhyserias, she might have held us, to shelter myself and Ter -'

'Foreign gods do not concern us,' Kris said.

Nureail's irritation at his dismissal of her worries, was far thicker in her voice than Kris's had been. '*All* I am saying, *Kris*, is that I think we should act as if we have only *four* days remaining and not six.'

'Act as you will, I intend my mission done today.' A sharp pain seared suddenly into the back of his head and it took great effort not to react to it. With passing suspicion he glanced around to where Thisian was standing, just on the off chance it was a prank of fire, but he was still conversing with the other Foreigners. No, the pain had been a reminder that his injury was far from minor. 'We will search this temple quickly and without pause,' he said to the Scholars, his dark eyes boring a hole into Tereail. 'We look for nothing other than a way to the Temple of Ice or any other of the Great Temples. Tereail, if I catch you examining something that is not immediately beneficial to our goal, I will cut off your thumbs.'

'And how am I to know if it is immediately beneficial to our goal if I cannot examine it?'

'You will know, Tereail, because he will have cut off your thumbs,' Nureail said, doing her best to keep from grinning.

Kris's control was being tested greatly this day. Looking up to the unseen sky he gave thanks to Frehep for all Scholars, Tellers, and Flameborns named Thisian, sent into the world to test his strength. His patience had run out however, so for the safety of those around him, Kris did not say anything, he simply turned and left.

Following one of the pathways that weaved in and around the piles of gold, weapons, and other useless junk, Kris soon passed a larger heap that blessedly took all others from his view. The chamber was vast, and some mounds of relics were so tall that the exits were not readily visible so he continued walking. Nureail had said Brijnok committed the ritual to banish all this wealth and items of power out of the mortal world and into the Great Temples, but it certainly seemed that significantly more ended up in this one.

An archway soon revealed itself to his brisk pace, and if he were more confident that no others were present in the temple, he might have moved faster. The sooner he was able to find the platform, the sooner he would be done with his quest, and done with damned Scholars. The next chamber opened up before him, and it was a stark contrast to the one he had just left. There were no mountains of treasured goods, there was nothing at all but the flickering movement of torches fixed to the walls. Some chambers within the Jhakral temple had been bare too, but each room was much smaller than the ones in this temple. The result of an empty room so large was almost dizzying.

Nine archways greeted him in three directions. They were all a distance away, with three on each side towards the centre and three more at the very end, so Kris broke into a run. The physical release, albeit a small one, was welcome as his feet echoed off the stone floor. The room was not as well lit as the Jhakral chambers, but the torches were likely just as unnatural. How else would they remain lighting in an abandoned temple? The flames even flickered from side to side from an unknown breeze that Kris did not feel. He did not care. Needing an outlet for his boiling rage, Kris would have laughed in gratitude at seeing another Jhakral wander through one of the large archways. But Kris never laughed.

Maybe he would run into one of Thisian's companions having strayed off instead. Kris almost enjoyed the idea of fighting the large one. He seemed a capable warrior despite being old and fat. Either way he needed to kill someone soon. Perhaps it was best if he had more time to recover from his injury but he did not want it. The throbbing at the back of his head was ignored for the run. He could ignore anything that was not immediately important.

A flash of movement appeared to his right and Kris stopped with a small skid, his sabre flashing out to greet whatever it had been. The empty chamber laughed at him with its silence. From where he stood, the archways were still a distance away, and if something had been in the hall, they would not have been able to reach any of the exits in time.

Kris returned back to a careful stride. Holding himself so aware and so ready took its toll on his speed, but eventually he reached the centre of the chamber, with the open arches leading into more halls on either side. Both were of equally daunting size, and both were equally void of anything at all. He should go back and send Tereail and Nureail through the barren rooms, letting him search the one filled with endless trinkets. He doubted the two Scholars had made it two steps away from where he had left them.

Turning back to look at the doorway he entered by, something flashed again into sight and immediately disappeared. From his injury, dizziness assailed Kris any time he moved his head too quickly, so he turned his head slowly back around to see if it would present itself again. Nothing happened. Closing his eyes to ease his frustration, Kris turned on his heel to swiftly be rid of the cursed room, but with his sudden movement came the sudden return of an image once more.

A shadow had appeared on the ground further down to his left, appearing only in his peripherals and never remaining in sight for more than a blink. But knowing its location now, Kris thundered towards it, sabre ready, to confront whatever it was.

Foreign magic was not beyond creating craven illusions, Hane's final act had been proof of that. A Fureath'i sabre could stick still into the gut of a Foreign mage though, and they had yet to find a spell to prevent it. The hidden figure causing the shadow might even have been Hane, perhaps tricking his way free of Jherin's brutal power, but Kris did not think it likely. He had a feeling that Jherin was too much to be fooled by an act like that.

Kris reached the location where the image had flashed and gave one strong swing of his sabre in test. It glided through air and nothing else and Kris eyed his surroundings with suspicion. There was no doubt he was in the right place, his only question was how to view the shadow again to strike it. Looking around the chamber, Kris did not grin as he reasoned the two ways every Fureath'i would deal with a situation: fight it or burn it.

Making his way to the nearest torch, Kris wrenched it out of its decorative wall-hold, breaking off the artistic pieces of stone that weaved around it. Holding the torch in the same manner he held the sabre in his other hand, Kris approached the empty floor space as he would have a squad of Prae'surlas. Swinging down the torch against the stone floor, Kris brought up sparks as he struck, and as the blaze moved away, the faintest of shadows appeared. Looking at it from that proximity, Kris thought he now knew what the shadow was.

Looking around at the other torches in the chamber, Kris considered for a second that he could always return and ask Thisian for assistance. Kris did not laugh but he felt that Dallid or Phira would have laughed if he had spoken those words aloud. So, breaking into a run, Kris moved from torch to torch and ripped each one free of its binding, leaving a trail of debris as he went. When he had a sizeable bundle in his hands, he jogged into the empty chamber nearest to him and deposited the burning lights to the side of the archways. It was slow work but with time Kris stood in a darkened room, filled with only one remaining torch and a swarm of moving shadows.

Quickly returning to the first chamber, Kris was surprised to find Thisian and the Foreigners gone. He had no other feelings on the matter. If Thisian had returned to Rath'Nor it was good, but more likely he had fled Kris's judgement. There had never been an Exile Powerborn before and it was a difficult concept to accept. The idea that Hane had been responsible for the trickery was still not disproved though. Thisian had not tried any tricks in front of Kris in the short time since the magician's demise.

He was not surprised, however, to find both Scholars exactly where he left them and with Tereail kneeling down engrossed in something completely useless. Nureail at least was moving while she searched, but kept craning her neck back to keep an eye on her brother. When she saw Kris she smiled warmly in reaction before gaining better composure of herself. Seeing how Tereail was positioned and knowing Kris's mind, she quickly moved to stand between the warrior and the Scholar.

'What have you found, Tereail?' Kris asked with interest. Nureail eyed him and even placed a hand over her sabre. Tereail was not as careful in preserving his own wellbeing.

'Kris, this place, if anything, is even more a paradise than the Temple of Jhakral. In this room alone, it is more than several chambers from the last temple combined, I could spend my entire life here.'

'It is a Noan candle,' Nureail said to stop her brother further condemn himself. 'That is what he has found.'

'Does it take us to the ice temple?'

'Of course not,' Tereail scoffed at him. 'What it can do however is draw away power as it is used, much the same way the Lae Noan prison can hold Powerborn in its cells. These are far older than that monstrosity though. That entire mountain is false.'

'There were only three of these thought to be in existence, Kris,' Nureail elaborated. 'One is in Rath'Nor, and the other two are in Foriton. All nations have pleaded audience to study the one in our possession, even knowing our distaste for Foreigners. That is how valuable these candles are. And now we have found another.'

'So it cannot help us get to the Temple of Ice,' Kris continued and Nureail bore her teeth at him in much the way a Fureath'i might.

'It can be used to kill a Prae'surlas Powerborn if we encounter one.'

'Is that our immediate goal?' Kris challenged.

'Killing Aerath? Yes. And killing Prae'surlas is the immediate goal of every Fureath'i that burns and bleeds, Kris.'

He stared at her. Nureail's larger eyes blinked and faltered under his cold, dark gaze, but she did not speak. She did not back down. Eventually Tereail interjected, the gravity of the situation suddenly entering his scholarly mind. 'You were not going to cut off my thumbs for this, were you?'

The disbelief in his voice was almost enough to make Kris smile. For a Scholar, Tereail often proved himself to be profoundly stupid.

'Where are the Foreigners?' Kris asked instead. He fully included Thisian in that assessment now. The man was more Prae'surlas than the Prae'surlas. If his thoughts lingered on the Flameborn power now running through Thisian's veins, it made the injury to Kris's skull pound even worse. So he did not think on the matter.

'Gone. The big one, Krife, told us to give you his farewell. He did so with quite an obscene gesture. Thisian Flameborn then,' she began and halted when Kris bristled at the honorary, 'wanted me to relay an even more obscene farewell. I trust you will accept my judgement on not delivering it.'

'The item they took, do you know of it?'

'Yes. I think so, but I cannot allow myself to believe it.' She bit her bottom lip with irritation. 'If I could just lay a hand on it then I would know all there was to Tell. But I at least know that the sword the treasure hunter carried was Jhakral. If they had stayed longer we might have even bartered for it. With the clasp we found, having the strength and power of a Jhakral would greatly aid us in our quest.'

'We will just have to continue to survive with our own strength then,' Kris said before adding, 'But I would have liked to witness you barter with a man standing in a room full of treasure.'

Nureail did not find Kris's joke amusing and Tereail continued to operate with a time delay to the rest of the world. 'We found a Kel Sheran power clip for a Jhakral sword, did we not, Nureail? We should have acquired the sword.'

Perhaps the man's absence from reality was all a part of his greater connection to time. Kris could not decide between frowning or clenching his fists. The Noan candle he had found could be useful if they encountered Iceborns though. Chances were high that was how Tereail had witnessed Kris killing one. It seemed odd to him that something so small could take away an Iceborn's power, where did it go? Kris did not care.

'I imagine it goes into the candle,' Nureail said to him. Kris had not known he had spoken out loud, and frowned at the idea he had asked an idle question. Worse still Nureail was not finished in her answer. 'Although, I once held an arm brace that had two circles in design, one black, one white and where they met a small jewel stood. Looking at the history of the piece I saw a warrior using it with a sword that had a hilt very similar to a Noan candle. There is supposed to be a similar design on the Jaguar and the Lion swords too, I wonder if the life and power they respectively steal goes into the holder of the blade. Anyway, in my viewing the man gained power from the arm brace and took it away from the being he fought. It could be that the Noan candles are really broken sword hilts, as we have not seen enough to know what a whole one looks like. Of course, that does not explain why fire activates it then, and I cannot use my talent to look back at the history of the candles obviously since it steals any power it encounters.'

'Obviously,' Tereail nodded. 'But it does make sense that power cannot be stopped and only diverted. The candles could not possibly stockpile an infinite amount so it would have to let it flow out through another device. Once we take this back to Rath'Nor we can certainly test the theory with the brace we have there before the King takes the piece away from us. It would make you wonder if the Noan prison works in a similar manner, and all the power from the captives were somehow going to Aerath. How else could he become powerful enough to turn the world to ice?'

Kris frowned at what his muttering had let happen. Rather than make him better in any way from knowing those things, Kris only wondered if the Noan candle would work on Aerath if he was somehow already connected to the Lae Noan prison. He had no other plan to kill Aerath though than try to cut his head off, so the Noan candle would do. If Kris died trying, there was not much he could do about it, but he would still need to reach his destination first.

'Come with me,' he ordered and marched back towards the room of shadow. By some blessing of the gods the two of them even followed.

Their pace was not included in the blessing though, and Kris waited patiently while Nureail arrived first, stepping cautiously into the darkened room. Tereail followed absently and seemed caught by surprise by the absence of light in the chamber. Kris frowned to see that they both still had their packs from the Jhakral temple. Had they really grabbed those bags while fleeing for their lives? He remembered then the stones that had kept the Jhakral separated from them. Perhaps the bags of useless trinkets were not as useless as the Scholars that carried them. Kris led them to where he left the torch lying on the floor.

'Read this,' he told them, not caring which of them obeyed. He picked up the torch and moved it to better reveal the circle of shadow that was now almost completely visible on the stone. It held the same runes and script of the platforms from the Jhakral temple.

Tereail peered down on it from the top of his nose. 'This appears to be the markings of a dais, Kris.'

'I did not say describe it, Tereail, I said read it.'

Tereail tisked at Kris's poor manner and looked around vainly. 'Perhaps I could if there were better light.'

Kris took a deep breath.

'This is not a dais, Tereail,' Nureail said, deep in her own study of the circle. 'This is a shadow path.'

'Really? In the Temple of Wind?' Tereail found the statement much more important than Kris did.

'Perhaps if, as Jherin said, and Lord Kr'une destroyed the platform,' Nureail bit her lip while lost in thought. 'Maybe the power destroyed the other platforms too.'

'Do you think the paths of power and the paths of shadow are linked like that? I know you think they already press upon our world trying to reach the other but can they both exist in the same location like this?' Tereail seemed to be speaking to himself rather than to his sister, she answered him anyway.

'Well I am simply saying that if a path of power was destroyed here and has revealed a path of shadow, then what does that mean? If Lord Kr'une's destruction of one platform linked to destroy all the others, then they can be connected to other platforms of one power, so why not other powers?'

'Read what it says,' Kris repeated patiently.

Tereail's eyebrows went up as he shook his head and said, 'Well, believe it or not, it reads the Temple of Ice.'

Kris had heard all he needed to hear and stepped forward onto the circle.

CHAPTER THIRTY FOUR

Darkness

The absence of light pressed on Kris from all sides. He still held the torch but could barely see the thing, the surrounding dark suffocated him so greatly. Of floor or walls or unseen enemies, Kris had no way of knowing, so tracing a soft arc with the side of his foot first, Kris took careful steps forward. In one hand he had the dim glow of the torch, and in the other, he had a steel sabre that did not even catch a reflection from the light. Kris considered outing the flames, because it did not gain him any additional vision but would likely alert any other occupants in the oppressive dark.

A breath sounded behind him and Kris turned with his sabre ready. The blade made gentle contact with something solid and brought forward a yelp, 'Burn you, Kris! Is that your sabre?' Tereail's voice was shrill with distress. 'If you have cut me how are we to bind the wounds in this complete night? I do not even know why you bother to ever sheath that sword you have it in your hand so often. Likely it is just so you can draw it as threat when you attempt to intimidate me. Is this blood?'

Kris calculated if he could quickly kill the man and let Nureail assume it was an accident. A familiar smell came to Kris's attention then, and the soft sounds of careful boot steps. He was able to picture perfectly her positioning, to match sound by sound her every move: the subtle movement of flesh over steel as she tested the hilt of her blade in their new surroundings; the sway of her hair as she immediately checked to see any sign of light from some direction; and finally the release of breath through her nose as she committed herself to their circumstances, ready to fight it head on. Kris clenched his jaw in irritation of what he was doing. Best to kill Tereail after all and with it gain eternal hatred from Nureail, granting Kris freedom of her.

'Is this the Temple of Ice?' Kris asked, knowing that it was not. He would tolerate a patient answer from Nureail, or a

contemptuous one from Tereail, as long as one of them gave him
the information he needed.

'Can you see any ice here?' Tereail said with contempt. Kris had
several dry responses to the Scholar's own flawed statement but
waited with great control for the man to continue. When the fool
did not, Nureail at least had the intelligence to elaborate for him.

'The shadow paths, Kris, do not bring you straight to the temple
as the flowstones did. Instead it gives us a path through the
shadows of our world bridging great distances quickly.'

'So we are walking to the temple,' Kris surmised.

'In a way, yes.'

'Then let us go.'

Kris turned and left, judging that the distant light of his torch
would be enough to let them follow. Hurried footsteps and
muttered curses soon followed as predicted, and Kris kept his ears
sharp for any sound of company upon their path. The throbbing in
his head had not lessoned in any way, but Kris had come to an
acceptable level of ignoring it. New pains for his skull soon arrived
from the Scholars.

'Kris we must be careful,' Nureail said, her breath close behind
him. 'These paths are not travelled for good reason. Ignoring the
variety of demons that survive in the world of darkness, these paths
also create new monsters from existing powers. Where a being
unwittingly walks through this unseen path in our world, if the
power is great enough, an impression is said to be left behind.'

'A shadow?' Kris said derisively.

'Yes, Kris, you could call it a shadow,' Nureail replied just as
dryly. 'Look, there are endless books theorising on these paths, but
the shadow creatures that are left here from passing powers are all
agreed to be savagely dangerous.'

'Are we leaving shadows as we walk?' Kris knew there was
nothing he could do but fight what there was to fight, but the idea
of a creature of shadow being formed from his own soul was not
something he wished to unleash to the world.

'Nureail,' her brother cut in before she could answer. 'It is
pointless trying to explain years of philosophy to a warrior. Just
keep it simple. If you meet anything here, Kris, kill it.'

'I can only hope the absence of light does not result in more mortal wounding for any Scholars during such a fight.'

'Kris, Tereail, stop acting like youths. To answer your earlier question though, no I do not believe we will leave a shadow here: Firstly, because we are not powerful enough and secondly, because we are actually *in* the shadow path and not walking *through* it.'

Kris did not understand but was content to leave it that way. He had always believed there were some things that a man did not need to know, and since meeting Nureail and her brother, that list of things had expanded immensely. If Phira were there then she would interrogate both Scholars exhaustively until every possible item of knowledge had been extracted. She was relentless when it came to obtaining information, to be stored away until a moment arrived where it might be used to gain advantage. It was differences like that where Phira excelled beyond Kris's own abilities. He had never allowed himself to admit to being physically tired, but mentally, the idea of listening to Nureail and her brother explain the endless knowledge they possessed, it was fatiguing even to conceive of the idea. Silence would be his shield against their onslaught, showing his blatant indifference to their useless explanations.

'If you can imagine, Kris,' Kris refrained from sighing as Nureail began, 'A road being built from the Temple of Zenith to the Temple of Dawn. Now I am not saying the shadow paths are simply between temples, in fact we were both surprised that one could even exist in a temple of power, but if you can picture the road, then that is what a shadow path is. While you walk it you are not going through it, you are on it, or in it, whichever the case may be.'

'Clearly it is in. We are consumed by shadow, not strolling along its top,' Tereail decided. 'And I think a road is the wrong analogy, better a river that we have dived into and are being swept along by its current.'

'A road will do for the point I am making,' Nureail said back sharply. 'Keeping in mind the creatures of shadow, if a Lord Fireborn walked from the forest on one side of the road, to the hills on the other, then *he* would be walking through it and not in it. Do you understand?'

'Yes,' Kris said. Silence was no weapon to fight the Scholars with. If they did not need to stop for food, sleep, or torturing warriors, then they would talk endlessly to themselves for years without end. Frehep forbid what Powerborn Scholars could do if they did not even need to stop for food or sleep.

'I do not think you do, Kris,' Tereail informed him. 'These paths have been the topic of complex debate for centuries. The fact that we are in one is remarkable. Nureail do you think you could connect in here? The knowledge you might gain would be significant.'

Nureail hesitated and Kris's shoulders bunched with tension. He did not want her to risk anything in this place.

'I do not think I should attempt it. I think that with our bodies moving so quickly over the world of light through shadow, that I would only receive a blur of several histories of constantly changing locations. More importantly though I do not want to release any power in this place, no matter how small ours might be.'

'I think it is an opportunity wasted. I would try it myself but my viewings are precisely that, what could I view with such darkness? At least with your connection comes certainty from things that have been firmly imprinted.'

'She has told you she does not wish it,' Kris said a little too harshly. Even in the darkness he could feel both their eyes on him because of the outburst. 'We will not waste any time or risk any venture that is not the direct concern of our quest.'

'You repeat yourself often, Kris,' Tereail stated, needlessly.

'That is because Scholars do not seem to know how to listen or remember.'

'That is absurd. Those are precisely the skills that define a Scholar.'

Kris closed his eyes for calm. It did not make a difference with the darkness anyway, and when he reopened his eyes, Tereail reopened his mouth. 'There is a difference between not listening and deeming something stubborn and self-important, hence dismissing it.' Kris did not respond so after a few moments of blessed silence Tereail's mind rambled onto something else. He was likely fearful of the dark and needed to hear his own incessant voice for comfort. 'How do we know we are walking in a straight line?'

Kris did not respond and simply continued walking in a straight line. If he had to guess, Nureail was either grinning at Kris's silence towards Tereail, or else she was frowning at her brother for becoming irritating. But secretly she would be wishing that she could answer him and begin a debate.

'I wonder how far wide of the path we could walk without it changing our direction. I doubt there are barriers, I am even surprised there is something as mundane as ground beneath us.'

'Tereail you open your mouth without taking time to craft thought,' Nureail said but could not help herself from addressing those voiced thoughts. 'What I believe however is that it does not matter which direction we travel, the path was crafted from the Temple of Wind to the Temple of Ice, whether it was linked to the flowstone or not, so those are the only destinations. I would even go so far to say that we do not even need to walk at all, that with enough time the path would bring us to our goal and by walking we are simply speeding things along.'

Kris wished she had not told Tereail that. The Scholar did not seem to be as lazy as Thisian, but Kris very much knew the man would prefer to sit and talk as a better means of passing the time than walking.

'An interesting idea, Nureail,' Tereail said. 'But where in that concept do multiple entities come into it. Let us say all three walking in completely contradicting directions, do we all then arrive at our end together?'

'Depending on who walks the faster perhaps, or perhaps two of us would become lost to the shadow.'

Kris heard the smile in her voice and was pleased at least that she was not taking Tereail's important topics as seriously as he was.

'What about you, warrior?' Tereail had taken to calling Kris that in return for Kris's own disdainful use of the word Scholar. 'What are your martial thoughts on this place?'

Kris did not respond. It seemed there was nothing in the world that could stop a Scholar from speaking endlessly about nothing, but Kris would by no means encourage or endorse such behaviour with verbal participation.

'It is true, Kris, that often the mind of a Scholar aims too high and can miss the target of a concept,' Nureail said diplomatically, trying to elicit a response from him by using her voice softly, implicating inappropriate affection. 'Many temples could benefit with the presence of at least one warrior among their minds.'

Yes but only so the warrior could kill all the priests and Scholars, Kris thought to himself before saying aloud, 'The only useful piece of information that I have taken from your theories is that we could benefit our mission by running instead of walking.'

'It was only a theory,' Tereail muttered.

'Yes, there is no way to know if running will get us to the ice temple any faster and it would also make us less aware of any,' Nureail paused to think of the right word, 'company.'

It was not as if they would see any worse while running, but Kris did take that minute to test their surroundings for sound. Tereail stamped like an infant just learning to walk and although Nureail's step was lighter, her thighs brushed together often. The smouldering of the torch was faint, and Kris was able to identify each of these and discard them, searching for anything out of place that could alert them to a possible creature of shadow, or *company* as Nureail called it.

Judging where his two Scholars were positioned behind him, Kris swung out his sabre to the side as a test. The blade itself did not make a sound cutting through the darkness, but the slightest sound that could have been a hiss was heard in sudden reaction. It did not come from the direction of his two companions.

Kris did not want to alert the creature he was aware of it, so he casually swung his blade out the other way too. If the thing was stalking them though, then it would be difficult to judge its position while constantly moving. With enough concentration Kris was confident he could he evaluate a direction to launch an attack but it would take time. His ears quickly began itemising each and every sound again, listing and dismissing with professional skill.

'What was that Lord Flameborn doing with those thieves?' Tereail asked loudly, but it would not distract Kris. 'I mean a lord of power can go where he chooses, but it is highly unorthodox that they take company. I believe I have never heard of such an instance. Apart from their fleshborn swords, all Powerborn ever travel with are others of their kind or they travel alone. He is from your village, Kris, yes?'

'He is an Exile, Tereail. It brings me no surprise or disappointment, and I believe Furea is the better for not having Thisian remain, especially as a Flameborn.' Kris wanted silence, even more than he usually wanted it, but did not want to alert their stalker to his awareness of it.

'You believe it is better for Thisian Flameborn to walk the lands of the world as our representative of what a Fureath'i Powerborn is like?' Kris could hear the smile in Nureail's voice again. Any topic that had the potential to cause him pain of heart or pain of head, seemed to bring delight to the Teller's lips.

'What a Foreigner thinks and does not think is of no concern to me or to Furea,' Kris answered. Let Thisian do as he pleased; Kris would do what he must. His voice was spoken calmly, without any hint of concentration. His mind was drawing closer to the shadows of sound that he craved though. Tereail's breathing, Nureail's footsteps, the torch that he held, the baggage that they carried, all of it was marked inside his head as right and proper, leaving still a sound that was not. Kris bore his teeth as he prepared to dive into the darkness.

'There is no need,' a voice sounded from behind, completely away from where Kris had been certain the creature stood. 'I will do you no harm, travellers.' The last felt like a whisper in his ear, but from the opposite side again from where the voice sounded first.

'You will retreat back to your pit of shadow, creature, or you will die by my sword,' Kris replied.

'You threaten while drowning helpless in a sea of dark. If I had not been guarding you then you would have already been overwhelmed by the beasts that dwell here.' Every different part of the sentence came at Kris from a new direction. Unless the creature was swimming within the shadows, then it was just its voice that was moving. It was a trick born of fear by a creature that recognised a warrior capable of killing it. Kris returned to the first location he had decided upon. If there is breath to give life to words, then there are lungs that he can plunge his sabre into.

'If you truly mean us no harm, then prove it to us.' Nureail spoke the words in a tone that Kris recognised as when she was feigning ignorance. She had spoken similarly to Jherin, asking questions Kris would guess she already knew the answer to but was testing a theory of hers first.

'If your lives are not proof enough, then perhaps this will calm you.' The voice echoed again and suddenly Kris was assaulted with light. Holding his sabre arm up over his eyes, Kris squinted to see that the brightness was slowly dimming, the surrounding shadow already creeping its way back towards them before slowing to a stop.

Opening his eyes fully despite their protest, Kris spun around to see the creature but found only Nureail and Tereail both still shielding their eyes. They were all three standing in a dome of white that faded grey towards its edge, showing exactly how black the darkness was that stood outside the protective dome. Kris's torch had gone out, the light somehow extinguishing it, so he stowed it away in his pack and gripped the sabre with two hands.

'Show yourself, creature,' Kris demanded.

'I cannot.'

'Why not?' Nureail asked, eager to engage her new fascination before Kris tried to kill it.

'Your eyes are not strong enough to see me.'

'Step out from the darkness and we shall be the judge of that,' Kris said back.

'I am standing right before you but my skin steals all light that would reveal me to you. Most creatures of your world have not the power to see me, but some do.'

'Powerborn?' Nureail asked.

'Yes those of your kind have eyes strong enough to take for themselves the light that my body feeds on.'

'But not us,' Tereail nodded, readily accepting the creature's tale. 'But if your body feeds on light, then how can you survive in a place of darkness?'

'I do not survive here; I endure here.'

'Why?'

The creature did not answer straight away. When it finally replied, the words danced all around them again. 'I am here for a time to watch. To keep sentry on the terrible creation you encountered in your temple.'

'Jherin,' Nureail said.

'Yes, Jherin,' the creature of darkness said the name with hatred.

'What is your name?' Nureail asked. 'I am Nureail, this is my brother Tereail, and this is our protector Kris.' That was the second time she had described him as her protector in an apologetic way. Needless to say, Kris did not like it.

'It is pleasant to meet you, Nureail,' the creature returned. 'My name is Fin'derrin.'

'You are a demon lord,' Nureail stated.

'If that is what you wish to call me,' Fin'derrin said back.

Tellings of demons were not exactly popular as Fureath'i Tellings went, since they did not often contain the deaths of Prae'surlas, but Kris had grown up with tales of Fin'derrin. In the stories the creature was not invisible, but described as a cloud of swirling darkness. In Furea, Fin'derrin is the demon that tries to devour the sun, when every few years a black power covers its heavenly light. Frehep always wins through, and the sun always returns, but the name Fin'derrin did not warm Kris to the invisible enemy.

'Why do you watch Jherin?' Nureail asked, and Kris eyed Tereail to see why he was he remaining so quiet. Perhaps he was content to let his sister address the demon only because it was potentially dangerous.

'I watch the creation of Fearie because of the destruction he will bring to all our worlds.'

'Fearie? That is Jherin's creator?' Again Nureail sounded like she was asking questions she already knew the answer to.

'Fearie is a beast more ancient than any other, with so much power that she had to create a way to prevent her own omnipotence. Fearie created an equal to her power in order to stop it. Where hers was the power of creation, her creation became the power of destruction. Jherin is that power.'

'Fearie,' Nureail said slowly, 'Jherin destroyed her?'

'No. He could not. He destroyed her power but not her life. Even then, she needed to help him, creating the lock that holds both her and her power.'

'So he protects the lock?'

'Jherin cannot tolerate being near that power. He does not protect it, he curses it. Sometimes, beyond his control, the curse calls him to the holder of a piece of it, to bring his destruction upon them, but Jherin fights his own creation as much as he fights all other creation.'

'So even though he has created, it is a curse of destruction that he has formed,' Tereail mused to himself, finally feeling the need to speak. 'So all he can do is destroy and you claim that he hates himself for it. It is a wonder he does not destroy himself.'

'I do not believe he can,' Nureail said with a hint of sadness.

'I would agree with you,' Fin'derrin said. 'But his power is not to be mourned, it is to be feared. Over the centuries, many armies have risen up to rid our worlds of this being. Jherin destroyed them all. His mind has not weathered the passing of history well. When you encountered him, it was with lucidity. Many others have not been so fortunate. When his mind falters, the result can be catastrophic. So I watch, hidden in the shadows, and I do what I can to guide him from our annihilation.'

'It is a dangerous task you have given yourself. What of Fearie? Can she not stop him? Where is she now?' Gone was Nureail's initial subtly, she now had a willing source of previously unknown knowledge, and her questions would only grow in number if they did not leave soon.

'Fearie cannot kill her son, the same as her son cannot kill her. She is creation and he is destruction, with both so equal in power and opposite in nature, there could never be a victor.'

'Why are you telling us these things?' Kris demanded. 'Why are you speaking with us at all? How is it that you even speak our tongue?' If any did at all, then these were the questions that needed answering. He did not trust why an invisible demon would happen to know the Fureath'i language and freely divulge intoxicating tales to two willing Scholars. Kris could not see anything, but there was something that told him the demon lord was now staring at him. Silence built up, and his two companions added their own disapproving glares at Kris's insistence they put an end to their current waste of time.

'A thing of power will communicate its wishes without need of tongue, warrior. Did you think that a creature as ancient as Jherin spoke your language too? What you hear and perceive is simply your inadequate mind trying to make sense of something far beyond it. Does not the fact you cannot see me prove how limited you are? Even understanding is just another invention of your flesh to attempt sense of an external world too complex for your comprehension. I could create such an illusion to your mind that you would never suspect that it was not reality. Because your senses, fleshborn, are all the reality you will ever know, never truth.'

'Perhaps my inadequate ears are mistaken, but you failed to answer why you still grace our humble minds with your mighty words.'

Silence again and along with it the feeling of violence to follow. Kris's senses were complex enough that he knew when a being feared him. Why else would it not have attacked?

'Very well,' Fin'derrin's voice sounded. 'I will tell you if you wish it. I speak because I feed off the light of a world, young warrior, but I can also take nourishment from the light of a life. It is not light as you can conceive it, but it exists all the same.'

'So you impede our journey in order to feed off our energy?'

'No, young warrior, not from you.' That made Kris uncomfortable, but only because he would wish it to feed from his strength rather than sully Nureail with its dark hunger. 'There are few of my kind that do not project their light to me, but never have I encountered one of your species that had nothing to give out to the world. If I did not know better I would say you are a demon in a man's skin or you are dead in all but appearance.'

The creature's statements did not have an effect on Kris but Tereail had the incongruity to laugh. 'Did you hear that, Kris? This demon cuts to the bone of your ways. You are the just a theory of what a Fureath'i should be as I have said, you walk and you talk as a Fureath'i should, but you do not live!'

'Be silent you fool,' Nureail snapped at her brother. The Teller looked at Kris with her soft eyes, moist from the too bright light the demon created, and Kris wished she would look anywhere but at him. When she spoke it seemed intended for the demon. 'He does not give you his strength, Fin'derrin, because it is all focused inward. Do not tarnish him with such quick assumptions.'

Kris frowned at Nureail's words, angry that *she* would make such assumptions, quick or otherwise. He was equally angered that she felt the need to defend him to some passing demon. Kris's own self-belief, that he is constantly more than he is, could not be damaged by some poorly thrown words.

Nureail held her chin high while waiting for the demon's response, and her demeanour was spoiled by darting her eyes slightly towards Kris to see his reaction too. He gave none. Her description of his battle was not so far amiss, all it avoided was the dark heart and darker thoughts that Kris used his will to keep locked away. Birth, blood, and desire were not what made a man. The choice between to do what felt right or to do what was right, that was what made a man.

'It drains me to fight back the shadow like this,' Fin'derrin finally said. 'I have enjoyed speaking with you. I will admit that the words I gave you did give out much life in return, but it is rare that I am granted the opportunity regardless.'

'It has been remarkable speaking with you also, Fin'derrin, I only wish that we were on more leisurely business. Our companion Kris is right however and we must press on.' Nureail looked around as if she might suddenly see the demon then, her eyes lingering on Kris for a moment too long.

'You travel to the Temple of Ice.'

'Yes,' Nureail replied, suspicions weaving through her tone.

'It is no coincidence that you happened upon this gateway. It was my wish to guide you here, to show you the shadow that would have otherwise remained hidden.'

Kris did not like that. 'Why would you wish us to reach the ice temple?'

'There are those that would not see the Iceborn Aerath succeed in his plans. He has captured one god and slowly kills another. What he does within the Temple of Ice affects every world.'

'Captured? Where has he captured a god? Which god?'

'He has captured Aerune, caught in one of the creator's hives. It swallows power to give to her but since she is sleeping; it goes to him.'

'Goes to who?'

'Aerath.'

'Are you saying he has captured a god in the cells of Lae Noan? Is that the creator's hive? What of the Temple of Ice? What do you know of the ritual there?' Nureail asked.

'I know that you will die there,' Fin'derrin said plainly.

'No, she will not,' Kris said back, just as plainly.

'Do you know how far it is?' Tereail asked then, as if he had not been paying attention to anything else. *Aerath has the power of the god Aerune?* 'I suppose it would be difficult for you to know that with regards to time or distance, since both move so differently here.'

'I can take you there now.'

'No,' Kris said just as Nureail and Tereail started giving thanks for the kind offer. It was of course the Teller that turned to argue with him. Either she thought her supposed fondness for Kris would soften him to her reasons, or else she was much smarter and knew to protect her brother from the grievous injury he would sustain from challenging Kris.

'Our goal is to reach the Temple of Ice as quickly as possible, is it not?'

'Our goal,' Kris replied, 'is to not trust an invisible demon to envelope us with its power in the dream that it will help us.'

'It is not without reason, young warrior,' Fin'derrin interjected. 'As I have already said, I simply endure this place and its absence of light. The nourishment I have taken from your companions will sustain me for some time to come.'

May your light burn brightly, Kris thought then. It was always just a Fureath'i saying that he had figured meant to achieve as much honour and glory in this life so you may shine as you ascend the heights of power in the next. The demon was making him think that something larger was hidden deep within the Fureath'i folklore. It was a good thing he was not a Scholar or he might have considered giving it more thought. But for now it was simply a good thing for the demon that it was invisible because Kris would like to kill it.

'My refusal does not change. We continue as we will,' Kris said with a hard look towards Nureail and Tereail. If they continued to conjure arguments with twisted words and spiralling reasons, he would have to leave them. Fin'derrin's words whispered around him then, sounding just as cold and firm as Kris's had.

'I did not *ask* for your permission.'

CHAPTER THIRTY FIVE

Enemies

Dallid stood to his knees in the snow, but it would not be long before it turned to water. The heat that his body radiated was destroying winter where ever he stepped. During the last few days Dallid had run from Furea to the wildlands and straight into Surlas, still unable to fully accept the speed and strength that his new Powerborn body could produce. The scars that the demon had given him on his hands and face were already gone.

Although Dallid had the map given to him by Sindel, he was mostly using the presence of the demon in his mind to guide him. It burned brightly in his head with the desire to kill Aerath burning even fiercer in his heart. Sometimes the urge to go straight for Lae Noan would overwhelm Dallid, his hatred for Aerath becoming too much, but he stayed strong and stuck to his plan. So he followed the demon, running hard for days. He ran too fast for anyone to stop him, too powerful for anyone to even try. But because of the heat his body gave off, and the winter that had seemingly cursed everywhere in the world, his passage had been melted and burnt into the ground for all to see.

So unless they were far stupider and even more inbred than Dallid thought, he was certain he had a small army of Prae'surlas following him. Controlling his body heat was just one more ritual that he did not know, but it must have been possible. There were countless Tellings of Fireborn and Flameborn entering Surlas by stealth and not leaving a ready road behind them for all to travel. Turning around again to make sure no one had caught up with him yet, Dallid was reassured by one fact: Prae'surlas were as big as they were ugly. So looking back over the white wilderness, Dallid reasoned that he would be able to spot a north-man for miles.

Since leaving the Temple of Dawn - and the surreal visions that came outside it - Dallid needed to test his new strength. With the winding forests behind him, there was a time when all he had was open ground ahead and never had he believed that any creature could move so fast as he had over that ground. There were probably thousands of things he did not know how to do as a Fireborn, but pushing his energy into the muscles of his body did not seem to be one of them.

He stopped periodically to test his other powers, doing his best to create attacks of fire, but his failures at these only disheartened him. The time he spent sprinting however, was so exhilarating that it made him forget all the confusion and anxiety he felt over everything else. He could forget that he hunted a demon wearing the skin of the most powerful Fireborn in history and he could forget that he also hunted the Iceborn that had humbled that same Fireborn. His mind had not trudged through the pain and loneliness of his marriage once, and it had not returned to the fact that in all likelihood he was going to die without ever seeing his wife again. He could become lost in the ecstasy of his own power, and it was magnificent.

When he had reached the end of Furea, Dallid could see the line of border forts that guarded it. It had been a mistake entering one of them, but he had been tempted on the slim chance he would find word of Thisian. After the way the elders reacted to him at the farm, and the warriors at the temple, Dallid did not relish the idea of seeing any more of his betters bow down to him. As a fleshborn he had never given any thought to how a Powerborn thought of him as he knelt down in awe of their presence. Now he wanted to scream at his brothers and explain to them that he was not any greater than they were. No one should ever need to grovel in reverence. Dallid knew that entering the border fort had been a mistake.

Thank Frehep there had not been a blaze commander on duty, but having an ember class touch his head to the dirt at your feet, unable to meet your eye, and unable to speak save to answer your commands; it was unnerving. Dallid only remained long enough to discover that Thisian's squad was positioned days away in the north eastern most point of Furea, and it would take Dallid too long to make the diversion. It would have been good to spend even a few minutes with Thisian though, and know that Thisian would never bow to him or call him lord. It brought a smile to his face just thinking about what Thisian would say when Dallid explained his plan of hunting down Aerath and Chrial'thau.

So you have been given the power of a Fireborn, an immortal warrior of our god, and the first thing you do is to run off and get yourself killed?

Thisian would energetically mock him and curse his luck, claiming that it should have been him to receive the powers, that they were wasted on Dallid. He might even say the only worse person to receive them would have been Kris, a man even more humble and modest, traits never associated with a lord of power. Dallid wished he could be in the presence of a real lord though, just so it would be someone who would meet his eye. And truth be told, Dallid could not guarantee that he himself would not bow down in deference.

So he had quickly left the fort known as the Third Flame - counted literally from its position from the Fire Wall - and entered the wildlands to find it had been turned into another Surlas. It was awkward to run through all the snow and Dallid had even been glad at the beginning when his heat melted it all. Then the danger of that hit him and Dallid returned to running as strongly as he could manage.

His surroundings did not change when he left the wildlands and entered Surlas. There was not even a fresh snow fall to mark his entry into the abysmal land. All it had been was a systematic look on the maps Sindel provided him to let Dallid deduce that he was suddenly in the country of his hated enemy. With his small pack of supplies and his Fireborn's tunic, he felt almost naked in the vast white countryside. He had thought to bring a cloak, but it seemed he did not need one. He could feel it was cold but he himself was not cold.

It was just another thing that his body could not accept, causing his mind constant distress. The burning fire within his head was always there too, always letting him know that somehow he was connected to that demon and that he getting closer. While Dallid ran and powered over the land, the demon flew on wings of black flames through the skies, but for all the speed that it gained by flying, the demon lost more speed by stopping to create murder and destruction.

Whenever he felt the devil stop, Dallid would stop in reaction. He was getting better at controlling it, but every time it felt as if Chrial'thau was right next to him. Dallid used those periods to run faster, eager to ignore the feelings he could decipher when the demon was feeding. It felt like it was getting stronger, growing more powerful with everything that it killed and burned. But every time the devil got stronger, Dallid got closer and now finally he believed he would catch him.

Standing on a hill of snow, a circle of melt water already forming at his feet, Dallid looked down at the Surlas city of Dowrathel in the distance. It had been his plan to avoid the cities, but somewhere near the City of Towers he felt the demon.

Dallid's speed, as well as helping to catch the demon, should have kept him well ahead of any pursuers, but now that he searched for the black devil, he could not help constantly checking behind for an army of Prae'surlas to appear. It was perhaps possible Chrial'thau was inside the actual city, if his demonic fire could get past the towers and he was disguised. It was a large city, easy to become lost or unnoticed, and from his vantage point Dallid had a great view of it. He could see all four greater towers protecting the walls of the city, and the fifth largest tower at its centre surrounded by palaces. Being a city so close to Furea, it was built for war, but being built by the Prae'surlas it was built for a lazy, comfortable, war.

The Fureath'i had only one city and it was a fortress built into two mountain ranges with layers of outer and inner walls that made the entire structure impenetrable. The Prae'surlas on the other hand had actually built their city at the bottom of a hill, with the river running north of it, leaving no defence from the south. In their arrogance they relied on the magic of their towers and the incompetence of the Fureath'i. Dowrathel was the first city that fell during the long war.

It had been rebuilt since, with the magic in the towers perhaps strengthened, but in the stories it was the place where Chrial'thau had humbled Aerath. The Fireborn had been in the height of his power and Aerath was an unknown Iceborn in command of the city. The war had only just begun and battle by champion was still accepted as a means of victory. Chrial'thau's win had been so complete though that the Prae'surlas refused to believe some form of treachery had not been used. They did not surrender and in his disgust Chrial'thau let Aerath live with the shame of his people. For the rest of the war there were no more battles of champions, knowing that the Prae'surlas could not be trusted, and as punishment the Fureath'i never accepted any surrender from a single warrior that day onward.

Is there something still left of the old Chrial'thau that he has journeyed here? To remind himself of a time when Aerath was weak and he was strong?

Feeling the pounding in his head, Dallid knew that the demon Chrial'thau was strong beyond belief now. It felt like the devil's black fire was roaring all around Dallid's head and yet he could not see the vile creature. The four guardian towers around the city should be sensing the demon's power too. Those towers had enough ice magic in them to withstand days of assault from the Fureath'i army centuries ago. Whenever fire was detected it would create a terrible ice wind that tracked the fire down and destroyed it. Any fleshborns that happened to be in the path of that wind were devoured as an afterthought. The ice cut through and killed in seconds.

Dallid could not imagine the Prae'surlas being so stupid as to not increase the strength in those towers when they rebuilt the city, but he could imagine them being too arrogant to do it. Regardless, the towers should be glowing bright with the threat of Chrial'thau's fire, no matter how black it was. Dallid did not dare go any closer least he activate them himself.

Scanning the wide landscape of everything white, Dallid looked for something black. The smallest flame should have been visible to his eyes, but still there was nothing. Rechecking for signs of yellow hair, or shining spears, Dallid wondered how long more before his pursuers would arrive. By right Dallid should leave the devil to do what it may to the city, and he should continue to Lae Noan. But he was using Chrial'thau as a compass to lead him straight for Aerath and hoped to find advantage while the two villains battled. He needed to kill Aerath soon, every inch of his being screamed for the Iceborn's blood, and Dallid had never felt such strong emotions before. It seemed unnatural. The devil looked drawn straight to

Aerath almost as unstoppably as Dallid was, but why had it come here to Dowrathel?

Dallid began to feel a strange urge to go down into that city, even though everything told him it was beyond madness. There was nothing but death awaiting him in the form of a wind of ice gusting out from four guarding towers. At least there was not snow falling from the heavens to make it worse; would that flames could rain instead.

Only then did Dallid crane his neck up to the clouds and only then did he see the demon miles above the city burning as a blackened sun.

He could not be sure if the devil waited for Dallid to look up, as if it wished for an audience to what it was about to do, but right then small black things did begin to break off from the demon and drift slowly down. Perhaps the demon could read Dallid's thoughts because a snow of black fire began to fall on the Prae'surlas city of Dowrathel.

As slow as they appeared at first, each flake of fire grew faster the further it fell. Dallid's gaze was drawn back to the city then as four bright lights formed within each of the towers. They pulsed from dark blue to white and the same shifting colours began gushing around each of the towers in a stream of magic. The air around Dallid fell with a deathly chill and all earlier thoughts about him no longer being able to feel cold were gone.

A haunting sound echoed from all directions, like the sound of a dying man's breath being whispered into his ears. Over the last few days Dallid had witnessed a lot of things, and he felt each one had made him better and stronger, seeing that creature Jherin included, and still those towers terrified him to his bone. Even with all the power of a Fireborn bursting to be set free, when Dallid looked at those towers he saw an agonising death. Was it part of the ice magic to strike mindless terror into the minds of Fureath'i?

The dying man's breath stopped whispering into his ears. The silence that followed made Dallid's hands tremble, he wanted to crouch down and hide. Then the towers flashed and the ice wind moved with frightening speed. Dallid jumped but kept his eyes open, watching each one of the fire balls sent down get swept away and devoured in a white wind of ice that spiralled the city with violent speed. If the people of Dowrathel did not know they were under attack before, then the arrival of their defensive magic streaking across the skies informed them quickly. Bells began to sound but before the first of them rang out, Dallid was sure he had heard laughter coming from the devil in the sky.

Dallid checked his surroundings again before looking back up. He did not want any Prae'surlas sneaking up on him unaware, but he was too fascinated by the scene before him. One Fureath'i, albeit poisoned with demon blood, was attacking an entire city of Prae'surlas. More bizarrely, Dallid suddenly had the unreasonable urge to join in. Even if he had been as skilful, clever, or strong as any of his friends, Dallid still would not have considered such a thing. The devil above him shouted out then and the light of the sun disappeared.

A gigantic creation of black fire hurtled toward the city. All four towers lit up without delay and all four ice winds shot straight out to meet it. The vast ball of dark magic was not aimed towards the centre of the city though, so all four winds did not hit at once. The devil's magic was aimed at only the nearest tower and so only that wind reached the fire before the fire reached the tower. The giant ball of flames burst apart, trying to devour the tower of light and ice, and a new pain arrived in Dallid's head. The feeling could only be Chrial'thau but did it mean the demon was in pain or could it be that it was actually feeding off of ice magic designed to destroy it?

When the three other winds arrived and clashed into the flaming tower, Dallid was further horrified to not see the flames smothered, but to see the winds catch fire. The black flames travelled back along the ice towards the other three towers. Dallid had already guessed that the devil's fire somehow fed power back to the demon from whatever it burnt, but what he was witnessing was too much. It meant the more power the towers would use to destroy the fire would only feed back to Chrial'thau and make the fire stronger. How could such a thing be stopped?

The pain in his head grew sharper and when the black fire reached the remaining three towers, Dallid dropped to his hands and knees from the force of it. Whatever reservoirs of ice power the Prae'surlas had stored within those towers - designed to fend off an army of Fireborn - the demon's fire looked immune and savagely fed on it. The blue and white light from each of the towers still shone, but it was surrounded by a dancing black evil. No longer did they represent the defence and safety of the people within the city, but all four towers burnt with a devil's fire to announce their destruction.

Dallid was conflicted. Any Fureath'i should love for an entire of city of north-men to be burnt to ash by a single Fureath'i, but if the black fire fed the demon with everything it touched, then he did not want to imagine how much power the thousands of lives would give the thing. With every death the devil would grow in power and as it grew in power it would only cause more death. Such a creature could destroy anything. How long before it turned its attention to Furea again?

Dallid's duty was to kill Aerath, and to better Furea. Killing the demonic remains of Chrial'thau would better Furea, and the fact that Dallid did not want to fight the creature only made the decision clearer. He could continue to hesitate, humbled by his weakness and fear, or he could stopping thinking about it and just act.

Setting down his meagre supplies first, fire burst to life from Dallid's skin. It travelled up his arms and around his head. The world went red from the fire burning before his eyes. As a fleshborn, he had never fully understood what it had meant that a Powerborn did not use magic, but that they were instead Connected to it. He understood it now; he was magic made flesh. They were one and the same. He drank deeper and deeper from a well of unending strength, and his body begged for more.

The red fire consuming him began to grow hotter and it was with shaking hands that Dallid saw his flames turn white. Panic, terror, exultation, his mind scrambled for every piece of sense it could grasp. Finding any kind of familiar physical concept, to label his completely non-physical sensations, Dallid was able to worry about what a lack of control could do to him. He was able to worry about the ice-wind of the towers somehow finding its way free of the demon blaze and coming for him. More, he worried about the bright white fire around his flesh being in any way connected to the demon or to Aerath, and suddenly Dallid was able to let his power go.

Pulling himself further and further back from the lure of infinity, Dallid first turned to look up at the demon, and then down to see a flash of white appear from the city below. Reducing his red fire back down to just his arms, Dallid watched as another flash of white appeared from the central tower of the city. It vanished again and strangely he thought he saw a figure standing there. A third flash then appeared as a bubble of white grew out from that figure. Four more bubbles appeared simultaneously and all five towers suddenly held spheres of ice trembling around them.

The black fire was trapped inside the bubbles of ice now and Dallid did not understand why the fire was not feeding off the new magic as it had the winds, but looking up to the demon in the sky, he saw a sixth bubble of ice also consumed Chrial'thau. Again he could see flames of black lashing out at the prison but the ice did not look to be breaking. Feeling foolish, Dallid put out the fire on his arms and crouched down in case anyone had seen him. He looked around once but then went back to stare at what real power was.

The pain in his head was still as intense as it had been, so Chrial'thau still possessed all the power of the four towers. Yet it looked like something was able to contain both the power within the demon, as well as the power again in the towers. If it was not Aerune the god of the Prae'surlas, then Dallid did not know who it could be. He had never heard of the northern god intervening in the lives of Powerborn or fleshborn, but then again Dallid had also never heard of a demon devouring an entire city of Prae'surlas before either. Then the white spheres disappeared as did the black fire that had been beneath them. Looking up Dallid saw the body of Chrial'thau fall from the sky.

Tired of hesitation and inaction, Dallid ran down to where the creature would land. If he could kill the beast while it was injured then at least he would have done one service to better his country. It would mean he would need to rethink his plans to kill Aerath but saving his country from this particular horror was worth it. Especially since he had only just realised the potential devastation the demon could cause.

He left a path of melt water in his wake and, as he approached the site, Dallid looked nervously up at the towers. He was still too far out to be in danger of spears or archers, but he did not know what range the terrible magic in the towers held. Unless the demon had damaged them for a time, but Dallid would not get complacent and he was just as careful to approach the fallen devil. Chrial'thau's body lay sprawled in the snow ahead of him.

There was no radius of melted earth, and with alarm Dallid realised that he could not feel the demon in his head any more either. Was it done already then? Was the demon dispelled from the world of light by one of the gods meant to protect it? It did not seem too unlikely to Dallid, but it did seem too easy. Why did Frehep not do the same when Chrial'thau was defeated? Or why did Aerune not act when Chrial'thau and the Fureath'i army laid waste to the city of Dowrathel centuries earlier?

Unsure what to do and growing angry because of it, Dallid looked around vainly again. There was no movement from the city, and still the same white blanket of snow everywhere else, so he walked over to stand directly above the demon. Streams of melt water flowed under his feet and when he stopped over the body of Chrial'thau, the demon looked a broken thing. It looked like an old man lying dead in a Foreign place of snow and cold. His white wet hair was matted down over his face and the leathery skin no longer looked tough, but thin and brittle. The thing almost looked Fureath'i again, perhaps regaining his humanity in death. Dallid's hand reached across for his sabre and was stopped by a spear of ice punching out through his stomach.

CHAPTER THIRTY SIX

Spears

Dallid's body erupted with flames. The fire melted the ice-spear and Dallid could disgustingly feel it turn into water inside him. The wound did not disappear though and he turned around numbly to see the owner of the offending weapon. Twenty five Prae'surlas had apparently grown out of the snow, their long white cloaks still hiding them to even Dallid's Powerborn eyes. The hole in his stomach might have been contributing to his distorted vision though.

They all stood in separate groups of five, each with four men carrying spears of steel and one carrying spears of ice. Every one of them were so tall that their legs should have snapped from trying to move, and each one got uglier as Dallid looked to the next. He had never been tall when compared to other Fureath'i, but standing alone in that field of snow with twenty five Prae'surlas looming over him, Dallid had never felt so small in his life.

He looked into the eyes of the man who had stabbed him and saw blue and white spirals looking back. He had a tunic similar to Dallid's except under his white cloak it was blue, decorated with what the Prae'surlas would have claimed were spears of white ice. All Dallid could see was white fire. Giving the hole in his stomach one last look, Dallid roared out his anger and blazed his fire brighter.

The Frostborn in front of him conjured another spear of ice and swung it for Dallid's neck. Using his small height to his advantage, Dallid ducked underneath and pulled his sabre free. The Frostborn dodged back and as he moved, a throwing spear flew forward from one of the others. Dallid spun with unnatural speed, swerving to the side and going back quickly to try hacking the Frostborn closest to him. Larger spears were thrust in from multiple opponents and every time Dallid tried to stab a single north-man, he was forced to deal with twenty four others.

Screaming out his frustration he swung his sabre hard against every wooden spear he saw, using his superior strength to knock them away. The spears of ice did not move as easily and every time his sabre met those it only bounced away without effect. The heat of his fire had already created a scorched battlefield in the middle of the snow, but it did not melt the ice weapons as it had the one through his stomach.

That wound was forgotten for the time, although he could feel it weaken him with every move, it would just have to wait until after the fight. Chances were that he would have many more to keep it company. He did not know how many wounds a Fireborn could take and still live, but he had a feeling he was about to find out.

The metal of his sabre finally found Prae'surlas flesh and their frozen blood splattered onto his burning face. Dallid had never moved as fast or fought as strong, his Powerborn agility making up for his average skill with a sabre. The Prae'surlas he fought though were experienced soldiers and, unimpressed by Dallid's show of steel or fire, thrust forward their spears once more. The Fireborn swayed to the side and caught a hold of one of the spears, snapping off the head and slamming the tip back into a warrior's skull.

The next spear slid harmlessly to the side of an arched back before the Fireborn gripped burning fingers into the wielder's throat and emptied his neck. His sabre found the stomach of a fleshborn that had edged too close, and in his withdrawal of the blade, Dallid cut it deep into the shoulder of another. Two more came straight at him and without thinking Dallid pushed out his empty hand, sending a fiery impression of it towards the next two victims. The hand shaped fires seared and melted the heads of his targets and they died screaming on their knees, clawing at their faces.

But for every fleshborn he managed to catch with his blade or flame, he had not yet touched any of the Frostborn. Dallid felt that they would be the instruments of his death if he could not find a way. How did other Fireborns do it? His opponents appeared to be just as fast and just as strong as he was, even though they should not be when compared to a Fireborn. If they were Iceborns facing him then it would be different and he would already be dead, but one Fireborn should be a match for five Frostborn. What was he doing wrong?

His sabre hissed past a Frostborn's neck just out of reach and Dallid had his answer.

Going against every instinct he had, Dallid threw down his sabre, lashing out with the fire from his fists instead. A Frostborn's hands went up to protect himself and a large shield of white formed. The fire broke through the shield but it gave the Frostborn enough time to fall out of the way. Dallid smiled that he was at least now making progress fighting other Powerborn when he was stabbed in the side by a fleshborn. The man did not withdraw the spear point but held onto Dallid while others ran in. He was quickly pinned from all sides with spear heads tearing up his sides and through his lungs. Blood gurgled out of his mouth as he tried to cry out his agony and Dallid could see his fire begin to fade.

His power had to retreat back inside his body to stop it from dying and so could no longer burn out in attack. But if all he could do was heal himself while north-men stabbed him at their pleasure then he would die anyway. So somehow he demanded that his body not heal the wounds, and instead called it all forward to push out from his skin. He burned furiously and his pain burned just as strong, but the fire rushed out to run down every spear made of wood and jumped onto every fleshborn holding them.

The Prae'surlas screamed and some wrapped themselves in their white cloaks, rolling around on the ground to put out the flames. Had there been any snow left in Dallid's vicinity then maybe they might have succeeded but he had scorched it all, evaporating even the water it left behind. So the Prae'surlas screamed and they died and their flesh burned until their bodies could no longer stand it. How fleshborns thought they could kill a Powerborn was laughable. He was a lord of fire with the blood of gods in him and they were just things of meat and blood waiting to die. Dallid caught hold of the spear heads still embedded in his flesh and cast them out. His own blood and meat gushed out of him but he assured himself that he did not need it.

All five Frostborn took the opportunity to advance on the wounded Fireborn then and Dallid cursed that if he could only fight them one at a time then he would have some chance. His body fell as he pushed out his power again but he did not need his flesh, his power was enough. Flames roared up in a circle high on all sides, creating a barrier of fire keeping all the Frostborn away from him, all but one. That was the one he would kill first. Giving a quick look to see all of his comrades separated from him, the Frostborn did not hesitate as he continued towards Dallid's fallen figure. Neither did Dallid hesitate as he forced his weak flesh to stand back up.

A spear of ice did not form in the Frostborn's hands this time, instead two long points of ice grew out of the soldier's closed fists. Dallid laughed and wished he had not thrown away his sabre. Now he had no choice but to use more of his power out toward his enemy. The Frostborn dropped and rolled underneath the fire attack, spinning back up with speed to stab Dallid right through the ribs with his spear-headed fist. Dallid grunted and felt his vision start to fade but not before he reached up and pushed two flaming thumbs into the eyeballs of the bastard Frostborn. He dug them deeper and deeper, and the frozen orbs melted softly and wetly. The Prae'surlas screamed but still managed to hammer in his other fist into Dallid's side and so the two held each other, the Frostborn spearing Dallid's innards and Dallid melting the north-man's face.

Neither looked like they were going to win and neither looked like they were about to die, even if Dallid did feel like as soon as he let go of his fire, all life would vanish with it. More pain stabbed up from inside him and he could feel the spears of ice shifting and moving. Viciously Dallid gripped harder at the man's face and then moved down to his neck. His burning hands sizzled and cut through the skin, blood pouring out and covering them both. Dallid's hands gripped further and further in until the Frostborn brought back his own hands in a panic to stop what Dallid was doing.

It was too late and all at once his fiery hands came together having burnt and melted through the neck, leaving only strings of flesh and bone. Catching the head again Dallid kicked the body and tore it from his enemy's shoulders. He stood there for a moment, surrounded by a circle of roaring fire, holding the head that he squeezed and ripped from another life. The fire from his hands continued to melt the flesh he was touching and Dallid threw the thing away.

What had he become? This was not him. Was the fleshborn he had once been, now destroyed to become Fireborn?

His barrier was still keeping the other Frostborn away but looking down at his bleeding body Dallid did not think he could even run from them, let alone fight them. For a time his power and body seemed in a teetering balance; as long as the flames stood around him, so too did his body stand. He did not think either would last for much longer but something caught his eye then by the edge of the flames and Dallid laughed weakly. Stumbling over and, unable to bend down, he dropped to the ground to close his hand around his Fureath'i sabre. Maybe he could kill one more before they finished him.

'My only regret is...' he said and laughed when he turned the wrist that held the coin of his wife. The leather had been ruined again, but the gold had also melted its way into his skin. Phira's face could no longer be seen and he had not even felt the pain, he had so much other pain to attend to. He would have loved to see her face again, but, worryingly, she was no longer his only regret.

His regret was not to kill more Prae'surlas either, but to kill only one: Aerath. Becoming Fireborn had changed him much for him to feel more hatred towards a Prae'surlas, than he felt love for his wife. *This is not who I am*, he reminded himself, *I am not this Fireborn*.

Seeing how much he had struggled with a single Frostborn, Dallid laughed at how he would fare against the Iceborn who had defeated Chrial'thau. He reminded himself fiercely that Phira was his heart and the only thing that kept his body living. She was his only regret because she was his life, without her there was nothing to live for. Dallid tried to deny how much she meant to him sometimes, to protect himself from the hurt of her absence, but he loved her more than anything else.

The fire from Dallid's body faded, and despite his walls of flame around him still burning, everything became very cold again. It was a terrible place to die, in a land of snow. The only thing that made it look better was the scattering of dead Prae'surlas that would be there, their spears broken and their blood colouring the world. As a Fureath'i he could not regret dying while killing so many, but he could not accept dying yet either.

He was still the man of flesh he had been born, and had to accept that he was also now the Fireborn he had become. Dallid needed to unite the two and amended that he could have two things that he would do before he died.

He would see his wife one last time and he would kill the man who destroyed his village. His need to kill Aerath gave him strength that he should not possess but it was his need to see Phira again that gave Dallid the will to use it. Standing up unsteadily, Dallid waited to see if his wounds would get any better. He had heard that Powerborn healing was quick, but of the multiple wounds he had received, none of them looked any better. The fire roaring around him was probably responsible for that, but if he let the fire go, then he would very quickly be given more wounds from the Frostborns that waited. It was a dilemma but not one to which he gave much thought. His plan was to run now, and hide until his wounds had healed. It might have been a cowardly plan, but it was his. Dallid let his walls of fire disappear.

There was an almost peaceful moment where he and the Prae'surlas stood still, the slightest time between action and reaction. But it was not he or the Prae'surlas who acted first. His small walls of red flame had vanished only to be quickly replaced with towers of black fire enclosing them all. The corpse of Chrial'thau sat up and turned its head towards them. The demon's body slowly drifted up into the air before dark fire erupted to scuttle all over him. The creature looked a far more fearsome opponent than Dallid did so at least the Frostborn were distracted by the scene. Dallid barely stood, his body a mass of holes and leaking fluids, his red fire burning feebly around his skin. The demon was a dark god of death and it held all of the remaining Prae'surlas frozen in terror.

One of them managed to move from the trance and it triggered twenty more towers of black fire. Each man was turned into his own creature of black flames as Chrial'thau killed them all. Dallid was left untouched and could only watch the north-men scream and writhe, some dropping to the ground, others held paralysed on their feet. He could feel Chrial'thau in his head again, and feel the power of the demon grow and grow, the more life and power his fire consumed. Dallid watched as Prae'surlas were killed and took no joy in it, he was sickened by it.

When the fires vanished and the charred skeletons dropped, it was with great relief to Dallid's heart. Even though it meant the demon's attention would now be on him, at least he did not have to witness the terrible deaths any more. There was still a black ring of flames burning on all sides and within it only two figures now stood. The centres of the demon's eyes still shone green in one and spiralled red and blue in the other, but the whites of its eyes had now become black like its flames. They stared at Dallid.

'You are a fool to have followed me here,' the demon hissed. 'Are you so eager for your own destruction?'

'I will kill you, monster,' Dallid returned, weakly, 'and then I will kill Aerath.'

The demon laughed. 'You are almost dead already and you hope to kill me? You are fortunate that I find you so pathetic. Perhaps it is nothing more than the torment I see in your eyes every time you look at this skin I'm wearing, maybe that is why I do not kill you.'

Dallid had no idea why the demon did not kill him. It had certainly come close when it brought the Tower of Frehep down, but the creature had also spared him at the farm. It did not make sense. Was it that they were both equally driven to destroy Aerath? Or was there a deeper Connection and Chrial'thau had indeed Transferred to Dallid before his death. Was some small part of the demon still the Fireborn of legend?

Dallid feebly lifted up his sabre and opened his mouth, but his words were cut short by the appearance of a flash of blue and white fire. It was a similar flash to the one he had seen in the central tower of the city, only this time he could see the Iceborn Aerath suddenly standing before him. The white and blue flames flickered out and before anyone else could move, Aerath crouched down and hunched his shoulders together. A bubble of ice formed around his body and when the ice giant stood back up, he thrust out both arms. The sphere expanded and shot out with speed, knocking the demon to the ground and hitting Dallid with equal force. It continued past and hit the walls of black fire, the sphere having grown to a height to match it, and once the two magics touched, both vanished with a deafening crack.

Dallid's body felt frozen, his skin glazed white with frost, but he was still able to move, even if every move caused him incredible pain. He pushed himself up to a crouch and only saw Aerath flick his eyebrow in question once before turning his back on Dallid to face the demon. If the Iceborn was confused why there was a Fireborn in his lands, or if he felt threatened in any way by him, then Aerath had a strange way of showing it. Prae'surlas saw everyone as beneath them but to disregard a Fireborn, it was a whole new level of conceit.

It crippled him to do it, but Dallid lashed out with his power and sent a fierce spray of red fire down on the back of Aerath. White arcs of ice magic appeared and disappeared until the fire dissipated and Dallid laughed at how ineffectual he had been. The Iceborn did not even turn at the failed attack and was speaking with Chrial'thau.

'You should not be here,' he spoke with a rich voice, full of authority. 'Return to Furea and burn your fellow rats.' The command had been so powerful that Dallid almost struggled to his feet to obey. For once the hesitation of his mind saved him from doing so. Was the Iceborn so strong that even his words held magic in them?

Chrial'thau at least, did not appear affected. 'But I have had a taste for ice now,' it laughed, 'and I like it! I think I will feed on Surlas instead.'

Aerath sighed. 'If you do not serve me then you do not belong in my new world. Return to Furea and kill your own kind,' he said with more force, Dallid's ears began to bleed at the power behind them. 'Get rid of them all. There is no place for vermin of fire in a world of snow.'

'My own kind?' The demon said softly, as if Aerath's words had finally worked. 'There are none like me! You made sure of that when you fused the demon's magic into Chrial'thau's, and thoughtlessly mixed it with your own! Will I take the rest now? The old Chrial'thau spared you here the last time you fought did he not? Is it not a fitting place for me to devour you?'

The devil's hand flew out but instead of a torrent of fire, only a single stream appeared. The same white arc flashed up to stop the dark magic, as it had stopped Dallid's, but the thin stream of black fire did not vanish. Instead it twisted and burrowed into it, making Aerath grimace with effort. The Iceborn lifted his hand and Dallid saw Chrial'thau's neck turn to ice. Both beings struggled to defend themselves while trying to kill the other at the same time, and Dallid knew he would never have a better time to attack either one. Aerath, it had to be Aerath. As much as the demon needed to be purged from the world of light, every ounce of flesh in Dallid's body burned with the need to kill Aerath. He stood up from where he knelt and stepped forward with his sabre in hand.

A scream came out from Chrial'thau as the demon brought its free hand up to its frozen neck. It looked about to shatter. Aerath was going to win, and Dallid needed to get to him now. But then the burrowing stream of black fire turned around to bore into Chrial'thau's own neck instead. This made Aerath roar instead of Chrial'thau and the demon even started laughing hysterically at what was occurring. And, before Dallid had taken two steps, the Iceborn was gone. The demon's laugh had not stopped and it looked around in expectation. When the creature found Dallid it smiled in delight and squealed:

'I have tasted his power and he flees in terror! I have seen his secret and he knows that I will now make it mine!' The devil's fire blazed out while he screamed his ecstasy and the beast started to float up into the air. Chrial'thau began to sing, 'The more I taste, the more I crave, the larger my teeth, the bigger my meals, the devil will bite down deep to the god, and all of that power will be mine to wield!' Great wings of black fire roared out from either side as the demon drifted higher and higher into the sky. Then the air in front of Dallid became a spectre of black flame and the scene vanished before his eyes.

When he reappeared Dallid was back upon the hill where he had first witnessed Chrial'thau's sacking of the city below, and next to him stood a spectre of ice instead of black flames. The demon was still below and now he was attacking the city with greater force. With large bat-like wings of demonic fire, Chrial'thau sent hundreds of missiles raining down upon the city of Dowrathel. The pain in Dallid's head became greater than all the other pains in his body. The four towers did not glow with blue or white light anymore, they all burned with black fire, and the terrible flames spread out with too much speed. The demon still continued to thunder more and more down on the city below it, and everything the flames hit ignited like a spreading disease.

A few small images of ice magic meagrely drifted up towards the flaming devil, but Dallid knew that the city was doomed. Aerath, who claimed to have killed the Prae'surlas god Aerune, had tried to stop the demon and had fled in fear. What chance would lesser Powerborn stand? The demon had sang it itself, the more the fire burned the stronger it became, and the more the fire could burn again. It was a horrific circle that Dallid could see no way of stopping. He turned to the spectre of ice accusingly.

'There are creatures like this in the world and you would have me try to kill Brijnok?'

The spectre did not look at Dallid, but it seemed fascinated by the destruction of the city. 'Destroy this creature if you wish.'

'How?' Dallid shouted in frustration. He had barely enough strength to be angry, but the spectre had brought it out in him. 'Why do you think I am capable of such things? You are asking a fleshborn to fight against gods!'

The spectre turned to him, the faceless crackling of ice forming and reforming constantly. 'Brijnok created the gods, destroy him and they will follow.'

All energy left Dallid then. He had taken too many wounds and the tasks ahead of him were too great. He just watched while Chrial'thau burnt alive a city full of screaming Prae'surlas and felt the power of the wretched creature grow in his head. Dallid had never felt weaker, and only a few days ago he was a simple fleshborn.

He had for no reason been given the power of the gods, elevated to the highest form of creation that walked on the earth and become Fireborn. He did not know how to use the power, he did not know how he had been given the power, all he knew was that he felt powerless. A Fireborn could face an army of a thousand men and the army would turn and run. Dallid had been nearly killed several times already in the last hour. The spectre of ice, a being with seemingly more power than him, thought Dallid was powerful enough to do something that the being could not.

His voice was weak with exhaustion as he spoke to the spectre.

'I will not do as you bid, I cannot, and please do not ask me again,' he turned his back on the spectre of ice and on the destruction of Dowrathel.

'If you do not then all life in this world will pay for your inaction. Everyone will die.'

'There are too many stronger things in this world for it to be my responsibility. Let them save it. I am not enough.'

The spectre of ice did not reply to that and neither did Dallid turn around to look at it. Fireborns were heralded as the most powerful things that could walk the world of light. Dallid walked stumbling, and headed north for Lae Noan. He tried to smile when he saw he no longer created a path of melt water under his feet. Instead he left a path of his own blood and yet he could not stop and rest until Aerath was killed. It was the Fireborn in his mind that forced him to keep going, and Dallid cursed the day he was blessed with all the power that could be given to a man within the world of light.

CHAPTER THIRTY SEVEN

Will

The world returned to darkness and Kris swung his sabre the moment the demon lord uttered its words. If the devil was looking for some emotion to feed from then Kris would give it rage. All he needed to do was unleash the darkness that lived inside his own heart and he would see how much the demon lord could stomach. His sabre sliced through emptiness though and Kris immediately returned to calm in order to locate the devil.

Crouched and ready, he was able to contain his own breathing down to inaudible but he knew that Nureail and Tereail would not be able to do the same. The fact that he did not hear their panicked breaths anymore told him they had been taken somewhere. Kris fought back his frustration and wrapped tighter the chains that contained it. He needed unerring focus if he was to best a demon of shadow that could control surroundings.

An image appeared to Kris's left. It was a doorway of light and beyond it sat Nureail and Tereail, huddled together in fear. Kris ignored it and strained his senses to determine where the coward demon lord was positioned. Somehow the light conjured from the door did not enter the place of shadow where he stood. It did not matter. There were no other sounds that Kris could mark and dismiss from his perception, so all he waited for was the slightest sense, and he would pounce.

The doorway was brought closer to Kris then and it became more difficult to ignore. Still the light ended at the image, either unable or unwilling to enter the black of the shadow path. Allowing his eyes to dart over to the door, he could see that the two Scholars were back in the Jhakral temple again. But instead of examining useless relics their eyes were focused on something out of Kris's sight. The demon lord was trying to distract him and his attempt would fail.

A second door then opened up to Kris's right and this one contained Thisian of all people. If Kris ever allowed himself to laugh he would have done so at the flawed attempt the demon had made to divert him. Kris already possessed the fire of ice needed to stop Aerath's ritual, so his need to keep the Scholars alive had lessened significantly, but his need to aid Thisian in any way was non-existent.

His other childhood friends, Dallid and Phira stepped into view then, their weapons drawn and their eyes focused on another unseen enemy. Trying to keep his reactions sharp, Kris scoffed at how unrealistic the distraction was. It was possible Fin'derrin could have taken Nureail and Tereail somewhere and placed them in danger, but Kris had just left Thisian. The likelihood of him running into both Dallid and Phira was too co-incidental to bear any considering. Perhaps the demon lord could read his thoughts, because the other Foreigners who had been with Thisian stepped into view to bring back a small hint of possibility. Everyone had their weapons out and they all faced the same unseen foe.

Kris did not bother trying to see it and went back to waiting. Often when it came to battles of will, strength of commitment was just one part, endurance and patience were equally as important. If Fin'derrin was displeased with Kris's lack of reactions so far then he would have to continue in his displeasure. To Kris the demon was showing desperation by bringing up more doorways to distract him. It simply meant that Kris was stronger and that he would win. A third doorway appeared. This one was right in front of Kris. The demon lord might have been growing in desperation, but he was at least growing to know Kris a little better. The newest doorway showed his squads.

If each vision was calculated to lure Kris through it or elicit some emotional reaction, then the doorway with his squad was the most likely to succeed. The main reason that Kris conceded this was because his squads were engaged in a battle, fighting a host of Prae'surlas and they were badly outnumbered. His eye straight away spotted an absence of each of the squad leaders he had assigned, and Kris clenched his teeth at the lack of organisation with which his men fought. Kris's sabre would not have helped his men much, but a voice of leadership to regroup and command them could mean the difference between death and victory.

Kris clenched his fist. Even if it was possible to join the battle and rescue his men from defeat, his mission was to reach the ice temple. All that stood between him and that temple now was a demon of shadow wishing to play games, trying to drag up something from Kris that he could feed on. He would give it nothing. If his men were to die then they would die killing Prae'surlas so he watched calmly as more and more got cut down. Soon Kris was able to identify the bodies of some squad leaders; the Sword That Walks was notably among them.

A movement to his left and Kris spun his sabre with savage strength. It sailed through nothing and Kris saw the source of the movement. Nureail and Tereail had started running and the door in the darkness followed the scene conveniently. The two Scholars were being chased by Jhakral, and without him there to fight the beasts, it would not be long before they were run down and killed.

More movement to his right, but Kris did not catch himself reacting as foolishly as he first did. The doorway containing his friends had increased its own dramatic pull as expected, and Kris was only mildly intrigued to find that it was not Jherin who they were battling. It was another kind of demon by the look of it, long black hair and dead grey skin. The thing's eyes burned bright green and it fought with a sword made of bone.

The two Foreigners, Krife and Griffil were cut down by it soon after the fight had begun and as Phira and Dallid fought sword to sword with the demon using remarkable skill, Kris raised an eyebrow at Dallid's increase in speed and strength. He had not been so skilled the last time they had met. Then Kris saw that Dallid was wearing the tunic of a Fireborn. It was only noticed so late perhaps because he was busy ignoring the Flameborn tunic that Thisian wore. Fin'derrin's visions were becoming increasingly flawed and inaccurate if the demon thought Dallid was a Fireborn. The green-eyed demon in the doorway cut through Thisian's neck with surprising ease. It moved as just another strike within the battle and the fighting did not pause to consider the fact that Thisian was now dead. Kris did not react. Even if the scene was real, then Kris would not have reacted.

Thisian had been the first to find him back when Kris lived with his grandfather. After his grandfather was killed, Kris did not think he had spoken out loud for many years. He had simply worked and trained each day in silence, never needing to speak. So when Thisian found him, the bombardment of words was disorienting. Thisian had been kind then, eager to help Kris become just like him. After spending some time together of course, Thisian gave up and instead changed to constantly ridiculing Kris's odd ways. That changed to fearing him soon enough.

After Thisian had seen Kris kill those women, he had been different for a time. Kris had almost killed Thisian then too. He walked into Thisian's cabin while he slept and rested the blade of his sabre along his neck as he had done to the three women. All it took was to draw back the blade and let the life pour out. But there was something about the way Thisian had looked at him when he saw him killing the women. There had been no horror, no judgement, Thisian did not care that Kris had killed three women. There had just been ready acceptance and immediate plotting of how to hide what had been done.

It was still unclear to Kris why Thisian acted so strongly in concealing the three killings, but he did it. If he had not, then Kris would have been killed himself by the elders for being an abomination.

Someone who killed his own kind.

It had seemed the right thing to do at the time. He knew that living with the memory of a terrible act was hard. He wanted to help those women by setting them free of the burden. When Kris was younger he had often wished someone would set him free the same way, but in weakness he had let Thisian talk him into not confessing. For someone who spoke so much, Thisian had never spoken to him about the incident afterwards. It was a bad time in Kris's life, he was much weaker then.

Looking back to the direction he had first faced - in Kris's judgement, still the direction of the ice temple - he went back to watching the images of his squads getting speared and killed by Prae'surlas. They fought respectably, and had anyone asked him then Kris would have agreed that he was proud, but the numbers were too great and the leadership was not there. They were all going to die and Kris accepted that fact. In the end there were seven of his men left fighting back to back. A ring of north-men held them pinned in with spears lowered. Kris waited for the moment when his men would make their final charge, hopefully taking out double the number of ice-men with them, but the charge did not come.

Instead his men dropped their sabres and began to slowly kneel down in surrender. The demon lord Fin'derrin was indeed trying harder because Kris was close to feelings of outrage upon seeing that sight. He somehow managed to withhold that emotion from the devil. If the thing fed on life energy and feelings, then let it starve while waiting to find it in Kris.

The doorway to his left came to a conclusion also but impressively with Nureail fighting back against the giant beasts. She must have discovered some way to make her wooden sword work, because she was swinging it with great effect. Every time she struck thin air, an arc of energy lashed out strongly, damaging the Jhakral that surrounded them. She moved well for someone not in the army, and attempted with some success to cover all directions from where the stone-skinned creatures were coming.

The task was too difficult of course, and Kris was only slightly disturbed to see one the Jhakral swords hack straight down and remove Nureail's sword arm. She would die from that wound if it was not closed immediately but she would die anyway without any other means of defence or escape. Kris did not want Nureail to die and he justified that she was still needed for them to complete their mission. He had the artefact to stop Aerath's ritual but he did not know how to use it. He needed Nureail.

He was gambling that was what happening was not real, risking the life of Nureail simply to not give Fin'derrin the satisfaction of his reaction. If she was really about to die then he needed to intervene. He could pick her up and run to safety where he would close her wound. Then they would find a way to continue their mission. But it was what Fin'derrin wished him to do. So Kris did not move.

Expectantly the doorway to his right concluded also, the green-eyed devil fighting extremely skilfully against Phira and a Fireborn Dallid. There may have been some flaws in Fin'derrin's images but Phira's skill was not one of them. The fact that a single opponent was doing so well was perhaps the largest flaw in Fin'derrin's concoctions. Dallid was the first to die, his head being cut off with similar ease to Thisian's. Whatever kind of sword the demon was using must have been formidable. It did not look especially sharp, the bone even making it look primitive and clumsy, but it sliced through Powerborn skin with ease. Phira disarmed the same sword almost immediately after the deed had been done. The green-eyed demon stood shocked, unarmed and waiting for the killing blow. It did not come.

Phira stood equally shocked, looking down at the dead body of Dallid. Kris was irritated at his own surprise when she threw away her sword instead of killing the beast. She just knelt down by Dallid's severed head and body, not knowing which to hold, not believing that he was dead. The green-eyed demon did not pick up his fallen sword, but instead grew another one from the palm of his hand. Blood sizzled from the wound and as soon as the sword was fully formed, the demon had no hesitation in killing Phira.

It was another mistake on Fin'derrin's behalf. Phira may not have as little emotion as Kris did, but she was much stronger than the vision portrayed. She would have perhaps felt as much devastation as she expressed in it, but never have dropped her guard like that. She would have killed everything in sight and only then allowed herself time to grieve as any real person would. She was stronger than most people Kris knew, and was invaluable to him when they were younger, Dallid even more so. Kris was so busy frowning at how Phira had reacted - unwilling to accept that love could weaken someone so dramatically - that he did not let himself react to Dallid's death. Even though Dallid was probably the only person in the world that Kris would admit to calling friend.

Kris's relationship with Thisian had always been a complicated mix of mutual confusion and irritation, and his respect for Phira often made Kris uncomfortable around her, seeing someone so much better than he was, but with Dallid it had been so different.

Dallid did not notice the differences that Thisian would mock or that Phira would try to improve, Dallid always accepted Kris as he was. He would not try to force conversation or lecture Kris on how other normal people would act. Dallid enjoyed Kris's company exactly as it was, he never tried to change anything. If Dallid was truly dead then he would miss him greatly.

But none of it was real. The likelihood that so many dramatic events would happen together at the same time, with all of them connected in a way to Kris, was too improbable. Fin'derrin had somehow drawn something from Kris to give reality to Phira and Dallid and his squads. It did not make sense as the demon lord had earlier expressed his inability to draw anything, but Kris would not concern himself with doubts. Whether any of the scenes were truth or not: did not matter. Kris would wait until his opportunity to kill Fin'derrin, or he would wait for the demon lord to give up his attempts and allow Kris to return to his goal.

His eyes on the door in front, Kris watched impassively as a particularly large Iceborn stepped up to his kneeling squad members. The Iceborn placed a hand on the head of the first Fureath'i warrior and did nothing that Kris could see. When he removed it, the squad warrior stood up, not even coming to the chest of the giant Prae'surlas, and strangely he was handed a spear.

Thinking it might be invitation for a duel of some kind, or trial by combat, Kris thought it even stranger when the Iceborn turned his back on the armed Fureath'i. Kris's warrior did nothing though, and stood attentively like he was a soldier who had held a spear all his life. The Iceborn placed his hand similarly on each of the kneeling warriors and every one of them stood up to accept a spear and stand as if they had become Prae'surlas. If disgust was an emotion, then Fin'derrin might have fed, but Kris did not think so. If anything to him, disgust was just an opinion. It was the correct opinion but still just an opinion. Kris could not admit if he did not wish to watch the scene or if he was concerned for Nureail, but he turned away and looked to the other door.

Nureail still lived but not for much longer. She had one hand pressed over the gushing stump of the other. Kris gave her little more than minutes left to live. Even if he did rush over he would not save her, he might only give her some heart by seeing him try to rescue her. These were images designed to distress, not realities to remedy. Any reaction would only serve to feed Fin'derrin. Needlessly, the Jhakral left Nureail watch as they took turns beating Tereail to death. Kris's eyes did not watch. His vision was fixed on the detail of despair the scene placed on Nureail's face. For a figment of magic, it was quite thorough. He could see first the heart fade from her face, the hope fade from her body and finally the life fade from her eyes. It was an unpleasant experience, but one that he kept to himself. The doorway closed.

The one to his right had closed earlier and all that remained was his surviving squad members who had been made into Prae'surlas. There had been some action take place already but he ignored it while he was focused on Nureail. As a result three of his warriors lay dead, and he saw with revulsion that the other four of his men were fighting each other with spears, while the audience of Prae'surlas cheered their entertainment. It was not a thing Kris had ever thought he would see, Fureath'i killing Fureath'i with northern spears, but now it was something he made himself watch. He would accept whatever Fin'derrin gave him and wait for the thing to grow weary of waiting. Kris wondered if such a magic did exist, where an Iceborn could turn the mind of a warrior to fight his own brother. Perhaps only on the weak minded, but he did not think he had any in his squads that were weak.

Kris did not frighten easily but the idea of such magic existing frightened him greatly. That his will could be taken over by another was perhaps the worst thing he could imagine happening and it was only then, when he worded it like that, he realised that it already happened to him. Every time he lost control there was a demon inside of him who did not care who he killed or how he did it. The devil whispered to him every day to do terrible things to men, women, and children, without discrimination. It was not always just to kill them, the darkness inside wanted to do worse. Kris had only his own strength to stop his greatest fears coming to life. He had created another person to show the world, and that person was simply the strength of will that stopped him from becoming the person he had been born. His will was all he had, it was all he was.

Kris continued to watch as his four remaining warriors became three, until one of them killed the remaining two. In victory he turned to the Iceborn like a serving dog and knelt for praise. The Iceborn even patted his head like a beast, and the joy on the Fureath'i face was almost as hard to watch as the sight of them killing each other. His reward was to be abandoned to his deeds as the host moved away, leaving a confused hound who did not know why his masters did not take him with them. Kris assumed the magic would wear off and the impact of his actions would be horrendous.

Cursing Fin'derrin, Kris began to remember the last time he had killed his own brothers. He did not want the demon lord to feed from his feelings on the event, but he had always thought it the greater weakness to shy away from responsibility of those acts. So Kris let himself remember that day rather than cower from it.

There had been no magic to take away his will when it had happened, Kris had known what he was doing and he had not cared. His will was strong enough that he could have stopped the sabre flying down upon his first warrior but he did not want to. The man was weak and undeserving of a place in Kris's squads. If Kris had not killed him, then he might have gotten a better man killed by his incompetence. The second warrior Kris had killed then was not weak.

He had been an exemplar warrior and an honour to command. Kris killed him because of the way he had looked at him. Rhysak was right next to him when he killed Polrin, watching as Kris's sabre cut open the blood of his Fureath'i brother. Then he turned those eyes on Kris and Kris could not stand it. So he killed Rhysak, as he had killed Polrin, and if anyone else had been near him at that time he would have killed them too.

Others from his squad had seen the deed, but they were far enough away to be relatively safe. They had rightfully avoided Kris until he was back in control, but what they should have done was kill Kris for his actions. He would have killed himself if he did not consider it the weakest option. It was much harder to continue living.

The doorway closed and Kris closed his eyes in thanks. When he opened them again all was still darkness. There were no sounds beyond that of his own breathing and no presence beyond the ghosts of what he had just seen.

'Why do you not just kill me? Would that not release my life for your pleasure?' His question was met with silence. If the demon lord would try to elicit an emotional response from Kris, then now it was Kris's turn to get one from the demon. If he could provoke

Fin'derrin into becoming angry then he would make a mistake. He would reveal himself in some way, even if it was to try killing Kris.

'Would you like me to kill you?' Fin'derrin finally whispered in his ear, the sound starting on one side and spinning around to the other.

'I would like you to try,' he said back.

'No,' Fin'derrin replied. 'You crave your own death. I believe you cannot stand your own company just as much as you cannot stand the company of others. You long to find someone who can take it all away, but you kill everyone who tries. You remind me of him, of Jherin.'

'Our only similarity is that you fear us both. Why else do you hesitate?'

'Perhaps I hesitate because I do not wish to give you what you desire, much the same as you do towards me.'

'Then let us stand here in silence until we both die.'

He thought he heard the demon laugh, but the sound faded quickly. Kris continued to stand ready. He almost laughed himself as another doorway opened up in front of him. Was Fin'derrin going to repeat the same failed attempts? The doorway grew closer and Kris frowned to see a temple made of ice in its picture. The chambers were of a style to match that of the previous temples, only with these rooms smaller and all in ice. In this room spirals of frost replaced the pillars of stone and everything was layered with a thick shine instead of dust. It was very probable this was the real Temple of Ice that he sought to get to. Kris did not move.

After a time, Nureail and Tereail appeared in the scene. They arrived startled and looked around anxiously either for enemies or for Kris. They found neither but remained where they were, deciding the best course of action was to wait for Kris to join them. All in all it was clever bait for Fin'derrin to place. How was Kris to know when he had been freed from the demon's games and really in the Temple of Ice? The two Scholars had not been overrun by Jhakral yet in any case, nor had they been turned into Prae'surlas or killed by a green-eyed demon. It reasoned well for it to be the real destination since it was not already filled with melodrama. Kris waited.

Tereail gestured and might have been suggesting courses of action to Nureail. She ignored them all with a scowl. Tereail paced about the chamber for a time and Nureail decided to use her time by examining their pack of remaining artefacts. Remembering that Kris was not there to stop him, Tereail too suddenly realised he could begin squandering his time with self-indulgence. He settled himself down to a cross legged sit, and began investigating their findings. While he stared at the candle they had found, Nureail took out the wooden sword just as she had done in Fin'derrin's last vision. For a time she stood and stared at the thing, but then smiled and said something to Tereail. There was no sound in these visions, but Kris could tell Tereail was not listening and waved her away from his intense examination of the candle shaped piece of ice.

'Why do you remain? I have given you your freedom.'

Kris did not reply.

'You are leaving your companions in danger,' Fin'derrin continued. 'I have masked their presence from the Prae'surlas left to guard Aerath's temple, but I will only do so for a time.'

Kris said nothing and enjoyed the silence it created.

'You believe it a trick? That I wish to spend my time further fooling your limited perception? I have concluded my amusement. I have taken what I wanted from you and it is time for you to leave.'

Kris did not believe the demon lord had been able to take anything from him. 'Why do you not make me leave? You have told me that you do not require my permission. So do it.'

It was Fin'derrin's turn to remain silent. This pleased Kris and he waited for the demon lord in what he knew to be his last moments in the shadow paths. When the words came he could hear the demon's irritation.

'Do you wish me to take you to your destination, warrior?'

'Take me there,' Kris commanded.

His surroundings changed. A dome of light formed first as before and the shadows retreated further and further back. A new wave of vision followed after the light and it created pillars and walls of ice. The temperature dropped fiercely, and every muscle that lined Kris's body was tensed to stop him from shivering. The two Scholars were as they had been pictured with the one difference that they were now huddling for warmth. Nureail was trying to bury herself in her cloak and Tereail was even trying to join her under it. They both looked up with relief at seeing him.

'Kris!' Nureail ran over and could not stop herself from embracing him. He frowned at her outburst, gently removed her arms and began surveying the chamber.

'Fin'derrin can fool our perceptions,' he warned her. Mist underlined the words from his mouth and Nureail looked at him and then back around to their location.

'I do not think he is here, Kris. I think he is still in the shadow paths. He said he remains there to keep watch on Jherin.'

The demon lord had said it could create such an illusion for them that they would never be able to distinguish it from reality again. The visions it had shown had been intricate in their detail but the one Kris was engulfed in now felt real. What could he do if they were trapped? If that had been the demon's pretence from the start then why would it bother to explain the possibility? Kris did not want to exhaust his mind with futile suspicions. What more could he do than act within the appearance of whatever world he perceived.

Kris listened to the shivering breath of Nureail and the rattling teeth of her brother, who was shifting his feet from side to side to keep blood moving in his body. He felt the cold of the ice-lined chamber crackle against his skin and try to pollute its way into his own blood. The walls and the floors were so smoothly glazed that they reflected his vision to rebound off each other without end. If there was not a clear archway at the end of the room, it would have been difficult to distinguish any definition to the ice chamber where they stood. There seemed a soundless echo that pressed on his ears from the Temple of Ice, but there were no actual sounds that he could identify. If it was an illusion, then it was a perfect one.

'Let us complete what we have come here to do,' he said levelly. 'Tereail, lead us to where your vision saw our victory.'

Tereail raised his head to look around, and nodded weakly toward the archway of ice. Kris took a step in the direction, and a sudden trembling began immediately after. The ground shook slightly, but it was with the sound of boots approaching. Kris guessed it was another Jhakral by the weight the boots seemed to be sounding, but instead ten other giants ran into view. Each one had yellow hair, blue eyes, and spears as long as two Fureath'i; Prae'surlas were not difficult to recognise.

While Tereail looked around in a panic to see where he could run, and while Nureail held onto a wooden sword with absurdity and fear, Kris had his real sword already out. Thick and curved in the Fureath'i fashion, the steel sabre was designed purely to kill Prae'surlas.

There were ten of them, the match for maybe five Fureath'i. Kris reasoned that he would just have to be five times the man that other Fureath'i could be. A seldom smile was allowed cross his face. This was no illusion. This was ten real Prae'surlas for him to kill or for him to die trying. There was nothing more in the world that he would want to do and there was nothing more in the world that he was better at. Gently unloading his pack and handing a delicate looking fire of ice toward Nureail, he smiled at her too. She was startled by it.

Letting that be her last memory of him only made his smile broaden before it opened wide into a roar and he ran for the ten giants. It was time to let go now. If Fin'derrin still watched then he would see what manner of creature he was dealing with. Let the demon watch from its shadows. It was time for Kris to release his own darkness.

• CHAPTER THIRTY EIGHT •

Destinations

The first Prae'surlas that Kris reached jabbed out strongly to finish the contest in one blow. Kris ducked and rolled forward, slashing both shins before stabbing up to the groin. Rolling free and to a stand, Kris kicked the injured giant into two of his comrades.

Two more spears swept for his head, and while he avoided one, the other grazed his cheek. Kris caught that spear in anger and pulled the giant who held it off balance. The blue eyed northerner stumbled so low that Kris was able to catch hold of his head and smash his own into it. Twice more he crushed his forehead into the nose and eyes of the Prae'surlas, before grudgingly pulling away to meet the next attack.

His sabre rang against stabbing spear heads, his body needing to turn or lift every second heartbeat to avoid their swings. It was an exercise that could only last so long and had only one outcome. So turning suddenly and running back to the warrior with the smashed face, Kris stabbed him in the side. It was not a mortal wound since Kris wanted him alive enough to get in his comrades way. He shoved the wounded giant forward and then swiftly deflected a spear thrust from his right. The spear was knocked down low and ended up getting caught in the feet of the man Kris had just pushed. That grounded the giant with an awkward roll, knocking over even more of the long-limbed northern warriors.

Down to a level of his liking Kris launched himself to that heap of flesh and stabbed aimlessly with savage repetition. Gore drenched his every stab and it was purest chance that enough blood splashed into the eyes of a Prae'surlas that tried to stick him from behind. The partial blindness, accompanied by Kris's reactions, resulted only in a deep cut along his ribs rather than right through his back. It further ripped up the inside of Kris's left arm as the northerner dragged his thrust back after.

That injury would slow down Kris severely but for now it only decided who was the next to die. The Prae'surlas responsible had moved back far enough, and used his spear's length skilfully, so Kris found it difficult to get past in his rage. His mind was telling him he was exposing his back to numerous other spears that at any moment would kill him, but Kris could only care about killing this one.

He threw his sabre at the man, who managed to skilfully spin his spear around and block the blade. But the manoeuvre had removed the spearhead from Kris's way and with nothing but his bare hands he attacked the giant. Using one hand on the lifted spear as leverage, Kris launched himself up thundering his other hand into the giant's neck. When he landed he kicked out the man's left knee, and dived on top of the Prae'surlas as he fell. Once mounted on top of him, Kris punched again and again into the giant's throat, roaring his hatred as he smashed all life from him. His fists were wet by the time a movement behind caused Kris to turn.

The spear thrust was already completed, and Kris threw himself to the side but knew that it would hit him somewhere. Instead of the pain and fresh anger that should have arrived though, the Prae'surlas suddenly went sailing forward through the air, his back arched in injury. Kris and the remaining Prae'surlas all turned to see what had caused the unexpected force, and to his view stood Nureail holding a long wooden sword in shaking hands.

With a look of determination on her face, she swung the wooden sword down again. An arc of energy pulsed out from the weapon, tracing the line of attack with a force of what looked like shifting air. The Prae'surlas were able to dodge to the side of that one, but Nureail had already changed her grip, swinging it horizontally instead. The resulting wave of force was not something the tall warriors could avoid as easily. One that attempted to jump the wave was caught in the shin and foot, sending him crashing to the ice floor. The other Prae'surlas that did nothing other than roar and block the force with his spear, was blown off of his feet, the spear cut in half.

Three others that had been out of the targeted area all ran as one towards the greater threat Nureail now presented. Kris had never gotten to his feet quicker, nor sprinted with such intensity. He did not have time to retrieve his sabre, as all that filled his focus were the three northern giants bearing down upon a terrified Nureail. His shorter legs, pushed with far greater strength and frantic speed, and managed to catch up to the Prae'surlas. Without plan Kris dove forward and wrapped his arms around a leg each of two warriors.

He received a heel into the chin for his trouble, but the attack tripped up both of them, with fortune even favouring one of the falling men to grab a hold of the third warrior in an effort to stay standing. All three tumbled to the ground and Kris did not care that it was simple luck the manoeuvre had worked. Spying a belt knife attached to the central warrior, Kris grabbed it, ripped it free, and ran it swiftly along the neck of the man to his left. In the same fluid movement Kris twisted the knife in mid momentum and pounded it down into the turning face of the knife's owner. The blade punctured the skull but cracked in the process.

The Prae'surlas to the far right was already up to his knees by then, reaching for his fallen spear, so Kris discarded the broken blade and rushed him. The longer arm of the northern giant smashed a fist into Kris's head in mid-charge, knocking his neck back painfully, and a second fist hooked into the side of Kris's skull, breaking the skin around his temple. Kris grabbed the arm the third time it struck for him and sank his teeth deep into the ice-man's flesh. The Prae'surlas grabbed Kris by the hair and tried to pry him loose, but Kris only let himself come free with a mouth full of meat. He then dug his fingers into the fresh hole, causing the northern giant to roar out in agony and leave go.

Once released, Kris pounced, landing his own punches into the giant's face. The force of his leap sent the man to the floor again, and the speed and ferocity of Kris's punches left him no room for defence. When the first of the skull bones cracked, it became softer on his fists as he punched and punched, but Kris did not stop. Bone and brain broke away in pieces from his onslaught and Kris's eyes were glazed over in rage, his mind roaring in unison with his voice, thought and awareness became things unneeded to the bloody task at hand.

The head of the Prae'surlas was all but gone when Nureail placed a calming hand on Kris's shoulder. Kris swung a savage back fist that cracked across her face and sent her sprawling to the floor. He roared as he attacked, and launched after her, hating her, punching her again and again in the face with vicious blows. She was screaming in tears and he thought he heard his name being called. He knew it was Nureail he was about to kill and still he wanted to do it. His entire body shook with the control it took for him to stop.

Nureail lay under him, cowering and bleeding, and all he could do was kneel where he was and not kill her. When more control returned to Kris, he managed to lift his legs away but remained on his knees, panting heavily.

Then the pain of it buried Kris to nothing, and it was not his wounds that he felt.

Shame and rage held him to his place, unmoving, uncompromising. He should not have hit her but she should not have been near him while he was lost in such a state. He needed to stand up. He needed to retrieve his sabre and kill the rest of the Prae'surlas that were only injured. He needed to take Tereail and Nureail to where they needed to be, so they could do what they needed to do. Whatever happened after those tasks were not his concern.

Kris stood up.

Nureail's eyes looked at him without accusation, but it was from behind hands that sheltered her face. Her brother was by her side, and his eyes would look anywhere but at Kris. The Teller pushed Tereail away from her and let her hands drop, showing how quickly the bruises and swelling had come. The blows had been powerful and there was good chance more than one bone in her face was cracked. Nureail held her chin high however, blood streaming down it, and spoke with confidence.

'I am fine,' she said to her brother who did not know what to do. Kris felt the statement aimed at him but he did not allow himself to believe it. Nureail had to swallow blood before speaking again. 'Let us go quickly before more come.'

She picked up her wooden sword and repositioned it before she was able to stand up again. Kris let his gaze linger on her, to see her strange mixture of strength and weakness that he found so humbling. But all he could see was what he had done to her. Kris turned his head swiftly and strode over to his sabre.

He stabbed into all of the other Prae'surlas one more time, drawing screams from some, and silence from others. The ones that had been hit by Nureail's sword were already dead. Whatever forced it emitted was more deadly than it looked. Kris's sabre made their death a certainty just in case. The two Scholars waited and watched as Kris methodically went from body to body. When he finished he stayed standing motionless, letting them see how drenched in blood he had become. Kris would not wipe himself clean, or shy away from their stares. This was who he was.

Anything else he might pretend to be; was just a man waiting for someone to kill.

***

Phira stood over the dead man and wondered if she looked the same as every other warrior in her squad. Although it had been two days since the first attack from the assassin Valhar, both nights he had been able to sneak in and kill her men right in front of her. She saw his face behind every mask in her squad each day, but still the bastard always waited until night to act. At least she now knew what had happened to the men who did not return after the previous day's excursion with the Ihnhaarat and Prae'surlas. She had Valhar to thank for that, he had given her back their ears.

It was a madman's mockery to deface her every solider with the removal of their ears. She would not have been surprised if he had tried to attach all the ears to his own head in the hope that it fit. The most recent ones that he had cut off at least had not been left as gifts right beside her. The lunatic must know that Phira had not slept since the first attack. She would never sleep again if it meant she could kill the man. *I am becoming Kris*, she thought absently to herself.

The constant paranoia was not something Kris would be bothered with though, and it was more tiring than anything else. The fatigue on her mind and spirit was worse than the lack of sleep or even the energy spent during battle the day before. Neither the

Ihnhaarat nor Prae'surlas had been seen to follow yet at least. But she and her squads were travelling hard, to try in vain to keep ahead of Valhar as well as escape the snow. Absolute exhaustion would not set in for another while, but desperation was creeping closer.

She had ordered every man to lie awake last night, setting up the inviting pretence of a sleeping camp. Her warriors had been in pairs so if one fell, the other would raise alarm. Two had gone out to the latrine trench when Valhar set upon them. Having already gotten past her scouts and sentries, the assassin had murdered both her warriors without a sound. Their necks were sliced across and presumably at the same time since there had been no cry of alarm.

Phira had no choice but to continue onward. She had no choice but to ignore the murderous looks of her own men, and the burning need for vengeance in her own heart. She had to ignore everything else in her own heart, so how could this be any more of a burden. All it meant was they had two more dead to burn now, after already leaving a bonfire of corpses at the Surlas border the previous day.

That had been their only diversion from solid travel but there would be no more sleeping now, no more stopping; they could no longer afford to give Valhar any opportunities to pick off her warriors one by one. They would not stop until they reached Amidon City and there could be no more scouts along the way, it was too risky. They would all need to travel as a pack, and even as few as their numbers were, Valhar would not survive an open assault.

Being the madman that he was, she almost hoped he would stride right in front of their party and demand their surrender. She would give almost anything for the chance of another duel with the bastard. His unnatural speed would not throw her again. But it appeared his speed or skill was not limited to swordplay as twenty dead Fureath'i told her strongly. She wondered if Valhar was waiting until he picked off everyone else one by one, before finally trying to kill her.

Even with two possible enemies searching for them from behind, Phira had to decide there was no need to cover their tracks or scout back. Theirs was a one way trip now but she could not lead her men forward blindly into the unknown. Neither could she send out scouts to leave them vulnerable to that bastard. She had imagined that he tracked them from behind, finding some way to sneak in at night to cause murder, but the bastard could have gotten in front of them too.

Twenty dead warriors, she repeated to herself in a craze, twenty dead and killed right under her watch. If the man was not a god amusing himself as a madman, or a Powerborn driven simple by his own power, then she dreaded to think how one mortal man was besting her.

She looked up into Lei's eyes and, although ragged with fatigue, they shone with a clear course of action. Drop everything and hunt down Valhar. Valhar the Madman who had assassinated twenty highly trained Fureath'i warriors. Excluding herself and Lei, she had only ten warriors left, both squad leaders Pellix and Drayilus were blessedly counted among them. Looking around to all of the surviving warriors now, they each echoed Lei's silent screams.

Possible plans included remaining in place until Valhar grew frustrated and challenged them directly, risking either the Prae'surlas or the Ihnhaarat to catch up on them, or they could continue forward but without scouts, and risk any number of other certain deaths. Phira could only think of one plan that she would consider, and it would either mean the death of Valhar or the death of her entire blaze command.

'We continue as we have been,' she started and saw the flash of disbelief and outrage in every warrior before she continued, 'With one difference. The pack will stay together, never separating for any reason without exception. We will watch each other shit and piss, and we will thank Frehep that we are still alive to enjoy the experience. Not one of you will do a single thing unless there are nine others watching you do it. But the scouts will need to continue ahead in a pairing of two, and those two scouts will be Lei, and it will be me.'

Her ember struggled with his desire to confront Valhar and his desire to protect his commander. To Phira the decision was obvious: he would follow her orders. She made the commands so others would not need to wrestle with choices of any kind. Lei would obey.

'If you are certain, blaze commander,' he said in compromise, obeying but still voicing his disapproval. Pellix and Drayilus seemed just as torn, but Phira knew that was because of the conflict of command it would leave them. Both were equal in status, but the Unseen Blade squad had more surviving members, so from pure strength of number, that put Drayilus in charge. Pellix could see it as any kind of slight that she wanted as long as no one else got killed. Phira was now the only person that should be in that position and it was the way it should have always been.

'Drayilus, you are acting ember until our return. Pellix, Lei will be leaving the markings of your squad to signal what we find. We will reach Amidon City before night fall, and there you are to seek out the *Brother in Flames* Inn. All will stay together in the common room until you regroup with either one of us.'

Pellix opened her mouth as if to say something but then thought better of it. Phira nodded to Lei.

'Speak, Pellix,' he said.

'Forgive me ember, blaze commander, what are your orders if...' she looked to Drayilus for help but the man did not even turn his head to register her. Pellix took a breath and fed more strength to her fire. 'What are your orders if neither of you return, if the madman kills you both.'

That possibility was not one Phira thought likely, but nothing Valhar had done so far had been remotely likely.

'You will wait at the Brother in Flames for one day,' she answered, 'and then you will travel south to the nearest border fort and have them send a raven to Rath'Nor informing them of what we have found. Order them to kill Aerath immediately by my command and to send a full ember of squads to Coruln to investigate a possible attack. I believe the ember command of Kris Fureath'i is situated near it and will suffice. Either way, after Aerath and Coruln have been addressed, inform Kris Fureath'i of what Valhar has done. That will seal the madman's fate if I do not do it first.' With any luck Valhar might even follow her squad back to Furea. Even if the assassin was able to elude some of Furea's top trackers in a Foreign land of snow, if he entered Furea, he would be quickly cleansed from the land. She turned to Lei.

'We leave immediately.' Her ember nodded and vaulted back to his horse. Phira climbed onto hers and fed more certainty to her plan of action. She would draw Valhar to her or he would risk losing her forever. Once she had him drawn out it was just a matter of making sure she cut off more than his ear this time. To stop his preternatural speed, Phira had a surprise in store for Valhar, courtesy of the vaults of Rath'Nor.

It was a necessary compromise that magic was sometimes needed to battle magic, and Valhar had to be some unknown kind of magic. She would have already used the item entrusted to her but she did not have the time to stay in one place and hope to bait the fiend while lying still. No, she would be the bait herself and if Valhar was not lured by it, then she would reach Amidon City instead and be back in Rath'Nor that very night.

***

'We should swerve south-west now if we're to make for Rath'Nor,' Griffil said. 'The order was quite clear and I don't mean to disobey it.'

'I don't think we can afford to wait until now, we should go sooner,' Krife returned. 'Every moment we waste is a moment we could be going to Rath'Nor straight away.'

Thisian started with a sigh but ended up with a laugh. He even thought he saw his miserable horse Kris smile at his hardship. The rutter never smiled though, even with the relentless mistreatment Thisian received from his companions since leaving that temple.

At least when leaving, the exit tunnel had been far less problematic than the entrance. It was just a normal hole in the rock again and neither of the three took any more time wondering about it longer than a casual shrug. They had headed straight for Amidon City then, and would be there by noon if Krife and Griffil were to be believed. But as he knew, Krife and Griffil were both filthy lying horse-rutters. *I'll let them rut you Kris*, he said silently to the horse, *that might get a smile from ya.*

'How about I give you a Telling about that lunatic Kris?' Thisian offered to steer the conversation. 'Then we can see how quickly you mock him.'

'Go ahead, Fireborn, but I must warn you, I'm pretty quick.' Krife winked at Griffil as they rode side by side, staying close to better mock Thisian.

'Well how about this one. We had just joined the army, and myself, Kris and another friend Dallid, were explaining to everyone how, since we were trained by Yiran the Unconquered - have you heard of him? Well never mind, suffice to say it meant we would be good enough to get promoted within days. So we were diligently informing everyone of this and a group of western recruits came over and had the audacity to call us a bunch of lying horse-rutters.

'They said they had some western youth called Gravren that tried to challenge Yiran and the so-called legend had retired in fear rather than fight him. To me, all of that was just good banter, but one of those fools made the mistake of prodding Kris in the chest saying that all easterners were weak, including us *and* Yiran. Well Kris prodded him back, but he did it by taking out the westerner's own sabre and prodding it straight into his chest.'

'Do you hear that, Griff? If we don't behave ourselves, the Fireborn's friend is going to prod us! Well, you'd like that wouldn't you, Griff? So let me tell you about this time, I was prodding the fattest, hairiest, dirtiest whore you can imagine...'

Thisian drifted away from that story as soon as he heard hairiest, even if it was about whores. He just shook his head still remembering the sudden murder Kris had committed that day. Thisian had even thought he was used to the murdering habits of that blood-crazed psychotic, losing count of how many Fureath'i the man had killed since Thisian met him. But Thisian had always felt somehow responsible for Kris, and deep down always thought he could teach him how to behave normally.

He had stood up for Kris again that time in Rath'Nor, to the elder's enquiry, explaining how the westerner had attacked Kris and that Kris defended himself. He may have used some exaggeration and during the Telling Kris had said nothing, simply staring at Thisian as he spoke. Dallid wisely stayed out of it, doing his best instead to make sure Phira did not find out and would not stick her almighty nose in.

When the elders asked Kris if everything said was true he still did not speak. He only turned his death-black stare on the Rath'Nor elders. They took his silence for agreement but Thisian knew they were all too terrified of him and wanted to be rid of it. Thisian had gotten rid of him that day too.

After the Telling, Kris asked Thisian why he would lie and lessen himself as a Fureath'i to stop Kris from being justly punished. Thisian of course pointed out to the idiot that he did not lie, but merely used what little truth he had and created something better. How was that not the Fureath'i way: to strive always to be better? Kris stared at him and then it was Thisian's turn to get angry. What kind of a friend was he that he did not thank Thisian for saving his life, for always looking out for him, helping him fit in with other people and trying to make him better than what he was?

Kris was silent again for a time, trying to stare Thisian down, but he did not break under that stubborn gaze. Thisian was in the right for once, having gone out of his way to save his friend. Finally Kris just nodded and formally thanked Thisian for his help. Then he calmly explained that he never wanted Thisian's help again, that if he did something he deserved to be killed for, then he should be killed.

That was when Thisian washed his hands of the dark-eyed killer, and by no connection, was the same time Kris's career in the army had taken off up the bloody heights of power. Thinking back on it Thisian was at least happy he was able to drag Dallid down with him for a few more years after that. Dallid was surely the lowest ranking of all of them now. Even as an Exile, being a Flameborn was much better than any rank within the army. Kris could go rut that horse those westerners had suggested. Thisian had much better things in mind that he would rut.

'Hey,' Thisian said, interrupting Krife's story about his awful whores. 'Tell me about nice whores, about the Fantaven whore houses.'

'Do they have Fantaven whore houses in Rath'Nor?' Griffil asked Krife with fake concern. 'I don't think so. And that's where we have to go, isn't it?'

'I'm surprised you have both hands visible you spend so much time dreaming of whores, Fireborn,' Krife said while shaking his head. 'How don't you Fureath'i have any whores in that country of yours? Is trying to kill each other the only form of entertainment you've got? Didn't think ye tried to kill your own Fireborns though.'

'Believe me, to Kris, that is a compliment,' Thisian admitted. 'If I was not a *Flameborn*, he would not even consider me worth killing.'

'I've actually read a lot about the adoration the Fureath'i people display towards their Powerborn,' Griffil said, nodding thoughtfully. 'It was a rare pleasure to witness such a showing of reverence in person. The respect he showed in his commands to you, the adoration in his murderous eyes, I nearly wept at the beauty of it all.'

'Would he have been faster, Fireborn? With his little sabre?' Krife asked.

In truth Thisian did not know. Kris was not as fast as Phira, but he certainly had an unstoppable viciousness that Thisian would not like to test, at least not before he was more experienced with his powers. Changing the subject he said, 'He wouldn't have been faster than Jherin either way. Is he a god? It was strange that he spoke Fureath'i.'

'No, Fireborn, not a god,' Krife said. 'The gods all run in fear of that one.'

'He didn't speak Fureath'i either, Thisian,' Griffil said, also being suspiciously civil. 'Things that powerful, they communicate with you no matter what you are or where you're from; the power just permeates into your head, and usually you don't even notice they're doing it, you just understand what they've said without remembering how they said it.' He turned to Krife then, 'And here we are carrying around a piece of rock that's cursed to draw that kind of attention down on us.'

'If you're going to piss your pants, Griffil, at least stand up and do it like a man.' Krife winked at Thisian. 'If he starts crying, we're leaving him here, Fireborn, just you and me from now on.'

Thisian half-laughed politely before asking, 'That rock we took? That's not going to make Jherin come find us? Is it?' *It had better bloody not.*

Krife shrugged his massive shoulders, 'Jherin, a plague, an army of demons or Powerborn, that dangerous friend Fureath'i of yours, it could make any of those instruments of destruction come find us at any moment.' The old treasure hunter looked at how Thisian's mouth had opened in mid-protest. There were far too many things to wildly complain about for any reasonable place to start. The grizzled giant burst into laughter at the look on Thisian's face.

Thisian in turn tried to frown some sense back into Krife to elaborate how he was not trying to be funny, and then looked to Griffil for any kind of salvation. The young thief did his best Krife impersonation with a heavy shrug, mimicking thick muscled shoulders, heavy with the effort of lifting them, and then followed the gesture with a comprehensive scratching of a patchy white beard and thick hairy arse.

Thisian cleared his throat and ended up spitting up some phlegm to the ground on one side of his horse. Krife raised an eyebrow in disgust at Thisian's lack of manners, and Griffil just laughed. Did those two ever take anything seriously? They were infuriating company.

'If it is as you say,' he started, slowly trying to reason out the severity of their dilemma, 'And that rock is cursed - and I remember Jherin saying that it *will* bring ruin and destruction on whoever holds it - then *why* do we have it?'

'To sell for gold,' Krife said with clear logic, bringing an approving nod from Griffil.

'Gold,' the thief echoed with satisfaction.

'Gold...' Thisian repeated also. 'Such as the mountains of gold that were in the same temple where we took that rock?'

'The very same,' Krife said back.

'I just wanted to clear it in my head,' Thisian said as he wondered if it was too late to follow Kris and join whatever quest he had embarked on. He would not mind bedding Nureail. She was pretty enough for someone with Foreign blood in her.

'Don't worry, Thisian, we'll be dead long before we manage to sell it for any gold,' Griffil said reassuringly.

Krife grunted and frowned at his friend. 'Do you think I would be as old as I am if I was as stupid as I look?'

'Or act? Or smell?'

Krife lifted up a lumbering arm and buried his squashed face into his own sweaty armpit. Thisian took the moment to curse Frehep for blessing Powerborn with enhanced senses. When Krife was finished drinking in his aroma, he decided not to challenge Griffil's accusations.

'The curse only works when the holder actually wants to find all three of them. Jherin said it himself. We're doing him a favour by taking it away. We'll sell it to some rich lord and let him suffer the descending horrors that will arrive to destroy him.'

Thisian choose to accept the explanation for the time, if only because it made him worry less about getting killed right that minute. He needed to get at least one Telling out into the world before he got destroyed by some ancient curse. Nureail had seemed interested in his story, so she might very well make one with him and Kr'une. He hoped Kris was not given any input to the story. He very well might not paint Thisian in much of a positive light at all. But Thisian needed a better adventure and a different Teller to compose it. 'So after we sell the piece of rock, where are we going next?'

Krife and Griffil both looked at each other, smiled, and said in unison, 'Rath'Nor!'

Thisian shook his head and cursed at them in Fureath'i. He got a raised eyebrow from Griffil at the obscure oaths - that a Foreigner should not have known - but Krife as usual appeared to have not heard or cared.

'Fireborn,' Krife said, irritatingly. 'I don't want that little fella coming after us because we didn't do what he outright told you to do. I have enough murderous bastards out to cut my balls off.'

Thisian sighed, and when a sudden thought came to him he started laughing too. 'You know, there's a woman who's twice as dangerous as him and hasn't half the control. If we ever meet her she will definitely kill me just for being a Flameborn.' It was a good thing he was never going back to Furea then. He would be safe from Phira and every other disapproving Fureath'i once they got to Amidon City.

'We'll look after you, little friend,' Krife said warmly. 'I know being a Fireborn can be dangerous.'

'Well I've never been stabbed or shot before becoming a *Flame*born,' Thisian said, while scratching the half-healed scars in his chest, 'And Phira would kill the two of you too just for knowing me.'

Krife pushed out his chest and lifted up his chin. 'I haven't been killed yet. Don't think I'll start doing it anytime soon either.'

'It's true,' Griffil confirmed, hitching a thumb towards him. 'He hasn't been killed.'

Thisian opened his mouth to say something insulting back when a sudden wind gusted through them. Both Krife and Griffil held onto their thick furs, pulling them tighter around, and Thisian did the same with his thin little cloak. He bloody hated the cold. It was almost enough to make him miss Furea, if not the people who lived there. Looking miserably at Krife and Griffil trying to wrap themselves away from the wind, and then looking at all the snow that covered absolutely everything around him, Thisian wondered was there any place in the world that was colder right now.

He doubted it.

***

Dallid stood in the centre of the raging snow storm as it besieged him from all sides. The sky was dark, and white spray was being flung everywhere in his view, but still Dallid could make out the lone mountain in the distance. The only promontory for miles of flat snow, the Lae Noan mountain prison stood out like a spear thrust against nature.

The entire climate of the land seemed severely against nature. How could any people, even as warped as the Prae'surlas, live willingly in such an environment? Snow and ice had no place in the world of light. They brought nothing and provided for no-one. If Dallid ever found a way, he would burn the land to ash and destroy every last trace of cold or winter.

The demon Chrial'thau was no longer in Dallid's head. He was not sure what it meant beyond that the demon might not be of help in his attack on Aerath. Unable to watch the butchering of an entire city, Dallid had set out on his own for Lae Noan. He had felt the demon follow in time, the presence in his head bloated with sickening new power. Dallid had even thought he saw a darkness in the sky to signal the devil's passing. But if Chrial'thau had reached the mountain, then he had disappeared. If it was possible to kill the demon, and if its disappearance meant just that, then Dallid would at least be free of regret for not ridding the world of Chrial'thau's obscenity. He could almost take comfort that he could now die in the killing of Aerath.

Knowing he wished to see his wife once more, Dallid still felt his death would free Phira also. Free her to pursue the betterment of her career and country without the buried guilt of discarding Dallid. She would be the wife of a dead hero, the Fireborn that avenged Chrial'thau. She could be King within the week.

Dallid shook his head. He would not dishonour her like that. Their love fed the fires in each of their hearts and was responsible for each of their strength. Phira's pain in her choices was simply folded into determination to make her decision worth it. Dallid knew he should do the same. To enter Lae Noan was to die, but not before Aerath. He had no idea of how he would accomplish such a thing, but he would do everything he could to tear the Iceborn's head from his shoulders.

'I have never wanted to kill anyone, only to love you,' he said quietly to Phira. The howling blizzard battered his gentle words to nothing. Dallid stepped forward towards Lae Noan and towards Aerath. There would be an end to it soon, one way or the other.

CHAPTER THIRTY NINE

Appearances

Valhar had not taken her bait.

As she approached Amidon City, Phira tried to focus on the fact that she could be back in Rath'Nor in a matter of hours, but all that gnawed its way into her was that Valhar had not taken her bait. Should she have made herself more of an inviting target? Should she have stripped herself of all weapons and clothing, to stand naked and willing in the snow for him?

Phira liked to think she was good at predicting things, she liked to predict how people would react and she liked to predict how she could use that to her advantage. But trying to predict what Valhar would do, or even where he was, it was impossible. Phira hated feeling so helpless and the more she thought about it, the angrier she got about everything. If Thisian was there he would tell her she needed a good rutting to calm her down. The thought made her laugh out and Lei turned to look at her with concern.

'Be quiet, Lei,' she said, and continued her self-analysis. Phira had not always been so angry about everything, but she would put her foul humour down to being surrounded by snow for the past months, that and having all of her men killed right in front of her. If only she could kill Valhar, or Aerath, then she was certain she would feel better. She would even settle for killing Thisian at that moment. Maybe it was too much time without Dallid that had burnt away all the joy she used to take in everything. That thought of course only turned her mood worse. Phira turned her ire on the Foreign city they trudged towards.

She tried to look upon the sprawling mess of scum, snow, and stone without caring or disgust, and even though the setting sun at least gilded everything with a golden shine, the city still looked like a battle had destroyed it, and then vomited snow and ice all over. Amidon City was a city without walls but possessed nothing that any army would wish to seize. It was an infection that had festered and grown over time, revealing new hovels and buildings every week like warts and sores on the living earth. Her lip curled in a sneer.

'Your smile brings warmth to my heart, blaze commander,' Lei said with a grin. 'Did I not know better I would guess you are trying to seduce me or else you contemplate retiring here as an elder.'

'I have an estate in mind in northernmost Surlas where I plan to start a village instead,' Phira answered, 'And believe me when I say you do not want me to seduce you. If you think I am violent with you now, then you have much to learn.'

'It is well that I have such a skilled blaze commander to teach me.'

Phira's hand fingered the hilt of her blade and Lei edged his horse away from her, brushing the side of his face that held the scars she had already given him. Maybe Thisian was right, she did need sexual release, maybe then she would stop tormenting Lei so much. Amidon City was full of whorehouses, such a Foreign concept, but maybe she would try one. It would be interesting to see what skills another woman might have to please her. Phira had only promised Dallid that she would not lie with other men, she somehow reasoned that he would not mind it if she lay with a woman.

It all depended how long it took to secure the star markings for Rath'Nor. It was not as if she would want to spend any time strolling around and admiring the city. As the buildings got closer, they only got uglier. She had not yet been to the cities of the Mordec Empire, but had heard they were a thing of beauty. There were elaborate bridges that spiralled over countless canals and there were inner cities of palaces and towers that had been carved with an artist's hand. If those Foreign cities were designed to delight the eyes, then this Foreign city was designed to shit on them.

'I cannot conceive, blaze commander, how so many can live in such a place.'

'Amadis the Powerful once ruled this city, Lei. He gathered armies from every land without a sovereign and gripped them in his power. This was little more than a camping ground for an incredible host of warriors then. It was when the camp followers began building temporary dwellings, and small towns arose from the families of his army, that this monstrosity was born. His adopted daughter Eva tries valiantly to clean the streets and create a respectable city, but the task is too great. Perhaps Lyat's absence is more to blame, his own missing control of the crime lords let them all flock here to nest and fester.' Phira turned to look at her ember. 'So many live here and survive, Lei, because they are all stuck together by the same adhesive filth.'

They entered the city then, not passing under any gates, or even finding a road worthy of the name, but just suddenly became surrounded by rundown dwellings. Keeping one hand resting on her Mordec blade, Phira kept her eyes keen. She did not want the occupants of Amidon City thinking two Fureath'i an appetising target. They still wore the thick black Ihnhaarat cloaks, but were free of the masks, with the hoods pulled back and the cloaks thrown wide, so they just looked like any other Foreigner. Lei had his sabre ready also but he had scarce let it leave his hand since they started out from the squads. Valhar had not taken her bait, but it no longer mattered to Phira. She was where she needed to be, and she would soon be back in Rath'Nor.

During her training in Rath'Nor she had studied every map she had come across. Her time as Yiran's apprentice had given her a solid base of geography to begin with, but Phira's time in the Scholar's quarters had burned the entire world into her mind. Even without knowing the streets they rode down now, using the direction they had entered she would be able to navigate towards their destination. Eva Yeda, the Lady of Amidon, was Phira's destination; the quickest way to secure the star markings for Rath'Nor.

She had never travelled by Spike before, but Yiran had, and so Phira knew enough of what to expect. A scroll showing the stars above Rath'Nor would give her the markings to press into the metal plates, and once thrown to the earth, it would open up to swallow its owner and reappear at the encoded location. The powers it travelled were similar to the powers that magicians touched or Powerborn were Connected to, and for some reason neither of those could use the Spikes because of it. Yiran had told her about flowstones within the Temple of Zenith that worked in a similar way.

Lady Eva would have access to Spike codes from her father or from her other connections, or else she would know where to find them. She was an impressive woman by all accounts; the very apex of the heights of power set firmly in her sights, much like Phira. But from the appearance of the city, the Lady Eva seemed to lack any urgency for achieving such goals. Perhaps if their meeting went well then Phira would return and discuss some plans of her own to burn order into the chaos.

As such a young blaze commander, Phira achieved a reputation for always having a plan for every occasion. Male warriors found it difficult to accept that she was better skilled than them so they conceded that she was just more clever and more cunning. It was okay for a female to be sly and crafty, but not stronger or faster than them, oh no.

In her own mind it had always been raw arrogance that won her through most circumstances though. Yiran had taught her that appearance was one of the most important things a leader can have. With Lady Eva, he explained that there was truly a woman with a plan. In his dealings with her he had come to the judgement that Eva always had a hundred different schemes unfolding at the same time, and most of those had plans within plans. He surmised that despite so many different factions appearing to rule within the crime ridden city, that underneath it all Eva was in control, even if no-one else in the city knew it. Phira did not know if that was true and would judge for herself when they met.

'Such a lovely place, blaze commander,' Lei said after passing a man lying either drunk or dead on the road. 'Perhaps we should not wait under we are elder, perhaps we should Exile and come to live here now.'

Phira smiled at his attempts at humour but her eyes marked every man and woman they passed, assessing their worth and threat before moving on. Even children did not escape her judgement. To live in such a place would be a life of constant defence of your self-worth, or a life where you had given up on caring about living. Either way she was no longer in the mood for amusing conversation. The threat of Valhar still shadowed the possible threats of the Amidon citizens. It was more than probable that the madman tracked them and only waited for the right moment to strike. She was so close to her goal now, she could not risk failure through indolence.

'You remind me of a boy from my village, Lei,' she said without looking at him. 'He always thought to laugh at life instead of fight it.'

It was unfair to compare Lei to Thisian, but she needed her ember to have his balls on today, this was no place for his female frivolity. More and more of the ragged looking locals seemed to be paying attention to them now, which did not surprise her since a Fureath'i's golden skin was easy to recognise in a city full of Foreigners.

Theirs was the only nation she knew of that had skin the same colour as the sun, but as seldom as her people left the holy nation of Furea, the Fureath'i people also carried a sharp reputation. The rumours that they carried copious amounts of gold were born of the truth that it was indeed plentiful in the country, due to the mines within the Fire Wall. That alone was bad enough to announce your arrival in a city full of thieves and murderers but the fact that most Fureath'i had little use of gold, preferring to be as self-reliant as they could, made it worse. It meant if someone would not try to take it by stealth they would try to take it by trickery or false barter. So she hoped the other well-known Fureath'i reputation would win out, and that was the one for extreme and unpredictable acts of fire and violence.

'What if you were to laugh at life while you were fighting it, blaze commander?' Lei continued. 'A recognition of the way it can often be beaten so bravely and yet never defeated.'

Phira sighed and this only caused Lei to broaden his grin. He took pleasure in her irritation much the way Thisian would, much the way she did at unmanning him as often she could.

'Lei, if I wanted to laugh then I would order you to strip, but I did not bring you for your pitiful nudity and I do not need to hear your every whining thought.'

Lei nodded, his orders understood, his personal feelings put aside. Phira was pleased with his reaction until he spoke to confirm it. 'You need me to protect you from an entire city, blaze commander.'

She closed her eyes and thought about not replying. She was not Kris however. She could not spend an entire day with a person and never speak. Memories from her youth were coming back more and more frequently of late, perhaps it really had been too long since she had seen Dallid. But she remembered spending a journey through the forests with Kris that had lasted three days and the boy had not once offered a single word beyond a direct answer to any of her questions. Sometimes strength was forcing yourself to be personable rather than just silently tolerating the presence of others. She could always slash Lei across the face again to shut his mouth from talking.

'I need your eyes, nothing else. Not your protection, not your sword, not your company and definitely not your mouth, so shut it.'

'I will shut my mouth at once. It is an ember's duty to obey his blaze commander,' Lei replied, failing to completely stop the grin from appearing on his face.

The man was getting better at keeping his horse out of striking distance so Phira decided she would just ride in silence. They stepped their horses carefully down the icy streets and watched while everyone stared at them. Ironically it was safer to traverse the hard packed earthen roads of the Foreign city than any made of stone when the weather was so cold. It was an odd thing to think Amidon City safer than Rath'Nor in such an instance, but she could never imagine the Fureath'i fortress covered in ice or snow. Could Aerath's ritual be that strong?

Looking to the snow-capped houses, with roofs that looked close to collapsing under the weight, and seeing people wrapped in as much as they could, Phira feared it just might be. How one Iceborn could possess so much power was inconceivable. Working her mind to come up with solutions, the first that sprang to mind was that Aerath had been invoking the ritual for years.

'Blaze commander, ahead.'

Phira turned away from the group of men she had been studying in the shadows, and saw in front of them armoured soldiers marching loudly. The shine of their breastplates and crunch of their boots tried to stamp righteousness on the scum ridden streets with every step. Their swords were short and straight, made for stabbing from behind the large rectangular shields they carried. Phira did not possess one of the Shakara swords yet, but hoped that she might include one in the bargain she would strike with Eva Yeda momentarily.

'Warriors of the Shakara!' she called out in king's tongue, with her arm lifted and palm faced out. 'The sun god sees you and wishes words!'

The officer in charge eyed her and seemed to give some thought before ordering the march to a halt.

'What brings two Fureath'i to our city?' he asked suspiciously. All of the soldiers had hands resting on their swords, but they had been that way even before she had stopped them. Phira did not yet take offence.

'I would speak with your Lady Eva Yeda. Tell her that Blaze Commander Phira the Unrivalled seeks audience.'

Phira did not presume the Lady to know her name, but she would know enough to respect the rank of her title. The officer took more time in deciding what to do and if he were a man in Phira's command, he would be taught to make his decisions much quicker. As it happened she was only moments away from cutting one of the soldiers to show them she expected to be obeyed faster.

'Very well,' he said grudgingly, saving the need for blood, for now. 'I will take you to my lady's office, but whether she will be available to meet with you has yet to be seen.'

Phira nodded her acceptance and waited as the officer split his force, leaving a rather young faced man in charge of the group remaining behind to continue the patrol. When they set off, it was at a painfully slow pace. Gone was the sharp march of the impressive soldier, it was replaced with the discontented trudge of men having their time purposefully wasted. She held her tongue that their time would be less wasted if they took a swifter step, and went back to her survey of the city.

The Shakara soldiers themselves did not escape her critical examinations, but as they travelled, Phira began to see more and more buildings of larger construction. Proper Inns and taverns of passable legitimacy could be seen, although buried in snow like the rest. Trade shops and markets appeared, often with guards standing over them as well as workers within. Soon two remarkably larger constructs loomed into view.

The first was what could only have been the Amadis Arena: a theatre where warriors fought each other for gold and glory, to the roar and entertainment of a crowd. When Yiran spoke of it, it was with distaste, although the skills of the combatants were not to be disrespected. As a youth Phira had toyed with a fantasy where she would be the undefeated champion of the Arena. It was soon explained to her that it was no dream fit for a Fureath'i, and she became brainwashed with the tradition that her only dreams should be to hate the Prae'surlas and to die trying to kill one. Phira shook her head at how much her country was held back by their stubborn culture.

The last time traders had arrived in Rath'Nor, Phira heard that there was a Jhakral that fought in the arena. She did not know if that was true, since the beast could easily break out and run riot through the city if it was a captive, but then other such powerful warriors like Ithnahn Berenger and Protharik the Demonlord had fought there apparently of their own free will. Who was to say that a Jhakral would not enjoy the blood, food and riches it received from the Amadis Arena? Even the disgraced Prae'surlas champion Frind'aal had taken home there. Spending his days fighting without any reason Phira could find other than to wait for death. Such a death had not come of course, even though he had been Exiled by Aerath, the man was still Iceborn.

To her mind Aerath should have killed Frind'aal when he had been bested. The news that a man claiming to be the Prae'surlas god reborn, and one that had defeated their champion, had reached Fureath'i ears with concern. Frind'aal had been the strongest of the Iceborn, although he and Lord Chrial'thau had never faced each other in combat. The fact he was not only beaten by someone stronger, but was then let free and not killed, was yet another threat toward Furea.

It was rare for a Powerborn to be allowed Exile from a nation but the Prae'surlas had a very complex structure of rights and ranking. Every north-man needed to be above another in some way and it was possible that Frind'aal had been only allowed Exile due to the great dishonour that accompanied it. How lowly the man must rank, to be below fleshborn even now, would be a harsh punishment for a fool Prae'surlas.

Pushing her personal curiosities aside, Phira drew her attention back to the second structure they were approaching. It looked to be part-palace and part-fortress, with the defensive walls that one might expect to find around the city, but within it spiralled the palaces that Amadis had created when he was the ruler. The Palace of Amadis had been renamed the Shakara barracks, but to Phira the military additions only made it better. Along the walls archers strolled, and at the gates stood a full squad of guards. Admittedly an army would not be assaulting the palace and all they had to protect against were thieves and criminals, but Phira was pleased with the precautions Lady Eva was showing her. The officer escorting them spoke a few words at the guard post and one of the runners went off to deliver the news. He waved them inside, and once at the stables he spoke again. 'You may wait here with your horses until word returns from the Lady.'

Phira took a breath but managed a smile of gratitude. If it had been the Mordec Empire she was visiting they would have been offered their own apartments to wait in, with a large fire and given hot baths and refreshments. There would be servants massaging them and cleaning their clothing, they would even be offered other servants as bed warmers while they waited. For a nation that condemned slavery, the Mordec Empire certainly had a lot of servants. Phira's focus to her goal dissipated the anger building, and the man's obvious ignorance was all that stopped her from kicking him to the ground.

Turning her scowl of irritation towards Lei, the man was grinning at her again. Nothing that she could identify specifically, but he had a way of looking at her like he was always on the verge of breaking out in laughter. Suddenly though, she found her reactions as funny as Lei must. Any Fureath'i of rank would of course not expect any of the courtesies Phira had just demanded within her own head. It was the excessive knowledge that Yiran had drilled into her - and her own almost Scholarly dedication - that had created so many Foreign thoughts within. A Fureath'i needed nothing more than the sabre in her hand and the fire in her heart. All else can burn to ash.

'Be quiet, Lei,' she said in Fureath'i, so the officer would not hear her words.

'As you command,' Lei replied in what could be seen as clear disobedience to a direct order. The Shakara officer did not like their secret conversation and cleared his throat roughly to show his annoyance. The man had a large white moustache but if it were shaved off she would not have thought him an old man. Phira saw her own ember stroking around his mouth in contemplation of perhaps growing some facial hair too. She would never allow it.

Looking up at the setting sun, Phira needed a distraction from Lei's insubordination. It was possible that the Lady Eva would not be in a position to see them immediately and would ask them to return in the morning, but spending a night in Amidon was not something Phira wanted to do, no matter how curious she was about bedding a woman. She wanted to be in Rath'Nor the instant she received the markings for the Spike, baking in the Fureath'i heat instead of shivering in the Foreign cold.

When footsteps came scattering from behind, Phira was pleased at how swiftly the runner had returned. The boy was completely out of breath but spoke without delay. 'The Lady will see the Fureath'i ambassadors immediately,' he panted, sweat dotting his forehead despite the freezing cold.

If the officer was surprised they were to be seen so quickly, he gave no indication other than a gesture for the two Fureath'i to dismount. 'We shall see to your horses while you are away,' he said with a bow, perhaps coming to realise their importance finally.

'Do not touch our horses,' Phira said. 'We will be returning quickly.'

The man looked shocked at the authority in her voice. Giving another awkward bow, he marched away with the barest of gestures that they should follow. The boy was left to stare at them and the horses, not sure what he was to do. As he was passing, Lei crouched down and whispered something that Phira could not hear and passed the boy what was most likely gold. The boy looked relieved at the words and terrified by the coin. When they were both a few strides away Phira growled to her ember once more. 'I thought I gave you an order, Lei,' she said, still in Fureath'i.

'I did not say a word, blaze commander,' he said loudly and without a grin. He did not meet her eyes. It was probably for the best that she could not see the amusement in his and that he could not see the violent intent in hers.

Once they entered the compound fully, the officer set a brisker pace to be rid of the Fureath'i savages. For a palace in outward appearance, it was pleasantly clear of decoration or wealth on display inside. Instead it was built for practical and military purposes. Replacing wall hangings, there were arrow slits, and instead of intricate tile designs on the floor, there were murder holes in the ceilings. Phira did not expect anything else from the abode of the great Amadis and it seemed his daughter had changed little.

As an adopted daughter, Phira had a fascination with Eva for as long as she knew of her. Phira herself was the adopted daughter of Yiran the Unconquered so she wondered if she would connect with the Lady Eva that way. Of course Amadis the Powerful was a great deal higher in importance than Yiran, from a world view at least.

Large double doors appeared at the end of the corridor and more soldiers snapped to attention at the arrival of their party. As she reached the doors, her escort departed with the briefest of bows. She was ushered into the lady's audience chambers and Phira's first impressions were that this was no lady she was visiting. This was a queen.

The throne room, as it could only be described, was vast. All the austerity of the palace hallways seemed now designed to only give this chamber greater impact. Two monstrous statues of Amadis the Powerful stood threateningly on either side of the room. They each mirrored the other, with the warrior's sword drawn and eyes that followed you as you walked. Shakara soldiers lined the walls, every second one holding short sword and shield, with the ones in between holding crossbows. One other warrior of note was in the room, and his was the role of guardian to the throne.

This man wore light clothes, in contrast to the weather, not even wearing armour and had three swords attached to him: the one at his left hip was the same size as the Shakara short sword, although it looked thinner and lighter, as did everything about the man; the sword at his right hip was longer by a hand, with a recognisable hilt of the Mordish katana that Phira herself preferred to use; and the third and final sword was longer than both combined and hung across his back. It was not a broad sword - a thick clumsy thing that Phira would usually associate with a length like that - but it was thin and curved like the others. The southern parts of the Mordec Empire used those long swords, but only the warrior servants of royalty. Such swords were used for fighting and beheading Powerborn.

Phira had heard of this man who acted as Lady Eva's guardian and who did all of her killing for her. His name was Brenit.

The man had his head completely shaved giving the look of a bird of prey, and his small eyes glistened at Phira as if recognising her own deadly ability. Her hand longed to rest on her sword, but she would not let the warrior think she considered him dangerous. She glanced again at all his weapons and threw her eyes in derision. Even though she did possess a rig full of swords on her saddle, there was no need for a warrior to carry three. She herself had only her favourite sword strapped to her hip, with one additional weapon strapped over her shoulders, hidden by her cloak. The Jaguar sword was on her back, and Valhar's Spike was also attached to her belt, both too valuable to be left unattended in Amidon City. She only had one other item secreted about her body, the King's gift from the vaults of Rath'Nor.

Ignoring the warrior servant, Phira was pleased to see his irritation at being dismissed so easily. His bird-like eyes glittered at her, knowing how dangerous she was and knowing that she did not consider him to be. It was petty but if it meant he was distracted with rage then it would give her an advantage if it came to killing him. With so many crossbow men lining the walls, Phira guessed she might just have time to kill him before she was filled with metal bolts. It would not come to that. She fixed her attention to the throne.

Mounted up high above a sparkling pool of water, the Lady Eva very much sat like a queen before her subjects. She had a grand robe of white that flowed out from her shoulders high and draped far back along the throne room floor behind her. It was an impressive piece of clothing, made better that Phira could see it easily unclasped from the lady herself. Underneath Eva was wearing what looked like a warrior's leather clothes, partially hidden under the theatrics of the robe. Eva's sword was not hidden though, that was clear for all to see.

The hilt was white with two circles on it just like the Jaguar blade Phira possessed. Although not sure how they were connected, she knew that Eva's blade was called The Lion. It was not as well-known as the Jaguar blade, nor was Phira sure what powerformed qualities it possessed. Perhaps it was just a tribute to her father's sword of legend. The message it gave was clear though, if she was to be seen as a queen then she would be seen as a warrior queen. She would not be the daughter of Amadis Yeda otherwise.

Eva Yeda had beautiful long blonde hair that danced in curls around her shoulder. Her face was just as beautiful but had a hard look to it. Phira was often told her own face held the same hardness, with tight muscle burning away any beauty that might once have been. Eva's cheeks and lips were pressed in tight and her eyes were blue; as cold as the snow covering her city. When she spoke the room itself seemed to get even colder still.

'You have come to declare your intentions towards my city?' she began. 'I have taken measures towards rectifying your situation. The culprit has been killed and his body sent out towards your army.'

Phira had heard that Eva Yeda was so clever that she would have you agree to whatever it was she wanted long before you knew what had happened. If this method of confusion was part of her ploy then Phira would not bite. She would step carefully. It was difficult to know that she spoke with someone so much smarter than her. Phira's sword hand twitched with indignation at the prospect. Lei thankfully did not react either, and as much as Phira wanted to find out more, she would first get what she came for. Meeting Eva's cold voice with one just as commanding, Phira replied, 'I do not yet wish to discuss those matters.'

The Lady Eva raised an eyebrow. 'Is that correct? Then what, may I ask, do you wish to discuss that is of more importance?'

It did not feel like the woman was warming to her, but Phira did not think the woman warmed to anyone. Maybe she was turning the world to ice and not Aerath after all. 'What I wish for, Lady Eva, are star markings for a Spike.'

There was a pause then, more likely to make Phira feel uncomfortable for demanding something so boldly than for any hesitation Eva might be feeling. 'And where would you wish to go, Blaze Commander Phira?'

'Rath'Nor.'

'Then I shall have the markings for you by morning.'

Phira was immediately disappointed that she could not have them now but would be willing to wait if she must. She was suspicious however at having her demands met so quickly. 'My gratitude, Lady Eva, to what payment would you like in return?'

Eva flicked her fingers to wave away the thought, 'None. Instead answer me this, how is it a fleshborn blaze commander, so young and female, has come to command a host of Fureath'i Powerborn? With no less than twenty Fireborn in their midst if my sources are correct.'

Phira's mind spun. Twenty Fireborn? Was that the army she had mentioned earlier?

'A lord of power can often become a warrior to command when given the right general,' Phira quoted back from Yiran's words, but she worried if she would still be given the Spike markings if it was found out that she was not who she was leading the Lady Eva into believing. With a sigh she regretted her need to get the markings was more important than the need to develop intrigue with the Lady of Amidon City. 'But I must tell you that I am not involved with the Fureath'i army that you have spoken of.'

Eva nodded as if she already knew as much. 'Well then, I do not believe you to be Exiles and from your entrance from the west I can only assume that you have come from Surlas,' Phira opened her mouth to object but Eva lifted her hand to stop her, 'It is no concern of mine what the Fureath'i do in Surlas, as long as you did not kill so many that they can no longer buy my farm workers.' Phira suppressed a grimace for the euphemism she used for the Chuabhotari slaves. 'All is not lost of course, perhaps you may be of some worth yet. Let us exchange other information in return for my kind gift to you.'

'Perhaps I may be of some worth in that regard,' Phira said without commitment and tried to keep her irritation at the words from flowing free.

'Shall I go first, Blaze Commander Phira? Please try to follow though as I will not repeat myself. The host I have spoken of, and mistakenly lead to believe that you are the ambassadors of, are a small army of no less than fifty Powerborn, including as I have said, twenty Fireborn warriors.' She paused to gage Phira's reaction. Such a force could level the entire city to the ground in less than an hour if they wished it, but Phira did not move. Eva gave the smallest of smiles then, maybe taking her non-reaction as reaction enough. 'You can see my concern, but let me first tell you their motives behind the march - if it is as I have guessed and you have been isolated in Surlas these last few weeks without news of Furea. It seems a demon has entered your lands, Blaze Commander Phira, I know little more about it apart that it has bright green eyes, that it has killed your Lord Miral'thau the Wise, and that it did so right in the middle of Rath'Nor.' To this both Phira and Lei did react. 'It gets worse I'm afraid. I have people who can gather information for me, even from Furea, and if they are to be believed this same demon has killed your Lord Miral'thau, your Lady Jaiha, a Flameborn by name of Lord Kr'une and, unbelievably, Chrial'thau the Great. An impossible thing, I know, but of Miral'thau I am at least certain, for fifty Fureath'i lords of power now march towards my city seeking retribution.'

'How has this demon been considered your doing, my Lady?' Phira asked with a dangerous tone to her voice. The bird-like warrior at her feet tensed at the sound of it but Lady Eva deemed not to notice. She answered in the same matter of fact way she had just described the deaths of three of the greatest Fureath'i Powerborn in history.

'I have in my city a number of undesirable people, and I had thought Protharik the Demonbane the least of my troubles. But alas the Fureath'i have decided that since Protharik is the only one in the world of light that can summon demons, then he must be responsible for the creature that attacked Furea and killed Miral'thau. I will admit that it makes a certain simple sense. One that would appeal to the need to seek violent retribution, but I do not believe Protharik is responsible. Regardless we have killed him and sent his corpse towards your people to stop the destruction of my city.'

Phira nodded. It was said by Foreigners that Fureath'i liked to burn anything at the best of times without reason. Fifty Fureath'i Powerborn then, with very strong reason, would burn a hole in the earth where once a city stood. The lady was faced with quite the dilemma, but surely she did not think that sending Protharik's corpse would stop the host. After all, most of Protharik's power, despite his summoning or hunting of demons, was the fact that he could not be killed. Eva followed Phira's eyes as if reading her thoughts and smiled that she was following.

'So this comes to my exchange,' she said coolly. 'I have already agreed to provide you with the markings you desire, but I would also like your answers to some questions. I will get to our options regarding the host, but first I must enquire as to why a lone Flameborn would be travelling with two non-Fureath'i and be staying at an Inn in my city called the *Dancing Whore*?'

Phira wondered if the Lady was so clever that she sought to throw Phira's mind off by preaching complete nonsense. Plans raced through her mind, with solutions to the various problems not coming smoothly. Thinking herself clever for securing the star markings so quickly, Phira reconsidered that she had now trapped herself by announcing her need for the Spike codes. If she could not repay Eva in one way, then she was sure there would always be some other. Phira did not like the idea of being in debt to such a woman.

'I accept your terms, Lady Eva,' Phira said confidently, pleased at the small traces of irritation on the lady's face. 'In return for your great kindness, I will travel to this Inn and uncover why this Flameborn is here. Then we shall make contact with the approaching host of Powerborn, and I am confident we can resolve this matter peacefully.'

There was silence for a time. Eva's sharp eyes seemed to read every thought that Phira was calculating and Phira's thoughts were moving too fast for even her to keep up with. Then there was the slightest nod of approval from the queen of the chaos city. 'If you could do such a thing I would be greatly indebted to you, Blaze Commander Phira.'

Phira just smiled and left. Turning her back on both the lady and the man Brenit, she could feel their eyes on her back as she walked. Lei shadowed her as he should, and once they had left the throne room, they found the original moustached officer waiting to guide them back to the horses. The officer's dislike for Fureath'i let him dispense with any unwanted pleasantries about their meeting and they walked in contemplative silence. The intense look in Phira's eyes did not invite conversation regardless. She had received a lot of information suddenly and was trying to wrestle them into something manageable. Already one plan was decided on but she would continue to create new ones for as long as she could. The path she had set herself on was one of deceit but necessary, and it painfully side tracked her from her primary goal.

When they returned to the cold of the courtyard, it had already darkened to full night. The boy Lei had paid to watch their horses was still there and on first inspection everything seemed to be as they had left it. Few words were spoken and they were both soon out of the Shakara complex. The area around the barracks had an impressive amount of lanterns but already Lei was busy glaring at every shadow. The news they heard would not have hit him as hard as it had Phira, he would be confident she would have a ready plan suited to match the occasion. He would be able to concentrate on his orders and avoid thinking about the deaths of their nation's greatest Fireborn, or about the army of Powerborn about to destroy the city.

A wild fire in the city would kill her just as easily as everyone else, but that impending danger was trying to contend with her thoughts about Lord Chrial'thau. If he had been killed, then Coruln could have already been attacked. But the Frostborn said Aerath was planning on doing that, so why would a green-eyed demon be involved at all? Her thoughts suddenly wondered if Yiran was alive. The idea that he could have died with Chrial'thau stole all the confidence Phira usually relied upon to get her through times such as these.

It could of course all be Foreign lies and misinformation. The only thing Phira should be confident of was that the Lady Eva was much cleverer than she appeared, even more so than Yiran had surmised. So that meant there was one other thing that Phira could be certain; it was going to be a long night.

CHAPTER FORTY

Love for gold

He had run out of gold. He never thought there could possibly be anything in the world that he could spend so much gold on, but in one short night Thisian had found it, and it was whores. Krife had them staying in an Inn appealingly named the Dancing Whore, but the minute he had dropped his saddle bags in the room, Thisian had insisted on going to a whorehouse. The grizzled old treasure hunter had even kept his promise, bringing him to a Fantaven house, and the Fantaven house was not just filled with women, it was filled with goddesses.

Thisian had asked enough questions about it while they were travelling, and according to Krife and Griffil, the Fantaven goddesses were the most beautiful, most skilled and most expensive women in the entire world. They were even guarded by other women called the Guild of Gelders, or to use their official name: the Cock-Cutters. Strangely though, despite the fact that they were hideous in appearance, there was still a certain perverse appeal to those gelders. Everything in the entire building held a perverse appeal. Thisian had never been to any other whore house, but after five minutes in the Fantaven house, he never wanted to be anywhere else at all, ever again.

When he walked in the doors, and was disarmed by the fierce looking gelder-women, Thisian had then immediately been swept off his feet by two identical looking women with red hair. He had never seen hair that colour before. Every Fureath'i woman either had brown or black hair, and he knew Prae'surlas women had the same piss coloured hair as the men, but the fiery red hair of his two women had been perfect. It spoke to his heart, and to many other places, and even with his Powerborn strength and energy he had been quickly worn out by them.

It could have just been his heightened sensitivity that wore him out so quickly, but by the same dazed grin of idiocy and stupor that beamed on every other man he saw, Thisian guessed it was more likely the skills of the Fantaven women. He had begun by charming them with his best smiles and amusing conversation, but they had placed gentle hands over his lips. There was no need for the game of charm, all he needed was a purse full of gold - which was now of course completely empty.

He had emptied the contents of his purse right after the two red headed women had emptied the contents of his balls. The red hair between their legs had fuelled his imagination and afterward he had immediately asked for a woman of every different hair and skin colour that the house held, insisting on having them all at the same time. The result had been... *traumatising*, but in the absolute very best of ways.

Thisian stretched out his arms with exhausted satisfaction and journeyed down the stairs to a lounging room, where men and naked girls lay around smoking pipes or partaking in what Griffil had called narcotics. Krife and Griffil were both sitting on some cushioned seats. The big man was fast asleep and the younger thief was looking around with amusement on his face. He spotted Thisian and cheered out for him, 'Is it true? Have you run out of gold before the parlour has run out of girls?'

Thisian grinned proudly, but shrugged his acceptance. There had been so many girls - all doing so many things to him and to each other, with their hands and with their mouths, and with their breasts - there had been so many breasts. Thisian gave his thanks to every god that ever gave life to women and their breasts, and to all their other many wonderful assets, he loved them all. 'I have never lived before I came to this place, Griffil. I feel I might be indebted to you both for a lifetime.'

'Well as long as you don't let Krife hear you say that. He would hold you to that oath.'

'How did he fare?' Thisian asked, remembering Krife's graphic description of exactly how fat and hairy he had wanted his woman. 'Did he manage to find a whore as fat as he is?'

'Fatter!' Krife said from behind closed eyes and patted his massive stomach loudly. 'But I'm not that fat.'

'You are too fat for me to carry anyway,' Griffil said as he stood up from the cushions. 'We should return to the Inn. You are charged by the heartbeat here, whether it is sleeping or otherwise, and our Fureath'i friend here is out of gold.'

This made Krife open his eyes and burst out laughing. 'You had enough gold to live here for a month, Fireborn! How many girls did you end up with?'

'I have never needed to count so high before, there were so many...' Thisian drifted back in memory of all the things that had just happened to him. His balls began to hurt at the thoughts and he snapped back to reality. 'There were enough. It will keep me smiling for a month.'

'Yes, until you wake up tomorrow and want to come back.' Krife stood up then and rolled his shoulders with a roar. 'Come on, we must make one stop before we settle down for a long night of drinking at the Inn.'

Thisian blinked and assumed that they would go straight to the Inn to fall asleep. Griffil certainly looked tired enough. But Krife had led him true to the Fantaven palace of treasures, so Thisian would willingly follow him anywhere after that. He was indebted to the man after all. They walked out of the house, having retrieved their weapons from the fearsome Cock-Cutter women who had taken them. Thisian gave them a second look and tried to recall if he had been with any of them during his blur of pleasure. It didn't look like it. They had faces of rock, and Thisian had never thought a woman could look so strangely appealing and yet so wildly unattractive.

In fact he was not sure he had ever seen a woman that he had found unattractive before, apart from the beasts that had bred with Kris. Every other girl though, no matter their aesthetic deformity, each one could always have a special quality that he wanted to explore. His mind was probably just numb from exhaustion.

It was dark when they exited and Thisian was not confident if he had been in there for one day or three days. A rumble in the sky made him think of how Krife's stomach would be growling had they been there so long, but a clash of thunder ahead made him jump out of his daze. There was snow everywhere, and it was still unbearably freezing, but up in the skies it looked like a thunder storm was coming.

The thunder made Griffil look at Krife instead of the skies, and the big treasure hunter just laughed. 'A storm will not destroy us, Griffil. But come on, we're selling the damned thing now aren't we?'

He had forgotten about the bloody piece of rock that was cursed to bring destruction down on them. It did not matter though, as Krife said they were going to sell it and that was where they headed. Thisian felt drunk as he wandered through the night. He left boot prints in the snow and saw movement everywhere in the shadows between buildings. Either three people were too many to attack or Krife's size alone kept the lurkers away. They walked unhindered whatever the reason and Thisian began letting his love-drunk eyes admire the fire burning in the street torches. All the fire lit up was snow, but it was still fire. That was him now; pure fire. Thisian the Conqueror of Whores, the Exiled Flameborn, the one Fureath'i that could not stand to be Fureath'i, and he was fire made flesh.

A flame burst to life from his fingers and Thisian grinned with satisfaction before the damned thing caught on his cloak. Trying to put it out only made things worse since his hands were still on fire themselves. Krife and Griffil turned to frown at him and Thisian began to panic before suddenly Connecting with all the fire and forced it back inside. The torches near to him flickered at his command, almost disappearing with his own, and he began dusting the smouldered bits of fabric from his cloak. Krife and Griffil were still staring at him.

'Ah go rut a bloody horse,' he said. 'Frehep's balls, when you've got as much power as I do, you can't be expected to keep it all inside.'

'There I thought those Fantaven girls emptied out everything that you've got inside,' Krife said with a grin.

Griffil curled up his lip in disgust. 'Krife, really, must you be that vulgar all the time?'

In answer Krife turned away from Griffil mid-sentence, not listening, undid his breeches and began pissing in the snow. For an obscene few minutes Thisian and Griffil were left speechless as Krife emptied out the entire Midanna River before their eyes. When he was finally finished, the old giant placed his hand on Griffil's shoulder before saying, 'Let's keep moving.'

It was enough to sober Thisian up from whatever whore-induced drunkenness he was experiencing. He watched as Griffil turned his head to look at the wet hand print that Krife had left on his shoulder, and Thisian was too appalled to say anything. Opening his mouth once or twice, he soon gave up and started walking after the treasure hunter. Griffil followed in a daze of his own disgust, but Thisian could guess that it was more that he should have known not to expect any less from Krife. A soft squelch from under his boot, let Thisian know that he had not taken the care he should have to avoid Krife's creation of piss. He heroically ignored it and continued their pleasant trek down the fire lit city.

The buildings got better the further they went, but the Fantaven house had been in a good part of Amidon City anyway it seemed. A looming shadow behind some of those buildings made Thisian wonder if it was the Amadis Arena they were passing in the darkness and looked forward to maybe venturing there in the morning. He would need to find more gold he guessed, but selling the cursed stone was going to give them gold, was it not? So he would have plenty to purchase entry to the Arena, as long as he did not go back to the Fantaven house first. He would just have to go there after.

Turning back to the direction they walked, Thisian saw in the distance something resembling a border fort made of stone. It was larger than the forts he was used to - apart from Rath'Nor - but that was all it was. Amidon had so many differences to Furea, the first being all the stone instead of wood, and then it was all the cold instead of heat, but most importantly were the women willing to do anything he could dream of for simple coins instead of disapproving glares from Phira and any western women. He could almost picture Phira's face if she had witnessed what he had just been a party to.

They came to the gates and Krife clapped the first guard on the shoulder in greeting. Luckily it did not leave a wet hand print, and they all seemed to know Krife well. Some of the guards threw Thisian - the dangerous Fureath'i - some suspicious looks, but were not overly interested in who Krife's new companion was. They were allowed into the great fort without challenge, and were even guided through the complex by a man with a gloriously fluffed up moustache. He conversed pleasantly with Krife and Griffil, and Thisian followed along to the conversation enough to know that he was not interested in it. The moustache man looked old and soft, but he did manage to get Krife talking in a manner other than rough grunts, loud abuse or roaring laughs.

When they entered the building, Thisian was loudly disappointed at how drab and austere the place was. He nudged Griffil and spoke in Fureath'i, 'It looks like there's nothing at all here for a thief to steal that he could spend on whores.'

Griffil smiled but eyed the arrow holes in the walls before answering. 'Don't underestimate Lady Eva's ears that they don't understand your tongue, Thisian. Only a fool would try to steal from her.'

Krife roared out laughing at that moment, more than likely at something he himself had said. Thisian had nothing to keep him so entertained. His hearing could pick out some words from their conversation but his understanding of the king's tongue still faltered when people spoke too quickly. He was much better at speaking it than listening to it. Griffil was the only one he could understand all of the time, and that was because the slender thief made an effort when it came to teaching him.

In the absence of amusement however, Thisian's mind wandered to fantasy. Not a fantasy of females though - his whore-lust was well and truly satisfied for the time being - no his mind returned to grandeur. Amadis the Powerful had ruled these halls, his strength and speed greater than any Powerborn, his other powers seemingly endless. It was said he grew a new power every day and the great man often demanded that the world needed to come up with a better title to describe him, somewhere between Powerborn and god. Thisian liked to believe that the man had founded the first Fantaven house in his greatness.

When Thisian came back for air from his musings, he was startled by the sight of a man looking to kill him. The man's eyes were small and fierce, and moved down to Thisian's partially hidden, tattered - and now badly stained - Flameborn tunic. The man's head was shaven clean, and he had a sword strapped to his back even longer than Krife's beast of a thing. Being such a close friend of Kris, Thisian was used to men with the intent to murder him shining brightly in their eyes, but the warrior in front of him looked particularly deadly.

Krife stomped up next to him casually, and as he did with everyone he made the man look as small as a child. He nodded down to the dangerous looking warrior with a grin and just said, 'Brenit.'

If Brenit responded to his name, Thisian did not see it in the detailed murder the warrior was staring at him. The man with the moustache cleared his throat nervously. He did not appear to be any more comfortable about the shaven-headed killer than Thisian was.

'They request an audience with our lady, master Brenit.' All the response Brenit gave to that was a darting look from his bird-like eyes. They rested on the moustached man for a moment making him squirm uncomfortably before Brenit returned his glare to Krife and Thisian. It was almost as if he could not decide who he hated more. Thisian wondered for a moment if Kris had grown taller, shaved his head and gotten a big long sword for himself. The skin was wrong though. The moustached Foreigner coughed again before speaking, 'Our lady has always seen master Krife and master Griffil in the past...'

Brenit turned and disappeared through the large doors before the man was mid-sentence. He smiled with embarrassment at Krife. 'Brenit, ah, does not seem to like, well, people.'

'No people at all?' Krife asked. 'What about me?'

'I do not believe so,' the man smiled back. 'But do not take it to heart.'

'Too bloody late,' Krife said.

'Forgive Lady Krife, he gets offended easily,' Griffil added.

The doors opened again but it was a different servant that stood behind. This one smiled, bowed and gestured for the guests to enter. He was smaller, friendlier and less dangerously decorated with swords than Brenit was. Thisian definitely preferred him. When he stepped confidently into the chamber then, his good mood vanished. Brenit was still there of course, standing up by the throne, but along both bloody walls leading up to that flaming throne, stood lines of cursed rutting crossbowmen. They had better not try to shoot him with any of their cowardly bolts. Thisian had developed an extreme dislike for bows and crossbows and getting shot by them. It would not be his legend that he was to be the most shot Flameborn in history.

His mood soured, Thisian snorted at the needlessly big statues of Amadis the Powerful looming in the chamber, and almost laughed at the size of the Lady Eva's cape. The long white garment stretching back behind her throne might have impressed some people, but to Thisian it was as pointless as the pond she had in front of the throne. Who was she trying to impress with her army of crossbow men and her body guard Brenit with his three swords. The biggest of those he was even holding by his hip now, pretending it was sheathed but Thisian could see it was not. The over-long thing made him look like a giant rat with his tail stretched out behind him. All in all Thisian was profoundly unimpressed by the famous daughter of Amadis the Powerful and her obsession with things being so large. He examined her as they got closer to the throne, and after noticing she had no cleavage at all on display, Thisian saw her face.

He was in love.

For a man who had spent the last few hours, or days, waist deep in whores, all energy was suddenly restored to Thisian when presented with such beauty. Her hair was gold and fell in wondrous curls past her shoulders. It created the perfect frame for the picture of her face as the line of her cheeks led beautifully down to her pursed rose-coloured lips, which complemented perfectly the dazzling blue of her eyes. He was so bewitched by her that Thisian almost considered never looking at another woman again in his life, unless perhaps if they were whores specifically chosen because they looked like her.

'Krife, your Fureath'i stares at me as if I were a whore,' the Lady Eva said coldly.

'The man likes whores,' Krife said back simply with a shrug. Every man in the room jerked to attention, ready to kill Krife for his words. Brenit was moving his shoulders with anticipation and he looked to Eva eagerly for the order. She did not move however, simply staring down at the three travellers without expression. Thisian tried to make his own gaze less of a leer and more mysteriously inviting.

'Forgive us, m'lady,' Griffil interjected. 'Both my companions are damaged in their minds from exhaustion of the body.'

Despite his polite words and elegant bow, Eva ignored Griffil's gesture with an impatient flick of her hand. 'What do you want, Krife?'

'Why? Are you busy with something else?'

Again every soldier shifted their position in outrage, waiting for Eva's command to kill all three of them. Raising up her two fingers the men relaxed but the looks in their eyes did not. Eva's own eyes shot towards Thisian for a moment before she continued. 'My apologies, Krife, shall I just sit here until you are ready? Would you like me to send for some serving girls? Food? Wine? Other pleasures?'

'Gods no,' Krife said. 'Don't get the boy started again.' Thisian dropped his head with a proud smile. Scratching the white and grey bristle of his beard, Krife looked like he thought about the right way to explain what they wished to sell. 'I have in my possession, Lady Eva, an item that you will wish both to have and to be rid from your city.'

'If you speak of your thief, Krife, then you are correct. I both have work for him and a place in the gallows for him, or better yet the Arena.' Griffil opened his mouth to protest and Eva cut him off, 'Do not pretend, *thief*, that I could not name a full dozen items of extreme worth that you have stolen from me or someone under my protection. Be thankful I do not have Brenit kill you immediately.'

Krife bristled at the threat but then turned to Griffil to mouth the words, *"a full dozen?"* The thief shrugged both with shame and pride, and, before Krife could continue, Thisian felt he needed to interrupt. 'What job would you have us do my lady? Would it pay gold?'

Eva eyed him sceptically and those blue eyes were starting to look less like an inviting pool and more like a storming ocean. Frehep's balls but she was beautiful though. He wondered what she tasted like.

'A Fureath'i that wishes for gold? And a Flameborn by the tunic? Should I call him Lord or Exile?'

Krife cleared his throat to say, 'He prefers to be called Fireborn.'

Eva sighed. 'Yes, Lord Exile, I will pay gold for you and your thief to steal something for me. It is an orb that belongs to the crime lord Hrothlar, that can produce scrolls with the star markings for Spikes on it. Will you do it?'

'Yes,' Griffil said immediately, while Thisian answered: 'How much gold?'

Both Krife and Griffil were staring at him now with looks of disbelief, but Thisian tried to remain serious. Eva was not interested in discussing the exact terms of their agreement though, instead she waved to dismiss them. 'It is agreed then. Have it back to me within the hour and I will forget the thief's past indiscretions and keep Lord Exile in enough gold for a month.'

'You would be surprised how much he could spend in a month m'lady,' Krife rumbled but then reached inside his shirt to pull out the small stone segment that he had attached to a strip of leather cord. 'But as you are hurried, I would address the matter of this item.'

Eva's eyes locked with the stone segment and her lips pressed together tightly. That was all the reaction she gave but the rage was plain in her eyes if not on her face. It was an impressive talent to be able to look both perfectly composed and to look ready to kill all three of them that instant.

'You have brought this into my city, Krife?'

'And would see it removed swiftly for the right price,' he said back without shying from her fury.

'You hold my city as hostage and negotiate a ransom,' she said coldly. 'Why do I not kill you and remove the piece myself?'

'Because I didn't take it, it was given to me, and that could make all the difference when it comes to the safety of your city. But let's not fight. I'm only offering to sell you an item of power, a little worse than any other.'

Thisian looked into the bright blue eyes that were staring hatred at Krife and saw them working to plan a way for advantage. She began to remind him of Phira when she did that, and that almost ruined his attraction towards her. Almost.

'You have doomed my city, Krife, but perhaps you can save it also.' The big treasure hunter nodded that they understood each other and that no one was going to get shot, especially not the

Flameborn. Thisian bet that all of the crossbow men would even bloody aim for him first too. 'Return in one hour with the orb and I shall have the agreements written up and ready to be accepted in return for that stone.'

'How do you know what I want?' Krife asked.

'I know you long enough, Krife, to know that gold and riches do not interest you. I will have exactly what you wish for when you return.' The elusive answer seemed to satisfy Krife greatly. 'Go now before that thing begins its curse and if it does begin, Krife, then I will have to kill you for it. I can no longer be a friend to a man that threatens my city.'

Krife shrugged and turned to leave. Thisian thought he should say something else to impress himself on her, but the words would not come, not with a room full of crossbow men all looking to shoot him anyway. They would be back in an hour. That should give him enough time to find the right words to win her heart, and if he could not win her heart then he would settle for other body parts instead. Flashing her one of his best smiles, the lady raised an unimpressed eyebrow back at him. She may pretend to be unimpressed, but Thisian knew she was impressed alright. Gladly following his two companions, all three treasure hunters left the throne room of Lady Eva Yeda.

'A full dozen Griffil?' Krife shook his head as soon as the doors were closed. 'Men have been castrated and crucified for even thinking of stealing something important from that one. Well I suppose what need do you have for balls? You never use the bloody things.'

Griffil did not respond and Krife grabbed his own balls for a rummage while the subject was being discussed. The soldier with the bushy white moustache returned and Krife placed the busy hand around the man's shoulders instead. It was strange to see the big man so pleasant with anyone, and Thisian heard them start talking about a time when they were younger. Perhaps they grew up together. Those relationships could be complicated as Thisian well knew, with at least two out of his three close friends likely to kill him the next time he saw them. Phira would kill him for either being an Exile or for just being a Flameborn, he did not think she would care which reason she used, and Kris would probably kill him, well because he liked to kill people. Thisian missed Dallid.

Looking at Krife and his friend ahead of them, he tried to imagine the old treasure hunter as a youth. It was hard to picture him ever being younger though, particularly because of his size. As a gruff old man he was almost acceptable, sometimes, but the idea of a young man of the same size and strength, and with the same habit of angering people so greatly, it was a lot for Thisian to accept.

'Griffil,' Thisian whispered.

'Yes?' he answered, with a clear show of pushing his eyes towards the walls to make Thisian show caution about what he was about to say.

'How much gold do you think she will pay?'

Griffil laughed. 'You're focused, Thisian, I'll grant you that. Let me put it this way, to save her city, Thisian, she would give Krife half the world. Does that make sense to you?'

Thisian scowled. Of course it did not make sense. 'But how much gold will we get for stealing this orb? Do you know who Hrothlar is?'

'Yes and I think you'll like him, Thisian. He's Prae'surlas.'

• CHAPTER FORTY ONE •

Weapons and words

Griffil was wrong. Thisian did not like Hrothlar the Prae'surlas at all. He did not like how the crime lord's estate was more heavily defended than the Shakara barracks and he did not like how Hrothlar had given all his men bows. Prae'surlas were supposed to use spears. Thisian felt he could dodge a spear, so why was it now that he was Flameborn, everyone decided to carry bloody bows and crossbows?

He didn't know what he should curse which god to rut, so he cursed them all and had them rut each other.

Maybe he should start praying to one of the Foreign gods instead of cursing them all of time. Frehep never listened to words from a fleshborn but Foreign gods did. So which one should he thank for becoming Flameborn? If he became an avid worshipper of that god then maybe he could get more gifts. Rhyserias the goddess of time had been the one to mangle poor Kr'une, apparently. That had certainly been a big factor of the Transfer. It was hardly Frehep in any case, the god of looking and doing nothing. *Do you see me now sun god?* Thisian shook his head, he was supposed to be Connected to the god as a lord of his power, and still he could feel nothing for him.

Going back to his new list of gods, Thisian dismissed Oranin and Trabus, even if Kr'une's death had saved Thisian's life, he did not want much to do with the gods of life and death. He could also dismiss Am'bril the goddess of tempest, unless giving Thisian all day access to fire was her way of apologising for the cold weather. Brijnok the god of battle enjoyed giving people gifts to claim them as his own, but he could not have influenced Kr'une to Transfer his powers. Di Thorel the god of fortune was looking like the most likely.

Settling on the god that probably suited him best anyway, Thisian right there and then became a warrior priest of Di Thorel.

He didn't know if Di Thorel even had warrior priests the way Trabus and Brijnok did, but if there were not any, Thisian would be the first. His newly formed order would further confirm his proud title of Exile and he could use it to kiss goodbye to Frehep's balls.

Frowning at the poor choice of words, Thisian tried to concentrate on his current circumstances. He would have to come up with a new curse to replace his favoured one of Frehep's at a later stage. Right now he was busy keeping still and being quiet. The looming bulk of Krife stood next to him, pretending to hide in the shadows of an alley, but he would have had more success pretending to be one of the buildings. Thisian had told them both earlier, in no uncertain terms, that he was not going anywhere near the archers that patrolled the walls. To that Krife had just told him to calm down and Griffil had flown into Hrothlar's compound alone, scaling the wall with surprising ease. The man did weight less than one of Krife's fingers so maybe it was not so hard for him as for normal people.

And I am calm, Thisian thought to himself fiercely, and he was better hidden in the shadows than Krife was. He would probably have been better at scaling the walls too, being one of the few Fureath'i skills he was good at. Even when it came to staying still and being quiet, Thisian had years of practice from his time in the Fureath'i army. Well, he had years of practice being told to stay still and be quiet at least. The success rate of accomplishing those orders was a different Telling. Leaving out a sigh, Thisian went back to doing nothing and Krife turned his big fat neck to scowl at him for making noise. When he opened his mouth, to protest that he did not make any noise, a loud thunder clap sounded in the skies. Krife frowned at him again.

That noise had nothing at all to do with Thisian though so he frowned right back at Krife with one of his best Kris frowns. It was the type of frown that told you Kris was slowly crossing off the number of reasons in his head why he shouldn't kill you. Soon getting bored of the intense frown though, Thisian went back to looking around in the dark. It sounded like a storm was gathering overhead, and the ground was still covered in bloody snow. All this Foreign weather was giving him a pain in his head, or else it was all the frowning he had just done. Either way it felt like there was a crowd of people pressing in around him. It kept calling for his attention making him look in a direction expecting to see people, but all he could see was more snow under foot, a dark stormy night over head and Krife's big fat back everywhere else.

A crowd of people did appear then, on the street in front of Hrothlar's estates, which gave Thisian something else to look at, but they had nothing to do with the pain in his head. That pain was making him turn south. It must simply be some great new power he was developing. Thisian might have to use some of his old powers soon if the group on the street saw them though. As old as his new Flameborn powers could be called in any regard.

Looking close to see why they were all just standing about in front of Hrothlar's estates, Thisian almost turned away at how revolting they looked, and standing to the front of the group, pushing their weight around as if they were the leaders, were two of the ugliest.

One at least had an excuse; he had his face burnt off. Thisian doubted the injury would make him very friendly towards a Fureath'i, and definitely not to a Flameborn. The other one had no such excuse and just had a squashed nose, one eye higher and wider than the other, half of one ear bitten off and of what Thisian could see of the man's teeth, they were either all cracked or they were shaped like the fangs of an animal. They were both awful enough to look like brothers and both awful enough to make Thisian want to vomit. He had never thought he could look at Krife and think the man better looking than another human being, but the grizzled old treasure hunter was a portrait of beauty when compared to the two Foreign monsters out there. Listening in carefully, he could make out their ugly voices.

'Prae'surlas scum, thinking he can make us wait out in the cold. Just because he likes this snow doesn't mean anyone else does.' The uglier of the two was the louder also, with the scarred man not really saying much that Thisian could hear. Ugly kept on talking enough for the both of them anyway. 'I'd like to slap that mask right off of Hrothlar's face one of these days with the killing side of my sword. And maybe when he stops paying us so much, I will!'

Thisian wished the man would put on a mask himself. Krife was watching the men with equal interest, if not disgust, but did not seem alarmed. The rabble continued to wait outside the gates - shoving and bickering amongst themselves, waiting for the gates to open - and watching the burnt man closer, Thisian did not see him speak at all. Maybe he was just being paranoid but Thisian could almost swear that the man was even eyeing the shadowed alley that himself and Krife were both hiding in. It was unlikely but still Thisian held himself ready to run. Unless he could figure out some ritual to heat up the skin of everyone's hands so much that the ruffians on the street all dropped their swords and the archers on the walls all dropped their bows. The next Powerborn he met, that would be the first piece of magic he would demand to learn.

An Ihnhaarat stepped out into view then and Thisian quickly rephrased his declaration. The next Fureath'i Powerborn he met, then he would ask for some training - before admitting he was an Exile. The Ihnhaarat that strut into view did not even look like a Powerborn anyway, and definitely did not walk like one. The man in the thick black robes and white mask, swaggered as if he was on a stroll and needless to say the appearance of the Ihnhaarat warrior got the attention of the group of street thugs. Thisian did not know much about the Ihnhaarat but he thought that their warriors had the designs of skulls on their masks. The one that was strolling straight towards the group had a blank white one.

'Hey Ihnhaarat, you got any tits under that robe of yours?' the ugly man called out in greeting. The Ihnhaarat did not respond but turned the dead white mask towards Krife and Thisian. This time he definitely was looking right at them and it was not Thisian's imagination. Maybe the man was Powerborn and he could sense another great lord of power nearby. Thisian could not sense anything of course, unless you counted the sensations trying to crush his skull. 'Well?' the ugly man repeated. 'The last time I killed an Ihnhaarat, she had tits under those robes. She was almost too dead to rut though and I've never had me no live Ihnhaarat since. Can you understand what I'm saying?'

The Ihnhaarat took off his mask and replied, 'Of course I can't understand what you're saying, I don't have any ear you idiot.' The man underneath the mask pulled down his hood and revealed long shoulder length hair, shining silver under the street lights. The ugly man recognised him and smiled with amusement.

'Well look who it is: Valhar the Bastard. What did you say, madman? You got your ear bitten off like me did you?' The man Valhar did not reply, only frowned in confusion. 'Well never mind, if you're here to see Hrothlar you'll have to wait. Me and my boys are here first you see?'

'Of course I can see,' Valhar replied tersely. 'I still have one ear left, don't I? But I'm not looking for that snow-growing Prae'surlas-bastard Hrothlar, I'm looking for bloody ghosts. Do you know how bloody hard it is to look for them when you can't even see the bastard things? They cut off my ear and now I can't find my sword without it!' He screeched the last words and the men waiting around the gates started shuffling nervously. Thisian felt very uncomfortable watching the strange man, and one of Ugly's men must have felt even worse.

'Ephraim, maybe we should let him go in first, you never know what he'll flaming do.'

'No,' Ephraim growled. 'We will not *let him go first*. I don't care what he'll do, there's fifteen of us! Is he going to kill us all? Well, bastard, are you? Not bloody likely.'

'You can't kill ghosts you fools,' Valhar said absently. He was staring at thin air and the gods only knew what hallucinations held his attention so raptly. Then he pointed straight at Thisian. 'There's one of them now.'

All the men turned to look into the shadowed alley, but neither he nor Krife moved a muscle. There was nothing to see, only darkness. Having turned in the direction though, one thing that was clearer to see, was Griffil slowly climbing down the walls of the estate. The burnt man pointed to him and everyone turned to stare at the thief just as he stopped in mid-climb and stared back at so many people looking right at him.

Krife mumbled a curse and started unclipping the beast of a sword he had strapped to his back. Thisian slowly started scratching the back of his head in solidarity. Should he fight fifteen men with a sabre or should he try to set himself, and maybe something else, on fire to scare them off. It was a tough call since setting himself on fire would only give the archers on the wall a nice well-lit target to aim for.

A loud thump then sounded as the wooden gates of Hrothlar's estate were kicked open to reveal a slightly more presentable group of warriors, headed by one big tall rutter with a mask on his face. Standing head and shoulders above everyone else marked him as Prae'surlas just as much as his bright yellow hair did. Thisian wanted to laugh imagining how ugly a Prae'surlas needed to be before he covered his face with a blue wooden mask. Well he supposed none of it really mattered right at that specific moment in time, since the new arrivals brought the total number of men staring at Griffil on the wall to probably forty. It would be interesting to see what kind of plan Krife would have. The man was the most antagonising, annoying, anger-provoking man in the entire world, so he had to be pretty smart to have survived so long.

Krife charged out of the alley and ran straight for the forty people.

Thisian panicked. What was he supposed to do? Stepping out of the alley, he fidgeted with his hands still not sure whether to use his sabre or try magic. An archer from the wall spotted the commotion and notched an arrow straight for Thisian. What! Why should he be the bloody archer's first target when Krife was the big bastard running with a sword? Either way it answered Thisian's dilemma and he threw his hand up at the archer violently, hoping some magic might happen.

Unbelievably a flash of fire appeared in front of the archer's face, knocking him clean off the wall. Smiling in triumph, Thisian looked around to see if anyone saw that but all he could see was Krife swing his sword into forty men and cut down what looked like half. Round and round he spun, the speed and size of the attack too much for anyone to really do anything other than get out of the way - apart from those who got batted aside with large chunks of their body missing.

Griffil arrived next to Thisian then, watching with distress as Krife spun deeper into the crowd of men. 'Thisian! Create a distraction.'

'What? What do you mean a distraction?'

'Magic, Thisian! Use some magic so Krife can get out of there.'

Thisian's mouth hung open, unsure of how to explain that he didn't really know any. Krife's fearsome swings did not lessen in their intensity but the men were staying further and further back from him now, waiting for the moment to close in. More archers were running along the walls to take aim. Thisian wondered did he really like Krife that much? He was not sure.

'Frehep's bloody balls, fine!' Thisian shot his hands up at the archers first and amazingly more fire blasts appeared in front of them. They were only small bursts, but it was enough to startle them, making some drop their bows or fall off the wall. *Take that, archer bastards!*

Turning to the ground thugs next, Thisian's first target would be Valhar and his bloody Jaguar blade. He looked around for him but the feared assassin was gone, and so instead Thisian shot his hands out to the edge of the group, not wanting to get Krife. More small blasts of fire appeared at his command and the shouts from the men they hit were enough to distract others. Krife did not have to be told when it was time to leave and he turned heel and ran without delay. The group of men followed just as quickly, but with Krife out of the way, Thisian was free to make more blasts of fire appear in front of all of them. But as he created more and more, Thisian started to feel the scars in his chest hurt, and suddenly decided he had done enough magic. Some of the men had been hit right in the face, hopefully blinding them, and others had even caught fire on their clothes. There were a lot still standing but he had done his job, now it was time to run for their lives.

Krife nearly trampled Thisian as he barged past, and looking to his side Thisian cursed that Griffil had already fled too. So turning his back on the host of angry men, possibly with archers among them, and one Prae'surlas so ugly he had to cover his face with a mask, Thisian ran as fast as any Powerborn had ever run. He spotted Krife's bulk up ahead before it disappeared between buildings and followed likewise. Sometimes skidding in the snow, Thisian still managed to catch up to the two fleeing thieves and together all three of them weaved and dodged their way between streets and buildings until Thisian was content that they were good and lost. He did not think either of them were skilled enough to have that good a map of the city in their heads, but was impressed that neither had broken their necks slipping on ice. After a time they did stop, and looked around to confirm to Thisian they indeed had no idea where they were.

'Okay, Fireborn, Eva's barracks are over there,' Krife said, not even seeming out of breath. 'You're the fastest so take the orb to her straight away. Tell her to send the letters with you to our Inn. I'll hand over the segment then so she can do whatever the hell she wants with it, but tell her she has to move fast. Hrothlar knows us and knows where to look for us. In case Eva decides to send her own small army to meet us, then it's your job to know which of her servants is holding those papers. We'll have our packs and horses ready, and once we get those, all that concerns us is getting as far away from this place as we can. Understand?'

Griffil hesitated but did not speak straight away. Thisian was the fastest yes, but in no way the most reliable. The orb was made of glass, what if he dropped it? Instead of raising those concerns, Griffil just took out the orb and placed his palm on top. It began to glow light blue in colour.

'What are you doing?' Thisian asked before turning to Krife, 'And what do you mean all that concerns us? What about the gold?'

'Forget gold, Thisian, we have that. We only got this orb to win back Lady's Eva favour so she doesn't put a bounty on our heads,' Griffil said while staring at the glowing orb. 'And what I'm doing now is using the star marker. I have a friend I've been meaning to free for a while. These marks should be just the way to do it.'

Krife let out a laugh. 'Are you talking about Lae Noan?' Griffil's face stayed serious though as the orb continued to swirl strange clouds in the drifting shades of blue, so Krife answered for him. 'You see, Fireborn, Griffil here, before becoming the companion of the great Krife the Treasure Hunter, he was the special friend of none other than Ithnahn Berenger.'

'The travelling hero?' Thisian asked with delight. He loved stories of Ithnahn. They were not as grand as Amadis, or the older heroes like Brijnok or Moi'dan, but Ithnahn was a modern day hero, who was still alive. He had no army to command or anything like that, but would journey from land to land using his powers to fight evil and bed women. Much the way Thisian intended to use his. If Ithnahn were to join their group of adventurers they would definitely make a Telling out of it within the month.

'The travelling fool,' Krife said back. 'Always sticking his head into places it had no business. He's in the Prae'surlas ice prison now because of that, never to be seen again.'

The colour of the orb changed suddenly from blue to brown, the glass texture crinkling under Griffil's hands, then the thief pulled away one hand and took with it the top layer of the orb that turned out to be paper. The glass sphere still sat in his other hand, and was back to looking dull and inactive. Griffil was extremely pleased with the crinkled piece of brown paper though.

'No one has ever escaped Lae Noan, Griffil,' Krife reminded him.

'How can it not work?' the thief said back. 'We Spike in, free Ithnahn, and Spike out. If there are any Iceborn there they won't have time to do anything.'

'Then why hasn't it been done before?'

'Because people are lazy and stupid, Krife. Maybe it has been done but the Prae'surlas need to protect their reputation and no word has spread. If I was the one who escaped I wouldn't tell anyone and risk being put back.' He pushed the orb at Thisian. 'Here, take this before Hrothlar's men find us.'

Thisian took it and wondered why no colours began swirling for him. Did he need to think of a place? If he became the only one to free someone from Lae Noan, then he would definitely tell everyone. What would be the point in doing it otherwise?

'Don't you need the star markings to get back from Lae Noan?' he asked.

Griffil shook his head. 'Everyone should know the marks for this city, mainly because you don't need them. Amidon is the central line of marks on every Spike, because some people believe it's located at the centre of the world. Could be why Amadis created the city here.'

He was not sure how much to believe that, but Krife and Griffil were turned and leaving. Thisian watched them break into a run and go down separate routes without even discussing it. The plan was all well and good apart from the fact that Thisian was now the one all the crime lord's men would be looking for. It would have been simpler to just have all gone together, unless they were testing if Eva would kill Thisian once she got the orb. *Bastards.*

Trying to look over the buildings where Krife had pointed, Thisian sighed. He couldn't see anything. That meant blindly trusting in Krife. But with little other choice, Thisian set out. He broke into a careful run, trying to simultaneously look around at the night shadows as well as down at the snow and ice underfoot. Also while running he was very conscious of the smooth sphere of glass he was trying to hold. The glass was not the best kind of surface to get a grip on while bouncing around at a run and Thisian had a strange feeling that he was definitely going to drop and smash the thing. Wrapping it in the ends of his cloak, and then wedging it under his arm, Thisian felt no better about his odds, but at least it would be his cloak's fault if it fell now.

With fortune it was not long before the giant structure of the Amadis Arena came into view. Despite the darkness, there were enough street lamps to give his eyes light, and the shadows in the distance could even be recognised as the palace. He said a dutiful thanks to Di Thorel, but then Thisian wondered why there were not more wild fires with such a disastrous combination of thugs and street lamps in the city. Perhaps the Foreigners that lived in the city were not as brainless as he assumed. It was a pity the fires burning in the lamps were not enough to melt some of the snow. It would take burning the entire city to the ground to get rid of all of that much snow. Thisian was suddenly proud of himself for the thought, because it was very much a Fureath'i one.

As the warrior priest of Di Thorel, Thisian felt much more Fureath'i than ever. Maybe if he announced himself as a priest when he got to the Shakara barracks then his order would grow. The barracks walls came into view, and the palaces inside got clearer the closer he got. Looking at the guards on the main gates, Thisian tried to remember the ones who had known Krife. The man with the fluffy white moustache was not there and the others all looked too similar to distinguish. Surely one of them would remember letting a Fureath'i in earlier. It was likely after all that no Fureath'i ever ventured into the city, and his golden skin and godly looks could not help but strike notice.

The closer he got, the more confident he became, delighted that he might even have a private audience with the Lady Eva herself. He waved in friendly greeting at the guards, palm empty and facing

out in Fureath'i fashion. The soldiers all drew their swords in
friendly reply.

'State your business, Fureath'i!'

'I am here,' he started before faltering over how to say it. On
more thinking, perhaps he was not the best person to send. Not
until his king's tongue was a bit better in any case. He started again,
'I am here, I am seeing Lady Eva Yeda.'

'The Lady is busy,' the guard grunted. 'Come back in the
morning.' One of the other guards nudged the one talking and
pointed to what Thisian was holding under his cloak. 'What are you
hiding, Fureath'i?'

Thisian blew air from his mouth. On the plus he was able to
understand what the guards were saying, at least he thought he did,
but he still did not have the right words to explain himself. Should
he show them the orb? Or just remind them about Krife. The last
time he mentioned Krife's name to a Foreigner he got slapped
across the face. Maybe the word was a curse in king's tongue.

'Krife,' he started and the men all drew themselves up in anger.
Yes, definitely some kind of curse word. 'Krife, Griffil, me, we all
seeing Eva before. I like seeing her again.' Archers appeared on the
walls to see who was seeking entry at the late hour. Always bloody
archers!

'You go get Krife, Fureath'i, tell him we want a word with him.
No one calls the Lady of Amidon City a whore and lives. Not while
there are Shakara here to kill him. You tell him that Fureath'i and
you come back.'

Did he have enough king's tongue to explain that he did not
really call her a whore, only implied it? Thisian did not think so and
figured that even mentioning the word whore to the men would
only get him shot. The scars from his old wound still throbbed at
the thought and the earlier display of amazing power did not help
matters. He briefly played with the idea of fighting his way through
with more fire magic. The idea was cast aside and Thisian left. What
was he supposed to do now?

In the Tellings and legends the hero never had a problem with
speaking the right language. He never had to turn around and go
back to his friends saying he was not allowed in. Even if he did go
get Krife and Griffil, the guards seemed angry enough to not leave

them in regardless. If he was a hero in a Telling, he would sneak into the palace anyway. He would scale the walls and find a way into the Lady Eva's private bed chambers. She might even be so pleased and surprised that she would use her wide-open, aghast-mouth to suck his cock there and then. Thisian could add a Lady to his list of rank and station since he already had a squad leader, so if he could add a Lady then all that was left was ember, blaze commander, general and queen. Eva could count for Queen too if he thought about it hard enough, Phira-bloody-almighty would have to count for all the rest. She would be general and King sooner or later anyway.

His plan of action solved, to marry Eva and rut Phira, Thisian circled around some buildings to see what the walls looked like away from the guard house. Even at night they looked like he thought they would, they looked bloody big. With a sigh he took off his cloak and wrapped the orb a bit better. Then he deftly tied it in a line around his chest with the orb in front. At least that way if it fell while he climbed, he could see it fall and not get surprised by a sudden smash on the ground below him. Stretching out his cold fingers, Thisian reminded himself that he had hand-climbed walls dozens of time while training in Rath'Nor. Fureath'i swarming over city walls was an image any Foreign city shuddered to think about because once the magic was countered in Surlas cities, that was exactly what happened. Tens of thousands of Fureath'i climbed up and in, and once they got in, bloody mayhem.

Wondering if he was going to have to cut hand and toe holds with his sabre every step of the way, Thisian gave another prayer of thanks to Di Thorel for the barracks walls being old and poor. To be fair, why would anyone want to sneak into a barracks full of soldiers anyway? But still it seemed since he had pledged his worship to Di Thorel, Thisian's fortune had never been better. Forgetting idle wonder, Thisian committed himself to the climb. New strength in his arms made it easier at first, but having to keep a close eye on the bloody orb of fragile glass wrapped in his cloak, quickly made it hard. Lightning flashed overhead, thunder sounding soon after and the last thing Thisian wanted was for it to start raining on him. It would more than likely be sleet or hail judging by the cold, but he did not think thunder and snow could happen together. Could they?

Not caring too much about whatever Am'bril wanted to do with the weather while she was in the mood she was, Thisian reassured himself that he did not need the heat of Furea anymore. He had that heat inside his flesh now and could create it at will. Let Aerune, Am'bril, Creedus and every other Foreign god of weather do whatever they bloody well pleased, as long as it did not start raining. Slipping and falling might not kill him, but it would certainly stop him from bothering to try climbing it anymore.

Keeping an eye and ear for archers, Thisian got closer to the top. There were no sounds of boots or talking that he could hear, and no sight of archers further down the walls. But that did not mean that some bastard was not sitting and waiting for him to climb all the way up just so he could shoot Thisian off at the very top. He could picture the man now, crouching down, trying to hold back his laughter, imagining how funny it would be when the thieving Fureath'i got all the way to the top and then got shot right through the face with an arrow. Would that kill him? Thisian did not think it would kill a Powerborn before he became one, but he was not anxious to find out. Taking one last breath he launched himself over the top of the wall and crouched down behind the ramparts. There was no one waiting for him.

Slipping over the edge in a flash, letting himself fall to the ground below, Thisian closed his eyes in preparation for the impact. Once his feet touched the ground, he rolled on instinct, but turned his shoulder to protect the orb strapped to his chest. Coming all the way over and landing one hand out to stop himself, Thisian waited for all the pain to arrive. The sprained ankles, the twisted wrist, the jarred shoulder and bruised ribs, they were all about to hit him and Thisian clenched his teeth waiting. Why did he slide off the ramparts so quickly without thinking? The pounding in his head - that an army was marching on top of him - still hurt but after some time Thisian cautiously stood up. There was no other pain.

He patted his limbs to double check but he also wanted to shout out in delight to Di Thorel how being a Powerborn just kept getting better. He thought injuries would still be there but that he would heal them quickly. It turned out instead that his flesh was just that bit too strong now and his reflexes that bit too agile. Taking off into the shadows, Thisian's next stop was Eva's private bed chambers to show what else a Powerborn's stamina could do. He imagined she had bright pink nipples and vivid blonde hair between her legs, and his balls began to hurt again to remind him that he was all whored-out from earlier.

No, he reassured himself, *I am a lord of power and there are no limits to my whoring.*

His strength returning, Thisian started creeping around the courtyards but the mixture of army barracks and decorative palace was confusing. Not that he would have known his way around anyway, but it was good to have an excuse. He could see the main gates alright, and wondered if he should just try to follow his previous path to Eva's main audience chamber and find his way into her bed chambers from there. It was the only plan he had so Thisian made his way over to the gates but not so close that any guards might see him. Trying to remember which way they had been led the last time, Thisian picked a likely door and crept inside. The corridor was painfully bright and clear of anything to hide behind so Thisian just lifted his chin confidently and marched his way down. There were no Shakara soldiers yet, but if he did find any he would just say that the guards at the gate left him in and that he was to see Lady Eva immediately. It was not a bad plan, unless the bald headed Brenit was waiting at her doors again. There was something about the crazy look in his beady little eyes that told him Brenit would not listen.

But what else could he do except keep walking? There were still no soldiers about anyway. Maybe the late hour kept them away. The corridor he was following split into two then and Thisian scratched the back of his head to remember which one the fluffy moustached man had taken them down. Relying on his god friend Di Thorel to steer him right, Thisian went left. He kept his confidence up as he marched down the open corridor and reassured himself that fortune favoured the handsome. When another split came in the corridor, Thisian was about to curse his useless god when he recognised the large double doors down to one side. And even better than there being no Brenit, there were no guards at all. It was suspicious, and so squinting to see closer, Thisian thought he could make out that the doors were slightly ajar.

Creeping quickly down the corridor, Thisian could confirm the doors were indeed open. When he got to them he was even able to peek inside and see the reason. The guards that must have been standing at the doors were all inside the audience chamber, with their backs to Thisian, staring at five Prae'surlas standing in front of Eva's throne. Everyone in the room had their swords drawn, including Brenit who had chosen his over-long sword that looked more like a whip than a blade. Did the Prae'surlas barge their way into the hall? How did they get past the gates outside? They hardly just appeared, unless they used a Spike. Did the Prae'surlas use Spikes? Thisian had no idea but it would explain why everyone in the room was so angry. Either that or the Prae'surlas had just called Eva a whore.

Not liking his back to the corridor behind, Thisian risked sneaking through the doors and crouched down behind a small statue just inside. It was another one of Amadis, but just a block with his face on it. The two giant statues that dominated the room must not have been enough to keep the man happy. Everyone's attention was on the five Prae'surlas so Thisian felt his entrance had not been noticed. Somehow he did not feel like announcing his presence just yet either. Once everyone had put away their swords maybe, and more importantly their crossbows, then he would approach Eva. It might be best to wait for the Prae'surlas to leave too. He at least could understand perfectly what the filthy north-men were saying, sticking to their native tongue. The Lady Eva appeared just as well versed in the northern language.

'Tell me why I should not kill you for arriving in such a way,' she said coldly in Prae'surlas.

Of the five north-men, Thisian noticed one of them was wearing a bloody Powerborn tunic. The blue and white one was for Frostborn he was sure, but Frostborn could not use a Spike, so how did they get there?

'Daughter of Amadis, in killing us we would only breathe further glory to our god. We have come with his word and he offers you mercy.'

'Does he.'

'He does, daughter of Amadis. The great Aerath is creating a new age for this world, a glorious one of ice and it will be the age of the Prae'surlas. Lesser nations are being offered this mercy to submit willingly to his rule. Not all of your people will be spared, but some may be of use. The weak and the unworthy will all die when the ice comes, but you are being allowed to select some to save, so that they may serve us.'

'He would have me bow down and worship him as my god?'

'All will bow down and worship him as the only god. All others will die. Only the Prae'surlas will survive under Aerath's power. He would have me return your answer, daughter of Amadis.'

'Would he,' Eva said with the same cold look she always gave. The beauty of it of course warmed both Thisian's heart and his loins, but he could see how others might find it foreboding. 'Tell me, Frostborn, how do you feel that he makes you address a woman? How does it feel knowing that this woman could kill you right now?'

'It does not matter how beneath a man you are, I carry out my god's will without waver.'

'So Aerath is behind the unnatural cold and plans to turn the entire world to ice. He would need a lot of Chuabhotari farm workers to feed his people if this were the case. Are you telling me that he does not wish to negotiate a treaty for my slave contracts, that he simply demands I kneel down to his arrogance? Tell him to come to me in person or tell him that his beloved Prae'surlas will starve under his godly rule.'

The Frostborn turned around and placed a small piece of ice on the ground between the four fleshborns that were with him. He did it slowly and carefully, before standing back up to face Eva. 'You speak of arrogance and yet you show more than even your father had. Our lord Aerath will take what he must from the Ihnhaarat for slaves. He needs nothing from you. So is this your answer, daughter of Amadis? That you have not the sense to accept our lord's mercy even though you are undeserving to receive it?'

'You have heard my answer, Frostborn. I will not repeat myself to you. I will speak directly to Aerath.'

The Frostborn smiled at her words. 'You will have your wish, *woman*.' He said the word like it was an insult and turned around to place his hand on the small piece of ice he had placed on the floor. 'Those that are unwilling to accept our mercy shall be given our -'

Eva held out a hand and the Frostborn stopped in mid-sentence. With her other hand she waved a finger at Brenit and the shaven-headed warrior lashed out his long sword whipping the head clean off the Frostborn. The other four Prae'surlas did not move and Eva still held her hand out in front of her. Thisian wondered what the hell sort of powers she had, to hold five men still, while he also wondered how quickly he should turn and run, after seeing how fast Brenit had just beheaded a Powerborn. The bloody thin sword did lash out as if it was a whip but even a whip would not remove a head like that. The hand Eva held in front of her suddenly clenched to a fist and the four remaining Prae'surlas dropped to the floor. There were five Prae'surlas dead, one of them a Frostborn and all faster than Thisian could utter a curse. By Frehep's flaming balls, it was time to bloody go.

Something caught his eye then, as a flash of blue light came from the middle of the dead bodies. It was the piece of ice the Frostborn had placed and as it flashed out brighter Eva lifted a hand again but it did not stop the light. The image of a man came to life from the flash of blue, and it looked like a faded picture made of frost. Eva's fist clenched at the image but nothing seemed to happen. Instead the image spoke, his voice crackling like if the ice itself were talking.

'If you are looking upon me now then you have doomed your people with your pride. Where once you may have been a use to our new age, now you will never see it. May your deaths show others the folly of your ways, kneel and weep before your god.'

A ball of blue light starting forming in front of the image, and Thisian could see it shine clearly through the ice of the man who had spoken. The sphere grew bigger and bigger, and began pulsing from blue to white and back again. Eva lifted her hand to unclip the robe that draped back behind her throne. When she stood up without it Thisian saw she was dressed like Phira would be: a blouse and tight leggings, with a sword wrapped around her waist. It was hard not to admire her figure, even though Thisian knew something bad was about to happen as the pulsing ice magic grew faster and faster. Eva did not look panicked though. She calmly stepped down from her throne and drew her sword.

The blade was white all over, with something that looked like black circles by the handle. Thisian did not have time to examine it further though as the growing ball of magic flashed out violently and Eva stabbed her sword straight into the heart of it. All traces of power and light vanished into the sword, the thin figure of ice disappearing also.

The audience chamber went silent, looking completely empty with that sudden burst of light gone, despite it being filled with anxious soldiers all around and dead bodies at its centre. Those dead bodies had now become the same ice the image had been. They were now hollow statues of blue crystal and when Eva slid her sword back into its sheath, all five shattered to pieces. She repositioned herself back upon her throne.

'Have the ice destroyed and send word that my men are to report any Prae'surlas they see. Summon Frind'aal from the Arena and have him attend me at once.'

Two guards with their backs to Thisian moved to obey, going to the ice and sweeping it into the decorative pool at the bottom of the throne. All of the fragments were pure blue without any red of frozen blood or flesh. What kind of magic did Eva possess that she could turn Prae'surlas to ice? Or had it been whatever magic the picture of the Iceborn was creating? A figure rushed past Thisian's position then, sounding out of breath, and spoke, apologising for his sudden intrusion.

'M'lady, forgive me, I have ill news.' It was the man with the fluffy white moustache from earlier.

'Speak, Macire, it can hardly be more ill than an impending war between my city and Surlas.'

The man Macire ran his hand over his long moustache before answering. 'I fear it may be worse. It seems the Ihnhaarat have come for war with our city also. More than a hundred are reported seen approaching the eastern gates. The ones we have captured insist we have stolen a herd of Chuabhotari slaves from them and they have come for retribution.'

'So we have hosts of both Ihnhaarat and Fureath'i bearing down on our city in one night, with a war against Surlas soon to follow. If this is not the curse of destruction Krife has brought to us, then we have simply run afoul of every god's favour instead.'

'I have word of the treasure hunter also, m'lady, the word is out that he attacked Wolfram and Ephraim's men outside Hrothlar's estate, before attacking the crime lord with a Fureath'i Fireborn. Everyone under Hrothlar's and Ephraim's command are out in force now, searching the city for them, murdering anyone that gets in their way.'

'Very well, Brenit take as many soldiers as you wish and find those three imbeciles,' Thisian thought that might have been a good time to announce his presence but Eva's next words changed that. 'Kill them and send their heads to Hrothlar and the brothers. Maybe that will stop some of the violence in the city tonight. Krife signed his own death when he threatened my city, but bring back the heavensphere intact and he will have a piece of rock with him also. I want you to shove it down the throat of a corpse of Protharik and sent the thing out towards the Fureath'i host, let them deal with its curse.' She turned to the men lining her walls.

'Form a squad and start evacuating citizens from the surrounding buildings. They can take sanctuary here but it will mean enlistment to the Shakara army in return for the safety of their families. Explain to them the circumstances they will be facing if they do not, including the coming war with Surlas.' She pointed to the next officer. 'Form another squad and direct a herd of slaves as best as you can towards the Ihnhaarat. It will slow them down if nothing else, but if they are not satisfied by it then do your best to lure them towards the Fureath'i host.' Both officers saluted and left immediately. Eva was not finished and turned to Macire.

'I want a squad to go out with specific orders to find that Fureath'i, Blaze Commander Phira the Unrivalled. If we have the orb to give to her well and good, if not she will have to do what she can to stop the Fureath'i host regardless. I will give her little choice on the matter. Find her quickly because I intend to release Brute from the Arena and command him to kill all Ihnhaarat and kill all Fureath'i. A Jhakral rampaging through the city is not something I would normally allow but if it will distract the Powerborn from destroying my city then let it be so. If Fia Kasia and Lyanti are in the city then I want them sent to me also. They will be able to help stop the blaze if the Fureath'i do decide to burn the city to the ground. There are too many people looking to threaten my city tonight and every one of them will pay, even if I need to go out and kill them all myself.'

Phira-bloody-almighty is here? Could things get any rutting worse! Thisian decided that it was not the right time to approach his future wife Eva. Instead he turned and he ran, hoping that no-one spotted him. He sprinted as quickly as his power fuelled legs would carry him and did not stop when he managed to get outside. It was time to go back to Krife and Griffil and warn them about everything that was about to happen. Cursing his bastard of a new god, Thisian decided that it was not a good night to be a Fureath'i in Amidon City.

· CHAPTER FORTY TWO ·

Killing

It had taken Phira and Lei some time before they found anyone willing to give them directions to the Dancing Whore. Most had turned and ran at the sight of them, which turned Phira's mood worse, which in turn made her look even less inviting to friendly conversation. She was growing more tempted to take out her sword and demand the information that way, but it would not be fitting. The people ran because Fureath'i had the misguided reputation for being violent savages, so trying to get the information using savage violence would only have been further damaging.

They found the Brother in Flames Inn easily enough and left their mounts there, but had then set straight out into the night. She wanted every minute she had to secure those Spike markings, and once she had them Phira intended to use them immediately. She would let Lei look after their horses and link back with the squads. That was of course if Valhar had not killed them all. The madman still made her look at every shadow as if it would suddenly become a blur of speed or a knife in the dark.

Steering back to her main focus, she had to solve two problems. She first needed to find the Flameborn, and then depending on who it was, Phira would send them or Lei towards the oncoming Fireborn host. First predictions would make it Lord Kr'une, known as Kr'une the Ranger, who travelled outside of Furea frequently to remind raiders of the power the Fureath'i nation possessed. But the Lady Eva had bluntly told her that Kr'une was one of four Fureath'i Powerborn recently murdered, along with Chrial'thau, Miral'thau and Jaiha. The world was always changing but could it change so much in a few days?

If Kr'une was dead or if the Flameborn turned out to be a hoax, or worse, then Phira still planned on returning to Rath'Nor first, delivering her message and then coming back to Amidon with orders from the King to stop the destruction of Lady Eva's beloved city. Of course the timing would have to be precise and several factors would need to align correctly. First the Fireborn host would need to be at least a day's march away, and for Fireborn that would have to be a considerable distance. Secondly, she would need to get the Spike markings sooner than first light, and then it would take time to explain the seriousness of Aerath's ritual and the need for action, followed by a less heartfelt plea for sparing Amidon City.

To be direct about it, Phira did not think it was likely she would succeed in all areas of the plan, and if she failed in her attempt to stop the destruction, then she would not give it a second thought. There were advantages to forging a strong alliance with someone as influential as Lady Eva, but Phira would be satisfied that her primary mission was complete.

One other alternative was of course that the host of Fureath'i Powerborn reached the city before Eva could give her the star markings. In that instance Phira would try to convince them to accompany her back into Surlas immediately to kill Aerath. Without a direct order from the King that might be difficult but Phira would try none the less. Using the star markings and Spike to return to Rath'Nor to get such a decree from the King was still the best option though.

Looking up to the sky, Phira noticed the storm clouds rolling above her, but gone was the biting wind that she had been accustomed to over the last days of travel. Snow and ice still sullied the ground and buildings, but with fortune she would be surrounded by heated stone and burning sand soon enough.

'Your king's tongue is a little fierce, blaze commander, if I may say so,' Lei offered, thinking of how she had finally gotten the directions she wanted. She had not threatened the man, but she had strongly implied that he had no other options in his future than to answer her.

'I could make Kel Sheran sound fierce if my mood was sour enough, Lei.'

'I do not think a Jhakral could make the Kel Sheran language sound fierce, blaze commander. It is full of weak sounds and limp meanings, like the people who speak it. Yet I believe it when you say *you* could.'

Phira said nothing. Was the man saying she sounded worse than a Jhakral? She did not exactly share Lei's opinions on the Kel Sherans either, since Yiran had influenced her in that regard. He had considered one, a man named Dagen, his close friend. The Defenders were admirable warriors, if not fool-hearted for fighting without weapons, but then again it was said that no weapon could kill a Jhakral, so maybe they had the right of it. A guild of warrior fools in a nation of genius scholars. Yiran said they fought with rope and nets, to bind and tangle the large beasts, and when bound simply drowned them. She had to admit it was a simple solution to a serious problem of trying to kill a thing that could not be hurt. The only problem of course was: what if there was no water around?

A hand appeared out of the darkness and grabbed Lei's shoulder. Phira's blade was out of its scabbard before she even heard the words whispered, 'Thisian?'

Lei adeptly seized control of the shadow attacker as soon as the hand shot out too and wrenched his arm around to hold him immobile. It was a slender youth, with curling brown hair, and a small beard around his mouth. Once he was caught he did not try to struggle free.

'You search for a Fureath'i named Thisian?' Phira asked the man in her fierce sounding king's tongue. Then she was shocked when the youth responded in passable Fureath'i.

'Apologies. I simply thought you were someone I know. Please there is no need for any violence. May the sun god see you both killing Prae'surlas instead.' He even turned the empty palm of his free hand.

'You speak Fureath'i well for a Foreigner,' she said with consideration. 'But there is always a need for violence. What is your name? How is it you know a Fureath'i named Thisian?'

'My name is Griffil. And I shared cups with Thisian once, when I journeyed to a border fort for trade.'

Phira nodded for Lei to release the man, and he slowly stood straight working his shoulder. The slender man eyed her drawn sword, resting peacefully by his neck, and looked around furtively as if to bolt.

A roar sounded from the distance and froze everyone to the spot. It was the hostile scream of a beast, and loud enough to belong to something very large, yet still far away. Griffil looked at her and offered his opinion, unwanted. 'It sounds like Brute,' he said amiably, no doubt trying to get her to put her sword away. 'The Jhakral that belongs to the Arena. Have you ever been to the Amadis Arena?'

'It sounds like he wishes to break free from there,' Phira said while waiting to see if more would follow. Instead what followed were a group of men running down the street. For a moment Phira thought they might be running from the Jhakral, that it had indeed broken loose, but then when Griffil suddenly disappeared before she could catch him, she began to think otherwise.

The approaching group had weapons out ready and the two leading them looked so much alike as to be brothers. Their eyes had noticed the youth's quick departure but then focused on Phira and Lei. She wondered if they were going to slow down or if they would simply march straight into the end of her blade. One of the brothers put his sword in front of the other though to bring him to a stop. The few men behind him skidded to a halt too, and did not seem happy to be standing still.

'The sun god sees you warriors,' Phira offered the Fureath'i greeting in king's tongue. She did not raise her palm and instead tilted her blade.

She could see one of the brothers had very bad burn scarring, but it was the other, whose face looked badly beaten, that frowned with a sneer of amusement as he spoke. 'Do you hear this yellow bitch? The sun sees us? It's flaming night you dog-brained whore.'

Lei drew out his sword at the words, but Phira did not feel insulted by the remarks. She only felt irritated that she would have to waste her time killing these men if they did not leave.

'The greeting is to say that you are seen for whatever it is you have made yourself to be,' Phira explained pointlessly. 'It is up to the receiver to take pride or shame from the judgement, whether or not they have made themselves better in any way. I will offer you one chance to leave here and become better men.'

Predictably, the brother who had talked was not content to leave it at that. 'Wolfram, my brother, it was a yellow little Fureath'i who burnt your lovely face now wasn't it? Do you think it made *you* a better man?'

The burnt man named Wolfram just smiled disgustingly. His brother joined him and showed a mouth full of fangs. The name might have been common, but she knew of the two brothers named Wolfram the Fire and Ephraim the Beast. They were strong and they were brutal, and they were supposed to be impossible to kill, shrugging off any number of wounds that would have slain someone else.

'Well then,' Ephraim continued, 'we can't have you bettering my poor disfigured brother without a chance to do the same to you, now can we?' His leering eyes drank in her body. His fanged smile made her want to grimace. 'I know of a lot of things we can do to make *you* better, bitch. I've never had me a Fureath'i before.'

It seemed they had made their choice so Phira was done with talking. She stepped forward before he had finished his last word and her first strike knocked the sword clean out of his unsuspecting hands. The coward then had the reaction to grab for the man next to him and throw him forward into Phira's following thrust. Lei engaged the other brother, Wolfram, but did not possess Phira's speed or skill and so became entwined in a fight. Then everyone else did too. With one man dead, Phira spun and ducked beneath a sword to stab a second man. She was probably the only one there not interesting in fighting this night; she was only interested in killing.

Ephraim had taken a sword from one of his colleagues, but instead of coming back for her, he circled around to help his brother attack Lei. Her ember was doing well against the stronger opponent even with one or two others trying to distract him. Wolfram's sword was much thicker and heavier that the Fureath'i sabre, but Lei was managing to keep it rolling away with speed and skill, giving anyone else that got near small cuts to keep them back. Phira thought to move in but was made to kill a different man that hacked down at her. All she needed was to sway to the side and she had her choosing of where to stick her sword. He died with a short scream.

The two brothers were on Lei now and Phira darted over before they killed him. Wolfram had the sense to turn his attention to her, but Ephraim was still focused on Lei. She could not risk Lei dying, so was forced to glide around the silent brother Wolfram and slash a small wound onto the arm of the louder Ephraim. He spat and cursed at her, but Lei was experienced enough to move away and let her take the two of them unhindered. Her ember would take care of the remaining men, only three left and who were now standing off in fear of engagement. Both of the brothers were very strong, and had enough skill that they would have killed Lei had he stayed.

The same was not true of their chances against Phira. They fought in unison to their credit, and used full advantage of their greater strength and size, but Phira was too fast. Their over-powered swings became a hindrance as she moved just out of reach and threw them off balance. She was still unable to strike or wound yet, since the other brother would always be on top of her before she took advantage of frustrating one. The large broad swords swung down or across, and Phira deflected and dodged gracefully. Great roars accompanied Ephraim's attacks, often giving prior warning, but the scarred brother Wolfram fought with grim silence. His movements were smarter, and he held back once he saw Phira was making them step off balance. Ephraim only used his frustration to swing harder and stronger and go further off his balance.

Using that, she began moving so that she was making the loud fool step between her and his brother as often as she could, despite Wolfram's best efforts of trying to double behind. It was only a matter of time before she frustrated the beast-toothed warrior into doing something rash, and just as she knew he would, Ephraim lunged forward with a mighty jump. It covered more distance that she expected and might even have caught another fighter, but with Phira she only shifted to the left - as Ephraim's sword hammered down hard into the dirt - and she slipped her slender blade between his ribs. Without looking she withdrew and thrust the blade into the stomach of Wolfram coming to his aid, and narrowly avoided his sword hacking off her shoulder. Despite the mortal wound, the fire-scarred man tried to lift his weapon again for one last swing but Phira twisted her blade and the man's fingers flew open in spasm, dropping the weapon.

Withdrawing, Phira made quick slices along both brothers' throats. If they went on to survive that, she would be impressed. The Beast and the Fire were not Powerborn though, they were just two more dead lumps of flesh littering the streets of Amidon City. Phira turned to see that Lei had killed one of the remaining men, but that the others must have run off since their bodies were absent. Her ember was smiling at her.

'I sometimes forget,' he said.

Phira raised an eyebrow in question.

'Your sword, blaze commander, even though we all live in constant pride of it I sometimes forget how fast it can be. It is astounding to behold.'

She grinned back at him, but turned quickly as one of the men Lei had chased off seemed to be returning. It was only a shadowed figure of the man so far, but he walked well with a fighter's grace, and even called out to them with one hand in the air, palm turned out in Fureath'i fashion. Phira thought the man might be Valhar, until she heard his voice.

'The sun god sees you, Fureath'i,' he shouted. 'I wish you no harm.'

Phira laughed at his overconfidence. 'Then I suggest the sun god see you turn around and perhaps no harm will come to you.'

'What is your name?' the man said, ignoring her fair warning. As he got closer she took note of his strange garb. He was dressed for battle certainly, but in clothes she had never seen. Weapons of every kind were secreted somewhere, so many that they should impede the cat-like walk he was demonstrating. A demon's face attached to his belt made Phira wonder if this was Protharik, but he had not the white hair for it. As more and more light came upon him, she saw his face and a single scar that went from his mouth to his ear and back through his hair, turning it white. It looked a mighty blow to leave a wound like that, and one not easily survived.

'I am Blaze Commander Phira, the Unrivalled,' she answered. 'And you?'

The scar made him look like he was always grinning, but his skin pulled tighter as he smiled fully. 'My name is Brijnok, the god of battle.'

Alarm and scepticism rang with equal weight in Phira, and she could not decide which to pay heed. The man did move like a warrior, but not a god. If he was not skilled, then naming himself Brijnok would invite swift death, and under all the reasoning Phira had a base feeling that she did not experience often: fear. Fear that this man was better than her.

'Fureath'i do not worship Brijnok,' she said testing. 'We have one god and need only one.'

'Ah Frehep, yes,' he said and spread his arms out wide. 'Where is he? Have you ever seen him? The sun god sees you but you never see him. You think he cares for fleshborn? He does not even protect his own Fireborn.'

'He protects Furea from a winter that will kill everyone else. Why are the other gods not doing the same for their realms? Why does mighty Brijnok find time to wander the streets of Amidon City?'

'Furea is small, Blaze Commander Phira. Frehep can focus his stubborn might on one plot of land for as long as he wants before it overwhelms him. The real gods do not give themselves limits over which realms they rule.' Brijnok smiled smugly.

Phira met his smile. 'As I have said, Brijnok has no worshippers in Furea, despite his claims for limitless rule.'

His smile this time seemed genuinely amused rather than smugly confident and he gave a small bow to Phira. If Powerborn were anything to go by, then a god should not bow. 'Forgive me if I have offended. I have not come for battle, if you can believe me. I have come to offer praise. The brothers Wolfram and Ephraim have long been valuable worshippers of mine and have given me many battles.'

'Those two were no soldiers. They have seen no battles.'

'Not all battles are war, my dear Phira. My power comes from violence, whereas your violence is your power. You were magnificent. It makes me wish to treat with Frehep so I may see more of your country men if they are anything like you. But what made me take notice of you in the first place, dear Phira, is a familiar sword that you hold strapped to your back and yet do not use. It does not harm the owner of the blade, only their enemies. I should know after all, I created it for my brother.'

'Valhar is your brother?' Lei asked without thinking and the man calling himself Brijnok just laughed at his stupidity.

Phira did not feel the need to mention that it was said Brijnok killed his brother with such a sword. Betrayed in the last to seize the full power of godhood for his own. 'If you are truly Brijnok, why are you here? Why are you speaking with us? Are the gods so bored that you need to amuse yourself with mortal conversation?'

The man's face darkened. 'Ephraim and Wolfram were mine, and you killed them. Valhar is mine, and you stole his sword from him. If you were not so impressive I would be here to kill you, my dear Phira. As it is, I will instead claim you as mine. You will bring me much power from your blade, even more if you had courage enough to hold The Jaguar. Think of the names that have been linked to it, Amadis, Valhar, yours dear Phira could be the next, could even be the greatest, all you need do is to embrace it.'

'My blade is for Furea, *dear Brijnok,*' Phira said simply and left. It was difficult turning her back on such a dangerous man, one that claimed to be a god, but she had no time to waste with him. She would never be his. She was her own, and no-one else's. That would never change. The truth of it hurt her as she thought of Dallid.

She felt Lei fall in with her as she marched and could even feel Brijnok's gaze burning a hole into her back. She did not care. If he was truly a god then let him kill her, and if he was not a god then let him die trying. Lei threw her uncertain glances, clearly rattled by the meeting, but after all had she not given her men a warning of such a thing days earlier. The wilderness outside Furea was not to be trusted. A peasant in rags could as easily be a god or a Powerborn, or some fool magician trying to be both. Even if that peasant was fleshborn, being Foreign they could still stick a dagger in your back. The more she killed of these Foreigners the better the world would become.

The burning feeling in her back changed then as Brijnok seemed to start following her. Phira did her best to ignore it and wanted Lei to turn around in her stead to judge the threat. While she maintained her confident dismissal of Brijnok, her ember did indeed turn around, his experience ruling over his discomfort at the unfamiliar situation. Lei muttered the word no before grabbing her arm and forcing her to turn also.

While Phira frowned her disapproval at Lei, the ember was already placing himself between her and the approaching Brijnok. It was his duty to do so, but Phira moved him to the side with her sword. Ready to shout challenge to the would-be god, her breath caught short and her teeth clenched down. The man following them was sauntering down the street as if enjoying a summer's day through a meadow and it was not Brijnok.

This man had shoulder length hair that was grey at the sides, and looked lean like he was made out of leather. His eyes were grey but they shined with madness. He looked around and marvelled at invisible beauty that surrounded him. Turning to the two Fureath'i he smiled with warm greeting. 'Isn't this the most beautiful city in the world?'

If Phira ever had any doubt that Valhar was a madman before, then that statement settled it. Of Brijnok there was no sign, and Phira began to wonder if he was in truth the god and Valhar's ability to appear and disappear could be of the battle god's doing. Her sword arm shook with a creeping madness of her own when she saw he held an Ihnhaarat mask in one hand. The bright white of it clashed against the thick black cloaks he was wearing. Had he truly been hiding as an Ihnhaarat in her squad as she suspected, or was it just some crazed taunt to wear the clothes of one of her men that he had killed.

'You got past my squads,' Phira said flatly, already positioning her feet and sword to be ready for the madman's otherworldly speed. She had given Lei his own task should the assassin show up.

Valhar looked confused. 'Did I? The last I remember I killed them all. But my memory has not been the same since I lost my ear. Things have started to fall out. Have you any idea what that sounds like? To have things fall out of your head through an ear that isn't there? Without my ear I can't even hear what that bloody sounds like!'

'It sounds like madness,' Phira said back, pleased that Lei had begun to move behind and away. She needed to risk palming him an object she had been gifted from the vaults of Rath'Nor, and if Valhar was waiting for the perfect time to strike, it was then. Instead he looked crestfallen at the accusation of madness.

'Madness?' He sounded truly scandalised. 'Do you think so? If the ear was attached to part of my brain then maybe you cut out an important part. How am I ever supposed to know now?'

Lei had taken the small object and was slowly backing towards one of the street lamps. Despite the object being made of what looked like ice, it needed fire to work.

'I give you my word, Valhar,' Phira said solemnly. 'You are indeed mad.'

The assassin just blinked rapidly for a moment, either trying to process her statement or becoming undone by his insanity.

'How can I take the word of an indecent Fureath'i, who dresses up like a bloody ghost, who has the indecency to *steal* my favourite sword *and* my favourite ear! And then does not even have enough indecency left to kill *herself* because of it. Even if you did, it would not stop me from killing you!'

Lei returned and Phira was happy that she could now stop stalling the lunatic standing in front. She could feel nothing of what Lei did, but then she did not have any power other than her own flesh. There was a risk that if the enchantment around Valhar belonged to Brijnok, and was not his own, then the Noan candle she had Lei set, might not work. But the madman was currently standing without any visible weapons ready anyway. She would kill him this time.

'Have you heard of a Noan candle, Valhar?'

His face twisted with rage. 'Of course I haven't heard of it, you cut off my bloody ear!'

Phira stepped forward. Safely behind her on the street, guarded by Lei, sat a small lump of what looked like ice but burned as a candle. It had been found in the Temple of Zenith and given to Phira by Lord Miral'thau himself when she began her mission into Surlas. Although she prized her own strength greatly, the candle was welcome as it took away the power of a Frostborn or Iceborn. It made everything into a fair fight. A fight Phira would not lose.

'The Noan candle, uses the same power that the Lae Noan ice prison does. It steals unnatural power and makes everyone fleshborn, free of magic.'

'We aren't in Lae Noan you insane woman! I know it's bloody snowing but this is Amidon City. My vision might've been halved because you cut off my ear, but you have two ears that work perfectly, you should be able to see fine!'

Phira was almost close enough to finish the fight with one swift blow. 'It means, Valhar, that your speed is gone.'

Valhar looked at her then and his grey eyes seemed to shine with understanding. He nodded in acceptance and said, 'I'm still faster that you!' He screamed and reached behind him, pulling free a crossbow that was already coiled. He fired before Phira could attack, and she barely had time to swerve to the side, her sword coming up to deflect the bolt if her dodge failed. Her speed was enough though and the quarrel sped inches past her. Using the same reactive movement her sword swung down towards Valhar who managed to avoid her attack also. It was not the same speed of blurred movements from before, but he appeared still highly skilled. It did not matter to her, he would lose.

Two knives appeared in his hands then and flew forward just as she spotted them. The first she met with her sword. The second was thrown low and she barely managed to move her leg in time. Trying to gain ground once more, Phira saw two more knives appear in Valhar's hands. He would run out of them eventually and Phira would get close enough that they would be ineffectual regardless. Darting forward she feigned to one side before sliding to the other in order to throw off his aim. Valhar looked at her as if she had gone insane, but decided to throw his knives low again towards her stomach and sides. They were both flung wisely, with a distance between them to compensate for her movement, and as a result she did not avoid them both. One grazed her hip giving a shallow cut but she could feel blood begin to pool beneath her clothes.

Sprinting forward now her blade came up to knock away one more knife before hammering down to take the madman's head. He threw himself back in reply and fell to the ground with a roll. Phira hacked down angrily but Valhar was too fast and frustratingly out of reach. He laughed as he rolled away, sounding like he was greatly amused by her attempts. If he continued what he was doing then it would make Phira do something rash and foolish, until she let her guard down in her haste. It was exactly how she had just fought against the two brothers.

Composing herself, Phira made slow careful steps forward. Valhar had no weapons again but that could just be part of his design to enrage her. She held herself ready both to react to him and to attack. He had killed unthinkable numbers of her best men; he needed to be killed in return. His grey eyes glittered as he smiled at her, genuinely looking like he was enjoying himself. His eyes then shifted to something behind Phira, it was a cowardly trick and she would not fall for it.

But when the roar bellowed out, it was all she could do not to jump. Instead Phira half turned and retreated back some steps so she could view Valhar to her left and whatever new creature to her right. What she saw was too much.

A beast twice as large as any Prae'surlas stood panting in rage at the end of the street, and as if to prove the point a Prae'surlas in the garb of an Iceborn stood beside him. At least she though he was Prae'surlas. His hair was not the usual long yellow as most northerners, instead it was cropped short and had a much darker look to it. The description fitted Frind'aal the exiled champion, which made the beast standing next to him Brute the Jhakral of the Arena. Ridges of bone lined the body of the beast that had bulging muscles underneath trying to break free. The slender man she had encountered earlier had been right after all, the beast had been freed.

Both were looking at the Noan candle burning in the middle of the street, almost buried in the snow, but Phira's eyes were focused on her ember Lei, kneeling down beside it, clutching his stomach. She turned back to Valhar with accusation. He quickly nodded and said, 'Alright. I will kill the Jhakral, you kill the Prae'surlas, then we can kill each other, yes?'

Almost paralysed with rage, Phira might not have been able to act if it was not for the Jhakral removing the decision from her. He let out a roar and charged for the Noan candle burning half-way between them. Her feet powered her in the same direction and she had little time to wonder what effect the candle would have on a Jhakral. Would it make its skin soft enough to pierce and sap weakness from its strength? Or would it not have any effect since a Jhakral's power was its flesh and not magic. It was a debate for another time as they both reached the centre at the same instant. As the Jhakral's bulk looked to stamp and shatter whatever was on the street in front of it, Phira had the barest moment to decide whether to save the candle or save Lei.

She dived for the candle but was beaten to it by a gigantic foot stamping down and crushing the thing. The Jhakral followed the act by kicking a smashing blow to Lei's head which sent the injured ember sprawling with a cry. His stomach was soaked with blood and more began flowing from his head where the Jhakral foot had hit. Without the candle Phira would be killed from behind by Valhar or from in front by the Iceborn, never minding the Jhakral, a beast impossible to be killed by a weapon anyway. There were too many impossible enemies to conceive fighting any of them. Phira sliced her sword across the creature's thigh regardless. She would kill them all.

The beast swung for her and she was too fast, sliding away only to cut down on the exact same spot on the Jhakral's leg. The targeted leg kicked out at her and she rolled away, coming up only to duck back down to avoid a fist. She hacked down again on the same spot on the creature's leg. There was no sign it was doing any damage but the Jhakral reached behind its back to take out his own gigantic sword with which to fight. Content that she was at least annoying the thing, Phira risked a quick glance back for Valhar and found him gone.

Doing the same for the Iceborn, she could see no sign, and then had no time for further search as the weight of the massive sword came crashing towards her. She dived away, rounding to her feet and jumping out of distance all at the same time. She did not risk matching swords, as hers would simply be snapped in half. The second sword strapped to her back then began to feel heavy. The Jaguar blade killed anything with one touch, perhaps even a Jhakral. It was the only way she could win and still Phira would not do it. Only part of it was the concern that it would kill her if she touched it, but most of why she would not use the sword was in defiance of Brijnok and Powerborn everywhere. She did not need magic or power to be great.

Another clean slice along the Jhakral's leg sounded like running steel against stone, and the same dance continued. As long as Valhar or the Iceborn Frind'aal did not return, she was grimly determined to wear the creature down. It would have to die by exhaustion if she could not find any other way to kill it. Another duck, a skilful spin and once more she landed a strong chop against the leg of the beast. A mark had begun to appear now, the smallest of indents but it was there.

A groan from Lei made her look to see him try to rise. She could not be certain where his stomach wound had come from but she suspected the bolt from the crossbow had done it. She was a fool not to have noticed, but her concern was in killing Valhar. The Jhakral heard Lei's groan and turned its head. Small eyes twinkled from underneath the thickly boned face, darting from Phira to Lei and a cruel intelligence made the Jhakral go for the injured man.

Phira screamed at the beast's cowardice and chopped viciously down on the same leg she had been working on. In her fury, she did not see the brute arm spin around and make heavy contact with her body. Lifted from her feet and thrown straight through the air, Phira was sent flying over Lei and landed badly, knocking all of the wind from her. She jumped back to a stand just in time see the Jhakral chop its giant sword straight down on Lei. He was killed instantly but the Jhakral did not stop. It swung down again for the midsection and twisted its giant sword sidewise to rip Lei's body in two.

Phira sprinted forward screaming. The Jhakral had a cruel smile on its face when Phira placed her first foot on the flat of his sword. She managed a second foot hold before the sword was moved but she had already sprung upward toward the creature's head. The beginning of a roar and the slightest sign of fear could be seen on the Jhakral's face before Phira plunged her sword deep into the twinkling eye of the beast. The narrow Mordec blade slid straight through until it hit the solid wall of the skull at the back. She fell with the Jhakral, her sword still caught, and jumped free without it.

She stood trembling then, at the monstrous death of her friend, and at the justice delivered to the monster that had done it. There were no tears. It was always something that worried her before, that she could not cry, but such a thing only made her stronger. Yes Lei was dead, but men die. It took only a few moments of shock before she reached down and pulled her narrow blade free. Wiping it clean on the Jhakral's loin cloth, she examined it to see how badly damaged it was from when she was striking the thing's leg. She would need a new sword. Phira wondered if she had time to return and retrieve one from her saddle bags. Looking down to her dead friend, she knew she needed to burn his body too. *Lei is dead...*

'You astound me.'

Phira turned savagely, ready to kill whoever dared to intrude on the scene and did not change her mood when she saw it was the fool who claimed to be Brijnok.

'You will turn your heel and run if you do not want to be killed this very moment.'

Brijnok ignored her words. 'Never has a Jhakral been killed by a sword and you did not even use the Jaguar blade. My dear, Blaze Commander Phira of Furea, I stand humbled.'

'Instead of standing humbled, you will be lying dead if you do not leave,' she repeated, her voice shaking.

'That such a talent has been kept hidden from me, for so many years, makes me furious at Frehep for hiding you so. And your fleshborn frailty makes me despair that you could be killed at any moment by a coward's arrow or a beggar's sickness. It must not be so. You are mine now, Phira, and you will only die by a sword.'

'I am not yours!' she yelled out. 'I am Fureath'i! I am my own!'

Brijnok stepped back, fearing her anguish and spread his arms in peace. 'It is already done, dear Phira,' he nodded behind her and said, 'Look.'

She turned and saw Valhar right in front of her, his crossbow levelled at her head. There was no way she would escape without injury, but she was certain Valhar would die before she did.

'You have no decency,' the madman said, the hurt raw in his voice, his arm shaking with incongruous emotion. 'We agreed. *I* would kill the Jhakral, *you* would kill the Prae'surlas. Isn't that what you Fureath'i spend your lives doing, and still you betray me! Your ghost heart is so cold that I now know you've made all this snow. How *could* you?'

Phira no longer had any energy for his madness. 'Shoot me, Valhar, if that is what you wish but I will no longer listen to your ramblings.'

Valhar stared at her, tears ridiculously glistening in his eyes. Phira wished she could cry for Lei, wished she could prove that she cared about someone other than herself. The emotions were there, her loss, her anguish, the injustice that he had died because of her, but she could not make herself feel them. She was hardening herself to the tasks that needed to be done, she needed to stay alive, and she was ready to move when Valhar did, but the bastard did nothing. *Very well*, she thought fatally, *I will make the first move then.*

A laugh from Brijnok made her turn, it was foolish but she was surrounded by fools tonight. 'He cannot. Do you not see? It is already done, you can only die a sword now, dear Phira. The power I have given you will not allow anything else.'

She looked at Valhar again and saw the struggle he seemed to be going through. Sweat was breaking out on his forehead and Phira did not think there was anything else that could make her more livid.

'I do not want your power,' she said with a growing heat inside her. 'I did not ask for it and I reject it! I am what I am because of my own doing, not by magic given to me and I will not have you take credit for my achievement.'

'It cannot be undone, nor will I try.' Brijnok was moving further and further away, knowing that Phira was about to attack him. Let the god taste his own gift and have him try to kill her with a sword.

'This is madness!' Valhar shouted out. 'How can I kill her with a sword when she has my sword? If she had any decency-'

Phira cut him off short and lashed down with her blade. She was too close and too fast, and even his abnormal speed could not save him. When the sword passed down into his neck, Valhar was suddenly gone. Turning around wildly Phira rounded on Brijnok who still tried to appease with his arms spread out.

'He is mine and I yet have need of him. I will not let you kill him.'

'Valhar will die by my sword and there is nothing you or any other god can do to stop me!' Phira said before deciding she was finished with talk and charged the god of battle. For a moment he just smiled, the scar that pulled up his lip making the gesture grotesque, and when Phira thought he would explode into attack, he too disappeared.

For a time she remained ready, thinking either opponent could reappear at any time. But soon she knew that both were gone. The curse Brijnok had put upon her tried to take up her attention but she was drawn back to the red stained street that was her only company apart from the snow. It was a terrible thing for a Fureath'i to die outside of Furea, even worse for them to die in the snow. *Worse again when the Fureath'i was such a man as Lei.* Phira only felt then how much strength she had taken from him.

There had been the moment, when she could have taken Lei away from the Jhakral. The beast had been focused on the candle and she could have pulled him to the side, and protected him. There was good chance that from such a distance the crossbow wound would not have killed Lei. It could have been healed by a Scholar back in Rath'Nor or with enough rest. But she had chosen the candle as it would have meant her own survival, and the betterment of Furea. It was hard for her to feel that Furea was better now.

Wishing she could fall to her knees in despair, Phira could only stand defeated with her head hung low. It was not possible for her to stand there, in the falling snow of a Foreign city, and weep simply as a woman who had killed her friend. She could not afford to be just a woman, and she could afford no friends. She was Phira the Unrivalled, blaze commander of thousands, and she still had work to do this night.

CHAPTER FORTY THREE

Surprises

The storm began while Phira saw to Lei's body, and it brought with it more sleet and more snow. She could feel her face reddening against its bite, the bruising she had received days earlier still painful when she winced against the cold. She had a new injury on her hip that needed to be ignored now too. Focusing on the task, Phira bundled both halves of Lei's body into his cloak. She needed a place to burn him and continuing her journey to find the Flameborn would achieve just that.

The body of the fallen Jhakral, despite its size, was quickly becoming covered in snow. A drifting thought made her wonder if their rock-like flesh would even rot or if the body would just remain there as a part of the city. She had left enough other bodies on the streets to rot. Putting her sword back into its sheath, Phira crouched down and picked up the bundled remains. Sticky with blood, the cloak leaked the red fluid on her as she stepped forward. If anything she felt like the fresh pouring of blood almost served to clean the Foreign blood and snow that had already stained her.

Muscles tired from fighting began to hurt under the weight of the flesh she carried. Her steps did not slow though and her arms did not lower. A Fureath'i was a fire, and a fire only looked toward the next thing it could burn. The night was not over. Her mission was not completed. She would keep going.

***

Thisian gave up. He was sick of running and he wanted to spend some time sitting instead. He slid down the wall of some building and soaked his breeches in the muck and snow. Ignoring the lack of dignity it provided, it was good to be off his feet. Not only was running tiring but it was dangerous too, often knocking over innocent civilians in his way. The civilians were as innocent as they could be in this city anyway, simply out enjoying the night storm, basking in the deadly cold of a shadowed alley. They could have stabbed and mugged him for all the attention Thisian gave to them. But he held tightly onto the glass sphere tied around his chest and he held onto the idea that he could find the Inn eventually too. He needed to warn Griffil and Krife, and they needed somewhere to hide. A whorehouse would probably do until they left the city. He would suggest it at least.

More than the threat on his life by Eva, someone he still hoped to bed and marry, and the fact Eva said Phira-bloody-almighty was in the city too, Thisian's distraction was amplified by the pressing sensation in his skull that something else was closing in on him. He felt like there were people all around him, but could not see any - apart from the occasional murderer minding their own business in the shadows. A few started to wonder what Thisian was doing sitting down in the snow then, so he cursed and stood up, reluctantly going back to a run.

The sensation in his head flared again and Thisian spun to stare accusingly at an empty snow-damned street. It had started to piss it down in greater quantity, making him spit routinely whenever the floating filth drifted into his mouth. He wondered if there could be such a ritual, if all of the Fureath'i Fireborn combined their powers, to make it snow down fire on top of some Prae'surlas city some time: gentle flakes of crystal fire, one to burn each and every north-man to the bone. Maybe not the women though, he was still unsure whether he needed to bed one of those. The conflict within him was severe.

Thunder cracked again over head, but Thisian had missed the flash of lightning that should have come before it. He had never heard of a thunder storm while it snowed, but then again if someone had tried telling him about it then he would not have listened. The thunder only reminded him of the roar he had heard earlier too. It sounded like a demon beast was loose in the city, so maybe running around blindly as fast as he could was not the best idea after all. He never knew what he would run into. The sensations in his head drew him on though.

The growing pressure brought him right to the end of the current street he waded through, and around a corner near the end.

It was not a demon that he saw. Instead, Thisian was delighted to see a familiar brightness. Someone had clearly gotten as sick of the snow as he was and started burning buildings to melt the white fungus. The feeling within his head must have been his god-like Connection to the fire and it was calling him toward it, to embrace it as a brother. He would much rather be embracing a whore though, even a Prae'surlas one. No, surely not. Could he do it?

Thisian struggled on with unbearable inner turmoil, and found himself wandering towards the flames. That was definitely the feeling that was pressing inside his head, the fire was calling to him. He felt foolish wasting his time just to get closer to it and might have tried to argue that it was completely the wrong direction away from the Inn but he had no real idea where the Inn was anymore. He was just not used to cities. His navigation in a forest or a whorehouse was far more skilful.

The sensations grew intoxicating as he got closer to the raw glory of the burning buildings. He had not yet turned the corner to see how many were aflame but could feel it had to be several. The feelings were getting increasingly overwhelming, and Thisian was feeling very small in power compared to the fires he approached. The thing felt alive, as if it was a creature of purest element and was getting ready to devour the city whole. Would the snow get in its way? Thisian did not know enough about snow to guess for sure, but from the power he was feeling in his mind he did not think anything could stop it.

He turned the corner and saw a scene of both glory and horror. The glory bathed him as the entire street was alight with flames. Never in his life did he think something not female could be so beautiful. But the horror of seeing dozens of other Fureath'i Powerborn on the street completely ruined the moment for Thisian.

It was a battle that he watched, Fireborns and Flameborns were fighting strange animals and a Foreigner with hair as obnoxiously white as the snow. Turns out the roar he had heard was indeed some demonic beast, several of them in fact. The creatures the Fureath'i fought looked like scaled bears, or winged bulls, some with necks as long as serpents, some with as many legs as a spider, each one a monstrosity, twice as large as a man. Raging fires lit up the scene from either side of the street, but the fights often entered into those burning buildings with little hindrance to any of the combatants.

Dead bodies lay about the street, all of them looking like they had the same bright white hair as the single swordsman. The hair went down to his waist, held unbound but perfectly straight, and it was a marvel it did not hinder his fighting. How he fought Fireborn with just a sword was a marvel in itself, and one soon solved as the man became engulfed in flames. His screams were wild but his death was quick. At least that was what Thisian thought.

Blinking to be sure, Thisian stared as the same man now stood over the still burning corpse that he had been. If the Fireborn who killed him was surprised he was still alive, he had no time to express it, as a thing of darkness seemed to jump out of the swordsman's shadow. The beast was black and covered in spikes and horns, with arms almost twice as long as the rest of its body. Vicious talons lashed out at the Fireborn, but then also lashed out at the white-haired warrior. Both dodged the attacks, but if the man was Protharik the Demonborn as Thisian suspected, then why were his own demons attacking him?

He was compelled to watch on, fascinated how each dead Protharik lying on the street still held a sword, and how the lone fighting Protharik held the exact same. But an upsetting thought came to Thisian then, that it had not been the fire he had felt, but the host of Fireborn and other Flameborn. They must have been the crowd of people he felt pressing against his head the closer they got to the city. He could feel each one of them, and those closest even turned to look at him when not immediately engaged in a battle. It was a brotherhood that they could not help but accept him into by power of blood and fire, and the bond and sensations he felt were too strong to ignore. He should run in and join the fight, help bring his brothers to victory, and likely get his head torn off him by a hellborn demon.

Clarity descended on his soul and Thisian knew it was the right thing to do; to turn and run as bloody fast as he could. Looking around to be sure he would not be seen fleeing first, a blue flash caught his attention in the middle of the chaos. The street burned on all sides and Fureath'i Powerborn fought against demonic beasts and a man that could not be killed. Bodies of Protharik and bodies of the demons were scattered around in the snow, and Thisian thought he could even make out the still forms of one or two fallen Flameborns now. But with all of that happening, the one image that held his attention was of a giant Prae'surlas appearing in their midst.

He had long blond hair slicked back over his head and blazing eyes of blue light. He wore a white and silver tunic, and stood in a circle of his own blue ice-fire. Thisian had never seen an Iceborn in real life before, but the fool had somehow appeared in the middle of what looked like forty to fifty Fureath'i Powerborn. Thisian even spotted a lot of red and gold tunics meaning there were a great number of Fireborn there as well as lowly Flameborn. It looked like the same Prae'surlas from the image that had appeared in Eva's throne room, but all those northern bastards looked alike. Either way he had seen his first Iceborn and was now about to see his first Iceborn get blown to pieces from the fire of fifty other Powerborn.

A few of the Fureath'i lords stopped to look in confusion at the new arrival but the demons did not stop and so the chaos had to continue. All the Fireborn at least seemed to recognise the greater threat and tried to leave their current entanglements as best they could, running as one towards the giant Iceborn. The insane Prae'surlas turned his head around slowly to look at everything that was going on, and Thisian ducked his head back behind the building to stop those eyes spotting him. When he peered back from around the corner the same Iceborn was crouched down with his arms wrapped across his chest. A bright blue light began to glow from him and the strange circle of ice-fire flared at the new magic. The Iceborn stood up just as half a dozen Fireborns were about to reach him and threw his arms, releasing a bubble of ice shooting out and knocking them all. The bubble did not stop there though and grew bigger and faster, hitting more and more of the combatants in the strange scene. Thisian dived back behind the safety of his building again in case the bloody thing hit him too.

Looking around for a good direction to run, Thisian could not. With an idiotic curiosity he had to stick his head back around the corner and see what had just happened.

As surprising as the first scene had been to him - to see fifty Fureath'i Powerborn fighting a pack of wild demons in a burning street - the new one was worse. The Iceborn at least had vanished, but it looked like the few Fireborns that were closest to him had gone too. Everything else on the street then had suddenly become frozen, completely covered in a thick layer of frost. One or two houses still burned near where Thisian stood, but all of the rest had become structures of ice.

Fireborns and demons were caught in mid action, frozen with a heavy sheen of white all around them and icicles dripping from their limbs. From the look of the frozen sword he could see one warrior holding, Thisian thought he could spot the only Protharik still standing, albeit as a statue of ice. Maybe he could not be killed, but freezing seemed to solve that problem. As long as did not die he would not reappear and so he was trapped. Thisian had no idea what he should do, should he try to melt the ice around some of the Fireborns?

The blue light returned and the giant Iceborn was once more on the frozen street. He stepped over to a crowd of ice-covered figures clustered together and stretched out his hands towards them. Then he, and all the blocks of ice he gestured at, disappeared in a flash of blue light. Where and how was he taking them? Why was he even doing it? Why not just kill them? Thisian did not necessarily want any Fireborn to die but it made sense to kill your enemy while they were weak. It was all happening too quickly so Thisian really didn't understand what was going on. The Iceborn returned again and choose new frozen targets to take with him and Thisian finally had the sense to get the rut out of there. Wherever all those demons and Powerborn were being taken, Thisian did not want to bloody go there too.

Turning and fleeing, Thisian skidded to a halt when he saw someone walk into his view at the end of the street. With just as much urgency as trying to escape the Iceborn, Thisian turned into the nearest alley and sped for his life. If his powerful eyes were not mocking him, then that had really been bloody blaze commander herself, Phira, bloody, almighty, marching straight back into his life. If those other Powerborn might not have beheaded him for being an Exile then she would do it quicker than even Kris. Dodging down through the alleys, he tried to keep an equal distance from both the ice-damned street of frozen Fireborn, with the ice-damned giant Iceborn who was stealing them all, and the ice-damned blaze commander who was the worst of all.

Looking up to Di Thorel, his new god of fortune, he asked, 'Is there anything else you think you could do to make this snow-cursed night any bloody worse? You dog-rutting son of a tit-less whore!'

The next street he ran onto was filled with warriors dressed in black robes, with their faces covered by white masks. The masks that turned and looked at him were skulls, at least two of them with flows of blood painted on as tears. Thisian's first thought was that he should probably stop cursing his new god, but it was quickly dismissed with thoughts that his new god deserved far more cursing for what he was making Thisian go through in one night.

Reaching down deeply for every scrap of power Thisian felt he might have within his Flameborn body, he gave the group his most charming smile and turned to run away even faster.

***

Phira saw the building on fire down the end of the street and marched grimly towards it. She had not expected to find a place to burn Lei so quickly, and wondered what had happened to start the house fire. It was possible that the Fureath'i host of Powerborn had arrived much quicker than anticipated. Fireborn could outrun a horse at full gallop, when the need arose, and if that was true then the city was finished.

Going straight up to the burning building, something pulled at the edge of her vision, but she did not become distracted. She needed to be rid of Lei's body so she continued with her mission and everything else was secondary. Getting as close to the building as the heat would allow her, a cynical thought made her think about what Brijnok's curse would do if she tried to jump into the burning building. It was certainly not a sword, but how could it not kill her? If she ever did reach a point where it would be acceptable to die, then she would make it her final act to ensure that it was not a sword that did it.

Using reserves of strength she was not sure she still had in her arms, Phira tossed the packaged body into the fire and stood waiting to make sure it was in deep enough. Satisfied, she then turned to be confronted with a street of ice. Every other street in the city was deeply covered in snow, with more howling down from the skies every minute, but this was the only one frozen solid. How could such a thing have happened? Is this where Frind'aal went? She was in no mood to try fighting an Iceborn.

Stepping carefully onto the abandoned street, Phira saw some lumps of shaped ice lying on the ground. Wiping snow from one she saw a dead man underneath. His hair was white and his eyes were open to reveal the red irises. Moving over to another frozen mound her suspicions were confirmed that it was Protharik, since the new body was the twin of the first. Were all the frozen mounds the corpses of Protharik the Demonlord? Some looked too large to be but Phira would not waste her time investigating.

Not everything made sense but it made sense that the Fureath'i host of Powerborn could have arrived and sought to slaughter Protharik as often as it pleased them. That would explain the scattering of bodies, but how was the street frozen? Could Frind'aal have done all this? If he happened upon the scene then the Fureath'i Powerborns would have killed him too or maybe the fight was still running through a different street. The howling wind made it hard to hear.

A blur of movement from behind made her spin and Phira saw what looked like Thisian of all people. She had thought it was too much coincidence for that man Griffil to mention his name before. Thisian - and it was definitely him - was rushing out of one alley and into another, down the very street she had just come from. He had been cradling something in his cloak, not wearing it against the cold, and she even thought he was instead wearing the yellow and orange of a Flameborn tunic. Perhaps her mind was addled with exhaustion or grief, but she did not think so. Her wits had never failed her, and one night of chaos would not unhinge them.

As if to add insult to her insistence, a band of Ihnhaarat took that moment to appear, chasing after the idiot Thisian. One skull mask turned to see her, the two burning houses behind and the frozen street that curved beside. Almost as a passing thought the warrior decided to run forward with a lazy swing of his serrated sword. No commitment or effort was put into the attack. Phira apparently was just something standing in the street that a passing Ihnhaarat might like to kill.

She did not even dodge the attack. Instead Phira stepped forward and stuck the fool through the stomach while they still had their sword raised high above their heads. Kicking the skullwarrior free, Phira sighed as the others stopped their chase to see what she had done. There were ten of them who had not yet disappeared into the alley, and it would be pushing herself beyond her limits to survive it. *Would dying by ten swords count as to die by a sword,* she thought bitterly. If her plans for Furea were not so important, a part of her wanted to get killed just to frustrate Brijnok. She would not be his creature.

Turning her blade, Phira wondered how many she could take down before their numbers proved too much. The black robed warriors spread out to circle her and she kept her balance poised with careful steps of retreat to stop them. Keeping her back to the burning buildings instead of the frozen street was not especially wise, but she was not in the mood to be wise anymore. Shifting her weight slightly, she was within distance to kill the first now.

No commands in Ihnhaarat were given, or sounds or gesture of any kind, but suddenly the skullwarriors withdrew. A childish part of Phira was disappointed but the blaze commander within her was grateful. The black robes swept back into the alley towards were Thisian had fled. One by one they disappeared until a single warrior remained. He looked back at Phira through the skull mask, and even in the shadows she could make out the red streams of blood decorating it. Not a skullwarrior then, but a stormwarrior. With a similarly lazy dismissal, the stormwarrior reached a fist towards the heavens and cast it down on Phira.

Phira launched herself out of the way, but there was no need. Nothing happened. The stormwarrior had already turned to leave, confident that the lightning would have obliterated her, and when it did not, he turned back sharply to see why. Anger at Brijnok for the unwanted protection battled with smug satisfaction in Phira that the stormwarrior was so shocked. *And how causally they thought to kill me,* she mused, *a simple hand gesture and away to more important matters.* It was a pity that she could not see the stormwarrior's face, but the cold smile on Phira's would have to be enough. She lifted her own fist up and threw empty air at him in mockery.

Throwing out his hand with more force this time, the black gloved palm of the stormwarrior shook with effort as he tried to call lightning from his fingers instead of the heavens. When a light appeared, Phira's confidence faltered, but the light grew so slowly that she did not panic. Unless it was a ritual of great and sudden power, Phira reserved her concern, since again, even from behind a mask, the stormwarrior seemed baffled. His stance and startled attention were enough to lead Phira to believe this was not intentional. Gradually the light grew and took shape, and a sword formed. It was jagged and serrated, like the other Ihnhaarat blades were, but this one was also twisted and white. When it was completed the stormwarrior examined the blade, showing clear concern despite his face being covered. It was a blade of lightning.

'When I kill you, I will take that blade for my own,' she spoke in clear Ihnhaarat and added her own Fureath'i growl to it.

The stormwarrior looked at the sword he just created, and at the Fureath'i warrior that seemed responsible. The Ihnhaarat then turned his palm in imitation of Fureath'i greeting, letting the magic-wrought sword fall soundlessly to the snow. It happened only in sparring matches and other test fights, the gesture a sign of surrender, but never in battle. It did not seem possible the Ihnhaarat could know so much of Fureath'i custom to make mockery.

'Fureath'i do not accept surrender,' she said simply as she walked towards the disarmed Ihnhaarat.

At her words the stormwarrior lowered slowly to his knees, now with both palms raised in submission. The action baffled Phira. The Ihnhaarat were mysterious to a fault, but it stood to reason that a Powerborn who could command storms and lightning would not be so humble as to kneel before a fleshborn.

'Fureath'i do not take prisoners,' Phira said as she stepped closer and closer. What did the stormwarrior hope to achieve? A quick death was the only thing Phira could bring to mind and it was all she planned on giving.

She was close enough to slit the man's throat now and the stormwarrior even took that moment to lift his chin up so his blood painted mask could face the sky above. Pale white skin was revealed in a small glimpse between the mask and the high necked coat, and as confused as Phira was, it was time to kill. She would kill the man for no other reason than he had the audacity to try to kill her. His current defenceless state was irrelevant. Phira turned the sword in her hand and everything exploded into white.

She felt herself flying backwards through the air and landed first on her injured hip, and then rolled over her shoulder, straining awkwardly to keep hold of her sword. The Jaguar blade on her back dug into her and if she had been less distracted she might have worried about it cutting into her skin as she landed. Instead the only sword that concerned Phira was the one in her hand, drawn ready to slay the next Foreign creature that faced her.

But the stormwarrior was gone. A ring of fire and a blackened pit of earth replaced where the Ihnhaarat had knelt. The strange sword still lay where it had been dropped but the strange man who created it was no more. *Would he really give his own life to take mine?* Phira was not sure, but it was definitely lightning that had blasted down on his body and nearly killed her with the proximity. Brijnok's curse might not be as powerful as he thought.

Turning around to the street of ice behind her, Phira's next move should be to find the Powerborn host. She had thought they might be days away but now that they were here she needed to assume command and take them to kill Aerath. If there were as many as Eva had implied then it would be more than enough to kill a single Iceborn and leave Surlas before the army retaliated. Looking back to the blade of white lightning, she stood up and moved over to collect it before leaving. It was incredibly light, and Phira tested it in her hands while all the time searching for more Ihnhaarat treachery. None came from the alleys or the shadows and she had no inclination to hunt them out. She gave the lightning blade a testing strike on the ground and was pleasantly surprised at how strong it was. Phira had expected it to shatter as glass, but would only keep it as a collection. Like the rest of her assorted weapons, few of them saw combat since one sword was enough for anyone who knew how to use it properly.

She hoped that the same collection had not already been looted from her saddle bags at the Brother in Flames, but that was a thought for later. Moving over to the skullwarrior she had killed, Phira indulged one last curiosity before she returned to the night of death and violence. Using the tip of her sword, she flicked off the skull mask the dead warrior wore and revealed the pale face of a black-haired woman. Although surprised, Phira was glad to see that women could be considered warriors in other lands - maybe not good warriors, since this one had certainly not been - but warriors none the less.

Crouching down, she stripped off the scabbard and attached it to her own waist. The lightning blade did not exactly fit as snug as her movement would need, but it would not easily fall out while clipped in either. Taking one last look at the dead woman, Phira could still not make out her female frame through the thick coats and cloaks, much the way she herself had been disguised while travelling through Surlas. There was much mystery still in the Ihnhaarat, but it was not her job to discover them tonight. She marched towards the street of ice to find sign of what direction the host had gone.

Walking over to one of the frozen corpses again, Phira examined the man Protharik. He was strangely handsome, for a Foreigner, his face looking too perfect, almost beautiful. Dallid's face was shorter and wider, with stronger cheek bones and an iron jaw; the face of a fighter. Lei's then had been a mixture of the two, combining a beauty of inner light with the hardness necessary for the external world. Bending down, Phira saw one of the demon hunter's swords lying next to him, not as affected by the ice as the dead man had been. Too many weapons would soon become cumbersome, but Protharik the Demonlord's sword was something to keep. The same was true of the cursed blade of lightning, even if it was created in a grotesque manner, it was likely the only sword in the world of its kind.

The real Protharik must have fled when Frind'aal arrived, and his demons with him. The Powerborn would not stop in their pursuit and Phira wondered if Protharik would ever die in full. Because if she knew the Fureath'i, then they would not stop killing him until he actually died, and if she knew the stories of Protharik, then he never would. It was a paradox that would have been amusing had she been of better mood. As it was, all she could think of now was that if she was in charge of that host then she would command no more deaths, and keep the man alive to be tortured for a few years, perhaps forever. Old age might achieve what Fureath'i fire could not.

Seeing no footprints, despite her own being clear, there seemed little to follow in order to find the Powerborn host. Phira wondered as to what purpose she should continue to find the single Flameborn either, especially if that Flameborn was Thisian in costume. As for the host, she had to admit also that she might not be able to convince them to come with her into Surlas. She might have the same rank as them, but it would take an order from the King to commit an act of war like that. She needed to return to Rath'Nor.

Considering a journey to the Brother in Flames and waiting there with her squad until morning, Phira wondered if it was enough. Would Eva be in the mood to deal with a trifling agreement when faced with the demolition of Amidon City at the hands of Fureath'i? Would her Inn even survive the fires if they started spreading? The lone Flameborn, if it was genuine, became an option again. She would outrank him and could order him to Connect with whatever fires they could find. Putting those out and saving what she could, would be useful in creating a future relationship with the Lady of Amidon City. It would even leave the Lady Eva in her debt. Having a power like Eva Yeda in your debt was something Phira was keen to possess. She set out to find the Dancing Whore.

***

Thisian stood outside his Inn finally, after sprinting for what seemed like a year to find the Dancing Whore. A worn painting of a topless woman dancing a jig with skirts held up greeted his eyes, and Thisian bowed respectively. He almost tried to look up those skirts as he leaned over but thought it improper. At last he was at a place of comfort and safety, however temporary it was, and did not think anyone was going to show up and want to kill him in the next few minutes at least.

Those Ihnhaarat had been mad savages and really looked like they wanted to kill him - as much as they could look like anything with those stupid bloody masks on. One of them had nearly caught him at the start, despite his Powerborn speed, but that one disappeared soon after. Thisian had heroically outrun the rest with graceful ease. Nodding his head again in recognition for his great victory, Lord Thisian Flameborn walked into the Inn.

An inviting chair, a warm drink and a warmer woman, was all Thisian wanted for a minute's peace, so he could forget about the night of chaos outside. If there was not a group wanting to kill him for the stolen orb he was holding, there were groups that wanted to kill him for being Fureath'i and more still for being Krife and Griffil's acquaintance. The gods alone knew why those Ihnhaarat had wanted to kill him. Maybe it was the way he had smiled at them. Or, of course, his new god Di Thorel could just be testing him, to see how much ill luck one Flameborn could take on one night. Thisian entered the Inn and saw what was inside.

'Let Di Thorel rut a rotted bull's corpse! And let a live bull rut him up the arse while he flaming does it!' Thisian exclaimed as he looked at Krife and Griffil. Krife laughed at his outburst but other than that the two were sitting quietly, which was strange in itself, but of course they were tied up. A Prae'surlas wearing a blue mask to cover his ugly face was standing near them, along with a number of rough looking thugs.

His back was still close to the door and two of the thugs tried to sneak their way behind. Thisian put a hand up to stop them.

'I have seen some arse-ugly Prae'surlas in my time, but I have never met one so bad that he needs to cover it with a mask,' he announced proudly in Prae'surlas, staring down every man in the room with confidence. 'And if you all don't run for your lives right now, I promise that you'll end up looking far worse.'

He desperately hoped they would run. It was not that he did not want to fight, but he just did not look forward to the prospect of getting stabbed or shot. He'd win eventually of course, he was Powerborn after all, but still. Setting down his covered bundle first, with slow careful movements, Thisian kicked it under a table and then threw his hands to either side to set them ablaze with awe-inspiring fire. His terrifying threats and supernatural display would be enough to send any man running with a coward's piss trailing behind him.

The only problem was: nothing happened.

There was no fire. The tingling feeling that he had constantly under his skin was gone, and even the sense of Connection with the fires or other Fireborn was gone. The sensation of people crowding in on him from all sides had vanished when in reality it was actually happening. He threw out his hands again and was suddenly paralysed with panic. The swords and daggers the men were holding all looked a lot sharper now.

'You do not speak like other Fureath'i, yet you still speak like a fool,' the Prae'surlas Hrothlar said back in king's tongue. Thisian was further distraught by the comment as he had thought his bravado had been very Fureath'i. The tall man continued from behind his mask, 'Your fire will not work when you are near me, instead it makes me stronger.'

The man tapped his mask to imply that the thing was responsible. So all Thisian had to do was get past every blade in the room and punch off that bloody thing so he could get his powers back. It was plausible at least. If he took some wounds his healing would deal with them once the mask was smashed, right? Or if he was able to free Krife and Griffil, together they could win out, but how had the two been captured in the first place? There did not seem enough men to restrain Krife, unless the mask was responsible for that too, or else the small room had hindered his fight. More likely he had just been asleep and had woken up to a dagger at his throat.

The men edged closer and Krife spoke up. 'Just give him the blasted orb, Fireborn. Hrothlar here, even if he does like dressing up as Moi'dan with his masks, he won't kill us. Well, he might kill you, he is Prae'surlas after all, but he won't kill me and Griffil. We can be too much use to him, isn't that right Hrothlar?'

The Prae'surlas did not respond but just watched as his men edged closer and closer to Thisian. Perhaps they were certain that his Flameborn powers would not work, but he was still a Fureath'i, a savage of lethal skill to be approached with caution always. Perhaps he could use that to his advantage. Choosing his timing just right, Thisian launched into an impressive run out of the Inn and back into the snow-damned night.

All he seemed to be doing was running lately, and his latest flight was cut short to a halting skid as a bald-headed, three-sworded, Powerborn-decapitating bastard was waiting outside with even more people that wanted to kill Thisian. Hrothlar's men burst out of the Inn after him and stopped when they saw the new arrivals too, and alarmingly - for the first time that night - Thisian had no idea which way he should run. What was he supposed to do if he had nowhere to run? Brenit and the Shakara with him were less in number than Hrothlar's bandits, but they circled the Dancing Whore effectively. There was still no feeling of fire from his treacherous veins either so Thisian doubted his run would be that fast any more regardless. The door to the Inn was still open and Thisian heard Krife bark out a laugh.

'You're in trouble now, Hrothlar! Eva's sent her pet dog to fetch us.'

'Actually, Krife,' Thisian shouted over his shoulder, 'Brenit's here to kill us too.'

'That bloody stone, Krife!' Griffil hissed at him. 'Did you really think something like this wouldn't happen?'

'Don't get your skirts in a tangle, Griffil. If Eva wants us dead then the fault is bloody yours, not mine,' he said back before shouting out the door, 'If you want to kill me yourself, Brenit, you'll have to kill Hrothlar first. You can't hear it from under his mask but he thinks you're nothing but a bald-headed scraping from a whore's arse, and I agree with him!'

Hrothlar ignored Krife and spoke to Brenit directly. 'Neither of us wishes for a war, Brenit, there is nothing to be gained. We will leave here with what is ours and you can have the treasure hunter and his runt.'

Brenit eyed the Prae'surlas for a time, and then eyed every other man present. Each was just a darting look from his bird-like eyes, but he seemed to weigh, judge and dismiss each man as a threat. Thisian began to wonder if the man would ever speak when finally he just shook his head. It did not really answer Thisian's wonder, but it gave Hrothlar his, and by the sound of his voice, one that he really did not like.

'Has a slave no mind to think for himself?' Hrothlar grated, his throat thick with anger. 'Then let your blood begin an ocean of death for this city.'

Brenit stepped back but never did it look like retreat. His eyes were enough to hold everyone frozen as he stared death at each of them. It was not until his eyes stopped on Thisian did he reach and unfasten the long sword he had strapped to his hip like a rat's tail. It was so much longer than Krife's beast of a sword, and so narrow.

Looking down in horror Thisian saw that he had actually drawn his own sabre. With a start he almost threw it to the ground to avoid provoking any violence, but looking around there was still no place to run. Whispering up to the snow-shitting sky, where storm clouds raged, Thisian made one last prayer to Di Thorel. 'You horse-rutted, piss-drinking, snow-bearded bastard, what have I ever done to you to deserve all this?'

Brenit strode forward and Thisian jumped to the left just as all of Hrothlar's men rushed out from the Dancing Whore. They provided good distraction for the whip-sword warrior, but Thisian still only jumped right into another one of the Shakara soldiers. A short sword stabbed for his stomach and Thisian barely swung his sabre down to deflect it. His arm already felt tired from the effort and he cursed Hrothlar for his blasted mask. Moving without endless reserves of power to fuel him was completely exhausting.

The soldier held up a rectangular shield and butted Thisian with it before stabbing forward with the short sword again. If that shield had not knocked him to the ground the sword would have gone straight through his face. He was too handsome to die in such a gruesome way. Scrambling to his feet, Thisian finally had a direction to run in front of him but before he could launch himself toward it, Brenit stalked into view.

'I'm not Powerborn at the moment, Brenit,' Thisian attempted while looking around to make sure he did not get stabbed in the back. The sound of metal cracking against metal, and of men shouting or screaming, meant Thisian had to raise his voice considerably to try reasoning with the ex-slave. 'Hrothlar's mask is stopping my power. It would be a waste of your time killing me! Kill him first and then we can have a real fight. Isn't that what you want?' He hoped Brenit understood Fureath'i, but the words did not seem to effect the shaven-headed warrior in the least. His bird face didn't even smile as he moved to kill Thisian.

The window between them smashed to wooden pieces then as a man was hurled out of it. He landed in a heap and did not get up. Thisian had no opportunity to look inside to see what was happening, so he only assumed Krife had somehow freed himself. *So how had the big bastard been captured in the first place?* Brenit's sword lashed forward and Thisian's sabre went up to meet it in reaction. The strength and speed of the man's swing knocked the Fureath'i blade clean out of Thisian's hands. He dove to the ground to retrieve it which ended up saving him from Brenit's return blow. Kicking into what he planned as a running escape turned into a tackle against another Shakara soldier. His weight fell on top of the shield as they crashed to the ground and he heard the crunch of the man's face underneath. There was a softer sound as he knelt onto the shield getting up and then stamped his foot on it without thinking while starting his run once more.

The shield slipped from under foot and sent Thisian sprawling yet again into the disgusting snow, further wetting his already soaking clothes. All that stood between him and freedom suddenly was just one more man trying to kill him, this one without shield or armour - only one of Hrothlar's murdering thugs. He had a big ugly sword that had enough notches missing to make Thisian wonder if it was even sharp enough to cut him. So, running at him, Thisian swung down with his sabre making the man lift his sword to meet him and then move back in a stance ready for fighting. The only problem with such a stance however was that Thisian had no intention of fighting. Instead he sprinted to the right and away out of reach of anyone wanting to kill him.

'Thisian!' Phira shouted as he ran towards her. She was completely covered in blood from head to toe and from the determined, angry way she moved, none of it looked as if it were hers. He tried not to be surprised by her arrival. Why should she not join in? Everyone else was trying to kill him, so all that was missing now was Kris. The only difference was that Phira would actually do it. Could the curse on Krife's small piece of stone really have drawn so many people to the one location, all to destroy the person holding it? He felt like shouting out that he did not have the bloody thing, but it would have been more useful to curse Di Thorel again.

'Blaze Commander Phira,' he tried to say seriously with a formal bow. 'We should leave here. Quickly!'

A sound from behind him made Thisian turn to see a head roll along the snow. The man he had just dodged now tottered headless for a moment before collapsing. Thisian thought that one good thing about Brenit's sword being so long was that it meant the man at least had to be far away. But then intelligence reminded him that the sword meant he could still bloody kill you from that far away. The long-sworded bastard marched straight towards them, his metal whip-blade dragging in the snow to his side. He stopped though when as he saw Phira.

Thisian could see the shaven skull of the warrior tense when looking at Phira, and he watched as the man's small bird-eyes darted between the two of them. It seemed he could not decide who he wanted to kill first and Thisian thought he should make his decision easier. So he ran. He ran straight past Phira which was dangerous in itself, but she could not yet know he was Flameborn or Exile so she would have no reason to want to kill him right then. She simply stared with disbelief at his cowardice and he felt like shouting at her did she not know him at all?

Something that felt like shame but that could have been fresh terror, welled up inside Thisian as he came to the corner of the street and vanished from the violence behind him. But once safely out of view for a time, Thisian stopped and spent that time cursing. Had he really just left Phira to be killed?

He could not go back of course, that would be complete idiocy. But instead he crouched down in the shadows and looked around to see if Phira would be alright. She had always been obnoxiously skilled with a sword, but Brenit's sword was miles bigger than hers.

It seemed she wasted little time wondering about him anyway and had moved in to meet Brenit without delay. The larger warrior was stepping back, most likely to give himself enough room to use the longer sword and Thisian had time to notice something amusing. Phira was wearing more swords than him. She had at least three scabbards on her belts, although one looked empty, belonging to the sword she held probably, but she also had a forth one strapped to her back underneath her cloak. Brenit swung for her.

Phira's sword flicked up to meet it lightly, letting it glance past safely before coming back again. She blocked that one too and had already gotten so close inside his guard that she was able to spin and kick the man in the stomach. His own foot went to sweep her legs from under her and Phira danced back with grace, taking the opportunity to strike Brenit's sword so he would be off balance for a moment. She used that moment to smash her hilt into the exposed forearm that held the sword, but Brenit did not waver. His fist flew forward, followed by a high boot, and finally his sword swing, the further back he pushed her. Phira avoided each attack but had been moved out of striking distance for her shorter sword, which was still much longer than a Fureath'i sabre.

Brenit's long sword whipped down again with terrible speed and reach. It forced Phira further and further back until Thisian began to wonder how she would be able to get close enough to strike back. Maybe if he ran in to distract Brenit, nothing so close as to invite any harm, but just enough to be a nuisance and give Phira advantage. The cracking sound the whip-sword made as it slashed through the air made Thisian come to sudden clarity about that plan. Even if he had his Powerborn speed and healing, he would be a madman to get involved. That thought then made Thisian aware of a familiar tingling back beneath his skin. Was he finally out of range of that stupid mask?

Shielding one hand behind the other, Thisian gave a small test of fire. He was anxious to see if he could do it again, but did not want Phira to find out, even if she was about to get killed. He spread his fingers and a flame sprang into being, burning beautifully. He quenched it straight away and went back to watching Phira dodge desperately for her life. She did not necessarily look in danger of getting struck with the long sword, but to Thisian's eyes there was no way she could strike Brenit either. It could only be a matter of time before her sword was swatted from her hands from the raw strength of Brenit's strikes. After all, hers were only womanly muscles trying to keep hold of the blade; his had been hardened male muscle and his sabre had been slapped out very easily. He had to help her.

Looking around to make sure there was no sign of that masked bastard Hrothlar, Thisian could not be sure if the man was out of reach or dead. Either way he did not want to suddenly lose his powers again if he ran in to help Phira. He would distract Brenit first with a fire flash. That seemed to be the only thing he could actually do besides setting his hands on fire or running for his life. So, taking a breath to steady himself, Thisian clenched his fist around his sabre, ready to run in once Brenit was distracted. Holding out his other hand, Thisian closed his eyes and sent out a flash fire in front of Brenit's face.

The man's head shot back and his hand went up protectively, and as Thisian was about to run forward, Phira launched herself into the air like an animal. It looked as if she flew from where she had stood towards to Brenit, gliding in slowed motion with her sword already coming down in mid-movement. When she landed it was with her sword plunged in the chest of the warrior. The fight was over, she had killed Brenit. Of all the things that had surprised Thisian that night, Phira's ability to jump was one of the most surprising.

Brenit managed to look into Phira's eyes before he fell, and she withdrew her blade before he dragged her down with him. She had to place her foot up on his chest to haul the sword free and she did it with an acrobatic flip backwards. It seemed to Thisian she was showing off now, but he was still amazed at how she had jumped that distance with such speed.

As he slowly walked towards her, she was picking up Brenit's long sword and examining it. The thing was longer than her entire body and looked ridiculous in her hands, she must have thought so too since she tossed it to the ground before looking at his other two blades. When Thisian approached her, he heard her say something about only needing one sword and it made him laugh accidentally. She turned fiercely.

'Peace!' he said as he hastily put his sabre away and turned up his palms. 'I only laughed because you said a warrior just needed one sword and yet you have four.'

'Why are you here, Thisian? And why are you wearing the stolen tunic of a Flameborn?'

'The sun god sees you too, Phira, and seeing you warms my heart,' he said and even smiled to try melting her severity. She just looked at him with impatience and then around towards the Inn for further danger. Thisian's own eyes went back there as well to see nothing but dead bodies. That seemed strange as surely there would have to be at least one still alive to have killed the last. Phira looked like she would kill him if he did not talk. 'Alright. Let me introduce you then to Lord Thisian Flameborn.' He bowed as he spoke - even thought it should have been her bloody bowing to him - and when he rose, both his hands sparked aflame.

She looked unimpressed. 'That was your fire against Brenit? I do not need help from magic to kill a man, Thisian.'

'Lord Thisian,' he said with a smile and Phira's sword slashed his face before he saw it even move. He could feel blood tickle down his cheek but could also feel the wound begin to heal as it formed. Phira's eyes stared at it with disappointment.

'So at least you do not lie,' she said while examining his eyes. He forgot to think that they would be different now. 'Explain to me quickly how this has occurred. There is much I still need to do tonight. And much I will need of you also it seems.'

Thisian was not sure how much he liked that but he told her of Kr'une and the raiders. He had to tell her he was Exile, but at least she might leave him out of her plans once she knew. When he finished she looked around impatiently. 'There is much that we will speak of but now is not the time. Your story, it does not seem real yet. It will be difficult to come to terms with your power, Thisian, but I must return to the Lady Eva with you. We will explain how to save this city from the fire of our brothers, maybe then her men will not interfere by making us kill them.'

'Why don't you just go straight to the other Fureath'i? You're a blaze commander after all. And why do you want to save this city anyway? I can think of a few dozen reasons why I'd want it saved but not you.'

Phira sighed. 'I would not have authority enough to order the Lord Fireborn in charge from desisting from their efforts, and I need to save the city so that the Lady Eva will keep to her word and give me the star markings that I need.'

'Star markings? Do you have a Spike? Can I see it?' Thisian asked, his boyhood wonder returning with embarrassing suddenness.

Phira rightly frowned at him, her severe face looking even more severe. 'Do not be a child. Come, let us return to Lady Eva. The night is dangerous here, Thisian, stay close to me if you do not wish to get killed.'

'I'm a Flameborn now, Phira, I don't need you to protect me. And wait, I'm not going with you. Eva wants me dead. Although I'm tempted to try changing her mind at some stage, tonight is not the time. But if we're lucky,' and he stopped to scowl up to heavens, tempting them, 'the orb that we stole is still in the Inn. You'll be able to get your markings from that!'

Phira looked at him with a mixture of irritation and suspicion but nodded all the same. 'Thisian, I find all of this difficult to believe, but very well, perhaps my mission will finally be at an end.'

Thisian lead the way cautiously and did not feel comfortable with her at his back. Even more so that he was not confident what he would find back at the Inn, since Hrothlar could only be gone because he had killed everyone and taken back the orb. All he might find were bloody corpses. Stepping around the dead bodies that decorated the street outside the Inn, Thisian jumped at a sudden cry from behind. Phira was stabbing the dead as she walked past them and one had not been fully dead. She looked at him questioning why he had stopped and he shook his head at her. Did the woman ever stop killing people? She was worse than Kris.

But Phira could do what she wanted as long as she did not start killing him. Thisian prayed to Di Thorel that nothing would happen to make her want to do that. The useless god owed him that much after the night he had.

Pushing open the door to the Inn carefully, Thisian was both surprised and relieved to see Krife and Griffil as the only two standing, their bindings gone. He could not see a Prae'surlas body anywhere but no-one else lying on the ground seemed to be moving and that was the important thing. Krife smiled at seeing him and then again at seeing Phira.

'Burn the gods, Fireborn, during all this fighting you still found the time to find a whore, and a Fureath'i whore at that!'

Thisian slowly closed his eyes and waited for Phira's sword to kill them all.

CHAPTER FORTY FOUR

Loss

Kris's side burned. Every step he took brought fresh pain and he had enough everywhere else that he did not need the wound in his ribs calling for special attention. The back of his head still felt like it was a broken shell, and the rest of his head did not feel much better. His nose was broken, the slash on his cheek pulled his face, his jaw and temple were both swollen, and he could not move his left hand, the arm badly torn, with the hand itself bloodied and broken. So instead Kris clenched his right hand around his sabre, using the strength that it still possessed to drive the rest of him.

'Kris will you stop and listen to me!' Nureail repeated, 'Your wounds need to be cleaned and stitched. You will bleed to death, or they will become infected, and they will kill you!'

Kris did not listen. He could not stop because he could not face her. Even the sound of her voice brought the image of him striking her and how close he was to killing her. If Tereail had stood beside her, Kris was certain he would have lunged for the man and killed him anyway, weapon or no. That he wanted to kill the useless man was a given, but that he actually would have done it in his blood-lust was unacceptable. Keeping his eyes and ears fixed on the Temple of Ice instead, Kris drove both Scholars from his mind. What was important was making sure they achieved their goal before running into any more Prae'surlas. Kris was eager to kill more, but he was not a fool. Fire in his blood could only drive his body so far past its limits. Nureail was right, his wounds needed to be tended to, but not yet.

'Kris if you do not stop I will make you stop! I would rather knock you unconscious and save your life than let you keep walking and die.' He did not turn but he could picture her waving her wooden sword in what she hoped was a threatening manner. That picture then focused on her face. The skin had broken on her cheek and the swelling had closed her eye, the entire right half of her face was coloured with bruising. Kris was strong enough to knock a Prae'surlas twice his size with the first blow he had given her. She was lucky to be alive.

'Let the fool be stubborn,' Tereail offered. 'My visions only saw that he succeeds, not that he survives after.'

'Now you speak like a Fureath'i,' Kris said in reply. He meant it as an insult but knowing the Scholar he had probably taken it as praise.

'Be silent,' Nureail snapped at her brother. 'He has already saved our lives twice and he can burn if he thinks I will let him die when I can save *him*. Kris, it will only take a few minutes, why do you not stop?'

'What then in those few minutes, Teller, if another group of Prae'surlas arrive?'

'Oh so I am back to Teller now? Does that make it easier for you? That you did not nearly kill Nureail, but only a Teller?'

Kris rounded on her so fiercely that she jumped, almost dropping her sword. She tried to regain some defiance, holding her chin up, but his dark eyes could have burnt her alive.

'What fool are you to touch a man when he is like that? I was this close to killing you, woman.' Kris wanted to rage at her for what she did, for what she made him do. No, he wanted to rage for how he was reacting. What he did was no one's fault but his own. He tried to divert his mind away from her, but she did not make it easy. Indeed she began to laugh at him.

'So finally I am a woman now,' she said before her voice went soft. 'Kris as much as you do not like to admit it, I am still Fureath'i. Yes, I am a Scholar, and a Teller, and a *woman*,' she smiled saying that, 'but I am Fureath'i, if not completely by blood then wholly by heart. And I have been hurt before. This,' she motioned painfully to her ruined face, 'will only make me stronger, make me better.'

Kris wanted to say that she was already better than anyone else. He was beginning to understand what she had said before about fighting for strength when weak. If you had no strength to begin with: what did you use to become better? She looked too perfect to be anything but fragile and helpless, and yet she was Fureath'i, if not a soldier then still a warrior. The men in his squads would laugh at her wooden sword, but with it she had saved his life. If he was to view her as a Fureath'i though, then she would have to do the same for him. He would keep going until Furea was safe.

'As you speak for your injuries, so do I for mine,' Kris said the words coldly. He did not leave room for argument. Turning his back he was grateful that Nureail seemed to accept his words. Tereail of course did not, but his objections were restricted to hushed whispers between brother and sister. Although Kris could not completely hear, nor did he want to, it sounded as if Nureail came out as victor. It was rare that she did not. Kris's body cried out for him to reconsider her council, the strength of his flesh fading with every step, but that only made him harder of will. The bleeding was slowing, so the wounds were not deep. He would keep going.

The next chamber of ice they entered shone as if polished metal. A fountain of water, frozen in mid-stream, was all the chamber held. Its spray went as high as to touch the ceiling and the icy sculpture that it had become looked as brittle as Kris felt. A childish impulse almost had him shatter the fountain purely as an outlet for his frustration. He did not do it.

Once past the thing, Kris's eyes were brought down an archway glittering to their left. The fountain of ice had clearly amazed Tereail's focus, and Kris could hear him theorize excitedly about physics and magic. Even to his own simple mind, Kris knew there was nothing of physics or natural order to the temple. The most obvious reason was that it was not as deathly cold as it should have been to justify so much to be so frozen. All three were shivering as they moved but it was not enough to cause them immediate harm, only discomfort.

Leading his party towards the left most archway, Kris eyed the room warily. He had seen a similar one in the Jhakral temple and had felt an instinctive need to stay away. This time however he was drawn to it. Tereail continued to speak to himself, loud enough to draw every Prae'surlas within roaring distance down on them, and Nureail had sense enough to remind him to quieten. She sounded distracted to Kris however, as he himself had become when full sight of their destination came into view.

He had thought the glittering was just more ice, but it was a room full of mirrors, of varying sizes lining the walls in odd shapes, or standing alone in sudden outcrops. Nothing looked to support the glass rectangles, and each one seemed to reflect the room differently, but the strangeness of the reflective glass was not what held his attention.

A woman was suspended in the air at the end of the chamber, her legs crossed by her feet, her arms held out by her sides. Her head was tilted back and if Kris had ever thought a woman beautiful before, he had been profoundly mistaken. Her hair streamed as long as her entire body, which was naked and perfect in every way. That she was a goddess, there was no doubt, and if she did not look like she was carved out of ice, Kris would have knelt and devoted his life to her.

More mirrors stood beneath her forming a circle by her feet. Each mirror did not reflect the room however. Instead they shifted visions of different lands, visible both on the side facing Kris and the side facing the goddess. The snow-covered cities of Surlas looked suited to the ice temple when they appeared, but the jungles of Tari, and the deserts of Furea came into view also and looked as out of place as could be.

Duty to protect his nation brought Kris's eyes back to better inspect the frozen goddess. He walked unsteadily towards her. Getting closer, Kris saw that she shone blue because of a second skin of ice that surrounded her. Managing a step to his right, followed by another step that was almost a fall, Kris was able to view the woman from a side position. Her back arched backwards slightly, her breasts pushed out as if in pain. The flowing hair, bright green in colour, wove out and down to her feet and was also wrapped in individual bindings of ice. Looking up to her ageless face, Kris stared into the frozen eyes that in turn gazed to the ceiling without life. Her eyes shot down to Kris then and made his heart explode with shock.

She stared at Kris, making him feel self-conscious about how tainted his own eyes would look. Hers shone with a light that he was ashamed he had not noticed before they moved, and all the ice in the world would not stop him from adoring her.

'Am'bril...' Nureail said, her voice cracking and hesitant. She sounded like she had not spoken after weeks in the desert and when Kris tried his own tongue he found it as dry. Nureail was able to speak again before he could, her words gaining a measure of strength the more she did. 'This is how Aerath is turning the world to ice.' She stepped back then, and reached out a hand to grab her brother's robes. 'We should move away. Her power is strong even now and we could become as trapped by it as she is by Aerath's.'

They had not gotten as close as he had, and Kris watched them move further away in horror. He could not contemplate leaving Am'bril's side. Kris already felt humiliated that he was not kneeling in her presence and wondered wildly why he was not. Looking up to her, he met her eyes again and stood captured by their divinity. It was difficult to pull his attention away when Nureail spoke.

'Come over to us, Kris, her magic is too strong to be near.'

Magic. Kris almost wept as he steeled himself and moved away. His had always been a life of struggle and yet as he dragged himself further away his heart claimed to have never felt such pain as he now experienced. The pitiful state of his body became an echo of a different life. Pain at betraying the goddess stabbed his soul. His traitorous feet pulled him backward like a coward, and he contemplated taking his own life in order to stop them. It was as if there were several parts to him, each with their own mind, every one of them howling in anguish at what was happening, all but one. One had taken a merciless grip of the rest and squeezed their throats to the point of murder, all so it could command his feet to keep them moving.

'I am sorry...' he whispered, his jaw clenched fiercely to stop tears from forming. But with each step that brought more torment, the strength to bear that torment also came. The further he got from the goddess the more lost he became and greater his satisfaction. When he was finally back to the entrance of the room with Nureail, Kris's mind reeled in outrage at how he had been bewitched. The pain of his heart and soul was once more usurped by the burning torture of his body. He was becoming weak. It was not just weakness from injury, but weakness that the magic of a frozen goddess, one dying by all accounts, could dominate him so completely. Being a mere fleshborn suddenly did not seem enough when faced with the magnitude of powers they were facing.

'I believe it is part of Aerath's ritual to have her power surge outward, Kris, so it can pass through each of the mirrors,' Nureail said, trying to avoid looking at Am'bril but constantly having her gaze dragged back. 'He has driven ice into her so deeply that her power over the weather can bring nothing else. Her Connection to it alone would have achieved his goal eventually, but using these mirrors will make it a reality much sooner than even Tereail has seen.'

'I did not have the time to study further into the future,' he said with regret. 'There were too many possibilities with this task that I could have spent years without going further.'

Kris believed him about how he could have spent years doing nothing. Disgust at the Scholar brought him back to some regain of composure though. 'These mirrors, I saw them in the Jhakral temple, what do they do?'

'More than one?' Nureail asked. 'I would have thought Aerath gathered these here to focus his power. The Temple of Zenith has only one and Lady Jaiha would not let us near it.'

'She feared we would become lost in them as Am'bril is now,' Tereail put in. 'They feed on life and power aptly for the vacuums that they essentially are.'

'You know of the shadow paths, Kris,' Nureail began to explain, 'how they walk along a different world, one of darkness, while linking to our own. We believe these then are from above rather than below, from the world of power, where the gods are. The same way Powerborn are Connected to that world, these mirrors are not. They remain detached from us so much they are not even in one physical location, but several, at the same time. It would not surprise me to discover that the ones in the Jhakral temple are the exact same as these, and even the one in the Temple of Zenith is here among them.'

Kris looked at her with disinterest. 'I did not ask how they did it, Nureail, just what they do.'

Nureail grit her teeth but held her calm. 'They are connected to everything, because they are everywhere. They are holes in our world caused by the tears between the world of flesh and the world of power, the same tears that allow magic to occur and allow Powerborn to be Connected with the world of power. And because of what Aerath has done to Am'bril, they are turning the world to ice, Kris.'

'Then we should smash them.'

Tereail laughed. 'I am almost tempted to let you try. Your sword would swing straight through it and drag you out to another part of the world. They are everywhere and nowhere, Kris, the fact that we can even see them in the Great Temples is because the temples themselves are Connected to the higher plain of power.'

'So the mirrors are not our concern,' Kris concluded for him, 'and we use the artefact now to stop the ritual. Tell me how it works, and I want only the briefest of answers, Tereail.'

'Then you shall have one,' he said snidely. 'I do not know how it is to work, only that you are here when it does.'

Kris flexed the fingers gripping his sabre, and worked his shoulders to test how well they could still swing it. 'You are telling me, Tereail, that your sole purpose in this mission, to explain how you have seen us save our nation, that you cannot do that.'

Nureail moved between them, as her brother replied oblivious as usual. 'Do you think you would be here if you had not been the only clear part of every future that I have visited? There were often others, but their images were insubstantial, their certainty to be involved too thin. If you cannot play your role now, Kris, the fault lies with you and no-one else.'

Taking a deep breath, he fought not to kill the man for another minute. Turning to Nureail, his eyes drifted from her face for a moment, before forcing it back to look at her. 'Nureail, will you connect with the item? Travel back and see how it has been used before. Tell me how to use the item to unfreeze Am'bril and stop Aerath's ritual.'

Before she could answer her eyes drifted behind him and Kris spun to see what it was. She was looking at one of the mirrors. The reflection of the room it gave was shifting and everything faded away until for a moment Kris could only see his own image. It was a fearful sight, his battered body, his blood soaked clothes and the black as pitch eyes that showed everyone what intentions lay behind. He grimaced at the sight and almost turned away but did not. Then his clothes in the mirror started to change, swirling around until they became the tunic of a Fireborn. Before he could frown, his face changed then showing that of someone else, but not someone he knew. The Fureath'i was young, but he had the spiralling red and yellow eyes of a Fireborn. The description did not fit any of the current lords that he knew and he turned to the Scholars to see if they could identify who it might be. Nureail shook her head at his unasked question, so Kris went back to see what else the mirror would show him. The idea that it was more of Fin'derrin's lies crept into Kris's mind, but he let it sit there without indulgence.

The young Fireborn had turned his back on them and the rest of the scene around him became clearer. He was in a place of ice but it looked more of a cave than a temple. The Fireborn walked to the end of the cave where a large structure of ice dominated the area: an altar on the floor and behind it, a giant winged beast. Only the smallest part of the head and wings were visible, the rest buried in the mountain, making it larger than anything he had ever heard of. The Fireborn kept going until he reached the altar and placed an item on top of it. Kris's eyes saw straight away that it was the fire of ice relic that they themselves held. The Fireborn waited for a minute and then grabbed the item with both hands.

It exploded into life and a fire floated up with both red and blue flames intertwining. Stepping back and watching, the Fireborn looked around as the strange flames drifted to touch the ice of the altar. Where ever the fire touched ice, it did not melt but seemed to turn the ice into fire, all with intertwining red and blue flames.

The blaze of magic spread, revealing the giant face of the winged beast that looked like a fossilised skeleton. On the altar though, as the ice became fire and spread out, it revealed a person lying underneath. What it revealed was no skeleton or fossil, what it revealed was Jherin. The white-skinned creature lay sleeping on the stone altar underneath the beast, and the Fireborn foolishly approached him to see if he lived. When Jherin opened his eyes the Fireborn exploded into a mist of blood, and the white-skinned creature sat up as if nothing had happened. Kris watched Jherin turn and stare at the skeletal head of the giant before the scene faded. The mirror returned to show their three reflections. The two others stood as speechless as he. Any other time it would have been a blessing.

'This thing needs a Fireborn to activate it,' Kris said sceptically.

'That is your first thought? Kris, what we have just seen could change our entire perception of the world! These mirrors truly are connected to everything, past and present, so we can learn all there is in creation with it!' Tereail almost clapped his hands with excitement.

'Well we could stand here until the mirror kills us at least,' Nureail said with a scowl toward her brother. 'Or have you forgotten that just by standing this close to it, the thing is already killing us. Every minute we stay here we are losing years of our lives. You know that is how quickly it consumes life and energy, Tereail.'

'The same as Fin'derrin,' Kris said with a growl. The reality still seemed too true however.

'Not quite the same, Kris, no,' Nureail corrected him. 'Fin'derrin looked to just take nourishment from our life, I do not think he took it away from us. These mirrors though, they will visibly age us if we stay here long enough.'

'Then we will stay here long enough to complete our mission,' Kris said turning back to the reflective surface. 'I asked how had the item been used before and the mirror showed us that scene. But if we need a Fireborn to activate the thing, then why was it so imperative that no Fireborn come with us?'

'Because they could not use the flowstones, or the shadow paths, and because Jherin would have likely destroyed them,' Nureail said. 'And us too.'

'These mirrors, Tereail, you said I could go through them, to another land? If I go through, will it be able to bring me back?'

'They might if one of us reached through to pull you back,' Nureail started before rounding on him, 'but you cannot! As much as these things take from you by just standing in front of them, they will kill you if you enter them. They will take everything that is good from you and leave what's discarded, withered and feeble.'

Kris turned away from them and towards the mirror. There was little good in him that the mirror could take but he would see what his options were. He readied himself to order the mirrors as he would any soldier under his command - as long as that soldier was not a Scholar.

'Tell me how we can get a Fireborn to this place.'

The mirror swirled again only this time it brought back a scene within the Temple of Ice. The very room they were standing in was filled with Prae'surlas soldiers and they were marching through the mirrors into what looked like the forests of eastern Furea. The scene shifted then to confirm his thoughts and Kris wanted to bear his teeth at seeing so many north-men enter his home land. The Prae'surlas that entered the mirror from the Temple of Ice had been young and strong, but the ones that came out into the forests of Furea looked old and haggard. It seemed Nureail was right in what the mirror did to you, but not right in that it would kill him. Kris failed to see how this answered his demand though. He wanted to know how he could get a Fireborn to the chamber to activate the ritual needed. Then he saw Rhisean the Scarred walk into view.

The man was large of chest and arm, and would have been an impressive figure even without all the extensive burn marks that covered the skin of his body. With those scars though, Kris believed that he looked even more impressive and upon seeing so many north-men appear from thin air into his forest, Rhisean went about killing them immediately. The speed of the Fireborn was exceptional, shooting what looked like long ropes of flames from his hands and piercing through the flesh of every Prae'surlas there. They were all dead within moments, such was the vast difference between fleshborn and Powerborn, but when more north-men stepped out of mid-air in front of Rhisean, he charged at them and fell back through the invisible mirror that he could not see. He had fallen straight into the Temple of Ice.

The scene shifted again and showed Rhisean on his hands and knees, suffering from the effects of travelling through the mirror. When he lifted his head Rhisean stared at so many Prae'surlas waiting to invade eastern Furea. Every inch of the temple was infested with them. The Fireborn even glanced at the frozen figure of Am'bril for a moment before pushing to his feet and he then began lashing out his signature whips of flame. Kris would have enjoyed watching him kill so many Prae'surlas, but a larger one stepped into view, dressed in a tunic of silver and white.

The whips of fire lashed out to burn through the neck of the Iceborn, but a white arc flickered in the air to counter Rhisean's attack. The fleshborns backed away and the Iceborn kept walking forward as Rhisean increased the intensity of his attacks. When his body erupted into flames, Kris thought for sure that the Iceborn would be killed, but he could see the fire of Rhisean's body drift back towards the mirror he had just come through. The thing looked like it was stealing his strength just when he needed it. The Iceborn's hand shot out and gripped Rhisean by the throat and then both men were gone. All that remained was a circle of blue flame underneath where they stood. The mirror returned to show them their own reflections again but Kris was not satisfied.

'Where did they go?' he demanded harshly.

The mirror dutifully went back to showing what he wished, but what he saw was Aerath throwing Rhisean into a cell of ice and sealing the door behind him. Kris had never seen the place but he knew what Lae Noan was: a mountain of ice where Powerborn could be sent and stripped them of all their power. If Rhisean truly was in that place, then the King would need to know immediately and mount an assault. Kris was so angry he could not bear it. Wondering for a minute if the mirror was already depleting the strength he needed to keep control, he took a step away and towards the Scholars. They stepped back from him in fear without thinking, and Kris thought that it was one of the wisest things he had seen from them yet.

He did not feel the need to hear their conclusion nor would he voice his. To him, the mirror had shown that a man will not die when he goes through, and more it showed that a powerful Fireborn could go through it with less effect. Standing further back, he faced the thing again. It looked like he would only get one shot to go through the mirror before it killed him, and he would be certain it was the correct place that he would go. They would need the most Powerful Fireborn now, and they were so close to their goal that it did not matter whatever unknown destruction would arrive to intervene. Nureail may have been right and Jherin may have been what they were sent to avoid. So now they could recruit a lord of power to finally finish the task. If Aerath showed up, then Kris would gladly help the Fireborn kill him.

'Show me Chrial'thau Fireborn,' he ordered and the mirror obeyed by shifting to a scene of storming snow. Through the storm he could see something black like smoke, but the clearer the image became the more the black smoke looked like fire. It was a demon that propelled itself through the sky on wings of flame, and there were flashes of colour coming from its twisted face. Kris could see green shine through, as well as blue and red, but why was the mirror showing them this? Then the demon turned its head and it was Chrial'thau. The two Scholars behind him gasped, and he thought he heard Tereail faint. Nureail cried out her distress.

'What is this? How has this happened?'

The mirror changed scene again and this time it showed the inside of the Tower of Frehep. There were dead Prae'surlas and dead Fureath'i scattered around the floor, Kris's eyes picked out the still forms of Yiran and Dallid straight away. They were dead. There was a large Iceborn, the same one that captured Rhisean and he was placing a sword into Chrial'thau's chest. The green-eyed demon from Fin'derrin's visions was held bound against a wall, watching the Iceborn with interest. There was a flash of light from Aerath's hand and then the scene vanished, before showing a new one with Dallid standing over the fallen body of Chrial'thau. Not only was Dallid alive, but he was also wearing a Fireborn's tunic, again, just as he had in Fin'derrin's fantasy. Kris would not give in to paranoia. Chrial'thau woke up and burst into black flames. Nureail gasped and Kris did not need to watch anymore.

'Show me Jaiha Fireborn.'

The demon of black fire disappeared, and as pleased as Kris had been to see Dallid alive again, he tried not to wonder if his old friend had survived the scene. There was no time for personal curiosity. The colours swirled and when it showed the Fireborn Jaiha, it showed her fighting Fin'derrin's green-eyed demon again. Kris insisted this was no illusion, he knew what was real. He knew his pain was real, he knew his struggle not to kill Tereail and Nureail was real. The frustration and rage that he held back was so real that his sword hand shook.

The green-eyed demon fought Jaiha sword to sword, her fire attacks not affecting it, but the priestess showed herself to be very skilled with a sabre. It was not enough. In one moment they were fighting through the corridors of the Temple of Zenith, and the next the Fireborn's head had been cut off. Nureail was beside herself with the sudden loss, and Kris felt the urge to try calming her. There must be something he could say to make her stronger, but the words would not come. So he spoke to the mirror instead.

Rhisean was widely accepted to be the strongest Fireborn after Chrial'thau, but Kris had already seen the lord was imprisoned in Lae Noan. Jaiha then was considered to be next in rank as well as power. If they needed the strongest Fireborn after that, then it would be Chrial'thau's brother. 'Show me Miral'thau Fireborn.'

The minute the image began to form and a green-eyed demon could be seen, Kris did not need to see any more. Was it an entire species of the same type demon that was killing the most powerful of Fireborn, or was it the one single creature?

'Whoever has loosed an Attro'phass demon into the world of light has committed as much an evil as Aerath has by turning it to ice.' Nureail's voice was trembling with tears. 'Both are as likely to kill everyone in it. It is said that nothing can kill an Attro'phass demon, only another one of its kind. But there are no others like it. They have all killed each other. If that is the last one, then what can possibly kill the thing?'

Jherin could kill it, Kris thought to himself, *and I would kill it too*. But that answered his question if it was just one demon doing all that devastation. It was able to travel quickly to kill the three famed Fireborn like that. He wanted to know who else the thing had killed. But right then, all he needed was one Fireborn that it had not.

'Show me the strongest Fireborn that is still alive.'

'No, Kris, we need to know who else that thing has killed. Our nation has been crippled with those deaths alone!' She shouted at the mirror as if accusing the thing of the deed, 'how many more Fireborn has it killed? Tell me!'

The mirror shifted back to the image of a snow storm. Kris wondered would it repeat itself showing the demon Chrial'thau again. Instead it showed a single Fireborn doing his best to run through a blizzard. The mirror focused closer and closer, giving as much clarity as it could underneath all the gale-thrown snow. Before it rounded on the face though, Kris had an idea of who the man was. It was Dallid. He did not know why Dallid was in Surlas trying to make his way through a snow storm, or why he had apparently become a Fireborn, but Kris did not look forward to seeing the green-eyed demon appear to kill him.

'Show me the strongest Fireborn that is still alive,' Kris repeated, ignoring Nureail's emotional pleas. If Dallid was to die, then he would miss him, but Kris needed a Fireborn to complete his mission.

The mirror did not change its scene and he turned to show his intentions to Nureail. He had his plan already decided, but did not like how easily the mirrors reflected Fin'derrin's own illusions. If it was not Fin'derrin's dream that he was in, then what powered the mirrors to answer his demands.

'The gods, do they control these things?' he asked to either Scholar. It was Tereail who answered.

'If they did, would they not stop the ones killing Am'bril? I believe these mirrors consume thought and intention as they do power. As I have said they are empty of reality here in our world, so they claw hungrily for anything they can use to connect to it, maybe even create false realities with what they take. It might be that Jaiha and Chrial'thau are not dead, but just the construct of our thoughts and fears.'

'No Tereail,' his sister said. 'Those scenes had the feel of history about them, all but the one we see now. This one may or may not be happening, but I knew instantly those others were things that had. I believe the mirrors can take our life and will, and use it to connect to the reality that concerns it. Maybe it has taken part of my connection to time, maybe it can take yours Tereail and show us what is about to happen. But if we stay here too long we will die as surely as Am'bril will, the mirrors will steal everything that we have.'

Kris grunted. Perhaps the mirrors had already stolen his patience. He certainly felt weaker than he could ever remember, but his injuries and his company were as much to blame for that. 'If we stay anywhere too long we will die as surely as Am'bril. The world turns to ice. Aerath's ritual freezes the goddess of tempest, while these mirrors create a new reality in our world.' It had finally happened; he had started to sound like a Scholar. But there was no time to despair about it, he needed to act. If the mirrors stole life and will and made it shape reality, then Kris would show them how he did exactly the same. Every day was a demonstration of how his will created the world around him, forcing his dominance onto things to make them better.

'That Fireborn, Kris,' Nureail said. 'He is from your village, is he not? He is married to Yiran's apprentice, Blaze Commander Phira.'

'Dallid,' Kris said.

'He is not Fireborn,' Nureail said simply as if the statement needed to be spoken aloud. But if Thisian could become a Flameborn, then why could not Dallid become a Fireborn also? He wondered dryly what Phira had become, but Kris did not care about how these things happened, nor did he care that he had never before heard of any fleshborn ever becoming Powerborn. It had happened now so he would take what he was given and bend it to his will. Action should dictate reality; not the other way around.

'Kris, no.' Nureail grabbed his shoulder just as he was about to march into the mirror. He looked at her, waiting for an explanation, and saw the turmoil in her eyes. She did not want him to go, but she must know it was the only solution. 'The mirrors, Kris, they will take nearly all of Dallid's power, if it is true he is Fireborn. You saw how easily Rhisean was captured after going through it. And it will do worse to you. You have no power for it to feed on so it will take you instead, your strength, your life, it will take all that lets you stand. If you give up your strength to these voids, Kris, there will be nothing left to keep you alive.'

'What can it take from me, Nureail?' Kris said as he gently removed her hand. 'If these things are like Fin'derrin, then you heard what he said about me. There was nothing of life within me for him to feed upon. Tereail said it himself: I am just the idea of what a Fureath'i should be, forced into being. I am not a thing of life, to exist naturally; I am a thing of will, to exist as I decide.' Her face dropped with each word. She did not want to hear them. In a moment of weakness he put away his sabre and let his only working hand cup her face with tenderness. Her skin was so soft and she hugged his hand tightly. But if ever there was not a time for weakness it was now.

'Perhaps it will be as you said,' he added finally. 'Perhaps because my life is so hardened within, the mirrors will not be able to take it. This might be why the futures chose me, that I might be the only one who *can* walk through these mirrors without harm, even as weak as I now stand.'

He removed his hand and his eyes went dark. Not at her, but she recoiled as if they were. He darkened himself to the world around and without another word turned and entered the void.

CHAPTER FORTY FIVE

The power of a god

There was sudden movement beside Dallid and in reaction he burst into flames. It was impossible to see clearly with a full storm of winter battering him from every direction, but he could make out a figure lying face down in the snow. Running over, Dallid expected to see the demon Chrial'thau, or strangely, even the Attro'phass demon - his eyes had been playing tricks on him during the storm of late, showing flashes of green among the white and the darkness.

Pushing demons from his mind, Dallid put his foot under the fallen figure and turned him over with a kick. He was stunned to see it was another Fureath'i, and even more so to see it was Kris. The man was known from desert to forest as one of the hardest men in the army, as well as one of the fiercest killers of Prae'surlas, so perhaps it should not have surprised Dallid to find Kris in Surlas looking to kill more. But seeing with alarm that he wore only the scant battle-garb of a soldier, Dallid cursed that he himself wore no cloak or coat. His brain worked to think of what he could do to save his friend from freezing to death, if he was not already dead. Kris answered that thought with a grunt and began getting up.

Kris's head was the first thing to rise and he simply nodded with grim acknowledgement that Dallid was there. Should he not be surprised by Dallid's own appearance in the middle of Surlas, or even that he wore the tunic of a Fireborn and that his arms were dancing with flames? Kris was never one to react to things like others did, but his ready acceptance of the situation was too much even for him. It took Dallid some time to realise that Kris's mouth was moving, but he could not hear him over the wind.

Crouching down closer to better hear, Dallid thought he should first put out his fire so as not to burn his friend, but then scolded himself that fire was exactly what Kris needed. He looked older than when Dallid had last seen him, his face battered, his clothes soaked in blood and more than anything he looked deathly tired.

Kris was strong, but he would die from the cold like any other man if Dallid did not do something. He needed to act.

Sending his arms out first to his left and then to his right, small bursts of fire broke free and took purchase in the snow. Kris had stopped trying to talk to him and just watched now with his unreadable dark eyes. One of Kris's arms was hanging limp, and Dallid shook his head as he saw the man trying not to allow his body to shiver. Dallid continued planting fires as quickly as he could, arcing out in a circle around them. He had thought it took years of learning incantation and ritual to perform any manner of pyromancy, but perhaps that was for acts of greater complexity. Right now all he needed was to use his power as he used any other muscle. He did not think about doing it and just did it. Soon a line of roaring fires surrounded them, but despite their size - and the unreality they provided to the snow storm - it would not be enough to shield his friend from freezing to death.

Dallid could see the flames around him, even feel some degree of their heat, but it was his other awareness of the fire that he latched onto. In his mind Dallid took a hold of that Connection, and in body he raised both arms up together hoping that it would achieve what he wanted. When his hands were only able to move a fragment upward, feeling like they were trying to up-root a tree trunk, he was first disappointed that it was not so easy, but pleased that his plan might work. Dallid would raise a shield of fire, but while trying to do it he felt like he had to lift a man standing on each of his hands, both in terms of weight and of balance. The Connection that he gripped thrashed about like a flame would. But slowly he moved his arms higher and higher, trying not to think of how his power could be linked to his strength of muscle, yet it seemed it was the flesh in his arms doing all of the work.

Each of the fires around them rose up with the motion and it spurred Dallid on even more. The strength he had in his arms often bested other warriors in training from their brute force, but right then, lifting those fires upwards, Dallid felt as if his arms had never known a muscle to ever power them. There was no other choice but to keep pushing them. If he could not do this, then Kris would die. *How had he gotten here in the first place dressed as he was?* His face was a mess of bruising and dried blood. One arm hung unmoving at his side, and the little clothing he wore was crusted with blood. Dallid wondered if Kris might die from his wounds regardless of whether he saved him from the storm or not.

He forgot about Kris then as his arms threatened to fall and he shouted out to keep them rising. The fires roared as he roared and he would achieve what he had set out to do. His hands suddenly touched each other over his head and before he let them drop, Dallid looked around to see a dome of fire had been created. If he thought he was tired while raising his arms, it was nothing compared to the exhaustion he felt after dropping them. But there a comforting heat now, and gone was the roaring wind and the invasive flurry of snow and ice. It was all replaced by a crackling of flames that reminded him of heart fires and better days. He felt safe from the rest of the world, alone with an old friend in a place of comfort. The arrival of Kris reminded Dallid of the friends he lost in the fight at Coruln. He missed Jathen and Emylias, and he almost hoped that Thisian would show up out of nowhere like Kris had just done, but by all the gods he missed Phira more than anything else.

'It pleases me greatly to see that you are a Lord Fireborn, Dallid.' Kris said to him. It would have been better accompanied with a grin, but Dallid did not think Kris ever smiled - or laughed, or slept. Without the grin his words sounded like he already knew Dallid was a Fireborn and had known for some time. Dallid shook his head.

'How are you here, Kris? You look like you are already dead and you are dressed to surely die in this winter!'

'I would say the same of you were you not a lord of power. Lord Dallid, I do not jest when I say I would bow, but I fear that I might not be able to rise again.'

Dallid waved his hand vigorously. 'By every flame of Frehep, Kris, do not bow, and do not call me lord! It is too difficult for me to accept this as it is. I am not worthy of your awe, you were always so much more than me. Even now if I were to meet a real Fireborn I myself would bow down and yet I cannot accept that others should do it to me. If I were a real Fireborn, Kris, I could heal your wounds, but I do not know how. I would even explain how this has occurred to me, but I do not understand it, and I fear we will soon be short of time. A dome of fire in the middle of Surlas will attract swift attention.'

'You forget the Prae'surlas are stupid,' Kris said and almost grinned that time, but at least he did not call him lord.

Dallid laughed. 'You've been practicing your jokes! I knew myself and Thisian would influence you eventually.'

'I fear my mind has merely gone slack from exhaustion,' Kris returned. 'But you are right when you say we have not time. I am here under orders from Lady Jaiha.'

'So she is not dead?'

Kris frowned before answering. 'I believe that she might indeed be dead. But regardless, her orders stand. Aerath has enacted a ritual that will turn the world to ice, Furea included. He does this by killing the goddess Am'bril. Lady Jaiha believed that we had to save the goddess within ten days or all would be lost. I thought we had six days remaining, but Nureail thinks it might be much less. Upon seeing the frozen goddess myself I am likely to agree.'

'Nureail?' Dallid said. 'The Teller? The one that would visit with Yiran?'

'Yes. She and her brother Tereail accompanied me so we could acquire an item of power, a fire shaped out of ice, that they believe can stop the ritual. But we need a Fireborn to use it.'

'Where are they? Where have you come from?'

'The Prae'surlas Temple of Ice. There are mirrors, holes in the world, that can connect to a piece of our reality but it comes at a cost. I already feel that price on myself and am not confident I will survive the return. You should know that if you follow me to this place, those mirrors will feed on your power, perhaps reducing it permanently.'

'Better to flare brightly for a day than spark limply for a year,' Dallid smiled back at him, but then he frowned. 'I cannot. I have come to this place to kill Aerath. Kris, he came to Coruln, he killed everyone there, my squad, Yiran the Unconquered is dead by his hand, even Lord Chrial'thau, although he is worse than dead. Chrial'thau is a demon now because of Aerath, wearing the skin of our greatest legend and committing atrocities in his name. I have chased the demon here in the hope that I will kill them both, or that they might kill each other.'

'You believe that you can kill Aerath after he defeated Lord Chrial'thau?'

'I cannot explain it. There is nothing in my mind or heart that believes I could defeat even an ordinary Iceborn, yet I cannot stop moving towards Aerath. I do not know if it is Chrial'thau's power inside me, or something else, but every time I decide to seek out Rath'Nor, or Phira, or anything that takes me away from Aerath, I am driven back to the single goal. I have to find Aerath and I have to kill him.' Dallid felt like he was abandoning his friend, abandoning his country, and yet his shame was still not strong enough to overpower his need to keep going to Lae Noan. Kris saved him from his torment.

'When we stop his ritual, Dallid, it is almost certain that Aerath will come to us,' Kris said simply. To him it would be a clear decision, what was best for Furea was the thing that he would do. Dallid jumped at the reasoning before the Fireborn inside him could argue.

'Let us go then, Kris, quickly, before my mind is changed.'

Kris nodded and looked around at the dome of fire. 'I do not know if she can reach us through this. I think we might need to let it go.'

'Who will reach us? If I drop this, you will freeze.'

'There are several more pressing matters that will kill me first. I will not be killed by snow.'

Dallid agreed reluctantly and let the ritual disappear. He had not even known he was still holding onto it and felt remarkably stronger with its release. It was good to know he had been exhausted from holding the fire and not just from creating it. But the winter storm battering back down on him took away any other thoughts he might have had. With all fire now gone, Dallid stayed as close to Kris as he could, partly not to lose sight of him in the blizzard, but partly to ensure he could create more fire if his friend looked like succumbing to the cold. Kris ignored the storm that assaulted him though, and he simply stood still and waited.

Dallid's eyes would be sharper than Kris's, so he kept them looking around for one of the mirrors that he had spoken of. Kris's hand clasped onto Dallid's then and he was jerked forward before he knew it. He had not seen anything but his eyes followed Kris's body disappearing into nothing and soon Dallid's own flesh vanished. He screamed.

Something dug claws into his heart and pulled savagely to tear it out. The core of him was being dragged through blood and bone by an unseen force, and every inch of him was paralysed in pain. He had no hands to clutch at his chest and stop the act. He no longer even had a voice to roar with. With no eyes he saw only in his mind the heart ripping free of his chest and before he could die, it was over.

He was on his knees, gasping for breath and shaking from trauma. His hands touched a floor of ice, but there was no feeling of cold from it. Raising his fingers up to his chest Dallid expected to see his ribs burst outward and gore matting his body. There was no wound, but memory of the attack did not fade.

'Kris!' A woman's voice cried out and she scrambled down to cradle the man lying next to him. Dallid craned a neck that felt like it had been broken and saw Kris lying motionless on the floor. The woman's hands pressed everywhere on his body to find wounds or maybe a heartbeat, and finally gripped his jaw to shake him vigorously. 'Kris! Wake up! You are not done here yet! Do you hear me? Burn you! You are not allowed to die!'

Dallid heard tears from the woman's voice, and was vaguely aware of someone else standing apart from them. If Kris had just been through what Dallid had been through, in his injured state, then he was dead.

'Open your eyes! Burn you, Kris! I said open your damned eyes!' It was Nureail. Dallid recognised her now. Her face looked savagely beaten, but she moved with more strength than anyone else in the chamber.

'Stop.'

It was a whisper, pushed through closed lips, but Dallid heard it.

It was too soft for any other ears to notice and Nureail kept shaking and shouting at Kris in a fit of hysteria. How was the man still alive? It shamed Dallid into rising.

When he slowly managed to stand, the entire room shined too brightly with ice around him. There was a haunting image of a woman frozen in ice, floating in mid-air at the end of the chamber.

She pulled at him like the journey through the mirrors had, so immediately he lowered his eyes to the floor and shifted them to Kris.

'Stop.'

Louder this time and Nureail froze where she was, her breath caught.

'Stop shouting at me, woman,' Kris said with more strength and opened his eyes to smile up at Nureail. She laughed in disbelief, tears flooding down her face.

'You have a beautiful smile,' she blurted out at him.

'I simply have not the energy to frown,' he said back and incredibly began to get up.

'No! For the love of the gods stay where you are and rest! Your friend is here now, we will do the rest. Tereail help me stop him from rising.'

Dallid laughed and the two looked at him accusingly. He turned his palms in apology. 'Forgive me. I am laughing because even when dead, Kris needs two people to stop him from getting up.'

Nureail tried to laugh but was still too shaken to collect herself. The man Tereail strolled over without urgency and just looked down at Kris, with his sister pressing both her hands on the warrior's shoulders.

'If he wishes to rise then let him, he still has to kill Aerath remember.'

'Kill Aerath?' Dallid asked while Nureail began cursing at her brother.

'Yes,' Tereail said back. 'Aerath will come here as soon as he feels his ritual come undone. With fortune our own ritual will be too far gone for him to do anything about it.'

'How do you know this?'

'I have a connection with time that allows me to see visions of the future. In nearly all of them Aerath has come, but in most Kris cuts his head off.'

'Kris?' Dallid said. 'The man can barely breathe, and you expect him to kill an Iceborn? I will kill Aerath when he gets here. Will you be able to give me warning?'

Tereail looked Dallid up and down like he was studying him, after a few frustrating minutes he just shrugged. 'Perhaps you will, you are supposedly Fireborn after all, but I am afraid I have never heard of you. Nureail tells me that when you were youths with Kris you were just a fleshborn? That cannot be, so you will forgive me if I am less than optimistic about your chances of success, or that you are even Fireborn for that matter, and not just some imposter using magic. We've already had one person claim to be a new Flame-'

Dallid punched the man in the face, knocking him on his ass and felt much better for it. He heard Kris begin to cough in what could have been a laugh. The man Tereail held his jaw in purest shock and his face almost made Dallid burst into laughter too. 'You tell me to my face that I am not a Fireborn when Kris almost died to get me here. Well at least you do not call me lord or try to kneel. I think I would only hit you harder if you did.'

'I also hold the title of lord...' Tereail muttered but at the look Dallid gave him, he silenced again immediately.

Standing over his friend, Dallid saw warring expressions of concern and anger on Nureail's face, but all he could see on Kris was pained amusement. 'I have wanted to do that for some time, my friend, and am pleased that it has been done for me.'

It was not like Kris to smile and look so content but he had not seen the man in some time. He looked older again than he did back in Surlas, his face worn and his hair gilded silver. Perhaps twenty years older than the last time he saw him before that. His eyes were still as black as ever though, no amount of years could soften those. 'That you have been in his company for so long without doing so only shows you still have as much control as I remember.' Perhaps that he was so near death, Kris had allowed himself to show emotion for once, to try and feel what it was like to be happy. 'Rest, Kris, I will do what needs to be done now.'

That was of course if his powers had not been ripped out of him like he had felt. His eyes went to Kris's hair and Dallid frowned to see so much grey. Now that he noticed it, even the arm Nureail had used to pull them through was shaking, though she was making an effort to hide it. Those mirrors took much from the user and it was time to find out what it had taken from him.

His closed his fists and relief flooded through Dallid as fire crept up from his skin. It took its time to grow, but steadily it flowed around his arms, stopping only when it reached his tunic. In appearance the fire looked strong, but underneath Dallid still felt dangerously weak. He let the flames vanish.

Maybe Tereail's vision had seen Dallid as the one who killed Aerath, both he and Kris had similar length hair even if Dallid was slightly shorter. To someone who did not know them, it was possible they could be mistaken for each other. Especially if the man saw Aerath die by a sword, Tereail would not have expected to see a Fireborn use a sword to kill an Iceborn, since he had probably never heard of a Fireborn who knew no magic. But if Tereail had seen Aerath die by a sword, then at least it was possible.

Turning to Tereail and then changing his mind, Dallid addressed Nureail. 'What must I do?'

'Of that you must ask my brother, if he is still willing to give you a straight reply.'

The look of smug satisfaction on the Scholar's face was irritating but Dallid would not unfairly judge the man. 'Lord Tereail?' he asked, trying to sound as if he was not mocking. 'What must I do?'

The man did not seem to care if Dallid was mocking or not, he just looked pleased at being called lord. Well if the man truly had the status of lord then there was no reason why Dallid would not. Rummaging first in his Kris's belt pouch, Tereail pulled out a glass object before replying. It was a small orb of glass intricately carved into the shape of fire.

'Of what I have seen, there is little that is certain. In most, Kris decapitates Aerath in this room while flames of blue and red surround them on all sides. An image in the mirrors showed us a Fireborn from centuries ago clasping his hands over it before it worked.'

'What of you and your sister,' Dallid interrupted. 'Where are you during the visions?'

Tereail made an impatient face at the interruption. 'We are not in the visions. If the chamber becomes consumed with fire like I feel it must, then we would be wise to be elsewhere.' Or dead, Dallid added without saying. Aerath could kill a fleshborn in a heartbeat. 'I imagine that you will need to be underneath the goddess Am'bril for the ritual to work.' Dallid slid his eyes over the floating goddess and looked away uncomfortably. He did not like the idea of getting closer.

'Be wary, Dallid,' Kris said while Nureail tried to hush him without success. He sounded so tired. 'There is a power seeping out of her that can capture you when you are too close. But perhaps as Fireborn you will not be as affected.'

Tereail was frowning at Kris for the second interruption. The man clearly had a lot more to say. So why was he taking so long to say it? It almost made Dallid want to take the glass item from his hands and just go down to the goddess that very minute. He needed to be more wary though, as Kris had advised, he needed to know as much as he could. Dallid felt like Phira then, a warrior who hungered for knowledge as much as others hungered for blood. He himself had never been interested in anything other than Phira, so could seldom find the energy to give his attention to learning. He needed to concentrate. Tereail had already continued talking without him.

'… a different Connection than you may have known. According to what I have read, and what I now think it must be, it cannot be fire that the object wants, but power. Once it has power then the ice magic will burn by its own volition, if that is what you can call it. I would call it the negation of ice magic if I had to give it a term. Not in the way Lae Noan negates magics, but this will balance and counter the magic rather than rendering it void; a burning of the ice to stop the world from turning to ice.'

Dallid nodded as if he had understood a single word, and Tereail eyed him sceptically. Instead of trying to wrap his mind around how it would work, Dallid moved forwards to what would happen after it had worked.

'These mirrors, they can show me where Aerath is now?'

'Yes, but do not get too close,' Nureail answered for him. Tereail ignored his question and tried to bring Dallid back to his lecture.

'Dallid you do understand how you will power this thing don't you? Not with fire, but with power itself. You will have to Transfer to it, much the way a Fireborn dying of old age does to a younger one.'

'Or a dying Flameborn might do to any passing Exile,' Kris added strangely.

'Yes, yes,' Tereail said, 'but the consequences of Transferring are severe. Once it is unleashed I do not believe you can stop it. All of your power will rush out so strongly that it will be impossible to control. You will lose it all. Become fleshborn.'

It had not been so long since he was fleshborn. The loss would not be so great. It did mean he could no longer possibly kill Aerath though. Kris had not the strength to even try, no matter what Tereail insisted, but he was far stronger a warrior than Dallid was. If at full potential Kris had a slim chance to kill an Iceborn, then Dallid had none. Something in his head screamed at him to forget the ritual, that Aerath needed to die, but Dallid was able to silence that for now. He felt contented that he would die for a noble cause. The mirrors might even be able to grant him his last regret. They could show him Phira.

A mirror to his right swirled into clouds of different colours, and became the image of his wife. Dallid smiled at the sight of her even though she was covered in blood. It would not be her own. She was always too fast, too skilled. Some Fureath'i thought of Phira as too arrogant, but Dallid knew she was just superior. How could she help not talking down to people when she was so clearly above them? He smiled again.

The building she was in was odd, it was not one from Furea, and there were two Foreigners with her, a small slender man and another that looked like a fat Prae'surlas, but with black and grey hair instead of blond, and a giant sword instead of a spear. Even stranger still there was a Fureath'i with her that looked like Thisian. She seemed like she was ready to kill all three, but Dallid knew it was simply a dangerous air she had around her all the time.

As much as it overjoyed his heart to see her again, Dallid frowned at the mirror's sudden imagining. His mind had only brushed on the thought of his wife, when he was about to ready himself for the Transfer. He should have been focusing on how he would lose his powers and likely be killed by Aerath soon after. How much good would it do to deny the ritual and yet leave the man responsible alive? The Iceborn could simply do it again and again until it worked. The dilemma was not easily solved, but to Dallid it seemed killing Aerath was back to being the best thing he could do for Furea and for the rest of the world too. Phira's picture vanished and Dallid eyed the magic with suspicion. Anything from a temple of ice was not something a Fureath'i should readily trust.

A scene of more ice materialised this time, in what looked like the inside of a cavern. Aerath sat on a throne of white in the centre, which would make it the inside of Lae Noan. The blue eyed giant sat alone, unmoving, either transfixed with inner thought or involved in some other cursed conjuring of magic.

'Why does he just sit there?' Dallid demanded. The mirror changed then to show a corridor of prison cells. Bars of ice lined holes in the walls of either side, and the majority of them showed occupants. For hundreds of years Lae Noan had been collecting criminals of power, or anyone the Prae'surlas deemed deserving of captivity. Tereail stepped closer to the mirror, as if searching for something within it.

'Your last words, you asked the mirror why Aerath sits on his throne?' Tereail did not wait for Dallid to answer and continued anyway. 'It could be taken literally, I imagine, that he sits there as protector of the mountain, and these cells are what he protects. But I do not think it is so. Have you ever heard of Noan candles?' Dallid sighed and wondered why Tereail asked questions if he was only going to answer them himself. 'There is one in Rath'Nor that is greatly prized and we have discovered another here with us now. But when lit, it steals away all magic or power, and I have always questioned, where does that power go?'

The mirror shifted back to where Aerath sat on his throne and Tereail let out a laugh of triumph. 'And to think Lady Jaiha would never let us study the mirror we had all along. This is remarkable. It can only confirm what I have assumed. That throne was created by Aerath, and no other keeper of the mountain has had one. Of course you could imagine that it was simply his arrogance, and self-proclamation that he is a newborn god, that merited his need of a throne, but how did he come to acquire those god-like powers? How can a single Iceborn turn an entire world into ice?'

Multiple scenes drifted through the mirror then. It showed Aerath holding a man that looked exactly the same as him by the throat. It showed him placing that man into a cell within Lae Noan and sealing it with a wall of solid ice, the only cell without a window. It showed Aerath gripping Am'bril by the throat next and freezing her solid before bringing her to the Temple of Ice. The way it showed Aerath travelling, it was nothing Dallid had ever heard described before. He looked like he dissolved into blue flames and reappeared again at will. The mirror kept showing more and more scenes of Aerath that he only guessed were answering Tereail's question about how a single Iceborn could turn the world into ice. It showed him in the Tower of Frehep taking the stone segment from it. Then it showed an image of that white-skinned creature Jherin that Dallid had seen in the visions the fire spectre showed him. It even drifted to an image of Brijnok grinning back at Dallid. Where these two beings the only ones able to kill Aerath, or were the two of them assisting Aerath in turning the world to ice.

Finally the mirror began flicking between different cities. Dallid did not recognise any of them until Rath'Nor appeared, but the images continued on quickly. It looked like the mirror went into those cities, but in the same quick flicking succession. It showed groups of Prae'surlas, usually five that Dallid could see, at least one in each group wearing the tunic of a Powerborn, and they seemed to be negotiating with the city leaders. Different throne rooms appeared and disappeared until he saw Rath'Nor again and laughed to see the five Prae'surlas being cut down and killed the minute they appeared in the fortress. Dallid spotted the strange blue fire on the floor of each scene, which meant Aerath was able to transport his people the same way he did himself. Cycling through more places in the world, Dallid smiled to see the Prae'surlas killed in more than a few of the locations.

The Ihnhaarat with their strange masks shot lightning from their hands to kill the north-men. The Powerborn with the group was twitching uncontrollably on the ground by the assault, allowing a man with a skull mask to chop down and remove the head. Another location saw a man with a shaved head behead a Frostborn with the longest sword Dallid had ever seen. He was just beginning to like the mirror when pictures of Aerath started coming back again.

It still ran through each place, some with the Prae'surlas dead, others not, but in nearly all of them a picture of Aerath appeared as a thin sheet of standing ice. It reminded Dallid of the mirror he was watching now and it was maybe how the Iceborn managed to show his image in so many places at once. But as quick as the images appeared, bubbles of bright-blue ice magic also appeared. Scene after scene the bubble expanded and froze everything in the room. When it came to Rath'Nor, a room full of Fireborn destroyed the image with a whirlwind of flames. It looked like they destroyed everything else in the room in the process, but at least the ice magic was smothered.

The cycle went back to the Ihnhaarat and when the ice magic expanded, a cage of lightning formed around the blue light and for a time the ice looked like a beast trying to break free, before eventually fading. An image of what could have been Kel Sherah, for the dark skin of the people in it, also negated the ice magic by a means Dallid could not understand. Even in the place with the shaved-head man - who had killed the Frostborn so quickly - the ice magic in that instance was thwarted by a powerformed sword a woman on the throne held.

But for every scene that the ice magic was stopped, there were three or four where it was not. The cities in the Mordec Empire would have no magic to protect themselves and Dallid imagined a lot of those he was seeing just had all of their leaders killed. The way the mirror was cycling through each scene so quickly made Dallid think that all of the attacks had happened at the same time. For some reason the idea of one Iceborn slowly turning the world to ice was not as hard to believe as the same Iceborn killing every world leader in a single act of power.

'How can he attack so many cities at the same time, and look like he was not even there?' Dallid could not understand the magnitude of power that Aerath was showing. How was he to kill a thing like that? Irritatingly the mirror just shifted back to the scene where Aerath sat on his throne. If that was supposed to answer Dallid's question, then he should ask the damned thing show him how to kill the Iceborn.

'He has the power of thousands, Dallid,' Nureail said from where she knelt. 'Every single Powerborn he has inside Lae Noan, now gives Aerath their power. We only just saw through these mirrors that he has captured Lord Rhisean and fed him to the mountain. The gods only know how many other Powerborn he has captured before or since. The more power he gathers, the greater his ability to capture more.'

'Exactly,' Tereail said with excitement. 'Thousands of prisoners, with all of their powers stolen by the cells of Lae Noan, and fed into a throne of ice connected to Aerath.'

'So that is how he defeated Lord Chrial'thau,' Dallid said, the fight suddenly making sense. During the fight it looked like the Fireborn legend had the better of Aerath so many times, and to Dallid's mind delivering absolute killing blows even to an Iceborn. But always Aerath stood unaffected, his stolen power keeping him alive beyond the means of a normal Powerborn.

'It is true then that Lord Chrial'thau is dead?' Nureail looked defeated at speaking the words. If there were time, Dallid would have detailed to her what had happened, the country would need to be told of Yiran's death and his bravery right to the end. But there was no time.

At Nureail's words Chrial'thau appeared in the mirror they were viewing, but impossibly it was in the same ice cavern where Aerath sat on his throne. The demon rippled with black fire and distorted the air to shimmer around it. Aerath simply looked at the devil with indifference, not even stirring from his seat.

'Is this happening now? Tell me!' He grabbed Tereail by his robes.

'We are not sure!' he said in a rush. 'It has shown us what Nureail believed to be the past as well as demonstrating the present when it showed us you. But there is no way to be sure unless we can somehow demand an answer from the mirror.'

'This does not feel like history,' Nureail whispered. 'I believe this is happening now. Is that demon truly Lord Chrial'thau...'

Dallid could not answer. He watched as Aerath rose from his throne and walked forward to meet the burning demon. It was too much to ask that the two would actually kill each other. The devil looked to be laughing and its black wings of fire spread out behind it as Aerath walked. Then the same bright blue light appeared from Aerath as he had witnessed in the other scenes. Only this time it was not just one explosion of ice magic, it was multiple bursts in quick succession. Every wave of the ice power blasted Chrial'thau backward, until the devil's fire went out under the onslaught. More and more expansions of light and power exploded out from giant

Iceborn and when the magic stopped, all that remained of Chrial'thau was a layered lump of ice attached to the floor.

Aerath wasted no time and clenched his fist over the ice before opening his hand again with a violent wave. The frozen remains of Chrial'thau cracked and separated, sending what would be its severed limbs flying across the cavern of ice. It happened so quickly. How easily Aerath had dismembered and killed what Dallid had thought to be an unstoppable demon. The Iceborn seemed to have so much power that there would be nothing he could not do. Dallid had foolishly hoped to kill Aerath while he was distracted fighting the demon, but it had not even been a fight. Then the floor shattered underneath and Chrial'thau flew up from a hole it had burrowed to save itself.

The demon had no time to return an attack however, because as soon as it reappeared, Aerath's arms pushed out to the walls, floor and ceiling around him. Huge spears of ice grew out of every side of the cavern and pierced straight through the body of the demon pinning it in mid-flight. More and more spikes and icicles arrived to spear through the burning flesh, until the cavern looked like it would become filled with solid ice. The devil's fire still burned, but with Aerath's control, Dallid imagined he could now explode the shards, tearing Chrial'thau to pieces in truth this time.

It did not happen. Dallid waited to see the creature's demise and still the burning thing struggled. In much the same way the large spears of ice were weaved in and out of the demonic Chrial'thau, the creature had sent its own magic weaving in and out of the ice. Dallid could see it now, like a snake or a worm eating through rotted flesh. The black fire must have hollowed out Aerath's creations because the giant spears of ice did indeed shatter, but it was under the devil's weight. The demon stayed in mid-air when they fell, but this time by its own suspension of hellish flames.

The same snakes of black fire that had eaten through the ice also remained visible, all connected to the devil and waving like tentacles through the air. The tendrils of fire shot out towards Aerath and met angry flashes of white and blue from an unseen shield of magic. From everything Dallid had witnessed from the Iceborn so far, nothing had ever penetrated that invisible shield. Perhaps Chrial'thau knew this too, because more snakes of black fire lashed out, and they wrapped themselves around Aerath's throne instead.

Dallid could see the alarm on the Iceborn's face at the fate of his precious throne, and he could even see the snakes of black fire burrowing further and further through the Iceborn's shield. Conflicted, Dallid did not know who he wished to come out as victor. Part of him wished for Aerath's death so badly that he did not care how it arrived, and then another part of him raged that he himself should be the one to kill him. It was as bereft of reality or reason as the scene of power he was witnessing now. A tendril of black fire broke through Aerath's shield at that moment, and wrapped itself around the Iceborn's neck. But before it could touch the skin, Dallid saw blue fire flash out from Aerath's feet and he disappeared.

The scene was deathly still for a time, with the floating demon and its tendrils of fire drifting lightly in mid-air. The devil did not search for where its prey had fled, instead it just sneered a lustful grin at the throne of ice waiting below.

A familiar bright blue light appeared then and another bubble of ice exploded outward, pushing back the hundred snakes of fire reaching for the throne. More and more explosions started again, but by the time they got past the fiery tentacles of Chrial'thau, it had grown back its wings. The devil wrapped those around itself to protect from the bubble of ice, and no matter how many more Aerath sent, they had no effect on the creature's new magic. It appeared the demon had learnt how to avoid Aerath's tricks, and with two such immensely powerful beings, Dallid wondered how long such a fight would go on for. It could last for mere moments or it could endure for years, either seemed as likely.

Dallid could see Chrial'thau's mouth moving now, no doubt taunting Aerath into making a mistake, but there was no sound coming from the mirror. Dallid still did not understand how and why the mirrors were able to show him any of this. If the strange scene was to happen in the future then perhaps he would still have enough time to join in and seize advantage. If it was happening right now however, there would not be a better time to destroy Aerath's ritual. While the Iceborn was battling for his life, Dallid would burn away the evil he was trying to condemn upon the world.

It was a difficult decision to make, but he would have to rely on the demon to kill Aerath. The devil looked more than capable of doing it and as much as he desperately wanted to kill the Iceborn himself, Dallid knew that he had nothing that could match the power of either of those two beings.

Snatching the artefact from Tereail's hand, the Scholar jumped at the sudden movement, and Dallid did not waste time explaining himself as he strode over to the frozen goddess. He would Transfer his power to the item and free the goddess Am'bril, maybe she would be able to aid them in destroying Aerath if Chrial'thau did not.

As he stepped closer Dallid found it easier to look upon the frozen form of Am'bril, no longer feeling uncomfortable to do so. Moving between the oddly arranged mirrors that circled her, Dallid could feel a pull from them that immediately sapped away his strength and energy. Standing next to a single mirror at the end of the chamber was nothing compared to being so close to so many. It felt like all his life was being bled out of him, but Dallid could not give it any more thought. His head was now directly in front of the goddess's feet.

He looked up to bask in her elegance and became lost. Her divine beauty was so extreme, that Dallid was trembling with excited pleasure he would soon be freeing her. All he had to do was Transfer all his power to an object of ice magic. But what was his power when compared to a goddess? He moved his gaze down to examine the piece and struggled not to crane his neck back up just to stare at holy Am'bril once more. He would have time to revel in her greater glory when she was freed, when his powers were gone and he was fleshborn once again. He was already less than nothing when compared to the glory of the goddess, becoming less again did not matter.

Words from Dagen drifted back into mind as he was about to give away his power. The idea that it could have been a gift from Frehep, or the dying Transferral from Chrial'thau, or a curse invoked by higher powers solely to destroy Aerath, and now Dallid was about to give it all up. But what better use could he have for it than stopping the world from turning to ice? He could use it to kill the man responsible.

Kill Aerath.

The pressure of the command within him was so great that Dallid felt like he was being pulled apart from every direction. The mirrors pulled and tore at his power and body, the goddess consumed his soul with her divinity, and his head and heart roared at him to kill Aerath. It even roared at him to kill Brijnok, but then the smallest part of his heart whispered in the voice of Phira:

'The sun god sees you, Dallid, so what will he see you do? Will he see you hesitate or will he see you act?'

Dallid Connected to his power, Connected to Frehep himself, and instead of letting it burst out from his skin, he pushed it into the fire of ice that lay in his hands. It needed his power. It hungered for it. As soon as the Connection touched the artefact, something grabbed a hold of Dallid himself and began to devour everything within. It was so much like what the mirror had done, he was not sure it was them he was bleeding all his life to give. Instinctive fear gripped Dallid and after a heartbeat of hesitation, he snapped his Connection shut.

Dallid dropped the object on the floor and stepped back in shame. It landed hard, rolling slightly but did not break. Nothing had changed. Nothing had happened apart from Dallid hesitating again at the moment of truth. He had failed in his role and did not know if he had the courage to try again. He turned around and hoped Kris was not looking at him. He hoped the mirrors would not suddenly all conjure up the image of Phira staring her disappointment at him. He hoped even more they would not show his own reflection.

Turning back to the frozen goddess with dismay, Dallid's breath caught as the smallest flame appeared from the item underneath. Blue and red fire sprang to life and danced around the small glass and instead of growing bigger as Dallid had thought it might, it grew wider.

A circle of flames ringed out and in places bunched together to create another small fire similar in size to the original one. The floor of the room was ice but when the fire touched it the ice did not melt, it turned into fire. Kris had called it a fire of ice, and that was exactly what it was; it was a thing that turned ice into fire.

The flow passed under Dallid's boots without pause and he could not Connect with it, or sense it, or even feel heat from it. Looking over to the other three, Kris's head was turned and watching as the blue and red fire trailed out past the ring of mirrors and into the rest of the chamber. Nureail did not object when he tried to rise, and even hauled Tereail over to help. Supporting Kris to stand with an arm over each of their shoulders, the short fire passed underneath their boots without reaction also and Dallid wondered what would have happened had it hit Kris's skin while lying down.

When the trails hit the first of the outer mirrors around the room, small fires burst up in front of each. Looking back closer to the goddess, Dallid saw the same had happened for the nine that surrounded her. Scenes of varying lands opened out to meet him, most of them already deeply buried in snow. Only Furea and one or two others were still holding out to some semblance of normality. The blue and red fires were larger in front of the mirrors than anywhere else, even greater than the one underneath Am'bril herself. That first one had not grown at all, but already Dallid could see trickles of melt water begin to form on Am'bril's prison, the only ice that was not turning to fire. Flows of water streamed down her face to remind him of tears of gratitude. He felt like weeping tears of joy himself but was too distracted by the alien flame that consumed the chamber.

The other three Fureath'i watched the blue and red fire more with concern than fascination, and Dallid wondered if they could feel heat from the strange flames if not him. Was he still Fireborn? He had stopped the Transferral but did he stop it soon enough? He was fearful of finding out. When he worked up the courage to clench his fists, pure red fire burst free and Dallid laughed. He let the magic climb its way up his arms and around his body, adding himself to the bizarre occurrence that was happening.

The walls and ceiling of ice were now stone again with a thin film of red and blue fire covering them instead. As the fires in front of the rest of the mirrors grew around the room, Kris and the others moved out of the chamber. As unnatural as the fire was it could still look for other fuel to feed it. The little power that Dallid had given the artefact might only bring the ritual so far, and that could mean the fire might look for flesh to melt or even the air itself to burn.

Since he was still Fireborn he would not need air to survive in the chamber, but the three weaker fleshborn would. *Weaker fleshborn*, he repeated back to himself with contempt. Kris was stronger than any person he had ever known, born of flesh or born of power.

The three were looking at him now, with Kris and Nureail's mouths moving, shouting something. He could not hear them, they were too far away and the roar of the blue and red fires next to him too great. Dallid pointed at them to get further back in case the fire spread. There was no smoke but that did not mean the three could still not choke or suffocate. They responded by pointing towards the mirror they had used to view Aerath and Chrial'thau. Surely they did not mean to use the mirror as a means of escape? Kris would not survive another trip. Dallid was not even confident that he himself could endure another passage through the life stealing objects.

'Leave through the archways!' he tried to shout over to them, 'I will remain here!'

The thought of moving away from the goddess behind him was unthinkable, but he was also able to reason that he needed to stay and see the ritual through. He was enthralled with the living fire that swayed all around him. Had the goddess not been there Dallid felt he might have remained just to experience it in totality. Perhaps the other three felt the same and that was why they hesitated to leave. The dancing flames were mesmerizing, but more so to him. He felt as if he should be looking at a brother. A feeling of kinship ran through him if not the same Connection he had expected. Kris and the others still shouted to him and gestured towards the mirror, but Dallid ignored them. He would stay to be close to the flames, and he would stay to greet the goddess when she awakened.

Dallid's eyes went wide then and felt suddenly awake after a year of sleep. Strangely it was not alarm that filled his veins, he was simply alert. He had feared the moment, but anticipated it also with a consuming need. The blue and red fire around him faded to a mere backdrop. The goddess behind him disappeared from his senses as just another thing of ice to be gotten rid of. All that kept

Dallid's focus now was the man who had suddenly appeared within the chamber of ice and fire. Aerath stood as a giant in the room and stared solely at Dallid.

The flames of red grew stronger up from Dallid's skin, moving in the same swaying motion as the blue and red fire on all sides. The trip through the mirror and the Transferral would have made Dallid weak, and Aerath would have the experience of decades, if not centuries, of ice magic to his advantage, and of course all the stolen power of Lae Noan. It did not matter though. The power of a thousand others might fuel Aerath's frozen heart, but Dallid was going to kill the man. The Fireborn smiled dangerously at the Iceborn he was about to kill. With a roar he pulled free his sword, the blade dancing with flames in reply, and he charged.

CHAPTER FORTY SIX

Death

Aerath folded his arms across his chest and threw them out with an explosion of magic. A sphere of blue ice was sent out and grew larger with speed, before parts of it suddenly turned red and then the entire thing became fire. Dallid stopped his charge, holding up a hand to meet the wave of magic, but the fire passed over him without effect. The Iceborn frowned, looking down at his hands with accusation, and then turned his glare to Dallid.

Dallid smiled.

It was not any new-found brazen courage, but Dallid smiled because the artefact turned all ice to fire. That meant Aerath's power was meaningless if every ritual of ice magic turned to flames. Fire could not hurt Dallid. He wanted to roar with laughter at the good fortune, instead he roared out for battle and continued his charge.

Aerath flicked his hand to create a spear of ice but it turned into a flowing spear of red and blue flames. The Iceborn threw away the creation and it dissolved into air as he did. Dallid was almost on him then, and was overwhelmed with excitement that he would actually be able to kill the man. The power of a thousand others ran within those veins of ice, and it could do nothing but create fire. Dallid swung his sabre down at the unarmed Prae'surlas, anticipating the satisfying crunch of blade through bone.

'Kneel.'

Dallid stopped his run dead and dropped to his knees at Aerath's command. He bowed his head in deference and awaited his god's will. He was greeted instead with the upraised boot of Aerath and was knocked back with such force that Dallid wondered if every bone in his body had just been shattered.

He slid along the ground through the blue and red fire, his limbs trembling, trying to keep a hold of the sabre in his hand. His other hand twitched uselessly in front of his damaged chest, which was dented inward from the force of the kick. Whatever spell Aerath had just used on Dallid to make him kneel had disappeared and was replaced with immobilising pain. It felt like every one of his ribs was now piercing his lungs and that his sternum had fractured inside of his heart. Dallid knew a Fireborn did not need these things to live, but his body told him he was already dead. Unable to move or breath, blind panic threatened to take him.

Somewhere underneath the pain and panic, Dallid reasoned that Aerath still had all the power of Lae Noan, and if he could not use it to power his ice magic then he could use it to power his words and flesh. It was still an impossible fight.

Aerath walked forward but it was not to finish the damaged Fireborn. His eyes were focused on the small item underneath Am'bril's feet that was causing the chamber to swarm with living fire. Dallid watched as the giant strode through the flames without hindrance and spotted something hanging from his neck as he walked. It was the stone segment he had taken from the Tower of Frehep.

As if invoking the name of the Fureath'i god summoned fresh power to his limbs, the shattered bones in Dallid's chest suddenly cracked out with great pain but it was an act of healing. Drawing in shuddering breaths, Dallid could use his lungs and his heart again to pump blood and air. It was absurd that a Fireborn should care about such things, but the comfort of familiar life gave Dallid the power to stand back up.

As he did, Aerath was almost at the artefact, and there was no way Dallid could reach him in time. With no other option, Dallid lashed out with his own fire as he ran. The fire blast travelled with far greater speed and crashed into the back of the giant causing him to stumble. Aerath turned around to deal with the attack and Dallid sent another fire blast ahead of him. Bringing up his hands to protect him, the fire hit Aerath high around his arms and face. The force of the blast did not knock him back like it had before but it did melt and blister his skin. It burnt deep enough to reveal bone and Dallid sent more and more fire against the man. He knew that if he was to have any chance of killing Aerath it would only be while the fire of ice burned.

He arrived at Aerath with his sabre ready just in time to see the Iceborn heal with sickening speed. Dallid's own healing had been quick too, but seeing it done on another was disturbing. The Iceborn's hand snaked out to grab Dallid by the throat but he swung his sabre up to meet it. The blade cut into the flesh but not as deeply as it should. It should have hacked the entire hand off but all that happened was the sabre became lodged halfway. Aerath shook his arm away, taking the sabre with it, and then smashed his other fist into Dallid's face. The blow made his neck snap back so fast he knew it must be broken, and Dallid found himself on a floor of fire once again, struggling to handle the mortal injuries that should be killing him.

He watched as Aerath tore out the sabre from his arm and threw it away. He watched too as the Iceborn once more ignored Dallid as a threat and continued to the artefact that was stopping him from creating ice. Dallid's neck crunched back into place and the bones that had been cracked on his face healed as well. He knew that Fireborns did not heal this quickly, not even the most powerful. So what did that make him? The spectre of fire told Dallid he was created for destruction. Even Dagen had suggested he was created from a curse attached to the stone segment that Aerath wore. Was the curse so powerful that it would do anything to destroy the person holding that stone?

Dallid stood up again and if he was to be given immediate healing to destroy Aerath, then he would use it and not think about where it came from.

Running over to pick up his sword from the flames, Dallid promptly drove it into Aerath's back before the Iceborn could retrieve the fire of ice. Aerath elbowed behind him, but Dallid's shorter height worked to his advantage and was able to avoid the blow. He stabbed again this time hitting a lung, hoping that it would make the giant falter. But if it hurt Aerath in any way, he did not show it.

With a sneer of irritation, he sent both hands out at Dallid, one catching his throat and the other catching the arm holding his sabre. Once the giant had a grip around Dallid's neck, he strode forward and lifted the small Fureath'i high into air. Dallid could feel the flesh of his neck and arm tearing, and the bones in both begin to crumble. He could feel his windpipe getting crushed and his body screaming for air. He could feel all of this but told himself that he did not need them. Whatever injuries the ice devil threw at him he would endure. He would heal. He would survive whatever it took to kill Aerath and with that to power him Dallid broke his arm free of the Iceborn's grip and began stabbing him in his stomach and chest.

The arm that held him in the air did not move, but Dallid could see the pain in Aerath's face as the first two strikes penetrated flesh. The Iceborn's other hand snaked back down to grab hold of Dallid's stabbing arm, and this time crushed straight through all flesh and bone in a single grip, making Dallid scream out in pain and drop the metal blade. Aerath's other hand gripped just as tight, hoping to squeeze through Dallid's neck in a similar way and remove his head from his body. He did not think any amount of unnatural healing would save him from that, so with nothing else that he could do Dallid reached out for every scrap of fire power that he could Connect with. The living walls and floor of the room flared at the call and Dallid's body erupted with flame.

It did not heal his flesh but he could see Aerath's arm begin to smoulder and burn under the intensity. Dallid cried out for more and, with his only functioning hand, he began to claw at Aerath's arm. The heat from his fingers raked into the Iceborn's flesh, but the strength and power of Aerath's grip did not change.

In desperation Dallid grabbed for the stone segment that hung around his neck. He did not know why he did it, but the moment he touched the stone with his hand, Aerath roared and flung Dallid through the air.

When he landed more bones broke but he was free. His momentum almost took him into one of the strange mirrors though, one that was showing a snow capped mountain range, and Dallid dug his fingers into the ground to stop himself. He stopped in enough time but being so close to the mirror Dallid felt weakness sweep over him. His body still burnt with fire, and he could see each flame drifting towards the mirror. Getting rid of the flames before they became lost, Dallid started to rise.

The unnatural healing of his damaged flesh did not come this time, but Dallid pushed himself away from the mirror anyway. His shoulder looked too far forward and the wrist of the same arm was still crushed from Aerath. Looking over to the Iceborn, Dallid saw with dread that he had finally reached the fire of ice.

Lashing out with anything he had, Dallid did not set himself on fire, but instead did it to Aerath. The giant Iceborn became a thing of red flame, and although Dallid knew his healing might fight it off for a time, that much damage had to hurt him.

Aerath did not drop to the ground and writhe in agony as he should though, and he did not scream as the flesh melted and fell from his bones, instead he kept moving. Dallid could see the Iceborn wither down to a blackened skeleton before his very eyes, but still the Iceborn was able to reach down and grab the fire of ice.

The goddess Am'bril above was getting burnt by the flames, the skin of her legs starting to blister just as Aerath's trembling fingers wrapped around the small artefact underneath. Dallid could not be sure but he thought he heard a crunch as Aerath held the item, and when the blazing blue and white eyes turned around to stare at him, Dallid was certain that he had missed his chance.

Blue light surrounded Aerath, and the red fire went out. More and more blue spectral power pulsed from the Iceborn and his flesh grew back whole. The man who had looked near to falling apart, from the frailty of his charred and blackened bones, was just a memory. The Iceborn who had humbled Chrial'thau was whole again, and he stood up slowly, walking away from where Am'bril was still held suspended. He stepped past the mirrors that surrounded her and looked around at the room filled with fire. The red and blue film of flame that covered every surface suddenly looked like such a small thing in the presence of the ice giant. He folded his arms across his chest and sent them out wide to create a room of ice.

The ice magic flew out destroying every trace of fire within the room, and when the wave hit Dallid he fought back with the paltry amount of fire he had left to stop it. He managed to burn a hole through the ice wave as it continued past, but everything else in the room had not been so fortunate. Every other flame had been frozen in mid movement. The larger fires that had been formed in front of the mirrors were motionless and glazed in ice. The floors, the walls, and the ceilings looked like they were full of daggers and spikes.

Turning around to Am'bril, Dallid saw that she no longer floated in mid-air either, but had fallen to the floor. Her body landed on the frozen fires of red and blue that had burned underneath, and Dallid saw those flames of ice now sticking up from where it held her impaled.

Aerath was looking at him. The giant stood and watched as all hope fled from Dallid's eyes. The goddess Am'bril was dead and Aerath had his full power returned. Dallid had failed to kill him when he had his only chance.

He had not been strong enough.

Besides being able to keep getting back up, only to get knocked down again, Dallid did not see what special power was within him that the spectre of fire thought he had. How could he kill anything like Brijnok or Aerath? Taking a deep breath, Dallid set his fists on fire with a weak blaze. His sabre was on the floor a short distance away, but he did not think he would have time to retrieve it, so he created the image of a sword in his hands, made out of fire. The strange looking sword made him smile for a moment before the floor came alive with spears of ice.

Long thin spears struck up from the ground all aiming for Dallid's flesh. He managed to slice through the first of them with his new sabre but there were too many. The ones that he could see he tried to dodge or attack, but soon an unseen one struck up through his foot. As he screamed another shot through his leg and then more and more stabbed into his body until he was held motionless and in agony with blood streaming out from every wound.

The sword of fire and the flames on his flesh had all disappeared to heal the hundred wounds he had just received and as much as Dallid tried to create more fire, the power would not come. Aerath walked forward to finally kill him and Dallid opened his mouth to throw one last insult to the Prae'surlas. Nothing but blood spluttered out from his mouth however and Dallid could not even move enough to laugh at his helplessness. Aerath kept coming.

Dallid met the Iceborn's eyes as he approached but he almost wished he could close them if only to picture Phira before he died. The precious time he had spent with her made him smile, and the news of his death reaching her made him smile wider still. She would kill every one of the Prae'surlas now, including Aerath, and all because of Dallid's death.

Watching Aerath walk towards him and seeing the stone segment around his neck made Dallid want to burst free from his prison one last time and kill the Iceborn, but he had nothing left. All he did instead was fill his last thoughts with Phira, drowning out all other thoughts of fear or vengeance, of hate or hope.

Aerath stumbled then as he walked forward and Dallid reaffirmed that Prae'surlas legs were too long that they trip over them. Aerath stumbled a second time and fell to one knee. Wondering what was happening, Dallid could not move his head to look around, but then Aerath fell to the floor and it revealed Nureail standing behind him in the distance, holding a wooden sword. Aerath pushed back up from the ground and Nureail swung the wooden weapon again. An arc of energy flew through the air and struck Aerath to knock him back down. Dallid wondered why Nureail did not just keep using the weapon over and over and not give Aerath opportunity to get back up, but either way Aerath got back up. She swung in response but Aerath had managed to get to his feet before the energy hit. He was knocked backwards but remained standing.

Now Nureail did swing her wooden blade as fast as she could to send more and more arcs of energy down at the ice giant, but Aerath's hand was already raised. The arcs were frozen and shattered in mid-air, blasting back closer and closer to Nureail before one exploded right in front of her and she fell screaming. Dallid could see Kris try to get up from where he was lying at the sound of her scream, and he could see the other Fureath'i Tereail clutching something to his stomach nervously. The sword that Nureail was holding went from brown to white as ice surrounded it but Dallid could see that the ice did not stop at the weapon and crept down to contaminate her hand as well.

Nureail screamed louder and a sudden spark of fire got Dallid's attention.

Tereail had a flint and was desperately trying to get a spark to catch on a strange piece of ice. It looked like a candle. Memory came back to Dallid of the Scholar talking about some Lae Noan candle that could stop all power. If that was the thing the man was trying to light then it would mean Aerath would be stripped of everything, not just his ice magic this time, but his strength, his healing, every ounce of power within him. It would also mean that the spikes of ice that crippled Dallid would kill him without his own power to heal, but when he saw Kris get back to his feet in the distance he knew what he had to do. He had to remove Aerath's power like the spectre had told him, and without any power, Aerath would simply become another man for Kris to kill.

Tears formed in Dallid's eyes as he was about to die and with a final burst of power he did not know he had, Dallid Connected to fire. His body burst to flames and the spikes of ice shattered just as he sent a spark to Tereail's hands and ignited the Noan candle. Dallid's fire vanished but the wounds did not immediately kill him as he had expected.

The entire chamber began to shake and tremble like it was about to be ripped apart. Aerath stood with his hand outstretched and with clear panic on his face. Nureail still knelt, with half of her arm frozen but took strength when she saw Kris stride past her. Tereail crept further into the room with shaking hands holding the candle that was causing all power to stop. Dallid wondered briefly what affect the candle and the mirrors would have on each other, with both trying to steal the same power, and perhaps even stealing that ability from each other. But he could not give much to that thought, all his focus was on Kris striding towards Aerath.

With the wounds he looked to have received and with the two journeys he took through the mirrors, Kris should be finished. That he stood unaided was nothing short of a miracle, but that he moved with deadly intent, his sabre ready to kill the Iceborn Aerath; it was too much.

The room continued to shake and the frozen shards of fire began to crack and fall. Aerath looked around in panic and Dallid saw him even consider going into one of the mirrors to avoid the Fureath'i that was walking forward to kill him. They no longer showed images of cities or different lands, they all looked blank and solid. Dallid did not know if the mirrors would work while the candle burned and Aerath must have had similar doubts.

So instead he decided to stand and face the Fureath'i that was half his size, but as he swung out his hand to grab Kris's sword arm,

Kris dived forward with a roar and stabbed him in the heart. Before Dallid could wonder if that wound alone might kill Aerath, Kris had already withdrawn the blade and stabbed again, and again and again. With only one arm, Kris drove his sabre savagely over and over into Aerath's flesh, until the giant Iceborn collapsed from the intensity of the assault.

Aerath twisted to fall on his stomach and Kris followed him down not giving an instant to be free of the brutal attacks. Aerath's back was cut into and hacked open, breaking through bone and tearing up flesh. Kris's face was a terrifying distortion of butchery and rage, and his eyes were so black that Dallid wondered if it was not a demon he was watching.

Dallid tried to open his mouth to tell Kris to stop but his throat was not working. His mind reeled at how the man could find such energy but if he did not direct the blows to the Iceborn's neck, then Aerath's power might still return. More and more ice shattered in the shaking chamber, and Dallid did not know how much power the Noan candle could hold. If Aerath held all the power of the actual mountain, then how could a tiny candle hold the same amount, as well as taking Dallid's power, and whatever power the mirrors might possess.

The giant's back was soft and limp, all but completely destroyed by the unending attack, and only when there was almost nothing left did Kris stop to inspect what he had done. Looking over to Dallid and then down to Aerath again, Kris finally moved his sabre over the back of the Iceborn's neck with a shaking hand, so weak that it looked ready to drop the sword if he tried to lift it again. But lift it he did. Here was the vision that Tereail had seen: of the strongest of Fureath'i fleshborn battling victorious and ending the life of the strongest of Prae'surlas Powerborn.

Ice was breaking all over the rumbling chamber, and suddenly Nureail screamed as the ice of her arm was shattered. She fell to the floor missing half of the limb, and Kris stood up and ran to her without thought. His legs gave away in mid-run and he fell, but pushed back up immediately. He fell on top of her when he reached her, hesitating to touch the ruined arm that looked like it had been torn off at the elbow. There did not look like there was any blood but Dallid did not know if such a wound would still kill a fleshborn.

If the ice had not sealed it then she could soon start bleeding and die just as surely.

Eyeing the still form of Aerath, Dallid tried to get up to finish off what Kris had started. He could not risk the candle breaking. It would allow Aerath to have all his power restored to him. If Aerath could heal from just a blackened skeleton, then he could heal from the mass of gore Kris had made of him too. Try as he might though, Dallid still could not move. All energy had disappeared the instant the candle had been lit. Still feeling the pain of his injuries, Dallid did not know why they had not killed him, unless his final blast of fire had sealed them. Either way it stood to reason that if his wounds did not kill him, then Aerath's wounds might not kill the Iceborn either. He needed to tell Kris to finish Aerath, to cut off his head, but the words could not come. Surprisingly the Scholar Tereail spoke them instead,

'Kris! You must finish Aerath while we have the chance!' Kris ignored him. The only thing in the world for the warrior now was the welfare of Nureail. She did not move and Dallid did not know if she was still alive. 'Kris, you fool! The Noan candle cannot hold so much! It is already cracking! Nureail is dead, damn you, and there is nothing we can do about it, but you need to kill Aerath now!'

He grabbed Kris by the shoulder and tried to pull the warrior away from Nureail. Kris spun back with a snarl and swept his sabre along the man's face. Blood came away from the strike, but the force of the blow had sent Tereail retreating back too fast for him to keep his balance. Kris jumped up to follow the man, his sabre lashing out to kill the Scholar, chasing him further back. Dallid watched with horror as Tereail stepped blindly backwards into one of the chamber's mirrors, still holding the Noan candle. A deafening boom filled the chamber as he fell inside.

CHAPTER FORTY SEVEN

Destruction

Kris stopped, reality descending on him, and he stood staring at the mirror Tereail had fallen through. His body heaved up and down with ragged breath, and Dallid saw the warrior's sword hand continue to shake. The mirror the Scholar had fallen through had gone black. Every other mirror in the room had returned back to shifting scenes of different lands, and with a sense of dread, Dallid felt power return to his flesh.

Looking over he saw the smallest of blue flashes and knew the giant was still alive. Dallid needed to rise first. If ever he had needed to find one last source of power then it was now. Aerath's hands lifted him up and Dallid's did the same. Both Powerborn were trying to stand, and both were without any trace of strength. Aerath's movements seemed as if without a body, his torso had been so butchered by Kris, but alarmingly another flash of blue light appeared and the Iceborn's movements became steadier, his body became thicker. As Dallid finally managed to push himself to his knees, Aerath had most of his flesh returned and was standing once more, albeit unsteadily.

The flesh that had been hacked to the bone before was now hanging in strips of wet skin and meat. Every part of him was a stream of flowing blood. The stone segment he had stolen from Frehep's tower was still tied around his neck, remarkably intact, just as the Iceborn's head should not have been. Aerath's blue and white eyes flashed and his skin healed further. They flashed a second time and clothes of woven ice began to decorate him like new. When he was fully recovered those same blue and white eyes looked down at where Kris had moved protectively over Nureail, and then they moved to Dallid.

Neither of the two Fureath'i were in a position to attack him or pose threat, so Aerath turned his back on Dallid and moved his gaze to where Am'bril lay dead on the floor. Aerath's eyes then moved past her to look at one of the mirrors, and Dallid recognised it as the one that had held the scene of Aerath and Chrial'thau in the throne room of Lae Noan.

Dallid could see the demon Chrial'thau still in the image and could see he was now sitting on Aerath's throne.

If it was as Tereail said, and the throne could Connect with Lae Noan's power, then Chrial'thau was trying to steal it from Aerath. Foolish hope began to burn in Dallid's heart again.

'All of your precious power,' he managed to croak from his damaged throat, 'and now you will lose the very source of it.'

Aerath's head turned around to Dallid and then back to the mirror, which changed to a view of a single prison cell. On either side there were bars of ice covering the adjoining cells, but on the one the mirror showed: it was completely sealed up. Whoever was in that cell, it had been covered to ensure no-one ever found out. The spectre of fire had told Dallid to look for that very thing. He said if Dallid could find that then he would find the source of Aerath's power. If Chrial'thau was already stealing part of Aerath's power, then perhaps Dallid knew a way to steal the rest. With one final effort of power, he lurched forward to his feet and dived straight into Aerath, pushing them both through the life-stealing mirror and into Lae Noan.

***

'Give me the orb that creates star markings.'

Thisian winced at how angry she sounded. She was ordering them as if they were under her command, and Phira clearly expected swift obedience. Thisian surprised himself by looking around to get it for her, checking under the table where he had left it but it was no longer there.

'We don't know what you're talking about,' Krife said, folding his thick arms across his chest.

'You are lying,' Phira said and Thisian saw her turn the sword in her hand. He knew from experience that she did that only when she was about to kill someone.

Griffil must have seen the motion too as he quickly jumped in. 'What he means is that we no longer have it. It was taken from us by a Prae'surlas of all people. His name is Hrothlar if you want to find him.'

From the way she eyed them both - actually no, she was eyeing all three of them - it made Thisian think that she did not believe Griffil either.

'This Prae'surlas, he did not try to kill you?' Phira asked instead.

'It seemed we were *beneath* him. You know how Prae'surlas are,' Krife said, spreading his arms out to display his grubby tattered clothes, and the big hairy stomach that pushed out from them. Phira eyed his hands, and the massive sword strapped to his back. They flicked to Griffil's feet then before finally resting on Thisian, clearly blaming him for all of it. He thought about smiling at her, but changed his mind. It was best that she would want as little to do with him as he could manage. A smile might only win over her female heart to helplessness. With fortune she would forget about all ideas of dragging him back to Rath'Nor and get on with her own life like she did best.

'It seems I've quite the talent for choosing friends, Phira,' he said with a smile, but it was not the charming one he saved for women he wanted to bed. Now was not quite the right time to try bedding her. 'I'm not saying Krife and Griffil here are the same standard as the friends of my childhood,' he said with a placating gesture to Phira, 'but this is my new life now, with Foreigners so low that they fall further beneath a Prae'surlas sneer than a Fureath'i. Have I not found worthy brothers?'

'Do not talk again, Thisian, or I will return your head to Rath'Nor instead of your body,' Phira cut him off rudely before he could continue to further antagonise her.

Krife elbowed him and whispered in a low rumble. 'Do all your friends want to kill you and send you back to Rath'Nor, Fireborn?'

'He is not a Fireborn,' Phira said sternly. 'At least there is that much to be said for the situation.' She pointed her sword towards Krife first. 'I have had a long night and wish to be done with it in the next few moments, so if you do not want to join a long list of other corpses, answer these questions wisely. Why would Hrothlar leave the two of you here after you killed so many of his men? Why also is there a blood-smeared blue mask behind Griffil's feet, the same as Hrothlar is reputed to wear, and your knuckles bloody from hitting it, Krife?' Krife looked down at the back of his fist and turned to Griffil with a shrug. The thief shook his head with disapproval and Phira went on. 'I then have two further questions, which you can choose to answer instead of any others. First, where is the orb? And second, why would you try to keep it from me? As soon as I have taken the co-ordinates for Rath'Nor from it, I will be gone from this city, leaving you all to roam free,' she said before adding, 'for a time.' The last she threw at Thisian. He cursed under his breath since it meant that she was indeed intent on hunting him down and hauling him back by his hair.

Of course she would not let him be forgotten, it could only better bloody Furea by having one more bloody Flameborn lost forever in the mundane ranks of army life.

Turning to Thisian again Krife grinned. 'I like her, Fireborn, as arrogant as Amadis himself. But I think I like that other friend of yours more. There wouldn't be as much talk from him I think, he'd have just killed us and been done with it.'

'You're bloody right about that,' Thisian agreed and got another lightning quick slash across the face from Phira as punishment. 'Burn me! Will you stop doing that?!' He held up his hand protectively to the new gash and stepped back out of sword range. She did not say anything to remind him she had ordered him silent and instead waited patiently for Krife and Griffil to hand over the orb.

The big treasure hunter just shrugged and Thisian wondered if moving those big shoulders was as exerting as it looked. 'Well, Griff, you heard the other lady, let her use it. Anything to thank one of Thisian's Fureath'i friends for not killing us.'

Phira eyed him for that remark, but instead of challenging it, she just watched as Griffil moved away to fish out where they had stashed the orb. She might have thought Griffil was leaving to pull out a throwing knife or crossbow for all the intensity she fixed on him. Thisian took advantage of the pause to think of anything he could say to stop Phira from coming back for him or spreading word to everyone in Rath'Nor about the Exile Flameborn that needed to be captured and returned for training. His mind was blank though, so he looked about helplessly.

He spotted the cut ropes by the chairs where the two had been captured and wondered how they got out. Griffil might have had a knife stashed somewhere and cut himself loose. Krife then would have wrecked his way around the Inn, but how had the two of them let themselves get captured in the first place? That and the fact that Hrothlar was missing did not reassure his trust in the two companions that had earlier offered his death as a bargain. Maybe he could return to Rath'Nor with Phira, she might be able to put in a good word on how he saved her life. Maybe even enough to make people forget about the attempted Exile.

'Hey, Fireborn,' Krife elbowed him again. There would be a flaming bruise on his arm if he was not a bloody Flameborn. 'You ever get between the legs of this friend of yours?'

'Krife, please,' he said softly and Phira's eyes glared at him momentarily before going back to keeping a watch on Griffil rummaging about. 'Can you at least try not to make her any angrier than she already is?'

'Do you think she likes big swords? Because I've got a very big one.'

Thisian saw Phira attempt to ignore him, but Krife had a way about him that made it very difficult. Heroically Thisian jumped in to stop the situation from exploding into more violence. Krife was always in the mood to pick a fight, but picking a fight with Phira would be his last. There had been far too much violence for one night already, and it was not exactly the kind of legend that he wanted to create. There had to be a less gruesome way to make a legend, one with more whores and maidens, and less people trying to kill you.

'Phira? Can I see the Spike before you go?' She threw him a dismissive look so he smiled as he added, 'I've just always wanted to see one, and I thought since I saved your life earlier you might humour me.'

'You are lucky I did not kill you for interfering, Thisian.'

'Lord Thisian,' he grinned back. He really couldn't help himself.

'Lord Thisian! You are a lord and protector of all you see now? And what lands do you protect here outside of Furea? I will have you chained and dragged down the streets of Rath'Nor as an example for others that might ever consider abandoning our nation as an Exile. There are ways to Transfer what should not have been yours and give it to another more deserving, Thisian, and it will not need your consent. A single Lord Fireborn could rip it free from you and take my word when I say I shall make sure it is done!'

So perhaps he would not try returning to Rath'Nor with Phira. Thisian pretended to ignore all those terrible things she had said and just asked, 'So can I see the Spike?'

With a contemptuous laugh she reached behind and pulled out the metal device, throwing it onto the table beside him. 'You are forever a child, Thisian. Here, if it will quieten you for even the barest of moments then it is worth the risk of you stealing it.'

Thisian eyed it, and eyed Phira too for a moment, to see if it would be a trick to get him close enough to slash with her sword again. From this distance the Spike looked like several daggers bent and bound together in a jewel shape, and when he picked it up with the quickest of movements, he was surprised by how light it was. Griffil had returned then with the orb and not a crossbow, and gave one last look to Krife before handing it over to Phira. Thisian quickly put down the Spike and offered his assistance.

'You simply put your hand on top of it and concentrate on the place that you wish to go. The top of the orb will then crinkle and become a kind of paper that you can peel away from it,' he stuck his hand to Griffil. 'Here, this is what it will look like.'

Griffil raised an eyebrow before taking out the parchment he created earlier. Phira just ignored him. 'I do not need to see what paper looks like, Thisian.' She held the orb in one hand, and placed her sword hand on top. She did not risk closing her eyes, staring intently at what she was doing.

Thisian would not have been as skilful as Griffil, but he believed he was able to move softly enough that no-one would notice. He placed the sheet of paper on the table in front of him and had no choice but to go ahead with his plan. What choice did she bloody leave him?

It was difficult to shift his eyes to make sure the right notches were being pressed, but there were not many thankfully. So he picked up the Spike as if weighing it in his hands again and Phira did not even look at him. All of her attention was on operating the orb and getting the star markings to send her back to Rath'Nor. She threatened to humiliate him in front of everyone there, even threatened to find a way to take away his new power. She threatened to kill him.

Thisian threw the Spike down at Phira's feet and stepped back as fast as he could. The metal landed on the very tip in perfect balance and opened out with a display of colour and light. The magic swirled up and around Phira, before swallowing both her and the orb into itself and vanishing. When it was done Thisian realised his hands were not even shaking.

It had to be done. He knew she would not have rested until she brought him back. It was not as if he had killed her, just, sent her away.

Krife grunted. 'Eva won't be happy we lost her orb.'

'You do know you've sent her to Lae Noan, Thisian, don't you?' Griffil didn't exactly say the words with accusation, but Thisian felt it anyway.

'Yes, I know,' he said and thought about explaining why he had no other choice. But knowing Krife he would not care and Griffil, well he deserved an explanation at some point alright, but privately. For now he turned to Krife. 'You do remember I said that Eva wants us dead, right?'

'Probably because we lost her orb,' he mumbled. Pulling out the Segment of Ahmar from around his neck, he added, 'she will still want to get this thing out of her city as fast as she can.'

'Yes and killing us will do that the quickest,' Griffil explained.

Krife rolled his shoulders - maybe they *were* sore from all the shrugging. 'Haven't been killed yet tonight, and don't intend on starting now.'

Thisian shook his head and cursed. He would have to change gods. Fortune had brought him nothing but bad luck and other Fureath'i, and he even had to send one to flaming Lae Noan, killing her in every way other than holding the sabre himself. For a frightening moment he considered trying to go after her, something suddenly drawing him to Lae Noan that he could not explain, but there was no way he could get there. It was foolishness. Taking a hold of himself, Thisian made an effort to forget about Furea and any embers or blaze commanders that would do their best to upset him. A stray thought about Dallid drifted into his mind, about the brotherhood he had at least shared with him, but sending Phira to Lae Noan had finished that. So Thisian burned away all thoughts of Dallid along with everything else that was considered Fureath'i.

Farewell, Dallid, my friend, we had once been brothers but now no longer.

***

Dallid's face lay on cold ground, wet with melt water from the heat of his body. *Lae Noan.* That was where he was, with Aerath. He opened his eyes and weakly searched for the giant. The figure was soon found, his bulking mass laid out on his back, blood still running freely from the wreck of wounds Kris had given him. Dallid thought they were healed but the mirrors must have ripped them back open. He looked no more able to rise than Dallid did. That fact made all his imagined energy disappear, the fevered hope that he could somehow find the will to stand again, vanished when he knew that Aerath could not either. Perhaps they would both rest unconscious for a time until their strength returned. The cowardly thought made Dallid laugh.

It seemed he had no greater desire in the world right then but to close his eyes and rest. All manners of treacherous reasoning conjured themselves into being and danced seductively to his mind. Dallid did not close his eyes though, nor did he rise. He could not. It was as simple a fact as any other. The second trip through the mirror had stolen too much from him, and he wondered if he looked as aged from it as Kris did.

Kris. A fleshborn who had been through twice just as a Fireborn had, and yet the fleshborn was able to rise when needed to kill Aerath. His traitor mind put forward the suggestion that the mirrors might take more from a Powerborn, since there was more to take, but he knew it for false. He needed to rise and, without a sabre, find a way to destroy Aerath once and for all.

A blue glow then appeared from behind Aerath's closed eyes. The blue and white light grew brighter as the eyes opened and then made its way down his body. Dallid had been a fool to think the mirrors would take away that source of power, and a greater fool to think that the demon sitting on Aerath's throne would take much more. Chances were that the mirrors took away everything else and only through desperate need had the power of Lae Noan been wrestled back from Chrial'thau's grasp to Aerath. The Iceborn giant awoke and rose to his feet.

Dallid had no choice but to do the same, he had only one chance left. Fuelling himself with a laugh of madness and futility, Dallid stopped thinking about how he could kill Aerath now. The two chances he had already been given, the fire of ice and the Lae Noan candle, had both failed. How could this last chance work instead? No, just because his mind could not conceive of a thing did not mean that it did not exist. He would look at it simply. It was a man of ice that he sought to kill and so he would do it by fire.

Flames burst into life along his skin again, possibly for the last time. The expulsion of energy from his body nearly brought him to the floor again, but the look of concern he saw on Aerath's frozen eyes was enough to keep him upright. There was fear in the Iceborn's face and such a man as could still fear was one that could still be killed.

Drinking in his enemy's trepidation, Dallid waited to regain an energy that was not arriving. The fire that covered his body was taking all that he had. If it had not been for the slightest change in Aerath's gaze, Dallid might have let the flames go. But if he had done that then the heat his fire was producing would not have begun melting the single cell of ice that was completely covered up - the only cell in the entire corridor that did not have bars to show the prisoner inside. Realisation sparked in the cold eyes of white and blue, and as quickly as he struck out, so too did Dallid.

Shards of ice appeared and exploded into Dallid's face and torso, piercing every vital organ his flesh had within him. He had sent his own attack before being struck, but it had not been directed at Aerath. Instead a ball of fire collided with the wall of ice that covered the cell, melting it completely.

In the hazed moments before consciousness left him, Dallid saw Aerath rush forward and wrestle with a man that looked exactly like him. It was as if Aerath was fighting with his mirrored reflection. Aerath stopped the other Iceborn from leaving the cell, but ended up barrelling both of them back inside. A smile gifted Dallid's face a moment then. It was a smile for the idea that Aerath was now inside one of his own prison cells.

***

Pain raged through the demon that was once known as Chrial'thau, but along with the pain came purest power. When it sat upon the ice throne, the demon felt like it was suddenly within a raging river. Power bombarded the devil and tried to wash it away, but it held firm and drank from that river. The power consumed, scalded the demon profoundly, being so complete in design to not be touched by its kind. But when Aerath created the trap to stop anyone usurping his power, he failed to account for a being of all worlds to do so. The glory of the shadow, still linked to the sickening light, and held together by the flesh that stood between. The demon of Chrial'thau had the potential for supremacy in all worlds.

Pain and power, more and more, it could not be possible how the mountain held so much. Looking down at its hands gripping the throne, the demon of Chrial'thau laughed when it saw them wither with blackness, the flesh rotting away before it lit with dark fire. The devil laughed even harder when the fire ran all three colours of blue, red and black. It only showed once more that there was no power that it could not have. The creature would have it all. It would take every drop of life from the mountain and then burn every world to ash. The devil's fire would devour all it touched and nourish the demon further, only making the fire stronger again. There was nothing that could stop it.

Then the demon felt a surge in the power that was rampaging into it. It was if all of the mountain's power had just been added again, not doubling what was there but multiplying it by itself. As seemingly infinite as the power was, it was still shared between Aerath and the demon. But Aerath had entered into the cells of Lae Noan, as Chrial'thau could somewhere sense him, and what began was an inexorable cycle of power. All the power of Lae Noan linked both to the throne and to Aerath, fed back into itself to increase its hold, only to go back into Aerath again which fed the mountain over. It would not stop.

The river turned into an ocean and the demon of Chrial'thau screamed as it swept through, abolishing the devil in a devastating release of power. Everything exploded in a storm of black maelstrom, streaked brightly with lines of red and blue. It consumed all that surrounded it, and hungrily searched for more.

The demon, the throne, and the source of Aerath's power, were all destroyed as one.

· CHAPTER FORTY EIGHT ·

Lae Noan

The ice was oppressive but not cold. There was no mistaking she was inside Lae Noan and worse she was inside one of its cells. Phira kept wary eyes on the man who occupied it with her, slumped in the corner, but he did not seem alive. There was no cot in the cell, or anything else, it was a blank cube of white. She had no way of knowing how long the man had been imprisoned there, as he just sat huddled, eyes open and stared at nothing. Was that to be her fate?

No, it would be Thisian's.

She would escape and Lae Noan would make a fitting prison for Thisian once she had finished with him. To be an Exile was bad enough but then to condemn a fellow Fureath'i, a blaze commander, and a woman he had grown up with, who was married to his best friend... it was too much for Phira to think about. If she began, the frustration of it, combined with the confinement of the ice cell, it could break her. She would survive this. She would escape and she would survive this.

The orb she was holding did nothing no matter how intensely she concentrated now. A brief thought about it never working, based on who had given it to her, was dismissed however. When she had used it in Amidon it had begun to materialise in her mind and in the feel under her skin, before the absolute coward Thisian sent her here to Lae Noan. It could be no other place, and the magic of the orb would not work within the cells. Neither would the Spike, which stood by her feet, still open. That she had been able to appear within the cell itself was strange since no magic should exist between its walls. It was fortunate so that she was not swallowed into Lae Noan as a part of the Spike. The metal device, held open as it was, looked like it was still feeding all of its power into the prison cell. She kicked it to the corner with her cloak and threw the orb with it, hoping it would smash. The cloak she had removed to feel less trapped, but no matter how she tried to perceive it, she was hopelessly trapped.

She should try to question the prisoner again, but the man did not appear cognisant. He had long hair hanging loose and dishevelled around his face, and more growing down from his chin. He was not old but looked haggard. Everything about him was the sight of a man who was broken.

'When I arrived,' she repeated. 'What did you see? Did the Spike work in this place?' If it did once then it might again, if she could get it closed to stop it losing energy.

The man did not even blink though. He was already lost to the mountain. It was precisely why Phira had not thought Lae Noan as much of a punishment. A person would simply lose their mind and become numb to its oblivion, unless they were of incredible will or power. The Prae'surlas certainly went out of their way to capture such, if only to demonstrate the supremacy of their prison.

Growing impatient with the dead man, Phira peered out through the gap of bars set along at eye height. Eye height for a Prae'surlas perhaps, but Phira had to push onto her toes to see out from the lowest part of it. She thought about calling out to the other cells but did not want to attract the attention of any guards yet. If the other prisoners were coherent then they would have heard her heated questioning of the man when she first arrived.

Her rage at Thisian had been at its freshest, and the mindless thing sitting near her was lucky to have survived it. Looking down at her sword, Phira hesitated. It was her favoured sword, a gift from Yiran, his name engraved on it but he had named it *Unrivalled* for her. It was already worn from the battle with the Jhakral and she did not relish damaging it further. That left the sword of Protharik and the one from the stormwarrior, neither of which she was keen to destroy. There was always the Jaguar blade, and although its power might not work within the cell, she still did not dare to touch it, not until Valhar was dead. She would consider using it to kill Valhar himself though. That murderer was one more man she would spend her every hour hunting down to kill, him and Thisian, when the time allowed.

She needed to get out of the prison first, and would not use the Jaguar blade. Brijnok's curse said that she could only die by a sword, and whatever false assurances he might have given her, touching the Jaguar might just be the sword that does it. Taking out the jagged weapon in the shape of frozen lightning, Phira decided she would rather destroy something that Brijnok's curse had created.

Taking aim, Phira swung high against the bars of ice. The impact jolted her wrists and elbows, and as she feared, the blade took damage, whereas the bars looked to take none. She swung again. It was difficult to commit the strength that was needed, knowing that she did not yet wish to attract guards and knowing how much the impact would hurt her. But she continued. On her fifth swing, she was halted in mid-stroke by the man's voice behind her.

'You waste your time,' was all the man said, speaking as if half asleep, he did not even look at her.

'You may spend yours as you wish, but my time is too valuable to spend any longer in here.' She had an Iceborn, a madman, and a Flameborn to kill, and in that exact order.

'You waste your time,' he repeated.

Phira went back to ignoring him and striking as hard as she could against the bars. The noise it made was significant, enough to alert any guards if the prison even needed them for the cells. Fighting her way free from Prae'surlas fleshborn was an achievable option, but Phira wanted to exhaust other possibilities first. The chance of a Frostborn arriving, or worse an Iceborn, was too likely. With a few squads of her best men she would eagerly fight them, but on her own it would be just arrogance beyond even her to consider it. She struck again.

The man behind her sighed dramatically as if gathering enough air for more words. True enough, his lifeless speech followed. 'This place takes your power, whatever it may have been. Accept that you are now powerless, or be driven mad by it.'

Phira would not waste any more time on the defeated man. 'I *am* my own power,' she said. She did not need to be born with something given to her by a god. Neither did she need to go clawing at their feet for other magic. And she did not need some god's curse to protect her from fleshborn weakness.

Phira struck again at the bars of ice and hacked off a chunk for her efforts. A small piece but a success none the less. She almost smiled churlishly at the man behind her, but then a torrent of fire appeared in the corridor and she jumped back.

Black flames with streams of impossible blue and red flooded past and did not look to have an end. Phira stepped further back from the heat, as far as she could in the cramped space and not trample the man with her. There was nowhere to hide from it. If the fire burnt through the ice doors then she would be freed but she would be dead.

No, that fire could only be magic, and magic could not exist within the cells of Lae Noan.

With forced confidence she stepped closer to the flames to inspect them. It was with both fear and elation that she saw the ice melt under the fire's fury, first the thin bars on top and then the solid wall of ice itself. Phira's fear was slowly pushed away by her mind when she watched as the flames did not travel inside the cell through the enlarging hole it created. If magic could exist in the cells then it was swallowed so quickly to make it look like it could not.

Such a show of power and fire could only have come from a hundred Fureath'i lords all attacking the mountain as one. But the black flames were not natural, and the streaks of bright blue were almost worse, hurting her eyes to look upon. No, nothing good could have created such a thing.

But good or not, the fire meant freedom and Phira was not the only one to realise it. The man behind her slowly got to his feet. He stretched out limbs that might not have seen movement in years and stared in bewilderment at the fire burning down his prison. Phira was also standing, but with her sword ready should the man come any further back to his old self. He looked only slightly more impressive now that he stood. Perhaps when he was well groomed he might have looked a man of worth.

'What is your name?' Phira asked.

The man did not turn to answer her, his focus too intent on the fire or else his mind was not yet recovered - if ever it would after such an imprisonment. She would not try to talk with him again.

There might be strength in numbers when escaping, but a departure of stealth was just as prudent.

When the fire abruptly stopped, Phira did not wait and grabbed the open Spike before leaping out of the hole the flames had created. Hoping for a reaction from the metal device, Phira shook the Spike to see if it would close and be used for escape. When nothing happened, Phira tossed the Spike away. There would be thousands of prisoners soon running down the halls of Lae Noan and she intended to be out of the mountain as quickly as possible.

Darting a quick look in either direction, Phira could indeed see similar damage on almost every cell door, as well as holes burnt through the floors and ceiling. Choosing the direction where the floor was not missing, Phira ran. She still held the lightning sword, already damaged beyond use and so she discarded this too it as she ran. She pulled free her favoured sword, Unrivalled, and held it ready. There was no telling what manner of fiend would soon appear from the melted prison cells. Keeping an eye on those she passed, Phira saw many strange creatures, one with a cleft down the centre of its head, one wearing a full metal helmet and dead-faced mask, but she cursed when she saw a Jhakral lurking behind one of the cell doors. The hole burnt into the wall looked too small for it to squeeze through though and if the prison still worked as it should then the Jhakral would be too weak to make it any bigger.

Either way she did not want to find out if she would have the same luck killing a Jhakral a second time. Something else crawled awkwardly out of a broken cell some distance in front of her then. It looked almost like a man but with arms longer than its whole body and thick with muscle. The man, if you could call him that, used them to walk as much as he did his legs, but Phira did not stop running. If the long-armed creature wanted to die straight away after how many years of imprisonment then he was welcome to do so. He need only move to hinder her and she would oblige him in his wish. His eyes widened at her darting pace but Phira did not have time to see if his intentions were violent or not. Instead the ground beneath her crumbled as the ice, too badly weakened by fire, could no longer support her weight.

She might have taken the fall skilfully had there not been a person lying in the corridor underneath. So instead of taking the landing with a roll on her shoulder, Phira had to spin in mid-air to land on her side, not on the injured hip thankfully, and she managed to keep her sword arm held up and ready to use. Then her sword nearly fell from her hands as she looked at the body that lay beside her.

It was Dallid. Dallid with dried blood covering his face and body as if he had been stabbed a thousand times, but his chest rose smoothly to show life in his veins. He wore the unmistakeable tunic of a Fireborn, although it was torn to shreds, and Phira's heart nearly sank when she considered that he had gone Exile with Thisian. But Thisian's story of the Lord Kr'une had not included Dallid.

So shocked by his appearance, Phira did not notice the two men struggling with each other in a cell close by. All others seemed to be empty but she would not dismiss them as so. Quickly making sure Dallid did indeed have a pulse, Phira kissed him on the lips before she knew what she was doing. She got up fast, glancing upward to see that the long-armed beast was not following and stalked forward then to see what kind of criminals were fighting each other in the cell closest. She stayed down low and it only served to contrast the two giants she witnessed wrestling within the cell.

Each one as large as the other, each one a Prae'surlas wearing the tunic of an Iceborn, white with silver spears arching up the borders. She had heard Aerath was described as one of the largest Prae'surlas in the nation, but why would he be fighting within one of his own cells with another Iceborn? Both looked exactly the same to her, and although the Prae'surlas were well known for inbreeding, the two would have to be brothers. Aerath had no brothers, so these two should not concern her. While in the cells however they would be without their powers and both extremely vulnerable to her sword; killing two Iceborn was too great an opportunity to pass up.

Looking back to Dallid, Phira knew she was leaving him open to attack. There would be vast numbers of Lae Noan prisoners running loose and looking to vent years of violent frustration. But her fight would not take long. It was worth the risk and still she hesitated. This was why Lei had died. She had chosen her own safety and the success of the mission instead of the life of another

Fureath'i. Bringing both herself and Dallid to freedom should be her number one priority. Otherwise there would be countless other Frostborn and Iceborn that she might pass and consider the same.

It was her life to make these decisions in a fraction of a heartbeat, and in the time she had spent hesitating the two would already have fallen to her sword. She blamed Dallid for tearing her focus and causing the dilemma. In many ways her life would be cleaner if he was not so deeply within her heart, but she knew also that without Dallid she could not really call what she did a life at all. He filled what would otherwise be an empty cavity within her chest and pumped blood and life to the rest of her body. But this was too great an opportunity to pass by.

Phira stood up and lunged forward into the cell. She pierced one of the Iceborns in the stomach before cutting back across and slitting the throat of the other. The one she had stuck through the stomach had a tunic as torn and bloodied as Dallid's had been, and the other Iceborn's tunic soon became just as bloody as all life poured out from his neck. Both giants dropped dead as they should. After all, within the cells of Lae Noan without their power, they were just flesh to be killed like any other.

Phira dug her blade into the neck of the one whose throat she had slit and meticulously sawed through the rest of it. The head rolled free and she turned to do the same to the other Iceborn but shouts from above told her that many more prisoners had finally broken free. They were as likely to crash down on top of her as she had if the ice holding each floor was as weak. Looking down at the Iceborn still with his head, she considered for a moment before sighing and running back out to Dallid. Beheading one Iceborn would have to satisfy her and Phira smiled when she thought that no other fleshborn had ever done that before.

Once back with her injured husband, Phira looked around quickly but saw no one else near yet, so she knelt down to inspect Dallid's condition. Seeing him again let the reality of how much she loved him wash over her completely. She was tired of pretending to be strong enough to live without him. Even her own heart had no idea of how much she missed him until she saw his face. It could not matter anymore if he would be a distraction, Phira would arrange a way for them to be together from now on. He could certainly take Lei's place as her ember. Why was he wearing the tunic of a Fireborn though? Why was he even here! She would kill him if he had gone Exile with Thisian.

Holding back her frustration, Phira picked up Dallid and balanced his weight over her shoulder. He was so badly wounded she winced as her shoulder pressed into the soft and bleeding flesh. But if it hurt him, he did not react.

It would be impossible to fight with him weighing her down so much too, which just meant there was no more time to waste. She started off in the direction that had the least of amount of roaring. Yiran had shown her maps of Lae Noan before, designed simply as a circle, of several floors, but all joining up at four central lines. Each line then either led to the core of the mountain where Aerath had built himself a throne, or it led to an exit. She hoped it was the southern exit she would find herself at, but there would be no way to tell until she was outside.

Knowing that any direction would bring her to an exit eventually, but also knowing that all four exits were the only places in the mountain that needed to be guarded, Phira picked up speed to get there first. She could discover how to get past the guards when it came to it, if they had all not been burnt alive by the fire.

Movement from behind made her turn her head slightly, just to see how immediate the danger would be, and she ground her teeth when she saw it was one of the Iceborns. The one she had stabbed in the stomach had not died within the cell, but had managed to drag himself halfway into the corridor. It was the one with the tattered tunic who looked already dead, but was regaining his healing power the more of his body he dragged out of the cell.

Further arguments began to burn in Phira's mind about focus and priorities, and leaving Dallid open to anyone who would find him in her absence, but Phira swept them all away. This was her focus. To better Furea, and there could be no better use of her time than to rid the world of one more Iceborn. When the war arrived, and it was all but imminent, every Iceborn not challenged by a Fireborn could slay hundreds of Fureath'i warriors. What was one man's life worth when compared to that?

She laid Dallid down, careful not to put him into one of the cells. If he really was Flameborn like Thisian, or even Fireborn like his tunic suggested, then she did not want whatever wounds he had received coming back to kill him. He could not be Powerborn though. The wounds must be superficial. Dallid was strong and he would endure. She allowed herself one more kiss to make her believe that her love for him was equal to the love she had for her country, then she sprinted down to make quick work of the crippled Iceborn.

The wounded giant supported himself against one of the walls and blood ran freely from the stomach wound she had given him. There would soon be more. The Iceborn saw her approach and instead of try to kill her, he tried to command her.

'Kneel,' he muttered through gritted teeth.

'No,' Phira said back and kept coming.

The Iceborn lifted a hand to destroy her, crying out in pain at the effort and clutching at the wound in his stomach with his other hand. The one raised to slay her did not falter, but neither did an attack of ice come forth. Blue and white light formed and solidified around the gesture, a haze of power moving slowly in her direction but with no chance of harm. The great sword of ice forming was nearly complete when Phira heard Dallid roar from behind. She was still far enough away to afford to stop and turn, and saw a figure hidden deeply in hooded robes standing above him. A yellow mist was seeping out from underneath the figure's robes, and when it touched Dallid, he screamed. Phira did not know what to do and for a moment she hated Dallid because of it.

There was no time for hesitation and yet there she stood, unable to decide which needed her attention quickest. Her heart soared then as the yellow mist burst into flames and Dallid rolled slowly to his feet. It was unthinkable. Dallid really was a Fireborn? She dismissed how impossible that was though, because she had just been given a solution that suited her wishes. Phira made the last steps forward to kill the Iceborn.

He had managed to get himself to a full stand despite his wound and Brijnok's curse stood ready in the giant's hands. It was a broad sword of ice, narrowing in the centre to form what looked like a spearhead at the top. The frozen corridors of Lae Noan gave just enough room for the Iceborn to use it, if of course he had the strength to swing it. The wound in his stomach still bled freely, but the hate on his face and the light burning in his frozen eyes spoke of energy still present. Before she engaged, the man even had the presumption to speak.

'I am all but stripped of my power, my throne destroyed, Aerune slain by a Fureath'i whore, and now I am reduced to this? Not even a spear?' He spat blood to the floor in disgust.

'You have Brijnok to thank for the sword, but you can thank the Fureath'i whore for killing you,' she replied in Prae'surlas. Her eyes darted to the body of the Iceborn she had just beheaded, before returning to the one she was about to behead. Weakness would soon make him drop his sword, but for now she would hurt him. Jabbing in at his stomach wound, the giant swung down to deflect her thrust, and the force of it nearly knocked Phira from her feet. He chopped again and she jumped back, unable to get close enough to cut him. It seemed the Iceborn still had some Powerborn strength left in him after all. His power would continue to increase as time went on too if Phira was not able to kill him quickly.

More prisoners appeared down the corridor behind the Iceborn and the surrounding noise of the battle for escape increased with each moment. A glance backwards let Phira see fire still burning brightly, but she could not see much else so went back to looking ahead. Further down she saw three men crawl out of cells and speak with familiarity to each other rather than hostility. They looked of no race, expect for maybe the Mordec Empire, but all three would have been suited to the streets of Amidon City.

Incredibly, an old woman, looking too frail to stand, appeared from a cell past the men. While still testing for the Iceborn's next attack, Phira calculated that killing the old woman would be more likely the three men's goal rather than involving themselves with two armed combatants. So she did not concern herself with them any further and lashed out at the Iceborn again.

For a man who had never used a sword before, he fought extremely well, using his size and strength to his natural advantage, but often leaving one half of himself exposed, no doubt used to the long end of a spear being there to cover. Striking down on the opening, and cutting into the bicep of the Iceborn's arm, Phira spun out of the way of a counter, ending up behind the giant Prae'surlas. Her back was now to the three men - who she could not hear killing the old woman over the rest of the noise the mountain provided - but she could see clearly Dallid fighting off whatever thing had tried to feed on him.

Streams of fire roared out from Dallid's hands and the impossibility of it still had Phira marvelling. Yellow tendrils of dark mist tried to dart out from the thing's robes and strike, but the creature was moving backwards as it did so. Dallid looked in command of the situation.

The Iceborn's blade swept for her again, but Phira's confidence was growing now that she wounded him once. Soon another opening appeared and although she was not in a position to seize it, Phira noted the manoeuvre and waited patiently. When fighting larger opponents, her elusive style would always cause great frustration. The Iceborn was no different, with his sword crashing wildly into the walls with rage. Each time the Iceborn's impatience got the better of him, so did Phira, diving in to deliver small but important strikes sapping his strength. The larger one for the stomach she sought was close in coming, the opening she had seen was bound to repeat and she would be ready.

The giant's eyes shifted behind her and Phira had no choice but to roll out of the way and turn in case someone new had arrived. As it happened it was not anyone new but the same three she had thought smart enough to stay clear. They moved differently now though, their steps awkward and halting. She had not noticed before that their eyes were blood red. The colour was only made fiercer by red streaks that trailed from the eyes and lined their skin like a wound. Looking past them Phira even saw the old woman was still standing, unhurt, and with the same blood-red stare looking back at her. The elder just stood there and watched, as the three unarmed men moved in their odd way to fight two armed warriors, one of them an Iceborn. No, she did not watch, she commanded. There must have been sorcery involved for the three criminals to let a defenceless old woman live and then challenge forward in a trance against two warriors that would surely kill them.

The Iceborn glanced down at where she crouched and grudgingly lifted one hand free from his sword towards the three new attackers. Phira watched ice creep slowly up from the ground and begin to bind the staggering feet of the on-comers, first one foot and then the other. The distraction gave Phira her opening though and she rushed in towards the Iceborn, managing a lightning strike against his open stomach. The result was exactly as she wished, with the giant crumbling in pain and bringing down his neck to her reaching. Fire exploded in front of her then knocking the Iceborn forward to the ground and Dallid's shout coming after.

'Phira! Praise Frehep it is you! Move away from him quickly, Aerath's power is too great!'

Aerath? The fact that he had just prevented her from killing Aerath rather than an ordinary Iceborn did not help to warm her to their reunion. It had been years since they had seen each other, and the joy was overflowing from Dallid's face, but she did not need the help of magic. Even if she was the only one from her village that had not suddenly become Powerborn, she was still a killer of Powerborn and she swung down to demonstrate just that. Aerath's hand swept up, free of his sword, but incapable of using magic on her. Phira was confident she would slice through it until the giant gripped hold of her blade in mid-swing and snapped it in half with a spray of ice.

So it appeared magic could still be used on her so long as it did not threaten her life. Did not becoming disarmed in a fight count as endangering her life? She would have to raise the subject with Brijnok, if she did not kill him the next time they met. Drawing free her last sword - the fallen sword of Protharik - Phira returned the gesture to Aerath, coming from the side instead of down and this time sliced straight through all of his fingers. Then Dallid barrelled into them, sending Aerath skidding along the floor from the power of another blast of fire.

Turning to the three entranced men with the glittering red eyes - who had already struggled free from the ice restrictions - Dallid set all three of them on fire. Impressed, the action settled in Phira's mind any doubt that Dallid was indeed Fireborn, and an extremely powerful one at that. For a Flameborn it could have taken an hour to prepare the ritual and then another hour to recover from it. But Dallid set three grown men on fire in an instant and looked ready to do it again to a hundred more. Phira's eyes spotted the old woman fleeing down the corridor, surrounded by even more prisoners, likely under her sorcerous control as well, and Phira barely refocused in time to see Dallid reaching over her shoulder.

'No!' she shouted and moved back out of reach so that his hand would not touch the hilt of the Jaguar sword.

'Quick, Phira! Give me a sword,' he said, confusion and urgency mixing in his voice. His large eyes and shaggy hair still reminded her of the boy she fell in love with, and even the hard muscle of his man's face was softened by his joy at seeing her. 'Let us cut off his damned head and be done with it once and for all.'

She smiled at him and he returned it lovingly. 'Yes, let us kill Aerath together, my heart.'

He opened his mouth and she knew that he probably had so much more to say, as she herself did, but there was not time. There was even less with more prisoners appearing, either looking down from above, or peering around from a distance either side of the corridor. One was a large man with a black beard who was striding purposefully towards them. She ignored him and turned to finish Aerath when suddenly a dozen Frostborn ran down the corridor. They were blasting prisoners back into the cells and creating new doors of ice when they suddenly saw Aerath on his knees. Phira turned around in alarm to see more Frostborn coming from the opposite direction doing the same. The large man with the black beard turned his head just as they approached him and suddenly the entire world dropped.

CHAPTER FORTY NINE

The power of a sword

It was as if someone had picked up the ground and slammed it back down again with the force pressing everyone with it. The ceilings above, two dozen Frostborn, a Fireborn, numberless other prisoners and a man who called himself a god, were all crushed down to the floor. Phira was the only one still standing.

'Lyat...' she whispered.

It could only be the Destroyer of Armies himself, held prisoner in Lae Noan instead of dead as was thought. There stood a man who had killed ten thousand men in a single act of power, and there Phira stood in defiance of him. She was too in awe of his appearance to be either amused or angered by the appearance of Brijnok's curse as the air in front of Lyat crushed itself into the shape of a sword in his hands. At first it looked as if the blade would keep the form of crushed air, as both Lyat and Phira stared in amazing at the creation. Then the air solidified into darkness, before creating stone, before melting to become liquid fire, before becoming steel.

'What is this?' he demanded. 'What have you done to me? I will kill you, Fureath'i, do not think I won't. I will bring the entire mountain down to be rid of this place, so I will not hesitate to kill a woman in my way.'

'Then kill me,' Phira said and walked forward. She had no wish to kill Lyat the Destroyer of Armies, but why would she not? As legendary as he was, the man was still a crime lord, albeit the ruler of all crime lords. He certainly looked like he wanted to murder Phira in any case. With his free hand he reached out towards her and she could even feel the world shake from the effort of his attack. But she was not an army and she could only be destroyed by a sword.

She walked up to him and he swung his sword at her with vicious strength. But the man was no sword fighter. Phira swerved to the side and used the man's momentum to knock the blade out of his hands. He stared up at her in a panic and she swung her blade across his neck - Lyat the legend killed by a little woman. But instead of going where she aimed it, the sword fell straight down. Phira tried again and was lucky that her sword was not pulled from her grip by the force it hit when she got too close. Lyat stood back up confidently.

'I may not be able to kill you, girl, but you cannot kill me either.'

'Perhaps I do not need to kill you,' Phira said back. 'Perhaps all I need is to touch you.'

'Aye? And what do you mean by that?' He said with a smile at first but then his eyes whipped to the black hilted blade strapped to her back. 'You have his sword...'

Lyat sounded shaken and Phira knew that his powers could not stop her from touching his boot. His powers would only accelerate her swing if she aimed it down. The Jaguar blade only needed to pierce inside to touch the skin and the great Destroyer of Armies would be no more.

The ground underneath them chose that moment to explode in fire and sent both flying backwards. A great weight lifted from the air and suddenly all two dozen Frostborn would be able to move again. With a shake of her head to regain her senses, Phira wondered if she had Dallid to thank for that idiotic attack. More explosions from the ground appeared underneath the Frostborns and she turned to indeed see Dallid standing up again. Aerath was still down but at that moment looked up to see both Phira and Lyat grounded too. The Iceborn's eyes turned to Dallid just as Dallid and Phira's eyes met for the briefest moment. Then a wall of ice appeared between them.

Her reaction was to panic but the commander in her reminded Phira that Dallid was a Fireborn. It was not her duty to protect a Fireborn. Instead she would use the time to kill as many of the fallen Frostborn that she could, her earlier caution of Powerborn now gone after seeing what Brijnok's curse did to them. She could even use the time to kill the great Lyat while he was down. Her ego had always wanted to see how many of the great fleshborn warriors she could best, but now she could set her sights on higher targets. She could become a slayer of Powerborn the world over; showing that to be fleshborn was not to be weak. She was not learning to enjoy the magic cast on her, but she would use it like any other tool. Besides, the spell did not give her any magic or power; it simply took it away from her opponents.

Keeping an eye on the Prae'surlas Powerborn that were still slow in recovering from Lyat's power, Phira stepped forward carefully. She could see Lyat getting up from the blast and wondered what he might try next. If she could only get her sword above him then anything he did with his power would bring it down on himself. She did not want to chance the Jaguar sword if she did not need to, but Lyat was dangerous enough to warrant the risk. More prisoners had started coming up the corridors but upon seeing all the Prae'surlas getting back to their feet, soon changed their minds and left again. One or two kept coming though, either through arrogance or curiosity.

One prisoner boldly walked over all of the rising Frostborn and Phira paused to frown at the new arrival. He was unarmed of course - having just escaped from a prison cell - and dressed in little more than a shirt, waistcoat, boots and pants, almost a mirror to Phira. He walked like her, and seemed to be heading straight towards Lyat just like her. He had a hard face with cold grey eyes, clean shaven and looked chiselled from stone. He had long hair tied back behind his head tightly, going down his neck in a braid, and he walked as if he thought himself more god than man.

Lyat did not see him though and when his eyes landed on Phira the entire mountain began to shake, with every Frostborn crushed to the ground again. Lyat's face was twisted with frustration and there was a sword being crushed out of the air and into his hands once more. She almost felt sorry for him that he had been imprisoned helplessly for so long despite his raw power, and now freed, he was so close to escaping and she was stopping his power again.

Phira had been so captivated by the power of emotion in Lyat's face that she had failed to notice that the newly arrived prisoner had also not succumbed to Lyat's power. In fact he had made it all the way to Lyat and stood right beside him without incident. He placed a calming hand Lyat's shoulder and when the big man looked up to see who it was, he let out a breath of relief.

If Lyat had been controlling his power, the arrival of the new prisoner had distracted him enough that every floor and ceiling above them now shattered with a deafening crack. The wall of ice that Aerath created to keep them separated was also smashed and Phira had to dive inside one of the empty cells to avoid falling wreckage. She covered her ears to block out the sound of stone and ice crashing all around. Then, risking a glance out, Phira had to duck back inside when the body of a man thumped down in front of her having fallen from whatever higher floor he had been on. Looking back out she could see many more such unfortunate prisoners lying dead from the fall, but the most striking image was the lone friend of Lyat still standing untouched.

Lyat himself had gone for cover inside one of the prison cells, but his friend had remained where he was. She watched him reach down and pick up the sword Lyat's power had created and there was no doubt in Phira's mind the man was a sword fighter by the confident way he held it. She could think of one friend of Lyat the Destroyer of Armies who matched the description of this man, and if it was true that Lyat was not dead, but held prisoner all this time, then why not the great Amadis Yeda. It was said the world did not touch Amadis the way it did anyone else, and here he stood apart from it all, yet could not be more dangerously involved.

Their eyes met and the most arrogant part of Phira wanted to test her skill against the best that ever lived. Some of Amadis's critics said that without the Jaguar blade he would not have been as deadly, others said that he used magic that rendered weapons useless. But Phira believed the only thing that rendered weapons useless was the skill with which Amadis fought them. If she could only die by a sword, then it was very likely that Amadis could be the one holding it.

Movement from both directions showed the Prae'surlas Powerborn digging their way up from the rubble that Lyat had created. Amadis turned his head to those behind him and Phira took the opportunity to get back to her mission. Killing Aerath and getting Dallid out of there was her priority. She could prove who the better sword fighter was some other time.

Slates of ice shifted underneath her feet as she raced down to where Dallid and Aerath had been. There was no sign of them at first, but she soon spotted the red of Dallid's tunic. She went straight to a white tunic lying next to it. There was no more room for distraction. She slipped her sword into the neck of the Iceborn giant and ripped it up. That cut one half of the neck away and she spun Aerath over to hack off the other half, only to find that it was not Aerath at all. Cursing, but still finishing the decapitation of the different Powerborn, Phira looked around for her real target. Kicking off more stone and debris, she saw only one other Prae'surlas lying underneath it all - another Frostborn - before the others starting getting up. Resting her sword on the Frostborn's neck she quickly stamped down to drive it all the way through to sever the head. But two others had gotten to their feet by then and she had to fight.

They laughed at how small the woman in front of them was, who wanted to fight them, the big strong Powerborn men that they were, and then during the following confusion of why their magic would not work on her, Phira sliced open their guts and throats. There was not enough time to hack off their heads unfortunately as more had also gotten up, including Dallid and Aerath. Great swords of ice began forming in all the hands of the bewildered Frostborn, and the giant Aerath glared his contempt at her. How dare a Fureath'i woman subject all these important Prae'surlas to the humiliation of impotency. She wasted no time in smiling back and instead went back to cutting her way through Powerborn flesh.

Aerath acted also. Instead of attempting his own ice attack at Phira he instead Connected with the ice under her feet and threw her off balance as the slates underfoot were whisked away. She fell and Aerath charged at her but not before Dallid got off a fire blast to stop him. A white arc of ice appeared, stopping the attack and Aerath continued unhindered, stamping his boot down onto Phira's head. She spun out of the way in time and barely avoided his next kick, but could not get back to her feet with the slates underneath her shifting. One of the Frostborn stabbed their new swords at Dallid like a spear, and another did the same to Phira. She managed to avoid that only to see Aerath's boot coming back down.

Her own boot found the solid footing of the corridor wall and she was able to push underneath Aerath's legs, and stabbed straight up into his thigh. Back on her feet she slashed him across the back before dealing with two Frostborn attacks from the other side. Dallid sent a blast of fire into one which allowed Phira to stab the other through the kidneys, but then Aerath shot a spear of ice through Dallid's chest.

Phira smashed the spear as soon as it entered Dallid, trying not to think what wounds might kill him, and then gave her attention back to Aerath who smiled at her. He backed away from her attacks and behind Phira could hear Dallid shouting out in pain again. She turned to see more spears of ice piercing him from the walls as he fought back against the other Frostborn. Aerath knew any magic he tried too close to Phira would fail but that did not mean he couldn't butcher Dallid to distract her.

It was working.

Every roar of pain from Dallid felt like a wound inside herself, but she would not let Aerath get away again. She swung at him and he moved back. He had no weapon, since his magic was not aimed at Phira, so she had an open target to carve up. Increasing the intensity of her attack, all the giant Iceborn did was continue to retreat. Thinking she was being set up for a trap, Phira glanced behind her swiftly to check and then back again. Aerath was gone.

Blue flames trailed on the ground where he had been and when she spun back around to Dallid she saw Aerath there instead. The same blue fire flickered around his feet and his same cruel smile was shining towards Phira. Another wall of ice shot up to keep her away and Phira rushed towards it.

There was no ceiling this time, as Lyat had collapsed all of it in the area, so with some luck Phira could find a way to climb over - despite it being twice her height. Using the momentum of her run, Phira jumped at the wall next to the barrier of ice, hoping to push off it to gain further elevation. But the wall was too slick and her foot slid straight down causing her to land in a tumble. She could hear Dallid screaming out in pain on the other side and Phira stood back up. She returned to the wall next to the barrier and began hammering the hilt of her sword into the ice knocking out a foothold. She slammed it over and over, until a chunk cracked free.

Not satisfied but with urgency telling her it would have to do, Phira moved back to gain some distance, and then ran at the wall again. This time her boot found the foot hold and she launched off it to just about grip the top of the ice barrier. It was thin and cut into Phira's fingers but at least it was not so thick that she would slip. Hauling herself up, she could see Aerath lift Dallid by his throat and fling him into one of the Lae Noan cells. None of the other Powerborns had seen her yet so she positioned herself and readied her jump.

Aerath was close enough that if she aimed it right, then in her fall she could take the bastard's head with her. Her own weight, as meagre as it might be, would add strength to the swing and should be enough to do it.

Aerath began growing a door of ice to keep Dallid inside the cell, while the Frostborns began investigating around the corner of the corridor. As soon as Dallid saw the ice door begin to form he scrambled to get out and Phira readied her jump at the same time. Then Amadis Yeda walked around the corner, his sword dripping in blood but the rest of him untouched. Phira could not waste time worrying about him though and jumped regardless. Aerath turned in alarm to see Amadis appear, and paused in his blockade of Dallid's cell. Dallid did not hesitate and launched himself out through the remaining gap.

The ice giant saw neither of the two Fureath'i descending upon him, but he saw Amadis Yeda was free once more and that Aerath was without the power of his throne, or his god, to fight him. In terror, he fled.

The steel of Phira's sword touched the back of Aerath's neck and the fire from Dallid's hands touched Aerath's chest. Then, the Iceborn and everything that touched him was swallowed by blue flame and dissolved into the life-stream. In one instant Phira had known Aerath's head was removed, and the next she was suffocated by brown and purple shadows. Spectres of hell flew all around and screamed in her ears. They dived right for her throat and then did not touch her. She still had her sword but the shadows passed through it. They passed through her. She was nothing to them. She had no power. Flesh passed unnoticed through the world of power. Phira sought for calm and looked around at the new world she had been brought to. She turned to see Dallid and Aerath, and both were being torn to pieces by the same shadows.

It looked like a hundred figures each pulled both Powerborn in a hundred directions. Images of Dallid came loose in the hands of one shadow, only to be jerked the other way by another. At one point there were a dozen separate Dallid's each being dragged a different way until returning to the centre again. A pulse came out from Aerath then, not ice, but some form of magic, and all the shadows disappeared. The scene became clearer even though her mind could not accept it. She stood, but there was nothing to stand on. She could see endlessly in all directions but there was nothing to see. Then Aerath noticed them. He did not speak but he smiled. He had found his way to kill her. He would leave her in this place forever.

Blue fire crawled out from his feet in slowed motion and before it could swallow him to return back to the world of flesh again, the flames turned red and flared. The fire disappeared and Aerath frowned in alarm but it was not Dallid who had stopped him from leaving. They had been joined by a fourth figure.

It was a spectre of red and blue flames, and if Phira did not know any better she would have said it was Amadis. The figure even had a sword at its hip, and when it drew the blade, the spectre slashed it down across Aerath's face. The Iceborn fell and the thick clouds all around them rippled with the power of the strike. Then Phira heard a man laughing. The spectre of fire turned in alarm and an all-too-familiar voice sounded in the air around them.

'So this is where you've been hiding.'

The spectre disappeared at Brijnok's words, and to Phira's alarm so did Aerath. The blue flames flew out and with immediate reaction Phira ran forward, grabbed Dallid and threw them both in its wake. The world of power dissolved and the world of flesh slammed back into place.

They returned to exactly the same location from before they left. The only difference being it was no longer populated by a small army of Frostborn. It was now populated solely with Amadis and a collection of heads.

Again it was only his sword that was drenched in blood, his clothes completely untouched. Of Lyat there was no sign, so it was down to just the four of them: Aerath, Dallid, Phira and Amadis. She knew Amadis was the most dangerous by far, something much stronger than a Powerborn, and here he was, presented with a Fireborn, an Iceborn, and a fleshborn woman, and Phira was the one he stared at.

'You have my sword.'

Before she could respond, Aerath did instead. Spears of ice fired out from the walls and Amadis smashed them the instant they were formed. With terrifying speed he cut apart the last spear and spun to slam it into the Iceborn's already ruined face. The spectre of fire had left an open gash removing Aerath's eye and nose, and the force of Amadis's blow did more, knocking Aerath into one of his own cells with a spray of blood. Then Amadis kicked Dallid square on the chest, the strike sending him sprawling into another cell, before turning his eyes lastly to Phira.

She knew his strength was greater than a Powerborn. She had seen how instant his speed was when he attacked. The moment he moved he would be on her. Phira turned the sword in her hand and waited.

Much the same as Valhar, there was only a flicker of movement to indicate that Amadis had attacked, and so Phira spun in response. Blind to see what form of strike he had chosen, she could only act to what she knew of his style and how she herself would have struck. His sword sliced down on empty air and her own raked up across his ribs as she spun free. Her body was tensed and ready to move again straight away but Amadis had ceased his assault. He stood with his back to her and touched the wound she had given him. He was in disbelief.

'Who...'

But he was interrupted by the arrival of even more Prae'surlas Powerborn from both directions, all Iceborn this time. The giant Aerath even chose that moment to join them, striding out and inhaling deeply. What followed was the walls coming alive again but not with spears. It came alive with hands of ice and the creations did not attack her or Amadis. Instead they grabbed each of the newly arrived Iceborns and threw them into the cells of Lae Noan. The ice-hands followed and became doors to stop the

Powerborn from escaping and when Aerath inhaled again, Phira understood.

He was re-growing his power. He was linked to Lae Noan and every power he fed to it became his to use. Phira's sword grew heavy and she looked around nervously for signs of Lyat, but she could not see him. Then she saw ice weaving its way around the metal of her blade and suddenly the sword was snatched from her hand. Ice grew out from the wall to swallow the sword and no matter how fast she reacted, Phira's blade was gone.

She looked in alarm at Amadis but his sword had been similarly stolen. They were both left unarmed and at the Iceborn's mercy.

Aerath ignored them. His eye flashed and a skin of ice pushed its way out from his flesh. The new frozen face was just as deformed and a second Aerath ripped itself free, before running past her down the corridor. It was the Iceborn's image in every way but made completely of ice. Three more burst free in as many seconds, one darting the other way and two climbing up the walls to the higher floors like spiders. Phira thought she knew what he intended them to do. They would capture more prisoners until Aerath had returned himself to full strength.

When no other images broke free of the Iceborn, he turned his only working eye on them, first Amadis, then her. Spears of ice shot from the walls and Phira dived backwards to avoid them. She landed outside the cell where Dallid lay bleeding and she jumped in with him. To bring him back out to the corridor was to invite more injuries but without his powers inside the cell, the ones he already had could kill him.

Hefting his bulk under her arms, Phira dragged him out and as soon as his head was free he opened his eyes. They were red with orange and yellow spirals going through them. They burned with power and as his energy returned, his first act was to shove Phira back into the cell. Then he ignited into the brightest fire she had ever seen. From inside the cell she could not feel the heat, but she could see its light, and she had never seen anything so brilliant.

She moved back at first but then circled around to the edge of the cell to get a better look. She knew it could not touch her and she wanted to see where Amadis and Aerath were. Dallid had completely filled the corridor with flames now and unless they had jumped into one of the cells there was no way they could survive it. If they were both inside the cells of course then they would be vulnerable and she could kill them if only she had a sword. The heat of Dallid's fire might have melted her sword free by now.

Dallid continued to burn, the fire growing stronger and brighter until it became almost white. The power reminded Phira of Aerath's and she hoped that Dallid had not somehow Connected himself to the ice magic of Lae Noan. Whatever was powering Dallid's fire, he did not look to be in control. She could make out his figure in the centre of the storm and he looked to be screaming in pain. Still the explosion of power continued to grow and Phira began to wonder if Dallid had been the one to destroy all the cells. Had he been sent by Frehep to destroy Aerath? So much power could kill a Fireborn, let alone one who had been fleshborn all his life.

She tried shouting at Dallid to tell him to stop but she could not even hear her own voice above the roar of flames. Weighing up her options, she was not left with many and considered stepping out behind Dallid to get his attention that way. Did she trust Brijnok's curse enough to survive the fire? There was only one way to find out.

Her foot inched outside the cell and as soon as it did the fire stopped. Dallid looked around in panic and then down at his hands. A sword made of flowing red flames was circling into creation, each stream weaving around the other and for once Phira saw Brijnok's curse as a beautiful thing. The sword of living flame shone as if it was the sun made into blade.

While Dallid was staring at the creation in amazement, Phira took the chance to see if Aerath or Amadis had appeared. What she saw was Aerath's burnt flesh still standing, severely wounded, but not as badly as he should have been. He was becoming too powerful again, his ice creatures recapturing prisoners too quickly. But then to Phira's surprise, the burnt figure of Aerath lifted into the air and was thrown down the corridor crashing straight into Dallid. The two Powerborn tumbled past her and she turned to see Amadis standing where Aerath had been. He had been using the Iceborn as a shield against the fire, and now that she had stopped the fire, Amadis rushed at her.

She had no weapon, and no way to defend herself, so she thought about going back into the cell. Without his powers she might be a match for Amadis, but before she could dive out of the way of the attack, it stopped. Amadis's elbow was inches away from her skull and his face was tight with strain. His arm was held suspended, shaking with effort, and when his hand opened a sword began to form.

She did not need to see Brijnok's curse activate to know that Amadis's strength would have killed her, so she immediately began looking for her own sword to see if it had been freed by Dallid's flames. There was no sign of it. She turned to check if either Aerath or Dallid had gotten back up and was surprised to see that they had not. Turning back to Amadis, Phira saw his sword was nearly finished and she was quickly losing the only advantage she might get. Amadis was possibly one of the only people where Brijnok's curse would cause the death of her, rather than prevent it. When she turned around again and saw the reason Aerath and Dallid had not gotten back up, it was too late.

Lyat had returned and stood with his arms folded, blocking her escape. Amadis's sword had finished creating and she was more than alarmed to see a sword of black, with a circle of white on the hilt and flames along the blade. Reaching back instinctively, she didn't realise she touched the handle of the real Jaguar blade before it was too late.

She did not die.

Her fingers wrapped around tighter and forced it out of the wraps she had held it in. The sword felt good in her hands.

'This one,' Amadis said, admiring his own sword. 'I wonder if it is real.'

'It is a creation of Brijnok's so I doubt it.'

He looked up at her sharply at the mention of the battle god. 'You are his creature then. He gave you your power.'

'I am no-one's creature, and I am my own power. Believe me when I say what Brijnok did to me is a curse and if he was standing where you stand right now I would drive this blade through his heart.'

Amadis smiled. 'Then we might not yet be enemies. Your name?'

'Phira.'

'That is all?'

She considered giving the name her squads had given her as Phira the Unrivalled, but she was not so arrogant as to say that to Amadis Yeda. She gave a curt nod instead.

'Well then, Phira, all you need do is return to me my sword and we can leave as friends. I will kill Aerath with it, and I imagine as a Fureath'i, you have no love for the Prae'surlas.'

'To kill Aerath is why I am here,' she said softly. Keeping the sword would not better Furea in any way. Not giving it back to Amadis would only risk him killing her to get it. Her death would not better Furea. There was no reason to keep it. 'But this is my sword.'

Whatever traces of friendship that had begun to appear on Amadis's face turned back to stone. His grey eyes stared so coldly at her. 'Then you will die.'

'All I need do is touch you once with it, Amadis,' she told him and nodded down towards where she had already cut across his ribs. He needed to be reminded that he was now facing the wrong end of the Jaguar blade.

His eyes squinted slightly in thought but she could tell he was done talking. The next movement either of them made could be their last. Both of their eyes shot down then to the gentle appearance of ice on their blades.

'No!' Amadis roared. 'This will not happen again. Lyat! The Iceborn! Kill him!'

Lyat made no reply and Phira could see a look of concern on the face of Amadis. She slowly stepped back and into the safety of an open cell before turning to see what new threat was now happening. Lyat had not moved. He still stood with his arms folded, but there was a subtle shine to his skin. Aerath had done the same to him as he was trying with the swords, to create a net of ice so slight as to avoid any notice until it was too late.

Amadis ran forward ignoring Phira and on his approach the ice giant got back to his feet. The iced figure of Lyat was sent flying into a cell with a door forming immediately to cover it. Then Aerath connected with the slates of ice on the floor to trip Amadis in his run, but the swordsman did not falter. A barrier of ice swiftly formed between the two but Amadis crashed straight through it. Then Dallid regained consciousness with an explosion of flames and blew everyone from their feet.

She did not want to interfere with Dallid's ability to attack again, but now that she was finally armed with the Jaguar blade the battle could be finished in moments. All she had to do was touch Aerath or Amadis once and it was over. She knew she had to kill Amadis now because he would never let her keep the sword if she did not.

Turning her sword one more time, Phira ran to join the fight.

Jumping straight back to his feet, Amadis swung down on Dallid to be rid of his fire. A flash of flames burst in front of the swordsman's eyes causing him to miss and allowing Dallid to dodge to the side but only to get stabbed by Aerath's spear. Dallid's hand punched up to send a blast of fire at the head of the Iceborn, but as the flames formed they were turned to ice in mid-air. Aerath shattered the frozen fire and sent the shards at Amadis to stop him from advancing. The swordsman deflected the missiles with his sword and swung for Aerath's body. A white arc of ice formed to stop the blow before it landed.

Two streams of fire whipped out from Dallid's arms, one going for each of the other men. Aerath did not turn this one to ice and had to settle for creating a shield with his hands. The torrent of fire twisted and burrowed its way into it though, going deeper and deeper. Amadis had spun to avoid the stream sent towards him and barely got up his sword to block Phira's attack. He hit back but Phira had already dropped to the ground and swung for his legs with The Jaguar. Amadis lifted his two feet into the air but could not do so gracefully with the sudden need. He ended up falling to the ground but managed to kick Phira in the chest with both feet as he did so. She felt like she had been had been hit with a tree. Her ribs groaned and her vision went white but she was aware enough to see the swordsman back on his feet again, standing above her. A blast of red hit him in the back just as she rolled out of the way.

Dallid turned his back on Aerath to blast Amadis, and he was stabbed with two more spears of ice because of it. His entire body became fire then and Phira ran away from it before she ended up interfering. It was too late though. The fire had already disappeared and another sword was beginning to form. Her flesh was just too weak to have any of his fire near her without risking harm so the curse acted every time. Aerath threw another spear of ice towards him, but for once Phira's proximity to Dallid worked in their benefit. She jumped in the way of it and the magic faded to nothing. A great blade of ice began to appear again in Aerath's hands and as long as she stayed close enough, the battle would be decided with swords.

Knowing Amadis was the greatest threat, Phira switched sides with Dallid. He had been trained by Yiran also and would hold his own in a sword fight with Aerath. Amadis on the other hand, Phira was not even sure if she would hold her own with him. The great swordsman had been about to rush in when Phira appeared in front and he had to change his manoeuvre. Killing her would be no good to him if she had any strength left to touch him with The Jaguar, so instead of fighting with strength he began fighting with skill, trying to disarm her. Phira changed her own style also while defending, no longer needing to pick vital targets for her aim but to touch his flesh in any way she could. The two mirror blades met and withdrew, neither committing to any single strike, until Phira tried to twist her sword around Amadis's and touch his wrist.

The move was reversed by Amadis with lightning skill and Phira ended up with her own forearm cut up from the exchange. A fresh wave of panic filled her body as the false Jaguar touched her skin, but it was not the real blade. The cut was not enough to disarm her either but she did have to change her lead sword arm. She fought double-handed anyway but the shift in her footing, to account for the change in leading hand, was the automatic reaction Amadis had been waiting for. As her weight changed from one leg to the next, Amadis dived forward with a lunge. She avoided most of it only taking a cut across her jacket, but Dallid who had been fighting behind her was not so fortunate. It caught him deep in the small of his back.

He arched in pain but Phira could only see her opportunity to finish Amadis. Her blade swung up for his wrist but Amadis withdrew the sword bringing Dallid back with it. She had to throw The Jaguar from her hands to stop it from hitting Dallid and the moment she let it go, both she and Amadis both dived to retrieve it.

Blessed fortune had Dallid fall into the way of Amadis, so Phira could gather her sword once more and roll forward to plunge it into Aerath's leg.

The Iceborn fell to the ground dead.

Not allowing her sudden victory to distract her, Phira turned ready for Amadis's next attack and then time slowed down. She had called it blessed fortune when Dallid fell to block Amadis from her sword, but now she saw Dallid had fallen to his hands and knees when he was pulled back on top of Amadis. The swordsman had gotten free quickly because he was now standing above Dallid with his sword raised high. Dallid's own sword of flame was in his hand and it made him powerless.

It happened so quickly.

Phira did not believe her eyes when she saw Amadis's sword slice cleanly down through Dallid's neck. His head tumbled clear and bounced twice before rolling to a halt. His eyes were open and they looked at Phira.

'Dallid...'

Amadis spared no time for grieving and rushed forward to kill Phira. The decision was instant in her mind that she would let him kill her this time but only so she could do the same to him. They were both about to die and they both knew it. Then a man with a twisted smile appeared and took Amadis away.

'No!' Phira ran forward screaming. 'Brijnok you bastard! No!' She screamed and tears ran freely as she trashed about the empty corridor demanding vengeance. She swung at the air and continued to shout her rage. She struck the walls and the floor, anywhere she could find until she finally broke down, her head falling, her entire body defeated.

'No... no, no, no,'

Her trembling hands were the only things that moved in the corridor. Prisoners could be heard in the distance, but Phira could only hear her continued denial as she whispered it over and over. She would have killed him. Why did Brijnok steal him from her? She would have killed the man that murdered Dallid... *Dallid*. The blaze commander inside her spoke sternly, saying that she would have to burn the body of the fallen warrior. Was it even possible to burn the body of a Fireborn? How could he have been Fireborn?

How could he be dead? If Dallid had not really been a Fireborn, then perhaps he was not really dead.

Phira lifted her head.

'No, no, no, no,' she continued to mutter softly over and over as she walked, her sword dragging along the floor as she stepped in a daze to Aerath's body.

The Iceborn was dead so the world was saved.

Phira did not feel like it was.

Resting her sword along his neck, Phira pushed her foot down to gain a purchase. It broke into the Iceborn's flesh easily enough, the power that might have once made it difficult gone. Sawing the rest of the head off was messy but quickly done and when she held it up to examine the villain, a chain of ice fell away from the neck, holding a broken shard of rock. She gave one last look to the dead blue and white eyes of the man who would have destroyed the world and then threw the useless lump of flesh away.

Kneeling down she picked up the chain of ice holding the stone and stared at it for a time. She put it into her belt pouch and slid the Jaguar sword into a sheath. Phira looked around numbly for other trophies that she could claim. The great sword of ice created by Brijnok's curse might be worth collecting, but it would be too large to carry. Her eyes kept drifting past Dallid as she searched the carnage of the scene, and finally she allowed them to rest on him. She stood there and stared.

Walking over to the body she carefully leaned over to pull the sword of twisted-fire out of Dallid's hands. That was the sword that had killed him, not Amadis's. If she had not been near him then he would have burned Amadis to ash with his flames. Instead he was dead.

Numbly, Phira slid the amber blade into her belt. It would remind her of what she had done to Dallid, and it was also all she had left of him anymore. Having a sword by her side that was made from him, would mean having him closer than she had in the last three years, but in her mind there had always been an end. There was always a time in her mind, when her duty to her nation would be complete, and she could retire as an elder with Dallid to raise the next generation together. That way, she could pretend she was happy, knowing that happiness waited for her.

Now she no longer had a plan. Phira pulled out the Jaguar sword again and stared blankly at the silver flames that ran up it. If she had only given it back to Amadis then Dallid would not be dead. Amadis would have slain Aerath with it, having no reason to attack her or Dallid, and they might now be allies.

Instead she would have to hunt him down and hurt him for what he did. She would kill Amadis and she would kill Brijnok, long before she would set her mind to Valhar and Thisian, Phira would kill everyone responsible for Dallid's death. She looked at the sword in her hand again.

Phira no longer knew which sword had killed Dallid, but she knew that she was the one responsible.

A group of men came shouting down the corridor then. They halted for a moment when they saw Phira standing by so many bodies, but upon seeing she was just a woman, they continued forward. Phira did not lift her head from her husband's body. The men approaching were shouting at her now, asking if she could spare a moment for a man who had been without a woman for years. They made clever jokes and good-natured fun about which one of them should rape her first. Phira just kept staring at Dallid until one of them grabbed her.

The blade of the Jaguar sword sliced up through the groin of the first dead man. The next had his stomach opened and Phira absently told herself she did not need to go to so much effort. The men were fighters and they tried their best, but after gutting that last one, Phira just nicked the arms and fists of the rest. More dead bodies lay around her feet and Phira went back to staring at Dallid.

It was not real. Dallid was not Fireborn and he was not dead. He could not be, because if he was dead then that would mean she was dead. It would mean she no longer had any heart to fuel her life, she no longer had any reason to have a life; if Dallid was dead then she would crumble to useless nothing and she would never be that. So her husband was not dead and she would figure out what had happened. A shadow appeared above her and Phira tiredly looked up to see it was the long armed demon she had passed before. He was peering down from one of the higher cells that still held some ice. He leaned further out to see what was down there with her, when the ledge of ice fell through. The demon scrambled unsuccessfully to hold onto some of the other cells as it fell, but instead he hit the ground hard in front of her.

The thing landed on top of Dallid and Phira lost her mind.

'Get away from him!' she screamed and cut straight into the thick neck of the beast. It died with a touch but she did not stop hacking at it. She cut apart the heavy limbs until they were separated enough that she could kick them away into the cells on either side. It left Dallid uncovered again and Phira leaned down to carefully place his head back above his shoulders. She sat him up against the wall and with Dallid's eyes still wide open, Phira almost did not know them when she examined the red and yellow spirals running through.

Dallid's eyes had been soft brown. 'What have you done to your beautiful eyes?' she asked quietly.

An Ihnhaarat stormwarrior ran down the corridor then, and this time did stop and run the other way when he saw the amount of corpses surrounding Phira. Phira would not stand for it.

She sprinted after him, passing the three bodies Dallid had burned alive earlier, and kept running with the masked Ihnhaarat in sight. The ceilings were still intact the further she went into the mountain and a dark skinned Kel Sheran floated down from the level above through a hole in the ice, falling with a speed too slow to be natural. When the man spotted Phira she saw a sword of glass form in his hand before she killed him. The Ihnhaarat was still ahead but Phira was catching up. Two men with robes spotted her coming and did nothing more than die when she passed them. The Ihnhaarat ahead had been stopped by a group of tiny silver-haired pigmies and Phira saw the stormwarrior shoot lightning into them. The pigmies were too many though and the lightning did not stop them all. They jumped on top of the Ihnhaarat, pulling him down and tearing at him with claws and teeth.

When Phira arrived they launched themselves through the air at her, but those she did not bat out of the way with her sword, did little damage to her. Some scraped her arm, others bit her leg, they all died in the end. The fallen Ihnhaarat craned his neck up and then spoke with a woman's voice,

'My gratitude, Fureath'i, I owe you my life.'

Phira took the payment owed and stabbed down into the woman's shoulder as she walked back towards Dallid. Her sword hung low as she made her way back down the corridors of ice. It brushed the dead magicians in their robes, it brushed the dead Kel Sheran and the three burnt dead men that Dallid had killed. Returning to where she left Dallid, Phira roared at seeing the demon of mist from earlier had returned too. Dark yellow tendrils of smoke were drifting out from a dark cowl, and touching all of the dead bodies Phira had left there.

'No!' she roared, hysteria making her voice shrill. The demon of mist looked up in shock, the red glowing orbs hidden under its cowl narrowing at the sight of her. That would have been its only chance to run but like a fool it stayed where it was. Phira would have chased the demon down and killed it in any case. An arm of dark yellow mist lashed out and stopped short of Phira's face. She could see it begin the turn and swirl and no doubt form a sword, but her own sword lashed up into it instead. The mist disappeared and the fabric that had covered its body dropped to the ground empty.

Phira picked the shroud up with her sword to examine the thing and then tried to shake it off with dismissal. The fabric became tangled on the sword and Phira shook the sword wildly to get rid of it. She threw the sword away instead and ran her hands up through her hair, gripping it painfully. She pulled it harder and began pacing around the corridor, no longer knowing what to do. Phira picked up The Jaguar again and unsteadily slid it into a sheath at her belt. Every move she made was so slow, and so tired, and she knelt down to examine Dallid again with shaking hands. She cupped his face and tears fell from her eyes.

'I'm so sorry, Dallid. I'm sorry I wasn't here to protect you. I'm sorry I wasn't with you. I'll never leave you again, I promise... I'm sorry...'

Her legs felt weak. She backed away from Dallid until she hit the cold ice of the wall behind her. When it touched her she sank down to the floor to join all the others. Dallid sat across from her, just looking. How she had often longed to see Dallid one more time and now she had her wish.

So she sat, and she stared at Dallid, and she wept.

CHAPTER FIFTY

A new life

Kris reached through the mirror and caught Phira by the shirt. He hauled her through quickly before there was a chance to feel the mirror's effects. But just because he had not felt it, did not mean there had been none. Tensing the muscles in his legs, Kris flung Phira through and let her slide to the ground as he himself dropped from the effort of it. Neither of them moved for a time after that.

He stood back up as soon as he was able and looked down at the arm he had sent through the mirror a third time.

He watched it shake with weakness, before trying to close the hand into a fist. The joints were enlarged and swollen, and would not close fully. The flesh looked rotted, and the fact it was his only working arm made the matter worse. Kris's left one still hung useless, the bicep torn to pieces. He stood there in silence for a time willing strength back into his broken body. There was no-one else that moved within the Temple of Ice.

'Kris?'

Phira was slow to wake from the passage through the life-stealing mirror, so Kris had let her rest. Now her voice was dry, her eyes red rimmed and bloodshot.

'The sun god sees you, blaze commander. You are safe here.' As safe as anywhere it seemed. Even if there were more Prae'surlas nearby, it had to be safer than Lae Noan. He would do what he could to protect Phira in her weakened condition. Looking back at the scene he had taken her from, Kris stared without reaction at Dallid's corpse. So many bodies lay close together, another of them was headless also and it was Aerath. That was good.

'Where are we?' Phira tried to rise, but was still not ready. He knew it was difficult to recover from the ordeal, it was best that she rested for longer so Kris did not offer to help. All she managed on her own was to twist her neck around and take in her surroundings. The chamber was littered with broken shards of blue and red ice.

All of the larger fires had shattered when the chamber was quaking. He did not know if they had stopped the ritual of ice or not, but Aerath was dead and that was enough. The goddess Am'bril had dropped from her suspension some time ago, and she looked as dead as any other thing, god or not. His concern was solely for Nureail, and as long as her frozen wound did not open or fester, then she should live. He would make sure of it.

His affection for Nureail had made him search for Tereail in the mirror that he had vanished through, but there was no scene that arrived. All it would show was a picture of blackness, as would any other mirror he ordered. It likely meant the Scholar was dead. It was frivolous to search, and duty had belatedly called him over to the mirror where Dallid had taken Aerath, only in time to see a Foreign swordsman kill his friend. He thought about jumping through the mirror to kill the man responsible but he could not leave Nureail. In Phira's rage that followed though, the chances were high that she would have killed Kris had he jumped through. So he waited and as soon as she came to rest he pulled her to safety.

Kris knew he should have checked on Dallid earlier. He should have ignored Nureail and run to help as soon as his friend disappeared. He should have cut off Aerath's head when he had the chance. But he did not.

It was not thought or conscious will that had made him forsake all reason when he ran to Nureail's aid. It was nothing that Kris could recognise as any part of him. Perhaps it was new, or perhaps his journeys through the mirror had stripped away too much of what had been him. Nureail had found a place to survive within the darkness of his heart, and it was a thing he now held so precious that nothing else mattered. As his actions had shown, it was also a thing that made him profoundly weaker. The mirror had indeed taken much.

Looking back to where the Teller lay unconscious, Kris considered moving closer to her again, to make sure the wound was clean, that she did not fever, to even give her the warmth of his body heat. Kris almost began that way when Phira managed to crawl to her feet.

'We are in some kind of Prae'surlas temple?' she asked.

Kris nodded. 'The Temple of Ice. It was here where Aerath centred his ritual to turn the world to ice.'

Phira eyed the mirrors, the images of different lands suddenly becoming more dangerous. One mirror still showed the corridor where Dallid was killed, but Phira did not pause on it. She continued her survey of the chamber, paying closer attention to the ones with shifting images that surrounded where Am'bril lay. Kris himself would like to find a way to smash the things. It was disturbing that a thousand Prae'surlas could file through one of them anywhere into Furea at any time.

The Prae'surlas would be damaged by such travel, some might even not survive it, but given the right location, into a secluded area with ample time for recovery, they could still arrive close to several targets worth attacking. There had to be a way to destroy the things. Perhaps when Nureail woke she would know. Phira's mind seemed to follow his own, but in the opposing direction.

'If only we had these in one of our own temples. We could wage an assault anywhere in Surlas.' She had not asked if he knew of such a one, so he did not volunteer the knowledge that a single mirror existed in the Temple of Zenith. It was no honourable way to fight a war. She finished her survey of the room and focused on him. 'You look like hell, Kris. But you knew of the ritual Aerath was completing? How? Did Gravren find a way back to Rath'Nor?'

'Of that, I do not know, but it was Lady Jaiha, the Decider of Fates, that quested me to this task. Nureail's brother saw it his visions of the future.' Phira took a cursory glance around for the man, and her eyes lingered on the fallen figure of Nureail for a moment. As for where Tereail had been sent, if he lived, Kris would have to find out at some stage. He did not look forward to another trip through those mirrors, but he would do what he had to. Even if the man was dead then Kris would find him if only to burn his body for Nureail's sake.

'I heard word Jaiha had been slain, by a demon with green eyes. As well as Chrial'thau the Great, Miral'thau the Wise, three more Fireborn dead, as well as...' she hesitated over what she was about to say but then quickly added, 'I have killed Aerath.'

Kris nodded that all she spoke was true, he had seen it, but she left her words open. Curiosity was not a trait Kris had ever understood, so he did not lead her to elaborate. Better questions would be how she had gotten to be within Lae Noan, and where were her squads? She also appeared to kill both the Iceborn and a score of others afterward with a single touch of her sword. Was it laced with poison? It was certainly the same colour as the Jaguar sword that Amadis the Powerful had used. They were all questions someone else might have asked.

'If you have no orders for me, blaze commander, then I will take Nureail and return to Furea.' His mission was completed. Aerath was dead and the goddess Am'bril was freed from her prison of ice. What did it matter to Kris if Am'bril was dead, his task had not been to keep her alive, only to free her. Perhaps there would be a dais that linked the ice temple to the Fureath'i fire temple. Kris did not think there would be or an army of Prae'surlas would have used it to rampage into Furea by now. When Nureail woke, they would search for it.

'Kris,' Phira said, her eyes suddenly uncertain. 'Dallid is dead.'

Kris nodded. 'I know.'

If Phira had expected more then she would have to find someone else to speak with. He cherished his childhood memories and his friendship with Dallid more than anyone else, but he died trying to kill Aerath, what other death could a Fureath'i hope for?

'He was Fireborn,' she said then. 'When he died, he was a Fireborn, and still he was killed. I...' She shook her head, speaking more to herself than to Kris, but focus returned to her. 'And Thisian, he is Flameborn, and an Exile, and I will kill him the next time we meet.' Kris said nothing. It had never happened before that a Fureath'i fleshborn killed a Fureath'i Powerborn. But she was his superior officer and it was not his place to tell her who she could and could not kill. If she said she would kill Thisian then he believed her. Phira laughed. 'What about you, Kris? Have you become Frehep-reborn since last I saw you?'

'I am without any power,' Kris replied and it was Phira's turn to nod. A sound from Nureail then made his head whip around. She was awake. He had not doubted that she would, but relief filled him to the bone. He looked to Phira first before he went to her, and she nodded her permission to go.

His legs still felt like they would give way at any moment when he tried to run, and now that his mission was over his entire body needed much rest. But he kept going until he reached the Teller, collapsing at her side. Her eyes looked up at him with delight and her lips parted, ready for words that did not come. Kris frowned to wonder if she was indeed well if she did not speak, he had never known her not to speak. His mouth opened first to ask her how she felt but then his head turned in alarm when a figure appeared next to Phira.

It was a man of middle years, a scar pulling up his mouth into a sneer, and he was armed with more weapons than anyone should have been able to carry and still move. All Kris's body wanted was to close his eyes and rest for a time with Nureail in his arms, but he pushed his legs back up, standing steady despite the feeling of dizziness that threatened to take him. Clenching the fist of his weakened right arm to ready it, Kris pulled free his sabre. Neither Phira nor the new man turned to pay him any attention.

'Where did you take Amadis!' Phira screamed at him, lifting up her blade to point it at the newcomer's throat. She looked even more exhausted than Kris felt, barely able to hold her sword, so Kris began inching closer as she continued to shout at the newcomer. 'Why did you take him? I will kill him no matter how long it takes me, Brijnok, and I will kill you for getting in my way! For giving me this curse! This curse that killed him!'

'Be at peace! I took him because he was about to kill you. You should be thanking me.'

'Thanking you?' Phira laughed weakly, almost sounding like a sob. Her voice lost all strength as she continued. 'Unless you have come to tell me where Amadis is or you have come to remove this curse upon me, Brijnok, then I would suggest you disappear, or I will have to kill you. For what you made me do.' She turned the Jaguar blade and stared at it for a moment. 'For what I did.'

Fire returned to her then as she bared her teeth at the man who called himself Brijnok. 'We will see how well your sword works upon its maker.'

The man smiled, the scar pulling the skin on his face. 'You cannot know how much it pleases me that you've decided to use the sword, Phira. For a time I'd considered you too stubborn, but I should have known there would be a need too great to pass up the power it provides. Already you have killed Aerune *and* Aerath. I'll admit I'm disappointed because Aerath promised to provide me with great battle, but with the deaths of Am'bril and Aerune, there is still reason to rejoice.'

'It is good to know, Brijnok, that a god can die.'

'Lesser gods can die, Phira, let us not be confused.'

'So Aerune and Am'bril were lesser gods? And what of the world now? Will the weather return without them to temper it?'

Brijnok spread his hands. 'I cannot see the weather getter any worse if that answers your question, unless another god tries to take Am'bril's place. Creedus, your Ihnhaarat's god of storms might enjoy that role, or even your beloved Frehep, although I doubt he would bother. But who can know. In my time the weather was ruled by nature alone, perhaps it will be so again. We shall have to wait and see.'

'For a god, you are remarkably ignorant,' Phira said with disgust. She had not lowered her sword in all the time Brijnok had been talking. Kris knew her muscles must be finished, especially after the drain the mirror would have taken. He spotted blood running down her right arm, and knew that the left with which she held the sword was not even her strongest.

'I am the god of battle, *girl*, not a soothsayer to predict the weather. I am the First God, the one worshipped by all even if they do not know it. From the moment you scream out as an infant to take your first breath, your life becomes a battle for survival. Even other gods cannot challenge me for to do so would only power me further by the battle it would insight. So do not presume to make claims of my ignorance, mortal, and give praise that I let you live at all.'

Phira waved the sword in front of him. 'So you do not want me as your pet then? To bring glory and battle in the name of holy Brijnok? Give me Amadis and Valhar and I will return the sword to them with pleasure. You say you are the First God? So were you not a lowly mortal like me at one miserable stage in your life? Or are all those tales of Brijnok's Empire lies fed down from above?'

'Reach into your belt pouch and you will find the answer, *fleshborn*. That is the reason I have come here, not your sword.

That is the reason Lae Noan is now destroyed. And that is also the reason why I was drawn to you in Amidon City.' Phira moved her bleeding hand, painfully, Kris could see, and fished out a small rock on a chain of crystals. He spotted Brijnok's hands flex toward it for a moment, but the shift was slight and whatever he had intended, the so-called god of battle changed his mind. 'Do you know what it is? Let me tell you. There are three of them in total and they are called the Segments of Ahmar, each one cursed so powerfully that even here destruction in one form or another will descend in time. You are fortunate to be fleshborn, because the more power that holds it, the faster and greater the destruction that follows, and it is a curse so absolute that even my enchantment would not protect you.

'Yes I was mortal once, but when I lived there were no gods, there were no beings of power, only men and the weapons that the gods had left behind when they had all been destroyed. And of those ancient gods, there was one so immense that she Connected to every other being; to everything. She had so much power that she could not contain it, and in her desperation she created a lock to be rid of it. You hold one piece of that lock now, the other is still in Amidon City and the last is in a place of my keeping, under the protection of a being of my choosing. If you were to possess all three, then you would be where I was so many hundreds of years ago.

'My brother and I tracked down the three, survived the terrible destruction that came with them, and once I held the lock for that incredible power, my first thoughts were: *with this I will become a god.* And by just thinking it, my will was created and the barrier between this world and the world of power was torn open once more. I became the First God then, but the realm of power I was thrust into bled hungrily into your world of flesh, creating unending Connections between men and power, breathing life to the first of the lesser gods, then the Powerborn and now countless others that inhabit this age. If you were to collect all three then you too might be able to create a new age, if you are not as foolish as I was. Imagine it, had I simply thought in the slightest difference that: with this I will become *the* ultimate god. *The* god that was only one person, *Her,* all of her power and with it the Connection to every living thing and every source of power conceivable.' He spread his hands out then with a shrug. 'But the risk is great. If you do not intend to hold the three quickly then destruction will find you.'

Phira laughed. 'Will my destruction be a sword, Brijnok? Or is this little rock more powerful than you?'

'It would be a thousand swords you arrogant bitch. Are you so conceited to think you would survive that? I almost hope that Jherin comes for you himself, but how do you think Aerath was so easily defeated even though he had all the power of Aerune, and of Amadis, and of hundreds more at his command? He was destroyed because the curse on that stone is so great it would bring the entire world to kill him given enough time. I watched him take the stone in the Tower of Guardians, I watched how the curse immediately created a demon out of your Chrial'thau and how the curse made the only fleshborn left alive into a Fireborn, all just to kill Aerath because he held that stone. Things that should never have happened, did happen, all to bring about the Iceborn's doom. The demon destroyed Aerath's throne and the Fireborn freed Aerune. It was you then, Phira, that was the final act the curse created. I wondered why I was so impressed with a fleshborn that I would give you so much power. The curse of destruction worked on even me in creating you. You were created to kill whoever held one of those stones and kill him you did.'

'So I am to kill myself now?'

Brijnok struggled to remain patient in the face of Phira's mockery. Kris wondered why he was speaking with her at all. He was trying to entwine Phira in one of his ploys, but Phira was not to be used. She would end up with the god of battle serving her, Kris knew, but Brijnok continued on oblivious.

'There will be a hundred others within weeks that will do it for you, Phira, unless you can collect all three. But believe me when I say that the curse increases when you hold two together. So, Phira the *Unrivalled*, if your conceit is not too great, I would recommend you quickly create a place where the stone can rest and keep the curse dormant. This is what I would advice, until you are in a position to hold them all.'

Phira examined the shard of stone and without showing her thoughts on it, put it back into her belt pouch. 'You would show me where these other stones are?'

'I would.'

'Why do you not take them for yourself?'

Brijnok smiled, his good mood returning, thinking that Phira was beginning to be agreeable to his plans. 'Destruction would find me quickest of all if ever I were to touch them again.'

'And if I were to achieve it, to slither under notice like a serpent, before holding all three at once, I would have power without limit?'

'Yes.'

'I could return the dead to life?'

'You could create anything your mind can fathom.'

'But not return to the past and think of better words for my first act.'

Brijnok snarled at her. 'Do not test me, girl, you do not grasp what powers were at work. But I do now, I know precisely where I went wrong and it was not just words. It was the creature connected to these stones, I tried to destroy him and it destroyed my chance at infinite power instead. But my patience is wearing thin with you. What I offer is beyond generous.'

'You offer me nothing, least of all reason.'

'What better reason is needed than the power in itself?'

'You offer me no reason why you would present me with such a gift.'

'Have I not already rewarded you enough, by taking away most of your fleshborn weakness? But yes, you are right.' He eyed her, perhaps finally beginning to realise she was not to be underestimated. 'I will not deceive you. The gift would not be the power for you to use, but the power of my reward once it is mine. I could give you anything that you wished for in return for gathering these stones for me. I have been nothing but honest with you. I cannot always control my temper but neither do you. I respect formidable warriors above all else, Phira. It should be clear that I can be trusted, and we should join together.'

'It is clear that I would be a fool to enter into such agreement. I have heard tale of a man named Moi'dan that took part in such a pact. His own brother killed him for it.'

Brijnok did not snarl this time, neither did he smile. His face was as much a mask as Moi'dan's might have been. 'You do not know as much as you think, *fleshborn*. And yet you mock the ignorance of a god. If I wanted to kill you then I would have already done it.'

Phira stepped forward making the tip of the Jaguar blade move closer to Brijnok's throat. 'I have already killed one god today. Tell me, god of battle, is it my arrogance or my conceit that makes me think this sword will kill you too?'

Brijnok laughed at her, but still he stepped back from the blade. With a sigh he tried to appear unaffected by her threat. 'Think on my offer, girl, or be destroyed by the stone you hold. The choice is yours.'

He disappeared then and Phira's sword fell down heavily from where she held it. Kris checked on how Nureail fared quickly before moving. The Teller met his eyes and her smile was too pleased for a woman who had just lost an arm and a brother. He would never understand her.

His legs protested when he began walking towards Phira.

'I have seen another of those stone pieces,' Kris offered, but Phira looked too exhausted to be interested.

'The one Brijnok claimed was in Amidon City or the one he claimed hidden under the protection of a guardian?'

Kris considered it. 'It did appear under the protection of a guardian named Jherin, but I do not think he is under Brijnok's control. The one I saw was in the possession of Thisian and two Foreigners of his company.'

'Krife and Griffil,' Phira said, the topic seeming to refuel her rage.

'Is it your intention to collect these stones then as Brijnok suggested?'

'No,' she said firmly and Kris was pleased. It was not a fitting quest for a Fureath'i, although Phira had never been conventional. That was probably what made her so brilliant, and it would have to remain another thing outside of Kris's comprehension. 'But I will give Brijnok what he wants, even if it is not what he asked for.'

Kris frowned and waited for her to explain. Her eyes were still fixed on the mirror holding the scene where Dallid sat dead in Lae

Noan. When she shifted them to Kris, he wondered if his own eyes ever looked so dangerous.

'I will not just bring him battle, Kris, I will bring him war. For the first time in a hundred years I will bring the entire nation of Furea to war and we will finally wipe out the Prae'surlas race.'

Her look let him know that she had a plan, something significantly more complex than amassing a hoard of millions and signalling the charge. The last war had adeptly destroyed both nations, with neither one victorious. Kris had yearned for such a war all of his life and now it was his, he wished it was not.

The mirrors had done something to him, changed him, let his control lapse for long enough to let Nureail into his heart. He had feared his darkness would contaminate her but it seemed the light of her heart was too strong. He looked away from Phira, back to Nureail and could already predict the conflict that his new life would bring. War would take him away from her, perhaps forever, but life as a Fureath'i would never have allowed them to be together in any case. Even if she followed him in the war, then she would die, possibly killed by Kris himself. He fought for strength and looked away.

Phira returned to staring at the dead body of Dallid through the mirror, perhaps also contemplating the change to her life it would bring. Kris could not guess at what emotions she might be feeling, but he did know one thing and that was she had meant what she said. Phira would bring the god of battle a war, and it would be one that created a new ocean in the world filled completely with Prae'surlas blood. From what Kris had seen, the Prae'surlas were not to blame for Dallid's death but that did not matter. Because of Dallid's death, everyone would die.

***

'So tell me, Griff, who do you think will kill the Fireborn first?'

'Well, it is a difficult choice, Krife. There are so many.'

Thisian sat quietly on his horse and did his best to ignore the childish remarks his loyal companions were involved with. A Flameborn had more poise and dignity than to lower himself to such a level.

'Well I reckon it will be Eva,' Krife said with a nod. 'I reckon we can blame the whole thing on the Fireborn here and she will let us back into her precious city.'

Griffil considered the proposal. 'He did lose her orb, and that would make Hrothlar out to kill him too. But based on our experience I think it will have to be a Fureath'i that does it. Every Fureath'i we've met has only barely stopped themselves from killing poor Thisian here.'

Thisian opened his mouth but shut it again. There was no point in arguing with them when they were being like this. They continued their ride away from Amidon City as a new dawn broke the horizon to the east. They were heading south and it was Krife's fault that they had to leave, not his. Thisian was not the one who brought some god-cursed stone into the city. There had better be more Fantaven houses wherever they were headed.

'Where are we going again, Griffil?' Thisian tried, hoping to change the subject and hoping to get a straight answer this time.

But both Griffil and Krife shouted in unison, and both with great joy, 'Rath'Nor!'

Thisian clenched his fists, frowning to suppress his anger and alarmingly realised that he had become Kris. Should he try to learn that language? Communicating only through fist clenching and frowns? Griffil must have seen the same murderous look in his eyes too because he held up his hands in apology.

'Alright, Thisian, I'll tell you, no need to send us to Lae Noan for making a few jokes.' Griffil grinned, waiting to see what reaction he would get. Thisian gave none and hoped to every god in the world of light that he really had not become Kris. The world did not need two of them. 'Well, Thisian, you may be pleased to know that we are going south.'

'South,' Thisian repeated without enthusiasm. He knew they were headed south. South was the Furea border and the great forests behind it, but they were heading more south-east at the moment, meaning they would avoid Furea completely. 'You mean past the Amalgamation of Sorcerers and off this continent to go where no-one has ever come back?'

'And why do you think no-one ever returned? What I think is there might be whorehouses there better than the Fantaven!' Krife offered helpfully.

As much as Thisian wanted adventure, he did not want an adventure that no-one would ever hear about, and no-one ever heard about anything south of the continent. 'But why, Krife? Why are we going south?'

'Well,' the big treasure hunter started, before pausing to rearrange his crotch, 'First I'm going to the Amalgamation of Sorcerers to demand tribute for Hane getting killed on us. Then I'm going to sell those magicians this piece of stone that caused so much trouble back in Amidon City. And then, Fireborn, we're going south to meet a man called Balfore Thane so we can get another one of these stones!'

Krife roared out in laughter at the look of pure disgust Thisian had for the entire plan. What point could there possibly be in getting rid of one of those god-cursed stones only to go get another one? If they wanted to die, then why not just go back to Jherin and piss on his face? Will all the gods descend personally to destroy them this time? Will the dead come back because of those blasted stones? Will Ahrthuru come back with a rutted army of Jhakral for them? Will Moi'dan and all nine of his bloody masks show up? Or will Lyat come back and bring the entire bloody sky down.

Even if none of that happened, Krife would go out of his way to make sure something just as bad happened. Forget Kris or Phira or Eva or Hrothlar all wanting him dead, it looked like Thisian was now actively looking for even more people that would want to kill him too.

'I have an answer to your earlier question, Krife, about who will be the one to kill me,' Thisian told him. 'You. It'll bloody be you.'

Epilogue

Rage filled his veins instead of blood. His fist crushed the metal of his false sword, only further reminding him of what he had lost. Tossing the thing to the ground, the worthless metal sounded loudly down the empty halls. He turned and left the blade where it lay.

Reaching the double doors, his impatience was so strong that he kicked open the entrance to the audience chamber, causing lines of men armed with crossbows to turn in alarm. He paid them no heed and continued his march ahead. Too much time had been lost already - much more than he had ever thought possible. Courtesy was no longer something he would concern himself with.

The queen upon her throne rose smoothly to meet the offending warrior that approached. A vast white cape spread back behind and flowed smoothly with her steps as she descended. Her delicate hands wrapped gracefully around a white hilt and the sword was drawn.

'Father,' she said, void of any indication of what her next action would be.

'I have come for my sword,' Amadis said back to her, allowing no trace of question as to who was the true ruler in the room.

Eva's eyes did not react as she took in his form, after so many years without seeing or hearing any trace of him. She would have created her own kingdom in his absence, commanding perhaps hundreds of thousands, wielding absolute power as he would have done. And now he has arrived out of nowhere to take it all away.

That she would give him the sword, Amadis did not doubt, but which end of it she would present to him, still remained to be seen.

It would be fitting to his current mood to have to kill his adopted daughter, but after already losing one of his swords to the arrogance of a woman, he would not lose another. Eva's eyes followed his mind as always, even though he did not feel her reach for him as she could, and she smiled.

The queen of the city knelt down before Amadis and presented the Lion sword to him. At the act, every other man in the room dropped to their knees, perhaps only now recognising who stood before them, despite his visage being carved twenty feet high on all sides.

Amadis wrapped his fingers carefully around the blade of The Lion, feeling its unique power mix into his flesh. He would never again be able to touch the Jaguar sword, but neither did it mean he would allow that Fureath'i girl to keep it.

'Rise, my daughter.'

Eva stood back up and Amadis could detect a trace of warmth in her smile this time. She had changed much to let her mask fall so freely. Memory had brought back to Amadis the truth of what power a mask could provide. He would find them all and return to the power he once had.

'What are your commands, father.'

Amadis swung his new sword in an arc and then scowled at his surroundings, feeling as trapped as he had within the cells of Lae Noan. A new sun was already rising outside and there was much to be done. His eyes met that of his daughter's, and he could see the hundreds of new plans his return had created. The entire world was about to change.

The time Amadis spent within the cell had stripped him of everything he had thought he was, but it had returned to him more. The communed magic that caused his mind to falter was expelled by the mountain, but they had not been one man's mind trying to press itself onto another's, nor was it poison or madness that he accused Aerath of afflicting on him. It was his old mind retaking control and memories returning to him as he became whole once more. Understanding of who he was and who he would be again came slowly throughout the years within the ice. In another age, he had been known by a different name, before he had been shattered into nine separate beings. The spectre of fire was one of those beings. He had been a fool to think the spectre a poison of Aerath's creation. His first action now would be to find the spectre and merge together the broken shards of his mind and power, and then he would find the other seven.

'It is time to become who I once was, my daughter, before I took the name of Amadis. Before I was betrayed, with my mind and powers scattered to the world. It is time I reclaimed what has been taken from me and time to kill the man who took them. It is time to kill my brother Brijnok and for Moi'dan to once again rule this world.

'May all my enemies die screaming...'

One to travel through life. In the shape of an eagle it stands on the mask, because with it the eyes of all life become known.

One to control power. In the shape of a demon it stands on the mask, because with it the light of all creation can be taken and used, leaving only darkness in its absence.

One to heal all wounds. In the shape of a scar it stands on the mask, because with it the wounds of flesh become the openings of power.

One to increase all motion. In the shape of a wolf it stands on the mask, because with it the movement of all becomes prey to its wearer.

One to nullify all violence. In the shape of a turtle it stands on the mask, because with it the rage of all life is trapped within.

One to control the will of others. In the shape of a helm it stands on the mask, because with it all become trapped within their own souls.

One to create power. In the shape of a hammer it stands on the mask, because with it all power can be forged into being.

One to blunt all magic. In the shape of a shield it stands on the mask, because with it there is no protection given to those who have only power.

One to blunt all weapons that may attack him. In the shape of a blade it stands on the mask, because with it all other blades and their users become useless.

69325288R00427

Manufactured by Amazon.com
Columbia, SC
11 April 2017